My Dear Illusion

SARAH READY

CROWN

W.W. CROWN BOOKS
An imprint of Swift & Lewis Publishing LLC
www.wwcrown.com

Published by W.W. Crown Books an Imprint of Swift & Lewis Publishing, LLC, Orlando, FL USA
Cover Illustration & Design: Elizabeth Turner Stokes

Library of Congress Control Number: 2025934024
ISBN: 978-1-954007-86-4 (eBook)
ISBN: 978-1-954007-87-1 (pbk)
ISBN: 978-1-954007-89-5 (hbk)

PRAISE FOR SARAH READY

PRAISE FOR FRENCH HOLIDAY

"Ready (The Fall in Love Checklist) whisks readers to the South of France for a saucy enemies-to-lovers romance...This is a winner."

— *PUBLISHERS WEEKLY* STARRED REVIEW ON

FRENCH HOLIDAY

"Ready has written a tale that deliciously taps into its French trappings...A charming dramedy featuring a promising sleuthing duo."

— *KIRKUS REVIEWS*

PRAISE FOR THE SPACE BETWEEN

"...emotional roller-coaster, but in the end true love prevails. For hopeless romantics, this one's got the goods."

— *PUBLISHERS WEEKLY*

"A touching tale of adult reckonings and reunions with some heart-tugging reversals."

— *KIRKUS REVIEWS*

"...a compelling novel of longing, betrayal, friendship, as well as the undying belief that love and music can heal the world. An original and deftly crafted novel that will be of special interest to fans of contemporary romance laced with humor, "The Space Between" is especially and unreservedly recommended for community library Contemporary Romance collections."

— MIDWEST BOOK REVIEW

PRAISE FOR GHOSTED

"Ready's twisty plot keeps readers guessing how this couple could possibly reach a happy ending."

— PUBLISHERS WEEKLY

"Ready brings her trademark blend of lively tone, amusing details, heart-tugging romance, and adept plotting to this paranormal tale."

— KIRKUS REVIEWS

MY DEAR ILLUSION

1

Life, my dear friend, is illusion. Some people will tell you different. Some will have you believe that everything you see and know is true.

But I'm here to tell you, everything—*everything*—is illusion.

What can you trust? Nothing.
Who can you trust? No one.
No one.
Except me.
Trust me.

THE SHELL GAME IS ONE OF THE OLDEST GAMES KNOWN TO MAN. YOU KNOW the one. It's a favorite of hustlers, thieves, and con men.

You need a gull (a gullible), a con man, and his compatriots. There are three shells—or bottle caps, matchboxes, whatever—and a ball. While the con man spins and whirls the shells in a dizzying dance, his fingers flapping like the wings of so many blackbirds, the gull frantically tries to keep his eye on the ball, eye on the ball, eye on the ball . . .

While he's concentrating on tracking that precious little ball, his wallet is stolen, his watch is pinched, and his car keys are in someone else's hands. Meanwhile, the ball isn't under any of the shells. By practiced sleight of hand, the ball is under whichever shell the gull *doesn't* choose.

Unless it's a game of lull the gull, in which case the ball *is* under that shell. But not the next time. Sorry.

You can find the shell game carved into the walls of ancient Egyptian tombs. You can read about it in letters from the Middle Ages. It's been played in every prominent civilization throughout history, this game of trickery, theft, and misdirection.

The shell game is a favorite of mankind. For some reason, gulls always believe they can win an unbeatable game. But trust me, no one can beat a game that *isn't* a game.

The shell game is closely related to what many call cups and balls.

But cups and balls isn't a ploy to hustle or thieve. It's an illusion to enchant and delight. It's the purview of conjurers and magicians. In fact, most magicians are judged by their mastery of cups and balls.

With three cups and three small balls, a magician can transport a roomful of people into a magical realm where the laws of the physical world don't exist. They can make the balls vanish, reappear, pass through solid surfaces, jump between cups, travel inconceivable distances, and transform into new objects and then back into themselves. A skilled magician seems to break the laws of space and time.

Whether you're playing cups and balls or betting on the whirring speed of the shell game, one thing remains certain: distraction, sleight of hand, and misdirection are key to the illusion.

They're the key to everything.

You're lucky if you only meet con men playing the shell game or magicians delighting with cups and balls. If you meet a conjurer—a true conjurer—and you recognize them for what they are, you're dead.

Sometimes I wake up gasping and sweating, grasping my sheets as I struggle upright. I dream my life is a shell game. The cups are whirring— faster, faster—I'm spinning and weaving—faster, faster—I'm dizzy and breathless—until . . . the shells are overturned. Everything falls apart. The game is done.

I've been having this dream for twenty years.

What am I supposed to tell you? What am I supposed to say? You said if I ever got the chance, I should start at the beginning. All stories have a beginning, most have a middle, and some have an end. Whether the end is all the shells flipped over, the ball vanished and gone, or the proper shell overturned and the ball exactly where it's supposed to be, I guess we'll both find out.

But you're asking me the same age old question: Will I be your hero, or will I be your villain?

Hero?

Villain?

Hero?

Neither of us can know. Not until this story is done.

You know me. I'm Mari Locke. I was born without a middle or a last name—not because no one cared to give me either, but because I was dropped like a parcel outside Hell Gate, with a note pinned to my tattered, bloodied blanket that read, "This is Mari. Take care of her. Debt incurred."

I'm not sure Jagger would've taken me in, except the east wind whispered to him that when it blew through a narrow, cobbled alley in Hell's Kitchen it had skated over the sharp edge of the knife Philoneas Ward held as he bathed in my nameless parents' blood.

The east wind claimed my mother had just given birth, my father had fought to protect her, and that their screams were a distant cousin to the wind's high-pitched, keening wail. A rag man, one of those shadowed, wraithlike half-men who never speak, had wrapped me in a piece of bloodied cloth and carried me to the mouth of Hell Gate.

Did the rag man write the note? I don't know. Did he name me? Perhaps. Or maybe it was the wind who told the rag man my name. The wind has been known to whisper secrets buried much deeper than the last words of a dying woman.

Regardless, my name is Mari. Jagger named me Locke because that's what I do. It's who he made me. A lockpick.

Jagger—wicked, horrid Jagger—is deviously smart. In this world, a lockpick is the best defense and the greatest weapon. If you control a lockpick, you can own the world.

I grew up on the edge of the East River, not fifty feet away from where the silent rag man dropped me. I wonder what would've happened if he'd left me outside a charity hospital or under the awning of a marble-lobbied apartment building on glitzy Park Avenue. I wonder what would've happened if I'd never learned about shell games, cups and balls, and locks that needed picking.

I suppose if that had happened, I never would've met you, and you never would've told me to tell this story. When we were kids, you always said that if something went wrong and we were separated, I should play out my part of the story and send the truth your way.

"Pretend we never met," you said. "That shouldn't be hard. And keep it light—you know I hate a tragedy."

So I forgot. If we haven't met, you'll want to know what I look like, how old I am, that sort of thing. Telling a story is more difficult than I thought. I'm bound to forget some things and omit others. I'll boggle tenses, jumble perspectives, confuse sequences. And yet I'll tell it all as best I can.

I'm twenty-two years old. My looks are average. Most people describe me as forgettable. Some spend years learning the art of becoming forgettable, but I was born with the ability. If you entered a room—say, the medieval art gallery in the Met—and there were five people in that room—an eagle-eyed docent, an anxious mother, her tired three-year-old daughter, me, and an older man in a navy suit coat—you would remember everyone in the room except me.

I'm not short, but I'm not tall either. I'm not thin, nor am I heavy. My hair isn't brown or black but an indifferent shade in between. My eyes can't decide if they're gray or blue. I'm not tan, pale, dark, or light, only an indeterminate color unambiguous in its resistance to conform. I don't have freckles, moles, birthmarks, or anything else to set me apart. No crooked teeth, curls, nor any other defining feature. When Jagger first laid eyes on me, he reputedly said, "Ah. Illusions dance in her blood."

That sort of talk is a death sentence outside Hell Gate. Inside Hell

Gate? It's an insult. No one has illusions dancing in their blood except for the conjurers. No one inside Hell Gate is a conjurer. Jagger only meant that my appearance tricks people's eyes into glossing over, makes them hurry on, as if I'm a stream moving quickly, rippling soundlessly—invisibly—by.

If you remember, when you first met me, you almost didn't see me even though I was right in front of you, chained to a dirty brick wall. You almost walked right by. You always said I took up less space, less air, than other people. I was your very own quiet, restful, shaded pool in the center of a silent forest, hidden in plain sight, right in the midst of a raucous city.

That's me. A whisper. A ghost. A not-illusion.

How did we get here?

I can't think about it. I don't want to think about it. If I do, I'll get lost in the illusion and not want to go on.

But you always said, "The only way you can see through illusion is to become the truth."

Most people in our world look without seeing. Hear without listening. Talk without speaking.

I'm going to become the truth. That way, maybe the horror, the nightmare, the despair of it all, will fall away, and I'll find the terror eating at me is merely a mirage in the desert.

I'll be your villain. I'll be your hero. But either way, I promise, I'll be yours.

So. Look. Listen. See. Hear.

It began, as best as I can tell, the night of my seventh death.

2

I WOKE TO THE SOFT THRUM OF THE GHOST TRAIN THUMPING RHYTHMICALLY across the uneven tracks of Hell Gate Bridge. *Whoomp, whoomp, whoomp.* The sound matched the heave and ho of my heart sloshing about in my chest. *Wake up*, it urged. *Wake up. Open your eyes.*

I didn't. Not right away.

As everyone knows, when you wake up after being clonked on the head and knocked unconscious, you never let on that you're awake.

Instead I lay still. I calmed my heart and my breathing by picturing myself as a scabby-kneed eight-year-old, my scrawny legs hanging over the East River balustrade as I kicked my feet through the open air and waved delightedly at the ghost train clackity-clacking past.

There are plenty of ghost trains in New York—they're just figments caught in a loop after all—but the Hell Gate train has always been my favorite. There's something irrepressibly cheery about a rust-bellied, graffitied diesel from 1962 clattering its way across the great stone bridge.

I'd always wave at it, charmed by its diesel puffs and good-natured clacking. I especially waved when I realized no one could see the train but me. At least, I waved until Jagger told me the conjurers could see them too, and if they caught me waving at something that wasn't there, I'd be dead before I could say "choo-choo".

So I stopped. But for now, at least, the familiar *whoomp, whoomp* calmed my heart and my breathing enough that I could take inventory.

I guess I was knocked out for just a few short minutes, perhaps only thirty seconds.

My arms and my legs were spread in a star shape, and I was sprawled face down on itchy, spiky grass. An acrid tang hung in the air, like the sharp scent of a struck match. The alkaline taste of battery acid and blood coated my mouth. There was the crackle of dry leaves and the clatter of dry-boned branches as the wind swept past, dragging a cold finger over my cheek to let me know that *it* at least knew I was awake.

No one made a sound even though I knew there were a great number of people circling me. I could feel them watching, like a giant murder of crows perched over a farmer's field, waiting to desiccate the crops.

The question was, which murder of crows was it? The Smiths? The Clarks? The Wards? The Bards?

The Smiths would make the most sense. After all, I'd just bypassed all their "infallible" security, nabbed a golden key from their "unbreakable" safe, leaped out of their "unopenable" third-story window. I'd made a fool of them all.

Slowly—ever so slowly—I opened my eyes. The night was curiously dark, the streetlights shrouded by a heavy veil of fog that left a sulfuric yellow taint in the atmosphere. The air was heavy, wet, too cold for late June in New York.

The fog wasn't natural—I knew it right away by the biting cold that sank into my pores, the weight of it pressing down on my bones. It was a fog born to hide and mask, to disorient and confuse. Someone had whispered this fog into existence.

At that thought, my stomach hollowed out and my pulse beat frantically against the vulnerable side of my throat. I'm not a coward, but I'm also not in the habit of brazenly inviting death to come and pick me up for a dance. I know death doesn't like to waltz. All the same, I kept still and quiet.

There was an unnatural calm, an unusual stillness, that left me muzzy-headed and confused. The dark and the fog smeared the ash trees, so they stretched like black-clad rag men haunting the East River's edge. That was where I was, wasn't it? At the black edge of the East River.

My sprint had taken me down Ditmars Boulevard and dumped me in the North Lawn of Astoria Park. Manhattan was just beyond the black waters. I'd flown toward the river, cursing Jagger with every pounding step. Why had he demanded the key this night of all nights? When every flipping Smith from around the world had been called home and was squatting in their hallowed mansion—that ridiculously barren, stoic-faced ancestral pile of bones.

Sometimes I got tired of Jagger's demands. Then I remembered what he did when he wasn't demanding, and I reminded myself to appreciate his demands for what they were.

A reprieve.

Slowly, I focused on the sound of the chattering river and tried to remember how I got here.

Untie the knot.

The thought swept through my mind as swift as a messenger pigeon. The words were spoken in a male voice, a whispered, hoarse plea.

Untie the knot.

I didn't recognize the voice or remember hearing anyone ever speak those words before. When I tried to concentrate on them, a sharp, red-hot spear lanced my temple.

Untie the knot!

The voice thundered through my mind. A vicious throb spread across the right side of my skull. I flinched, and when I did, a man spoke.

"She's awake."

I'd recognize that voice anywhere. It was a creaky, breathy voice that sounded as if the owner's windpipe had been violently crushed and only a narrow tube was left to leak his words through.

Herman Clark, principal conjurer of the Clarks, historian, scholar, and creepy son of a gun who had a fetish for snakeskin boots and plucking all the hair from his body, including his eyebrows and eyelashes.

The Clarks were definitely not the crowd I was hoping to run into.

The Smiths would've been okay. They lived by the philosophy "kill first, ask questions never."

The Bards might've been all right. They were the cruelest, but they also got bored or distracted easily.

The Wards were the worst. Instead of killing, they imprisoned people in hellish labyrinths within their own minds, the mazes so deep and twisted people went mad trying to escape.

I never want to run into a Ward.

The Clarks . . . let's just say, they loved history and all the freakish things that went along with it.

I'd not actually met any of the principal conjurers before now. Stolen from them? Yes. Lots. Darted in shadows and around corners, tiptoeing around them? Plenty. Watched them and learned about them from afar? Oh yes.

If you want to destroy something as great as the conjurers, first you have to know yourself, and second, you have to know them better than you know yourself.

So what did I know about Herman Clark?

That if he'd sought me out, I was unlikely to come out of this night alive.

"I'm awake," I agreed, pushing off my elbows and stiffly rising to my feet.

I was dizzy, woozy, and my heart was still sloshing around in my chest. The fog thickened even more, and not even the wind could brush the curtains of it aside. Maybe there were ordinary people in the park walking past, but if so, I couldn't see or hear them.

We were under the giant stones of Hell Gate Bridge, but now the fog had moved in, I couldn't see the metal train tracks spanning the river. Nor could I see the lights of Manhattan or even the yellowed streetlamps. In fact, I could only make out the graffitied bridge stones rising from the misty grass.

The chattering murmur of the river was muffled and distant even though it was only a dozen feet away. Slowly, I wiped my clammy palms on my jeans and took in the mess I was in.

Six. There were six of them. I might be able to lockpick my way out of two or three minds, but not six.

I let out a slow breath through my nostrils and focused on Herman Clark's thin lips and the flatness of his expression.

"You're the one who's been stealing from the families in New York." His accusation hissed across the clearing like air blown through a broken straw.

The six of them had me completely surrounded. You'd expect them to be wearing something creepy, like black robes and hoods, but no. They were dressed like professors, librarians, archivists. There was a lot of tweed and khaki and Oxfords.

I could play dumb and try to bluff my way out of the situation. Say something like, "Huh? Do you guys know how to get to Grand Central? I'm completely lost."

Tourists are always trying to get to Grand Central. And they're always lost.

But that probably wouldn't work. This was Herman. *The* Clark. I'd studied him for years. If he thought I was a lost tourist he'd probably do something horrific anyway, just for the fun of it. His five compatriots wouldn't bother to intervene. They'd likely join in.

"You stole a book from me last week."

Ah. The book. Apparently, he hadn't realized that last month I also stole a ledger, and last year a laptop from his son, Primus.

"We've been watching for you, little thief."

I shifted my stance and perched on the balls of my feet, readying to flee if the opportunity arose. My odds weren't good.

Jagger wouldn't come for me. None of them—not Roumelade or Winnie or Griff or any of the others—would come for me. Not even Justice, even though just yesterday he'd claimed he was in love with me. I was on my own, as I was every time I went out to pick a lock.

"I'm not 'little thief,'" I said, knowing naming things gave conjurers power. "I'm not anyone. I don't have a name. And I haven't stolen anything."

The conjurer next to Herman, his eldest son Primus, smiled grimly, held out his hand palm up, and then twisted his second and third fingers, connecting them to his thumb. I braced myself, expecting pain or death or horror.

Instead the gold necklace with the small key that I'd stolen from the Smiths floated from the hidden pocket in my jacket. I leaped forward and tried to snatch it out of the air, but my hand closed around nothing. The key was an illusion.

Primus held out his palm. The real gold key glinted dully in the weak sulfuric light.

"You're right about one of those," Herman agreed. "You haven't stolen anything. We have."

The cold of the fog gripped me, and a clammy sweat broke over the back of my neck.

Someone had told them where I'd be. Someone had told them what I was sent to steal. Did they also tell them who I was? *What* I was?

"I love it," Primus crooned, watching me closely with a small, delighted smile, "when they realize they're about to die."

"You can't," I said, cloaking myself in false bravado. "You can't kill me. The code says death may only be meted out in payment for death. I've not killed anyone. Let me pass."

The conjurer to my right, a shorter, thicker version of Herman, stepped forward. It was Secondus, Herman's second son.

Herman was not what you'd call original in naming his children. His only daughter—a gaunt, black-haired woman—was called Last, because he'd decided not to have any more children after her. She was here too, behind me, along with her uncles, Herman's younger brothers.

Secondus grimaced. "But you see, the code only applies to conjurers and their families. And you are not a conjurer. But you're also not human, are you?"

I swallowed, my mouth dry. "I'm human."

"No. I don't think so. If you were, you wouldn't be able to see us right now, would you?"

Crap.

They were using illusion. This fog? The sulfuric light? The thick, ghostly mist? If I were human, I wouldn't be able to see the conjurers through it. I'd walk right by them.

I hadn't realized. In my fuddled, dizzy state, I hadn't noticed the knots and threads of illusion. I hadn't—

"You're one of Jagger's creatures, little thief. Which means . . . you have no protection. We can do whatever we like."

Primus said that. It was then I remembered Elenor, one of Jagger's crew since before I was born. She was held up as a warning for us all. She'd been trying to lift a wallet from Philoneas Ward, just to prove she could. He frayed her mind and made her walk her own thoughts like a tightrope stretched over an endless abyss. Her mind broke, and no one could stop it from happening. There was nothing anyone could say or do. Jagger snapped her neck as a mercy.

I didn't want a broken mind or whatever the Clark version of torment was. So I decided it was time to use a bit of my own magic.

Pedantic. Ordinary.

Just a bit of sleight of hand and misdirection. The magic of mortals.

Quicker than the eye could track, I grabbed a thunderer from my jacket and threw it at Herman's feet. A thunderer is like a flash-bang, but the device is the size of a metal jack and much more powerful.

The boom cracked like a gunshot, and the flash was blinding. I was already running. I sprinted toward the weakest Clark—Last. Her illusion was a small stream compared to her father's power, a trickling tributary to his rushing river, the ability always diluted the farther the conjurer branched from the principal on the family tree.

While the light cracked and seared their eyes, I tossed a handful of serpents to the ground. These were Jagger's creations. They were as small as worms, tightly coiled bits of gray rubber, but as soon as they hit the earth, they transformed into six-foot-long rattlesnakes.

They were made from Jagger's blood, rattlesnake venom, and dirt. He didn't give them to everyone, and I hated using them, because once they were activated, they attacked whoever was closest. I'd been bitten once and didn't ever want a repeat of *that* experience. It was twenty-six horrible hours of feverish delusions while my blood felt like it was on fire.

Secondus was the first bitten. His scream shattered the fog. I tilted my shoulder and rammed Last, thrusting her aside.

If I could make it to the river, I could dive in and disappear under the water. I sprinted across the promenade.

The fog was gone. There were people again. Dog walkers. Runners. Couples walking hand in hand. The Hell Gate Bridge spanned above me, glistening under the crescent moon.

I shoved past a man yelling into his phone and jumped over a tiny poodle. The balustrade was *right* there.

I gripped the cold iron, boosted myself onto the railing, and stood like a gymnast on the thin strip of metal. The cold wind whipped across me, a knife in the moonlight.

The ordinary people, the dog walkers and joggers, shouted in alarm. They couldn't see the Clarks; they only saw a young woman in black jeans and a black canvas jacket perched on top of the East River balustrade, ready to leap to her death into the dark, tempestuous waters.

"Look, Mommy! A snake!"

I made the mistake of looking back, terrified a child had somehow seen one of Jagger's snakes and that the conjurers would end her life for her clear vision. But the girl wasn't real. It was Last holding an illusion.

The rattlesnakes were gone.

The conjurers can create, and they can also destroy. It had only taken them seconds to kill Jagger's snakes.

In that moment, while I perched on the railing desperate to take flight, Herman smiled at me. It was a grim, self-satisfied smile as he whispered in his empty-husk voice.

"Die."

3

____

The icy drench of water seized my limbs, and my lungs spasmed at the shock. I fought the urge to drag in a desperate breath as I sank into the black depths of the East River. The current clawed at me and shoved me deeper, away from the thin sheen of muddy light sitting on top of the water like an oil slick.

I was away from the Clarks, but I wasn't away from their illusion.

There were different levels of conjuring. The principals, the heads of families and their children, could make illusion reality. The cousins could make you *think* illusion was reality. The rest of them, down the line, had watered-down illusions, until the fourth and fifth cousins played nothing more than parlor tricks.

It was Herman who bound me. This wasn't a magic trick or an illusion to deceive the mind. If it was, I would've broken free in a moment. No, this was the work of a master. My arms were shackled, my ankles bound. I was wrapped in iron chains and plummeting headfirst toward the graveyard at the bottom of the river.

Do you remember Houdini? The Handcuff King who could escape from any shackle, straitjacket, or handcuff. Do you remember his water-torture cell, where his feet were locked into a frame and he was lowered headfirst into a tank of water and locked inside?

I felt very much in sympathy with Houdini as the iron shackles weighed me down and locked me in the dark, turbid waters. Just like good old Harry, I had to hold my breath, keep my head, and pick some locks.

This may have been the first time I'd tangled with a principal conjurer, but it wasn't the first time I'd had to unravel an illusion. When I was three, almost four, Jagger's on-and-off lover, Roumelade, took me to Central Park to tumble in the grass in Strawberry Fields. While there, the story goes, I laughed and clapped when a little boy turned a folded piece of paper into a swallowtail butterfly.

I didn't know it at the time, but that boy was a conjurer's son. He was three or four. Maybe he was there with his family—more likely, he was with a nanny. Roumelade thinks he was a Bard.

Luvic or Ragnor.

I don't know. I don't remember him.

Apparently, I ran after the butterfly, and when I touched it, the swallowtail fell back to paper and drifted lifelessly to the ground. With a touch, I'd broken the boy's illusion.

Terrified, Roumelade had grabbed me, tucked me under her arm, and ran.

After that day, for three or four years, I wasn't allowed outside without Jagger nearby. He realized I wasn't just a ward of Hell Gate; I was one of those rare people who could break illusions. A lockpick.

He spent the next twenty years making certain I could break any illusion thrown at me. It would keep me safe and keep me alive.

Before you think Jagger did it because he cared about me, I'd like to stop you. He did it because, with a lockpick, he's the most powerful leggerock in North America—maybe even the world.

Regardless, I've been in chains, I've been in handcuffs, I've been locked in tombs, and rooms with only fifteen minutes' worth of air. Some were illusion. Some weren't. Each time I followed the same steps to free myself. Reality is a rope, and illusion is a knot.

All I have to do is start at the beginning and follow the knotted loops twined together. Some knots are childish and easy to untangle, like a shoelace just waiting to unravel. Others are double-knotted and take longer to pick apart. The worst are like a thin gold necklace with dozens of tangled knots that only hours of careful prying, cautious loosening, and gentle separation can unwind.

The greatest conjurers can create a Gordian knot of illusions. No one on earth has ever been able to untie a Gordian knot. Alexander the Great cut through it with a sword, but a knot severed with a sword isn't truly destroyed. The destruction is an illusion, and it comes back to bite you.

The iron chains and shackles binding me were a double knot of illusion. To anyone else, they'd be real. That person would sink to an early grave. Whoever had told the Clarks about me either didn't mention I was a lockpick or didn't know.

I cleared my mind and flowed into that calm, meditative state where dreams and visions spawned, muses lived, hunches traveled, and instinct reigned supreme. In my mind I found the rope of Herman's illusion. It was a dull, matted gray, like weathered paint on a battleship. It coiled around me in a clove hitch and a sailor's knot. I sped down the line of it, walking tightrope over the slippery surface, and dove toward the first knot.

A tight burning began in my lungs. I'd been underwater for fifteen seconds at most. The current was vicious in this part of the East River. It tore at my clothing and flayed my skin with icy fingers. A time or two, I struck against a rock and a shock tore through me, but otherwise, my descent was uninterrupted.

I doubted the Clarks were watching. They wouldn't have any reason to expect me to emerge from the river, hale and hearty. Remember how I said the Clarks were historians and scholars—that they loved history and all the cruel tortures found within its depths?

Well, they'd made their little inside joke, and I imagined they were strolling from the park, chuckling at how the night had played out.

This is Hell Gate. They knew that too. Hence the iron.

Do you remember the history of Hell Gate? I'm sure you do. But if you don't, I'll remind you. Back when New York was a young city, the Dutch sailed the East River and found this particular stretch . . . deadly. There was a hungry whirlpool that swallowed ships by the dozen. There were jagged rocks that ate cargo and people too.

They named it Hellegat. The name was a warning.

Hell Gate lies between Queens and Randalls and Wards Islands.

Yes, that Ward.

Remember how Wards Island once held the largest asylum in the world? Remember the twisted paths people paced trying to escape? The Wards have always made cages of minds.

Anyway, between Queens and Randalls and Wards Island, there is the tidal estuary called Hell Gate (which preceded the Hell Gate that is Jagger's domain). It's a graveyard, with legends of shipwrecks and gold, treasure and death.

Back in 1904, a steamboat was hired by German immigrants for their annual Lutheran Church picnic. What do you think happened? I'll remind you. The boat caught fire at Hell Gate. There were more than one thousand women and children on board, and only about 150 men over the age of twenty-one.

Desperate mothers tied life jackets over their babies and toddlers' necks and threw them into the churning water, hoping to save their lives. The children sank. All of them.

Why? The life preservers were stuffed with iron. A new regulation had come out requiring a certain amount of cork in life jackets. To meet the required cork weight, the life preserver company had stuffed the life jackets with iron shavings.

As I sank, wrapped in chains, the icy, anguished, iron-laden souls rushed around me in a turbulent whirlpool. The roar of water clogged my ears, but the figments were still there, churning around me and dragging me through the underwater rapids, deeper and deeper.

I ignored them. There wasn't anything I could do for them. I could only work on unraveling the iron chains that held me. I traveled down the dull gray rope of Herman's illusion and reached the final knot.

Some call this skill "clear vision" or "truth-seer." Some call it knowing. Others just call it truth. I've never called it anything except lockpicking. I took the hooked tool that I made in my mind, shoved it into the tight knot, and pried it apart until the entire thing unraveled.

At the last loosening of the knot, the iron chains around me disappeared. A figment—one of Hell Gate's victims—dragged an icy finger down my cheek and then shoved the racing water upward, propelling me toward the black night sky.

In case you're worried for them, concerned at the tragedy of a hundred years ago, don't be. In reality, they're all gone, washed up to Heaven within a moment of their death. The figments in the water are just thoughts and emotions caught in the rapids, circling in an endless loop, creating a misty version of a reality already passed.

Like Roumelade always said: "Figments never hurt anyone. Mind your thoughts, though, else you leave a figment behind."

So I kicked my legs and pulled through the turbulent current, fighting to reach the surface.

My lungs were seizing, desperate to drag in a breath. My legs were cramping from the cold and the lack of oxygen. I was bruised after being battered by underwater rocks and rapids.

My mind was clawing at the walls I'd built up, shouting, *I have to breathe, I have to breathe!*

But I held the plea back and kept crawling toward the surface. Steady. Calm. I'd come up slowly, just in case the Clarks were still there.

I'd been under for two minutes. Jagger had routinely held me underwater for much longer than that. He'd only stop when I was able to break free of a wooden box locked and chained to the bottom of his swimming pool within three minutes flat. The first fifty-seven times, Griff had used an axe to break me out before I drowned.

When my head broke the surface, I kept my face tilted down, my dark hair blending with the black waves. I didn't want the moonlight to catch and reflect off the icy paleness of my skin. I'd be easy to spot from Astoria Park.

I crawled slowly over the waves, fighting the currents. Soon there'd be a coast guard boat, a police boat, maybe a helicopter, called by all the concerned dog walkers and joggers who'd witnessed my desperate leap. I needed to be far, far away.

A half hour later I dragged myself over the coarse rocks lining the coastal edge of Wards Island Park. My knees scraped against the rough, jagged boulders as the waves lapped over me, trying to pull me back into the water. I shivered in the damp evening air, my clothes clinging to my clammy skin.

The thought hit me: I was *alive*. I'd faced a principal conjurer, his family, and I'd survived.

I was alive.

I grinned, gripping the stones and the muddy sand as I pulled myself into the tall grass and woody shrubs lining the water's edge. The foliage was thick and hid me from view. Wards Island was dark, and Manhattan, while close, was hidden by a black line of locust and ash trees that folded over me.

I stood, my legs heavy and my muscles like jelly, and shook, as unsteady and vulnerable as a newborn lamb. As soon as I got home I'd luxuriate in a hot shower, eat an entire double-cheese pizza from Donatello's, and then sleep until noon tomorrow. Maybe I'd even spring for a pint of mint chocolate chip ice cream and eat the whole thing from the carton. Jagger would want to know why I'd failed to retrieve the key, but I wanted to know why the Clarks knew I was after it.

But. Shower first. I smelled like a hard-boiled egg left to rot for a year and then doused in kerosene and dressed in seaweed. My skin was sticky, and there were *things* crawling in my hair. I'd kicked off my shoes while swimming, but there was river detritus wrapped around my jacket and my jeans.

My skin itched as I peered past the shrubs and the trees toward the illuminated soccer field. This part of Wards Island was a park. I was standing in the towering shadow of Hell Gate Bridge.

If I hurried, I could be home in fifteen minutes.

"Mari!"

The whispered hiss cut through the sound of lapping waves and summer cicadas. I froze, my muscles tense. I was three feet from the river's edge—I could always dive back in and disappear in the depths.

"Mari! It's me!"

I squinted at the cluster of black locust trees and the tall grass rippling like a snake in the wind.

When I saw him, my shoulders sagged and I let out a quiet, relieved sigh.

Griff.

Of all of us, he was the only one I'd expect to come looking when someone didn't return. Jagger's rule was every man for himself. It was enforced with strict brutality. Which made sense. If one person died, that was just one person dead. But if one person died and then another died trying to save them, and another, and another, well. Then there'd be no one left. In this world, helping others got you killed more often than not. So Jagger's rule? Don't help anyone.

Griff grinned, his white teeth flashing in the moonlight. Gosh, he was young. Well, he was older than me, but he *seemed* young, somehow still managing to smile and laugh and have this childlike way of looking at the world.

Everyone let the rules slide when it came to Griff—even Jagger.

He popped his head over the grass and waved, motioning me toward him. He was in his usual black beanie, his shaggy brown hair sticking out from the ends. He always wore black pants, black shirts, and jackets, just like the rest of us. Just like me, he had two black lines tattooed across his forearm. But unlike me, since I was forgettable, everyone remembered Griff. It was his eyes. They were big, brown, and so warm they made you want to smile even when there was nothing to smile about.

"Am I glad to see you," I said, walking toward him on wobbly legs. "You won't believe what happened. Who I ran into. Griff—"

I stopped mid-step, the cold river water dripping in black rivulets onto the tall grass. The wind whipped around me, racing over me, whispering a warning. It had flown through the fog of Astoria Park, over the cresting, moon-clad waves, onto the rocky shore of Wards Island. It arrived here before I did, so it had seen what I hadn't.

"—in."

I lurched backward, toward the river. The wind shoved me. It was too late.

I reached out with my mind, slid my hand through the knot, and Griff disappeared. In his place stood a black-clad figure cloaked in shadow and darkness. This was an illusion that would take long minutes to unravel. I didn't have the time or the strength.

The figure held out his hand and twisted his second and third fingers, connecting them to his thumb. In a smooth motion that took only milliseconds to complete, he conjured a silver bow and an icy blue arrow glowing cold with neon fire. In a blur too fast to track, he shot the arrow straight at my heart.

There was no time to spring to the side or twist away. Instead I held my hands in front of me, untying, untying . . . If I was lucky, the arrow would disintegrate, the illusion broken by my mind.

If I was unlucky—

The arrow struck my chest. It cracked my ribs and sliced through my breast. The cold neon fire pierced my heart. I blinked. My heart quivered around the shaft of the arrow. It hurt. The pain speared through me as my heart struggled to beat around the shaft.

I choked on a breath. The air fell from my lungs, and I dropped to my knees. The ground was soggy, cold, wet. I lifted a heavy hand and gripped the cold fire of the arrow.

It was illusion made real.

The night dark spun around me, closing like a curtain in the final act. I shuddered. Struggled to stay upright. Willed myself to untie the . . .

Untie the knot.

Mari, untie the knot.

The male with that desperate, hoarse voice pleaded with me again. His whisper shook me as I fell, tumbling to the grass like the lifeless facsimile of a paper butterfly. My back hit the ground. My hands gripped the arrow, and I struggled to pull it free. There was no breath inside me. My heart had stopped beating.

Untie the knot!

I held onto that whisper. Followed it; raced after the pulsing golden thread of it. There was no knot, only a thread of golden light. A sharp red pain lanced my skull, and my vision blurred.

Everything was silent. No breath. No heartbeat.

The shrouded, shadowed figure stood over me. His form shifted and blurred, untraceable, like the cold waves of Hell Gate on a moonless night. I knew he was a man, although I didn't know how I knew. There was nothing of him but darkness. Real or imagined.

I couldn't move. My mind was sluggish and fogged. My eyes held the spot where he stood.

He nudged my side with the toe of his boot. I couldn't see his face. He was darkness and death. My hands fell from the fiery ice of his arrow, wet and warm with my blood.

The shadowed man leaned down and closed my eyes.

His fingers paused, resting gently on the cold, clammy skin of my cheek, burning me there.

Finally, I died.

4

THE FIREFLY GLOW OF THE STREETLAMPS LIT THE PATH LINING THE CONCRETE edge of Astoria Park in a warm, comforting yellow. To the west, beyond the water and the arching bridges, the buildings of Manhattan were a dark silhouette against the purple summer sky.

The night was warm now, the cold mist forgotten or never known. The air held a gentle early-summer warmth that beckoned families outside to playgrounds, couples outside for starlit picnics, and dogs outside with their owners to play ball. The park echoed with the shouts of children kicking a soccer ball across the grass, a toy poodle barking at a Doberman, and a mockingbird mimicking the sound of a car alarm.

The wind skated over the glossy river, muffling the sound of traffic rushing over the bridge and amplifying the song of the cicadas hiding in grass and mulch. In a quick gust, it caught a Yankees baseball hat and tossed it from a man's head. The hat tumbled down the sidewalk, flipping wildly in the gust. The man chased after it. The Doberman, tired of the poodle, decided to chase the man, his petite owner in tow. The kids abandoned their soccer game and joined the race too.

The wind sped down the path lining the East River, racing toward Hell Gate Bridge. It dropped the hat in the dirt and scraggly grass underneath a thin maple tree, and then, with one more blow, it sent the children's soccer ball thudding against the graffitied stone of the bridge.

A man, indistinguishable from any other, shadowed and leaning over the metal railing at the river's edge, turned and looked toward the noise. No one in the park had noticed him or the man next to him. In fact, everyone's eyes slid right over them, unseeing. When the man was satisfied there wasn't anything of importance to catch his attention, he turned back to his conversation.

"You're certain she's dead?"

Hang on! Hang on! I can practically hear you shouting at me. *But Mari, you're dead! You're all the way across the river, toes up, arrow through the heart, dead. How can you know what's going on in Astoria Park when you're dead?*

Good point.

How do I know? How can I tell this part of the story?

The wind told me.

Like I said before, the wind can go places most of us can't, and it knows more secrets than the worn wooden seat in a church confessional. I wouldn't say the wind is always truthful or reliable. You can't really trust something as fickle as the wind.

But while I've been trying to figure out what happened, and if there's a way or a reason for me to go on, the wind has been telling me secrets.

I'll tell them exactly as they were told to me—that way, you can decide for yourself whether you believe them or not.

So whenever the story goes somewhere I'm not and could never have been, just know, it's the wind telling that part of the tale.

Back to it.

"You're certain she's dead?"

The man speaking was the shorter of the two, although it was hard to catch things like height and heft, or even features like eye color, or facial expressions. It's like Jagger would say: "illusions dance in his blood."

"I'm certain. I watched the life drain from her." The second man spoke with a casual indifference, as if he were telling the first that he'd used a coupon to buy his coffee and bagel that day.

They were so thick in illusion that the only thing to distinguish the two men was their voices.

The second man had a deep voice, like a wire pulled taught over rock-strewn rapids, his syllables echoing as you fell into the depths.

The first man had a lighter voice, a tenor, the melodic sort well-suited for reading Byronic poetry or singing operatic love songs.

Even though no one looked at them or even noticed them, they both spoke in quiet tones, muffled even further by the gusts of wind riding the river.

"It's done then." This was the first man. He balanced his forearms on the metal railing and stared grimly over the dark night at the leafy smudge of Wards Island Park. "Her body is gone?"

By this question, I have to assume the men knew or believed I was in Jagger's service. Anytime one of Jagger's nines died, they returned to him shortly after their death.

"Yes. Do you know what she stole tonight?"

The first man tilted his head in ascent. He knew.

"And from the rest of us?"

"Are you asking what she took from me, or are you offering to share what she stole from you?"

The second man ignored the question. He pointed across the water toward the small island. "Jagger's greedy. He won't stop. Even with her death. He believes he can control the outcome of the game."

"Jagger won't win a game he can't play. Are you ready, my friend?"

"Friend? Do I have a choice?"

The first man turned away from the river and faced the darkened park. A dozen ash trees stood like black-robed figures silently watching them. The wind sifted through the leaves and whispered an indistinguishable message. The man narrowed his eyes at the noise.

Finally, his shoulders loosened. He turned away from the trees and the wind. "No. We made our choice a long time ago."

The second man nodded gravely. "The next time I see you, I'll try to kill you."

"And I'll do my best to end your life."

It wasn't a warning. It was a promise.

Then the two men, in a move that spoke of long practice and a lifetime of love and friendship, raised their hands to heart level, pressed their palms together, wound their fingers, and clasped them tight. For a long, silent moment, they stared into the dark, swirling depths of each other's eyes.

The second man leaned close. "Death won't come between us."

The first man laughed at his words. "Only life will."

"To the end."

"To the beginning."

5

It takes some time to come back to life. For hours, you're inside of yourself but unable to move, speak, or feel. You can hear, but you can't respond. Sometimes Jagger rages. Other times he's gloating and satisfied.

This time he was absent.

Instead Roumelade sat next to my prone form, humming the tune to my favorite epic poem about Odin gouging out his own eye in return for a drink from the well of knowledge. She tells it a little differently from the official version. Instead of journeying beneath the roots of the world tree, she claims Odin died and descended to the underworld to reach the well.

Unlike Odin, when I die, I never descend to the underworld. I've never had the opportunity to gouge out my eye or drink from the well of knowledge. Roumelade claims it's because I was born with clear vision, and that my own sacrifice will have to come in the form of something else.

To Roumelade, sacrifice is a normal part of life, and every day, we all make big and little sacrifices to keep the world turning.

Like her.

She sacrificed her beauty to spend 100 years with Jagger. She claims it was worth it, even though he stopped wanting her so much after she turned from a glinting, diamond-like beauty to what he cruelly calls his dried-out, wasted wishbone.

When Jagger told her she'd have to give up what she prized the most to spend 100 years with him, she thought she'd be giving up her looks, so that was what she sacrificed. In reality, what Roumelade prized the most was his love. So she sacrificed that too. I've never had the heart to tell her Jagger's love was always an illusion, and what really happened was that the illusion was shattered when she gave herself to him.

All the same, she loves him, and in her own way, she loves all the rest of us too.

I was stretched out on my thin mattress, the worn cotton sheets spread over me. The lamp on the nightstand next to my bed bathed my closed eyes in a soft red glow where shadows could dance and play a theatre of illusions and ghosts over the backs of my eyelids. There was also the faint smell of crushed spring violets—the perfume that always lingered on my skin for days after I came back to myself.

It would be a long, nearly endless night. Since my second foray with death, Roumelade knew I was terrified of the coffin of my own body, so she'd promised to make sure I was never alone in the hours it took me to settle fully back into life. I was sure she held my hand as she hummed. She would hum or sing or talk until her voice was as raw as a grackle's caw.

"She's back?"

It was Griff, his voice floating through a mist. Even though I knew it hadn't been him in the park, I still wanted to flinch.

"What happened? Mari, did you . . .?" He seemed to remember I couldn't answer. It wasn't as if he didn't have practice with this himself. "Rou, did she . . .?"

"She did. She just popped in—*poof*—landed on the middle of the kitchen table, naked as a newborn. That's the way it always goes, isn't it? Crushed my blueberry scones, spilled the cream, toppled my tea. Poor Mari."

There was the sound of shuffling feet over the worn wood of my bedroom floor, then a quick indrawn breath. "She's not gonna like how she looks this time."

Roumelade clicked her tongue. "What does it matter? Nobody'll notice. She goes through 'em fast enough."

"Don't say that."

"It's the truth, isn't it?"

"Not any faster than me."

"Ah, but Griff, accidents love you. You can't help it. Mari, on the other hand, loves dancing with death."

If I could've protested I would've. I do not *love dancing with death.*

"She can't help it either," Roumelade said. "Since that conjurer sent her parents to the afterlife, she has to chase after them all. Her parents. The conjurers. She won't rest until they've met their final death—or she has."

"Don't say that either."

"Don't say what?" It was Justice's deep voice. Seemed everyone had invited themselves for a party in my bedroom and I was the silent guest of honor. I heard his heavy steps, and then he whistled slowly. "Mari. You're beautiful this time around. Never seen anyone this beautiful. You look like Sleeping Beauty, gorgeous, dead-still, just waiting for a kiss . . ."

Kiss me and I'll kill you.

"But if I kiss you, you'll kill me." There was a smile in Justice's voice as if his fondest wish was to have me slide a rusty knife into his gut. He gave a low, appreciative hum and then, a moment later, said in a brisk voice, "Jagger's looking for you, Griff. It's about the game. Come on. He wants to—"

I strained to hear what he said, but both Justice and Griff had left my room, and their muffled voices and footsteps were beyond my reach.

Roumelade sighed. "The game. If I never have to see another game, I'll die happy. Not that being under the Bards has been terrible—they aren't as bad as the Wards or the Smiths—but the game always brings too much slaughter. If the conjurers kept it among themselves, that'd be different. But it always spills over to the humans, and then it spills over to us. You weren't alive for the last one—you don't know what it's like. Or the one before."

There was a shudder in her voice, the chilled sound of fear rarely heard from Roumelade. She was one of the most practical people I'd ever met, taking both cruelty and kindness as simple facts of life. Neither fazed her much—it was how she'd survived so long as Jagger's sometimes lover. Both his kindness and his cruelty were offerings at the feast of his table, and she'd willingly eat both, so long as she had a seat there.

"You might think Jagger only wants to win the game for power, but Mari, if he can control the outcome, then just think . . . just think what he could do."

I had. That was the problem. I'd thought long and hard about what Jagger could do.

Here's the thing. Jagger is greedy for power. And Jagger is selfish. And Jagger is what most people would call evil, although some would say he's the lesser of two evils when held against the conjurers. But I wouldn't say that. Maybe his evil has merely been curtailed by his own limitations and inadequacies. You cannot say someone is less evil just because they're incompetent or inadequate. Give him ultimate power and then see what he'll do.

Although, luckily—thankfully—he is selfish. When someone is evil *and* selfish, they have limits, they have caution, they have self-preservation, which at times gives them pause. Imagine if he was a selfless evil, spurred by a cause. That sort of evil is the hardest to fight, because the wielder has no sense of self-preservation or caution. They will commit the worst atrocities. Every day I give thanks that Jagger is selfish. And let's give thanks that the conjurers—at least this crop of them —all selfishly value their own lives too.

"Jagger has found a way to win the game," Roumelade continued, pride in her voice. "As soon as you wake, he'll tell you. Mari, you'll finally get to face the man who killed your parents. Kill him right back. Jagger promised you could. In less than two weeks we'll have the crown of illusions. *The crown of illusions*, Mari. Think on that."

I didn't want to think on it. What would we do with the crown of illusions? We weren't conjurers. We were discards and cast-offs, the forgotten children, the descendants of mud and bone and blood. Or, in Roumelade's case, the captured reflection of churning river water and a thousand tears. Jagger had seen her one day peering up at him from the whirlpool in Hell Gate and scooped her right out of the river.

Anyway, the fact remains, even if Jagger did somehow manage to win the game *and* the crown of illusions, he couldn't *wear* it. Only the eldest child of a principal conjurer can participate in the game, and only the winner of the game can wear the crown. Anyone else who dares lay the crown on their head dies a million agonizing deaths.

Literally.

It's happened a few times in the past. Fools try to steal the crown and plop it on their heads. Let's just say, their screams and the relaying of the endless agonizing torment are enough to keep thieves at bay for a few millennia after each botched attempt.

But the song of power is alluring. The conjurer who wears the crown rules the entire world for the next 100 years. They are the absolute power until the crown is passed on at the conclusion of the next game.

Maybe you're thinking, "Hang on, Mari, hang on. No *one* person rules the entire world."

I don't know. Maybe you've forgotten everything you once knew about conjurers and their history. Maybe you've learned a different history from the one I know. Perhaps you know the victor's version, while I know the hidden history of the oppressed and the defeated. I'm not sure what they've told you or what you think you know.

I'll tell you the conjurers' history as I know it. But as you know, history is easily altered; erased and rewritten to feed the hungry, egotistical hearts of the living. The only way you can be sure of the truth is to go back in time and watch events unfold.

But here's the history I know. Roumelade told it to me the third time I died, after a six-foot-tall jackaltooth caught me in the pitch-black abandoned subway tunnels underneath the Bard mansion. I was eight. I liked a good story.

(If you don't know, 600 years ago, Jackal Bard conjured a half-jackal, half-wolf creature to guard the gates of their home. The Bards have conjured these monstrous creatures ever since to rip apart any uninvited mischief scented person/being encroaching on their territory. Jagger, in one of his endless tests, told me I couldn't come home until I made it past the jackaltooth or died trying. The night after my third death, I made it into the front hall of the Bard mansion and stole a wooden-handled umbrella and a shiny bronze button from a rain-soaked trench coat.)

Here is the history of the conjurers.

Long, long ago, there was only God. God was everywhere and everything, nowhere and nothing. God floated in a vast and endless expanse that was larger than comprehension and smaller than anything known. It was a black, silent nothingness. Yet God was.

Then God *thought*, and with thought God created. God thought heaven into existence. God thought the world into existence. God thought life into existence. Finally, God thought mankind into existence.

God created both man and woman in his image.

And here is where history has been forgotten and minds have been clouded.

Because in the beginning, mankind, like God, could bring thoughts to life.

God created universes, worlds, life with thought. And in God's image, man created with thought too.

Whatever man believed, whatever man conjured in the vast halls of his mind, sprang up before him. Hasn't it been said that if only you believe, you can move mountains? In the beginning, mankind did move mountains. They envisioned vast cities and they sprang up before them. In their minds, they heard angelic music, and it filled the earth with sweet noise. They pictured art, music, riches, and abundance, and everything they thought was made reality.

To think was to create.

This is what it meant to be made in God's image. Thought was real—more real than the physical realm, because thought preceded the physical, and of course, thought never truly disappeared.

But what happens in every Eden? What happens in every garden?

Plants die. Crops wither. Flowers fall and rot. Weeds choke and kill seedlings, thorns and briars overtake the garden, and it all falls fallow.

The downfall happened when the first Ward saw his younger brother's wife. She was as beautiful as a drop of dew glistening on a red rose petal. He wanted her. He *wanted* her. So he thought himself into his brother's form, and he took his brother's wife and laid with her.

That was the first time thought had been used for ill. It planted a seed that took root and spread throughout the world.

When a son was born, it was clear he was not the second Ward's child. The boy had red hair, not black hair. Gray eyes, not brown eyes. The second Ward was enraged at the deceit. He thought of his brother's death, envisioned it, willed it, and then he killed him.

The second Ward gave birth to death. His wife had come to hate him and love his brother. She went to the underworld and visited the first Ward and promised him that since he'd tasted true death, she would make certain his brother found true death too.

She raised her son in the barren desert, only feeding him bitter fruit and thorns so he would grow up bitter and thorny, with only one desire. To kill his father's murderer. To kill the now eldest Ward—the most powerful man on earth.

And so, for 100 years, not-son and not-father battled by imagining ways to kill the other. They brought into reality earthquakes, tsunamis, wildfires, and hurricanes. They created armies that clashed in war, plagues that swept nations, droughts and famines that choked the life from entire continents.

After 100 years of conjuring countless horrors, the youngest Ward defeated his father's murderer and sent him to a true death. When he looked around and saw what had become of earth, he should have mourned, but he couldn't—after all, he'd been raised on bitter fruit and thorns.

The rest of mankind had been corrupted. The seeds of wrath and revenge, envy and greed, lust and vice, sloth, gluttony, and pride—they'd been sown and taken root. They couldn't be banished from the hearts of men. The world became a hell of evil thoughts made reality. Every minute, a new wicked thought was given birth to live and ruin as it desired.

This was the time of before. When all of mankind were conjurers.

If it had continued, the world would've been destroyed by the thoughts of mankind.

So God destroyed mankind instead.

With a thought, he swept a flood over the earth.

He destroyed every city, every village, every lone hut. He wiped our history from the earth. He left so few people alive that it would take thousands of years to recover. None of them remembered—no, none of them knew—that thoughts could become reality.

That ability had died in the flood. Completely extinguished by the waters.

Except . . . not quite.

When the floodwaters came, four families fled along a golden stream of light, down into the deepest, darkest cave in the world. It was so deep it reached the edges of the underworld. Roumelade claimed they stopped at the edge of the well of knowledge—the one Odin had sipped from. She believed the youngest daughter of the Wards took a drink. She says all the river folk know this, because rivers babble and share secrets that are eons old, but I think she made that part up.

Months later, the four families emerged from the cave. They found a new earth. One where mankind had forgotten the power of their thoughts.

After that, the four families took an oath that from that time on, they would only use their thoughts for good, they would protect the people of earth, and they would never bring war and destruction, famine and plague, disaster and devastation to the world again.

They would be the moral compass of mankind; the creators of destiny; the conjurers of mankind's fate; the guiding light for us all on the path of righteousness.

Ha.

Ha ha ha ha.

Excuse me while I laugh.

Okay. I'm finished.

Back to the four families.

There were the Smiths. They were the compass's north. They were skilled in weapons and combat, the shield and the sword.

The Wards were the east. They were the protectors and the jailers. They could build walls to keep out or in.

The Clarks were the south. They were the scholars and the scribes, full of wisdom and careful thought. The advisors.

The Bards were the west. They were the musicians, the poets, the oracles, and the artists. They connected conscious thought to subconscious knowledge. They were mankind's inspiration and muse.

All four compass directions were key to bringing mankind to a prosperous and peaceful future.

Each of the four families agreed to pass power between them. After the flood, their abilities changed. They soon learned that the head of the family held the most power; the first child was the receptacle for the family power and held the second most power, until their parent died and passed their power on; the second child had a lesser amount; and so on, until only a morsel of power was left for the offshoots of the family tree.

I think of conjurer power like a river. Each principal is the source, and they have a rushing river of power within them as wide as the Ganges, as long as the Amazon, and as deep as the Yangtze.

Each offshoot of their family draws power from that source. The eldest child—and heir—is the largest tributary, so the power that flows through them is like the Mississippi River. The second child is the Danube. The third child less. Until finally, the third cousins and fourth cousins are trickling streams, barely drawing any illusion from the principal's river of power.

Only children of the head of the family receive major conjuring abilities. That's why children of second, third, and fourth (etcetera) sons and daughters never have significant conjuring abilities. They're too far removed from the main river of power.

These relatives—cousins, second cousins, and so on—are employed by the family, put in positions of power in government and business around the world to serve the family's ends, but they're not included in the main power structure.

Conjuring families are very hierarchical. In the end, it all comes down to power. This is one reason conjuring families can be ruthless. The power isn't held by the firstborn per se, merely *the eldest*. So if a fifth born child becomes the eldest through a series of accidental or deliberate deaths, they will become the most powerful. (Historically, the mortality rate in conjuring families is very high.) Finally, if a conjurer has a child with a non-conjurer, that child is always powerless.

The greatest power comes with whoever is currently wearing the crown of illusions. When the four families came out of the underworld, the four heads of the families all combined their thoughts to create the crown. It's a receptacle of all their power. All four of them died from the effort it took to create this crown. Roumelade likes that part of the story best, because it's all about sacrifice.

Anyway, the original four's eldest children went on to rule after them. Every 100 years, a new conjurer is chosen to wear the crown, and for the next 100 years, they are the greatest conjurer on earth. (Conjurers live to be about 180 years old—the flood shortened mankind's lifespan significantly.)

The entire tone of earth and the path humanity will take is influenced by whoever is wearing the crown. Sometimes people wonder if there's someone behind the scenes, pulling the strings of all the events that happen on earth. Well, I can tell you, the answer is obvious. The only things pulling strings are thoughts made into reality. Illusions made real.

How do the conjurers choose who wears the crown? That's easy. The four heirs play the Hundred Year Games. The winner is crowned.

The world's fate is decided in this game. If the winning conjurer is evil, you'll get the Dark Ages (Ruithvain Clark) or the Black Death (Sicily Ward). If they're a zealot, you'll get a holy war (remember the Crusades? That was a Smith. All eight/nine/too many times). If they're artistic or intellectual, you'll get a renaissance (Owain Bard) or a time of enlightened philosophy (Arjuna Ward).

But this time around, the four eldest . . . There are no artists or philosophers or thinkers. There's only . . .

Darin Smith. The cold north. Suckled with a sword in his hand, and with a lust for world war.

Jacob Ward. The deceptive east. Connoisseur of secret plots and lies, fond of assassinations and toppling governments.

Primus Clark. The cruel south. Longs to return to the oppression and tyranny of humanity's violent history.

Celia Bard. The greedy west. Feeds off the vices and lusts of humankind, stoking passions until all of man's potential is sucked dry.

One of them will win the Hundred Year Games. It begins tomorrow night. And in less than two weeks, the fate of the world will be known.

Jagger thinks he's found a way to win.

Unlikely.

It's more likely he'll become one of those cautionary tales—one who experiences the million agonizing deaths.

But I can't help but wonder, what's his plan? All my life I've worried about the outcome of this game. A hundred years of Dagrid Bard brought us world war, disease, depression, and discontent. Whatever the next generation brings, I feel, will be even worse. I've seen the conjurings of their minds.

Is there a way to stop them? Is there a way to unravel their realities and make their illusions crumble? If there were, would I take the chance?

Do you know what you said to me when I was wavering? You put your hand to my cheek and said, "Mari. Every time you turn your back on a responsibility that is rightfully yours to bear, you make the world a darker place, and you make yourself a lesser person. I won't see you become less. You have to do this. I have to do this. *We* have to."

Those were your words of wisdom.

When I finally opened my eyes, waking up from my seventh death, Jagger was smiling down at me with sharpened teeth and boastful eyes.

6

By the time Jagger and I arrived at the northwestern edge of Hell's Kitchen, the night had nearly given its last gasp. As we stalked the shadows of 12th Avenue, I looked over the battleship-gray Hudson and the long piers that extended like clawed fingers over the dark water.

We were only blocks from where my parents had reputedly met the sharpened end of Philoneas Ward's knife. For reasons that should be obvious, I didn't spend my weekends picnicking or frolicking through the delights of Hell's Kitchen. In fact, I couldn't remember the last time I'd been. Maybe when I was twelve, Jagger had sent me here on an errand, although even that memory was fuzzy, so maybe not. Perhaps I'd forgotten it out of self-preservation. That was entirely possible.

An itch crawled over my neck, and I had to fight the urge to look over my shoulder for whatever or whoever was watching us pass. Low gray clouds gathered over the Hudson, clutching the shore and moodily threatening rain. They crowded the road and pressed us closer to the darkened car lots and dirty brick and concrete warehouses lining the silent street.

It seemed to me there was an electric blue glow to the air and the ghostly whiff of static electricity. Every now and then I caught a pulsing blue light, and the hair on the back of my neck stood on end.

If I'd been on my own, I would've heeded the warning and gone back home to Hell Gate.

Instead Jagger and I strolled into the thick of it. There was no wind—it had died at 47th Street, like it was refusing to walk any further. Up ahead stood a three-story redbrick warehouse that stretched an entire block.

Streetlights lined the sidewalk, casting scraggly bits of grass that crept out of concrete cracks in a sickly yellow glow, but when the light touched the warehouse, the building seemed to gobble it up.

The warehouse was dark, with a row of foggy glass block windows lining the base. Most of the upper-story windows had been bricked up or smothered with plywood. The warehouse was spray-painted with graffiti—letters, numbers, pictures—nonsense to anyone who passed.

However, the graffiti was a simple illusion—one that could be made by even the weakest conjurer. If you looked closely, unfocused your eyes and then peered into the distance as if you were looking at one of those Magic Eye posters or random-dot stereograms, you'd see what was really written on the brick wall.

Painted in large gold letters, in old-fashioned italics, were the words: *"Welcome all who seek; find what you desire within the Night Den. Open Daily from sun death to sun birth; no figments, no water spirits, no judgment."*

Wonderful. Fantastic. Amazing.

We'd made it.

Jagger stomped to the only door into the building—a warped, rusted monstrosity—and glared at the flat gray metal. "Open."

A portion of the door, a small square the width of a hand, slid open, and a single red-rimmed gray eye peered out at us. In the dark it appeared disembodied, although I knew it was Jagger's cousin Eyetooth on the other side.

"What do you seek?" he asked in a creaky tumble of a voice.

Jagger bared his pointed teeth.

You know, I just realized I never described Jagger to you. Do you remember him? Do you know any other leggerocks?

If you do, then you'll know he's typical of his kind. He's average height, at six foot six. His skin is a worn, tumbled grayish beige, like a stone weathered and worn under a cold mountain stream. He's bulky and thick, with swollen joints. His arms are longer than a human's and his fingers are double-jointed, his gray nails thick and sharp.

Leggerocks have eyes of solid slate-gray and an obsidian-black pupil. They do not have hair, except for a small, stubbly amount on their heads, male and female both. Their skin weathers easily, and they collect wrinkles and sagging skin as proof of their longevity. Although Jagger has never told me his age, by his wrinkles and skin sags, I'd guess he's probably about 400 years old.

No one knows exactly where leggerocks came from or when they were thought into existence. There are too many contradictory stories to make sense of any of them.

It was either an avalanche that crushed a conjurer's lover and her tears brought the rocks to life, or it was a general who wanted an army of warriors as strong as the tallest mountains, or it was a greedy merchant who tried to disguise river rocks and sell them as diamonds, or . . . You get the point.

There aren't many leggerocks in the world. I say that's lucky for the world. They have a magic all of their own—one Jagger claims was given to them to balance out the power gifted to mankind and all of earth's other creatures.

Still, if there were more than a dozen leggerocks in the world, the world would be in trouble.

Jagger reached down and held his pointer finger over the sharp edge of the obsidian knife hanging from his necklace. Leggerocks use their blood to create. Who knows what nightmare he was considering bringing to life.

"You know what I seek, cousin. Let us in."

I have to give Eyetooth credit: he waited a full three seconds before I heard the groan of a half-dozen bolts sliding free. The door creaked open, and a weak light fell over the sidewalk.

Eyetooth, identical to his cousin except for the missing canine tooth in his upper jaw, gave a curt bow. "Welcome to the Night Den. By crossing the threshold, you acknowledge the owners hold no liability for death, dismemberment, or delight. Drop all weapons at the coat check."

Jagger swept inside, his black trench furling behind him. I followed, shivering at the feeling of déjà vu sliding over me. I didn't care for déjà vu. It reminded me too much of the feeling of reality and illusion colliding.

I'd never been in the Night Den before, although Justice came sometimes when hunting quarry. He'd told me all about the depravities involved in death, dismemberment, and delight and then suggested I never set foot inside.

You see, while I was raised under Jagger's thumb in Hell Gate, where greed and selfishness were a virtue, and had witnessed enough casual cruelty and disregard for the value of life to make me what most would consider . . . tainted by association . . . I'd been protected from the worst of it all by Roumelade and Justice, and even to an extent Griff. The rest of the citizens of Hell Gate—the pickpockets, the hunters, the slipshots, the servants—none of them had any desire to shield me. In fact, they were all eagerly awaiting my ninth death.

I pulled off my coat when Eyetooth held out his hands at the coat check. As I did, I couldn't help but notice the single black line tattooed on my left wrist. Yesterday I'd had two, but since my last death, I'd been left with only one. My stomach tightened at the reminder, so I dropped my hands and hid my wrist from sight.

If Jagger saw the lone tattoo, he'd smile, his slate eyes flat and anticipatory.

They always say "don't bargain with the devil," but they should've said "don't bargain with a leggerock."

"All weapons," Eyetooth said, glancing at my belt. He thrust a wooden box toward me.

Jagger had already dropped his favorite morningstar and dagger necklace into the crate. He nodded at me, giving me assent to disarm.

I unhooked the pouch of bloodworms, unstrapped a knife coated in Roumelade's tears (deadly), pulled free two thunderers and a canister of hell smoke . . . When I hesitated, Jagger tilted his jaw to the hidden pocket on my right pant leg. Apparently, we were playing it straight today. I pulled out the cluster of needle-size darts coated with Smith's Folly.

Luckily, and unbeknownst to everyone except Jagger, my greatest weapon wasn't a knife or poison: it was my mind. Jagger's greatest weapon was his blood. Neither of us could be disarmed of those.

I would never exactly be comfortable in Jagger's company or truly feel safe, but I did feel *safer* walking into the Night Den with him than alone.

He knew the way. He'd been before. After all, this was where the desperate and the dreamers came to dance on the knife's edge between life and death, reality and illusion. He made his best bargains with the desperate.

The entry to the warehouse was a barren, concrete-floored room with bare redbrick walls. The entire space was lit by a single flickering fluorescent bulb. There was the coat check, which was a long metal pole holding dozens of coats: a beige trench coat, a yellow raincoat, luxurious mink, cheetah, and rabbit fur coats, a black leather coat, a raggedy coat, filthy coats covered in mud and green slime, patched coats, worn coats—all sorts of coats. There was a large shelf full of wooden boxes holding every weapon imaginable and unimaginable. And there was a three-legged wooden stool by the metal door and a clock above it. A real finger inched across the clock. On one side was a golden and powder blue sky with a yellow sun. On the other was a black night sky with a crescent moon. The finger was slowly inching toward the sun side.

"Let's go," Jagger said.

He swept toward the back of the warehouse, where there was a hole in the concrete floor and a rickety set of wooden stairs leading down.

As we descended, a chill, wet draft scraped over my bare arms. Was it the wind, or was it just the breathy moans of the concrete walls? Was it possible that the Night Den was too hidden and deep for even the wind to reach?

There was a damp, musty scent in the air, and the wooden stairs creaked and heaved under Jagger's heavy weight. I followed slowly, letting my eyes adjust to the deep dark. There was no light to guide the way, no railing, so I let my hands drag over the damp, rough concrete. Suddenly, I was reminded of the conjurers' descent into the cave as the world flooded above them.

I listened to Jagger's heavy breathing and steadied myself as the stairs swayed, and still we kept going—down, down, down.

Then Jagger stopped. If I hadn't been so attuned to the groan of his footsteps, I would've collided with his back. Just beyond his shoulder, I could make out the dim smudge of flickering light, and beyond that, a door with a golden eye painted in the center.

Jagger turned to me, his gray skin sallow in the dark light. His profile was more angular than ever, and his gray-black eyes glinted with predatory anticipation.

"You're ready?" he asked in a voice that scraped over the tattooed line on my wrist. "You're ready, Mari?"

The eye on the door blinked at me, and goose bumps rose over my skin.

"Yes. I'm ready."

After I woke, Jagger had told me his simple, brilliant, unspeakable plot to win the game. He'd outlined everything I'd need to do over the next two weeks, telling me what I'd win if I succeeded. The death of the man who killed my parents. The defeat of the conjurers. My freedom.

I'd dressed in black canvas pants, a black tank top, and my canvas jacket. I'd French-braided my hair, refusing to look for too long in the mirror at my new face and body.

Every time I died, my face and body changed, shifted and reformed. I didn't know why. That was just how it worked. Jagger said it was the movement of mud and blood and bone; that none of them were stagnant. No one could pass along the outskirts of the underworld and come back unchanged.

I was still forgettable, unnoticeable by most, a shade between shades. Except, like Justice said, if you looked long enough, you'd find me beautiful.

When I'd seen myself in the mirror, my heart had lurched, and a dull ache had settled in my chest. This new face had the sort of beauty that made men and women feel as if they were reliving their fondest memories—the ones they'd forgotten and wished they hadn't. It was a face that made you *yearn*.

It was going to get me into trouble—I was sure of it.

Turns out I was right.

But at the time, I'd turned away from my new reflection, grabbed my weapons, and gone to the kitchen to eat the familiar, comforting chicken and saffron stew and dumplings Roumelade had made to get me "back in tip-top shape."

So although my legs were weak, my arms ached, and I was still getting used to being back among the living, I gave Jagger a resolute tilt of my chin.

He smiled appreciatively. He liked strength nearly as much as he liked deviousness. "Good. Then let's go say hello to your ticket to the games. Ah, Mari. You're going to love him."

7

THE GOLDEN EYE ON THE DOOR FOLLOWED ME WITH AN UNBLINKING GAZE AS Jagger and I entered the bowels of the Night Den. I'd heard of these eyes. They were called all-seeing eyes because they could peer into a person's heart and see the dividing line between good and evil. Supposedly, they prevented anyone without at least a sliver of good in their heart from passing through their door.

The eyes kept places like the Night Den from becoming dens of depravity—which, while a clichéd phrase, is also a real place you *never* want to visit. Jagger doesn't have an eye on Hell Gate because he has some truly terrible creatures visit, and he doesn't want them to feel unwelcome.

I guess I should've been grateful, but the Night Den's eye had a disconcerting way of looking right at me, as if it knew more about me than I did.

I shivered as soon as I stepped over the threshold, glad to be away from it, but as soon as the metal door swept shut, I wondered if it would've been better to stay outside with the watchful eye.

The thick metal door had blocked all sound. That was the first thing I noticed. The Night Den was roaring with noise. It was hard to separate all the layers of sound, and for the first few seconds, everything was just a loud, thundering boom. It was like being bombarded by a waterfall. But then my ears adjusted, and I was able to sort through the layers.

Music—not the harmonic scale with the octave notes that everyone knows, but a slippery sliding of notes that used the front, back, inside, and outside of every sound imaginable. It was a dizzying, whirling noise that fizzled my blood and tempted with a pounding beat.

Then there were voices—shouts, whispers, laughter, hoarse calls, and crooned suggestions. There were at least 200 or 300 beings in the Night Den, and it seemed all of them were talking at once.

Most of them were human. I imagined they had conjurer blood so diluted they were cast-offs and undesirables, or they had some other blood in their ancestry—like Griff, whose dad, according to Jagger, was the Jersey Devil.

(None of us hold this against Griff, because even though his dad is *really* not nice, you can't help who your parents are. Besides, it's not Griff's fault that the mind can think of all sorts of terrible things, or that sometimes those things take form and become real. A Bard made the Jersey Devil as a Halloween joke that never went away.)

Along with the clatter of voices and the slide of the music, there was the clink of dishes, the bang of metal cup against metal cup, the slap of plates to wooden tables, and finally, the pounding of feet against the concrete floor in a violent *thump, thump, thud*.

It took a moment after my ears adjusted for my eyes to adjust too. The Night Den was *dark*.

When I was younger, back when Jagger was still training me to be the best lockpick that ever lived, he'd sometimes lock me in deep, dark places where not even a whisper of light could reach. When the human mind is completely deprived of light, it starts to hallucinate fairly quickly. I have quite a lot of experience with the tricks the mind can play with you in the absence of light.

Luckily, the Night Den wasn't completely devoid of light. The walls were black, the ceiling was black, the floor was black, and over it all, a red and yellow glow flickered and licked, keeping the space disjointed and hazy. There was an overlay of mist or smoke, but there wasn't an acrid tinge. Instead the smoke smelled unusually sweet and tart, like crushed cranberries and allspice.

Over that sweetness were the normal bar smells of spilled liquor and beer, French fries and hamburgers, sweat and body odor. It was hot, and a bit of sweat trailed down the back of my neck even though I was in a tank top. There was no breeze, and I wondered if the owners purposely didn't have fans or air-conditioning because they didn't want to invite the wind into their abode.

Then again, not many people knew the wind was a Peeping Tom and an incurable gossip, so maybe they just liked stagnant air and sweat.

It took seconds for my eyes and ears to adjust, and in that time, a few people looked our way and then quickly looked away again. Jagger has that impact wherever he goes. Mostly, though, no one noticed our arrival. The Night Den was a big space. A huge basement of a warehouse.

Like I said, the warehouse was a block long, and from what I could see of the den, the open area was about half of that. There were darkened corners with booths cloaked in shadows. There were tables where groups drank and ate. There was a dance floor positioned around a silver stage, with long poles and ropes, where three men and three women contorted and moved in ways I didn't know were anatomically possible. Which meant they probably weren't entirely human. Not many people were watching them. Instead everyone's focus was on the ring at the center of the den.

It was a fight. A bloody, beat-each-other-to-death, fist-to-flesh, savage, primal, champion-type fight going down. This was why there was such a constant pounding of feet. With every sucker punch and vicious kick to the head, the people around the ring pounded their feet in mounting glee.

"There he is," Jagger said, nodding toward the ring.

I kept my muscles relaxed even though Jagger's pronouncement made me tense. There were two men in the ring. I wasn't sure which one he'd nodded to.

They were both giant. One was at least as tall as Jagger's six foot six, the other slightly shorter. The taller one had thicker muscles and a build like a leggerock, even though I think he was fully human. The shorter was rangier, faster, but had already taken too much of a beating. They were both bloodied, sweaty, and bruised. Over the music, I could hear the smack of bare knuckles against unprotected flesh.

They were completely bare except for loose pants. The muscles on their chests and abdomens reminded me of the muscles on the Spartan warriors who dealt in battle and bloodshed from birth on. The taller fighter jabbed the shorter under his jaw, and the shorter's head snapped back. Taking advantage, the taller one viciously slammed a fist to his head. The shorter fell to his knees and swayed unsteadily. I recognized the fogged look in his eyes. He was struggling to come back—to crawl back to lucidity and finish the fight.

The mob surrounding the mat screamed and pounded their feet. You could tell they'd come for blood, and they were about to get what they desired. You could smell it in the air.

"Which one?" I asked as we shoved our way across the room, closer to the ring.

I studied the two men dispassionately. The taller one was thrusting his arms in the air, gloating, revving up the mob. The shorter one was still foggy-headed and swaying on his knees. I wasn't sure which Jagger had motioned to. I didn't relish a braggart or someone who was unnecessarily cruel, but I also didn't want a weakling.

If I had a choice—which I didn't—I'd want a man who was strong, honest, humble, and loyal. One who never gave up, recognized right from wrong, and still had more than just a sliver of good in his heart. I'd want a man who would stand next to me even when all the odds were stacked against us. Of course, that's not the type of man you'd find in the Night Den—or really anywhere in this life.

Besides, all I needed was a ticket into the game, and the man who came with it didn't matter. Either of these fighters would be fine.

"Him," Jagger said, directing his gaze at the fight.

At that moment, the man on his knees surged upward in a lightning-quick leap. He slammed his fist into the taller man's throat.

The mob rushed forward, screaming with glee.

The shorter man launched into the air, snapped his leg, and kicked the taller man across the mat.

The taller slammed to the floor. He clutched his throat.

Then the shorter was on top of him. In one quick strike, the taller man was knocked unconscious.

The shorter man thrust his arm into the air, and the mob screamed with delight.

"That could work," I said, impressed even though I didn't want to be. The shorter one had taken a beating and he'd still managed to pull out a win. "I can work with a fighter."

Jagger's plan for winning the game was brilliant in its simplicity. As you know, every 100 years, the conjurer families come together and the eldest child from each family competes for the crown. However, there is a caveat written into the rules.

Thousands of years ago, the conjuring families realized the games were killing too many of their precious heirs. Some games went through four, five, a dozen conjurers before a winner was crowned. So the families decided an eldest child could "select" a paladin to enter the games for them. This paladin was a surrogate for the heir. They were blood for blood. Life for life. If the paladin died, no big deal: the heir was still alive. If the paladin won, then the heir received the crown.

The only requirement was that the paladin had to be a first-degree sibling, which meant they shared fifty percent of their genes with the heir.

Back in the Middle Ages, it was common practice for the conjurers to keep harems specifically for birthing paladins. This practice fell out of favor. During the bloody revolutions of the eighteenth and nineteenth centuries, families fell and rose as quickly as the shifting tide. With heads rolling, power jumped lines and knocked through second and third cousins and distant heirs like dominoes. After the Machiavellian power grabs and mass assassinations, the principal conjurers stopped spreading their seed so widely.

Nowadays the heads of families only have children after their political marriages. They typically kill any "accident children" born outside the marital bed. No spouse wants their husband or wife's accident child to become the eldest and gain the fount of power after succession. They especially don't want what happened in Russia or France to happen again, with the accidents killing off the heirs and staging a coup. So anyway. That's why there haven't been any paladins for a couple hundred years.

But there *could* be a paladin.

There's the *potential* for a paladin.

Jagger had told me he'd been looking for a paladin for more than 300 years. And he'd finally found him.

Apparently, twenty-five years ago, Wolfgang Smith, the head of the Smith family, had a minor indiscretion. He had sex with a human woman. A pleasurer at the Night Den. Nine months later, a little accident was born. Apparently, Wolfgang knew about him and let him live.

Like I told you, when a conjurer and a human have a baby, the child is a null. A dud. A zero. They don't inherit any conjuring abilities. The paladins of the past had conjuring abilities because the heads made sure to have sex with other conjurers.

I guess Wolfgang's baby was a null. Sort of. Sometimes, if the human has other traits latent in their genes, the traits are turned on when combined with a conjurer's blood. So these kids can crop up with all sorts of interesting talents. Jagger said this accidental Smith had useful traits.

Looking at him then, thrusting a hand in the air, blood and sweat running down his chin, I'd have said his talent was brutal strength and tenacity.

Jagger claimed this Smith would do whatever he wanted. He'd made a bargain with him, and as I knew, once you made a bargain with a leggerock, you weren't getting out of it. I wondered what hold Jagger had on him.

Not that it mattered. The only thing that mattered was getting into the game. Having this man accepted as a paladin. Winning the game. Then stealing the crown before the conjurers could set it on Darin Smith's head.

I'd be heading into the game with him.

Every player gets a body—or what most people call a servant/page/valet—to help them with all their needs during the game. You patch them up, you help them dress, you cook their meals and taste them for poison, you make their bed, clean their weapons—you do whatever they want or need—and you try your best to keep them alive. A body is the only other person who isn't immediate family that can be admitted to the games.

That was me. I'd be this Smith's body.

Sometimes bodies died or went missing. Jagger had warned me about that. I'd be careful. All I had to do was make sure this Smith made it to the end. And then I'd do what I did best and steal the crown right before the conjurers' eyes.

You're wondering if they'd recognize me.

No. They wouldn't.

No one ever does.

Every time I die, I look the same but completely and entirely different.

I felt like once, there was someone who could recognize me after I died, but that was more like wishful thinking than reality.

So anyway. Here we were.

If I succeeded . . . I was free of Jagger.

If I failed . . .

I didn't want to fail.

And if this bloodied, sweaty fighter could get me into the game, then I was all for it.

Jagger gripped my elbow in his clawed hand and tugged me through the screaming mob. People parted around us, shoved aside by his bulk. Anyone who had qualms quickly lost them when they saw who'd pushed them.

We neared the ring, and I could feel the heat of the fight and smell the copper tinge of blood and the bite of sweat. My ears were ringing from the jubilant roar and the stomping feet as the man grinned at the mob around him.

I could do this. I could see him winning the games.

But then Jagger was tugging me past the ring.

"But . . ." I nodded toward the fighter. "Isn't he our man?"

Jagger flicked his eyes over the ring and then curled his lip dismissively. "The human? No."

He drew me forward, deeper into the shadows lining the edge of the den.

The darkness was thicker here, the red lights weakly pulsing. This wasn't the raucous celebration found at the fighter's ring, it wasn't the sensual pleasure flooding the dance floor, and it wasn't the happy gluttony filling the bar tables.

The haze thickened, blanketing us in an opaque, red-tinged mist. The sweet, tart smell gathered around me, filling the air with the dizzying, cloying scent of cranberries and allspice.

"There," Jagger said in a self-satisfied purr. "There is our paladin."

8

I stared at the man, not sure if I'd heard Jagger right. He couldn't have meant this man.

This man? Him?

Him?

It wasn't possible.

If I went into the conjurers' game with this man, the both of us would be dead within the first day. No, within minutes. Seconds.

I checked again. Looked between Jagger and where his gaze pointed. But sure enough, he was looking exactly where I thought.

"Him?" I asked, my voice hinting at my dismay.

Jagger's mouth twisted into a delighted smile. "Yes. I told you that you'd love him."

"But he isn't . . . I can't—"

Jagger's grip tightened on my arm, his nails pressing into my flesh. "Don't say *can't* to me, Mari."

I remembered myself. Tucked away my dismay. Then studied the man we approached.

The red mist was thick in the Night Den, but it was even thicker around him, as if it loved him. Tendrils caressed his face and his arms, moving about him in a sensuous wave. The mist seemed to muffle the sound, and as we stepped closer, the noise settled into a muted whisper that sounded almost like ocean waves crashing in a conch shell.

It was no wonder I hadn't seen him the first time Jagger pointed him out, instead focusing on the fighters. This man was cloaked in mist and shadow. He was in a muted fog, hazy and shrouded.

My head was fuzzy, and the concrete floor felt as if it was sliding and swaying under my feet.

There wasn't any illusion here. Not many people in the Night Den were using illusion. Sure, there were small illusions here or there. Sparkling silver wings on a naked back. A unicorn horn. Purple skin. Nothing excessive though. Nothing dangerous.

In this corner of the den, though, there weren't any illusions at all. There wouldn't be. The air was thick with the cranberry and allspice smell. My head and throat were thick with it. I finally realized what the perfume was.

"He's an addict," I said, unable to stop the words. "Your paladin is a solange addict."

Jagger showed me his sharp teeth. "You know I love addicts. They'll do anything for the right price. Anything, Mari. Even kill. Even die. Yes?"

Oh.

Super.

Wonderful.

Jagger had partnered me with a solange devotee. How was I going to stay alive? How was I going to keep him alive? How was I going to make sure he won the games? There was no way.

"What's his trait?" I asked, suddenly worried I'd be seeing my ninth death before the week was out.

"Strength. He's as strong as a leggerock. He lifted a boulder in Central Park and tossed it a dozen yards just to prove he could. He'll do, Mari. He'll do."

Jagger always equated strength with skill. Unfortunately, no matter how strong someone was, they could still be taken down by cunning, talent, or a bullet. Swinging fists and throwing rocks wasn't going to do much in a game of conjuring.

Before the man noticed our approach, I took one last long look.

He was sprawled on a low red velvet couch. His arms were splayed, his legs hung over the side, and his head rested in the lap of a beautiful, long-haired, topless woman. He wore a black T-shirt, and it had ridden up his stomach, displaying the thin line of his abdomen and the jutting of his hip bones. His jeans were slung low, and his feet were bare.

There was at least three days' worth of dark scruff on his jaw, and I wasn't sure he'd actually moved from the couch in the entirety of the three days it had taken that beard to grow. Solange addicts could go for weeks without drinking, eating, or sleeping, not realizing the passage of time until they passed out from sleep deprivation or up and died from dehydration or starvation.

The topless woman's fingers drifted through the man's glossy black hair, playing with the ends that fell over his forehead and down his neck. His head lolled to the side and then fell back, his neck stretched out, exposed and inviting her kiss. His eyes were open, staring at the mist-shrouded ceiling, a look of placid ecstasy on his face.

There was a sensual curve to his lips—a just-kissed wetness. His eyelashes fluttered in the red light, and his skin glowed under the haze. He was lost in the solange. Completely, utterly lost.

My stomach twisted at the sight of his unfocused gaze. My heart pounded painfully against my chest, and my lungs seized as if I was locked underwater, drowning and scared, alone, and I hated him. I hated him on sight.

I dug my fingernails into my palms, piercing the skin. How dare he be a solange addict? How dare he? I wanted to stalk to the couch, yank him off the woman's lap, and shake him out of his bliss-filled stupor.

Didn't he realize he was putting us both at risk?

Didn't he realize that by running away from illusions, he was also running from reality?

Didn't he understand—?

No.

Wait.

Of course he didn't understand. Of course he didn't realize. He was just one of Jagger's shills. Another pawn. A desperate man willing to make a bargain and give up . . . whatever he loved the most for what he thought he loved more.

I uncurled my fingers and let out a calming breath. My heart settled, and my chest unclenched.

Then the man looked my way. His head dropped to the side, his cheek pressed to the woman's bare thigh, and he lifted his eyes toward me.

I stopped walking and held my breath.

Jagger and I were only a few feet away. We were deep in the mist that cloaked this part of the den. A few red velvet chairs and a low wooden table separated us from the man. The table held silver thimbles of solange. Golden eyedroppers. Candles to warm the drug. Melted wax dripping over the wood. A few glasses of what looked like sherry or brandy, and a plate of cheese and plump purple grapes that hadn't been touched.

I wasn't sure the man had seen me. His eyes were unfocused, his black pupils so large they nearly swallowed his irises. Just like anyone who uses solange, his eyes were no longer their original color (brown? Green?). Instead they were a deep navy blue, with swirling silver and cerulean striations. Supposedly, this deep blue was the color of the cosmos at creation.

His eyes caught mine and he stared at me—or rather, he looked through me, his gaze placid, unfocused. I shivered. I couldn't tell if he was looking at me or at something or someone else.

That's the thing with people who take solange. You never know what they see.

I understand why people use it. I truly do. It all started around 2500 BC when people were tired of all the illusions. One day, a group of priests discovered a plant whose leaves, when dried and prepared in a specific manner, could banish all illusions.

When a person ingests solange—either by drinking or dropping it into their eyes—they can't be fooled by a conjurer's illusions anymore. As long as they're under the effects of solange, all illusions take on the hint of unreality; the false illusions can't influence them in any way. Conjurers no longer have any control over them.

Unfortunately, with the good comes the bad. Solange is highly addictive. It also replaces illusions with . . . something else. It's not reality. You don't see the physical world as it truly is. You don't see the truth. It's not . . . Well, I don't know what it is, since I've never taken solange. It's an altered reality, a dreamlike mist, that leaves users with such a deep sense of ecstasy that they don't care whether they live or die. All they care about is the next dose of solange.

Almost everyone who takes it is a human with enough conjurer in their blood to know they're surrounded by illusion but unable to do anything about it. They take solange to hide. Or to escape. To save themselves. To save someone else. To find a way out of responsibility or to get away from the fear that plagues them.

Once in a while, you'll find an addict who took it to get away from a conjurer who had been using or abusing them. They use solange to escape. But you'll never find anyone who escaped from solange. Once you take the first dose, you'll take it until you die.

And this man? My paladin? For some reason, he'd chosen to travel the solange road.

Full-blooded conjurers rarely take it. First, it doesn't work as well for them. Doesn't halt illusions, but it does mute their own powers and weaken their abilities. Which is unacceptable to them. The high isn't worth the price.

But this half-Smith null? He'd found something he needed in the solange.

I studied him and his half-lidded gaze. He wasn't beautiful. He wasn't pretty. He looked like a Smith. A rough-hewn, hard-edged man. Even lying in that half-stupor, he was still a Smith.

A nose that was too long. Cheeks that were too sharp. A jaw that was too hard. Eyes with long, feathering lashes, and a wide mouth that on a Smith always curled into cruelty. A big body meant for starting wars. Calloused hands meant for holding a sword. A sharp gaze meant for controlling armies . . . except it wasn't a sharp gaze, was it?

I held his eye, and the strangest feeling came over me. I felt as if he was slowly stroking his hand over my jaw, feathering his fingertips over my lips, sighing as he pressed his mouth to mine. I could practically taste the sweetness of him, the cranberry and allspice flavor, the need and the ecstasy.

He was leaving a trail of fire over my skin.

I could feel his hands tugging my hips closer, holding me against the heat of him. I could feel the vibration of his need; hear the rumble of his voice as he moaned into my mouth.

And then—

I blinked.

And the corner of the man's mouth tilted up in a lazy, half-asleep, drunken smile.

The heat disappeared and was replaced with cold fury.

Strength? Yeah, right. This man's trait wasn't strength. He was a hedonist who played with people's thoughts and feelings. No doubt about it. His latent trait was mental, not physical.

I was taking a sharp step forward, ready to tell him if he ever pulled something like that again, he'd be sorry, when Jagger spoke.

"I was hoping you'd be ready to receive us. Did we not have a bargain?"

The man turned his fuzzy gaze to Jagger. He seemed confused for a moment, as if he couldn't understand who Jagger was or why he was speaking. His eyes looked like a broken kaleidoscope. The topless, long-haired woman leaned down and whispered in his ear.

At her words, the man's eyes focused slightly, and he slowly nodded. Instead of sitting, he settled back onto her thighs and gave Jagger a lopsided smile. "Care to join us?"

His voice wasn't what I expected. It was smoother, softer, like a summer thunderstorm that smelled of wet grass and clover and electricity.

The man gestured to the table—the solange and the food and drink.

I looked to Jagger. He nodded. We sat in the velvet chairs across from the half-Smith and the woman.

The mist had thickened even more, so it was practically a wall surrounding us. There were no noises, no smells, not even a rustle of air. We were closed off from the rest of the den, isolated and encased in a private world.

The mist wasn't an illusion like the Clarks had created. I didn't know what it was.

Jagger didn't seem concerned. Instead he leaned forward and placed his elbows on his knees, steepling his thick-knuckled fingers under his chin. Human chairs were always too small for his frame, but these were larger, made to accommodate all sorts.

"The game begins tonight at midnight," Jagger said, his eyes narrowing on the inebriated state of the man.

It would be sunrise soon. That gave us about eighteen hours to prepare. I wondered if this Smith could pull himself out of the depths of solange in time to convince his relatives he could be their paladin.

The man was already sinking back into his unfocused stupor. "Yes. Fine. I'll be there."

His words slurred together as if he was slipping back into a dream.

Jagger didn't seem to notice. "This is your body. She'll be with you at all times. You will listen to her. You will do what she says as if it is an order from me. Understood?"

The man didn't seem to hear him. Instead he was staring at a spot over my shoulder.

"Understood?" Jagger growled again. I'd never seen him have to repeat himself. It was a night of surprises.

The woman leaned down again and whispered in his ear. He reached up and absently stroked a hand over her naked breast. I clenched my teeth and glared at him. When I did, he turned his head and stared at me, eyes unfocused.

"Who?" he asked, still looking at me.

"Your body," Jagger said.

"Who is she?" the man asked, gesturing at me.

"The woman I told you about. Your body."

"That's not her." The man yawned and dropped his hand from the topless woman's breast. He closed his eyes as if he was going to take a nap.

Jagger narrowed his gray-black eyes on the man, and his joints bulged. I knew from experience that he was seriously considering snapping the man's neck, paladin or not. The rippling, bulging of his joints under his gray skin was always the physical evidence of a killing rage. Sometimes Roumelade could calm him down enough to avoid bloodshed. Sometimes not.

I really didn't want to have to witness Jagger tearing this man's head off his shoulders. An hour or two later, he'd be pissed he'd killed his first chance at winning the games in centuries, and he'd blame me for the lapse.

So I had to intervene.

Quickly.

"Excuse me," I said.

My voice always shocks people. That's one thing that doesn't change with my death. It's husky, low, and melodic. It comes out like an incantation that enchants people with every word. Roumelade claims it's because I'm part siren and my ancestors lured sailors to their deaths with the beauty of their song. Jagger doesn't ever say anything about my voice at all.

When I spoke, the man's eyes flew open and he stared at me, his cosmic eyes suddenly lucid and focused.

I leaned forward. "I am the one who will be going with you. You don't have to like it. You're stuck with me, and unfortunately, I'm stuck with you. You made a bargain, and that's that. Do we understand each other?"

The man couldn't seem to take his eyes off me. His pulse was pounding at his throat, and the silver striations in his eyes pulsed and shifted like lightning flashing through a navy sky.

Then, in a sudden move that I didn't anticipate or expect, he lunged off the woman's lap, fell across the table, and grabbed my left wrist. His touch was burning hot as he roughly turned my hand over.

Jagger had a knife to the man's throat before he'd even stopped moving.

Looked like we weren't playing it straight after all.

I raised an eyebrow, and Jagger showed me his teeth as he pressed the knife deep enough for a line of red to bloom on the man's throat.

The half-Smith didn't seem to notice the knife. Instead he was staring at the single black tattooed line on the inside of my wrist.

"You died," he said, still staring at the tattoo. He swallowed, and the movement caused the line of blood to swell. When he finally looked up at me, I almost jerked away. There was so much rage in his eyes that I was suddenly frightened. Of him. Of this place.

His eyes were a violent thunderstorm full of rage and anger, and the mist pressed in around us.

The man turned his head to Jagger, either uncaring or still not noticing the blade at his throat. "You didn't tell me she died. You didn't mention she was on her eighth life."

Jagger made a noise—half-laugh, half-grunt. "What does it matter?"

"It matters," the woman on the couch said, slowly drawing out the words like Jagger was dense, "because if she dies twice more, Finn will be stuck without a body in the games. If she's so careless as to die right before the game, what's to stop her from dying during them? Before, she had three lives. Now she has two. He doesn't want her. He can't win with her. She's a liability. Give him someone else."

The woman gave me a dismissive glance as if it was already decided that I was *out*.

Jagger bared his teeth in a pure leggerock threat. "You are not bargaining here. Unless you'd like to enter one of your own."

"Cora," Finn said.

At her name, the woman looked away. Then, after a moment, she bent down to the table, swept aside the items the man had spilled, and started to prepare another dose of solange, pointedly ignoring us all.

The half-Smith—Finn, I guess his name was—still held my wrist. There'd be a bruise from where he gripped me. I supposed Jagger was right: his trait must've been strength as well. I guess he didn't realize how strong he was, or he didn't care.

He was still staring at me, but the rage was gone. It'd been replaced by that vacant, half-glazed solange look I was familiar with. He'd retreated to some private dreamland the rest of us weren't invited to.

I took a deep breath. Tried to tug my wrist free. His grip was too tight.

I stood.

"Let go," I said.

Jagger scoffed and took his knife from Finn's throat.

I could get out of shackles, handcuffs, inescapable locks, yet I couldn't manage to get one man to let go of my wrist. Jagger grinned at me, sensing I was about to flip Finn over my shoulder and show him I meant it when I told him to let go.

I gave him one more chance. "Let go."

A dreamy smile filled Finn's face.

I was wrong before. I said he wasn't beautiful. And he wasn't. But he *was* beautiful when he smiled. Annoyingly beautiful.

I tucked my shoulder, twisted my arm to throw him off-balance, and flipped him over my shoulder. As he fell, I yanked my wrist free. Finn hit the concrete floor with a hard crack. The breath whooshed out of him. I'd managed to avoid hitting the table and chairs. That was impressive, considering how big he was.

He lay sprawled on the ground, staring blearily up at the ceiling. I walked close to where he lay and squatted down so he could look into my eyes.

"When I say let go, you let go."

"Rather not," he mumbled, staring drunkenly at the ceiling.

I shook my head. He was falling back into the stupor he'd been in when we'd first arrived. His eyes were glassy and unfocused. At the couch, the woman almost had another dose ready for him. She was heating a silver thimble over a candle, and the tart cranberry and allspice smell penetrated the air.

I leaned close to Finn and said in a low voice, "Get yourself cleaned up. We're in this together. I'll do whatever it takes to win this game. Do you understand? Whatever it takes."

He smiled blearily. "You're not as nice as I thought you'd be."

Why in the world would he think I'd be nice? I was one of Jagger's "creatures." None of us were supposed to be nice.

I narrowed my eyes at him. "By the way, if you ever use any thought or emotion manipulation on me, there will be consequences."

He just blinked at me. I wasn't entirely certain he'd heard me.

"Mari, are you done?" Jagger asked.

Finn smiled. "Hmm. Mari." He sounded like he was tasting my name and liked the flavor.

"I'm ready." I gave Finn one final hard stare.

And left him there.

Jagger stood and said to the woman more than Finn, "We'll be waiting at Hell Gate. Be there at dark."

He didn't need to tell Finn not to be late. The threat hung in the air.

As we left, the mist closed around us, but not before I saw the woman helping Finn up, and Finn reaching for another dose of solange. He watched me, his eyes full of lightning, as he tipped back the silver thimble and swallowed the destroyer of illusions.

9

THE ALL-SEEING EYE ON THE NIGHT DEN'S DOOR BLINKED AS THE DOOR SLID shut. The metal made a soft *humph* as a tendril of wind curled around the doorframe and blew along the concrete floor.

The wind wandered around the den, tickling ankles, sweeping hems of dresses, catching rides on undulations of laughter and the rockslides of shouted curses, until it splashed into a thick wall of mist.

Ahh. Mist. The wind loved mist—there were all sorts of interesting things to be found in its foggy depths.

It tumbled down the cold, red vapor until it found a thin slice, a small opening, near the ground—like a curtain, almost, but not quite brushing the floor. The wind gleefully slipped under it and found a small, mist-shrouded room—one with soft velvet couches and a table full of drinks and aromas that it could fan and carry around for days, teasing people's senses and making them look about, wondering where that memory-inducing smell had come from.

Now *that* was a fun joke. The wind could play that one for days.

It collected the cranberry and allspice perfume, coating itself in it, and then, satisfied, it brushed through the glossy, night-dark hair of one of the two people sitting on the couch. The wind rustled the man's dark hair, letting it tickle the back of his neck as if someone had blown a warm breath across his skin.

The black-haired man rubbed the back of his neck, his skin flushing red.

Both he and the woman with him stared at the opaque mist, the man with a shattered-eyes sort of look, and the woman with an angry curl to her mouth.

"She doesn't like you," the woman said, and although the wind had been about to leave, it decided to stay and swirl around the table legs, rub along the smooth velvet cushions, for a little while longer.

The man seemed unconcerned. He held a silver thimble in his hand, rolling it between his fingers. The corner of his mouth lifted in a small smile as he stared at the mist, toward the door with the golden eye.

"No, she doesn't," he finally said. He sounded happy about this.

"And she doesn't care about you." The woman's hands were clenched, her back rigid.

The man's smile grew. "No. Not even a little bit."

At his words, the woman stood and paced the length of the room. Her stride was quick and cutting. She jerked back around, and the wind caught her hair and lifted it.

"Then why," she bit out, "are you smiling?"

The man blinked at her. He tilted his head as if he couldn't understand the woman's anger. As if the effort of anger, frustration—anything but the vacancy of bliss—was beyond him. But then, slowly, his gaze sharpened and his smile turned predatory. Deadly.

"Because, Cora," he purred, "if she doesn't like me or care about me, then it makes what I have to do that much easier."

"Finn—"

He shook his head, one sharp jerk, and she cut herself off. Dropped her eyes and looked at the floor. Her shoulders drooped.

"You don't have to do this," she whispered. It was quiet, but the wind carried the words to the man's ears.

Slowly, he set the silver thimble on the table. The metal made a firm, resolved crack as it hit the wood.

"I do—"

"But you could die!"

"Then let me die," the man cut in viciously. "Haven't we already said goodbye? *That* nearly killed me. What else is there? Let me die if that's what it takes. You know this is the only way. You *know*."

There were tears in the woman's eyes, but she didn't blink. She refused to let them fall. Finally, she nodded.

The man's jaw clenched. He held his right hand in a fist as if he were gripping the woman's hand.

They both stared at the mist—one with tears in her eyes, the other with a resolute, determined set to his hard face.

The wind waited for them to say more. But after minutes of silence, it sighed, gathered a bit more cranberry and allspice scent, and then slipped out of the Night Den.

10

Jagger and I were almost back to Hell Gate before I broached the subject weighing on my mind.

There were no stars to be found. Even on the darkest night in the darkest hour, the only heavenly bodies that could be seen from Hell Gate were Jupiter, Venus, or Mars, battling it out in the sky. Otherwise the dusky city lights shone too bright, throwing a gray blanket over the heavens.

It had never bothered me before—it was what I'd always known—but suddenly, I wondered what it'd be like to live somewhere where the stars were more than a story.

Once, Justice, who has a pinch of conjurer in his blood, drew a starry illusion for me on the ceiling of the sky. We sprawled on our backs, on the scratchy tar paper roof of Hell Gate, staring at those false stars for hours, right until the sun came up.

But that was years ago. Justice and I were still little kids then. I had seven lives left, and he still had three. Now he doesn't have any, and I've only got two. I'd reminisce about how innocent we used to be, but I can't.

I was eight. Justice was eleven. Right after that night, Jagger sent Justice out to butcher a Growling that owed him a life debt, and he had me lockpick him into the Clarks' library. When I didn't lockpick quickly enough for his pleasure, he chained me to a wall for three days, telling me to use the time to contemplate the merits of speed.

Still, when I looked over the iron fence of Hell Gate at the old limestone walls coated in night-gray, I felt a wave of nostalgia for a night long ago, looking at stars that didn't really exist.

It was still dark—the sun wouldn't rise for another half hour. Hell Gate was always at its best in the dark.

It was built in 1815, well north of the downtown bustle of the time. It clung to the East River's edge, a hulking limestone monolith, five stories tall, with iron bars over the windows and iron gates barring the entrance. In the cornerstone, the original stonemason had chiseled out the words "Hell Gate—Home for Lost Souls—MDCCCXV."

Local history claims the Home for Lost Souls was a charity orphanage from 1815 until 1945, when it was bought by a real estate investor. Local history was wrong. Hell Gate has always been home to Jagger and those who live on the other side of reality.

It was the only home I'd ever known, and we were nearly inside the gates.

"Jagger," I broached, keeping my voice low, "how did Finn . . .?" I stumbled over his name, not sure if that was really what he was called. "How did he know I'm a nine?"

It'd been bothering me since he'd grabbed my wrist and flipped it over to stare at the tattoo. There was so much rage in his eyes.

"You died," he'd said, a violent storm brewing. *You died.*

Jagger shrugged, uncaring. He didn't look at me. Instead he stared at the bulbous-eyed grotesque that hunched over the eastern roofline. It was a misshapen stone dog, with long saber teeth, claws, and membranous wings.

There were two stone grotesques at Hell Gate. They hunched on the edge of the roof and snarled silently at all who entered. They were Jagger's guard dogs, although I'd never seen them called to life.

"When we made our bargain, I told him one of my nines would be his body. That he would follow your commands as if they were mine."

"Yes," I said, frustrated, "but how could he have known I died? We'd never met. He didn't know what I looked like—"

"Don't assume. Finn Alterra is a lifelong resident of The Night Den. Many secrets pass through those walls. I imagine he knew your name, your image, your history, within an hour of making our bargain."

I shook my head. That didn't account for the rage in his eyes. "He was enraged. I don't trust him."

Jagger laughed, a rockslide rumble. "My Mari. You don't trust anyone."

"Yes. But I especially don't trust him. What do you even know about him?"

Jagger held his palm out toward the iron spikes of Hell Gate, and the gates swung open, creaking noisily. We stepped onto the worn slate stones of the courtyard, and the gate noisily shut behind us.

"What's there to know? His mother was a human pleasurer. He was raised in the den. They kept his identity hidden. Until I found it." Jagger smiled, a vicious little light in his gray-black eyes. He enjoyed knowing things about people that no one else knew. "Blood doesn't lie."

Ah. I see.

Jagger can trace people's ancestry through their blood. Somehow, he must've gotten a taste of Finn's blood. Once he'd tasted it, he would've done anything to control him.

"Beyond that, he's the Smith's son. As a youth, he studied the classics. Philosophy. Languages. Military tactics. Typical Smith education. He wanted to impress his father. Hoped to be accepted into their hallowed halls. Instead, when he approached his father, he got a sword to the gut. Skewered him." Jagger chuckled at the brutality of a father gutting a son. "After that, he slunk back to the Night Den. Tangled with the pleasurers. Dove headfirst into the delights of solange. That was ten years ago. He managed to walk the razor's edge for a decade, but now . . ." Jagger shrugged and gave me a sly look. "Now he's fallen off the edge and is in free fall."

Free fall. I shivered at the words.

That was the term used when a solange addict was at the end of the road. They'd ingested so much that their tolerance was sky-high. They were Icarus; they'd soared too close to the sun and their wax wings were melting. The addicts had to keep increasing their doses and increasing them, flying with all their might, until finally, their minds combusted in a brilliant supernova.

The free fall was the plummeting headlong dive before the inevitable end.

"And what did you promise him?" I asked.

Jagger paused, his hand on the brass handle of the front door. He tsked. "Mari. Mari. You know better than to ask me what I've promised another man."

Of course I did. You never asked what Jagger had promised someone in a silent bargain.

"But what did *he* promise *you*?" I asked, tension gathered between my shoulder blades. The itch was still there.

Jagger gave me a pleased look. "He promised to win the crown of illusions or die trying. What else?"

I let out a slow breath and shook my head. Something wasn't right.

"The man who killed me. He used a bow of illusion. An arrow of blue fire and ice. Don't the Smiths favor medieval bows?"

My heart was thudding in my chest. Could it have been him? When he said "you died" with so much rage, was he angry because he was the one who killed me, and he'd expected me to stay dead?

Jagger gave a dusty laugh as he shoved open the front door. "They do. But our solange addict, he can't conjure a dust mote. Don't worry, Mari. He wasn't your killer. It was someone else."

I narrowed my eyes and stepped into Hell Gate.

Maybe. Or maybe, if Finn hadn't pulled back the bowstring, he'd been the urging behind the kill shot.

Someone had betrayed me last night. I'd lost the golden key to the Clarks. I'd died on Wards Island. And now I was entering the game with a solange addict that I didn't—*couldn't*—trust.

"Why didn't the Smith kill Finn? Why just gut him?"

Jagger kicked the front door shut. The weak light in the entryway glinted off his gray skin. Done with my questions, he pinned me with a cruel stare and asked, "Why kill someone when you can use them?"

That shut me up.

Except, what exactly was Finn being used for, and who was using him besides the Smith and Jagger?

11

————

WE ALL GATHERED IN THE WARMTH OF THE SLATE-FLOORED KITCHEN. ME, Griff, Roumelade, and Justice.

We sat at the thick oak table—a long, simple rectangle, with trestle legs and mismatched chairs. The table was older than Hell Gate and had been lovingly marred by knives and fists and mallets and singed by a few small fires.

Fifteen years ago, I'd lain under that table with Griff and Justice while Roumelade hummed a watery tune and stirred her chicken saffron stew on the Victorian-era cast-iron range. While the cook fire had crackled and orange shadows danced over the stone floor and tiled walls, we'd carved our initials on the underside of the trestle—the side farthest from Jagger's seat at the head of the table.

"ML," "GG," and "JM." That was us. Mari Locke, Griff Gilliam, and Justice Marr.

We were the only kids in Hell Gate. Even though it was supposedly once an orphanage, I think we were the only kids who'd *ever* lived in Hell Gate.

First there was Justice, then there was me, then came Griff. Sure, Jagger had nines before us, but they were all conscripted when they were adults.

Once, I asked Roumelade if it was because Jagger wanted to give her some kids to mother. Roumelade laughed and said Jagger didn't give gifts or care about wants. He'd made us nines as kids because he'd realized kids were easier to bend and shape and manipulate.

"Don't gift Jagger good qualities he doesn't have. That'll only boil up trouble," Roumelade always said. "See him as he is, Mari."

Which was her way of saying "don't go pretending darkness has light just because you want to see it there." You can't romanticize anything around Roumelade. She just doesn't allow it.

So when she plunked down a huge silver platter of crisp-skinned chicken, tiny, butter-glossed potatoes, and summer vegetables from her rooftop garden (slivers of sunny yellow summer squash, crescents of red and yellow bell peppers, and paper-thin cuts of sweet eggplant), I knew she wasn't going to romanticize my departure tonight either.

"So you're off to the games. You'll either end up naked-dead on my kitchen table or you'll win Jagger the crown. Or both. Hmm. Try not to land on my blueberry scones next time you die. Honestly, Mari." Roumelade shoved the platter of chicken toward me, gesturing with hot mitt-covered hands that I should serve myself.

"Don't say that," Griff said, staring morosely at the potatoes. "Mari's already on her eighth life. I don't see why she has to go to the games—"

Justice was leaning back in his chair, balancing it on two legs, quietly contemplating the range's fire, but when Griff spoke, he knocked his chair onto all four legs and scooted closer to me. He dropped his arm over my shoulders.

"She's going to the games because she's our lockpick. Who else could steal the crown from right under the conjurers' noses?" He grinned over at me, although the grin was dampened a bit by the deep shadows under his eyes and the worry lines on his forehead.

He looked tired tonight, his russet-brown hair messy, his gray eyes weary, his freckles standing out against too-pale skin. His shirt and jeans were wrinkled, and it looked like he'd come to the kitchen straight from an overnight and day-long job without going to bed. But still, he squeezed my arm, and the corner of his eyes crinkled with his grin.

"I appreciate the vote of confidence," I said, scooting closer when

Justice tugged my chair toward his. It felt good to be held this close by him. It felt normal, since there wasn't a week in my life that had gone by without my arm through his or his arm slung over my shoulder, tucking me against his side.

Justice, I think, had always had it harder than the rest of us. While I was slated to be a lockpick and Griff was a lurer, Justice had been made into something darker. He was the softest of us when we were kids, the one who cried when a moth burned itself to death in the ceiling light or stayed awake at night trying to catch mice to let them outside before they were caught in a trap and killed.

He used to tell me stories about how, someday, our parents would come and save us, even if they were dead and ghosts. They'd break Jagger's hold over us, and then we'd all go and live in a cabin together in the Catskills and have a vegetable garden and a picket fence—for some reason, the picket fence was important—and be a family. Sometimes we'd have a dog; sometimes it'd be two gray-furred kittens. But always, our parents would come, we'd be free, and there'd be a picket fence.

Justice stopped telling that story years ago. While I was valuable as a lockpick and Griff was . . . well, he was Griff . . . Justice wasn't so important to Jagger. He was just a weak, thin-blooded conjurer cast-off with a bit of illusion and a too-soft heart. So Jagger did his best to break Justice, and if the breaking killed him or his spirit, it didn't matter, because while Jagger didn't like killing something he could use, he didn't mind killing it if he couldn't use it.

So Justice had become Jagger's knife. Or, I guess you'd say, he'd become Jagger's killer.

Anyone who crosses Jagger eventually meets Justice. Or even anyone who doesn't cross him. Sometimes Jagger sends Justice out to assassinate people or beings, just to remind everyone in the city that he can. Deserving, undeserving, warranted, unwarranted—it doesn't matter, and Justice doesn't have a say anyway. I don't know how many people he's killed for Jagger. I suspect the number would make anyone sick, so I don't ask.

I still remember one autumn night, long after Justice stopped fighting Jagger, long after his first foray into death. He was about eleven years old, sitting cross-legged on the twin bed in his bedroom, just staring up at the ceiling light.

"What're you doing?" I'd asked.

He didn't take his eyes off the light. I heard it then—the noise of a moth banging against the glass lightbulb.

"Watching the struggle," he'd said, voice dead.

After a moment, the moth flailed one last time against the hot light and then it folded its wings and spiraled to the floor, like falling gray ash. Dead.

Justice's expression didn't falter. He didn't cry like he used to. He didn't even blink. He just stared at the dead moth on his bedroom floor.

"I'll get a tissue," I'd said, my heart pounding painfully in my chest.

"Don't bother." He'd walked past me on silent feet, out of his room, off on another of Jagger's assignments.

"Don't bother," he'd said. But I did. I folded the moth in a tissue and buried it under the grass in the park for the little boy who'd once cried for moths that died.

Now I leaned into his side as he grinned down at me.

"Of course," he said. "How can I not be confident? You're the best lockpick the world has seen in years."

"Save us from the flattery of friends," Roumelade said, taking her seat at the head of the table, opposite Jagger's empty seat. "If you want to know the truth, ask an enemy."

"I'd still rather you didn't go." Griff shuddered. "Even if this is the only chance to steal the crown. It's not a quick job. She'll be with *them* for weeks."

He was terrified of conjurers. They were the monster in his closet. The bogeyman under his bed.

"Anything can happen," he continued. "They could tear her mind apart. They could boil her in oil. Force her to live a thousand agonizing deaths. They could find out what she is and eat her soul—"

"That's folklore," I interrupted. "Conjurers don't eat souls."

Griff ignored me. "You could die your ninth death."

"And what if she does? So what? Is that such a terrible thing?" Justice took his arm from my shoulder and glared at Griff. "You weren't so worried when it was me."

Griff stared at Justice with his big, puppy-brown eyes. His lower lip trembled, and he looked down at his empty plate.

The thing is, Griff *was* worried about Justice. But he was even more worried about me because of what had happened to Justice after his ninth death. Justice had become . . . different. Colder. He wasn't exactly himself anymore. I mean, that was what happened. You lost yourself. You truly became Jagger's creature.

Griff was sensitive, and more than the rest of us, he'd seen Justice's final, wishful, hopeful light die. When he came back after that ninth time, his Justice light was snuffed out. It had scared Griff. Almost as much as conjurers scared him.

"It'll be all right," I said, reassuring Griff.

There wasn't any point in worrying about it. People worry too much about the things they can't change. I couldn't change the fact that I was a nine, but I could change how I went into the game.

"Justice, you go to the Night Den," I said.

"Yeah?" He gave me a sidelong look.

After tonight, I finally understood why he'd told me to stay away from the place.

I scooped a spoonful of vegetables onto his plate and then gave him a chicken thigh. "What do you know about Finn Alterra?"

Justice frowned and stared toward the fire, his eyes narrowing. "Not much," he finally said. "He keeps his nose clean. Never heard about any trouble. I've seen him around. He likes the pleasurers. A bit of an exhibitionist. The usual hedonistic type. Drinking. Partying. You know, enlightenment through excess—that kind of crap. I never paid much attention to him."

He gave me a sour look as if he was sorry for that oversight. But not paying attention in Justice terms meant he didn't see Finn as a threat or a target. He reserved that non-threat category for things like puppies, butterflies (although *not* death-axe butterflies), and spineless, worthless creatures that were too pathetic to bother with.

Hmm.

I passed the platter of chicken to Griff, having taken a chicken leg and as many of Roumelade's summer vegetables as I could. I was going to miss her cooking for the next two weeks. I didn't think about the fact that I'd miss it forever if the conjurers delivered me to a true death.

I frowned at Justice then said, "He's a solange addict. Jagger said he's in free fall."

Justice let out a whistle and raised his eyebrows at that. "He's sending you into the games with an addict in free fall?"

"A Smith," Roumelade said firmly. "He's sending her into the games with a Smith."

"Half-Smith," Griff said, taking a bite of his chicken. He loved Rou's chicken.

We all knew what was supposed to happen over the next two weeks. Jagger didn't trust anyone, just like me, but he trusted the power of fear and his absolute control over his creatures. The four of us in our cozy kitchen were the only people besides Jagger and Finn (and Cora, Finn's topless woman) who knew what we were about to do.

"You're going to have to be ruthless," Justice said, weighing me, deciding whether or not I could be as vicious as he would be under the same circumstances.

"I know," I said. "I'm going into the dragon's cave, planning to steal their treasure, and my paladin is a sloppy, drunk liability. Trust me, I know what I have to do."

"You'll kill him if it comes down to it?" Griff asked. "If that's what you have to do to get out of there?"

What Griff hadn't mentioned was that Jagger didn't care if I died in an effort to win this game. My life was a small thing in comparison to winning. I knew Jagger expected me to lose my life before I lost a chance at the crown.

But still, I lifted a shoulder. "Of course. I'll do what I have to do."

I took a bite of Rou's paper-thin eggplant. Somehow, she sliced it so thinly that when it cooked, it took on the flavor of caramelized air.

Justice cut his hand across the table, and Griff paused with his fork halfway to his mouth.

"Killing the fool is the easy part." Justice frowned at Griff. "What she has to do is keep him alive long enough to make it to the end of the game. To *win*. It's much easier to kill a fool than to keep him alive."

"And once we win?" Griff asked.

Justice shrugged. "Then the fool doesn't have any value anymore. Then you can kill him. I'm sure that's Jagger's plan. But until then, Mari has to use him. She has to use him to get close to the crown. To win."

"I don't know what this year's games are," I said. "I've studied the records of the games from the past two thousand years, but still . . . I don't know. I don't know what they're going to be, and I don't know how I'm going to get a sloppy, solange-drunk, half-Smith null to the end."

The Clarks recorded and collected records of the games. For the past ten years, Jagger had been sending me to break in and out of the conjuring families' archives to photograph the recorded histories of every game ever played. The records were spotty, contradictory, unbelievable, and probably more lie than truth, but they were all we had to go on. This morning, after we returned from the Night Den, I'd spent hours cramming centuries' worth of information into my head.

Even if I didn't know Jagger was going to send me into a game, it felt like I'd been preparing my whole life for this moment. I knew the conjurer families; I knew their prejudices and weaknesses; I knew history; I knew strategy; I knew how to unlock illusion. The only thing I didn't know was how to control Finn Alterra.

"It seems to me," Roumelade said, "that what you should be worrying about *more* is getting the Smith to the starting line. They have to accept him as paladin first. Otherwise"—she shrugged—"another hundred years pass. And so does Jagger's only opportunity. Just think, an end to the games. Just think."

"Just think, Jagger with the crown" went unsaid, but it was as if all of us heard it anyway.

Everyone was quiet for a bit, tucking the fire-roasted chicken and vegetables into hungry bellies. There was a last-meal somberness in the kitchen even with the cheery glow of the fire and the cozy orange light bouncing off the floral-painted white tiles. Still, the savory taste of herbs, vegetables, and chicken wasn't enough to banish the grim line on Justice's face. And even the sweet smell of sour cherry pie warming in the oven wasn't enough to wipe the worry from Griff's eyes.

Outside the kitchen, the maze-like halls of Hell Gate were full of pickpockets and slipshots, shills and shivs, figments and abominations—all mud and blood creatures who thrived in the dark and huddled under Jagger's cruel fist.

I could hear them through the thick plaster walls and over the soft hiss and crackle of the fire. When we left the kitchen, we'd have to watch our backs—there was no kindness or loyalty here. The only inhabitants of Hell Gate who had never tried to trick, maim, or kill me were the three people in the kitchen and Winnie.

Although, Winnie didn't have the heart to hurt any living creature, so she didn't really count. She was like Roumelade, birthed from tears and torment and pulled from thought into this world. I guess being the spirit of the executioner's tree (the one in southern Manhattan from way back in the seventeenth and eighteenth centuries) had soured her on the prospect of death.

Anyway, with dinner done, I scooted my chair back from the table. I was packed and ready to go. I had all the changes of clothes I thought I'd need. I had poisons. I had weapons that didn't look like weapons. I had my mind.

I was ready.

"Well, I guess I'll see you all in two weeks—"

"Wait," Griff said. He reached into his pocket and held out a small box. "For you."

I smiled and took the white box. The leather was warm from sitting in his pocket. It was about the right size for a ring.

I lifted the lid. I was right. There were two gold rings inside. They were braided metal, two threads twined together.

"They're callback rings," Griff said. "A matching pair. Whoever wears the other, you can call them back to you. When you put it on them, say their name and then 'whenever I call, you come.' And then, when you want them, say their name and then 'come back.' They'll appear right in front of you. They do the same with you." His cheeks turned pink. "They're my most valuable possession. I thought we could wear them, but then I wouldn't know when you were in trouble to call you. So . . . you can use them however you like. I just wanted to give you something that might help."

"Thank you. I'm sure they'll come in handy." I stood and moved around the table to give Griff a tight hug.

He wrapped his arms around me and squeezed. "Be careful, Mari."

Roumelade cleared her throat. "I have something for you too."

I turned to her. She held out two small diamond earrings on gold studs.

"I baked them. Solidified my tears." She smiled, her worn skin wrinkling.

Beyond baking scones and pastries, Roumelade also baked poisons. Both the natural and the unnatural kind.

"Wear them to the games. If you get into trouble, smash them. Or you don't have to be in trouble. You might just use them because you don't like someone." She gave me a twinkling smile.

Roumelade was motherly and sweet, but when she got like this, casually mentioning killing someone with her tears, she reminded me that sometimes she also could be as cold and cruel as Jagger.

Worn-out wishbone, twinkling, wrinkled mother, or tortured, once-beautiful water spirit—she was all of those and none. She was also what made my life and deaths livable. I could never judge her for her kindness or casual cruelty.

"Philoneas Ward will be there," she murmured, her twinkling smile still in place. It was then I realized this gift was her way of letting me quietly and easily kill the man who'd murdered my parents. "His wife too. Their son, Jacob. These two earrings have just enough tears for three deaths. Isn't that nice?"

I nodded and slipped them through the holes in my ears, fastening the gold studs into place. It seemed I'd be walking into the games wearing death.

Justice cleared his throat and stood, nodding his head toward the corner of the kitchen where the embers in the range glowed orange, and where the dirty pots and pans were piled in the old copper sink.

Roumelade sat back at the table and pretended to busy herself with drinking her iced tea. Griff sat with her and teased her, overly loudly, about how much he was looking forward to tasting the sour cherry pie.

I stepped into the heat and glow of the corner and wiped a bit of sweat sliding down my temple. It was summer in New York, hot and humid. The fire in the kitchen always felt hotter in the summer.

Justice's back was to the table, and when he looked down at me, the firelight moved over his face and a strained, desperate yearning flashed in his eyes for the millisecond it took for an ember to spark in the fire and then die. There. Gone.

He reached out and clasped my hands in his calloused ones. When he did, he pressed a slender knife into my right hand. It was the length of my palm, cold and hard. The hilt was matte-black and the blade narrow and sharp.

"It *never* misses," he said, his voice barely audible. "It's called Heart's Death. Use it only if you mean to kill. Through the heart, Mari. One hit."

I nodded, worried at the odd light in his eyes. "Are you all right?" I asked.

His hands loosened on mine, and he tilted his head in a slow nod. "You need to watch your back in there. Trust no one. Not even so-called allies or friends. It's always the friends who are the first to betray you. Don't trust Alterra . . . Smith. I don't have to tell you that." He reached up and brushed his hands over my cheeks. "Be smart, Mari."

"Always."

He nodded. Gave what looked like a painful swallow, his Adam's apple bobbing. "Betrayal comes when you least expect it. From the people you least expect. You have to be ruthless. Cunning. I wish . . ." He closed his eyes. His freckles stood out against the firelight, the copper highlights in his hair glowing in the warmth.

I reached up and brushed his hair back from his forehead. It'd been so long since I'd done so that he opened his eyes and looked at me in surprise.

"I know this," I said, reassuring him. "I know. You act like I didn't grow up here too."

He shook his head. "If you have to kill, don't hesitate."

I nodded. "I know."

"No matter who it is."

"I *know*."

He smiled at me then—his exasperated Justice smile from when we were kids and he would boss me around, telling me how it was. His eyes ran over my face, memorizing my new features.

"You're not going to tell me you love me again, are you?" I asked, wondering if that was what he was working himself up to.

"Maybe. If I did, would you kiss me goodbye?"

I slid the knife into my belt, and he dropped his hands from my cheeks. At the table, Roumelade and Griff were arguing about whether dandelions were supposed to be picked under the full moon or the new moon for dandelion wine.

"I'd rather you didn't love me," I whispered. I didn't know why, but I knew I'd never feel the same for him. I couldn't.

Justice lifted a shoulder. "I don't have much choice in my life, but I do still get to choose who I love. *That*, at least, can't be taken from me."

I nodded. I understood. More than practically anyone else in the world, I understood.

It was nearly time to leave Hell Gate. I took Justice's hand again. "Do you know who betrayed me last night? Someone told the Clarks where I'd be. A conjurer with an ice arrow of blue fire killed me."

Justice stared at me, his mind turning, thoughts churning. He knew more assassins, more killers, more snitches, than any of us. "I'll find out."

Those three words told me he'd find and then kill the betrayer.

"When this is all done," Justice said. "When the games are over, everything . . ." He paused, squeezing my hand. "Everything will be as it should be. Everything will be all right. Trust me?"

I smiled at him. "No."

He grinned back.

Then I stood on my tiptoes and pressed a kiss to his freckled cheek. He wrapped his arms around me and held me for a long breath.

When he stepped back, he was the cold, untouchable Justice again. And I was Mari Locke, Jagger's means to defeating the conjurers and controlling the world.

When I turned, Jagger was standing in the doorway of the kitchen.

His shoulders spanned the width of the entryway, and his gray skin wicked up all the light. He stared at me, a greedy, anticipatory gleam in his flat slate eyes. He wore the smile he always wore right before his clawed hands grasped something he greatly desired.

I stepped away from Justice. Walked past Roumelade and Griff.

Jagger bared his pointed teeth and rumbled, "Your paladin's here. It's time."

12

—————

The russet-haired, freckled, solemn man sat on the edge of Hell Gate's roof. The wind whipped around him, tugging him and pushing him, as if teasing a fatal plunge.

He ignored the gusts and stared at the lone man below, standing at the gates. It was dark. The sun had set, dipping beneath the Hudson, leaving a trail of fire behind.

The solemn man had a bird's-eye view of the black-haired man standing below.

"Standing" was perhaps a generous word. The man was actually wobbling, swaying, and stumbling. After a precarious tilt, he gripped the black iron bars of Hell Gate and hung on as if he was riding out a particularly tumultuous storm at sea.

The russet-haired, solemn man narrowed his eyes.

The wind knew he had the perfect shot. One quick movement and it'd all be over. It'd be easy. Quick.

The wind had seen this man perform the same effortless kill shot countless times. Except this time, it'd be obvious who had done it. It wouldn't be a secret.

The wind shoved a bit harder, and the man gripped the edge of the roof, scowling over at the stone grotesque. The misshapen dog also had his eyes on the lone man below.

"Finn," he growled, his mouth flattening. "I see you, Finn Alterra."

The wind knew the solemn man didn't hate many people. Really, he didn't hate anyone. He didn't have that sort of emotion left in him. It was easier to go through life dispassionate about everything and everyone.

But the black-haired man below?

He could hate him.

The wind had heard the solemn man's mutterings, carried down the five stories to the sidewalk. They'd lured it up to hear more.

"Stumbling, idiotic, solange-addled fool. He'll get Mari killed," he said, his voice hinting at anguish. "He'll put her in danger. Hurt her. *Worse.*"

The wind hadn't heard the solemn man so riled in a long time. Years. It licked around the knife he gripped.

When the man felt the hot lick of the breeze, he loosened his grip. He stretched his hand, and blood flushed back into his white knuckles.

He didn't look over when a small, dark-eyed woman slipped next to him and perched on the stone ledge. She peered down at the black-haired man at the gates and raised her eyebrows at his stumbling near-fall. Then she shrugged and kicked her legs over the side of the building. She swung them back and forth and stared happily at the gloaming. It was humid still, and the water vapor made the city lights waver and mist, like spirits lifting to the sky.

"Did you give her the knife?" the woman finally asked. She had a high, sweet voice that matched her petite frame, short hair, and innocent, heart-shaped face.

"What do you know about it?" the solemn one asked, finally taking his eyes off the swaying man at the gate.

The woman shrugged. "I know you took it out of your vault. I saw you."

"Following me, Winnie?" he asked, a dangerous note in his voice. "That could get you in trouble."

She fluttered her eyelashes at him. "Course I'm following you."

He scoffed, then frowned and dropped his chin to his fist.

She leaned closer and asked, "You think she'll be able to use it? If the time comes?"

He didn't respond.

The wind was growing, gusting and blowing around them. Out on the dark surface of the East River, waves were cresting and breaking. The wind held the scents of concrete and steam, river and exhaust, but also the memory of cranberry and allspice.

The man wrinkled his nose and let out a long sigh.

"She's never killed anyone," the woman said. "I'm not sure she'll be able to do it."

The man cut his gaze toward her. "How do you know?"

The woman shrugged. The wind usually stayed away from her. Years and years and years ago, it had swept through the leaves of her tree and rattled her bare branches and carried the wails and tears, but . . . it didn't bother with her anymore.

"That she's never killed anyone?" the woman asked.

The russet-haired, solemn man nodded.

"Well . . . I can see it. A person. They have a line inside them. It's like a silver slash. They cross it, they do murder, then they can't ever go back to the other side of that line. They aren't the same person anymore. They're a different person when they cross over that line. They can't ever go back to who they were. What they were. They're two people that don't ever meet. Once they do murder, that person on the original side of the silver line is dead. She's not dead yet."

"Ahh. Right," the man said. The wind caressed his face, wondering at the emotions of humans.

The woman didn't seem to notice the broken sadness in his voice.

"I think she might not be able to use that knife," she said, "even if she should. Even if she has every reason to."

They both looked down. The wide front doors of Hell Gate were swinging open. Two dark figures stepped out into the humid night.

"What are you thinking?" the woman asked, watching the figures make their way to the gate.

The man shrugged.

"You love her."

It wasn't a question. But he still nodded.

"How do you know?" she asked. When he didn't respond, she asked a different question. "What does it feel like?"

"Love?"

She nodded.

"Like pain," he finally said, staring at the figures below. "But more painful than all my deaths. More painful than poison. More painful than a knife to the heart. It hurts worse than anything I've ever known. It hurts, but it's the only thing that lets me know I'm still alive. That's what it feels like."

He stood suddenly. Turned his back on the figures below. Jumped off the rooftop's edge to the black tar paper. He landed silently on the balls of his feet and moved like a shadow. He strode toward the metal door and the staircase that led back into Hell Gate.

The wind rushed at him. It knew he was telling the truth. For the past year, when this man had stalked the Night Den, the all-seeing eye had barely let him inside. The only good left in him was the shard in his heart —that painful knife of burning love he refused to let go of.

The wind shoved the door shut behind him, the metal banging on the frame. The woman stayed on the rooftop staring at the spot where the man had sat. She wrapped her arms around herself and said to the wind, "It doesn't have to feel that way. At least, I don't think it does."

The wind rushed away, leaving her alone in the gloaming.

13

Behind me was the thick limestone of Hell Gate, with its rooms stuffed full of antiques and strange objects of power, and its halls crawling with Jagger's creatures. Ahead of me was the tall iron gate, with its spikes and foreboding appearance. Finn Alterra leaned drunkenly against the cold metal.

Jagger paused on the stone steps, his hand settling on my arm, stopping me. The night was humid; already, a wick of sweat tracked down my neck. My hair was in a French braid, but the little wisps at my temples curled in the humidity.

Jagger glanced over at Finn's slouched form and then leaned close. The yellow glow of the sodium vapor electroliers bathed Jagger's gray skin in an unearthly glow.

The old iron electroliers were from a time when electricity was something magical and wondrous. The glass bulbs were set in five brilliant globes perched on thin iron pillars that transformed the utilitarian streetlights into filigreed works of art. Two electroliers flanked us, and while the yellow vapor usually calmed me, that night, it felt like a cautious warning.

Jagger bent his head, leaning down to reach my shorter height. I could smell gasoline, rubbing alcohol, and chrysanthemum on his breath, which meant he'd had a glass of his favorite liquor before escorting me out the gate. It was a nasty drink called Furtig, made by distilling *actual* spirits. A teardrop's worth took a year to collect. It was incredibly expensive, rare, and Jagger only drank it when he had something to celebrate.

I'd never tried it, and I never will. Justice had a sip when he was fourteen, but he wouldn't tell me what happened after, even though I swear the small streak of white in his hair came right after he passed out from that lone sip. I stopped asking when he said, "Mari, there's some things I'm never going to talk about."

We've all got secrets at Hell Gate. I know when not to pry.

But the yellow vapor, the gasoline scented Furtig, and the heavy humidity that couldn't be chased away even by the howling wind—they all made me feel a sense of foreboding. As if there was something I should know; someone speaking, just out of range, and if I only listened harder, I'd hear what they were trying to tell me.

Untie the knot.

It was the voice again. The desperate, anguished, whispered voice. This time, I could tell, it was a teenage boy. Maybe thirteen or fourteen. Young. Someone I'd never met.

"I have one final instruction," Jagger said, his voice cutting through the echo of the boy's plea. "You may kill Philoneas Ward and his wife and son, but wait until after the games."

He waited for my response, and I nodded. I wasn't certain how I felt about killing two men and a woman I'd never met, but Jagger seemed to think he was giving me a gift, so I said, "All right."

"The conjurers will know you're mine. There's no hiding it. But whatever you do, don't let them know what you are. Understand? A nine, yes. The rest, no."

"I know," I murmured, staring at the dull gray of his nails on my arm.

"If they discover what you are, even I won't be able to bring you back."

"I understand."

He nodded.

Twenty-two years as his ward had left me with a healthy appreciation for the fact that Jagger was the only thing that stood between me and a conjurer torturing me and then delivering a thousand agonizing deaths.

The last recorded "true" lockpick died in 1792. By "true," I mean a lockpick like me—one whose skill manifests shortly after birth and doesn't have to be learned, more an instinct that can be shaped and strengthened. There are other lockpicks out there, but they aren't born with the skill, and they all spend decades training. Even then, they can never match the level of a born lockpick.

From the conjurers' recorded history, the nameless dead lockpick was gut-churningly tortured by the families for two years, and then the Wards twisted their mind into a maze and kept them locked for fifteen years in their little asylum on Wards Island. They were a prisoner of tortured illusions they could never escape from—until death.

So, yeah. I'm not interested in the conjurers learning that I'm a true lockpick and one of the few people on earth who can break their illusions.

"They may know Finn is under my thumb. Tell the truth, whatever they ask." He gave me his sharp-toothed smile. "As you know, the truth is often the greatest deception."

It was what Jagger believed. Me? I had a different view. I think what Jagger called the "truth" was a half-truth or quarter-truth that could easily be twisted into a new form called "a lie."

"So if they ask, I admit to being a nine. I admit that I'm there to win the crown for you?"

Jagger looked past the iron bars of the gate, toward Finn Alterra. "Yes."

I sighed. The straps of my canvas pack dug into my shoulders. I was weighed down with two weeks' worth of clothing and supplies.

"And what will he tell them? That he's bargained with you?"

"It doesn't matter what he says. The truth. A lie." He inched closer, pressing his nails into my skin. "You get him to win the final game. You get him on the dais, in reach of the crown. Then you take it, Mari. You take it."

"I will." My heart thudded against my rib cage as I stared at the iron bars and the shadow of Finn on the other side.

"I want him dead."

"What? Who?"

But I knew who. Jagger's flat gaze was focused on Finn.

The yellow vapor filtered over Jagger, giving him an eerie tint. "Once the game is done, once he's served his purpose, I want him dead. Justice gave you his little dagger, didn't he?"

My throat was tight. So tight I didn't think I could swallow even if I wanted to. Slowly, I nodded.

"Good. Then you get the crown, you kill Alterra, and after, I'll give you the Wards and your freedom."

I was uncomfortably aware of Finn only twenty feet away, leaning against the gate, his head lolling to the side as he stared with solange-filled eyes at the shrouded night sky.

"What if he's hard to kill?" I asked.

Watching him stare at the pillars of vapor rising off the electroliers made me think of the moths beating their wings against the hot sun of the ceiling lights.

Jagger gave a dismissive grunt. He viewed human life and death as dispassionately as bugs hitting the windshield of a taxi. An annoyance, yes, but not anything worth worrying about. "I'm sure when the time comes, he'll be easy to kill. Look at him."

I did.

Jagger was right. Finn's clothing was wrinkled, rumpled. He was loose-limbed and cosmic-eyed. His head was tilted back, with his jugular exposed. He had no awareness of his surroundings, no concern that an arrow or a knife could fly from the shadows and end him. He was just waiting patiently at the gate, lost in some cosmic dream.

"You're sending me into the wolves' den with a sheep as high as a kite," I said, unable to keep the disgust out of my voice.

Jagger chuckled. "I told you you'd love him."

"We'll be lucky to live through the night."

Jagger gave me a sharp-eyed glare—one he usually reserved for the lesser creatures that scurried in his shadow. "You'll do what I say. You'll do whatever you have to do to get that half-Smith to the crown."

All right.

In case I didn't mention it, you don't disobey Jagger. If you do, you'll end up without a head, without your intestines, or sitting at the dinner table where the meal is something like . . . your left foot. These things happen. Somewhat regularly. Even I'm not immune to his temper.

So I nodded.

"I'll do whatever it takes. And when it's done, you'll have the crown." I looked through the gate at the shadowed lines falling in bars across Finn's face. "And Finn Alterra will be dead."

Jagger studied the set of my shoulders, reading my resolve. Finally, he pulled his hand from my arm and motioned toward the darkened street. "I've spent centuries preparing for this moment. Don't disappoint me."

"I won't."

I didn't look back as I walked down the stone steps and out of Hell Gate.

14

FINN BLINKED AT ME OWLISHLY WHEN THE IRON GATE SLAMMED SHUT. THE clang echoed against the limestone and concrete, and then the howl of the wind swallowed the noise.

For a moment, I don't think he recognized me or even remembered who I was. I folded my arms across my chest and tapped my foot against the sidewalk.

"Ready?" I asked, my voice short.

Finn swayed a bit, listing to the side. I wondered how much trouble I was going to have keeping him upright for the next two weeks. Up close, he was bigger than I remembered. About ten inches taller than me, with the bulky, muscled build all the Smiths—even the females—had.

I guess not even solange and the lack of real sustenance that went along with it could obliterate centuries of breeding and the inherited physical strength of the Smith bloodline.

He'd shaved—his jaw was smooth now—but his dark green T-shirt and jeans were wrinkled, and his black hair was too long and messy. It feathered around his ears and hit his collar, and all I could do was picture the topless woman stroking her fingers through it while he stared stupidly at her.

I scowled, and when I did, a smile bloomed on his face. The humidity and the heat pulled a blanket over us. He stepped forward, swaying a bit. I grabbed his arm, dug my hand into the heat of his muscles, and steadied him.

He smiled down at me, his eyes a navy blue, with lightning pulsing and skittering over his irises. I wondered what he saw when he looked at me.

"Mari," he said, and I shivered.

Was I really going to be able to kill him? It was official. He was harmless. An idiot. But harmless.

"You're pretty," he said, slurring his words. "Were you always this pretty?"

A hint of cranberry and allspice clung to him. His skin was hot and flushed, and drops of perspiration rested on his upper lip and tracked down his forehead.

I narrowed my eyes. I had a suspicion . . .

"How much solange did you have before coming here?"

His smile grew as if he'd just let me in on a big joke. "Some." He held his fingers apart, indicating a thimble-full, then increased the width to two thimbles.

It pissed me off.

"What for? It's going to get us killed."

He shook his head, although when he did, it seemed to startle him, as if the movement made his head feel like a balloon floating on the end of a string. "It's going to save us. Solange."

He rolled the word "solange" around his mouth and then let out a happy sigh. He sounded like a true devotee.

I snorted. "The only thing solange will do is enslave you."

He blinked down at me, his eyes clearing, focusing on my scowl. "I know. The fruit of excess is always slavery. You either become slave to your vice or . . . hmm . . . you become slave to a tyrant. But can you become slave to a savior?" He considered this for a moment, as if the answer were a mystery that could only be found in the enlightenment of solange.

"Come on," I said, pulling him down the sidewalk. "We're going to take a taxi to the games."

We needed to walk west toward the shops and apartments on 1st Avenue, where traffic and taxis were to be found.

Finn grinned at my words, and I tried to squash the prickle that flushed over my skin at the way he looked at me, as if we were two good friends out for an evening stroll.

"Funny," he said, "going to the games in a taxi. Feels like we should be riding in on shadow or mist, or at least a white horse."

I snorted. "Well, this is New York. Here we have trains and cabs."

He blinked at me, then nodded eastward toward the distant form of Hell Gate Bridge arching over the river. The black steel lines crisscrossed and spanned over the mirror-black water. "We could take the ghost train."

"You can see the ghost train?" I asked, unexpectedly delighted that he could, and that he had the same name for it that I did.

He merely blinked at me again, momentarily shuttering the lightning bolts in his eyes. "Why wouldn't I?"

Right. He was half-conjurer, even if he was a null. Just because he couldn't conjure, it didn't mean he couldn't see figments or recognize illusions.

I shrugged. "Maybe the solange . . ."

"Solange unfolds illusions. The ghost train is real."

I nodded. That made sense, but . . . "We can't ride it though."

He shrugged. "Maybe. Maybe not."

Yeah. I'd like to see him try to ride a figment.

Finn leaned into my side as we walked down the sidewalk, past darkened townhomes and skeletal gingko trees surrounded by bloodred begonias. I kept a firm grip on his arm, steering him straight toward the lights ahead. There was a tiny deli on the corner—one that served cheap coffee and bagels with lox in the morning, and pastrami sandwiches at night.

Griff loved their bagels and snuck the lox whenever he could, because Roumelade refused to have seafood served in Hell Gate. She'd vociferously proclaim, "No fish! We aren't cannibals!" conveniently forgetting not all of us were born out of a river.

I guided Finn toward the soft glow and the pastrami scent of that corner deli, sure we'd find a cab there. It was late June. The sun had set a little after 8:30 p.m. We had about three hours until midnight, when the entry to the games began.

I took a furtive glance at Finn, wondering if he had a strategy. If he had anything in mind except his next dose. I couldn't decide whether I hated him or pitied him. The hate wasn't like me—I'd never felt so much unaccounted anger toward a person before—but it was there. It tasted like battery acid in my mouth and burned in my gut. For some reason, I wanted this man to be better than what he was.

"Before we get to the Bard Mansion . . ." I paused, and Finn blinked down at me. When I had his attention, I continued. "I think we should come to an understanding."

"All right." He dragged the words out, making them almost a question.

"You made a bargain with Jagger."

He nodded—one dip of his chin.

"And you have to obey me as if my words are his."

A smile curved on his lips. A quiver went through my belly. I ignored it.

"Yes," he said. "I have to obey you."

"Then I want you to stop taking so much solange."

He closed one eye, looked down at me, and tilted his head. "Except in that. I can't obey you in that."

"Is that what Jagger said?"

"It's what we agreed."

The smile on his face brought an angry niggle to my chest. "Fine. Do your best to keep it under control so you can at least walk in a straight line *and* think in a straight line."

"Is thinking in a straight line really best though? Or walking? I think circles get you there faster. True?"

Oh boy. This was going to be a long two weeks.

I shook my head. We were lucky he wasn't a full-blooded Smith. I couldn't imagine the crazy he'd unleash on the world. He'd be like a wacky two-year-old wanting cranberry ice cream to rain from the sky, and free rides on ghost-train carousels, and then, in a blink, he'd shift to a horny teenager wanting politicians to settle disputes with weeklong hedonistic orgies, all the while fondling breasts and spouting nonsense solange riddles. Then, probably, he'd go full Smith and demand a war fought entirely on white horses.

Thank goodness for him being a null.

"Or is it spheres? Mari?" He held out his free hand as if he were holding a sphere there and he was asking if . . . I don't even know.

We were almost to 1st Avenue. Up ahead, there were the lights of the deli and the neighboring barbershop, and across the street, a dusty, musty scented used bookstore that I liked to browse to find books for . . . no one. I guess, no one. But if I knew someone who loved to read, that was where I'd go.

"During the games," I continued, ignoring the absent sphere on Finn's palm, "you have to listen to me. Do everything I say. Even if it doesn't make sense. I've studied these games. I've studied the four families. If you want to survive to the end, you have to do what I tell you."

I felt a twinge at the fact that surviving to the end didn't mean he'd survive after the end. Even if I wasn't able to end Finn Alterra's life, Jagger would send someone else to do it. Probably Justice.

"Do whatever you tell me," Finn repeated. He snapped his hand shut like he'd captured the sphere.

"Even if it doesn't make sense."

He nodded.

I hated saying the last, but I needed to. "You have to trust me, Finn."

He stopped just short of the light of 1st Avenue. At the intersection, cars passed and people hurried by, not noticing the two of us standing still in the shadows.

I got the feeling Finn was weighing me. He looked into my eyes. His were backlit by the nebula exploding in the solange depths, and while he looked at me, I felt as if he'd lifted me up and tugged me into a star-filled sky where he could see all my secrets and all my yearnings.

I was naked, unguarded, and he could see everything in me—the very heart of me.

"Do you trust me?" I asked, my skin flushed, heart fluttering in my throat.

His eyes shuttered at my words, and I felt as if I'd fallen back to earth, back to the sidewalk by the deli, beneath the scaffolding at the edge 1st Avenue. A hot breeze blew across my cheeks and tickled the sweat on my neck.

Finn's gaze was solemn. His arm was rigid beneath mine. He was no longer tilting, stumbling, or weaving. Instead he watched the shadows play over my face.

Finally, he nodded. "Yes, Mari. With my life."

I barely stopped myself from flinching. Why'd he have to go and say that? Who trusts anyone? Who trusts them with their life? He was a dupe. A desperate dupe. Jagger really knew how to pick them, didn't he?

I smiled at him, although I imagine I looked a little nauseous. "Good."

"Don't worry," he said, patting my hand. My arm was still in the crook of his. "I'll do whatever you need. I'll win the game, Mari."

There was a "but" there—I could hear it in his voice.

"But . . . ?"

He grinned, his rough features transforming again into a man who was undeniably beautiful. "But . . ." he said, "you're my body. While we're there, you also have to do whatever I say. Whatever I want."

I narrowed my eyes. "Technically true."

He held up his hand and raised a finger for each item on his list. "Wash my laundry. Fetch me snacks. Draw my bath. Rub my feet—"

He broke off with a surprised "oomph" when I jabbed him with my elbow.

"You wouldn't—"

"Course I would. I like being waited on."

"I'm not—"

"You are. In the games, you are. You're my body, Mari. You do what I say too." His words were firm and demanding, but he was back to his vacant-eyed look, a small smile on his face. "I like my sheets untucked when I sleep."

I wanted to kick him. Would it be okay if I kicked him?

We were going into the games, and he was worried about untucked sheets and foot rubs?

I stalked to 1st Avenue, dragging him with me, and thrust my arm into the air. There was a taxi down the block. When the driver saw my raised hand, he veered across the traffic, aiming toward the curb where we stood.

"One more thing," I said in a low voice. "If it comes down to it and the Smith principal is in trouble, step in front of him."

"What?"

"Step in front of him. Shield him."

Finn blinked at me. The taxi slid to a halt.

"Why?"

"You said you trusted me."

Finn looked at the cab and then back to me. He stumbled a bit when he stepped off the curb and reached for the door.

"Finn?" I held my hand on the door, keeping him from opening it.

"All right," he said. "I'll step in front of the Smith."

His dad. We were talking about his dad. The one who'd gutted him as a kid when he'd introduced himself, hoping, I suppose, for a fatherly hug and some good old parental approval. Maybe that was why Finn had hesitated.

He opened the door to the taxi. A blast of cold air-conditioning hit me, along with the smell of leather seats and pine air freshener. The TV in the back seat played at full volume, advertising the latest blockbuster starring—who else?—Celia Bard.

I was about to slide into the cab when I heard a shout.

"Wait! Finn. Wait!"

I stopped, halfway stooped, Finn's hand on the roof of the taxi, his arm on the other side of the door. He was steadying himself, but also unknowingly exposing his back to possible threats while completely shielding me from harm. He was a tactical mess. A true disaster.

I slipped out from under his arm and waved a hand at the driver to give us a moment. Finn swayed a bit and half-tripped as he turned to see who was shouting his name.

It was the beautiful, long-haired woman from the Night Den—Cora. She was racing down the street, cheeks puffing as she gulped in air. When she was only feet away, she launched herself at him. He caught her

—barely—and stumbled again. I reached out and shoved him a bit to the left so he wouldn't fall over.

"You left. You left while I was sleeping! What the heck, Finn? What the heck." Cora buried her head against his chest.

His lips lifted in a half-smile, and he slowly rubbed her back.

I tapped my foot on the pavement and ignored the uncomfortable sunburn-type irritation prickling on my skin. "We need to go," I said, pointedly nodding at the rising half-moon.

At my words, Cora pulled her face from Finn's chest but left her arms around him. She gave me a hard stare, waiting for something. When I didn't say anything more, she shook her head.

"You're a piece of work."

My shoulders tensed. "You don't even know me."

Cora was beautiful. Long, curling auburn hair. Hazel eyes. Sun-kissed skin. That sort of voluptuous softness that men loved. She also had a flinty-hard stare and a lot of anger radiating off her. She clearly did not like me. Although, to be fair, I was slated to kill her boyfriend/lover/whatever.

Not that she knew that.

Finally, after she'd taken a long look at me and come to whatever conclusion it was she'd reached, she stepped back from Finn. "I wanted to tell you good luck," she said to him, pointedly ignoring me.

He nodded, still smiling his half-smile, and she pressed her fingers to his mouth.

"Good luck, Finn Alterra. All my luck is yours."

A warm, honey-sweet smell filled the air, and then a golden shimmer worked its way over his lips. I stared, unable to help myself. Cora was a good luck charm. She . . . I'd heard of good luck charms, but I'd never met one.

They came out of wishes and prayers and gold coins tossed into fountains. They were born of the most fervent hopes and dreams. They rose out of wishing wells and Roman fountains and fairy glades. I didn't know how strong she was, but if she was really strong, her luck could last for hours, even . . . days.

Finn slowly blinked and let out a soft sigh when she finally pulled her fingers from his mouth. He looked muzzy-headed and a little confused. Maybe that was how a good luck charm left you feeling, but I suspected it was actually the solange, or maybe lust.

I cleared my throat and nodded at the taxi. The driver wasn't going to wait much longer.

Cora gave Finn another squeeze and then turned to me.

"I'm warning you." She leveled me with her hard, flinty stare, her soft voice cold. "If you hurt him—even a scratch, a minor bruise—you'll regret it—"

"Cora," Finn said, shaking his head.

"If you hurt him," she continued, "you'll regret it for the rest of your life. You hear me?"

I stared back, taking in the threat and the promise in her eyes. She truly believed it. She truly believed that if I hurt Finn, she'd make me regret it. I wondered what other magic she was hiding. Or *who* she knew that could deliver on her threat.

I nodded, giving her the respect she wanted. "I hear you."

Cora didn't say anything more, just turned and stalked back down 1st Avenue.

"Nice girlfriend you've got. She's real friendly," I said, shoving my bag into the back seat of the taxi.

Finn gave me a crooked grin. "I don't have a girlfriend. I have a girl who's gonna marry me."

Great. No wonder she was so viciously protective. Rightly so.

"Get in." I gestured for Finn to slide into the cab.

It was time. We were on our way to the games.

15

THE HALF-MOON CLIMBED THE DEEP PLUM SKY, RISING FROM BEHIND THE behemoth of the Bard Mansion. Each of the families had a cloistered estate in the city, roughly in the area of their compass direction.

For example, the Wards were the east, and their little island sat in the East River. Although, they no longer lived on the island. Their current home was a stately marble mansion on 5th Avenue, not far from the Met.

The Clarks were the south. Their ancestral estate was in Lower Manhattan, near Trinity Church and all the long-dead graveyard secrets that lay buried there. The Clark Mansion had a hive of candlelit catacombs, carved out in the 1700s, where, years ago, I met my first real monster.

The Smiths were the north, and long ago, they had a home at the northern crown of Central Park. But with the population boom at the end of the 1800s, they decided northern Manhattan wasn't discreet enough for their martial activities. They moved their military-mindedness to Astoria, right across the river, into a block-long limestone mansion that looked like a cross between a Romanesque museum and a spartan government building. The façade was flat, most of the windows were glass block, and the security was "impenetrable."

Finally, the Bards were the west. They perched like preening eagles on top of their nest at the very northwesterly end of Manhattan, near Fort Tyron Park and The Cloisters. That far northwest, you have the steep-banked Hudson, the dense city-jungle foliage, and the uniform streets of tightly strung together yellow brick apartment buildings. Do you remember the jackaltooth that killed me underneath the Bard Mansion?

The subway tunnels this far north are all part of what's called the Washington Heights Mine Tunnel. They're the deepest, darkest, most inaccessible tunnels in the city, descending nearly 200 feet below the surface. In the early 1900s, the tunnels were all blasted out of the hard bedrock, and some of them were abandoned because of mudflows and collapses.

These are the tunnels where the jackaltooth roam. The Bards chose this section of the city to build their estate because they could use the tunnels to create all sorts of fantastic dreams and terrifying nightmares. Back in 1947, a Nobel Prize-winning scientist asked the NYC Department of Transportation if he could conduct experiments in the tunnels on radiation emitted from the rocks. This scientist discovered cosmic rays.

What are cosmic rays?

They're the clusters of particles that are born from our sun, the Milky Way, or even from distant galaxies. When they hit earth's atmosphere, they create a shower of particles that rains down on us. He believed the tunnels would be shielded from the cosmic rays.

I guess they were, but without the cosmic rays and the sun, all sorts of other imaginings grew like fetid mushrooms in a dark, damp cave.

So here we were. At the Bard Mansion. All glitz and glamour on the surface; all deep, dark, dank radiation mine underneath.

The taxi pulled away, and Finn tilted his head upward to gaze at the six-story yellow brick building illuminated by the half-moon rising behind it. Black metal fire escape stairs zigzagged over the front, and at the triangular-peaked roofline, umber-colored bricks were patterned in chevrons, like arrows pointing at the sun.

The air was less humid this far north. First of all, there were more trees. Their fat leaves provided shade as well as the cool water vapor released from over-plump stoma. A breeze wicked off the Hudson, smelling of wet basalt cliffs, diesel congestion from the 9A, and, of course, the cranberries and allspice of solange.

I blinked up at the estate and let my eyes unfocus, seeing beneath the illusion.

On first inspection, the Bard Mansion was an unassuming apartment building from the early 1900s. Twelve windows per floor, a rusty window air conditioner propped in each. Bricked-up windows at the basement level. Three squares of sidewalk. Evenly spaced rectangular dirt patches littered with cigarette butts, where thin maple trees grew. Three stone steps leading to the entrance. A locked glass front door with a video intercom. Nothing more. It appeared to be just another boring, middle-class apartment building. One among thousands.

"Can you see it?" I asked Finn, unsure of how the solange worked for him and whether it wiped away all illusion or only the illusions directed at him.

He hummed in the back of his throat, a soft rumble, and stared at the building with sleepy eyes. "What? The grand imitation of Paris's Palais Garnier? The gaudy ode to Orpheus? I see it."

I frowned at the Beaux-Arts-style mansion hiding beneath the unassuming apartment building illusion. It was crafted from white and 24 karat gold-shot marble and had columns galore. Arched windows. Scenes of debauchery were carved in bas-relief, and statues lined the roof. Beaux-Arts was big into symbolic statuary, with figures representing things like justice, industry, and agriculture. I wasn't certain, but I'd always thought the statues on the Bard Mansion were the different faces of dreams and nightmares.

"You mean an ode to Morpheus?" I asked.

Morpheus was the primordial Greek god of dreams. Orpheus was just a tragic musician and poet who descended to the underworld to save his wife.

Finn closed an eye and studied the white marble statue over the grand arched entrance. It was a man with his hands outstretched in the classic conjurer pose, a wild expression on his face that shifted between ecstasy and wrath.

"No," he murmured. "I mean Orpheus."

I thought of Finn's almost-wife, Cora. The woman who was going to marry him. Did Finn see himself as Orpheus, descending into the underworld of the Bard Mansion for the sake of his future wife? Was this all for her?

The expression on his face told me *yes*. His lightning-shot eyes took in the mansion as if he were preparing to descend to hell for the sake of the woman he loved.

The humid night air thickened, and a breeze curved around my flushed skin. For just a moment—the tiniest second—I let myself wonder what it would be like to have someone love me that much. To have someone love me so much they'd brave hell for me.

Finn Alterra may be an addict in free fall—a stumbling, cosmic-eyed, hedonistic mess—but he loved someone. If he was like Orpheus, he was loyal to death (and beyond), brave, true, and faithful for life. Orpheus loved his wife more than anything in the world. I wondered, for a moment, what that would be like.

I wondered what having Finn Alterra's love would feel like.

Just as quickly, I brushed the question aside. I was assuming things. Imagining. It was just as likely he was here for a truckload of solange. Who knew what Jagger had promised him? If Roumelade were here, she'd click her tongue and tell me to stop attributing good traits to someone who didn't have them.

Still . . .

"She must be someone special."

Finn turned to me. Shifted the small backpack on his shoulders. I wondered what he thought was essential to bring to the games. Not much, by the looks of it.

"Who?" He blinked at me, trying to focus. I was losing him again.

"Your Eurydice," I said. Orpheus's lost wife.

His lips curved at that, forming the smile that made him beautiful.

Suddenly, the cranberries and allspice were a bittersweet perfume. I didn't want to look at his smile anymore.

Orpheus failed, didn't he?

"Come on." I linked my arm through his and started toward the front gates.

The mansion beneath the illusion was glowing with thousands of sparkling lights—artificial stars winking in the night sky. Through the arching front windows, the entry's grand marble staircase and the diamond drop chandelier glowed bright.

I expected—and I was right—that we would be the last to arrive. All the other conjurers—the principals, the heirs, their siblings, the bodies—were already inside.

I didn't know if it was the statues or if someone was watching us approach, but all the same, I felt the weight of a dozen eyes on us.

Finn swayed, stumbling on the marble steps. He righted himself at the last second. I gripped his arm and prayed he wasn't about to get us killed.

"Ready?" I asked.

He didn't answer. Instead he looked up at the wrathful statue looming over us and smiled.

16

THE HUNDRED YEAR GAMES ARE RULED BY PROTOCOL. THIS HAS TO BE THE case, because otherwise they would end in slaughter, gore, and a Hamlet-style finale where everyone lies dead in the throne room, no head for the crown.

Not that death, murder, and mayhem don't happen during the games—they're just kept to a minimum.

Please note, "minimum" is relative. There has never been a year where less than two people have died. This includes relatives and bodies. It's not just the heirs who are in danger of losing their lives.

The Hundred Year Games are hosted at the ruling principal's estate. They last for a little less than two weeks, from just after half-moon to new moon. The night of the new moon is when the new principal conjurer is crowned.

As the moon ticks down, four games are played. Each family is in charge of a game. They spend years preparing a game that will test whatever conjuring ability, skill, or virtue they find most desirable in the next leader.

Typically, the game will play to the strength of the family that creates it.

For instance, the Clarks will have a game that plays into history or scholarly subjects.

The Bards will have a game of poetry, music, or entertainment (this is more diabolical than it sounds).

The Wards love mind games.

The Smiths—always—have games that involve brute strength, weaponry, or war.

When heirs die during the games, it's usually during a Smith game. They have a head sliced off, they're disemboweled, or they're eaten by a carnivorous war elephant in a macabre recreation of a Roman battle against Hannibal's forces.

There is a winner of each game. You must complete each one. If you don't, you're eliminated. Points are awarded, of course. Four points for first place. Three points for second place. Two points for third place. One point for last place. After the fourth game, a winner is crowned. In the case of a tie, the heirs fight in hand-to-hand conjurer combat.

And that's it.

For two weeks, the heads of the families, their spouses, the heirs, the siblings, any other relatives who choose to come, and the bodies all congregate together to witness the shift of power. Here's where the protocol comes into play.

Any conjurer or family member of a conjurer may request and gain admittance to witness the games. The host family must provide lodging and food for all admitted. (Not necessarily good lodging or food free of poison.)

Killing is allowed—however, once an heir enters the games, they may not be killed except by consequence of a game. Only an heir or an heir's paladin may enter. The heirs may employ a body of their choice. Once the games are complete and a winner is chosen, the winner will be crowned. No one may gainsay the outcome of the games.

The integrity of the games is of utmost importance. No matter the machinations and manipulations in every other part of their lives, the conjurers will do anything to keep the games pure and true.

Ritual. Integrity. Protocol. Honor. These virtues rule the games.

The wide brass double doors of the Bard Mansion swung open. The dazzling bright lights fell over Finn and me, and I blinked at the arching stairway, the naked marble statues lining the walls, and the sound of a raucous party echoing across the cavernous room. The last time I'd been in this entryway, I'd stolen an umbrella and a button. This time, I wasn't going to steal anything. Well, a crown—but that was later.

From the sounds of it, the families were having a wild bacchanalia in the ballroom before they got down to business. Discordant music, laughter, shrieks, and shouts all banged around the marble and jarred my ears. It was a sea of voices crashing into the entryway, amplified and echoing.

There was the sudden roar of a lion, an expletive, and then a laughing shriek. Over that was the smell of apple-tinted smoke, the sour note of champagne, and rich, honey-filled pastries.

"May I help you?" The crisp, impartial notes came from a gaunt, hollow-cheeked man who was the humanoid version of a jackaltooth. He had mottled skin and sharp teeth.

I did my best to repress a shudder.

Finn gave the man a surprised smile. He'd not noticed the doorman before he spoke. Instead, like me, he'd been taking in the statuary and the sounds of revelry. Apparently, Finn wasn't bothered by jackaltooth or their human relatives.

"Yes." Finn tilted a bit. Swayed. Then he grasped the muscled shoulder of a marble statue with a shield and sword to steady himself. Once Finn was fairly straight, he gave the gaunt doorman another happy smile.

When the man didn't smile back or speak, just stared, Finn wrinkled his brow.

"Excuse me. May I help you?" Finn asked.

"May I help you?" the man repeated.

"That's what I said." Finn frowned, looking offended.

"No. It's what I said."

Finn closed his eyes. Slowly opened them again. It was as if he expected the man to disappear upon their reopening. When he didn't, Finn shook his head, dumbfounded.

"May I help you?" the man asked again.

"Not likely," Finn said. "Not unless you give it without permission. Then it isn't help. It's hindrance."

The gaunt doorman tugged his sleeves down, pulling his black suit coat tight over his skeletal shoulders. I quickly stepped between him and Finn. I got the feeling if we didn't answer soon, the man was going to shift into a jackaltooth and tear his teeth through our throats.

"Yes," I said, nudging Finn back, careful not to push him so hard he'd wobble and tip over. "This is Finn Alterra, son of Wolfgang Smith. I'm Finn's official body. We formally request admittance to the games."

As soon as I said the words, the doorman gave a sharp, jerky nod and then gestured for us to follow him. He cut across the marble-floored entry.

"Come on." I grabbed Finn by his shirt and pulled him after the doorman.

"You could've been more help back there," I whispered as we half-walked, half-jogged down the long hallway.

I barely had time to notice our surroundings. It was very "gilded opera house." Gold-leaf plaster ceilings. Venetian plaster walls. Brass fixtures. Marble tables with porcelain vases, statuary, and oil paintings of all the famous Bards of the past. Just picture the gaudiest opera house you can imagine, mix it with a dash of gothic crazy, add a lot of nude Greco-Roman statues, and you've pretty much nailed the interior of the Bard mansion.

Finn tugged my grip free from his shirt and then took my arm. "I did help. He was the hindrance."

"He wasn't a hindrance. He was a doorman."

Finn stared at me blankly, so I tugged him after the doorman. The sounds of the revelry were growing so loud my eardrums were vibrating. The apple smoke was thicker, cloying in smog-like clouds near the ceiling. The air was feverishly hot.

Just ahead, a wide marble arch carved with vines and grapes opened into a grand ballroom. I was right. It was a bacchanalia. I'd witnessed some depraved revelries at Hell Gate, but this party was in a class of its own.

Long wooden tables were stocked with food, raw oysters and caviar spread on top of naked men and women who lay on the tables. The naked people were apparently the serving platters.

Cooked peacock, with colorful feathers fanned from golden skin. A wild boar—of course—had a steaming apple in its mouth. Champagne flowed in a meandering river around the ballroom.

Maybe once, it was illusion, but here and now, the river of champagne was real. A woman in a diaphanous gold dress kneeled down, dipped her champagne flute into the river, and took a long swallow of the bubbling liquid.

At the river's edge, the marble floor sprouted delicate chocolate towers, flower cakes covered in pink, violet, and blue frosting, and shot out a misty forest of apple-sweet smoke. I now recognized it as a smoke that, when breathed in, caused relaxation, lack of inhibition, and pain-filled pleasure.

Before I could warn Finn to stay close, not eat anything, and not breathe too deeply, he pulled free of my grasp and tipsily stumbled into the crowd. He elbowed Primus Clark (oh no), stepped on the long train of Celia Bard's turquoise sequin ballgown and caused her to trip (why?), and then, when someone shouted, "Oi! Who's that?" he spun around so fast he knocked Luvic Bard into the river of champagne.

At the loud splash and Luvic's shouted expletive, the music seesawed to a halt, the dancing stopped, the laughter and conversation died, and every single conjurer in the room turned their gaze on Finn.

He didn't seem to notice the danger he was in. There was death dancing in the air. I could feel the potential conjurings skittering over my skin. It was the sting of a rattlesnake bite right before the venom is shoved into your bloodstream.

We were dead.

Finn didn't even know it.

He stared around the ballroom, his navy eyes a spinning kaleidoscope. His shoulders were relaxed, his head tilted, a faraway half-smile playing on his mouth. Whatever he saw, it wasn't the same thing as me. All I saw was danger and death. Sixty, seventy conjurers dressed in silk, ready to kill.

I just had to announce Finn. Tell them who he was. Then protocol would steer the rest.

But before I could push through the crowd to get everyone's attention, Finn smiled at someone across the ballroom.

Oh no.

No.

I hadn't known him for long, but I knew that look. He was about to . . .

He leaned down, slowly dragged his finger through the violet frosting of a cake flower, and popped the sugary mass into his mouth. His eyes lit up, and he hummed in approval.

Someone in the ballroom gasped.

Finn smiled at the sound and, looking straight at the terrifying form of Wolfgang Smith, said, "Hello, Father."

17

I TENSED, MY HAND SLIDING UNDER MY COAT. I'D COME PREPARED. I KNEW the second I walked into the Night Den and saw Finn lying on that red velvet couch, starry-eyed and smiling, that this venture had a high probability of tipping sideways.

Griff had asked if I'd be able to kill Finn if I needed to get out. Justice had reminded me I needed to be ruthless. Cora had promised me that if I hurt Finn, I'd regret it.

I wasn't really thinking about any of those things though. Instead I was strung tight, frantically trying to anticipate every move the conjurers might make.

The trouble was, while the conjurers were by and large fairly predictable, Finn was a wildcard.

The ballroom was dazzling-bright and decadent. The bright lights and the apple smoke stung my eyes. I breathed a shallow breath and slipped unnoticed toward the edge of the room. Justice could move like a shadow, but I was more like a forest stream. People's gazes slid over me. Their eyes never settled; never quite caught my features. I used that to my advantage and whispered past the conjurers entirely focused on Finn and his father.

I inched to the edge of the ballroom, stopping next to a marble column I could duck behind and a ridiculously tall chocolate dandelion with yellow and orange sugar pollen coating the petals.

Every single person in the ballroom was turned toward Finn and Wolfgang. Have you ever felt the anticipation of a mob when they're lusting for violence? You can feel the craving—this sort of hunger twisting in the air, like a creature that needs to be fed, its jaws snapping, its maw wide, and . . . Hell Gate had this feeling a lot. Whenever Jagger pulled everyone together, there was always this violent, goose bump-raising hunger.

It pressed over my skin, and I quickly patted my hidden pockets, cataloging everything I'd prepared for emergencies.

"Father," Finn said, his voice carrying across the ballroom. Perhaps not everyone heard him before, because there were a few gasps and a muffled curse.

The violent hunger grew, pressing down on me. Finn was in the center of the ballroom and was so unlike every other person present it was jarring.

While the conjurers were in a rainbow of silks, satins, and luxurious ballgowns and tuxes, Finn was in torn jeans and a wrinkled T-shirt. He was rumpled, messy-haired, and solange-eyed. His shoulders were relaxed, his hands in his pockets, and he smiled at Wolfgang Smith as if they had a warm, loving father-son bond instead of a "come near me and I'll gut you" sort of relationship.

He looked like a harmless puppy in a den of wolves, completely unaware he was about to have a sword thrust through his intestines.

The Smith stopped in front of his son. He was tall, his hair dark with streaks of gray, powerfully built—exactly what you'd expect a Smith to look like. His nose was sharp, his cheeks angular, his jaw a long, slashing line. When he stood opposite Finn, it was as if a mirror had been slid between them; only thirty years and a tuxedo separated them. There was no denying Finn was Wolfgang Smith's son.

"Well, I'll be," someone said.

To which another someone said, "Shh!"

"I told you," the Smith said in a low voice that somehow carried to fill the marble ballroom, "if you ever approached me again, I'd kill you. What is so important that you'd die for it?"

Now that death was on the horizon, the conjurers pressed closer, aching to hear each word.

"It's his son," someone whispered.

"An accident? Who's the mother?"

"Never knew—"

The whispers were cut off by a sharp glare from Wolfgang.

Finn had that blank, solange-eyed look again. He stared at his father as if he saw something infinitely interesting.

"Well?" Wolfgang asked. He twisted his hand, pressing his first two fingers and his thumb together. A glowing blue sword—one made of fire and ice—appeared in his fist.

At the appearance of the sword, a sharp throb pinched my chest. The sword was eerily like the blue arrow that had pierced my heart.

Was it Wolfgang who killed me? His son Darin?

Finn didn't even blink at the flaming sword that had likely gutted him ten years earlier. He ignored it completely.

"I've come"—he smiled placidly at his father—"to be my brother's paladin."

At his words, Wolfgang raised his eyebrows. His gaze coursed over his son, judging and weighing. Then his mouth twitched. He pressed his lips flat. Then, finally, he laughed. It was a thundering, callous, awful sort of laugh.

With his laugh, the rest of the conjurers laughed too. I took in everyone in the room. There were the Clarks—they were all huddled in a corner. Dear dad. Primus, Secondus, and Last. The siblings were in black and looked like three crows hunched on a bare branch. There were other Clarks too— cousins or aunts and uncles. You could separate the Clarks from the rest of the conjuring families because they all wore black or dark brown and had pale, paperlike skin that came from studying in their catacombs for years at a time.

The Wards all stood opposite the Clarks. There weren't as many Wards as the rest of the families. Philoneas was slight, nondescript, wearing a tux and watching Finn with a small frown wrinkling his brow.

His son, Jacob, looked more like his mom—blond-haired and green-eyed. He leaned down and whispered something to his dad. Philoneas nodded, murmured something back, and then Jacob subtly pressed his fingers together in the conjurer's pose.

I felt the conjuring stir around him, but when he didn't make any further move, I looked away.

The rest of the Wards stayed behind Philoneas. They were a solemn, grim-faced lot. I wondered where his wife was. She was reputably a very unstable woman.

The Smiths—there were a lot of them too. They were all broad-shouldered and muscular. Even in suits and dresses, they looked like they might strip down and start wrestling or sword-fighting.

They were all closing rank around Darin, the heir. I'd never seen Darin up close before. He looked a lot like Finn—a lot like his dad—except lighter. His hair was chestnut brown instead of black. His face was wider, his nose shorter. He was more muscular than Finn, although the way he stood made me certain he could move like lightning. Darin's eyes were cloud-gray, just like his father's, and I wondered if that was what color Finn's eyes used to be too.

He stared at Finn—not with surprise, but with loathing. The edge of his lip curled, and his hands twitched as if he was a breath away from conjuring a knife to throw at his half-brother. Apparently, Darin knew all about his father's accident and wanted to be the one to end him.

Finally, the Bards made up most of the crowd. They were also the ones enjoying the show the most. They were the most animated, the most colorful, the beautiful butterflies flitting in amongst the crows and the wolves.

Celia held a glass of champagne and watched Finn with a seductively predatory gaze. Ragnor stood next to her. He was second-born and a musician to Celia's Hollywood glamour.

The one perhaps everyone had forgotten about was Luvic Bard. He'd been dunked in the champagne river by Finn's stumbling progression through the ballroom. Luvic wasn't a pop star or a movie star. He was third-born and mostly forgotten. Sometimes he played parts on Broadway, which was what Bards did, but mostly, he just caroused and drank and popped up in the media for some scandal or another linked to his brother or sister. I'd never paid much attention to him. There were many worse conjurers to be wary of than Luvic Bard.

But I realized quite suddenly that I should've paid more attention to Luvic. In a move faster than a blink, he was behind Finn. He twisted Finn's arms behind his back and held a long knife to his throat.

Luvic was dripping-wet, his tuxedo soaked and his black hair plastered to his head. Droplets of champagne slid down his cheeks. He gave Wolfgang a cocky smile.

"Illusion swords don't work on the solange-addled," Luvic said. His voice was a mellow tenor filled with a hint of laughter. "You have to use real steel if you want them dead."

Finn, for his part, didn't seem at all bothered to have a knife to his throat for the second time in twenty-four hours. Maybe this was a normal part of his life. What did I know? Maybe he was constantly being threatened with jugular slicing. Who knew what it was like growing up in the Night Den?

"Wolfgang," Herman Clark called from his corner of the ballroom, "I didn't know you had another son. What an *interesting* secret. Is he a conjurer? In line to be heir?"

The last questions were said in a taunting tone.

Darin cut his hand through the air. "He's null. He won't be my paladin."

"Ah," Luvic said. "Then perhaps I might . . ." He grinned and made a little sawing motion with his blade.

Wolfgang narrowed his eyes on Finn. I could see the scales in Wolfgang's eyes weighing 'kill him, don't kill him, kill him.'

"You gave the Smith a reason not to kill you, but give me one too," Luvic taunted. "This suit is handmade Italian silk, and you, my null friend, ruined it."

Finn tilted his head. A drop of blood formed a crimson tear and trailed down his neck.

My heart thumped wildly in my chest. I had to do something. I couldn't undo illusions—not without giving myself away. I couldn't stop a real knife from slitting Finn's throat. But I could do other things.

Roumelade had been right. The hard part was getting Finn *into* the games.

I saw the shift in Wolfgang's eyes. Knew he'd reached his decision, and the decision was death.

"Pomegranate," Finn said.

Luvic shook his head, staring at the people surrounding him. "Excuse me?"

"The reason you can't kill me. Pomegranate. Or was it apples? I can never remember . . ."

"Enough!" Wolfgang's sharp voice cut through the room. The blue fire and ice sword disappeared. He pulled a dagger free from under his tux.

He was about to deliver death.

That was my cue.

I yanked a thunderer free from my coat and threw it across the ballroom. It hit the marble floor. A dazzling light snapped brightly, searing the eyes of every single conjurer in the room. They'd be blind for a full ten seconds. The boom pierced the room, and someone screamed.

Another scream broke off with a gurgle. Then there was the sound of running, shouting, chaos.

I ignored the noise and the people shoving around me. I had to time this perfectly. This was going to be tricky, keeping both me and Finn alive *and* getting him into the games.

"Finn!" I shouted. "The Smith!"

I hoped he could hear me above the chaos. I hoped he remembered what I'd said. *"If there's danger, step in front of the Smith."*

I pulled my poison darts free. They were coated in Smith's Folly. I'd brought them with me when I was lockpicking the Smith Estate. I hadn't needed them then, but I needed them now. They were tiny. Barely the size of a sewing needle. I shot them with a three-inch tube, and since I'd been practicing for more than a decade, I never missed.

At my shout, Finn must've remembered his promise. He stumbled, tripping forward. Luvic shoved away from him, spinning in a circle, blinded by the thunderer yet searching for a threat. He held his knife in front of him, a snarl curving his lip.

I didn't know if Finn could still see. He didn't seem at all bothered by the chaos erupting around him. All the same, when he pivoted in front of his father, I sent the dart whistling toward him.

Wolfgang arched his arm back, a viper about to strike. He was going to shove the knife through Finn's right eye. But then—

The dart hit Finn in the neck.

Finn collapsed just as Wolfgang's knife arched down to where he'd stood.

If Finn hadn't pivoted in front of his father, Wolfgang would've been struck. He realized this at the same moment that I sent another thunderer through the arching ballroom window. The twenty-foot-tall window shattered. The lightning flash caused another blinding explosion. The boom popped my ears. The ringing and screams melded.

This was going to be the tricky part.

Finn was down. Wolfgang knew he'd saved him.

But now . . . the conjurers would be looking for an assassin. Me. Obviously me.

I prayed they'd think the assailant had jumped through the window or slipped out another way. In fact . . .

"There! They're at the window!"

"Look!"

I looked to the window, and sure enough, a shadowed figure cloaked in black leaped through the broken glass and sprinted down the sidewalk.

That . . . ?

Who . . . ?

A group of Smiths, a Bard, and a Clark jumped through the window and chased after the figure.

I couldn't focus on that—I had to keep on with the plan. I ran toward Finn, shoving past gaudily dressed Bards and somberly dressed Clarks.

"I'm his body. I'm his body," I said, pushing to the center of the ballroom. I dropped to my knees, hitting the hard marble, and grabbed the dart in Finn's throat.

I yanked it out and tossed it to the ground.

"I'm his body," I said again, when Wolfgang Smith jerked me aside.

Wolfgang's face held a vicious light, and his gray eyes were full of so much lightning I wondered if it was really the solange that made Finn's eyes spark or if it was the Smith in him.

Darin sprinted to his father's side, shoving people back. He flicked his hands, and a ring of blue fire surrounded the four of us. The fire twisted and shielded, a burning ice that cut the rest of the ballroom off.

"Who are you?" Darin held out his hand, ready to send me to my next death, I was sure.

"Finn's body," I said. Then, pulling on all the acting and games and manipulations I'd needed growing up in Hell Gate, I whirled to Wolfgang. "I saw the assassin taking aim for you. I shouted to Finn. He protected you. He's hurt because he protected you!"

At that, Wolfgang picked up the dart on the floor. Twirled the steel in his hand and then peered at the glistening tip. Then he stared down at Finn.

My heart raced, beating wildly against my rib cage. Nausea gripped me, and I didn't want to meet Finn's eye. For some reason, my throat ached and burned like it does when you're trying desperately not to cry.

All the same, I couldn't avoid it forever.

Finn had collapsed as soon as the dart had pierced his skin. The poison worked quickly. First it paralyzed. Then it sent a burning, fiery acid into your tissue. I was told it felt like a thousand fire ants devouring your flesh.

You couldn't scream, though, because your vocal cords had stopped working.

After the burning, your capillaries would start to burst. The first evidence of that would be pinprick blood spots in your eyes. Then they'd bloom over your skin until you were a mottled purple-red.

Finally, your organs would burst one by one, a domino of hell-fire pain that was unfathomable. And then you died. But you were aware the entire time. You could see and hear and feel.

The good thing was it only lasted thirty minutes.

The bad thing was it lasted thirty minutes.

I gripped Finn's hand and then finally looked into his eyes. He couldn't move, but I swore I could see the pain and surprise in those navy blue depths. As if, sure, he'd expected a knife or something like that. He'd take a knife for the game, but poison? *This* poison?

And death?

That was the thing. I didn't have the antidote. I couldn't fix this.

Finn could be dead in thirty minutes, and something in his eyes told me he knew it. The navy blue pulsed between dusk and midnight, while the silver threads of lightning flashed back and forth, pulsing with a frenzy that spoke of immense, unspeakable pain.

Wolfgang swore and then dropped the dart to the floor, melting the metal with a flick of his hand. "Smith's Folly." He said the name of the poison like it was a curse.

To the Smiths, it was. The poison had been created centuries ago by a Bard who wanted the Smiths to feel every sword, every stabbing, every battle scar they'd ever caused. It was an extremely rare poison, almost impossible to come by . . . and it only worked on the Smiths. To anyone else, it'd be like being poked with water.

"He is truly your son," Darin said, his voice harsh and angry.

Finn's lips were turning blue. His breathing came in gasping, rattling pants, shallow and infrequent.

"He'll die then," Darin said. "He's already dead."

I gripped Finn's hand. "Save him." I stared at Wolfgang. The man may be terrifying, like a wrathful general who only dealt in death and loved the chaos and horror of war, but Jagger, in his own way, was just as terrifying. "He saved you. He's dying for you. That is what he wants to do in the game. Blood for blood. Life for life. You owe him a blood debt. Pay it by letting him be your paladin."

I held Wolfgang's stare, refusing to look away, even though his gaze felt like a thousand pounds crushing my mind.

Finn took another gasping, dying breath.

"His eyes . . ." Darin said.

I looked. A red pinprick burst in the white of his left eye. The poison was moving quickly.

"He wants to be your son. To make you proud," I said, even though I didn't know what Finn did or didn't want. "He promised he would win the games or die trying. Let him. Repay the blood debt you owe."

I looked back to Finn. His eyes weren't blank or bleary anymore; they were swirling with a torture I'd never known. Yet when he found me staring down at him, his shattered gaze hooked mine, and I got the strangest feeling he was trying to tell me something.

Maybe it was that Cora would kill me for hurting him. Or that I should tell her, his Eurydice, that he'd tried his best. Or perhaps he was trying to tell me that I was cold-hearted and ruthless, and he never should've trusted me with his life.

"No," Darin said. "No. I don't accept him as paladin. Let him die."

I swore Finn's eyes crashed with desperation at that. I squeezed his hand. He took another wheezing, pained breath.

Wolfgang contemplated Finn. Stared at the sweat beading on his forehead, the sickly-pale pallor, the red pinpricks blooming in his eyes. He took in the way I held his hand.

Outside the column of blue fire, the rest of the conjurers waited to see what would happen.

"And if I don't have the antidote?" Wolfgang asked.

"You wouldn't—"

Wolfgang held up a hand and cut Darin off.

"Then he dies, and you lose a son," I said.

"A son I don't care about. An accident. A null."

"Still a son."

Wolfgang thought about this. Watched the sweat trickle down Finn's forehead. Pondered the twisting anguish in his eyes. He thought for sixty seconds, seventy, ninety, which to Finn probably felt like a thousand lifetimes.

I'd heard that when someone was poisoned with Smith's Folly, they screamed inside the cage of their own minds. I'd been poisoned by Jagger's rattlesnakes, but I'd been told they had nothing on Smith's Folly.

Finally, Wolfgang leaned close to Finn and said, "I accept. Blood for blood. Life for life."

"Father—"

Wolfgang narrowed his eyes. "We accept."

Darin dropped his head in submission. If the Smith told his heir to do something, the heir would obey. That was how the Smiths worked. It was a hierarchical military first, and a family second.

"Pick him up. Take him to our rooms. We have minutes before he isn't worth keeping alive."

At that, Darin picked up Finn, dropped him over his shoulder, and kept a moving blue flame spinning around us as we stalked from the ballroom. Finn was big, muscular, but Darin was strong.

No one followed.

No one objected.

As I hurried to keep up, I chanced a look around the ballroom. It seemed more than a few people had taken advantage of the chaos. There was a man lying dead near the wooden tables, and a woman slumped on a chair, with blood oozing from her shoulder.

I wondered if the conjurers who'd jumped out the window racing after the figure had found anything. Except . . . that figure . . . it hadn't looked right.

Now that I thought about it, I was sure it was an illusion. A good illusion. A near perfect illusion. But still . . . an illusion.

And an illusion so strong could only be conjured by a head, an heir, or a powerful second child.

Which meant someone important had purposely distracted, misdirected, and lied.

But why?

We were at the marble archway that led to the hall when I felt a tickle on the back of my neck. I took one last look.

There, still standing at the edge of the champagne river, was Luvic Bard. He watched me with a funny smile on his face, champagne dripping over his skin, a strange light in his eyes.

When he saw me looking at him, his smile widened, and then . . . he winked.

Yes. I'm sure of it.

He winked as if we shared a grand secret and he thought it was . . . delightful.

The blue fire licked warningly at my heels, so I turned and rushed after the Smiths. My gamble, I prayed, had paid off. Finn wouldn't die. He'd enter the games.

We just might make it through the night.

18

The Smiths had a suite of rooms on the top floor. Once we were out of sight of the ballroom, down the long hall and to a set of wooden stairs tucked behind a red-wallpapered door, Wolfgang snapped, "Now we run."

And boy, did we run.

The Smiths took the steps two, three at a time, practically flying as they raced up the stairs. I sprinted to keep up with them, my stride not even half of theirs. We wound in a spiral, circling a narrow wooden hall that climbed the floors. It must've been an old servants' passage, because it had none of the gaudy splendor of the rest of the mansion.

When we burst onto the sixth floor, my heart was banging frantically, my lungs were tight, and my legs were burning. Darin wasn't careful with Finn. In fact, during the sprint, Finn had been banged about, knocked against walls, and basically treated like a piece of luggage. His skin was even paler than before, the color of the moon reflecting weakly off the East River. He hung prone and lifeless over his brother's shoulder.

I barely noticed the palatial hallway with its scarlet carpet and alcoves with marble statues that watched our flight. I followed, the blue fire still spinning. Then we were in front of a wide wooden double door covered in gold leaf. The door was carved with scenes of battle, mayhem, and gore.

The Smith thrust it open and pointed to a leather couch in what looked like a sitting room. "Put him there."

Darin kicked the door shut and stalked across the room, the blue flames disappearing once we were inside. The room was spartan compared to the first floor. Navy wallpaper. Walnut paneling. Wood floor. The brown leather couch, two club chairs across from it. A coffee table that was three legs and a slab of slate. A bookshelf, an armoire that moonlighted as a bar, and three wooden doors that led off the main room. It had a rough-around-the-edges feel that I was sure the Bards had deliberately prepared for the Smiths. It fit them.

Darin dropped Finn on the couch and rolled him onto his back. Finn's body was lax, but tension radiated off him. You could practically feel the pain rolling from him, like the scent of sweat on a muggy summer day. His pain hung in the air.

I stepped close to him. He couldn't turn his head, but I wanted him to know I was still there. As soon as I was in his line of vision, I was caught by the red pinpricks in his eyes. They were blooming like a bloodied garden. His lips were the blue of a forget-me-not, and his breathing was so slow it had almost stopped.

I couldn't say anything. I'd done this after all. I could only hold his gaze.

His eyes were swirling like a summer storm over the Atlantic. Sometimes, when storms rose, lightning struck the indigo water and waterspouts sprang up, sending whirling columns of silvery water dozens of feet into the air. It was violent and beautiful, and it was exactly how Finn's eyes looked at that moment.

Wolfgang strode to a closed door and yanked it open. Five seconds later, he was at Finn's side with a small glass vial and a hypodermic needle. He shoved the needle in the vial, pulled up the liquid, and then, in one smooth motion, shoved the needle into Finn's carotid artery and slowly pressed the plunger.

Finn gasped. It was raw and painful. His back arched, his fists clenched, and then he screamed. I only heard it for a millisecond before

Darin wove a gag of illusion. But still, the anguish in Finn's scream tore through me with claws and teeth. I wanted to reach out and take his hand again, but instead I stood still, expressionless, waiting for the antidote to devour all the Smith's Folly in his blood.

After thirty seconds, Finn dropped back to the couch, his eyes closed, and took a succession of quick, deep breaths. Darin twisted his hand, and the gag fell away.

Both Darin and Wolfgang stood over Finn, watching dispassionately as he yanked in breath after breath. He was still sweaty, and his skin had a few small bruises and red splotches, but I think Wolfgang had managed to administer the antidote before any permanent organ or tissue damage was done.

"Are you whole?" Wolfgang asked, echoing the question I wanted to ask.

Finn swallowed, pressed his hand into the couch, and slowly sat up. He opened his eyes. Looked at his father, his brother, then back to his father. He ignored me.

Finally, he answered. "Yes."

Back at the Night Den, his voice had been the low rumble of thunder in a summer storm. Now it was ravaged and raw, the desolation after the storm.

Wolfgang studied Finn, measuring whatever it was that conjurers looked for in people. Viciousness, maybe. Ruthlessness. Callousness. I didn't know. Maybe they looked for what Jagger looked for in his creatures. If so, I wasn't sure Finn had what it took. I'd only known him for a few hours, and I felt he was too soft, too trusting, too . . . Finn. He belonged back at the Night Den, lying on a couch, making love to Cora, sucking down thimbles of solange. A flash of anger burned in my stomach.

"You can perform in the games?" Wolfgang asked. "They'll deliver more pain than the Smith's Folly did."

Finn tilted his head, staring at his father. He leaned against the back of the leather couch, too weak to support himself. His arms trembled, and he looked dizzy.

"Will they?" he asked, as if he thought the Smith might not know what he was talking about.

"Assuredly," Wolfgang said. "Would you still be paladin, knowing that?"

Darin didn't say anything. He only stood by his father, his shoulders stiff, face hard. The heirs who played in the games spent their lives training for the event. I wondered how Darin felt about having his rightful place snatched from him at the last minute. Angry? Jealous? Happy? Relieved? Or murderously furious?

"I would," Finn said, his voice gaining strength. "I would still be your paladin."

"You have to be strong," Wolfgang said.

"I'm strong."

"You have to be cunning. Are you cunning?"

"Undoubtedly."

Darin snorted, but his father ignored him. Instead he nodded slowly. "And intelligent. Did you inherit your mother's weakness and irrationality or my strength and wisdom?"

Finn's jaw clenched, almost imperceptibly. "As with all children, half of me is my mother."

"Yes. The weaker half."

For the first time, a glint of anger entered Finn's eyes. Apparently, he didn't like Wolfgang talking about his human mother.

"Weak?" Finn asked, his voice quiet. "Water is often thought of as weak. It gives, it flows, it yields. Yet water destroys the greatest of us all. Perhaps we must be weak to be strong."

Wolfgang leaned close, coming within striking distance. "A paradox, son?"

Finn smiled. "Truth is often paradox."

Finally, Finn looked at me. His bloodshot eyes flickered over me and then quickly away again. I felt his gaze like cosmic rays showering down on me. My skin tingled electric, and my heart pounded in my throat.

How did he do that? How did he look at me and make me catch fire?

"The Bard's game is first," Darin said in a quiet murmur that held meaning beneath the simple sentence.

Wolfgang scratched the silver stubble on his chin. Then, after a long, tense pause, he said to Darin, "You won't win this year. The Ward heir is too strong. The Clark is underhanded, the Bard a problem, but the Ward …"

Ah.

Aha.

It seemed Jacob Ward was the accepted favorite.

Darin clenched his jaw. He looked like an almost exact replica of Finn when Finn had clenched his own jaw at the insult to his mom. Their resemblance was uncanny. I wondered how Finn had gone undetected for so long. I supposed it was because people only saw what they wanted to see.

Wolfgang put a hand on Darin's shoulder. "Nothing is certain, except you will not win. Always know when to fight and when to retreat."

Darin bowed his head. "Yes, Father."

In the past, I'd heard Darin was the weakest Smith heir born in centuries. He was skilled at swordplay, shooting, martial arts—anything physical. He was immensely strong. From seeing him carry Finn up six flights of stairs, I'd say he was easily as strong as three men. But I'd heard rumors his conjuring was weaker than most heirs. I'd never believed the rumors until now.

Darin's mother had been a Clark. A third daughter of a third son of a third daughter. A last of a last. It was said her blood was so weak that she diluted the Smiths' line and then inconveniently died after giving birth.

That was what the rumors blamed Darin's weakness on. Maybe they were right. Who knew? Wolfgang Smith had never remarried; he just consoled himself with pleasurers at the Night Den.

All the same, Darin could still conjure a ward of blue fire, and he could still kill me or Finn as easily as blinking. I didn't doubt that. A weak heir was still an heir.

"We'll send him to the games then?" Darin frowned at Finn. "Maybe to his death."

Finn was still sprawled on the couch, his limbs heavy and his eyes sleepy again.

Wolfgang stared at Finn's drawn features. "If he dies, he dies. If he wins, you are crowned."

Darin nodded.

"Does it bother you, to lose a brother?"

Darin shrugged. "He isn't a brother of mine."

Finn let out a long sigh and struggled to sit up. He rolled his shoulders and then said, "Now that that's settled, do you mind? I'd like a short nap before the games begin."

Darin snorted.

Wolfgang watched Finn as if he were considering how he could stab him and still have him play in the games. He reminded me of a grizzled general who didn't remember what civilian life was like.

"What about the body?" Darin asked, nodding at me. "He should use Aska. My body. Not that one."

"Yes." Wolfgang barely glanced at me. "He'll use Aska."

Aska? *Aska?* I sent Finn a beseeching look, and then, when he stared at me blankly, I glared and bared my teeth at him.

"You may leave," Wolfgang said. He waved toward the door.

Leave? I glared at Finn. Made a motion as if to say, "Come on!"

He knew I had to be his body. He knew I was part of the bargain with Jagger. He *knew* this.

"Go on," Darin said impatiently.

"Finn—"

Wolfgang cut his hand at me, and I braced myself, waiting for a conjuring.

But then Finn said in a bored drawl, "One thing. She's my body, or else . . . deal's off."

Wolfgang's hand hung in the air between us. I held my breath.

"Aska has trained for years—"

Finn cut Darin off. "Doesn't matter. I want Mari. She's the only body I trust."

I held still, questions circling in my mind. He trusted me? He still trusted me? I stared at him, but he didn't look at me. Instead he stayed slumped on the couch, wearing an unconcerned expression.

"Fine." Wolfgang dropped his hand.

I let out a relieved breath.

Then Wolfgang pulled from his jacket the dagger he'd threatened Finn with in the ballroom.

"Hold out your hand."

Finn smiled and then slowly extended his palm. Darin thrust his hand out, holding it next to his brother's. Wolfgang slashed a line across the meat of his palm, then Darin's, and finally Finn's. A thin red line welled on each of their hands. Then Wolfgang clasped their three hands together.

"Second son for heir," he said. "Blood for blood. Life for life. It is done."

A jolt of power snapped over my skin and pulsed around the room. Wolfgang unclasped their hands. Darin stumbled back. Finn blinked and then shook himself off, as if he'd just emerged from a dunk in the river and was flinging off water droplets.

"That's done," Wolfgang said, a satisfied curl to his lips.

I wondered what it was that was done; what sort of conjurer ceremony he'd just performed. If he were Jagger, I'd say he'd just sealed a bargain with blood magic. But he wasn't a leggerock who used blood for magic; he was a conjurer who used illusions and lies.

"The opening ceremony is in two hours," Wolfgang said, clenching his hand so the blood wouldn't fall. "And you'll be our paladin." He turned to me, weighed me up, and tried to crush me with his gaze. "And you'll be his body."

"It's done," Darin said, sounding none too happy.

Then the suite door swung wide, and the Bard, the Clark, and the Ward were standing in the entryway.

"Paladin?" the Clark asked. He gave a paper-thin smile. "Isn't that interesting . . . ?"

The Bard stared at Finn for a long moment and then turned to Wolfgang. It was abundantly clear a body was something to be ignored. None of them looked at me once.

"In light of the events . . ." Dagrid Bard paused and then said, "And the death of Secondus Clark—"

I looked to Herman Clark, shocked. I wondered if he'd show a flicker of remorse, but there wasn't a sign of grief or even a hint of sadness. So it was Secondus who I'd seen lying dead on the ballroom floor. But who was the woman that had been stabbed?

"In light of those events and our failure to apprehend the assassin, I demand an inquisition of both your paladin—"

"An inquisition?" Wolfgang said in a dangerous voice. "In your blasted chair? I think not."

"Of your paladin and his body," finished the Bard.

And for once, all the conjurers turned to look at me.

I swallowed and waited for the Clark to say, "Wait a moment! That's the little thief! That's Jagger's creature!"

But he didn't.

I stood quietly and waited, preparing a thousand escape routes in my mind.

And then what though? Then what? I had to play this out. I had to finish the game.

"Section three, article forty-three, clause four," said the Clark in a scholarly voice. "'To maintain the integrity of the games, an unknown entrant may be questioned to the families' satisfaction before entry to the games. Questioning may include non-maiming torture, inquisition, or truth-telling.'" He smiled blandly at Wolfgang. "As you see, the rules."

There was a cold fury growing in Wolfgang's expression. I didn't think he was exactly concerned about Finn; I think it was more that he didn't enjoy being gainsaid.

Me, though? I was terrified of being questioned. I knew Jagger had said to tell the truth, but this was more than that.

The Bards had a chair. It dated back to the inquisition. I'd never seen it, but I'd heard of it. The priests who used it believed in the power of the inquisitor so much that the chair had been infused with the ability to make people tell the truth. The absolute truth.

The chair ripped all your secrets from you. It violated the depths of your mind. Whatever was asked, you had to answer with the truth.

I'd gotten Finn into the games, and he'd demanded I stay his body even when he had a chance to get rid of me. But now . . . if the conjurers asked the right question while I was in the chair . . . they'd learn I was a lockpick. They'd . . . they'd torture me . . . deliver a thousand agonizing deaths . . . they'd . . .

Sweat lined my forehead, and the spot where I'd been shot burned with an icy fire.

Finn caught my gaze and gave me a smile that was surprisingly reassuring.

"We submit to an inquisition," Wolfgang said, although the way he said it didn't sound like a submission. It sounded like a declaration of war.

"Come along then." The Bard gestured to the hall, and the conjurers followed him out of the Smiths' sitting room.

I stepped forward and helped Finn stand.

"It looks like the games have already begun," Darin said, a dry twist to his lips.

Wolfgang snorted.

Finn leaned into my side, although I could tell his strength was already returning. I helped him out of the room, bracing his weight as we followed the conjurers toward our inquisition.

As we walked, Finn leaned close, his warm breath fanning over my ear when he said, "Don't worry, Mari. Truth is in circles. It's paradoxes and mirrors. They can't recognize truth because it isn't in them. It'll be all right."

No, I didn't think so. If they asked me the right question and I was forced to answer it, things would certainly *not* be all right. But Finn, being Finn, didn't seem able to get upset about anything at all.

Unless someone insulted his mom.

"By the way," he murmured, trailing a few more feet behind the others, "next time you decide to kill me, try not to make it hurt so much."

When I looked at him, he was wearing a small smile, and his eyes lit with laughter.

He was *laughing* at me poisoning him. He was laughing at the pain.

"You're insane." He was actually enjoying this. I was sure of it.

"What would you have done if they hadn't given me the antidote?" There was genuine curiosity in his question.

I thought about it. "Ran?"

He laughed—a quick, quiet rumble. "Would you have felt bad?"

"Not really. Maybe for a minute. A week tops."

He grinned at me, his lightning eyes streaking. "I'm not the insane one here. Tell the truth, Mari."

I thought he meant for me to tell the truth about how long I'd mourn for him if he died, but then I realized we'd made it to a thick wooden door and all the conjurers were filtering inside a dark room.

It was time for our next test. We'd found the inquisitor's chair.

Just tell the truth.

No matter if it got you killed.

19

I'D NEVER BEEN INSIDE THIS PARTICULAR ROOM. REMEMBER, I'D NEVER MADE it past the front entry before today. If Jagger had known about this room, though, I was certain he would have sent me to plumb its depths years ago.

It was a treasure room of sorts. Or a junk heap. Or that one room where you toss all the things you don't use but also don't want to throw away.

The room was about thirty feet by twenty feet, and every inch of it was jammed with objects of power, objects of uselessness, and plain old objects. The difficulty was in sorting them out.

I was pretty sure the porcelain vases teetering on a wooden nightstand were objects of power, but the nightstand was just an object. The moldering striped couch was likely an object of uselessness, and the dozens of stacks of newspapers from the past 100 years were probably just plain old objects. But the trouble was, you never knew.

The hat rack with the flapper hats, the bowler hats, and the top hats . . . I'd be careful of that. But the mannequin with the Hollywood glam dress? That was probably kept because some Bard had worn it to an award ceremony and liked the celery color and the sequins. Then again, it might be an object that, if worn, would make you suddenly desirable to everyone who saw you. The catch being that they'd desire you to death.

You might be wondering how it is that ordinary objects gain power, or how beings like Roumelade are born. You might be saying, "Hang on, Mari. You said conjurers manifest their thoughts, but Roumelade wasn't made by conjurers, and neither was the inquisitor's chair."

Well, remember, all humans were once conjurers to one degree or another. Then the flood happened, and only the conjurers were left with the ability to conjure. But every human still has that primordial seed inside them. So when a large group of humans fervently believe something, whether subconsciously or consciously, it becomes reality.

That's why you suddenly have wacky placebos curing dreaded diseases. Or, for instance, sometimes the *sound* of the guillotine killed people. There'd be the crowd expecting death, the person under the guillotine expecting death, and when the guillotine malfunctioned, the person would still die. They died because everyone believed they were going to die.

Beings, though, like Roumelade, Winnie, Growlings, and more, they are created from a massive welling of emotion. The emotional thought is so great—for instance, thousands dying at once—that the thoughts all congeal and become . . . Winnie. Or Roumelade. Or a Growling.

Anyway, we all crowded into the small, cleared space surrounding the inquisitor's chair. I stood next to Wolfgang and a musty stack of newspapers that was three feet taller than me. Although terrifying, Wolfgang was currently the devil I knew, and his quick flash of rage at the mention of the inquisitor's chair, and then the short laugh at Darin's sarcasm, had made me feel he was at least a *little* human.

I know. I know. You're reminding me of Roumelade's rule. I instinctively want to give Wolfgang traits of kindness, humor, or compassion. It's a failing of mine. I've done it since I can remember. That's the trouble though. Living in a place as dark as Hell Gate, even the tiniest kindness seems like a bright light to me.

Suddenly, a short laugh makes a Smith a nice guy. A man who has spawned seeds of war across the world. See? This is a problem for me. I have to remind myself, one of the qualities of evil is that it does its best to have the appearance of good. Evil is the great mimicker.

Conjurers use this trick all the time. For centuries, they've had millions of people at once believing evil is good, wrong is right, and upside down is right side up.

Standing in close quarters, the scent of old newspaper and moth-eaten clothing tinging the stagnant air, I looked around for an escape route. No windows. One door. Five conjurers between me and the only escape.

And Finn, strapped to a silver chair.

It wasn't as if Finn had resisted. He'd sat in the chair as if Dagrid Bard were offering him a first-class spot on the Titanic and he wasn't aware it was going to sink. Then, when the Bard closed the silver shackles around his ankles, and then around his wrists, Finn didn't even blink. He just leaned back with a happy sigh and gave a little yawn, as if a metal chair that had tortured thousands was as comfortable as that red velvet couch in the Night Den.

When he saw me staring at him, he gave another half-smile. My stomach clenched. If the chair didn't have shackles, it would almost look like a throne. The legs were thick, the rectangular back tall, and the ornate silver filigree had been laid intricately over the metal. It was pretty, in a twisted way.

"State your name."

That was Philoneas Ward. It was decided that he'd be the one to do the questioning, based on the fact that a Ward's strength was mental prowess.

Tonight was the first time I'd heard his voice. I'd like to say it gave me the shivers or scraped over my skin like a skeletal finger, but honestly, his voice was ordinary and forgettable. He sounded a bit like how I imagined a guidance counselor or a concerned social worker would sound. Soft-voiced, caring, calm. Okay, fine. *That* gave me the shivers.

Finn smiled. "Finn Alterra."

"Good." Philoneas nodded. "And who is your father?"

"Wolfgang Smith."

This shouldn't have been shocking—not anymore—but all the

conjurers besides Darin and Wolfgang shifted with surprise. As if they didn't *quite* believe it.

"And your mother?" Philoneas asked.

"Lilith Alterra."

"Human?"

"Human."

Maybe no one else noticed, but I was watching Finn carefully. He looked relaxed, but there was the slightest sheen of perspiration lining his forehead, and while he was slouched, there was also a coiled tension just below the surface. As if it was taking all his effort to stay in that relaxed pose.

"Did she raise you?"

"Yes."

"Where?"

"The Night Den."

Philoneas tilted his head like a cat hearing the light step of a mouse tiptoeing in the walls. "What does she do at the Night Den?"

"She was a pleasurer."

"I'll bet she was," the Bard said with a hint of malicious glee. "Wolfgang always loved his little pleasurers. Perhaps I'll give her a go. But then . . . no. I don't care for yesterday's garbage."

I didn't see anything change in Finn's expression, but it was as if I could feel his rage. It pulsed around me and pressed on my chest. I could practically hear his threat: "Say one more word about my mother, and I'll slaughter you."

Even so, he only gave one of his vacant smiles. The effect was frightening, but none of the others seemed to notice the rage beneath his smile.

"Where is Lilith now?" Philoneas asked, ignoring the Bard.

"Dead."

"When did she die?"

"Twenty years ago."

"How?"

"Blood cancer."

"You've lived at the Night Den your entire life?"

"Yes."

"Enough." Herman Clark cut in. "Ask him if he killed Secondus."

"Ask him if he stabbed Morjorie," the Bard added. "Or if he'd like to stab Morjorie."

Darin leaned into his father and murmured, "If they don't shut up, can I kill them? Start a war? That'd be fun."

Wolfgang lifted an eyebrow as if to say, "You could try."

Philoneas hadn't bothered to look at anyone else; instead he'd kept his eyes on Finn. "You're a null?"

"Yes."

"No conjuring abilities?"

"None."

The Clark and the Bard shared a smug look, and then the Clark said, "Accidents do happen."

Philoneas cleared his throat. "Do you have a trait?"

Finn swallowed. Remained silent.

Philoneas reworded his question. "Human-conjurer children often have special abilities, called traits, like precognition, healing, audio clairvoyance . . . Do you have a trait?"

Finn closed his eyes. Clenched his jaw. A tic started beneath his eye. Finally, a single word was wrenched from him. "Yes."

The Bard and the Clark leaned closer, the fabric of their black tuxes whispering as if conspiring together, their shadows stretching toward the silver chair.

Philoneas tilted his head. "What is your trait?"

Finn stared at Philoneas, sweat lining his brow. Another word was wrenched from him. "Strength."

Philoneas considered this. The air in the closed room was growing stagnant and even more stale than when we'd first entered. The mustiness and the dust were pressing down on me, making my eyes itch. I watched Finn, his pulse pounding in his throat. My eyes were watery, so I blinked the dampness away.

"How strong?" Philoneas asked.

"I deadlift a . . . metric ton."

At that, Darin lifted his eyebrows and gave his half-brother a considering glance. It was the look one man gave another when he was wondering who would be the last man standing if they went at each other fist to fist. From the expression on his face, Darin wasn't quite sure which of them would walk away the winner.

But Philoneas merely nodded as if lifting a metric ton wasn't anything special. I supposed to most conjurers it wasn't. The greatest of them, the crowned, could move mountains with their minds.

Philoneas continued in his quiet, soothing voice. "You take solange."

"I do."

"Why?"

Finn looked toward me and then away. His eyes swirled, lightning skittering across navy. "Why not?"

"Why do you take solange?"

A drop of sweat trailed down Finn's forehead, and his chest rose and fell more rapidly, as if he was once again fighting the pain of the poison. But the poison was gone, so that meant he was fighting the pain of the chair.

But what was there to hide? Solange was solange. There were only so many reasons someone walked that road, and none of them were worth hiding.

Finn made a pained sound in the back of his throat.

Philoneas leaned forward and asked again, in that pleasant voice, "Why do you take solange?"

Finn stiffened and let out a ragged breath. Then he exhaled, and a long string of words were yanked forcefully out of him. "Solange is the light. In the light, I find the creator and the destroyer. Solange is the savior."

At the end of the ragged sentence, Finn gasped and dropped his chin to his chest.

For a moment, everyone stood in absolute stillness, taking in how much Finn had struggled *not* to say that.

The five men, all dressed in tuxes, formed a black semicircle around Finn. There was a beat of silence, the press of questions unanswered in the air.

Philoneas narrowed his eyes and asked again, "Why do you take solange?"

This time Finn didn't struggle; he only repeated in monotone, his chin down, eyes closed. "Solange is the light. In the light, I find the creator and the destroyer. Solange is the savior."

"Solange-addicted," Darin said, shaking his head. "It's what they all say at the end."

The Bard chuckled, happy with the evidence. At the sound of his schadenfreude, my hand curled into a fist. The musty air stung my eyes, and I blinked back tears.

"Are you in free fall?" Philoneas asked.

Finn opened his eyes again. They blazed with the light he spoke of. He stared at Philoneas with a disconcerting expression. "Me?" he asked. "We're *all* in free fall."

"But are you?"

Finn shrugged. "I'm either falling or I'm flying. Perhaps that's free fall."

"Are you in *solange* free fall?"

Finn smiled, leaned back in the chair, and took an unsteady breath. "Yes."

He looked tired. His skin was chalky and perspiration-lined. His eyes were red-pinpricked and bloodshot. There were pain lines bracketing his mouth and purple hollows beneath his eyes. I wondered if the bliss of the solange was wearing off, or if the poison had chased it away and now the inquisitor's chair was closing the door.

"How much longer do you have in free fall?"

Finn closed one eye. Peered at Philoneas. Opened it and then closed his other. He'd done that with the doorman too. I wondered if his cosmic eyes showed him something different when he did that, or if it was just a tic.

"No one knows how long their fall will last."

"Guess."

"A guess isn't a truth."

"If you continue in free fall, will you see the end of the year?"

Finn's chest rose. Fell. "No." This was said in a low growl.

It was June. That meant he had less than six months.

"Will you live longer than a month? Thirty days?"

The Bard smiled, tapping the steel watch on his wrist. "Ticktock," he seemed to say.

Finn shook his head. "I don't know." This was said unwillingly, I could tell, because it was uttered between clenched teeth.

For some reason, at those words, I wanted to comfort him. I wanted to walk the ten steps that separated us, push past the semicircle of conjurers, and get down on my knees. I wanted to wrap my arms around his middle and hold him.

Maybe it was the same reason I wrapped dead moths in tissue, bought Griff lox and bagels, or picked dandelions with Roumelade under the full moon even when I was almost too tired to stand. Maybe it was just one human wanting to comfort another. But it felt like more. It felt like I needed to hold him and then scream at him for even thinking about leaving this world.

That was an idiotic sentiment. Especially since less than an hour ago, I'd shot a dart into him that could've ushered him out of this world in minutes. It's just . . . there was something about him that turned everything inside me upside down. I couldn't say I liked it.

"Why did you come here tonight?" Philoneas asked.

"To be my brother's paladin in the games."

"Why do you want to be your brother's paladin?"

"To win."

The Bard gave a loud laugh at that. He seemed to think it was a grand joke. "You can try."

Finn stared at the Bard, although I'm not sure if he noticed the Bard was laughing. He seemed to be looking at something else.

Finally, the Bard's laughter died, but a smile remained.

"Hurry your questions." The Clark cut his hand impatiently. "The ceremony is in less than two hours, and all you've learned is that he's solange-addicted and the son of a pleasurer."

Philoneas waited for the mumblings of the Clark to cease. Wolfgang merely stared at Finn, his arms crossed, mouth flat. Darin still had the uncomfortable frown he'd worn since Finn spouted his solange prayer.

Finally, Philoneas continued. "Did your father ask you to enter the games as paladin?"

"No."

"Did anyone ask you to enter the games as paladin?"

"Yes."

I expected Philoneas to show a reaction to Finn's answers. Surprise. Interest. Anger. Concern. Anything. Instead he was still coolly polite, calmly soothing, strangely untouched.

When Finn admitted someone had asked him to enter the games, Philoneas nodded, unconcerned, and asked, "Who?"

"Jagger." Finn threw out the name as if it was of no concern to him.

I tensed, waiting for the explosion. But there was no explosion, no outrage, just a sort of amused indifference.

I flushed cold, a laugh caught in my throat. They didn't care. None of them. Not at all. The monster of my life, the bogeyman who ruled my world . . . he meant nothing to them. Jagger hated conjurers with an everlasting, burning passion, and the conjurers . . . they couldn't even work up a small emotion like distaste. Jagger was *nothing* to them. That would infuriate him.

"And what did Jagger ask of you?"

Finn lifted a shoulder in a half-shrug. "To win the games or die trying."

"You bargained?"

"Yes."

"What was the bargain? Say the words."

A muscle twitched under Finn's eye. "If I, Finn Alterra, win the Hundred Year Games with Mari Locke as my body, then Jagger Leggerock will grant me a lifetime supply of solange . . . If I lose, my life is forfeited."

The Bard laughed again. He had a robust, melodious laugh. It filled the room with mirth and glee. He was the principal—he currently wore the crown of illusions. Decades ago, he was a movie star, and you could hear the movie-star quality in the richness of his laughter. He wiped a tear from under his eye.

"I haven't had this much fun in ages. A lifetime supply? Your lifetime is limited to days. A month? Two?" The Bard grinned and chuckled again.

"Solange truly does cloud the mind." He waved a hand. "You have my blessing. Please. Join the games. Enjoy. You lose, you die. You win, you die. You die, you die. Ah, Wolfgang, your children do you proud. Weak. Both of them."

I expected Darin to object, but instead he looked bored, as if he'd heard the insult a thousand times before and it had ceased to have any power over him.

"Finish it," Wolfgang said to Philoneas.

"Would you have entered the games without the bargain?" Philoneas asked.

"No," Finn said. A simple answer to a simple question.

"I'm curious. What will you do if you win?"

At that, Finn's jaw clenched. His muscles strained. The lines around his eyes tightened, and I knew he was fighting the chair again. I wondered if this was where the truth about Finn would come out. I wondered what solange-filled secret he was hiding. Was this the end? My heart pounded, seeking escape, urging me to flee.

"What will you do if you win?" Philoneas asked again, his voice soft and eerily pleasant.

Finn made a pained sound, and his fingers curled around the arms of the chair, his knuckles turning white. His breath came in rapid pants, and as Philoneas spoke again, he strained against the metal shackles binding him.

Philoneas shook his head as if he was a patient, caring man and couldn't understand why Finn wouldn't answer the simple question. "Finn. What will you do if you win?"

"Cry."

The word burst from Finn so forcefully that I jumped.

No one noticed. Philoneas tilted his head in that catlike gesture again. Darin raised his eyebrows, and the Bard snickered.

"Cry?"

"Yes," Finn said, his teeth gritted.

"And what else? What else will you do if you win? After you cry." Philoneas smiled at the last bit.

Finn closed his eyes. Tilted his head toward the ceiling. "I'll have sex until I'm so weak I can't stand."

The Bard snorted. "And how long will that take?"

It wasn't Philoneas who asked, but Finn was still compelled to answer.

"Weeks." His voice was raw, and his words shivered over me. "Weeks of sex."

He exhaled raggedly and then dropped his chin. Opened his eyes. His gaze was cosmic-bright. His eyes were shining with silver lightning and the birth of a nebula. He was thinking . . . you could see it . . . he was thinking of weeks and weeks of sex. Sex until he was too weak to stand.

Justice had said he was an exhibitionist. A hedonist. I wondered if Finn would have sex with dozens out in the open, on a couch or on a table in the middle of the Night Den where everyone could see, or if he had a secluded room where he and Cora would lie with tangled limbs and rumpled sheets for blissful weeks on end.

I thought about him stroking Cora's breast . . . the vacant smile on his face. I thought about her pressing her glowing fingers to his lips. I thought about Finn having sex.

My skin was hot, itchy, and uncomfortable. There was a tingle working its way over me, and a tightening in my belly that felt a little like hunger and a lot like need.

I'd never had sex before.

To me, it had always symbolized danger, an unguarded, naked back, and the possibility of death.

But what would sex be like with someone like Finn? Weeks of sex?

He looked at me then, as if he could hear my thoughts. I felt it again —the press of his fingers to my cheek, the brush of his lips over my naked shoulder, the vibration of his whispered words against the shell of my ear. I flushed red, and Finn smiled.

"Will you do anything else besides cry, have sex, and gorge on solange?" Philoneas asked.

Finn didn't take his eyes off me. "No. Those are my only plans."

I swallowed, my throat incredibly dry, skin burning.

Philoneas nodded and then wiped his hands together. "And do you know what Jagger's plans are?"

"No."

"Were you sent to—or do you plan to—kill any conjurers, members of the families, dependents, or guests within these walls?"

"No."

"Did you kill Secondus Clark?"

"No."

"Did you stab Morjorie Bard?"

"No."

"Do you know who killed Secondus Clark or stabbed Morjorie Bard?"

"No."

"Did you attempt to kill Wolfgang Smith with Smith's Folly?"

"No."

"Do you know who attempted to kill Wolfgang Smith with Smith's Folly?"

"No."

The questions had come rapid-fire, with Finn's nos a quick staccato between questioning beats. But at the final no, I almost jerked in surprise. He *did* know. Except no. He didn't. Because no one had attempted to kill Wolfgang Smith. I'd always been aiming at Finn.

Finn had told the truth, because I hadn't attempted to kill Wolfgang.

That was what Finn was trying to tell me. *Just tell the truth, Mari.*

My shoulders relaxed.

"Will you attempt to kill anyone while within these walls?"

Finn gave a lazy smile to the room at large. "Even I can't predict the future. But I have no immediate plans."

Wolfgang snorted at that, and once again, I saw a flash of humor in him that I didn't expect.

Philoneas cleared his throat. "Fine. Last question. Who is Mari Locke?"

20

THE CHAIR WAS AS UNCOMFORTABLE AS IT LOOKED. MORE SO. THE METAL was hard, and the silver filigree had rough ridges that dug into my legs and my back. It was strangely hot, like a branding iron thrust from the fire. My skin burned, and even though I knew there was only musty dust and rotting newspapers, I swore I could smell burning coals and fire.

It hurt. Philoneas Ward had barely asked any questions. I'd answered right away, and still, it hurt.

I was beginning to appreciate the skill behind Finn's demeanor. It couldn't all be solange, could it?

Perhaps the stumbling, addled, blissed-out drunk was an act to cover up . . . the man who'd leaped across the table with rage in his eyes and grasped my wrist. The man who'd threatened slaughter with his eyes when someone insulted his dead mom. The man who'd laughed at being poisoned and withstood the sort of pain this chair was firing out without even flinching.

Because it hurt. I knew pain. This chair was in a special torture class of its own.

The fiery heat licked over the chair and sank needle teeth into my skin. Every time Philoneas asked a question in his calm, soothing counselor voice, the flames clamped down on me and poured a cauldron of boiling oil through my veins. At least, that was what it felt like.

So far, we'd determined my name, the fact that I didn't know who my parents were, and that I was one of Jagger's creatures.

"And what sort of creature are you?" Philoneas asked.

I decided I hated him. He was so bland, his features so forgettable. He was like a lurer pretending to be something he wasn't. He put you at ease with his gentle, soothing voice so you wouldn't realize he was a complete sociopath until it was too late.

"A nine," I said, clenching my teeth at the boiling cauldron fires rolling through me. The chair burned, but it also pressed a wedge into your brain and thrust answers from your mouth.

I didn't know how Finn had remained relaxed, and I especially didn't know how he hadn't immediately answered. To answer was to find relief.

Finn watched me from across the room. He was leaning against a stack of newspapers, his shoulders slumped, eyes at a sleepy half-mast. No one had paid him any attention since they'd unshackled him from the chair. They'd discounted him as a solange-addled hedonist who was in the games for solange and sex. A man too stupid to see the bargain he'd made could only end in death. When Philoneas asked who I was, Finn said, "My body."

That was all he would say. I was his body.

The conjurers weren't as interested in what I had to say. In fact, knowing I was Jagger's creature, they held me in lower esteem than even Jagger, which meant I had about the value of an ant or a centipede.

"A nine." Philoneas smiled, as if being a nine was amusing. "What life are you on?"

A hard metal hand was shoved into my skull, and I gasped. "Eight."

"Why are you here?"

"To be Finn's body."

"Why else are you here?"

Jagger had told me to tell the truth. He knew I wouldn't be able to fool the conjurers. He was right. A hot sweat broke out on my head, and my skin felt as if it would catch fire.

"To steal the crown for Jagger." The words were ripped from me.

Shoved from my mind to my lips. I couldn't have stopped them if I'd wanted to.

The Bard laughed, his melodious, gleeful mirth filling the room. "She thinks to steal the crown. Don't you know what happens to those who attempt to steal the crown of illusions?"

"I know." I answered before the burning oil could start boiling inside of me.

"No one can steal the crown. The leggerock is a nuisance." This was from Wolfgang, and not a question, so there was nothing for me to say even though the wedge pressed me to say *something*.

"Why else are you here?" Philoneas asked, his voice a soothing calm.

I didn't want to say it. I didn't want to say it.

Finn watched me, his gaze holding mine, a life raft in a sea of pain. He knew how much it hurt, because he'd just experienced it. I wondered, was this burning fire what the beginning stages of Smith's Folly had felt like, or was it less? Maybe this was instant karma for poisoning Finn.

But then, he didn't seem especially happy to witness my pain.

I smelled smoke and the acrid tang of burnt skin—either a hallucination or a figment from the chair's past—and I gritted my teeth in response. The wedge, that gauntleted hand, shoved viciously at my brain. I arched my back and strained against the compulsion to say it. Even the burning fires were whispering, "Say it . . . say it, and the pain will stop."

I stared at Finn. He held my gaze, lightning pulsing. *Tell the truth*, he seemed to say. *Tell the truth, Mari.*

The words wrenched from me. "To kill Finn Alterra."

The Bard gave a surprised laugh, and Darin let out a low whistle. "Some body," he said.

"Why?" asked Philoneas.

"Because Jagger wants him dead."

"When?"

"After Finn wins the crown."

Philoneas turned and smiled at the slouching Finn. "It seems Jagger wants his lifetime supply of solange to last only a . . . very short lifetime."

Finn didn't pay any attention to Philoneas. Instead he watched me.

There was a moment where he looked surprised, but then he gave me his bleary smile and nodded a single time as if he didn't expect anything less.

A single tear tracked down my cheek. It was hot, and the wetness tickled my skin, but I couldn't brush it away, because my wrists were shackled. Instead the wet trail stayed on my skin for all the conjurers to see.

Philoneas watched the evidence of my weakness drop from my cheek and then asked, "How long have you known Finn Alterra?"

"Since this morning."

"And do you like him?"

The wedge pulsed, twisted, not sure which way to push or where the right answer lay. So that was how Finn did it. There were more than two truthful answers to this question. I was still compelled to answer, but which answer could I give?

"No, I don't," I said, and the scalding pain lessened.

Finn grinned at me.

"Then why the tears?"

"Because," I said without needing the compulsion. "He's in love, and he's going to die."

At that, the grin on Finn's face disappeared. Wiped away as if it'd never been. He stared at me as if he was trying to pry inside my mind and discover if I was speaking the truth or some alternative version of the truth that the chair had allowed.

The Clark curled his lip. "Enough. Did you kill Secondus?"

"No."

Philoneas sighed, shook his head, and then continued the questioning the Clark had begun. "Did you stab Morjorie?"

"No."

"Did you attempt to kill Wolfgang Smith?"

"No." There was a hard push at that, a scorching of fire in my veins, but still . . . the answer was no.

"Do you plan to kill any conjurer, member of the families, dependent, or guest of this household?"

Here's the thing. Roumelade had given me the earrings to kill Philoneas, his wife, and Jacob. Justice had given me the dagger to deliver death in one strike. But I hadn't yet decided whether or not I was going to kill the Wards.

There was only one person I had to kill. "Only Finn Alterra."

Another tear squeezed out of my eyes and dropped down my cheek. The salt burned my skin.

Philoneas tilted his head. Studied me as if I was a puzzle with a missing piece. Suddenly, I was nervous he would delve deeper; ask more questions about Jagger and my role there. I worried he was going to land on the fact that I was a lockpick.

The wedge shoved at my mind, sensing an untold truth. The fire raced through my veins. I clenched my muscles, tensing against the pain.

"You're welcome to him," Wolfgang said finally, his rough voice calm. "But wait until after the games, won't you?"

All the conjurers but Philoneas laughed. He was still watching me, a wrinkle lining his forehead.

I couldn't look at him. Instead I kept my eyes on Finn. I know I'd just said I was going to kill him, but still, his steady gaze, relaxed shoulders, and half-smile were the only things keeping my head above water.

"I'm curious," Philoneas said. "What does Jagger expect to do with the crown?"

"Rule the world. Kill all of you. Rule the world."

The Bard's laugh rang loud. Again. "Splendid. A pebble wants to break a boulder."

Wolfgang stepped forward. "I've heard enough." He unbuckled the shackles at my wrists. "You may act as my son's body in the games. You may even kill him once the games are done." He raised an eyebrow as if he wasn't sure I had enough skill to accomplish the feat. "But be warned, once the game is over, I'll be ending you as well. Creature or not, you can die a final death."

I shuddered as he unclasped my ankles. Once unbound, the scalding fire in my blood vanished, and the painful wedge shoving at my mind disappeared.

Finn weaved forward, a little unsteady. He held out his hand to me, palm up, a wobbly smile on his lips. I stared at him, unsure of how he could be offering a hand when I'd just proclaimed my intent to murder him.

"Why? I'm here to kill you. Now you know the truth."

He shrugged. Smiled. "Yes. Now I know."

After a brief hesitation, I gripped his hand, and he helped me to stand. He was warm, almost feverish, and his pupils were blown wide. How much more could he take before collapsing and sleeping for days?

Finn's hand was calloused and comforting. He kept ahold of me while we walked out of the Bard's musty treasure room, back into the bright light of the hallway.

"Opening ceremony is in less than two hours," Darian said, turning to Finn and me. He frowned, looking over Finn, taking in his wrinkled clothes, messy hair, and bruised skin. He sighed and shook his head. "Come on. We have a lot to do if you want to stay alive until then."

Finn grinned at his brother as if he'd just told a particularly funny joke.

Darin scowled at me. "Try not to kill him until it's over, all right?"

I nodded. Insane. Insane family. Insane conjurers.

At that, Wolfgang stalked past us, and we followed him to the Smiths' suite to prepare for battle.

21

THE JAGGED, BLOWN-OUT GLASS TINKLED A SOFT MELODY AS THE WIND swept from the quiet, moonlit city street into the Bard ballroom.

It skidded over the sharp-edged glass, blew the shards like wind chimes across the marble floor, and slid across a cold stain of blood. The wind had been to the Bard mansion plenty before, for devilry and dancing and entertainments where scent and sound and touch were exquisite and pleasure-filled.

The wind liked the Bards. It ran along their chords, vibrated across their centuries of music, circled around rhyming verse and poetry, and bubbled in the drama of their theatre.

They were the most flamboyant of all the conjurers, and the wind enjoyed their excess. But even more, the wind enjoyed the games.

It always made sure to slip through, to linger, to listen. There were silent secrets, whispered secrets, and buried secrets that were aired at the games.

If you were invisible, if you were the wind, you could brush through a house full of secrets and carry them away on a barely noticeable breeze. Years—maybe centuries—later, you could air them out again.

The thing about secrets was knowing when they should be told. Tomorrow? A year from now? Twenty years from now? Never?

If you waited too long, a secret could become like parchment stored for centuries: at a single touch, the paper would crumble. However, if told too soon, a secret truth could become a lie. It could unravel like a sheet blowing in the wind, until only a single thread remained. Unwound, it was useless.

The wind liked to keep secrets to itself. Once in a while, it would bring a secret out like a prized morsel and slowly snack on the flavor. Sometimes it shared a small taste or a savory bite. Very rarely, the wind told many, many secrets to someone it liked very much.

Why?

Who knew? The wind was capricious and unknowable.

After millennia of witnessing the games of conjurers, the wind knew where to blow. It flew along the sticky pool of blood, floated in the bubbling effervescence of the champagne river, collected the scent of roasted peacock, and slid along the smooth marble tiles.

A woman—the wind didn't often concern itself with the names of corporal beings—wearing a diaphanous turquoise gown with a long train tiptoed along the hall and peeked around a corner. She wore the scent of citrus and pearl dust. She paused, held still, and then formed an illusion around herself so she became a part of the wall.

A second later, two men stalked past, neither looking in her direction.

"He died with a knife in his throat—"

"I know how my brother died."

"Yet it wasn't you who killed him?"

The woman stared after the taller of the two men. Both of them were Clarks—the wind knew this because they smelled of musty libraries, decaying things, and the wet stone of catacombs. The woman narrowed her eyes, pursed her lips, and then, when the taller man tapped his right hand against his thigh, she smiled and whispered, "Why, hello, Jacob. What are you doing pretending to be Primus?"

Although it liked the smell of citrus and pearl dust, the wind liked a mystery better. It rustled the woman's gown and rushed after the two men. The men separated at the grand marble staircase, the taller moving eastward. That was where the secret was, not with the other.

The wind followed, hot on his heels. He climbed to the second floor and then paused at a wooden door. Looked left. Looked right. The wind could've told him no one was there. It was only the two of them.

The man knocked quietly, his knuckle rapping against the wood. The wind slipped under the door and into the room before him. The space smelled of astringent soap, blood, and bandaging. The wind sorted through the silks on the bed, the slippery slide of pantyhose, and then tickled the nose of the woman lying on the bed.

She sat up. Clutched her chest. Took a shaky breath and quietly tiptoed to the door. She stood with her back flat against the wall. "Who is it?"

"Primus. We need to talk."

The woman closed her eyes. Her face relaxed, and her fingers uncurled from clenched fists. She opened the door and said in a rush, "Finally. He killed him. I saw—"

The man jerked his head. "Not here."

Quickly, the woman followed him from her room. The corridors were a maze, and under the veil of illusion, the man guided the woman to an empty room at the end of the hallway. The door snicked shut after them. It was dark, but the wind didn't need light to see. The room was small—a closet, really.

The wind delightedly ran over the mink and rabbit fur coats, breathing in the silky feel and the teasing warmth. There was the scent of mothballs and the closed, tight heat of an unventilated closet. The room was hushed and isolated.

"Who killed him?" the man whispered. His voice was muffled by the fur.

"I'm not sure." The woman smelled of perspiration. There was a bandage soaking the blood of a stab wound. "I thought . . . he saw something. He signaled me. It was our emergency signal. The one that meant he wanted to meet immediately."

"What could he have seen?" The man's voice held a different note—a tone more tenor than bass—but the woman didn't seem to notice. The wind noticed though. It was skilled at sensing the varying vibrations of voices.

"I don't know. I don't know! He'd been agitated all day. It was the stupid key you retrieved from that thief. The Smith's key. He said he was close to putting it all together . . . what the key was, why it was important. I don't know. He hadn't been right since that snake bite. He wanted the thief dead, and then . . ."

"Then?"

"When he saw the Smith's son . . . the . . . the . . ."

"The . . . ?"

"I don't know. He saw something. He went stiff, and his expression changed. Then he was signaling me. I swear he saw something important. I know he did. I think . . ."

"You think . . . ?"

"I think Secondus knew something about the Smith's son. I think it has to do with the key."

"Is that all?"

"No. Primus, I saw . . . I saw Jacob Ward . . . He was standing by his father, but there was a distortion by the tables, and I caught a flash of him. Like a reflection in the facet of a diamond. I think it was Jacob who killed your brother."

"I see." The man considered this. "You're sure?"

"Yes. Certain."

"Have you told anyone else?"

"Just you."

The wind paused at the cuff of a mink coat. The silence tickled, and then a shower of energy, like a thousand cold raindrops splashing over it, rained free. The man twisted his wrist, two fingers pressed to his thumb. The woman gave a startled cry and then collapsed soundlessly into the waiting arms of a dozen fur coats.

Then the man adjusted his suit coat, smoothed down his hair, and listened for any footsteps in the hall. Carefully opening the door, he stepped into the hallway. A moment later, he strode back toward the stairs. When a man called, "Hello," he nodded back.

The wind trailed after him, pushing ahead, down a hallway, up a stairway, down another hall, around a corner, up another stairwell, into a room, and then finally, like he was slipping out of a winter coat, the man stripped the illusion away. He shrank a few inches, lost the sharpness, and became someone else. The musty Clark scent that had fooled the wind was replaced by something sharper—something twisty and mazelike.

Oh!

Wasn't that clever?

The wind rattled the knob on the door, shook the wood with a laugh, and then wandered down the hall to see what other secrets it could find.

22

———

THE OPENING CEREMONY OF THE HUNDRED YEAR GAMES BEGAN AT midnight. The light of the half-moon glimmered through the thirty-foot-tall arching glass windows and spilled across the white and gold-shot marble, coating the room in a shimmery otherworldly glow.

Although there were at least seventy conjurers crowded in the great, echoing marble space, there was a reverent, solemn quiet that reminded me of a crowd standing silently in front of Michelangelo's David. Or perhaps it was the ceremonial hush that swept through and gripped a nation when a monarch dropped to their knees, bowed, and a crown was held aloft over their head. It was the breath-held quiet right before the crown began its descent.

I'd read about centuries' worth of games, but reading a record of something was different than living it. The Clark records always said something along these lines: *"The Heirs submitted to the Games under the witness of the Heads of Families during the opening ceremony of the 951st Games, 9510 C.R."*

That short, dry sentence didn't convey what happened in the opening ceremonies. Not at all.

Once in a while, the Bards or the Smiths would mention something interesting in the archived letters Jagger had me steal. Something like,

"Diogenes perished during submission to the games . . . wasn't the heir," or, "Candid flew to the opening ceremony with a battalion of shadows and attempted to steal the crown. RIP Candid."

None of the letters had prepared me for the pomp and solemnity of it all. At midnight, the principals, the heirs, and their siblings gathered outside the ceremony hall. It was a vast room with fifty-foot ceilings, white-gold marble panels and floors, and a dozen massive marble columns lining both sides of a mosaic-lined processional pathway. The mosaic was made of moon-glimmered tiles of gold, lapis lazuli, mother-of-pearl, and turquoise, set in scenes of conjurer achievement, destruction, glory, and disaster, all leading toward a marble dais that held a pool of still black water.

There was no light but the moon. No sound but the rustle of clothing and the shifting of feet on marble. No scent beneath the incense that burned on the dais and clouded the room with pungent, honey-coated fingers. No breeze, no wind, only a primordial stillness of the kind before wind or air were even thought into existence.

Then a sound began. At first, I thought it was the rushing of a cool stream through an autumn forest, then maybe the thrum of a hummingbird's wings. Then I was certain the sound was the mellow song of snow falling on a moonlit night.

But then I realized the sound was Ragnor Bard, and he was strumming a stringed instrument that looked like a guitar but wasn't. To my lockpick senses, his fingers glowed luminescent as they fell over the strings, conjuring a song that wasn't a song but a vanishing feeling or a never-held memory.

Finally, the thrumming, bubbling sounds shifted into notes, and then music. The notes were hollow but full, achingly sad but vibrantly hopeful, utterly terrifying, and absolutely beautiful. I wanted to block my ears but also never stop listening.

As Ragnor's song took on the beat of a throbbing pulse, his father, the Bard, swept toward the dais. All the conjurers in the hall turned as one to watch the procession.

First came the Bard, the current holder of the crown. He was dressed in a burgundy tuxedo with gem-encrusted gold rings on each of his fingers. His wife, Cressida, was a pale orchid next to his bloodied carnation.

Behind them strode their children. The heir, Celia, with her alluring 1940s Hollywood glamour. Ragnor, the chart-topping pop musician, still strumming his guitar. And Luvic, the on-again-off-again troublemaking Broadway actor, and the handsomest of them all.

The Bards, unlike the Clarks, didn't fight among themselves or vie with each other for power. Instead the heir held the leading role in their family drama, and the siblings willingly played their parts as supporting actors and actresses.

When they passed, I expected Luvic to wink at me again, or for his mouth to twitch, but instead he didn't glance at me once, even though I knew he'd calculated my exact location down to the inch. It caused an itch between my shoulder blades.

But then the Bards reached the dais, and the Clarks followed.

First came the Clark, Herman, in his black tuxedo and short black cloak. He was crow-like and severe. Primus followed at his heels, gloomy in a brown tuxedo and brown cloak. He looked like he was visualizing ripping the bloodied flesh free from a pile of bones.

I shuddered, thinking about the way the Clarks had surrounded me and taunted my death.

There was a noticeable space left empty for Secondus, and then Last followed behind them, her gaze picking over the conjurers lining the room. She wore brown like her brother, and her thin lips twisted as her attention landed on his back.

The Clarks, with their affinity for history, played out the roles of history's dynasties. In each generation, at least one sibling murdered another. There was no love between them, only a twisted, time-limited loyalty.

After the Clarks swept onto the dais, crowding the Bards, the Wards started forward. When they stepped into the hall, Ragnor's strumming sped up, and the music crawled over me, sending a vision of wilting flowers and ash raining from the sky. Jacob noticed the change. His mouth twisted until he looked like he was enjoying a good joke.

There were only three Wards. Philoneas was in front. He'd changed into a dove-gray suit that softened his already soft features. He strode sedately forward, his wife on his arm.

It was her I looked at. I'd never seen Uliea Ward—I'd only heard rumors. Unhinged. Mad. Violently insane. She was blonde like her son. Green-eyed. But while Jacob looked soft and gentle like his father, Uliea was hard like a blade, but brittle to the point of breaking. She clutched her husband's arm and stared around the marble room as if it wasn't a palatial hall but a mausoleum. Grief twisted her face.

A spurt of pity worked its way through my chest. I knew why she was grieving. I knew why she was mad.

Roumelade would sometimes tell us the story when Griff, Justice, and I were little and would hang around her kitchen begging for attention. She'd tell it like this: "You all know about the Wards. You know Jacob is the only son and the heir. But did you know that Jacob wasn't the *only* Ward child?"

Griff would always gasp at that, already scared.

"He had a twin," Roumelade would whisper, like it was still a secret even after the tenth retelling. "A little blonde-haired, green-eyed girl named Viola. She was her brother's mirror in every way."

"In every way?" I'd ask every time, not able to picture a person who was an exact mirror of another.

"In every way," Roumelade would confirm.

They did the same things. They liked the same things. They said the same things. They slept at the same time. They played at the same time. They were identical in every way.

Uliea loved her daughter. She loved her more than her son. More than anyone. Viola was her little doll. Uliea loved her with a mother's passion.

"Do you know what happens around the time of a conjurer's fourth birthday?" Roumelade would ask, with a dramatic pause.

"They come into their power," Justice had said one time, scowling at the jam and biscuits on the counter. He'd come into his tiny spark of diluted power when he was four.

"That's right," Roumelade said, pleased at his answer. "And on Jacob and Viola's fourth birthday, something happened. Something *terrible*."

"What?" Griff squeaked, even though he knew. After all, this was one of our favorite scary stories.

"Jacob made a wish on his birthday cake. Viola made the same wish." Roumelade pretended to blow out birthday candles, the breathy sound sending a chill over me. "And then . . . he started screaming."

"And screaming," I said, chills traveling down my spine.

"He couldn't stop. He screamed and screamed and screamed, until . . ." She waited.

A seven-year-old Griff was busy biting his nails. Justice, the eldest of us, tried to look bored but failed.

"Until . . ." I prompted, my heart thudding with each second's pause.

"He stopped," Roumelade said. "And little Viola, Jacob's twin sister . . . she exploded."

"I thought it was spontaneous combustion," Justice said, pretending not to be afraid.

"Well, that's the thing. No one agrees what exactly happened. Some say she exploded. Some say she spontaneously combusted. A few claim she just disappeared. But *everyone* agrees that when Jacob Ward came into his power, he murdered his twin sister and gobbled her power up. That's why he's the strongest Ward to live in centuries. And that's why you never want to be anywhere near him."

Griff had shivered. Roumelade had patted his cheek and given him a biscuit with an extra spoonful of blackberry jam. Justice—this was when he still tried to save mice and made wishes on dandelion seeds—worriedly bit his lip, but when he saw me looking, he bravely stuck his chin in the air.

And me? I whispered, feeling a little hollow, "Poor Jacob."

"Why poor Jacob?"

I didn't know. I couldn't explain it. I only felt there was something horribly sad about it all.

"It's not Jacob you should feel sorry for—it's his mother."

After Viola's death, she'd become . . . unstable. Lost in the maze of her own violent, unrelenting grief. She wasn't seen for a decade after Viola died.

Rumor had it that Philoneas kept Uliea under lock and key, stuck in one of those Ward mind labyrinths. Even now, she rarely came out.

So, as the Wards walked toward the dais, I watched Philoneas, my parents' murderer. I watched Uliea, the grieving mother. And I watched Jacob, his sister's murderer. They'd had a starring role in one of Roumelade's favorite kitchen stories, and now I was in the same room as them.

Finally, the Wards mounted the dais and took their compass position on the eastern side of the pool. The Clarks stood to the south. The Bards to the west. The north was the only direction without a family.

Then the beat of Ragnor's music shifted to a military march, and Wolfgang stepped forward. He strode down the column-lined path, not bothering to look right or left—a military commander in his prime. Behind him, Darin held his shoulders back, his head high. They marched as if they didn't know their spines could bend. Somehow, they made their tuxes look like armor and their bodies look like deadly weapons. I imagined yesterday, the Smiths had thought it would only be Wolfgang and Darin marching to the dais, but now they had a third Smith.

From the back of the room, I watched Finn sway, stumble, and then follow tipsily behind Darin. I was certain—almost certain—that the stumble and the sway were an act. He was dressed like his father and brother. Darin had thrown a tuxedo at him and mumbled that it'd probably fit. He'd also forced Finn to put on Kevlar beneath the tux, because as a null, he was especially vulnerable before being officially inducted into the games.

In the prep before the ceremony, Darin had almost been a mother hen in the way he'd drilled Finn on the pomp and protocol. "Blood for blood. I submit!" he'd shouted after Finn failed to repeat the exact phrasing for the ninth time. "I submit to the game as paladin!" Finn had only stared at him with wide-blown eyes and repeated it again, only forgetting one word. Darin had glared at me. "Make him learn it. The pool will kill him if he gets it wrong."

Now, at the back of the hall, pressed against the cold marble wall, I watched Finn trip over a step and then come to a halt at the northern edge of the pool. Once Wolfgang and Darin were standing with military precision and Finn was slouched next to his brother, Ragnor stopped strumming his guitar.

A moonstruck silence slid over the hall. I stood on my tiptoes, trying to catch the expression on Finn's face. I'd drilled him. I'd quizzed him. I'd made sure he'd remember everything Darin had told him.

But still . . .

I couldn't keep him alive if he said the wrong words and the pool decided to kill him. I also couldn't keep him alive if the pool decided to reject him. That was what happened to Diogenes in that archived letter I'd stolen. He'd claimed to be the heir, but it turned out he wasn't, so the pool had killed him.

I'm not exactly sure how the pool works. The original conjurers created it with the first game. Some say it's a piece of primordial essence ripped from the center of the universe. Others say it's the souls of all the conjurers who died in the flood. I think maybe the conjurers just thought a rule book into physical form, and when an heir thrusts their bloodied hand into the pool, they're agreeing to play by the rules or die.

My heart beat a painful tattoo as I pressed my back against the cold marble wall. I stood with the other bodies, all four of us in the drab gray uniform the bodies were required to wear: loose silk pants and long-sleeve shirts. While comfortable, they didn't have any secret pockets for weapons or surprises. Although, give me a needle and a little time, and I'd figure something out.

The Bard body was a short older man with gray hair who hadn't once looked up from the square floor tile in front of him. The Clark body was an extraordinarily tall man, with pale, loose-hanging skin and an oily, sickly feel. Then there was the Ward body—a wide, fleshy older woman with thick hands that looked like they could crush bones as easily as dough, and a permanent, spookily pleasant smile. And me. There was me. The Smith body.

I expected all of them, no matter their appearance, were skilled at deception, thievery, hand-to-hand combat, and murder. Just like at Hell Gate, I had to watch my back.

"Welcome, friends, families, conjurers," the Bard called, his voice magnified and echoing over the marble, "to the opening ceremony of the Hundred Year Games."

He was a showman. He held his arms wide, and his rings glinted in the moonlight. The crown of illusions flickered for a moment, appearing on his head and then disappearing again.

His wife stood next to him. His children flanked him, the three of them standing in an arrow behind him, dressed in peacock colors and sequins. Separately, they were all stunningly beautiful, but standing together, it hurt my eyes to look at them.

"The Games begin at midnight," the Bard said, playing to his fellow conjurers. "But first . . ." His expression shifted from benevolent monarch to mournful judge. "We have a murderer in our midst. And I find it my sad duty to flush them out."

I tensed. Held still like a mouse under the shadow of a cat's paw. On the marble dais, Finn stilled, his tipsy slide halting. He still looked drunk, bliss-eyed, and confused, but just underneath, I saw something watchful —something predatory. I don't think anyone else noticed. No one was paying him any attention.

Because as soon as the Bard said "flush them out," a man had shoved the conjurers behind him and sprinted toward the doors.

No one moved. No one attempted to stop him or help him.

It was a Bard. I was certain of it by the lapis-blue of his suit, the canary-yellow shirt, and his polka-dot bowtie. The Bards were the only conjurers who dressed with so much flash. He was young. Maybe twenty-five.

Before he'd taken three leaps over the mosaic floor, the man was twisted in the air and hung three feet off the ground. He was bound tight, thin metal cords wrapped around him like kudzu choking a tree.

The Bard sighed. "Phillip. What have you done?"

Phillip shook his head—kept shaking it. "I stabbed Secondus in the throat," he said, his voice strained. He shook his head no. No. No. No. "I killed Morjorie in the coat closet on the second floor." He kept shaking his head. No. No. No.

The Bard frowned. "Did you?"

"Yes," he said, shaking his head no.

"Why are you shaking your head?"

Phillip strained against the silver cords binding him. He looked around the room, at the Bards he'd been standing with. His family. He was searching, I think, for pity or aid . . . anything . . .

I peered at Phillip. Looked past what was there. Deeper. I looked beyond vision so I could see. And there, just there, buried deep behind a shell surrounding his outer mind, was a tiny glowing knot that was pulsing with a rhythmic insistence. It was tied tightly to his mind, woven from the thinnest thread. It was so small I'd almost missed it. But now I'd found it, I couldn't unsee it. Someone had placed an illusion in Phillip's mind. What was it that they'd made him see?

"I don't want to die," Phillip said. "Please. Uncle."

The Bard sighed. "By your own admission, you killed Secondus. You killed Morjorie. Was it you who attempted to poison the Smith?"

Phillip stopped shaking his head. The little worm of a knot pulsed hard.

"Yes," Phillip said.

I gripped my hands tightly. Looked to Finn. He held still. Preternaturally still. I had the strangest feeling that in a millisecond, he could erupt into a swirling fury of combat. It felt as if he was dancing on a razor's edge, waiting to see whether he should fall into quietude or spin into aggression.

Finn knew it wasn't Phillip who'd attempted to murder Wolfgang. We both knew. And so did whoever had tied the knot in his mind. It was a Ward, wasn't it? The Wards excelled at this sort of madness.

"I see," the Bard said. Then he twisted his hand.

There was an audible crack, like a twig snapping in half, and Phillip slumped in his chains. There was a flash of light, the glow and hum of illusion, and then Phillip was thrown on a gust of air from the room.

Dead?

I didn't know.

I couldn't be sure of anything.

Isn't that what you always told me? You can't trust what you see. You can't trust what you know. You can't trust anything.

"On behalf of my family, I offer my condolences and apologies," the

Bard said, smiling sadly over the hall. "Let his death be recompense. According to the code, life for life."

The three heads—the Clark, Wolfgang, and Philoneas—nodded in agreement.

Finn, who I'd been watching, relaxed. The movement was so subtle it was barely perceptible. But one second he was a sleeping volcano brimming with the threat of eruption, and the next he was back to a tipsy, dizzy fool. In fact, he took the opportunity, as the principals nodded their agreement, to stumble and knock into his brother.

Darin scowled and set him back upright, pushing him straight.

Finn grinned at Darin, then he smiled blankly over the gathered crowd. When he found me at the back of the room, his smile widened even further. Blank. Vacant-gazed. Starry-eyed.

A man no one would see as a threat. A man the conjurers wouldn't take seriously.

Well, I'll be . . .

As Roumelade would say . . .

Finn Alterra just got a lot more interesting.

When the moment came for Finn to enter the games, all the other heirs had already kneeled at the pool, thrust their bloodied hand into the black water, and sworn their oath.

Celia, with her lush, songlike voice and Hollywood smile. Primus, with his severe frown and cruel, unbending stare. Jacob, with his slight frame, soft features, and untold power. They'd been groomed their entire lives to play the game and to win. All of them wanted to rule the world.

When each heir stuck their hand into the water, a flash of golden light surrounded them, and a thunderous boom shook the hall. By the breath-held expectation around me, I realized the next few seconds determined whether or not the heir would survive the oath. But each time, the gold shivered, expanded, and then sank into the heir's skin, leaving a slight golden shimmer shining on them.

Celia raised her arms and waved regally at all the Bards spread out before the dais. Primus gave a cold stare at the gathered conjurers and then stalked back to his place at his father's side.

For Jacob, there was a blood-in-the-water anticipation running through the hall. Would he be accepted? *Was* he the heir? Or was Viola still alive somewhere, and *she* was truly the eldest?

Jacob smiled softly to himself, as if he could hear the questions and the dreadful hope that the pool would kill him. But in the end, when he thrust his bloodied hand into the water and swore his oath, the light shimmered over him and bound him to the game, just as it had all the others.

Last was Finn. Unlike the rest, he hadn't been envisioning this moment for decades. He also didn't seem to recognize the solemnity of the occasion.

With the other three, you knew they were there to rule the world. But with Finn . . . I didn't know why he was there. Definitely not to rule the world. And probably not for a lifetime supply of solange. I thought maybe it had to do with Cora—the Eurydice to his Orpheus—although I didn't see how entering the games had anything to do with their love.

I thought the conjurers didn't see him as a threat. Still, when the Bard lifted the ceremonial knife toward Finn, I caught a flash of something. An illusion spun as fine as a spiderweb, sneaking across the dais toward Finn. It reminded me of a poison mesh I'd seen once before. Nearly invisible, it attached to a person's skin, and then, over twenty-four hours, the mesh disintegrated, and the poison leached into their bloodstream and killed them.

My heart beat wildly, and I calmed my mind, letting my consciousness fly outside of myself, seeking the knot in the illusion. *Find it. Find it. There.* I began to work, unraveling the thread.

"Hold out your right hand," the Bard said as Finn stepped forward.

Finn turned his palm over and held it out.

The illusion crept closer, six inches above the marble floor, a spiderweb floating on air. A drop of sweat trailed down my skin.

There were so many knots—overhand and bowline—each link triple-knotted and double-backed, so there were dozens of knots to untie. The thread was oily, slippery, and difficult to pull apart. Someone on the dais was conjuring this; I could feel the immense power pushing it toward Finn. I just didn't know which of them it was.

It didn't matter. I had to unravel it.

There. I had one. The knot pulled free, and the web listed to the side. All the same, it kept floating toward Finn.

The Bard pressed the steel to Finn's hand and sliced through the meat of his palm. He'd cut deeper than the others. The slash caused a great welling of blood. It bloomed bright red and spilled over his skin.

"What are you here for?" the Bard asked.

Finn lifted his eyes toward the dark night sky and the half-moon shining through the windows. Then he looked back to the room and the black-night water of the pool. "To play the greatest game," he said in his thunderstorm voice. "To win the crown of illusions."

"And who do you play for?" the Bard intoned.

The spiderweb illusion was only a foot away from him now. The web was translucent, finer than hair, and invisible, I think, to everyone but a lockpick. It moved slowly, floating like a stinging jellyfish on a gentle current. I frantically worked the knots, untying, untying, untying.

I knew without a doubt that if this web touched Finn, he wouldn't survive. But the conjurer, whoever it was, hadn't noticed the unraveling of their web.

"I play for the Smiths," Finn answered.

If I timed it right, I could pull the entire thing apart and collapse the web just as it reached him. The conjurer wouldn't realize it had collapsed rather than sinking into his skin.

"And are you heir to the Smiths?"

"No."

"Then who do you play as?"

"I play as paladin."

There was murmuring through the room, a waterfall-like noise that echoed off the marble and rushed across the hall. The Bard held up his hand for silence.

The web was at Finn's legs.

"Kneel," the Bard said, that same gleeful laughter ringing in his voice that he'd had when Finn was shackled to the inquisitor's chair.

Was it him? Was he the one directing the illusion?

One more. I had one more knot to untie. I only needed ten seconds. *Just . . .* I gritted my teeth . . . *ten more seconds.*

Finn looked down. Tilted his head. Closed one eye. Then the other.

"Kneel, paladin," the Bard demanded.

Finn turned his head. Looked over the crowded hall, his starry gaze searching, searching. Then he found me. Smiled.

My heart skipped a beat.

Did he see it?

Could he see it?

He dropped to his knees.

I yanked the last knot free, tugging frantically and collapsing against the wall as the entire web disintegrated right before Finn's knees hit the marble floor.

Thank goodness.

Thank goodness.

He'd almost . . .

"Say your oath." The Bard smiled at Finn, and I was certain he expected Finn to die—if not in the next few seconds, then within the next day.

"Blood for blood," said Finn, his blood dripping from his hand into the dark pool. "I submit. I submit to the game as paladin."

Then Finn shoved his hand into the water. A golden cage of light snapped around him, glowing so bright my eyes stung and watered. But I wouldn't look away. If Finn was about to die, I had to witness it for myself.

His shoulders jerked; his back stiffened. The light crackled and twisted almost violently. It hadn't done that for the others.

Finn threw his head back. His eyes were wide, and the lightning and silver nebula in his irises pulsed and raged. Then zigzags of lightning crackled through the black pool, an electric storm born in water and blood.

The Bard leaned forward, gleefully anticipatory. The Clark's mouth twisted cruelly, a carrion feeder expecting to feast on roadkill. The Ward tilted his head . . . waiting. The Smith dropped his right hand to his side and tensed as if he were about to conjure his sword of fire.

This was when the pool chose whether a conjurer would live or die.

The cage of light became a golden column, consuming Finn in its depths.

I don't think a single person in the hall took a breath for five seconds. Ten.

The column extended from the floor through the ceiling. I didn't know how deep it went or how high it flew.

A clap of thunder exploded through the hall. The marble column in front of me cracked. My eardrums popped, and I stumbled, dizzy from the assault. The golden column expanded and then compressed, snapping over Finn and sinking into his skin.

There was no golden sheen like on the others. He'd swallowed all the light.

The silence in the hall was so deep it felt as if we existed in the time before worlds, before light, before sound. But then a high-pitched ringing began in my ears. I shook my head and steadied myself against the wall. Blinked to clear away the spots from the golden, sun-flare-bright column. The room no longer smelled of honeyed incense. Instead there was the hint of cranberry and allspice.

The Bard was shaken, but he pulled his tuxedo coat tight and stared, tight-jawed, over the crowd of stunned conjurers.

Slowly, Finn pulled his hand free from the pool and let the red-tinted water drip free. Then he clutched his hand into a fist and stood.

Perhaps he was unaware of what had happened outside the column of light. Or perhaps he didn't care. Either way, when Finn turned to look over the conjurers, he merely lifted an eyebrow at the cracked columns, the lingering marble dust floating in the air, and the drawn, shocked faces.

The Bard took control once more.

"Finn Alterra," he said in a loud, clear voice. "Welcome to the Hundred Year Games. You now play or die as paladin for the Smiths."

At those words, Finn looked at me and smiled.

23

The sweet, tangy scent of cranberry and allspice drifted through the room. The spice tickled my nose, and I fought hard not to sneeze.

Finn smiled at me as if he knew what the scent was doing to me. He rolled the silver thimble between his pointer finger and thumb, heating the solange over a small candle flame. The blue and orange fire licked his fingers. Didn't the fire and the hot thimble hurt? Or couldn't he feel it?

We were in his room in the Smiths' suite. He was a Smith. Their paladin. So, naturally, when the opening ceremony was over, Darin had led us back to our rooms, and with a last contemplative frown at his brother, said, "It's truly surprising, but I'm almost glad you didn't die." Then, when he looked at me, his frown turned to a scowl. "You're his body. Take care of him."

I was fairly certain Darin meant for me to get Finn some food, bandage his hand, and make sure he slept. I doubted he meant "give Finn a thimble-load of solange." But Finn had refused my offer of searching out food or drink, shaken off my desire to clean his hand, and just lifted an eyebrow at the single king-size bed in the middle of his room.

The bedroom lights were low, and the candlelight danced in a warm, flickering glow. The orange and gold lit Finn's face, highlighting the hollows of his cheeks, the sharpness of his jaw, and the striations in his eyes. He wasn't smiling, so he didn't look beautiful. He was only a man with too-long black hair, rough stubble lining his jaw, and shadows under his eyes.

The candlelight, though, made me remember what I easily forgot when Finn was swaying or stumbling or vacant-eyed. He was large. Muscled. A Smith whose body was a powerful and destructive weapon.

Didn't he admit to being able to deadlift a metric ton? And didn't I see the way he'd gone predator-still on the dais?

"I think you're a liar," I said, surveying his features.

Finn stopped rolling the thimble, stilling. He paused for only a second, and then he started rolling and tilting the solange thimble again.

The room was large. Where the main living room of the suite had been spartan and Smith-like, the bedroom was more extravagant.

It was thirty feet by thirty feet. The plaster ceiling was high. The walls were covered in rich walnut paneling and wallpapered in navy, with a swirling pattern of gold stars. There was an ornate limestone fireplace. Windows overlooked the street, with heavy velvet drapes. There were oil paintings depicting scenes of revelry and battle. A green velvet divan. Two matching club chairs. The antique walnut escritoire Finn sat at. A matching armoire, dresser, and nightstands. And of course, the giant four-poster king-size bed with the navy silk canopy.

The room was quietly luxurious and restful. It had been created with illusion made real. I could see the knots tied and the threads woven. A lot of the mansion had been crafted with illusion. The ballroom, of course. Most of the hall. Not the inquisitor's chair room. Not the hallways and entryway. But the suite's living room and bedrooms? Yes.

I'd looked for traps, tricksy surprises—anything dangerous or deadly —but I'd only found soft rugs, a plush bed, and a room with walls so thick it was practically soundproof.

"Finn," I said, tapping my foot on one of the luxuriously soft rugs.

His eyes were half-closed, and he was smiling at the thimble of solange.

"You're a liar. A lying liar."

His mouth lifted at the corner.

I crossed my arms over my chest. "I think this whole solange thing is an act."

Finn blinked at me, his navy eyes wide. Then he tilted the thimble back and swallowed the syrupy liquid. His throat worked, his Adam's apple bobbing. He'd closed his eyes, but once he'd swallowed, he opened them again. His pupils dilated, expanding and contracting, swallowing the lightning. A drop of solange glistened on his lower lip. He pulled his lip under his teeth and licked it off, leaving them wet-kissed and glossy.

A pluck of energy vibrated over my skin, and Finn made a soft noise, a happy sound, as the solange worked through him.

Goose bumps shivered over me, and a small string tugged in my belly at the noise he made. The room, with its luxurious furnishings and thick rugs, was suddenly overwarm. While Finn lounged in the chair at the escritoire, legs sprawled out and slumped, I stood scowling at the candle flame, the thimble, and the rumbly, happy noises he made.

At my frown, he clicked the empty thimble to the desk. "An act? We're all acting here, Mari."

My heart sped up, an involuntary racing, and then slowed like a taxi in rush hour, jerking quickly forward then slamming on the brakes, then repeating the same stop-go-stop-go.

"We're going to have to be honest with each other." I waved my hand when Finn's eyes drifted half-shut. "Finn." I snapped my fingers, and his eyes fluttered open.

He blinked at me, then he smiled. It was the smile that transformed his features from ordinary to extraordinary. "I'm always honest with you."

I snorted. "Please. I've been watching you. This whole stumbling fool, hedonistic solange devotee thing you've got going? I'm not buying it. You can fight. You're a Smith. I know you could fight three on one, four on one . . ." I paused, waiting for Finn to deny or confirm.

He didn't do either. Instead he sank further into the wooden chair and studied my face as if he were memorizing my features.

"Tell me you know how to fight," I said, desperate for confirmation we weren't totally without hope in the games.

"I know how to fight," he repeated, like he was only saying it because I'd asked him to repeat after me.

"You know how to fight well?"

He didn't answer. Instead he closed one eye and then the other, looking at me closely. That was another thing. Had he seen the slithering web on the dais? And when he'd smiled at me, did he know I was unraveling it? Except, that would've been impossible. No one can see the knots in illusions like I can.

"When you kneeled on the dais, did you see the poison web?" I asked.

"What poison web?"

I gave him a hard stare. "The one you looked at. The one under your knees that you nearly landed on."

"Ah." He nodded. "That. I thought of it as a malevolent matrix, but poison web sounds nice too."

"Did you . . .?" I paused. I couldn't tell him I'd untied it. He couldn't know. No one here could know. That would be a death sentence. The cozy luxury of the room and the soothing scent of cranberry and allspice were lulling me into a false sense of intimacy. No one knew my secret outside of Hell Gate.

"Did I know you were untying it for me?" Finn closed his left eye and studied me again. "Figured that was what you were doing. You looked like you were concentrating hard."

I kept a straight face, wiped of any emotion, although my heart banged violently, and a line of sweat popped up on my brow. My mind shrieked, *Run, run, run!* Finn knew I was a lockpick. He knew my secret. Whether he realized it or not, he held my life in his hands.

My hand involuntarily went to the thin strap under my shirt, where I felt the cold metal of Justice's knife.

Finn tracked my movement, the corner of his mouth tilting up. "I won't tell anyone. So maybe . . . you could wait to try to kill me until after the games?"

Okay. Right. Slowly, my heartbeat settled, and I loosened my fingers from the hilt of Justice's knife.

Finn waited until my empty hand had fallen to my side. Then he shifted in the wooden chair and reached for the small, amber-colored glass bottle of solange. How many of those had he brought? Two? Three? Or was this his only one?

He uncapped the bottle and tilted it so tiny iridescent raindrops of solange fell into his silver thimble.

"Right." I cleared my throat. Shifted my feet. "Right. I won't kill you until . . ."

Finn studied the drops falling into the thimble. It was a tiny rainstorm swirling in a thumb-size cup. "Have you ever heard of Prince Rupert's drop?" He gave me a quick glance and then went back to the slow drip of solange.

I shook my head. "No. What is it?"

Solange was clear. Translucent. But just like a soap bubble, it caught a thousand rainbows in its surface, so every color ever known was reflected there. It was beautiful in a mesmerizing sort of way.

Finn shrugged. "It's a piece of glass shaped like a teardrop. Just an ordinary piece of glass. But because of the way it's made . . . cooling from the outside in rather than the inside out, it's . . . it's stronger than—"

I curled my fingers into a fist. "Than what?"

Finn looked up, his starry eyes surprisingly clear. "Than practically anything. The wide end of this little piece of glass can withstand a bullet hitting it dead-on. It can be slammed with the force of a hurricane and survive unscathed. But Prince Rupert's drop has a weakness."

I leaned forward. "What?"

Finn studied me. He put down the bottle of solange and left the thimble half-full. The silence in the room was deep and thick. It coated me in its breath-held quiet.

"The tail of the drop," Finn said. "The narrow end. If anything or anyone touches the tail, even a small tap, the entire drop explodes. The glass shatters into a million pieces, and all the shards shoot out in a violent explosion."

I thought about this glass teardrop. On one end, it could survive an assault of bullets. On the other, a finger-tap shattered the entire thing. How could something be so implausibly strong and at the same time so dangerously fragile?

"We all have weaknesses," Finn said. "I won't share yours. I don't want to see you shattered."

"Why not?" We'd met less than twenty-four hours ago, and I'd already nearly killed him and admitted to planning on killing him later.

"Why would I?" he asked. "I don't like breaking things."

"That Bard. Phillip? I saw an illusion in his mind. I think he was compelled to admit what he did."

Finn didn't look surprised. He only nodded.

"What would you have done if the Bard had pointed to one of us?" I asked.

He smiled at me and said, straight-faced, "Ran."

I laughed. I couldn't help it. It was just what I'd said to him earlier today, when he'd asked what I would've done if the Smiths hadn't given him the antidote.

He grinned at my laugh, his eyes lighting. Against my better judgment, his grin made me feel warm and happy.

Suddenly, I wished Finn had never made a bargain with Jagger. I wished he'd never entered the games. I'd be here with or without him—I knew Jagger well enough to know he would've still sent me in regardless. I saw that quite clearly. But why did Finn have to be here? Getting to know him was going to make it harder to do what I was supposed to do. Help Finn win the games. Steal the crown. Kill Finn. Go home.

"Is your weakness Cora?" I asked, pushing away the thought. "Is that why you're willing to die in the games? For love?"

Finn took a deep breath, his shoulders rising. Then he lifted the bottle and finished filling his thimble. "Love isn't my weakness, but it is why I'm here. That's true." He lifted the thimble and held it over the flickering candle flame. A droplet of wax trailed down the thin white taper.

I followed the wax's slow progress and frowned at the tear shape it formed. "What is your weakness then?"

Finn rolled the thimble, tilting the solange. "Being born a conjurer but not. Illusion is my weakness." He blinked up at me, and I realized I'd been wrong. The solange wasn't an act. He was poisoning himself with the drug to shield his weakness. Only, he'd created another even greater weakness.

"Is the solange worth it? The free fall? You might not even have a month." My voice was ragged by the last sentence.

Finn's jaw tightened. He tilted the half-warmed thimble of solange back and swallowed it in one go.

"It's worth it," he said, and there was so much conviction in his voice that I knew he was thinking of Cora again.

Perhaps it was the yellow-gold glow of the flame. Maybe it was the fact that we'd both survived the ballroom, the inquisitor's chair, and the opening ceremony. Whatever it was, I decided I'd tell him something I'd never told anyone and ask a question I'd never dared to ask.

"When you talk about love . . ." I shifted on the thick rug, and the fabric whispered beneath my feet.

Finn looked at me and nodded. "Go on," his nod seemed to say.

"I don't know what it is," I admitted. "Not really. Not the kind you're talking about. I've never felt it. I don't think I'd recognize it. I'm not even sure if I could give that kind of love, or even receive it. If you don't recognize something, how will you know to let it in? Sometimes, though, I think love is an illusion. I really think it is." I paused. "Don't . . . don't look at me like that. It's not a bad thing. I'm not sorry."

Finn sat straight in his chair, his face pale, his expression one of a man looking at a seaside town destroyed after a storm. "I am. I'm sorry." His voice was that low thunderstorm again—the one that rocked through me and left me devastated.

"Don't be. It's not your fault."

Finn swallowed. Looked away from me. Gazed at the empty fireplace.

"So you're in the games for love," I said, trying to cover the strained silence. "You at least recognize it. I hope she's worth it. I hope she's worth dying for."

Finn's shoulders stiffened. The candlelight glinted off him, and when he looked back at me, his eyes were bright. "I met her fourteen years ago, when we were both still kids. As soon as I saw her, I knew right away I'd do anything for her."

"Did she feel the same way about you?"

He grinned, the whites of his teeth flashing. His expression was filled with restrained laughter. "No. She didn't want anything to do with me. I snuck out of the Night Den, followed her around the city. I'd leave her little gifts—packs of bubblegum, slivers of mica I'd found in the park, fistfuls of dandelions. She ignored them all." He laughed—a low, quiet, happy sound that vibrated through my chest. "After months of failed gifts and her ignoring me, I was following her through Times Square one day, not paying attention to where I was going. I fell down the subway station stairs. I got bruised and bloodied. But right away, she ran over and started yelling at me about how careless I was. She had a tissue she pressed to my knee, and she cried when she saw how much I was bleeding." He smiled as if he were reliving the memory.

"And after that, you were inseparable?" I asked.

"No. It took a while for her to trust me. But I kept making a nuisance of myself—keeping to the shadows, following her everywhere—until finally, she got so used to me that she was upset if I wasn't there. You could say I wore her down." He grinned, and he looked so young and carefree that I could imagine him as a scrawny, black-haired kid, following Cora around the city, leaving her dandelions on stone steps and bubblegum on the metal fire escapes. "I've always loved her in one way or another. By the time I was fourteen, I knew that if I had to, I'd die for her."

It was strange. Love was a strange thing. Why was it that people were willing to give up everything for it?

"But how do you know she loves you back? What if she doesn't?" I asked. "How do you know she'd die for you too? What if she wouldn't?"

Was that fair? One person willing to die and the other not.

But then, was love fair? There was the fairness of humans, where everything was equal. And then there was the fairness of God, where nothing was equal.

Humans demanded everything be given in equal measure, but God never gave in equal measure. He handed out talent, looks, wealth, and blessings in great amounts to some and paltry amounts to others. Human fairness and God's fairness were very different things. So maybe, if love was real, it wasn't fair according to human standards.

"She does," Finn said, his voice unwavering, gaze holding mine. There was absolute conviction in his expression. "She loves me. She'd die for me."

He was so convinced.

"How do you know?"

"She already has."

When I lifted my eyebrows, Finn said, "When I was fourteen, we were caught in a conjurer's trap. She could've saved herself and escaped, but instead she saved me. She died because of that choice, and I . . ." He shrugged. "I lived. If I didn't hate the conjurers before, I hated them for that. If I didn't love her before, I loved her for that."

"I didn't know good luck charms could reanimate."

There are a few beings who can reanimate, or who have multiple lives. Leggerocks, unfortunately. Roumelade, because she's water, and water can't be destroyed—it only changes form. Nines, of course. Figments, who aren't truly alive and therefore can't truly die. And apparently, good luck charms.

Finn stared at me, tight-lipped, unwilling to share Cora's reanimation secret. Not that I blamed him. As the saying goes, knowledge is power.

"What is it like?" I asked. "Loving someone so much. I'm only asking because . . ."

"Because you're sorry to have to kill me?" he asked, tilting his head.

Maybe I was asking because I wanted to know what it felt like to love and be loved. Or maybe I was asking because I wanted an excuse not to kill him. But then what? The task would go to Justice.

Finn slowly nodded when I didn't respond. He spoke in a quiet voice. "It's all right, Mari. You do what you have to do. I won't hold it against you."

"Thanks," I said, thinking Finn would do what he had to do too. "I'll try not to hold anything against you either."

He smiled at that, and I remembered, Finn wasn't here to lose, and he wasn't here to die. No matter how blissed-out or incompetent he appeared, he was here with an agenda.

"It feels like home," he said, watching me closely. "Love. Without her, I'm out in the cold rain under a dark sky, hungry, tired, and alone. She's home. Warm, bright, comforting, safe. She's open arms and the warm embrace after pain or struggle or nearly dying in the cold. When I found her, I recognized her as the home I'd always been searching for. Some people say you're each other's other half and you become one, but to me, it felt more like . . . when I was born, I forgot my home, and then, when I found her, I remembered it again. She helped me remember. That's what love feels like."

He watched me carefully as he spoke, gauging my reaction. When he'd finished, I nodded, smoothed my hands over my gray silk uniform, and shifted on my feet. I was uncomfortable, my skin itchy and tight.

Finn had that look on his face again—the one he'd worn when the Ward asked him what he was going to do after the games and he'd said, "Have sex until I'm too weak to stand."

Did he wear this look when he was kissing or making love?

My skin burned, and Finn raised his eyebrows. I was certain he could read my mind, because there was a slight twist to his lips that spoke of repressed humor.

Speaking of . . .

"I think you have a second trait."

"Hmm?" His eyebrows scrunched with feigned confusion.

"A mental trait. Stay out of my head."

Finn waved his hand. "Fine."

"So you admit—"

"I can't manipulate your emotions."

Huh.

"It's that you find me attractive—"

"No, I don't!"

He raised his eyebrows.

"I don't!"

"And you're sorry you poisoned me, and in apology, you'd like to fetch me dinner and draw me a bath."

"What?" I shook my head at the one-eighty our conversation had taken. "A what?"

Finn yawned and stretched his arms over his head. "I'm tired, Mari. It's been a long day."

"You want . . . ?"

He nodded. "You're my body. I'd like dinner with meat—I don't care what kind—and a bath, and then I'm going to sleep. Tomorrow is going to be a heck of a day."

I stared at him. He confused me. One second he was a philosophical solange devotee, the next he was seductive-eyed and talking about his love, and then he was demanding barbecue chicken and a bubble bath.

It felt like a diversion. Roumelade pulled stunts like this whenever she wanted us out of the kitchen. What didn't he want me focusing on? His reasons for being here? His preternatural stillness on the dais? Or . . . basically anything that had happened today.

"Am I right in thinking you aren't as solange-addled as you seem to be?"

"Solange-addled?" Finn weighed me up before answering. "No. You're not right. It's a second by second struggle to stay focused on this world. I'm walking a silver string suspended over the mouth of the universe. Earth below, solange above. If I'm stumbling here, I'm stumbling on that wire. Whatever you see in me, it's not what you think."

"Isn't that always the case?" I asked, thinking of the conjured world we lived in.

Finn tilted his head in acknowledgment. His eyelids sank, half-closed, and he leaned back in the chair again. He looked tired, drawn, and pale.

I remembered Darin's words. *"You're his body. Take care of him."*

Tomorrow was the first game. Finn was going to need to be in top form so he wouldn't . . . well, die.

"I'll get you some dinner."

"Thanks. 'Preciate it." He yawned again and closed his eyes.

"By the way, did you know the pool bathed you in a column of golden light?"

"Hmm? Did it?" He kept his eyes closed and yawned again.

"Finn? Did anything happen in the column?"

"Not really." His head fell forward, and his chest rose and fell in a shallow, rhythmic pattern.

I studied him for a moment. He looked different with his eyes closed and his head tilted as if he were already in a light, restful sleep.

First, he looked more like a Smith—like his brother and his dad—

because you weren't distracted by his eyes or his swaying and stumbling. You could take in the width of his shoulders, the size of his biceps, the tendons and muscles in his forearms. When he was still, you could finally see the power hidden beneath his own form of illusion. Because whether he'd admit it or not, Finn *was* creating a type of illusion.

Second, he looked different because his black hair had fallen gently over his forehead and his eyelashes were sweeping over his cheeks. The rough edges smoothed off his face, and he was left looking . . .

(If I'd admitted this, I wouldn't have liked myself very much, so at the time, I decided not to. But I can tell you now in the retelling.)

Finn was left looking like someone who could make me remember what it felt like to love. I thought maybe he could be the home I'd forgotten.

But he had Cora. He had love. And while I'd stolen many, many things in my life, I didn't steal people, and I didn't steal love. So I didn't admit to myself the second reason Finn looked different with his eyes closed. I didn't admit to myself that he might be the home I'd been desperately missing and had never found.

With his eyes still closed, he rolled his shoulders and said, "Meat, Mari. And potatoes. And I . . ."—yawn—"like apples too. With cinnamon."

I smiled at that. Even though I was tired. Sore. Gritty-eyed and achy. I'd go find him dinner and an apple with cinnamon for dessert. It was the least I could do.

"I promise," I told him. "You have my word. I'll do my best to keep you alive until the end, make sure you win the crown. So you have a chance of seeing your love, your home, again."

At least for the few days he had left on this earth. At least for a short time.

Finn smiled at my words, but I wasn't certain if he'd heard me or if he was dreaming.

24

DEEP, DEEP DOWN IN THE BEDROCK TUNNELS, WHERE DAMP, DANK
nightmares seeped from the stone, milky waterdrops *plop, plop, plopped* in
a hollow tapping noise that had echoed for centuries. The wind splashed
through the shivery-cold waterdrops and slid around the jagged stalactite
teeth lining the roof of the tunnel's mouth.

While it may have been content to play xylophone among the
stalactite and stalagmite (for a few minutes, at least), the wind had
another reason for creeping into the tunnels beneath the Bard Mansion.

There were watching things here, not listening things like the wind.
This deep below the earth air currents could become trapped, stilled, and
stagnant in the silent, watchful quiet. The wind liked the sweep of the
surface and the freedom found there. Down in the tunnels, where the
sun and the cosmos couldn't reach, the wind was slow and cautious.

Yet still, when the woman with the citrus and pearl dust scent swept
past, secrets written in her careful steps and cautious movements, the
wind caught ahold of the frothy turquoise tulle on her dress and hitched
a ride to the below.

The wind hated the idea of being trapped in the tunnels where
stillness and the watchful stone eyes reigned. The stone eyes gobbled up
secrets and never let them free, because stones couldn't speak.

Not speaking gave the wind an uncomfortable feeling, like the thought of diving into a wooden barrel and having the lid slammed shut behind you—forever. That had happened to the wind's cousin, and so the wind was especially careful to never travel somewhere it couldn't escape.

That was why, while it scurried in the wake of the citrus and pearl dust scented woman, the wind only took a moment to enjoy the hollow drip of water and the chill damp that coated the glistening walls of the tunnel. It was a creature, this tunnel, and the wind was whistling down its throat.

It rustled the woman's tulle and silk and kept close to the warmth of her secrets. She'd conjured sparks of blue and orange fire to wink around her and light her path. They were like fireflies on a summer night, gasping into existence, flaring bright, and then dying. The wind kept away from them.

"You're here. Finally," a man said.

A Bard, of course. There were four of them here, including the woman. The wind knew these four and liked them all.

"Yes, Father," the woman said.

Her voice sent a happy shiver through the wind. There weren't many who sounded like a cool ocean breeze singing over sand and seashells, tangling through seaweed and salt. She was a summer tide washing over a golden shore and sweeping the wind along.

It kept close, determined to stay with her, so that when she glided from the tunnels, it could ride the stirring of the air around her all the way back to the surface. Her summer voice would keep it safe.

"We don't have long," the man said, glancing down at the steel band on his wrist. "Which of you killed Secondus?"

The wind shifted across the four Bards in the room, stirring over cool skin, soft fabrics, and warm scents. There was the father and the one who wore the crown. The woman and heir. The man who pulled music from the center of the universe like a supernova birthing a star. And the last, the youngest man, who leaned against the watchful stone walls and smirked at the rest. The wind tickled his cheek, because he liked this one best of all. He was a trickster, just like the wind, and had many, many secrets.

The trickster twitched and then wiped the tickle at his cheek.

"Luvic?" the father asked, narrowing his eyes on the movement. "You?"

He laughed. "No. Not me. I had no love for Secondus, but . . ." He held out his hands and shrugged.

He tasted like champagne, sweet and bubbly.

"It wasn't any of you?" The father didn't quite seem to believe it. "It wasn't the paladin. Nor his body. I want her dead," he added as an afterthought. "Luvic, see it done. I want to see if she comes back."

The trickster—Luvic—tilted his head and stared at the sharp teeth of the ceiling. His sister's illuminations sparked around the dark, bulbous room. Not a room—more like a widening of the tunnel, where three paths converged.

"I hate killing pretty things," he finally said.

The musician snorted. "Since when?"

The wind moved to him, riding the calloused edges of the musician's fingers.

"Since . . . now?"

"Luvic," the father said.

The trickster flicked at a speck of limestone powder on the black lapel of his tuxedo. "Yes?"

"Soon," the father said.

The trickster slouched against the wall's rough stone.

"Soon," the father repeated, his melodious voice a forceful shove.

"Yes. All right," the trickster said.

After a moment of silence, interrupted only by the *drip-drip-drip* of the milky waterdrops, the musician spoke.

"It wasn't me who killed Secondus. Nor Morjorie. The Smith's Folly wasn't mine either. I had a dart for Darin if the opportunity arose before the ceremony, but . . ." He tilted his head. Shrugged.

"Perhaps it was Phillip after all," the woman said.

The father laughed. He enjoyed laughing, and the wind enjoyed riding his laughs. Then they all turned and looked at an alcove in the stone that the wind hadn't noticed. There was a body slumped in it, bound by icy metal. There was no warmth in the body. No spirit.

"You could've done better, planting the confession compulsion," the father said.

The musician nodded. "I know. I wanted it obvious. I wanted it to point to a Ward."

"Why Phillip?" the woman asked.

The musician's lip curled as he stared at the body. "He sent a note to the Clark before the ceremony. Told him he had the means to defeat you in the games."

The woman made a small noise of surprise. "Did he?"

"I wonder what that would be?" the father asked, contemplating his daughter.

"We all know what it is," she said. She looked down at the damp stone floor and the tips of her silver shoes peeking out from the feathering turquoise of her dress.

"But how did Phillip?" the trickster asked. "And who else did he tell?"

"Ragnor, protect your sister—"

The musician nodded. "Always."

"Luvic, kill the body. Find any other traitor to the family and be rid of them. Make it look like . . . a . . . Clark did it."

"Not a Ward?"

The father shook his head. "No. Too obvious." He narrowed his eyes on the dead man, then mused, "Did you get close to the cloaked man who leaped from the windows?"

The musician tilted his head in assent and straightened like a cat who'd enjoyed a successful hunt. "Yes. I nearly had him, but then—" He made a *poof* motion with his hands. "He disappeared. Like a shadow swallowed by the night."

"I expect it's one of the leggerock's creatures," the father said. Then, with a smile in his voice, he added, "He thinks the paladin will win the games and the body will steal the crown."

The wind waited for laughter, but no one laughed. There wasn't even the curve of a lip or a half-smile to ride along.

The air was heavy, and growing heavier every second the wind stayed in the deep dark. Soon, not even rustling skirts or swift steps could carry it back to the surface.

It shifted the woman's long hair and tickled her neck, urging her to hurry.

She looked back up at the dark, gaping maw of the tunnel and the rough, rocky sides of its throat. "I have to go. Creok is waiting."

"Creok is too demanding," the musician said.

"Creok keeps me alive," the woman replied.

The father looked again at the cold steel circling his wrist. "First, our plans for the games . . . With Darin removed . . . the paladin is a weak fool. A solange addict. He only cares for solange and sex."

The musician lifted his eyebrows.

The trickster slumped against the wall again and crossed his ankles.

"Should I worry?" the woman asked. "Sometimes an untrained foe is more dangerous than a trained foe. Their unpredictability and unexpected thinking can disrupt and cause chaos."

"Not to mention the column of gold that swallowed him," the trickster said. "In case you all forgot the pool's response to the solange devotee."

"Speaking of," the father said. "I thought you'd made a net to poison him. What happened?"

The trickster's jaw clenched. "It fell apart when he touched it."

The father nodded. "The solange. The destroyer of illusions. Well, no matter." He studied his daughter. Her cheeks were more flushed than when she'd walked down, her eyes glassy. He clicked his tongue at her feverish appearance. "The paladin's trait is strength. He plays for solange. He's in free fall and expects to win or die. Don't help him. Hinder him, if you like. If the chance arises, speed him to his death, but don't have a direct hand in it. Stay out of Jacob's way. If he's in the lead, let him have it. That will focus Primus's ire. If Primus is in the lead, hobble him, but make it appear the paladin is at fault. You know your role?"

The woman grimaced. "Siren."

The trickster grinned. "Aww, Celia. Would you rather damsel in distress?"

The woman stuck her tongue out, and her brother laughed.

The father cut his hand through the air, and the wind rode on the sluggish breeze.

"Tomorrow, it's expected you'll win. Do so. We're keeping the crown,

Celia. When you wear it, the world will put on the shoes I've spent a century crafting, and the people will gladly dance to our song until they die."

The woman gripped her dress and dropped her head as if she was waiting for the weight of the crown to be placed on the silk of her hair.

"Anything else?" the musician asked. "Has anyone seen anything? Anything we need to know before the games begin?"

The wind paused, clinging to the tulle of the woman's dress. It felt sluggish and weak in the stagnant, heavy air, but at the question, it rose higher, climbing up the lightly glinting sequins. It expected the woman to tell about the Clark that wasn't a Clark but was actually a Ward. It expected this dank, dark place was exactly where those kinds of secrets would be shared.

But the woman remained silent.

The wind laughed, a hollow sound echoing over the cold stone. So it was a secret. A *secret* secret. The woman didn't want to share whatever she knew about the clever Ward. Only she and the wind shared this secret.

The father smiled at his children. "Until tomorrow. You have your tasks. Ragnor. Luvic."

The men nodded.

"Celia? Win."

The woman clenched her dress tighter. "I will."

He swept past them, his dress shoes clicking loudly on the stone.

The wind thought about trailing him, jumping through the puddles of his shadows, but it was sluggish and tired. The three children stood in silence.

Then the musician nodded at his siblings. "Watch yourselves," he murmured, and then he followed his father.

The trickster and the woman were quiet. The eldest and the youngest. Her blue and orange firefly lights danced around them.

"I suppose . . ." the woman said, staring at the body on the rocky ground. She twisted her hand, and the body combusted, a quick indrawn flash, and then a snowstorm of ash swirling in the alcove. The wind clung to the woman's dress, too sleepy to stir the ash cloud.

"Do you need anything?" the trickster asked. He ignored the ash floating to the damp rock floor. "You're tired, Lia. I could get you a chocolate orange? A red-velvet cupcake from Lou's? Raspberry macarons flown in this morning from Paris? Anything."

The woman gave a distracted smile and then teasingly tugged on her brother's bow tie. "Creok'll take care of me. I'll be as right as rain come morning. Besides, you heard the Bard. You have mischief to make."

The trickster frowned. "Mischief can wait."

She clicked her tongue. "Mischief can never wait."

"It'll be over soon," the trickster said. "Don't worry, Lia. It'll be over soon."

The woman patted her brother's shoulder. "That's what I'm afraid of."

The trickster smiled, and the wind, knowing the trickster, recognized it as the smile he wore when he wanted to change the world and knew he couldn't.

Then the woman walked from the bulbous room, her firefly sparks trailing her. The wind tried to follow, but the air was heavy and stagnant, and it felt as if a thousand boulders were piled on top of it.

The dark came. The trickster stood still and quiet.

The trickster waited in the dark a long time.

For what? The wind didn't know.

The woman's lights faded. The stone eyes still saw in the dark, and they pressed on the wind.

The wind scratched at the trickster, clinging to the fabric of his tuxedo. But the trickster didn't notice. The wind lay down at his feet, falling weakly to the cold rock.

Finally, the trickster moved so silently, so stealthily, that not even a whisper of air stirred when he left. There was nothing for the wind to ride on.

The trickster was there. Then he wasn't.

The wind was left alone in the deep, dark tunnel. It was deathly still. Coffin-quiet. The wind was sealed in the dark, and there wasn't even enough air to breathe.

25

I DECIDED IT WASN'T SAFE TO BRING FINN FOOD FROM THE KITCHENS. IN THE records, at least one family member or body always died from poisoning during the games. Once in a while, even an heir was careless enough to eat or drink something that hadn't been taste-tested.

Even so, it took me a long time to wind my way through the mazelike corridors of the mansion and find my way to the front door. Hell Gate was a labyrinth, and as you know, if you just continue walking in a labyrinth, you'll eventually find your destination. But the Bard Mansion? It was a maze. Unlike a labyrinth, in a maze, you can be lost forever and just keep walking and walking and walking.

It was a little bit of illusion and a touch of architectural chaos, but it all resulted in the same thing. Me, wandering down dead-end corridors and wrong turns before finally, fifteen minutes later, popping out in the marble, statue-laden front hall.

It was two in the morning, and my steps echoed loudly on the marble floor. There were still conjurers awake—I'd heard some on my trek. Whenever I did, I ducked around a corner or quickly turned around to avoid meeting one alone in an abandoned hallway at night.

Conjurers were cruel, and I'd read enough to know bodies were regularly killed during the games. This was probably another reason it had taken me so long to reach the first floor. I was being cautious. Like a mouse. A mouse with teeth.

My hand inched under my uniform , and I clutched Justice's knife.

The doorman stood in front of the tall double doors, as still as one of the dozen statues. He still reminded me of a humanoid jackaltooth, and I repressed a shiver.

"May I help you?" he asked in his crisp, impartial tone.

"I have a food delivery."

I'd called a nearby diner that was open until four in the morning and ordered a steak cooked rare and a jacket potato with butter, sour cream, and chives. I usually ordered steak medium-well and potatoes with only butter, but this felt right. Finn seemed like a rare steak kind of guy.

A gong-like bell sounded, bouncing through the front hall. I gestured to the door.

"There it is."

The gaunt, mottle-skinned doorman bared his pointed teeth in a grimace, or maybe a smile. He swung the front doors wide.

"May I help you?"

A man in a reflective vest and a bike helmet looked at his receipt and said, "Order for Locke?"

"Here," I said, taking the delivery bag. The smell rose around me: charred steak and oven-broiled potato.

The man squinted at me. I was certain he could only see the boring apartment building, the glass front door, and the video intercom, but I still shifted under his stare. And then I caught the knot of illusion tied around him: a simple, loose-tied slipknot that I could've untied as a toddler. I nearly jumped in surprise.

That slipknot was classic Justice. Since he only had a pinch of conjurer in his blood, it was the only type of knot he could tie. Most of his illusions were bolstered by mundane magic. Makeup, misdirection, mind games. If I pulled on his illusion, it would fall loose, but he'd still be wearing the reflective vest, the bike helmet, and the makeup that made his eyes bigger, his cheeks hollower, and his nose longer.

I pulled a wad of bills from my wallet. I didn't bother counting them —I just handed him the whole clump.

"Havin' a good night?" he asked, a distracted frown on his face. He was in character, playing the harried restaurant deliverer.

The doorman sniffed the air and then made a strange rattling noise in his throat.

I nodded and held up the bag. "Now I am. Thanks for the food. It's a really good night. Really good."

Justice smiled at that and shyly ducked his head. It was hard to see him through his illusion, even as weak as it was. I'd never seen Justice on a job. Making constellations on the roof for me? Sure. Conjuring four-leaf clovers to wish on when we were kids? Yeah. Painting the scene of our mountain cabin with its white picket fence? Yes. But nothing like this. No wonder he could slip in and out of his assignments unseen. No wonder people were terrified of Jagger's knife. You'd never know when he was coming. You wouldn't be able to tell the difference between a harmless delivery person and death. I knew him better than anyone, and even I was having a hard time recognizing him.

Had Jagger sent him to check on me, or was Justice here for himself? Making sure I was okay and that I knew he was nearby if I needed him. I didn't know. I also didn't know what had happened to the actual delivery person.

"All right." Justice grinned and shoved the wad of money into his pocket.

I held back a smile.

"You take care of yourself."

"I will. You too." I hefted the bag of food and turned away.

The doorman shut the door, and the sound of his throat rattling cut off at the door's click.

I hadn't been sure before, but now I was. The doorman was part jackaltooth. That was the exact noise they'd made before they'd torn out my throat.

"May I help you?" he asked.

Goose bumps rose on my arms. The marble statues circling the room stared at us with milky-white eyes. Behind me, the curving double stairs were empty. Down one hallway was the ballroom. Down another . . . I didn't know.

"Do you know the fastest way to the Smiths' suite?"

The doorman leaned forward. Sniffed the air again. To me, it only smelled like steak, crisp potato, and butter, but there must've been something there, because the rattling noise began again in the doorman's throat.

I took a step back. I had a healthy aversion to all things jackaltooth.

The doorman pointed his long hand toward the hallway to the right. The one I hadn't been down before.

Was he being helpful, or was he sending me into a trap? I remembered what Finn had said. The doorman wasn't a help; he was a hindrance. Did Finn know something I didn't?

Yes. Probably.

But all the same, I took the direction the doorman pointed and hurried down the hallway, out of the marble entryway.

It wasn't until I was three dead ends, four turns, and five passageways in that I realized I was lost—again. Or walking in circles. I swore I'd passed that marble hall table, bronze-framed mirror, and wicker cornucopia full of fresh fruit two times before.

I frowned at the mirror, looking left and right. Then I focused on the cornucopia and realized I'd forgotten Finn's apple.

I reached out and plucked a deep red, pink-flushed apple from the top of the fruit pile. The skin was shiny, smooth, and the apple smelled like apple blossoms and crisp fall days.

This was exactly the type of apple I'd been warning myself about. It was probably poisoned. There wasn't any illusion on the fruit, but poisons were often from the real world. One bite, and game over.

I was about to set it back down when a man cleared his throat.

He had a soft tenor that was so sweet it could only come from a Bard. I turned toward the noise, bracing myself to either run, throw my knife, or untie a deadly illusion.

When I saw who it was, I didn't do any of those things. Instead I relaxed. Not because I wasn't still cautious, but because I was more curious than afraid.

It was Luvic. The youngest Bard. The handsomest—or prettiest, if you thought of it that way. He was twenty-two, just like me. He had raven-black hair and features that alone would be strange, but all together were beautiful.

His lips were lush and mischievously tilted. His eyes were an unusual brown-gold. His skin was a burnished bronze, as if he were the one that had been showered by the golden light of the pool.

Unlike some of the other conjurers, Luvic didn't use any illusion to enhance his appearance. His father, the Bard, used illusion to thicken his hair and hide the lines around his eyes. His sister used illusion to smooth her complexion. His brother used illusion to fix the ridge in his nose that hadn't healed properly after he'd broken it. But Luvic left himself exactly as he was.

"Hello," he said, his voice almost as melodic as Ragnor's. He put his hands in his tux pants pockets and slumped against the paneled wall.

He seemed to be waiting for me to reply. There was a ghost of a smile on his lips, and he raised his eyebrows in expectation.

"Hi," I said. I didn't say anything more.

Luvic grinned. "Are you going to eat that?" He nodded to the apple.

I held it loosely in my hand. "No."

"Ah. It's for your paladin then."

I stayed silent.

Luvic's smile grew. He looked up the hall, then down, as if he expected someone to round the corner and interrupt.

"I wouldn't," he whispered, his eyes widening meaningfully.

"Why not?"

He shrugged. "It's poisoned. It'll kill him in thirty seconds. Maybe less."

I couldn't tell if he was being serious. There was something strange about him. I had that tickle at the back of my neck again, as if a feather were brushing against me, trying to catch my attention.

"How do you know it's poisoned?" I asked.

He pushed off the wall and then walked toward me. Slowly. With his hands loose, as if to say he wouldn't do me any harm.

When he was close enough to touch, he leaned in and whispered, "Because I'm the one who poisoned it."

I dropped the apple. It hit the floor with a dull thud and then bounced a few feet. It came to a stop under the marble table.

I wiped my hand on my silk pants. "Well. That's nice. I hope you have a good night."

I took a step back.

Luvic snorted. "You're welcome."

I took another step back.

"By the way," he said, putting his hands back into his pockets, "you're going the wrong way."

I stopped.

He nodded behind him. "The stairs to the sixth floor are that way. Across the entry hall. Third door on the right after the clock. Gold filigree. Bas-relief of . . . who was it . . .? Orpheus?"

I frowned. What was it with this place?

Also, the doorman was a hindrance. He'd sent me in the wrong direction.

"Why are you helping me?" I asked, then I snapped my mouth shut. Luvic probably wasn't helping me. Maybe the third door on the right would open into a den of depravity and I'd be lost in it forever.

"Because you're pretty," he said, his mouth lifting and his eyes crinkling.

"Somehow, I doubt that's it."

Luvic held in a laugh. "How about . . . I like you?"

I shook my head. "Nope. You don't even know me. Try again."

He blinked. Held himself so still and silent it was as if he'd disappeared. Except he was still in front of me.

"Maybe you saved my life," he finally said.

"Really? When?"

I'd never met Luvic. I certainly hadn't ever saved his life. I wouldn't save a conjurer's life even if I was in thumbscrews and stretched on the rack. Nope. No.

He glanced at the ceiling, running his eyes over the ornate plasterwork. "How about . . . you saved it tomorrow?"

What?

"All right. Okay." I nodded. "Thanks for the tip on the apple . . ." I narrowed my eyes. Thought about what Finn had said when Luvic had a knife to his throat. "By the way, when you asked Finn why you shouldn't kill him, and he said because of apples, is this . . .?" I nodded to the cornucopia.

Luvic twisted his hand, and I flinched and launched my mind into the empty space where I could unravel knots. But he only made a pomegranate appear in his palm.

"Apple or pomegranate. He couldn't remember," Luvic said.

He held the pomegranate out to me. I pulled back into myself and took the glossy red fruit.

"He wasn't talking about poisoned apples," Luvic said, smiling at me as I held the heavy pomegranate. "He was talking about the tree of the knowledge of good and evil. Some people say its fruit was apples. Some say pomegranates. He figured I wouldn't kill him because I know the difference between good and evil."

"Do you?" I asked, raising my eyebrows.

Luvic grinned at me. "Maybe. Don't eat that pomegranate either. The seeds are death-axe butterfly pupae. You can keep it though. It's a gift."

I nodded and gripped the bag of food and the deadly pomegranate. I edged around Luvic, keeping my eyes on him. I felt a bit like a hiker trying to keep my eyes on a ravenous wolf as I tiptoed around it. *Don't turn your back.*

"You haven't said thank you," he said, watching me with an amused glint.

"Thank you."

He wrinkled his nose. "I meant for the ball. When I conjured that distraction for you. I thought having it jump out the window was a nice touch."

I stopped. My foot lifted halfway in the air. "That was you."

"Of course it was me. I winked at you, didn't I?" He winked again. "That's the signal. Wink. Wink."

Who?

What?

"Why?" I asked.

"I don't know. I didn't invent winking. It's been around for ages."

"No. I mean . . ."

He laughed. Of course he knew what I meant.

"I already told you. I think you're pretty. I like you. And—" He rolled his hand, gesturing for me to continue.

"I already saved your life sometime . . . tomorrow."

"Right." He smiled at me, and just like before, it was as if he thought we were sharing some inside joke, just the two of us.

He was strange. Very, very strange. I scrubbed a hand over the back of my neck, trying to get rid of that tickly feeling.

"I'm going to go," I said.

He nodded. "Sure. Go tend to your paladin. Ply your tender ministrations. I'm sure he'll love it. Try not to torture him too much with your soulful succor. He's in love, you know? All he wants to do is win the crown for his lovely lady."

I held back a scowl. "Okay. Thanks."

Did everyone know *everything* here?

I'd have to check the room again. There may not be illusions, but maybe there were listening devices.

"Third door on the right," he called as I hurried down the hall.

I held up my hand and waved the deadly pomegranate in goodbye. Once I was around the corner, I moved at a pace some would consider a run.

The suite was silent and dark when I returned. I assumed either Darin and Wolfgang were both asleep, or they were off on nighttime adventures.

In the bedroom, Finn was stretched out on the king-size bed. He'd stripped down to a pair of shorts and nothing else. He'd kicked the blankets off the bed, but the white sheet was twisted around his long legs. He lay on his stomach, the muscles of his back bunched and his head on a pillow. He was sound asleep. He didn't even twitch when I came into the room. The steady rise and fall of his chest didn't falter. Below his eyelids,

I could see the rapid movement of his eyes as he traveled through his dreams.

"I wonder what you dream about," I whispered. "Or who."

His brow wrinkled, and he wore a slight frown, his hand curling into a fist. Then he tensed, sucked in a sharp breath, and murmured in a sleep-slurred voice, "No. Don't let go."

I turned away and set the food on the nightstand. Maybe if he woke up in the night, he'd find it. If he was hungry, he could eat.

At that thought, I hid the pomegranate in my bag. I didn't want Finn to spy it and think it was a delicious snack I'd procured for him.

I looked around the quiet room and then sank my toes into the thick silk rug. The lamplight was low, spilling a golden hue across the room. Finn flinched again, so I walked to the end of the bed and yanked out the sheets, untucking them.

Then I methodically searched the room for listening devices. I found three of them. One on the underside of the escritoire. One tucked into the piping on the lampshade. One behind the headboard. I took them all to the bathroom and flushed them down the toilet.

When I came out, Finn's furrowed brow had smoothed, and he had a slight smile on his face. His hand curled as if he was reaching for someone. It hung over the edge of the bed, open and waiting.

I tiptoed over and grabbed a feather pillow. Picked up the blanket from the floor. Clicked off the lamp. Then I went and stretched out in front of the door. All sorts of things could come through a locked door in the middle of the night.

As soon as I had the thought, I sank into a restless sleep filled with cranberries and allspice, golden columns of light, and a voice that pleaded, "Mari! Untie the knot!"

This time, though, it wasn't a boy who begged me. It was Finn.

But no matter how hard I tried to untie the knot, I couldn't.

26

MORNING CAME TOO SOON. NOT AS A SLOW TRICKLE OF LIGHT TICKLING MY eyelids, but as a great, rushing flood that whooshed over me in a brilliant flash.

One moment I was lights out, struggling to untie a thousand knots of illusion in my dream world; the next I was sitting upright, heart banging, searching for the white light monster that had jolted me awake.

The white light was Finn yanking back the heavy velvet curtains. The screeching of the metal hooks on the curtain rod was the horrid alarm clock.

Finn was showered, dressed in dark, plain-woven canvas pants and a black T-shirt. He squatted down next to my nest of blankets and held out a steaming cup of coffee. The smell zinged through me and brought me back to the world of the living.

I loved coffee in the mornings. The blacker the better. This cup was as dark as the farthest reaches of Hades. Bless him. He was an angel.

"Morning," Finn said.

He'd shaved, and the soap he'd used tickled my nose and reminded me of clean sheets, late mornings, and walks through Central Park on cool autumn days. You'd think soap manufacturers bottled memories instead of scents.

I stretched, and something popped in my back. *Ugh.* Sleeping on the floor was not fun.

Finn smiled and pressed the mug into my hands.

"Where'd you get it?" My voice was scratchy and croaky. He must've snuck around me, and I'd been so involved in untying knots in my dreams that I hadn't woken.

"Darin."

"Ah."

Conjurers, the strong ones, could conjure edible food. It wasn't the best practice. Conjured food didn't have the same nutrients and life-giving qualities that food sown and grown in the dirt and raised under the sun did. But in a pinch, they could conjure a drink or a meal to snack on.

It was sort of like . . . say you're stranded in the middle of the ocean and desperately need water. You'd drink your own urine. It wouldn't be great. It wouldn't keep you alive for long. But you'd do it. Okay. Gross analogy. But that was pretty much what conjured food was. Urine in the ocean.

I only knew this because a few times throughout history, during times of famine, good-hearted conjurers (there have been *some*) tried to conjure food to feed the masses. It never turned out well. People just wasted away, like they were eating air.

When I grimaced at the cup—it smelled so good—Finn tilted his head and then, as if he understood my path of reasoning, said, "He brought his own beans. Sumatran."

"Oh, it's not . . . ?" I buried my nose in the cup.

"No. He made a pot earlier. The smell woke me up. Apparently, he likes his coffee as dark as night and strong enough to wake the dead. I thought you could use it."

Oh. Okay. Darin was a deadly, warmongering Smith, but he could make coffee. Why not? I took a long sip. The heat burned my tongue, and the strength shot through me and made my toes curl.

"I'm up. I'm awake," I said, coughing. *Wow, that was good.*

Finn laughed and held out his hand to pull me up. "I thought you'd like it."

I smiled at him in surprise. "You're different today. More lucid. Maybe both your feet are in this world, instead of one here and one in solange. I like you this way."

When I said that, his laugh broke off. He looked at me as if I'd burned him or attempted to shove him off a cliff. He dropped his hand and stepped back. The man I'd seen—the clean-shaven, direct, thoughtful Finn—disappeared, and in his place stood a remote, cosmic-eyed man with a distant smile.

"I didn't mean—"

"I don't need you to like me, Mari. I need you to help me win the games."

"But—"

He turned away, stumbled, and righted himself. I remembered what he'd said. He was walking on a silver wire between the world and the universe. When he stumbled here, he stumbled on that wire.

"It's not like I want to like you," I said.

It'd be harder to kill him if I liked him. I already knew that. Don't get close. Don't get attached. Just get in and get out. Preferably without dying.

I frowned at his back. He'd stilled halfway to the door, as if he was listening for something. A thought occurred to me. The conjurers had asked me in the chair if I liked Finn, but they'd never asked him if he liked me. And maybe, after the games, when Finn had had all the sex he could stand and all the solange he desired, he was going to try to kill me too.

So I asked the broad expanse of his back, "You don't need me to like you, but do you like me?"

Finn's shoulders stiffened. Then he turned and looked at me with his swirling navy eyes. Again, I had the strangest feeling he'd dragged me into another universe—one where we floated in the center of the cosmos while stars collided around us and he looked right through me.

My skin tingled, little fires lighting over me and licking my skin. I wanted to say, "Never mind. It doesn't matter if you like me. I have to keep you alive only to kill you."

It was like a farmer caring for and feeding his prize goose all summer, only to kill it and cook it for Christmas dinner. *Don't get attached, dear goose.* Unfortunately, my throat was too dry. I couldn't say a thing.

"You have to be ruthless," Justice would say.

"Don't go giving him good traits," Roumelade would chide.

"Mari, be careful," Griff would beg.

"Kill him," Jagger would demand.

Finn smiled at me as if he'd plucked all those thoughts from the air and heard each and every one.

"Wolfgang and Darin are in the sitting room," he said. "We're planning for the games today. Come when you're ready."

He left. And even though the coffee now tasted bitter and biting, I drank every last drop.

"You're not hearing me," Wolfgang barked, clearly exasperated.

It had been three hours of debate, strategy, and if-this-then-that scenarios. It seemed to me that Wolfgang and Darin were attempting to cram two thousand years of military strategy into Finn's brain in only a few hours.

For most of the morning, I'd stood against the navy-papered wall, ignored and unseen. Not even Finn had bothered to look my way, even when I'd clicked the bedroom door shut and walked to a corner of the room, behind the long leather couch. I liked having the wall to my back and the door to my front. Plus, if the Smiths decided they'd rather kill me than feed me, I'd be able to face it head-on.

But instead of mayhem, I'd had a sesame bagel, cream cheese, a bowl of fresh strawberries sprinkled with sugar, and another cup of coffee. All the food had been set out on the coffee table in individual containers, sealed with a lock of illusion that guaranteed no tampering and no poison. It seemed the Smiths were procuring their own meals for the duration of the games.

Finn had barely eaten any breakfast, although I'd noticed while getting dressed that sometime during the night he'd devoured the steak and potato. Even so, he'd made up a plate with a bagel and strawberries and pushed it my way, still not looking at me.

Not that he could. Wolfgang was drilling him on the siege of the citadel during the Mallian campaign. This was another of Alexander the Great's battles, and while I appreciated the history lesson, I wasn't sure it was going to do Finn much good in a game created by the Bards.

Sure, it'd help in a Smith game . . . but a Bard game? Not so much.

Finn was sprawled on the couch, his eyes half-lidded and starry-gazed. A daydream sort of smile played on his lips. I understood the Smith's exasperation. I didn't think Finn had been paying attention for at least two hours and fifty-nine minutes of the past three hours. There'd been a minute where Darin had made a joke about war elephants and Finn had laughed, but other than that, it seemed he'd been off in some other world.

Finn focused on his father. Wolfgang looked more battle-grizzled today, like a soldier on a long campaign. He was shrewd and calculating, a sharp wedge with brilliant insight that was a scalpel compared to the hammer and fist tactic Jagger usually employed.

Finn may not have been listening, but I'd been taking it all in. I'd never been this close to the workings of a conjurer's mind. I was focused. Know your enemy.

"Do I have to hear," Finn said, blinking sleepily at his father, "to listen?"

Wolfgang slowly scratched the stubble on his chin. I had the feeling that slow movement was the way he kept himself from lunging forward and plunging his illusion sword through Finn's gut.

"If you've listened, then what have you learned?"

Darin looked between his father and Finn with an amused smile. He sat in the club chair between them, although I doubt he would've stopped his father if he'd decided to gut Finn again. He took a sip of his midnight-black coffee.

Finn shifted on the couch, sitting straight. The clock on the wall *tick-tick-tocked*. With a final snick, it hit noon and began its soft church-bell chime. It was the tune great clocks all around the world played: *ding-dong-ding-dong-dong-dong-ding-dong*.

A shiver raced over me. The chimes were set to a rhyme. Not many people knew this, but at the softly ringing sound, Finn finally turned his gaze to me, and I was certain he was recalling the words.

"All through this hour, Lord be my guide. And by Thy power, no foot shall slide."

He was walking a silver string between worlds . . .

The clock made its final bellow. I wrapped my hands around my arms and stared back at him.

"I've learned," Finn said, turning back to Wolfgang, "that you've spent a lifetime studying war, while I've spent a lifetime studying myself."

Wolfgang stared at his son, the same lightning Finn had (the one I thought of as solange-tinted) shifting in his eyes. "You're a fool."

"Undoubtedly."

Darin cleared his throat and set his empty coffee mug on the table. "Wasn't it Alexander the Great who said, 'If I wasn't Alexander, I would be Diogenes'? Perhaps my foolish brother is merely Diogenes."

The Greek philosopher? The only thing I knew of Diogenes was that he claimed a man needed good friends or ardent enemies for self-preservation, because the enemies would instruct you, and the friends would take you to task.

I believed this to be true. My enemies had always taught me plenty about myself. And my friends kept my eyes wide-open.

I wondered how many enemies Finn had. I wondered who his friends were.

"I wonder," Wolfgang said, measuring his son with a thoughtful stare, "what you've learned about yourself. Have you learned if you're a quitter? Your mother was. In the end, she was a coward. She died rather than fighting to live. Have you faced all the dark corners and shadowed alleys of your heart? Have you seen the selfishness, the greed, the fear, and the malice? Do you know what you will do when faced with the choice to leap over the walls of the citadel to certain death, your army cowering behind you, unwilling to fight by your side? Will you leap like Alexander —storm a city and its waiting army alone, your death the most likely outcome? Or will you fall back—your shame, your cowardice, written in the stars? Have you seen your choice in all your learning? Certain death or cowardice—which is it?"

I watched Finn; saw the way he slowly curled his fingers into a tight fist. His father watched the movement too, a small, satisfied smile on his lips.

"I have no love for you," Wolfgang finally said, his eyes on Finn's fist. "I only ask that during the game, if you discover you are a coward . . . I'd ask that you die rather than slink back, the game unfinished. If you fail to complete the game, as you know, you are out. If that happens, you don't have to wait for the girl to kill you—I'll do it myself. I want an Alexander, not a Diogenes. Understood?"

Wolfgang waited for a moment, but when Finn merely stared at him with starry eyes and a line between his brows, Wolfgang stood, done with the strategy session.

"Darin," he said, "get him kitted out. He's not a conjurer. He has no defensive capabilities."

At least Wolfgang acknowledged that. The heirs had a huge advantage in the games: they could conjure, and they would. Whatever the games threw at them, they'd counter with illusion. But what did Finn have?

Solange, I guess. Riddles and philosophy. The burning desire to win for his almost-wife. He'd jump the walls of the citadel. I knew that, even if Wolfgang didn't. To me, it was obvious. Finn might play at Diogenes, but at heart, he was a Smith—an Alexander.

Wolfgang left. The clock struck another quarter hour. At one o'clock, the games would begin. One, for the beginning.

"You really know how to piss him off," Darin said, eyeing Finn with something like approval. "Look," he continued, "the Bards are showy, extravagant, a bit nuts. They like theater and drama. Their favorite virtue is cunning manipulation and playing parts. I'd suggest you hang back at first. Study the field. Let Primus or Jacob lead the way. Don't follow Celia —she'll use a strategy only fit for a Bard. You don't need to come in first. This time, just concentrate on finishing." He tapped his pointer finger against his lips and then said, "If you survive this . . ."

He didn't finish the sentence. He only went to the other room and then came back with an armful of black, plain-woven clothing—bulletproof, I was sure—and dumped them in my arms.

"Get him ready."

I did. Finn and I went into the bedroom and closed ourselves in the muffled wood and stone confines. He stripped down to his boxers, his clothing whispering over his skin. The rustle of him taking off and putting on his clothes was the only sound. I turned away and stared at the wooden escritoire with its candle, silver thimble, and bottle of solange.

"Do you need more solange before the game?" I asked—hating that I had, but wanting to give him any advantage I could.

"No," he said, his voice closer than I expected.

I whirled around. He was right behind me, dressed in a black shirt and black canvas pants. I tilted my chin, looking up at him. In this clothing, the Smith tactical gear, he looked more dangerous than I'd ever seen him. I could almost believe that he'd survive.

Heat rolled off him and seared my skin. I took a step back, distancing myself from the spark of him.

"I can't go into the game with you," I said, wishing I could. My hands shook, and suddenly, I was afraid for him. I'd read enough about the games to know they were tricksy nightmares, horrifying and deadly, even for full-blooded conjurers.

"I know," he said, staring down at me. "You'll stay here and keep me safe from traps and webs and poisons and . . . what?"

I ran to my bag and dug through it. "It's the Bards. I almost forgot. The Bards have jackaltooth under their mansion—these horrific wolf-jackal hybrids that attack anything not Bard. But . . ." I found it. I pulled out the brass button I'd stolen from the Bards all those years ago. Last night, the doorman had sniffed Justice just like a jackaltooth and then growled at his smell. "This is a button from the Bard's favorite jacket. What if it has enough of him on it to throw off the jackaltooth? Or any other magic set to attack anyone who isn't a Bard?"

I grabbed a needle and quickly sewed the button onto the underside of Finn's shirt. He watched me with a bemused smile. My fingers moved quickly as I looped the needle and thread through the buttonhole.

"There." I tied off the thread and flipped his shirt over, hiding the button. "That might keep you safe. Maybe." I smiled at him and shrugged. "Trust me though. If it works, it's worth it. You don't want to be mauled by a jackaltooth. Their teeth . . ." I shuddered.

The stars in Finn's eyes were swallowed by a dark cloud, and I felt something like barely caged rage rolling off him.

"Finn?"

He blinked, and the cloud was gone from his eyes. "Anything else?" he asked, absently touching the button on the underside of his shirt.

I shook my head. "Just . . . I think . . . the Bards like beautiful things. But even more, they like beautiful things that are deadly. I'd avoid anything that lures with beauty or song or . . ."

"What's that?" Finn asked, pointing to the pomegranate that had rolled out of my bag when I'd dug around for the button.

"Oh. Luvic—"

When I said his name, a line formed between Finn's eyebrows, and he frowned. "Luvic?"

"Luvic Bard. The conjurer who had his dagger to your throat at the ball. He sort of . . ." I shrugged. "Last night, he cornered me after I got your food. He claimed it was him who conjured the distraction at the ball, the shadow who jumped out the window, and . . . he told me not to feed you this apple he'd poisoned, and instead gave me this pomegranate as a gift. He said it was full of death-axe pupae."

I didn't know what I expected Finn to do, but I didn't expect him to smile as if this was the best thing he'd heard all morning. "Did he now?"

"Um. Yes."

He studied me like a cat curious as to what the mouse had gotten up to while it was napping. "I wonder why Luvic would do that."

I shrugged. "He claimed it's because he thinks I'm pretty."

Finn leaned close and studied the soft lines of my face, the indistinguishable color of my eyes, and the wisps of hair falling free from my French braid. This face was one that made people yearn. What did Finn yearn for when he looked at me?

"Pretty. Really?" He raised his eyebrows.

But the first time Finn saw me—just yesterday—he'd called me pretty too.

I shrugged. "Or he likes me. Or, apparently, I'm going to save his life. Who knows?"

Finn grunted, not looking entirely convinced about the last one. I understood. I wasn't convinced of it either.

"You should steer clear of him. He's not exactly trustworthy." Finn stared across the room at the pomegranate. He closed one eye, then he opened it and closed the other.

I narrowed my eyes on him. That feathery tickle had started at the back of my neck again. "How do you know he isn't trustworthy? Do you know him?"

"Mari, don't ever trust a conjurer." Finn turned to me and waited until I nodded, even though, being half-conjurer, that sort of included him. Not that I trusted him either. "Besides, everyone knows Luvic. He's always skulking around the Night Den looking for . . . fun."

I frowned. There was something odd about the way he'd phrased that. "Always at the Night Den? What, are you friends?"

Finn blinked. Tilted his head. Wrinkled his brow. "Why would Luvic Bard befriend me?"

I frowned. In my experience, conjurers didn't have friends. They also didn't hang around cast-offs, accidents, or anyone they considered a lesser sort. Luvic and Finn being friends was as likely as a coyote befriending a hare.

"He wouldn't," I finally concluded.

Finn nodded. "It's more likely we'd be enemies." It sounded like a philosophical statement—the sort Diogenes would propose. Maybe Luvic was the enemy who assisted Finn in self-preservation. An enemy to be thankful for.

"Do you mind if I take the pomegranate?" Finn nodded to the fruit.

I looked between the round, blush-red pomegranate and Finn's neutral expression and waved my hand. If he wanted it, he could have it. "Be my guest."

"Thank you."

He gave me a wide grin that sent a shimmery luminescence over me. Then he bent down and plucked the pomegranate from the floor. He tossed it in the air. It spun, catching the afternoon light, a hundred deadly pupae waiting to burst free.

When it landed in his palm with a fleshy thud, he smiled in satisfaction.

27

Maybe I expected the first game to have as much pomp and circumstance as the opening ceremony. Perhaps that was why I was surprised when it was only the heirs, their immediate family, and the bodies crowded in a small, barren stone room in the lower level of the Bard Mansion.

As soon as we arrived, Wolfgang shoved to the front of the gathering, using his physicality to move aside anyone in his path. Finn, Darin, and I followed in his wake, like fish trailing a shark.

I avoided the cluster of Clarks muttering at the back of the room. They were all in brown, except for their creepy, saggy-skinned body. His oil-slick feel gave me the shivers. I side-stepped around Uliea Ward, who looked on the verge of a breakdown. She kept flexing her bony hands, unflexing them, and then muttering to the thick wooden door on the far wall.

The Bards were the only ones who seemed completely at home in the rough-hewn stone room. They all had that relaxed, graceful posture that came from posing for the paparazzi or working in front of a camera. You'd think they weren't in a cold, damp, dungeon-like room, but instead having cocktails poolside at their sunny LA mansion.

The room, though, gave me the chills. It was maybe twenty feet by twenty feet. We'd descended to this level in an industrial elevator. The walls were rough, jagged stone with streaks of brownish red—iron, I hoped—and trickles of cold water.

The cold of the stone floor seeped through my shoes and through the thin silk of my uniform, dropping into my bones. The entire space had a rough, uncut look, as if the stone had been blown away with a large batch of explosives. That was what they did though, wasn't it, back in 1908?

Yes, I knew exactly where we were. I imagine you do too.

I'd smelled this mineral damp—like alkaline batteries leaching into icy water—and the stagnant, dry-bone mustiness before. It had a way of permeating your memory and filling your nightmares. I'd hoped the Bards wouldn't play their game in the tunnels beneath their mansion, yet here we were, the stone walls thick and the murmurings of the families echoing and bouncing around.

When we walked into the room, the back of Finn's hand brushed against mine. Was it on purpose? Did he remember what I'd said about the jackaltooth beneath the Bard Mansion? Was he trying to comfort me?

But no. When I looked at him, he wasn't even looking my way. He'd pulled his hand back and was staring at Celia Bard, closing one eye and then the other.

Still, I kept close to Finn. I was his gray shadow, blending with the slate stone walls and the rough stone floor.

While the heirs watched Finn—Primus with contempt; Celia with her come-hither allure; Jacob with the lazy curiosity of a predator at rest—none of them looked at me. I'd realized quite quickly that my status as body and my naturally forgettable presence made me even more invisible than usual.

It was to my benefit. You could argue invisibility was more useful than strength. For example, what did crowds want to see from a traveling circus? Did they want to see the strongman bending quarters with his teeth and lifting muscle cars, or did they want to see a magician disappear? I'd stick with forgettable, unimportant, and invisible, thank you.

Plus, for as long as I could, I'd stick next to Finn and unravel any illusions thrown his way. Granted, it was against the rules for anyone to attack, maim, or kill a player during the games, but I wasn't taking any chances. Jagger would have my head—literally—if Finn died in a preventable accident. He was Jagger's ticket to the crown, and I was his keeper.

The Bard held up his arms in a showman's gesture, and the conjurers quieted and turned their attention to him. His children stood behind him in their usual arrow formation, the sparkling jewels in his crown.

"Today is the first of our games," the Bard intoned. He wore a purple and indigo-blue tuxedo, and his hair was a thick, burnished illusion. He was a peacock, strutting and self-important.

At the time, I found a certain ridiculousness in his posturing. I almost found myself wanting to laugh at him. Was that the secret? Were you supposed to laugh at evil?

"For years, we have prepared our game. To delight. To enchant. To enthrall. It will test the greatest of our virtues. Have you observed . . .?" The Bard paused. Waited. Then he held out his hands again and gave a benevolent smile. "My friends, the world is starving. The souls of the people are a barren wasteland. Humanity has shriveled into marrowless bones and parched mouths begging for sustenance. *They are starving.* What do we do when the people are starving? We feed them. A starving person will eat anything. They will feast on garbage. They will glut on poison. They will devour their own child."

Darin stood on the other side of me. He let out a sigh and muttered, "Shut the windbag up and I'll buy you a pizza. Feast on that."

I held back a laugh. Turned it into a muffled cough.

Luvic stood behind his father. He'd ignored me the entire time we'd been in the bedrock room, but when I coughed, his gaze flicked to me. His left eye scrunched in a half almost-wink, and then he looked away.

What did that mean? Was it another signal? But for what? And why?

"Yes, a starving man will greedily grasp whatever you dangle in front of him," continued the Bard, nodding thoughtfully, "but we are benevolent. We are loving guides. We are . . ."

"Meat lovers," Darin whispered. "Pepperoni. Sausage. Your choice. Pizza. Just . . . make him stop. His speeches are *painful.*"

I wanted to elbow him. Step on his foot. Who knew the

warmongering son of the Smith was so sarcastically irreverent? Would he be like this when his father was extolling the virtues of invading and conquering all the countries of the world?

Somehow, I doubted it.

"The dazzlers," the Bard said. A little glow of illumination sparked around him, like an offset golden halo. "The beguilers. The world starves, and we will be the ones to feed it. In excess, they'll find ecstasy. The people are hungry. They hurt. We will feed them and free them from pain. It's easy to starve someone and make them hurt and then hand them the solution to their pain. The solution is the poison, but that's not so easy to see. The poison makes the hunger greater, the pain worse, and the cycle continues. You may be asking, what is the virtue I'm speaking of?"

Darin leaned close. "Not really. Not once have I asked myself . . . what does that crazed Bard think?"

I'll admit, I did elbow Darin after that one. I doubt he noticed. He was hugely muscled, and his side had as much give as a brick wall.

"Pepperoni," Finn said.

Both Darin and I looked at him.

He shrugged. "I'll have pepperoni pizza. Actually, I want two. Sixteen inches."

I raised my eyebrows, and then Finn stepped forward, closer to the front of the room where the Bard family stood.

Ragnor and Luvic moved as one to stand in front of Celia. They both held their hands in the conjurers' pose. Behind us, the Wards tensed. Jacob chuckled. Uliea stopped muttering to herself. The Clarks shifted, and the noise they made sounded like the fluttering wings of crows riding a storm.

"What is this?" the Bard asked, directing his question to Wolfgang instead of Finn.

Wolfgang cocked his head and flexed his hand in the move I recognized as the one where he was about to conjure his fire sword. Whether he'd use the sword on the Bard or Finn was yet to be seen.

"The virtue you speak of . . ." Finn swayed slightly, as if he were walking a tightrope between two skyscrapers on a windy day. "The virtue is hedonism."

The Bard smiled. Laughed his practiced movie-star laugh. "Ah, my solange friend. You've already drunk the poison, haven't you?"

"As you say." Finn tilted his head.

"I imagine you'll do well in this game. Perhaps you'll decide to stay in it forever." The Bard's eyes glinted, and suddenly, I had an even worse feeling about this game than I'd had only minutes before. "What do you have there?" The Bard nodded at the pomegranate in Finn's hand.

Finn stared at the fruit as if he'd forgotten he was holding it. "A snack. In case I'm hungry."

The Bard laughed again. "Our players can take one item into the game with them, and you chose a piece of fruit? Ah, Wolfgang. I'll bring out the wine tonight to toast your dead paladin."

"You'll be toasting it by yourself," Wolfgang said, a growl in his voice. I didn't know if he hated the Bard laughing at him, or if he hated it when Finn played the fool. "My son will beat your heir."

At Wolfgang's boast, the Bard coughed out a short, mirth-filled laugh. The Clark and Primus joined, and even their tall, gaunt body let out an oily cackle.

"Fools."

The room went quiet. It was Uliea who had spat the word. It was the first time she'd spoken above a confused murmur. She swept her gaze over the room, staring scornfully at the gathered conjurers.

"Uliea . . ." Philoneas warned, setting a hand on her arm.

She shrugged him off. "They're fools. If my daughter were here, she would kill them all. She would—"

"Uliea, please . . ."

"No." She swung a bony finger around the cold stone room, and I shivered when her wild gaze slid over me. It left an icy chill on my skin. "No. I hear you whispering. I hear you. You think Jacob is the strongest conjurer in centuries?" She laughed—a grief-stricken funeral laugh. "Jacob is merely the shadow cast by my daughter's sun."

I held still, not wanting Uliea's finger to land on me again. But finally, her hand paused, and her finger pointed at Finn.

He stared at her, his navy eyes pulsing.

"She'll kill you," Uliea whispered, her finger pointing dead center at his chest. "She'll kill you."

For a long, shattered-glass moment, no one moved, and no one spoke. Then Uliea sagged and let out a grieving whimper. Philoneas gathered her against him and turned her head into his chest.

An itch traveled over me, like a spider crawling up my neck. She was disturbed. Roumelade's story had nothing on this. Jacob Ward hadn't just killed his twin sister; he'd also sent his mother into an inescapable maze of madness.

I studied him, wondering what he thought of his mother's breakdown. It didn't seem to have fazed him at all. He stood casually, a far-off look in his green eyes, his right hand rhythmically tapping his thigh, as if he'd heard this "she's the sun, he's the shadow, she'll kill you all" spiel a thousand times before.

It was spooky, seeing him completely unconcerned by the fact that he'd exploded his twin sister into a million little pieces. Maybe he had gobbled up her power. Maybe I shouldn't have felt sorry for him for all those years. But I couldn't help it. I still felt sorry for him.

Maybe he felt my pity, because at that moment, the faraway look left his eyes. His gaze roamed over Finn and then moved to me. When our eyes met, I felt a hard jolt hit my chest. It was like a fist, tearing through the paper of my skin and grabbing onto me.

Oh. Holy. It was . . . Was this what Viola had felt when he'd ripped her apart?

I felt as if I might disintegrate. Float into a million tiny pieces.

He was doing something.

I could feel his conjuring stretching over me, poking and prodding and prying. His jaw clenched, and he leaned forward, no longer a lazy predator, but one on the hunt.

A whimper flew out of me. My heart boomed, trying to burst free from my chest. I felt as if I was being pulled apart. I couldn't find the knots. There was only a rope. A long cord tying around me.

Jacob stared at me, the far-off look back in his eyes. A screaming wail sounded in my mind. Maybe it was the same wail my mother had made when Philoneas Ward killed her the night I was born.

Where was the knot? Where was the knot that tied his rope to me?

I couldn't . . . I couldn't . . .

Black spots danced through my vision, a thousand nights of darkness calling.

Then, as soon as it began, it stopped.

Finn stepped close and blocked Jacob's gaze. He shielded me, crowding against me so his shoulder and side were pressed to mine. And just like that, the rope unwound and slithered away. I dragged in a shaky breath. My lungs were burning, and tears stung my eyes.

Finn's hand brushed the back of mine. I didn't pull away. Instead I moved closer.

I'd never experienced anything like that before. All illusions had knots to untie. Where was the knot in Jacob's illusion? And what was it that he'd been doing to me? It had *hurt*.

The only thing that had stopped it was Finn's touch. Did the solange dissolve the illusion? Did Finn standing in its path unravel it?

Perhaps.

I leaned back and took a quick, careful peek around Finn's shoulders. When I saw Jacob was still staring, as if he was trying to see through Finn to me, I ducked behind Finn's wide shoulders.

New goal: avoid Jacob Ward. Also: wear Roumelade's earrings at all times and use them if necessary.

The Bard was still talking. His voice pierced my thoughts, and I concentrated on his words.

". . . descend to Hadal, where you'll confront pleasure and pain, ecstasy and agony. Travel your chosen path. But don't tarry long. You must return through the golden door by midnight. The first through will collect the golden lyre as their prize." He raised an eyebrow. "If you can seize it from its guardian."

There was a surprised murmuring. The golden lyre was an object of power that had been held by the Bards for centuries. The ancient Greeks had believed its music was so beautiful it could make entire armies lay down their weapons or cause men to fall so deeply in love they would jump from clifftops chasing after the object of their desire.

"Get us that lyre," Darin whispered to Finn, "and I'll buy you pizza every night until you die."

I don't think Finn heard him. He was staring at Celia again, and Celia was making come-hither eyes right back. I scowled at her. *He's taken*, I wanted to say. *He's so far in love your siren glamour won't work on him.*

"There are three paths through Hadal," the Bard said, gesturing to the closed wooden door. "Melete. Mneme. Aoide. Choose wisely. Your choice will lead to success or failure. Life or death."

The Bard smiled first at Jacob, then Primus, then his lips thinned and he smiled at Finn. Finally, he turned to Celia and flourished a hand.

The wooden door groaned as it opened.

"Lead the way, my dear," he said.

Celia tilted her head regally. She was dressed in bright colors. Fuchsia, gold, turquoise. She wore a thick gold necklace—her one item, I supposed. Her shiny hair was wrapped in a crown of braids. She looked a bit like an erotic-movie version of a belly dancer, wearing a cut-off top and silk pants that cuffed at the ankles.

I wasn't sure that was the best outfit for a game, but she'd know, since her family had designed this one.

Primus swept forward, his brown scholarly pants and shirt clinging to him like dry parchment. He scowled at everyone he passed, pushing toward the door.

Jacob didn't look at any of us. He was in normal street clothes—an outfit a college student might wear on the subway heading to class. His blond hair, fair complexion, and slight stature were a deceptive camouflage. I shivered when he brushed by. He didn't look at me, but I could feel his attention.

Finn was about to follow, but I grabbed his arm and whispered as quickly as I could, "Hadal is the underworld. The tunnels are full of nightmare creatures. The most beautiful will be the most deadly. Some you won't see. Avoid anything that shines bright. The light is a lure. Use your instinct. The three paths are the ancient muses. 'Melete' means practice. 'Mneme' means memory. 'Aoide' means song. Whatever path you choose will be a twisted version, a perversion of itself. Just . . ." I held his arm tight, stupidly fearing for a man I'd only just met. "Please don't die."

He stared at me, seeing maybe more than was really there.

I swallowed, my throat aching. "I only meant . . ."

He nodded. "I know what you meant."

Funny. I didn't. Not really.

He turned away. Celia, Primus, and Jacob had already passed through the door. I stood still, barely breathing, as Finn was swallowed by the darkness.

Then the Bard twisted his hand, and the door slammed shut. Locked them in.

"How much do you want to bet he dies in the first fifteen minutes?" Darin asked, staring at the closed door.

"I think you should have a little faith," I said, not letting on that I was probably just as doubtful as he was. Maybe more.

"I'm a Smith. I deal in the concrete. If you want faith, go play with the Wards."

No, thanks.

"What now?" I asked.

Darin shrugged. "You go have fun with the other bodies. Skulk around. Be useful. Learn something interesting. Try not to get killed. It'll be at least . . . six hours before the first player comes through. Until then . . ." He waved a hand. "Go away."

I glared at him. Darin was an annoying brother. He wasn't even my brother, but still . . . he was an annoying brother.

He smiled as if he knew exactly what I was thinking.

At the door, I saw the short, gray-haired Bard body and Luvic in a heated whispered discussion. When the body left in a hurry, I decided to follow.

28

THE WIND LAY BREATHLESS AND WEAK ON THE COLD STONE FLOOR. THE stone room was its tomb, dark and silent. Inescapable. The stone eyes stared, relentless in their probing regard.

They pressed on the wind and mercilessly prodded until, exhausted, the wind curled into a tiny ball and hid in a crack. It hid beneath a trickle of icy water, near the gaping mouth of the descending tunnel.

Time wasn't linear for the wind—not like it was for humans. Humans viewed time like a strand of pearls, dropping in sequential orbs from beginning to now. But for the wind, time was *only* now, and because of that, the now was an eternity of torment. For the first time, it longed for the markers in the now that humans used to create past, present, and future.

The wind moaned to itself, listening for the company of an echo. It splashed around the icy waterdrop, rubbed itself between the tight walls of the rocky crack, and shivered weakly as it fell like a dying leaf back to the ground.

If it ever tasted fresh summer air again—full of sun-warm, loamy soil and dew-covered grass, magnolia blossoms perfuming park benches, and reality and illusions spinning whirlwinds to ride gleefully on—the wind would share its secrets. It promised itself it would share them with someone. It was a bargain it made with itself.

Deep in that dark, tomb-like abyss, the wind moaned and sighed and wished for freedom. Until finally, after promises made from fear, it heard the scuff of a heel against stone.

There it was again. Another scuff. A pebble rolling over stone. Then the sound, finally, of someone exhaling.

The wind shoved itself from the crack and crawled weakly across the stone floor. If it had a heart, it would've banged in anticipation and desperation. All the same, its currents prickled and shuddered as the sound of footsteps drew near.

Suddenly, there were shadows on the walls. They danced like moths, lit by blue and orange sparks. Then the scent of citrus and pearl dust floated near, and the wind nearly wept. She was back. The Bard heir was back. He would grab ahold of the waterfall of her silk clothing and—

No!

She moved too quickly.

The wind floundered on the stone, gasping as the fire lights faded and the woman hurried past, barely giving the wind enough movement to ripple even a grass blade's height above the floor.

It moaned, calling her.

But she was gone. The dark was back. The wind could feel the stone eyes pressing.

Then the sound of rustling wings and the smell of parchment filled the tunnel. The wind used the strength it had gathered from the Bard heir and floated higher, calling out a soft whistle to the Clark it knew was approaching.

It wasn't the hairless Clark—the one who smelled cold, like dried-out parchment and snakeskin. It was the other one. The sharp-boned man who the wind had seen torturing figments and sprites and other creatures in the catacombs below the Clark Mansion.

Sometimes the wind watched him in his catacombs. It liked the sound of ink pen scratching over paper. It liked the smell of old books and the feel of vellum and leather binding.

But it did not like the cold, metallic taint that clung to this Clark. He didn't have warm blood like most humans did. There was no warmth in his spirit. There was only cold, malformed, murderous intent. That intent sucked the warmth from his blood. Gobbled it up.

While the wind liked to feel all sorts of things, it didn't especially like the feel of this particular Clark. He didn't have many secrets. What secret was there in cruelty and torture? What secret was there in his desire to rule? None.

Still, the wind would gladly cling to his cold skin and bury itself against his woolen, parchment scented clothes. The wind would ride along with the parchment scented cruel one if that meant it could leave this tomb.

Then the cruel one was there, a dark splotch drifting on silent wings through the tunnel. He had no dancing sparks or light to guide the way. Instead his eyes glowed an eerie sulfuric yellow. He'd coated his skin in an armor of black and gray scales that sucked in the shadows and fed on his eyes' unnatural light. He scanned the craggy room. His upper lip curled at the plea-filled moan of the wind as it reached out toward him.

Instead of drawing nearer, the cruel one veered to the opposite side of the stone room and slipped through the tunnel without leaving even a tiny stirring of air for the wind to grasp and ride on.

It was hopeless.

The dark would swallow the wind. All its secrets would be buried here with it.

Then, after a dozen sluggish *drop-drop-drops* of water, the wind heard a light footfall that made it eagerly stretch with glee.

He was here!

He'd come!

The boy's steps were as light as a cat's paws on spring grass. He padded softly over rock in the silent darkness, his fluid movement a quiet whisper that was a cousin to the wind.

The wind reached out, stretched as high as it could—not very high at all—and whimpered weakly, calling to the golden-haired boy. No. Not boy anymore. Man. But the wind had known this boy since before he was born.

It had ridden his infant wails and baby giggles and stroked his downy cheek. It had rushed through the eaves of his bedroom and sung a gusting lullaby to push him into sleep. It had ridden this boy's breath as he'd blown out his candles on the birthday he'd come into his power. It had even slid down his screams as he'd shattered the girl—his mirror.

What did they call him? Murderer? Sister-killer? Dangerous one?

Ward.

He had come!

The wind let out another pitiful moan. It was so quiet it was barely louder than the drip of water on stone. It was so quiet there was no echo.

Still. The boy paused. He pulled his power around himself, a luminescent cloak—the sun behind a solar eclipse. The power pulsed and reached. He sent it through the room, solar wind fingers sorting and shuffling through the contents of an open drawer. He probed every crevice and crack in the dark stone room.

The wind rode the currents of power and let out a soft groan.

The boy tilted his head. The edge of his lips lifted in a soft smile. Then he walked to the small crack at the mouth of the tunnel.

"Wind?" he said in his soft tenor, squatting next to the wind and brushing his hand over the stone. "What are you doing here?"

The wind groaned and wrapped itself around the boy's ankles, rubbing and twisting in weak figure-eights. The boy smiled at its fluttering and twisted his hand, creating air currents for the wind to ride.

"It's not safe for you," he murmured, shaking his head at the wind. "Why would you come somewhere that doesn't have currents for you to ride? Secrets, I suppose. Did you find secrets here?"

The wind bathed in the light falling off the boy and strengthened itself in illusion's currents.

The boy stood, and then, at an echoing noise from the dark tunnel behind him, he shook his head again.

"He's close. I'm not interested in playing with the paladin." He frowned, and the wind tugged worriedly at the fabric of the boy's jeans. "Don't worry. I won't leave you. Look, I'll make you a current to ride. Hang on to me. Keep close."

At that, the boy pushed the wind high, boosting it with a surge of air and power. The wind wrapped itself in the boy's soft, forest-glade scent and clung tight as he sprinted on cat-light feet from the dark cavern.

The wind was free. The boy had saved him. The wind decided the promise it had made to share all of its secrets could wait.

29

I CREPT AFTER THE BARD'S SHORT, GRAY-HAIRED BODY, DUCKING FURTIVELY behind gilded brass mirrors, marble statues, and man-size porcelain vases. He wound through the hallways and stairways as if he could navigate the mansion in his sleep. Which I suppose he could, considering the body likely resided here with the Bards.

There were plenty of conjurers walking the hallways. None of them bothered to notice the Bard's body, and so, when I passed them by, I tried to make myself as inconspicuous as possible.

I often saw Griff do this when the slipshots at Hell Gate were in the mood for blood. He'd hunch his shoulders, drop his head, and make himself as small as possible. Usually, the slipshots would leave him alone. If not . . . well, Griff was a lurer, wasn't he? If they cornered him, they'd find out his hunched shoulders were a fishing line reeling unsuspecting fish in for a gutting.

Not that Griff routinely gutted anyone. But Jagger did. Griff was an asset, and no one except Jagger was allowed to do permanent harm to his assets.

So I hunched my shoulders, dropped my eyes, and made myself inconspicuous.

The Bard's body was definitely up to something. While he climbed the stairs and pushed through hall doorways, he kept glancing around in a furtive "is someone watching?" manner that screamed of hidden motives.

On the third floor, he paused, hidden by the folds of a velvet curtain as the Smith stalked by. I ducked behind another giant blue and white porcelain vase and held my breath.

The Smith paused only a half dozen feet away from my hiding place, and when he tensed and stretched his hand, I was sure he'd realized I was there.

But then a glass knife streaked through the air. He twisted his hand, and the knife melted in a stream of fire. Another flew at him. Another. A barrage of glass knives shot down the hallway. The Smith snarled and swept his hands out. He twisted, conjuring a fiery shield. The knives struck the shield and melted in a lavalike flow. They dripped to the carpet. It scorched and burned. Smoke curled around him.

"Try harder." The Smith bared his teeth at the empty hall.

But it wasn't exactly empty. At the far end, there was a knot of illusion. Someone had cloaked themselves. They were a fold in the curtain opposite the Bard's body.

The body's face was gray. His eyes flicked frantically between the Smith and the empty space where the knife had flown from. He pressed himself against the wall, keeping still and quiet.

Should I help the Smith? Should I unravel the knot at the end of the hall?

No.

The Smith's smile grew, and he twisted his hand. He conjured a bow of ice and fire. My breath caught, and my lungs burned. In a flash, he sent his blue ice arrow speeding down the hall. I watched the arrow spiral, fire trailing in its wake.

It hit the illusion with a sickly thud. A man grunted. Swore. A drop of blood fell outside the illusion and hit the carpet. It spread in a small red circle.

Wolfgang laughed. It was a battle laugh, filled with joy. My hands trembled. Was it Wolfgang who'd killed me with the ice arrow?

Was he the one who'd closed my eyes to death?

If so, did he know what I was?

The man beneath the illusion ran. His footsteps were muffled by the carpet. Then they faded altogether. For a long moment, Wolfgang stood in the hallway, bow in hand, a wicked smile on his face.

"Well-played," he said. Then he dissolved his shield and bow. Turned on his heel and stalked back in the direction he'd come.

I didn't have time to take a breath or consider my actions—the Bard's body was off again. He darted between the curtains and a statue, then he hurried down a stairway.

I chased after him, keeping just out of sight.

By the time we'd reached the fifth floor, my heart was pounding. A drop of sweat trickled down my neck. He'd zigzagged and backtracked so much I was certain he was wary of being followed and was trying to throw someone off his trail. Me, probably.

Finally, he ducked around a corner. I counted to fifteen and then followed.

I didn't . . .

I'd forgotten.

Sometimes, when you're following someone, someone else might be following you.

I was launched off my feet and slammed into the wall. My head cracked against the wallpaper and hit the edge of a gaudy brass mirror.

Immediately, warm blood slid down my temple. Black dots, like a swarm of mosquitos, flew across my vision. A sharp whining sounded in my ears.

Last—the youngest Clark—tilted her head. She was a gaunt, hungry crow staring at a bug she'd pinned to the wall.

My head spun. I'd hit the edge of the mirror hard. I thought I might be sick. If I was, there was nowhere for it to go. I was bound hand and foot, hanging three feet in the air. She'd gagged me, tying my mouth shut with illusion. There was only a thin hole for air to reach my nose.

If I were an ordinary body, I'd have been helpless.

But I wasn't ordinary. Her knots were simple. Just one loose thread over another, conjured in haste. I could unravel them in half a second.

But then what? She'd know. It was better to die my next death than to let her know what I was.

"Ohhh. How pretty," Last said, smiling grotesquely over her shoulder. "Lookie what I've caught."

Behind her, just to her right, was Primus's body. The tall, gray, gaunt man who gave me the chills. He had dead eyes and felt *wrong*. From someone who was raised in Hell Gate, that was saying something.

Last turned back to me and focused on my features. She moved so closed that I could feel the chill of her and smell the musty dust scent she carried. She was cruelly gaunt, bone-thin, and had sharp eyes that I'd mostly seen narrowed on her brother Primus's back.

I had to admit, I was struggling against her bindings. I knew thrashing about wouldn't do any good. I was caught, a butterfly stuck with a sewing pin to a piece of cardboard, my wings flapping helplessly. But still, when she leaned close and sniffed at the sheen of perspiration on my neck, I strained and pushed and . . . didn't move an inch.

She smiled at me as if she knew I was fighting her. As if she liked the struggle.

"You smell pretty," she whispered. "Like blood and violets."

She ran her cold finger over my temple and pulled back, showing me the glistening red of my own blood. She rubbed her thumb over her fingers, smearing it.

"I'd like to play with you," she said. Her voice was whispery soft, almost singsong. "But Father says I can't."

There wasn't enough air reaching me. The hole was too small. The buzzing mosquitos were growing in number, so my vision was almost entirely covered by their fluttering black wings.

"Do you like history?" she asked, stroking her blood-soaked finger over my cheek.

It wasn't a question. I couldn't answer. I couldn't speak.

I sagged in her bonds, hanging above the lush carpet.

If I was going to escape her, I had to do it soon, before I passed out. I could untie her knots. I'd brought a tiny, beaded needle of poison. It was in an inside pocket I'd sewn. But the poison was slow-acting—it took twenty-four hours to take effect. That wouldn't work. Instead I could pull Justice's knife free and stab her in the heart. But then I'd have to kill the body too. Could I, when I was already fading in and out of consciousness?

"Answer me!" Last struck me across the cheek. There was no give, because I was bound and pinned to the wall.

The blow jarred my teeth, and I bit my tongue. The copper taste of blood filled my mouth.

"Oh." She smiled. "Silly me. I forgot. You won't cry out, will you? If you do, I'll hurt you."

After a moment, she untied the illusion at my mouth. I sucked in a deep breath of air and fought the need to gag.

"Answer me."

I closed my eyes. Blinked away the majority of the black spots. "Yes."

I liked history. I studied it. I learned from it. I sought the truth in it.

Last raised her eyebrows, surprised and delighted. She looked like she wanted to clap her hands. "Oh, that's wonderful. What do you like about it?"

She watched me as if we were chatting at the library over a table of history books and we might very well become best friends. I'd never seen her so animated.

Behind her, the gaunt body shifted and then moved down the hall, investigating the distant sound of a closing door.

I swallowed, ignoring the sting of my tongue and the coppery tang of blood. "I like how it shows that even though evil often wins battles, good always wins the war."

She giggled. A high-pitched, happy laugh. "Oh neat. Do you think so?"

"Yes."

She grabbed the end of my braid, clasped it in her hands, and tugged until my hair pulled so hard my eyes began to water. "I don't think so. I think history is full of blood. My father sacrificed my mother. He carved her open right in front of us all. What do you think of that?"

She patiently waited for my answer. "I think that's sad."

She nodded slowly, her shoulders sagging. "Thank you. Do you have a mother?"

"No. She died when I was a baby."

Last let go of my braid, and my eyes filled with more tears at the sting of release.

"So you understand the pain," she said. "It hurts, not having a mother. Even Jacob has a mother. And the Bards." She spat their name as if she hated them more than anyone else in the world. "And what about Darin? His mother died in childbirth. A worthy death. Do you remember your mother?"

I was a *baby*. Of course I didn't remember my mother.

But there was something strange in Last's eyes. An odd yearning.

"No," I said slowly.

Last spread her small, bony hand around my neck. "But do you have someone like a mother?"

I wasn't certain she'd realized she was clenching my neck, cutting off my air again.

"Yes," I whispered, breathing through her grip. What did she want to hear? "When I was little," I said, "she baked me scones, told me bedtime stories, took me to the playground."

Last's hand loosened. Her cold fingers drifted over my pounding pulse, and she gave me a sad smile. "It must've been nice to have a mother who loved you enough to tell you bedtime stories. Was it nice?"

"Yes." I stretched against the illusion holding me tightly in place. Still no give. The body was slowly creeping back down the hall, rattling the knobs of closed doors and peeking into rooms.

If I was going to kill her, I should do it now, while the body was far enough away.

Last patted my cheek. "I thought it might be. Do you know why I like history?"

"No."

Her eyes lit up, delighted at my forced attention. "Because"—she leaned closer—"we're traveling in circles. Rounding the same mountain. If you're lonely, look to history. At first, I was upset about my mother. But then I peered into history. Humans have always had blood sacrifice. Even now. Look around. If you can't see it happening today, on a global scale, you're blind. It's celebrated, you see. That's when I realized my father was right. When Primus wins the games . . ." She smiled and rubbed her finger in the blood still running down my cheek. "Shall we be friends?"

No.

No, we definitely should not be friends.

"You remind me of my mother," she said, her crow-like gaze full of yearning. "You're pretty. Just like she was."

That was when I realized. It was this *face*. This stupid, eighth-life face that was achingly beautiful and made people see and feel their deepest, most hidden yearnings. It made them wish for forgotten memories and lost loves and missed opportunities.

Even someone like Last would fall victim to the promises of this face. She yearned, it seemed, for the love of her mother. Twisted? Yes. Sick and scary? Uh-huh. But here we were.

I knew this face would get me into trouble—I just didn't anticipate this sort of trouble.

"I wanted to kill you. I wanted to kill a body. But now I think I'll kill the Bard body instead. Isn't that nice of me? You and me? We'll be friends."

I couldn't help it. Even though I was pinned to the wall and the Clark body was too close, I said, "No. I'm not going to be friends with you."

Last's face twisted, and she reached up and slapped me again. My cheek throbbed and stung. The nausea climbed.

"That wasn't nice," she said. "Friends are supposed to be nice."

Okay.

Super.

It was time to get out of this situation. It wasn't worth dying for. Truly, it wasn't. And I wasn't going to untie her knot and attack. It was too risky. That left . . .

"I'm sorry."

Last nodded, her eyes sharp, mind working. "I don't believe you. You just don't want to die, even though you're Jagger's creature and you'll come back. I've killed his creatures before, you know. Some come back. Some don't. Would you like me to kill you after all? I can."

She waited for my answer as if she'd actually take what I had to say into consideration.

"I'd rather you didn't."

"Okay, so we'll be friends." She held up a hand, forestalling any commentary on my part. "And since I know you don't want to be, here's what we'll do."

The body came back and stood behind her, staring at me the way you might consider a bug twisting and jittering on the pavement right before you stepped on it and squished it dead.

Last reached up and pressed her cold, thin hands to my temples. "I'm going to make you a pretty little crown. It's going to sink into your head, and you'll wear it all the time. It's a memory crown. You'll have all these wonderful, lovely memories . . ." She smiled at me, waiting for me to be as delighted as she was. When I didn't move, she shrugged and pressed her hands tighter. "It's a history I'm weaving you. We're best friends in this history. We spend all our time together. You'd do anything for me because you love me. And I love you. As kids, we played at playgrounds together with your sort-of mother,"—she gave me a soft, sheepish smile—"and we ate her scones. Isn't that nice?"

No. It was not nice. It wasn't nice at all.

She twisted her hands. I could feel her weaving her illusion, tying the knots around my skull. It was tight and heavy, like thorny metal wires digging into my skin and settling into my mind. I saw the flashes she was weaving. Me and Last sliding down the granite slide at the 67th Street playground, gobbling blueberry scones while lying in the grass on the Great Lawn. My eyes watered and unfocused as she slid more memories into my mind.

I was sleeping over, and we were in her room, poring over history books and laughing together at the cruelties of the past. In this memory, I liked laughing with her. I liked her. Then she was showing me memories that I think she must have believed were things friends did. We were riding our bikes in Central Park; climbing the Statue of Liberty. It was spring, it was winter, it was fall. We did everything together—for years, for seasons—both of us inseparable. It was summer, and I picked a rose, the thorns piercing my fingers, and gave her the flower. "Friends forever," I promised, and she hugged me and whispered, "Friends forever."

What would I do for her?

Anything.

Did I love her?

With my whole self.

The thorny wire sank into my mind, knotting and tying, roping around me. A weave of illusion filling my past and rewriting my history.

"Mari," Last said, her voice liltingly soft.

I smiled at her, wondering why she was holding me in the air, against the wall, bound and tied tight. Was this a game?

I stared into her dark eyes, my beautiful best friend. She was the most wonderful person I'd ever known. The most kind. The most loving. I strained against the bonds. I wanted to give her a hug. I'd missed her.

"Mari? Are you my friend?" she whispered sweetly.

I gasped. "Of course I'm your friend. I love you," I assured her. I needed her to believe this. Desperately.

"But are you my *best* friend?"

"Yes," I said. "*Yes.* How could you believe anything else? I love you. I always have." A tear slid down my cheek. I was so lucky to have her in my life. So lucky to be her friend.

The body, the gaunt man behind Last—I liked him: he protected her —snorted into his fist.

"Bless you," I said, thinking he'd sneezed. "Last, are you okay? Do you need me to do anything for you? Anything?"

Last smiled. She reached out and took my illusion-bound hand in hers. "You would do anything for me, wouldn't you?"

"Yes," I said, smiling at her. "What are best friends for?"

Last nodded. "Exactly. Oh, Mari, we're going to have so much fun. What is it like being the paladin's body?"

"Uncomfortable," I said.

Last laughed as if this was the funniest thing she'd ever heard. I frowned, my skin itching and my cheek aching.

I should tell her I was a lockpick. Did Last not know that? I was sure it was something a best friend should know. She'd probably find that funny too.

I opened my mouth to tell her, but then the knots around my arms and legs loosened, and I fell to the floor. My knees cracked against the carpet, and my head swam. A drop of blood hit the floor.

I stared at it. I vaguely remembered Last hitting me. But that couldn't be right. Last loved me.

"What happened?" I asked, woozy and dizzy.

Last nodded to the gaunt body, and he yanked me upright. "One of the Bards . . . Luvic, Ragnor . . ." She spat both their names, and I tensed, hating them, because she clearly hated them. "One of them attacked me. You tried to stop them. They hit you."

How dare they?

I hated them. I would hurt them for harming Last. "I'll hurt them."

"Good," she said, patting my hand.

"Can I hug you?" I asked, my eyes wide. They still watered. Teared. "I've missed you. I don't like being away from you."

Last held open her arms and patted my back when I wrapped my arms around her. Her smell was one I loved: parchment and deep, dark catacombs.

"Mari," she said, stepping back.

I smiled at her. I loved it when she said my name. I gripped her hand. "Yes, Last?"

"Why are you here with the paladin?"

I frowned at her. Didn't she already know? "Because Jagger wants him to win the games."

She nodded. "So my father told the truth."

"What? You mean the chair?" Why didn't Last stop that? Didn't her father know we were best friends?

Last waved my confusion away. She leaned forward, clasped my hand, and whispered, "You want to hurt the Bards, right?"

"Yes." There was no question. They'd hurt Last. I'd hurt them.

"I think . . . poison is a good option. You aren't very strong. You can't sneak very well. But poison—do you have any?"

"Yes. I have some here." I patted my silk shirt at the little secret pocket I'd sewn.

She grinned. "This is why we're friends. We're so much alike."

I nodded. "I know. We really are." I squeezed her hand back.

"We've been preparing for years. You want my family to win the games as much as I do."

I nodded and continued nodding. I did. The Clarks winning the games would be the best thing the world had ever seen. It would be an era of wonder.

"We can't kill the players," Last continued. "But . . . you might . . . hobble them."

"Hobble them?" I looked around the hall, suddenly worried someone might overhear. "I don't want you to get in trouble. If it's against the rules—"

"Don't worry. It won't be me doing it. It'll be you."

Oh. Me. I smiled and nodded happily. "That's good. That's smart."

It'd be all right. If I was caught, I'd be punished, not Last.

"I want you to water down your paladin's solange. Poison it too. Not a lethal dose. Just enough to make him . . . lose. Badly."

"I can do that. Easy."

Last reached up and wiped the drying blood from my face, then she brushed back my hair. "Mari?"

"Yes?" I leaned into her hand.

"Kill Darin, if you can."

"Okay. Why?"

"He's not nice."

I nodded. He really wasn't all that nice. That was true.

"And Jacob?"

"Yes?"

"He drinks wine every night before bed."

"Ah," I said, understanding immediately what she was requesting. Hobble him.

"And Celia?" I asked, wanting to do all I could.

Last shrugged. "If her brothers die, she'll be dead soon after."

That was odd. "Why?"

Last shook her head, her black hair flying about her. It reminded me of the day we'd walked in the park together and a windstorm had suddenly started, carrying orange and yellow leaves past as we ran for cover, laughing the whole time.

"It's something Secondus said before he died," she said, but I wasn't paying attention. I'd fallen into a happy, fuzzy-warm memory. It wrapped around me, and I felt all glowy and lovely. I smiled softly at her. I was drunk on happiness.

"You hit her too hard," the gaunt body said. "Her brain's mush now."

"She's fine," Last snapped. She turned back to me and patted my cheek. "You're fine, Mari. Aren't you?"

"Oh, yes. I feel wonderful." I rocked back and forth and hugged myself tightly, smiling widely. "I was just thinking about how we used to walk in the park. Remember the day it stormed, and we sat under the oak tree while the leaves fell? We had a rain picnic with tea and blueberry scones. I was so happy that day."

Last blinked back a tear, wiping her eyes. "You're a good friend, Mari."

"Do you think after all this, we could go on holiday somewhere? Maybe you could—" I wanted to say "kill Jagger and free me," but I couldn't say it—not even to Last. "Go on holiday with me?" I finished hopefully.

"Yes." Last sniffed tearfully. "When this is finished, we'll go on holiday. You and me. We're friends for life."

I nodded. Of course we were. Hadn't we always been?

"Did you know, there are lots of friends in history?" Last said. She stared at me with her watery, luminous eyes. "Henry II and Thomas Beckett, Napoleon III and the Viscount of Persigny, Caesar and Cassius."

"But . . ." I frowned. "Didn't those friendships end in betrayal?"

Last clapped her hands and laughed. "You do like history!"

"I won't betray you," I promised, my head throbbing, a heavy weight on my skull. "I would never."

"I know. It's all right." She gave me a quick hug. "Tell me, what will you do to keep my friendship?"

"Anything."

"Kill Luvic and Ragnor?"

"*Yes.*"

"Poison Jacob and the paladin?"

I nodded, my head aching. "*Yes.*"

"Will you help my family win? Will you always desire my happiness?"

"Above all things," I swore.

"Mush," the gaunt body said.

Last glared at him and then smiled at me. "Come to me in two days. At ten o'clock at night. My room is on the third floor. The blue door next to the statue of Caesar."

My heart pounded painfully. "Can't I see you sooner?"

"No." She shook her head and patted my hand reassuringly. "No, friend. When you see me in the halls and at the games, pretend you don't know me. That shouldn't be hard."

"You're right. I'm a good actress. I'll pretend we've never met."

"Good. Don't speak to me. Don't look at me. You're my *secret* friend."

"I like secrets," I said.

"Me too," Last said. She tilted her head. "By the way, do you like chocolate?"

"Yes. You know that, remember? I especially love dark chocolate."

"Oh! That's wonderful!" Last pressed her second and middle finger to her thumb and twisted her hand. She held a gold box full of chocolate truffles. "For you. Eat them all. You'll love them."

I sniffed, holding back tears. "You are so nice. I really love you. I'm so lucky. I'm so lucky to have you."

Last pushed the chocolate box into my hands and patted my cheek. "You are, aren't you?"

An off-tune whistle sounded from down the hall. A lazy sort of song, with no rhyme or reason. Last stiffened, and the body swung toward the sound, narrowing his eyes.

"Go—quickly," Last whispered to me, gently pushing me away.

I took one last long look at my best friend. Life was so good, so much better, when you had a friend you could count on. One who loved you and cared for you and knew you.

I smiled at her and then spun, the box of chocolates pressed to my chest, and hurried down the hall. Before I went far, I cracked open the lid, and the delicious smell of dark chocolate and rich liqueur assaulted me. I grabbed three truffles and shoved them into my mouth.

The taste of them sprang over my tongue, covering the flavor of blood. The liqueur was spiced and strong, and it zinged and zapped through me.

I moaned. They were . . . they were delicious. I shoved another two into my mouth, chewing quickly and swallowing them down. I was floaty and happily dizzy. I felt like a glazed cherry floating in a pool of melting chocolate ice cream. Delicious. Happy.

Last was so good. So kind. So wonderfully thoughtful.

I turned back to wave at her, but she'd already gone. I stumbled, tripped over my feet, and rounded the hall's corner, dizzily taking the turn.

I slammed into a hard male body. The chocolate box flew from my hands, and the rest of the truffles tumbled across the floor. I cried out. Before I could drop to my knees to chase after them, Luvic grasped my arms.

He frowned down at me.

I swayed, staring up at his scowling face.

I hated him, didn't I?

I was supposed to kill him.

But first . . . my chocolates.

I tried to kneel, but Luvic's grip tightened.

I scowled at him. "Release me, fiend."

He choked on a laugh. "Fiend?"

He squinted and ran his gaze over me. The chocolate's zappy effervescence floated through my veins, and his touch made me tingle. I was still happy. So happy.

"What sort of trouble have you gotten into?" he asked. "You're mighty bloody."

"You should know. You did it." I scowled at him.

He lifted his eyebrows. "I did?"

"Don't play dumb."

"Ah." He nodded. "Right. It was me smacking you about. Bloodying your head. Bruising your cheek. Hmm." He pulled a white handkerchief from his tuxedo pocket and dabbed it against the blood on my temple.

I flinched away from him, and he growled.

"Hold still."

"Why?"

"Because if you die, you idiot, then you can't save my life, can you?"

"Die?" I blinked. He was glossy and glazed in a white golden light. His black hair looked soft, his jaw smooth-shaven, his eyelashes too long for a man.

He glared down at me. "You're drunk. Do you know how easily I could kill you right now? Just snap your pretty neck?"

I nodded, my head floating around on said neck. "But then I wouldn't save your life."

His hands loosened on my arms. It seemed he was seriously thinking it over. Wondering if it'd be better to kill me now or wait for the possible eventuality that I'd save him from some unknown assailant.

"Probably, I won't save your life," I said, "because I really don't like you. *Bard.* Bad, bad Bard boy."

Since his hands were loose, I reached up to touch his cheek, just to see if it was as soft as it looked.

"Mari?"

"How do you know my name?" I muttered, feeling spinny and drunk.

Luvic sighed. "Go to your suite. Do not pass go. Do not collect 200."

"What?"

He stepped back and waved his hand. "Right. Right. Left. Stairs. Right. Left. Right. Repeat it back."

"Mmm. No."

"For crying out loud." He sighed and muttered to the air. "Kill her, Luvic. Noooo, don't kill her. Kill her soon, Luvic. No, don't kill her. It'll make me saaaaaad." He scowled at me, his bottom lip impossibly lush. "You are a *pain*. Pretty, but a pain."

"Thanks," I said. Then I groped around for the interior pocket of my uniform. I pulled free a tiny copper bead from its sticker patch. It had a millimeter-long needle coated in poison. I stumbled into Luvic. He caught me, and I pressed the tiny, hair-thin needle into his neck. He didn't even notice it sliding in.

I smiled at him. "I'm going. Goodbye. Not nice knowing you."

I waved, backing away.

He watched me with a half-angry, half-annoyed scowl. "When you get to your room," he called, "you should clean up. Brush your hair. It's full of knots."

I patted my head as I rounded the corner. Luvic didn't know what he was talking about. My hair was smooth and knot-free.

It didn't matter. What did he know? He'd be dead by tomorrow anyway.

30

They descended deeper into the tunnels, the wind and its boy. The throat of the tunnel narrowed as they plunged downward, until the walls were so close the boy had to duck his head, trailing his hands over the walls on either side of him.

The wind knew the boy preferred the dark. There was no light in this tunnel, and the boy hadn't created any. He was comfortable in the quiet eclipse, not feeling any need to call fire lights, eerie eyes, or luminescence. His breathing was soft and soothing, and his steps padded steadily downward.

The wind rode with him, clinging tightly. Now that it was with the boy, it wouldn't let go. Not for anything. But every now and then, it would slide down the boy's arm and squat on his fingertips so it could rub against the wall. The rock walls were slick, wet like an esophagus. Surely they were being swallowed by a giant beast, and the hard, smooth, narrowing walls were leading them to the creature's stomach.

The deeper the boy crept, the colder the stone grew, until goose bumps rose on his skin. Down, down they traveled, deeper than the wind had ever been. It couldn't feel the memory of sunshine or the reflection of moon glow or the whisper of cosmic showers this deep. It could only feel cold stone eyes pressing.

A rumble worked through the stone, vibrating and shaking. It sounded like the growl of a beast when you were *inside* it. It shook the wind, and the boy pressed his hands to the walls as rock dust rained over them. The growling thunder faded, and the vibration stopped.

The wind gave a soft, fearful moan.

"Figment," the boy whispered. "Don't worry, Wind. Just a figment of the blast that carved this place from the depths. Men were injured in the blast. Some were trapped. It's just a figment of their terror."

The boy's tenor was soothing, and while the wind prided itself on not having human weaknesses, it decided this place was a fearful place, and clinging to the boy's reassurance was a natural thing. After all, hadn't the Wards and the wind been confidants and companions for thousands of years?

"The Bard called it Hadal," the boy said.

Cold skittered over the wind like a nor'easter gusting over the icy gray sea. Hadal? This was Hadal? The wind whimpered and skated up the boy's arm to hug his shoulders.

"You've heard of it?"

Of course the wind had heard of Hadal. It was the deepest, darkest place on earth. It was cast below twilight, flung past the darkness of midnight. It was down below the creeping black of the abyss. Hadal was the underworld, the deep, dark trenches where eyeless, earless, mouthless things slept. The sleeping things dreamed, and their nightmares spawned the creatures that lived in Hadal.

How did the wind know? The wind was related to the ocean current. While the wind knew the sky and the sun and the surface, the current knew its home, the water, from the sunlight zone all the way to the deep, dark, still depths of Hadal.

Shipwrecks sank to Hadal—battleships from human wars, merchant ships from human greed, exploration ships from human striving—all the sailors sank to the deep. The wind knew Hadal was where sirens were born. Their song was like the wind's but not. The Greeks had named them—entangler, rope, tie—because their song enchanted and lured.

But what other nightmares were born in Hadal? And why had the Bards pulled a mirror of Hadal to this deep stone trench?

The wind sighed. The boy would have to be careful, or else he and the wind wouldn't see the sun again.

"Have a little faith," the boy said, laughing into the darkness.

Ahead, a throat rattling echoed through the narrow tunnel. It ricocheted off the walls, and then the wind was thrown back as a hairy, wolflike creature launched itself on the boy. The boy braced himself, but the ferocity of the creature punched him down.

He slammed to the ground. The air whooshed from him, and the wind spun in a dizzying circle. It shrieked as the creature—a jackaltooth—snapped, its hot breath lashing the wind like a toothy whip. The wind smashed against rock. Fell to the ground.

The jackaltooth lunged at the boy's neck. The wind used all its meager, almost used-up strength to shove at the jackaltooth's maw. The boy twisted his hand. The wind fell, crumpling on the boy's chest.

Then, three seconds after it attacked out of darkness, the jackaltooth was consumed. It howled in pain. A screaming, rattling noise that pierced the tunnel. The jackaltooth contracted. Shuddered. And then violently exploded.

Fur. Bone. Blood.

The jackaltooth vaporized into dark mist. The particles were as fine as glass powder. Without wind, they rained over the tunnel, dusting the boy and the wind in the residue.

The boy sat up. Sniffed. Then—

"Ahh ... achoo!"

He sneezed.

Then he wiped his hands on his jeans, bent down to create a current for the wind, and whispered, "Thank you."

The wind settled on his shoulder and began to whisper what it knew about Hadal.

But before the boy had taken three steps, a voice called from the darkness, "Bless you."

The boy paused. Held out his hand, two fingers touching his thumb.

It was the woman—the citrus and pearl dust scented Bard.

She took a silent step toward them and lit the tunnel with her blue and orange sparks. She glowed, radiant and silky smooth in the darkness. Her colored silks were a flaming torch, her skin golden-smooth, the necklace a burnished collar around her throat. The wind knew her skin was soft, and human men loved running their hands over the slant of her waist and the roundness of her hips.

She smiled at the blond, slight, dusty boy. Man. She saw him as a man. A Ward. The heir.

Siren.

That was what the father had told her to be, wasn't it? Was she the siren who would lure the boy to his death? Would he drown in Hadal diving after this siren?

But if that happened, the wind wouldn't see the surface again. No one had promised to carry it to freedom but the boy.

The wind blew in the boy's ear, tickling him and urging him on. *Pass by quickly. Go.*

"I always wondered," the woman mused, running a hand over the bare skin of her midriff, "what it looked like when you blew up your sister. Now I know."

She made an illusion with her hands. An explosion of mist and vapor. It was gold and violet, and it rained over the tunnel.

The boy watched the gold and violet glitter shower over the stone ground. It settled like ash. His face remained impassive, as unfeeling as the stone walls. The wind liked it better when he smiled or laughed, but the boy only laughed or smiled when it was just him, a book or a movie, and the wind. No one else had ever heard the boy's laugh.

It was a secret, the wind supposed.

"Yes," he said, keeping his hand out, ready to conjure. "Now you know. Only . . . it was quicker. And messier. I was four, after all. Not as practiced."

"So you really killed her?" The woman's hand moved to the burnished gold of the necklace at her throat. Would the metal be cold like the air, or would it be warmed by the woman's skin? "Some think it was a ruse. That you didn't really murder your twin."

A dark shadow flickered over the boy's face. The woman's fire lights sparked around him, dancing close and then flitting away.

"No. I killed her," he said, his voice as unyielding as stone. "I shattered her into a million pieces. No ruse. No illusion. Just . . . gone."

A coldness seeped into the narrow tunnel, and the woman's fire lights dimmed. She took a step back, although the wind didn't think she was aware that she had.

"Do you regret it?" she asked.

The wind knew she was asking because she loved her brothers and would regret harming them.

The boy smiled, but it wasn't his real smile. "No. Not at all. If she were here today, I'd do it again."

The woman shivered.

"Are you here for something?" the boy asked, stepping forward. "Or shall we continue?" He gestured for the woman to precede him.

She paused, studied his shadowed features, then came to a decision. "I wanted to warn you. Don't take the Mneme path. It's certain death."

She spun around and hurried into the darkness, her sparks winking after her.

The boy watched her with a small frown. "How likely," he murmured to the wind, "is it that she's telling the truth?"

The wind laughed, and the boy nodded.

"My thoughts exactly."

~

The tunnel narrowed into a tube so tight the wind was certain the boy would have to crawl on his stomach before reaching the end. It was just like the craggy rock tombs of old, where only those crawling could enter, and only sun, wind, and spirit could exit.

But before it came to crawling and scraping knees and elbows on cold stone, the boy ducked one last time and then stepped softly out of the tunnel's maw.

He'd stopped almost immediately at a cliff edge. The rocky ground dropped away only feet from the tunnel's end. It was a sheer cliff, so deep the wind was certain that if it fell, it would fall forever.

It was the trench of Hadal. The birthplace of nightmares. This was the universe they spawned in. There was light here. That was unexpected. But when there was darkness, some creatures made their own light. A mimicry of the sun. It was warning, lure, or siren call.

The wind shivered and settled on the boy's shoulder, clinging to his soft T-shirt. It reassured itself by taking in the forest-glade, oak and maple scent of him, and by tumbling in his cool, calm, steady breath.

The boy shifted, and something with many legs skittered away, hiding under a pile of rocks. The boy let out a sigh.

They were in a giant, hollow, echoing cavern. It was an expansive universe, all darkness and spots of pulsing blue-white light. The wind didn't measure distance, but at a sharp gust, it would take as long to cross the expanse as it would take the wind to blow from the stones of the Smith Mansion to the cold iron fence barring the doors to Hell Gate.

The Bards had created a giant, domed cavern beneath their home and filled it with nightmares. The others—the woman and the Clark—had arrived before the boy. Only the solange-eyed one wasn't here yet.

There were three paths to cross the cavern. The boy studied each, not concerned that the Clark and the Bard were swiftly moving away.

There was the highest path. It was accessed by rough-cut stone stairs in the sheer rock wall. The stairs were slick, narrow, dizzyingly high. If this were a sunny place, the wind would amuse itself by tumbling down the stairs and knocking rocks and pebbles free. But here, tumbling down those stairs would send it into the trench. The wind shuddered.

"Mneme," the boy said, pointing to a wooden sign at the bottom of the stairs.

They wound impossibly high to end at a silver wire strung across the cavern. Whoever took the stairs would have to walk the wire to the other side. On the far side was a golden door, a barely visible light shining in the distance, but to reach it, they would have to dodge the creatures floating in the sky.

They were large, translucent, dome-like creatures, round and jellied, with tentacles moving in a nonexistent breeze. There were thousands of them—they congregated like constellations, bumping and shifting in the night. Inside of their bodies were tiny blue and white orbs of light that mirrored the cosmos. Poisonous. The wind could smell the poison leaching from their skin.

"Memory's path," the boy whispered. "I imagine you'll have to walk the wire of your memories." He smiled ruefully. "I think we should pass on that one. I'll let my memories stay in the past."

The wind didn't understand him. Memories were as real as the present. They weren't left behind even when forgotten. But it didn't want the boy to walk a wire he might fall from. The trench terrified the wind. It sighed its agreement.

"Melete." The boy pointed to a wooden sign at the edge of the middle route.

It was a narrow stone path, wide enough for a man walking one foot in front of the other. It curved, dipped, and climbed. There were blind corners, hairpin turns, and plenty of places for creatures to ambush an unsuspecting man.

"Practice's path," the boy said, narrowing his eyes on the Clark. "It'll get harder the farther he travels."

The wind nudged the boy's hand, and he looked out over the stone bridge, where the steep climb held a surprise. There was a pack of jackaltooth crouched behind the first rise. But worse, at the second rise was a giant worm the fleshy gray color of rotting skin. It had no eyes, and its mouth gaped wide. Dozens of tentacles surrounded its mouth, tasting the air, pulsing in the direction of the unsuspecting Clark. It had dozens of legs and thick, wrinkled flesh.

The wind didn't know what waited beyond the third cliff of Melete. What could be worse than a worm twenty times the size of a man?

"Zombie worm." The boy wrinkled his nose. "They drill through flesh to suck marrow from bone. I've never seen one created. I've only read—"

A scream sounded, sharp and frantic. The wind knew the sound. It was a death scream. The curdling fear, the desperate vibration. It was knife-edged and terror-stricken.

The boy tensed and spun toward the sound. He thrust his hand out.

The last path, the lowest, traveled over silent black water. There were no ripples, no waves to mar the surface. It was as slick and opaque as mercury, likely just as poisonous and deadly. There was a stone bridge, cobbled and covered in strange glowing things—nightmare limpets and barnacles that snapped and growled.

Then there was the chasm and the trench that fell forever. And the wall of water, contained by an invisible bowl. The water spread in a smooth black lake to the opposite shore.

The woman—the Bard heir—had chosen the lake route. When they'd emerged from the tunnel, she'd already been standing tall in a reed boat, gliding through the waters. Her sparks flew around her but didn't cast any reflection in the lake's mercury waters.

The woman screamed again.

"Aoide. Song," the boy said, his face drawn.

There was a creature in the lake. It hit the boat. Knocked the woman down. She clasped the edge of the reed boat, stood, and began to sing.

It was a death song. A siren song. A bell-like ringing. A melody that skittered over the wind and called to it to swirl and spin and rush through the cavern. The wind had never heard a song that held the notes that began the universe. It had never heard the collision of the stars. But surely that was what this was.

Three notes. Three cries. A throaty, desperate call.

And then the creature rose from the water.

No, it wasn't that it rose from the water—it was that it *was* the water. The mercury liquid congealed and wrapped in a whirlpool around the woman. She flung out her hands. Conjured a shield. The creature snapped it away. She conjured light and power and lifted the boat free. The creature flew into the sky and ripped through her illusion, capsizing the boat.

She conjured another boat. The creature formed a long, black, eel-like body. It flailed. The black water frothed and boiled.

The wind tugged on the boy's shirt. It liked the woman. She was citrus and pearl dust. She wore silk for it to run on. She had a robust, hearty laugh. She sang for her brothers, danced when she was alone, and her voice reminded the wind of the sea, her tears its salt. It liked her.

The wind tugged harder.

"No, Wind," the boy said. "She'll be fine. I'm not going that route. I'm not here to play rescuer."

The wind tugged again.

"No. She'll be fine."

The woman made herself a pair of wings. They were wings of blue and orange fire. She was fighting to lift free of the creature, but its mercury teeth tore at the wings, shredding them. She sent fire and missiles, bullets and explosions. Heat and sunlight. The creature devoured it all. She sang a luring song, but it was ripped from her throat.

The wind shoved the boy. He stumbled. "She'll be—"

The creature swallowed the woman.

One moment she was there, barraging the creature with hell fire, singing her dirge, and the next, she was gone.

The black lake was a smooth, deathly mirror, not a ripple scarring the surface.

"Fine," the boy said. "Fine. Okay. Fine."

The wind shoved him again. How long could a human survive in the mercury water of Hadal? Was she dead already?

"But Wind, you owe me, okay? Deal? You'll tell me a secret. A *good* secret."

The wind shoved at the boy again.

"Yes. I'll save her."

He kicked off his shoes. Shrugged his shoulders and flicked the wind free. "Stay here. I'll be right back."

He sprinted across the bridge, his bare feet cat-paw soft. Faster. Faster. The glowing barnacles and limpets snapped at him. He leaped into the air and dove into the black water.

The was no splash. No sound. The water swallowed him as if he'd never been.

Above, on the stone pathway, the cruel one laughed. A jackaltooth rattled in reply. A pack growled behind it. The Clark—the cruel one— conjured a wooden staff and ran toward the waiting creatures.

The wind crept to the edge of the rocky slab. It was cold. The trench was deep. The water was darkly silent. The wind watched, and the water watched back.

Time. What was time? How much time had passed? The Clark

fought, knocking jackaltooth from the ledge. They yelped and were swallowed by the water or the trench.

Was it ten jackaltooth? Twenty knocked over the edge?

The wind didn't know. The wind couldn't count. It only knew the boy and the woman were still beneath the dark waters. It crept closer, trembling. The stones of the bridge were slippery, like algae-coated rock. The bridge smelled like decaying fish and rusted metal.

Closer. *Closer*.

The boy burst from the water, flailing to the surface. The water churned around him. He drew a violent breath, looked sharply around, and then he was yanked back below the surface.

No!

No!

The wind rushed to the edge of the bridge. It sent a tentacle of air over the water's edge.

Its boy.

Its boy!

The wind sent out a soft wail. It pushed at the water, sent ripples and currents.

The water moaned back, and the wind wailed again.

Then the thick black water began to boil. It became a tar pit, sucking and groaning and bubbling. It ate creatures. It devoured them and left only bones. Would it eat the woman? Would it eat the boy?

The wind wailed again. Louder. It wailed the song it had wailed over still, red battlefields, across sun-scorched, famine-wrecked plains, across the bones of ships pierced on rocky shoals.

High above, the cruel one laughed again, now battling the giant, groaning worm.

The wind would be lost here forever. Lost in this airless, desolate, dark, deathly place.

The water exploded.

The wind lurched away. But still, a hurricane of icy vapor assaulted it, slamming it against the rocky bridge. The water screamed, thrown in a gale so violent the entire cavern was consumed. Black rain, dark sleet, it flung outward, rushing on a conjured cyclone.

The wind huddled against the bridge, wedging itself into a crack between two slabs of jagged, frail slate.

The boy rose from the cyclone. The black water drove from him, fleeing in vapor and violent rain. He levitated on a whirlpool of illusion. The eye of the storm.

Above, the cosmic sun and star jelly creatures pulsed and glowed. The water vapor crystallized in the cold and began to fall like black snow.

The boy's forest-green eyes focused on the crevice the wind was hiding in. The corner of his mouth lifted. The wind tumbled from the crack in a rush of joy.

The boy held the woman in his arms. She wasn't moving. The boy wasn't as big as a Smith, or even a Clark, but he was still larger than the woman, and he was strong. Strong in body, and strong in illusion.

He'd help the woman. If she wasn't breathing, he'd breathe wind into her lungs. That was what humans did. The wind had been the first to show them this secret.

The boy floated to the bridge, stepped down from his whirlwind, and dropped the woman to the cold stone. The lake was gone. He'd disintegrated it. There was only empty air and trench now.

Cold, black snow fell around them.

The wind brushed against the boy's wrist. He was cold, his skin wet and icy. A pool of sticky water fell around him, and the rotten, fish scented limpets snapped their shellfish jaws.

The wind felt the woman's chest. It wasn't moving. There was no breath in her. The wind pushed at the boy.

"I know," he whispered.

Then he bent down and pressed his hands to the woman's chest. Push. Push. The wind added its breath to the boy's. The boy's mouth was cold, but the woman's was colder. Her lips were dark blue, pink, and indigo, like August blueberries. These were death lips.

The boy pushed again. A rhythmic, songlike pressure. He gave her his breath.

There wasn't anything to conjure. The wind knew this. The conjurers could create anything with their minds—but they couldn't conjure health. Like food, it was a facsimile that fell apart as quickly as it was made. These were the providence of heaven, and conjurers, even if they wanted to, couldn't steal them.

Instead the boy's hands glowed golden-white. As he breathed wind into her lungs, he sent warmth into her skin. Her lips turned pink, her skin flushed rose gold, and finally, the wind felt the fluttering of her pulse.

It was slow. Drunk. Tilty and unsure. But it was there.

The boy sat back on his heels. Stared at the woman.

Overhead, on the towering stone path, the worm let out a gruesome shriek. It slid off the wall and twisted as it plummeted past. The wind waited to hear it hit the bottom. There was nothing. After a time, the wind couldn't even hear the shriek of the creature.

"Jacob! Take note!" the Clark shouted. His echo bounced around the hollow cavern and was swallowed by the abyss. "While you play, I win!"

The boy's mouth flattened, but he didn't turn to watch as the cruel one climbed to the third level of his path. Instead the boy watched the woman, setting his hand to her wrist and frowning at the sluggish pulse.

The wind rubbed against the boy's hand, thanking him.

"You're welcome."

The woman's eyelashes fluttered. Her brown eyes were glazed, and she stared at the boy with . . . the wind didn't know. Was this the look people gave right before they said words of love? Was it the look they gave right before a kiss—one under the stars on the day of the first snowfall?

The wind thought it was. It couldn't be sure, but it thought that was the look the woman gave.

"You . . ." She swallowed. Her voice was raw, jagged rocks on a seashore. "You came after me."

The boy stared at her. His face was hard, his skin still cold. A black snowflake fell on the woman's cheek. She reached up and brushed it off.

"Can you sit up?"

She nodded and pushed herself upright. The barnacles snapped again, and the wind sniffed at the woman. The citrus was gone. Now she smelled just like the black water. Both she and the boy did.

"Help me . . ." She coughed. "I can't breathe. Help me take off my necklace."

The boy frowned, but when she trembled, the wind nudged at his leg. The boy reached around and unclasped the gold.

"Here." He handed the necklace to her.

She took the cold metal in her hands. She dropped her chin and looked at him from below her thick eyelashes.

"All right." The boy frowned. "I'm off—"

The woman leaned forward and brushed a kiss across the boy's cold cheek. He stilled. The wind felt his heart pound. One hard lurch.

Then, before he could recover, the woman whipped the necklace at the boy. He jerked back. Twisted his hand. But it was too late. She clasped the gold around his wrist and slammed it to the stone. As soon as the metal hit the rock, it fused with it, melting sharp spikes into the stone.

The boy's wrist was chained to the rock. The wind whistled across the gold. Its power zapped the wind, sending a sharp electric buzz over it.

So the woman had brought an object of power. A binding object.

The boy jerked at the shackle. It held tight. The gold tightened around his wrist and shoved his hand against the stone. The gold band was thick now, digging into his skin and melding with the rock.

"Celia," the boy said, his voice a low warning. "Release me."

Objects of power were tricky things. The wind had seen many conjurers trapped by them. It took strength and power to break them. The boy was strong, but it would take him time to break the shackle.

The woman scrambled back. "Thanks for saving my life." She smiled at the boy. "But it's a game. I'm playing to win."

"Are you?" He kneeled on the ground, holding his hand against the cold rock. His gaze was ice. Cold and deadly.

The woman backed away, edging around the boy and working toward Melete. Aoide was no longer a viable path. She'd follow the cruel one, perhaps even overtake him.

"Of course," the woman said, stepping off the bridge. "Isn't that why we're all playing?"

The boy stared at the woman. There wasn't warmth in him. His heart was back to its calm, steady beat. The wind curled against his side. It could jump onto the woman's silks, follow her to freedom. But the wind didn't want to leave the boy. Besides, it had promised him a secret.

The last black snowflake fell into the trench, swallowed by the abyss.

"No," the boy said. "It's not. Watch out, Celia. It's better to have an enemy in front of you than at your back. I'm not playing to win. I'm playing for something more."

The woman shivered and then ran from the bridge. She leaped onto Melete.

The boy turned away from her and stared at the gold cuff. Thinking. Thinking.

The wind nudged him. Apologized.

"It's fine," the boy said. "You like her. I get it. She smells nice, doesn't she?"

The wind hummed.

"Right. And she sings well." He sighed. Tapped the gold shackle. It tightened, and he winced.

Across the cavern, a tumble of rocks sounded. The wind whooshed out a surprised breath. It was the solange-eyed one, the black-haired Smith. He was perched at the top of the winding stairs. He tilted, wobbled, swayed as if he were being buffeted by a breeze on all sides.

The boy glanced up. Snorted. "That one's going to die. And I'm *not* saving him. One's enough."

But then, after swaying and tilting and nearly falling, the solange-eyed one kicked off his shoes. The boy gave an interested humph. Then the solange-eyed one took a running leap and landed catlike on the wire.

The cosmic, poisonous jelly bulbs swarmed him. Sparks of lightning and flashes of memory cut at him. They swirled in a poisonous cloud, a deadly storm, but the Smith ran as if he *was* the lightning. As if he *was* memory. He was an electric current riding the wire. He dodged, jumped, swayed, and *moved*.

The wind recognized it for what it was. The solange-eyed one was dancing between worlds. He was conducting illusion and reality, an electric current carrying messages between worlds. He sped across the chasm. Untouched. Unhindered. He was a spark of gold flying through the air.

"What . . ." The boy stopped. Blinked at the Smith. "He's going to pass Primus. Wind! Do you see this? He's going to win!"

The boy laughed. He laughed so hard that tears leaked from his eyes.

Overhead, a thunderous roar sounded, shaking the cavern walls. A giant scaled creature detached from the stone. It had hidden itself until now, wrapped around the ceiling and the walls of the cavern. It was dark green, almost black, and it glinted metallically in the cosmic light.

The wind rode on its roar and fluttered at its violent hiss. It was a snake. A water creature from the Hadal, where neither sight nor smell nor hearing was needed, only a mouth to eat. Fangs to poison. A jaw to bite.

"He's not slowing," the boy said, frantically working at the cuff. He flicked his free hand, conjuring, prying, prodding. "Look at him! He's not slowing."

The Smith ran at full speed. The wind remembered men like this. It had seen them race over cold, bomb-ridden beaches, plunge through narrow cliff paths under volleys of arrows, leap off stone walls into besieged cities.

The wind tugged at the cuff, whistling over the boy's bound hand. "I'm hurrying. I know!"

The snake unwound itself from the wall. It consumed the air of the cavern, standing a hundred men above them all. The wind could smell the diamond-hard stench of its scales and feel the malevolent sizzle of its blood. Venom dripped from its fangs. When it hit the stone far below, the stone hissed and smoked.

The snake reared its head back, ready to strike. It unhinged its jaw and shot at the Smith.

Instead of dodging, the Smith leaped into the air. He landed in the snake's mouth.

"What?" the boy shouted. He twisted his hand one last time, and the shackle exploded. He jumped up. Shot a pulse of power outward. "Hold on. We're running fast. I won't be first, but you better believe I won't be last."

The boy sprinted across the bridge. Ran twenty leaps at a time over the stone pathway. The Clark had cleared the jackaltooth and the worm. The only remaining creature was a giant armored bone spider that the Clark was battling.

The woman was just ahead, running toward the armored spider. The boy flew past her. He conjured a flame wall, shoving her back.

"Jacob!" she screamed.

He kept running.

High above, the snake shook the cavern. Its tail swung with violent force. It hit the rock wall, and a slab the size of an apartment building slid into the abyss.

"What's he doing?" the boy said, jumping over a boulder. A lone jackaltooth tore at him, and he twisted his hand. The jackaltooth disintegrated. He sprinted past.

The cavern shook. The boy stumbled, and the wind moaned. It clung to his wet shirt, burying against his cold skin. The poisonous jelly creatures shuddered and began to fall, blue and white shooting stars. They missiled over the cavern. The boy conjured a dome over his head. Every time a cosmic creature struck the dome, it exploded in a mass of shattered glass.

The boy skidded next to the cruel one. The armored spider blocked the path.

"Not today." The cruel one shoved at the boy with his power. But the boy dodged.

"It's not me that'll win," the boy said.

The Clark flung a bolt of fire at the armored bone spider.

Another crash shook the cavern, and then the giant snake's jaw gaped wide. The Smith leaped free. He slung himself onto the snake's flat triangular head. The snake snapped. It tossed its head and twisted violently. But the Smith sprinted over its scaled back as easily as he'd crossed the high wire.

Another violent shriek ripped through the space. The Smith jumped off the snake's tail, landing at the golden door. He scooped up the prize lyre in one graceful move and then dove through the door.

It slammed shut after him.

The boy laughed. The snake's head exploded. A hundred glowing blue and white death-axe butterflies erupted into being.

"Time for us to be going," the boy whispered to the wind.

The wind agreed. It didn't like the poison-drip feel of the butterflies' wings.

The boy flicked his hand. A giant raven appeared, flapping its wings overhead. It dove at the bone spider, opened its beak, and swallowed it whole. The boy ran to the bird, arm high, and as the raven soared over him, he reached for its claw. Grabbed ahold.

The wind laughed as he and the boy soared over the abyss. The raven's wings pushed the poison jelly creatures and the death-axe butterflies far away, down toward the cruel one and the woman.

The raven dove toward the golden door, a gust carrying them the final stretch. The wind rode the illusion, exhilarated. The bird vanished in black mist as the boy and the wind dropped to the stone ledge.

"All right, Wind?" the boy asked, reaching for the door.

Yes. The wind felt wonderful. It would warm itself in the sun. It would ride over midnight waves and roll in morning dew and summer grass. The boy had carried it to freedom. Just like he'd promised.

So the wind kept its promise too.

Before the boy left Hadal, the wind whispered a secret.

It was the woman's secret. A deadly secret. People had died for this secret.

"Well," said the boy, "that *is* a good secret."

He smiled. It was his real smile. It was gone by the time he stepped through the golden door.

31

I SWIRLED AROUND FINN'S ROOM, SPINNING AND PIROUETTING, LIGHTER AND happier than I'd ever been. *Last, Last, la-la-Last. Best friends forever, la-la-Last.*

The suite was empty, and the bedroom Finn and I shared was glazed in the greenish-gold glow of summer sunlight filtering through maple leaves and rippling glass. The stars on the navy wallpaper shifted as I spun. I was effervescent. My blood was sparkling. I was a star too. A happy, cosmic . . .

I smiled when I spied Finn's bottle of solange on the walnut escritoire.

"Mayhem, madness, mischief, fun," I sang, skipping over to the desk. "Spin it, stir it, till mayhem's done."

I uncorked the amber cut-glass bottle and sniffed at the cranberry and allspice scented solange. Then I dug through my backpack and pulled free my little book of poisons. It was a paperback copy of *The Grapes of Wrath*. The center had been carved out, and my needles and vials and powders were tucked inside.

You'd think lots of people would suspect a book might hold secrets, but no, you'd be surprised. People instinctively shy away from *The Grapes of Wrath*. Unless they think it's a book about wine—in which case, they open it right up. But only Griff had made that mistake.

I sorted through my supply. There wasn't as much as you'd think. Smith's Folly. That wouldn't do—she didn't say to kill Finn. Sleeping Beauty? No. That put people into a deathlike sleep. The Assassin's Hourglass? No. That was what I gave Luvic. It killed too. What else?

Aha! I smiled as I pulled free Dainty Drink.

This poison only killed in very large doses, or in small doses spread over months. Its more common use was for its side effects. It made people feel like a five-foot-tall, ninety-pound female named Dainty who'd just chugged four cosmos and a slippery nipple at the corner bar. Dainty had no tolerance.

When administered, the poison made people uninhibited, loose-tongued, and stupid-drunk.

"Mayhem, madness, mischief, fun." I poured six drops' worth of poison into Finn's solange, then I added a splash of water from the bathroom sink, because Last had told me to water the solange down.

That done, I set the solange bottle back in its place on the desk.

The effervescent bubbles were still popping and fizzing in my veins. I licked my lips, trying to grab a bit of the chocolate flavor. I tugged my lower lip through my teeth and groaned at the spiced chocolate-liqueur taste.

Maybe Last would conjure me more chocolate the next time I saw her. I'd always thought conjured food was like pee in the ocean, but it *wasn't*. It was wonderful.

I hummed into the heavy silence of the room. It was quiet when Finn wasn't here to fill the space with his presence.

I stared at the window and the late-afternoon light splicing the thick carpet and spearing Finn's bed. His sheets were rumpled and tangled. Untucked and kicked about. He hadn't made the bed. I narrowed my eyes. Was I supposed to make the bed?

I ran my hand over the white cotton sheets. They were cool and silky-smooth. My eyelids felt heavy, and my head hurt. My cheek throbbed where Luvic had slapped and bloodied me. Slowly, I climbed onto the king-size bed. The mattress was luxuriously soft. I sank into the cloudlike give of the feather mattress topper.

Oh. Wow.

I sprawled on my stomach and took a deep breath. The sheets smelled like Finn. *Mmm.* I rubbed my cheek against the silken weave of the fabric and rolled around in Finn's summer-thunderstorm and spiced-solange scent. The sheets slipped against the silk of my uniform, and I twisted and stretched, a cat rolling lazily in the sun.

The silk ran over me, a waterfall of sensation. Finn's thunderstorm scent fingered raindrops over my sensitive skin, plucking and pulling and lighting my insides. I gripped the sheets and stared at the navy and gold studded canopy above.

My chest was tight, and my breath came in short, desperate gasps. My skin was so sensitive. Achingly so. I wanted to roll in Finn's bed. I wanted to breathe in the stormy smell. I wanted to—

Untie the knot.

I shot upright and looked around the room.

"Who's there?"

Mari, untie the knot!

It was the boy. His voice shoved at me, desperate and fearful.

I stumbled out of bed, shaking and dizzy, and peered around the empty bedroom. It had sounded as if he was just outside the wooden door, calling me.

As I hurried to the door, I passed the mirror by the walnut armoire. A flash of gold in the glass made me stop. I turned. Stared at my reflection.

It wasn't the purple and red splotched bruise on my cheek. It wasn't the dried blood and the half-inch-long shallow cut on my temple. It was the thick rope of illusion knotted and woven around my skull that had me reaching up and pressing my fingers to my head.

"What..."

My hand trembled, and a shaky breath left my lungs. Someone had crowned me in illusion, and I'd forgotten they had. My face leached of color, and the glittery, dizzy happiness fizzled away.

Untie it. Untie it. The mantra rolled through me. I brushed my hand over the gold rope. There was no feeling. No heat, no cold, no hard, bunched knots or slippery, waxy thread. No physical evidence of its existence. Only ... someone had conjured a reality for me.

Luvic, when he'd grabbed me in the hall?

Darin, when he'd shoved me out of the basement room?

I leaned close to the mirror, my breath fogging the glass, and studied the knots.

I think—I'm sorry—I think I've been remiss in my explanation of knots to you. Knots, rope, and illusion.

What is the world without knots? Where would we be? Did you know that knots predate the wheel, the discovery of fire, and perhaps even human beings? But of course they do. Who was the first knot-tier but God himself?

We overlook the wondrous and the wonderful—it is invisible to us—but take a moment to look for the knots that hold our world together. Not the knots of illusion, but the knots mirroring illusion through reality.

You lie in bed, and the weave of your sheets and pajamas are knots knitted together. Every fabric, every stitch, is a knot. Every morning, you tie your shoes—what is that? It's a double-slipped reef knot.

Braided hair? Celtic braid knot.

Necktie? Windsor knot.

That salted pretzel you bought me from the vendor in Central Park? Stafford knot.

When I stitched you up all those years ago, staunching the flow of blood? Surgeon's knot.

The nets that catch the fish Roumelade refuses to eat? The Carrick bend. The weaver's knot. The sheet bend.

The steel cables supporting the bridges that span our city waterways? Knots. Lots and lots of knots.

The walls of your home? Skyscrapers? The fiber cables that run under our streets? The electrical wires gridding the world? All constructed with knots.

When I was four, Jagger gave me a book. It was called *The Ashley Book of Knots*. It was a bible of sorts, and it contained nearly 3,900 different knots and seven thousand illustrations.

"Memorize them," he'd said. "Memorize them all. You have to know how to untie them."

That book became the doorway to a world of rope and knot and imagination. Knots are the entry to creation and eternity—the only limit is your imagination and the length of your rope.

The first fossilized knots found by archeologists date back nearly seventeen thousand years, but they reach much further into our past. Bone needles have been dated to 100,000 years old, and what do you think they were using bone needles for? To knot. The first written record of knots was by Heraklas, the ancient Greek physician. He described the reef knot, the overhand noose, true lover's knot, and the clove hitch.

I dragged my hand over my forehead, touching the knots piercing my skull. Clove hitch. Tom fool's knot. Friendship knot.

The clove hitch is supposedly the oldest knot used by humans. The knot is two hitches looped and tied around an object, with the purpose of securing the middle of a rope to, say, a fence post. You should deeply distrust a clove hitch when it's used alone, because it freely slips *and* easily binds. Most often, it's used in theater for stage curtains, or for mooring boats.

Usually, I thought of clove hitches as the purview of Bards because of the theatre connection, but sometimes the Clarks used them because of their ancient history.

Not that conjurers knew the names of knots or could even see what they were tying. For them, I think, conjuring was instinctive. Like swallowing. No one thinks about how to swallow, but as soon as you concentrate on swallowing, it becomes incredibly difficult to do. The same can be said for breathing, walking, sleeping. From what I could tell, conjurers couldn't see their own ropes and knots. Instead they felt them, like the wind on a breezy day, or like the hot sun pressing on your skin.

You couldn't *see* them, but you recognized them for what they were.

Regardless, I think conjurers merely called their purpose to mind, and the knots formed the rope of illusion. They didn't need to see the knots to tie them.

But I could see them. And thanks to Jagger's book, I knew what they were called, and I could use both instruction and instinct to untie them.

Each conjurer family favored certain knots.

The Smiths liked the type of functional, basic, no-nonsense knots often used in the military: bowline, square knot, overhand knot, reef knot, rolling hitch, half-hitch, cleat hitch, figure-eight.

The Clarks leaned toward ancient mariner knots and the knots decorating the pages of illuminated manuscripts: clove hitch, sheet bend, angler's knot, sailor's knot, granny knot, true lover's knot, bottle sling, Solomon's knot, beautifully ornate Celtic knots.

The Bards were song and theatre and poetry, and their knots were lyrical: butterfly loops, lark's head, Prusik knot, blood knot, and the simple overhand and bowline. They were the only family that regularly spliced: back splice, chain splice, eye splice, pigtail.

Finally, the Wards were the prison-keepers, the wardens, and constructors of mazes and labyrinths. Their knots were the most dangerous and the most binding. I'd only seen them use the basic knots: bowline, reef, figure-eight, and one other. The most difficult knot to escape. The constrictor knot.

The constrictor knot is an unyielding knot. A shackle. A squeezing, tightening, harsh prison of a knot. It is meant to bind—permanently.

It's a simple knot, similar to the clove hitch, but one end of the rope passes under the other and forms an overhand under a riding turn. It can be tied quickly, with little effort, but once tightened, the illusion is tightly bound and near impossible to escape.

The Wards tend to use thinner rope, because then the constrictor exerts even more pressure and ties a tighter knot. If an unusual binding is needed, a Ward might progress to a double constrictor or a cross constrictor. If the Ward wants the illusion to eventually break, they'll conjure a slip constrictor.

This isn't a firm rule. While each family favors knots, they can and do use all of them. It's more a guide. Maybe the conjurers don't even realize they're tying knots. Maybe it's only that their thoughts are knotted symbols on the thread of illusion.

All the same, my head was roped in a bevy of knots. They coiled through my hair and sank into my skull. There were at least 100 knots, all of them one of three types: clove hitch, tom fool's knot, or friendship knot.

I mentioned the clove hitch—the oldest knot in history.

Tom fool's knot is also known as the conjurer's knot. It's used for trickery because it can be tied quickly, and it's often used as a handcuff. Clarks love this knot because it was one of the knots described in the first century AD by Heraklas.

The last knot is the friendship knot. This knot is unusual, because it's more decorative than binding. It's a beautiful winged cross, and the knots on my head were tied in silver and gold. It was developed in the Tang or the Song dynasty in ancient China as one of the eleven basic knots. This knot is an artform and a history. Before writing was developed, knots were used to record events and histories: complicated knots for big events, and small knots for minor events. The people wrote with knots, exchanged stories and emotions in knots. Even memory was preserved in knotted cords.

Looking in the mirror, it was clear someone had tied a history to my mind. A slipping, binding, trickily beautiful, handcuffed history.

I exhaled slowly and then worked the clove hitches free. They easily unraveled as soon as I twisted the clove to the inside and pulled. Once untied, they disappeared. The pressure of the rope loosened, and the heavy weight on my head lightened.

For the tom fool's knot, I grabbed the loose running ends and pulled. They unraveled in seconds. I concentrated in that space outside myself, working the illusion free.

Finally, the friendship knots. They were the last of the rope, silver and gold, digging into my skull. There were sixty, maybe seventy. A decorative knotwork, almost like macramé. I tugged on the first. It held, tight and resistant to untying.

My breathing quickened, and a dizzy nausea raced over me. That tingling, effervescent pop sizzled again, trying to come back to life. I wondered . . . Last might help me. She might know who did this. But no. She'd said not to come to her until two nights from now.

I was impatient now. I formed my thoughts into a metal spike—like the marlinspike used by mariners—and pried the first friendship knot free. It fell apart like an autumn leaf, drifting free and crumbling to dust on the ground.

The throb in my skull lessened, and the heaviness lightened. I sent the spike through one knot, then another, and another, and one by one, the dry parchment leaves of a long history blew free from my mind.

At the last, there was one friendship knot left. It glistened over my right temple. I stared at it.

Last.

Last had built us a secret history. I'd pulled the illusions from my mind and my past, but I could still bring them out, like photocopies of something that was once there. Since my conscious mind had read Last's illusions, the facsimile of them would remain.

I clenched my fists, digging my nails into my hand. I wanted to hate her, but I couldn't. Do you know why? Because an echo of the emotion was still there too. I remembered the feeling of loving her. I remembered how it felt to care for her.

I glared at the remaining knot. It was a bright, vivid memory. It was us lying on our backs in a rowboat in Central Park, drifting under Bow Bridge. The breeze tickled my nose, and a bee drifted lazily by. Last, fourteen years old, looked at the bright blue sky and said, "I miss my mom." I took her hand and held it.

I wanted to drive a spike through the memory and unravel it. I wanted it out of my mind.

But while conjurers couldn't see illusions, they could feel if they were there. If all the illusion was wiped away and the rope completely dissolved, then Last would know it had been removed.

Conjurers couldn't remove illusion. They could destroy it. Explode it. Melt it. But they couldn't carefully, intricately, surgically remove it. If a conjurer tried to remove an illusion on a person's mind, their brain would —for lack of a better word—implode. Turn to mush. Jellify. Illusions that entered a person's mind weren't ever meant to be undone.

It was why the Wards were so feared. What Last had done to me was child's play compared to what a Ward could do.

I unclenched my hand. Took a deep breath.

Outside the bedroom, a shouted "hello" and a response sounded. I jerked. Noticed the bright green-gold afternoon light had shifted to the pink-hued gold of a summer sunset.

"The game!"

Hours had passed since Finn had entered the game. The first conjurer could already have left Hadal. I raced to the bedroom door, flung it open, and ran through the suite and out the door.

Hall. Stairs. Left. Right. Stairs. Hall.

No.

No, no, no.

Did he make it out? Was he okay? Did he win? Did he lose? Did he live? Did—?

I skidded to a stop. Crushed myself against the plaster wall.

"I will kill you!"

The words came out as a snarled roar, barely discernable over the palpable rage. A crash sounded. The shattering of ceramic. A vase? And the crunch of wood splitting as a body hit it.

I was on the first floor, only a few twists and turns from the elevator to the lower level. Past the marble entry. Down the gaudy bronze and gilt hallway full of chandeliers and man-size vases.

There were a few marble statues here and there, and I imagined whoever had been thrown was grateful they'd hit a fragile vase and not a statue.

I crept toward the corner. Slow. Quiet. Careful.

Someone on the other side of the hall's turn was choking. Gasping for breath.

I inched closer, tiptoeing over the marble, careful not to scuff my shoes or make any noise. The stupid mansion was echoey, with all its marble and plaster and gaudy metal. That echo could spell the end for me.

"Dead," the man said. "There is no rule against killing family members, is there? You're dead."

I paused at the corner, muscles tense, thighs flexed, ready to run at a moment's notice. My heart slammed, echoing in the hall of my chest.

I was dizzy. Woozy. Tired and achy. It had been a day. The enraged man wasn't killing Finn—that was clear. Finn was a paladin and therefore safe from random, rage-filled hallway attacks.

I could back away. Tiptoe down the hall and turn another direction. Pretend I'd never heard a random slaughter occurring.

But then—

"Pomegranate, Luvic? Don't tell me the death-axe pomegranate wasn't your creation. I lost the game because of your little trick. You think it's funny to play games? You think it's fun?"

Ah.

Okay.

So here's the thing.

I was in the middle of backing away. I'd already taken half a dozen careful steps. I hadn't made a sound. Not a squeak or a breath or a scuff. I was easily going to escape the murderous conjurer on the other side of the wall.

But . . .

Luvic.

Did I like him?

No. Not really.

Did I trust him?

Absolutely not.

Did he deserve to die for giving me a pomegranate?

No.

Jagger would shout at me, "Never help another! Leave them to die!" That was the number one rule at Hell Gate. If someone was foolish enough to die, leave them to it.

Justice would shake his head. "Ruthless, Mari. Saving Luvic isn't being ruthless."

Roumelade would say, "Don't romanticize him. He had his own reasons for giving you the pomegranate."

Griff would just say, "Be careful, Mari."

I decided to take imaginary Griff's advice. I crept back down the hall and flattened myself against the plaster wall. Then, quickly, I peeked around the corner.

Just as quickly, I jerked back.

Crap.

Luvic was flattened against the hallway wall, one of his hands clutching his throat, yanking at a noose. He twisted his other hand frantically. He was desperately trying to conjure. A blue and white porcelain vase was shattered on the floor beneath him. A mahogany table was smashed.

Bits of porcelain and wood shrapnel had hit Luvic. Blood sprouted from scratches on his skin.

That wasn't the worrisome part.

The worrisome part was the red of his face. The wideness of his eyes. The clear sign that he was being strangled by a hemp noose hanging from an illusion-constructed gallows.

Courtesy of Primus Clark.

Luvic clawed at the rope. He gasped, throat constricting for breath. His other hand flicked, attempting to conjure a knife. Blade. Fire. Flame. A stool to stand on. Each attempt was knocked away by Primus.

In the game of power, Primus was stronger by far. He was heir. Luvic was a third-born. On a full-on frontal assault, Luvic would be dead in minutes. Seconds.

I peeked around the corner again.

Primus's back was to me, but Luvic, in his desperate gasping, locked onto me.

His eyes widened.

I could feel his plea.

I could hear him.

Mari. Mari!

I had to be fast. I had to be sneaky. I had to make it so Primus wouldn't suspect I was there.

"Take note, I've had enough of Bard trickery. You won't be interfering anymore. You didn't think I'd notice? You conjured a death-axe butterfly pomegranate for your fifth birthday. I recorded the event in the archives. Fool! Dead, stupid fool. What will the archives say now? Luvic Bard. Worthless. Powerless. Fool. Failed understudy to his sister and brother's star. Dead for attempting to manipulate the games. Too bad your sister lost too. Was that your plan? Do you want her to lose, or just me?"

The rope tightened, and Luvic lifted off the ground.

His eyes held mine. He'd stopped gasping for breath, his face shaded from red to purple.

He still wore his tuxedo. The white handkerchief he'd used to wipe the blood from my temple was stuffed in his pocket.

Crap.

I centered my mind. Took a deep breath. Studied Primus's noose and gallows illusion.

The illusion was a clove hitch—untrustworthy—flanked by a half-hitch. They'd slip, and the more you struggled, the tighter they'd bind.

There was no time for finesse on my part. I had to hope that when I pulled them loose, Luvic would be aware enough to conjure himself out of this mess.

One.

Two.

I winked.

Three.

I yanked the rope, pulling the clove hitch and the two half-hitch knots free.

The gallows and the noose disappeared. Luvic conjured a gunpowder explosion. It burst outward with a violent, fiery pop.

Luvic slammed against the wall and then slid to the floor.

The explosion hid the fact that I'd just made an illusion unravel. Instead it looked as if Luvic had marshalled some unknown talent and defeated Primus's noose. Unfortunately, he'd also knocked himself out. His head had hit the wall so hard I'd heard the crack of it twenty feet away.

He slumped to the littered ground, the flames of his explosion winking out.

Black singed the plaster walls. Little fires licked at the splintered wood hallway table. Smoke curled around Luvic and rose in an acrid smudge.

"Luvic, Luvic," Primus murmured, crouching over him. "One last trick, hmm? Too bad it failed."

Primus held out his hand, and I was certain he was preparing a death blow. Could I be fast enough? I held still. Concentrated my mind.

I could see the illusion forming, a thick rope looping over itself—

"Luvic!"

I yanked back into myself.

Celia flung herself across the hallway. She'd entered from the side opposite me. She threw herself in front of her brother, flinging her hands out.

A shimmery glow erupted in front of her. It was a wall of frothing water and misty haze. It shrieked with moans and melodies, wretched songs and grieving murmurs.

It reminded me of Roumelade when she'd kneeled at the edge of the East River and cried. Was this what she'd been before Jagger had scooped her out of the water? Was this a wall of poison tears?

Primus seemed to think so. He took a step back.

His brown scholar's clothes were torn and dirty. I could see blood and bruises and scrapes on him. Suddenly, I realized he'd had a hard time in the games.

But Celia hadn't fared any better. She was pale. Bruised. There were bloodied cuts down her arms and black singes on her torn silk clothes.

Still . . . she flung the wall of mist toward Primus and stood, snarling, in front of Luvic's unconscious form.

"Touch my brother and die."

I stood frozen. Celia's voice was an ocean current, a rocky shore, a tempest crashing across the ocean, rising to sweep a city away.

Primus held out a hand, holding himself ready. "You can't kill me. We're in the games."

Celia laughed, and a chill shivered over me. "The games don't last forever. If he's harmed, I'll know it was you. I will bury you in the ocean. I will drown you in the siren depths. Bring you back to life. Drown you again. Bring you back. Drown you again. I will make your torment last centuries. Record my words, record-keeper. I vow it."

Holy.

Could she do that?

Was she that strong?

Primus brushed his hands together. Straightened his torn brown shirt. Considered Celia's wall of mist. "Perhaps I acted hastily. Perhaps it *wasn't* your brother who provided the paladin with the death-axe pomegranate. Perhaps he *doesn't* want you dead. Perhaps?"

Celia tilted her head. Narrowed her eyes.

Primus smiled. A cold snake smile. He nodded at Celia. Stalked down the hall.

My heart banged, and I pressed myself closer to the wall. He went in the opposite direction. Thank goodness.

I had to leave. I had to go. Now.

There was no way I was staying within twenty feet of Miss I'll-drown-you-a-thousand-deaths.

When Primus's steps faded, Celia kneeled and bent over her brother. Her shoulders slumped, and she sighed tiredly. Then she brushed her hand over the mottled red and purple ring lining his throat.

"Oh, Luvic," she whispered, "what are you doing?" Then she conjured and spoke into a tiny device. "Ragnor. Luvic's hurt. I'm near the elevator, by the old Ming vase. Get here."

And that was my cue. I crept down the hall, tiptoeing as quickly as possible and then speed-walking down curves and corners, until I reached the steel industrial elevator that went to the lower levels.

I hit the down button and let out a sigh of relief as the bell chimed and the doors slid open.

"*Where* have you been?" Darin shoved out of the elevator. He scowled at my appearance. "Come on."

Wolfgang was there too. And Finn.

He was alive. *Thank goodness*, he was alive.

A rainstorm of happiness flooded over me. I hadn't realized how worried I was. The fear I'd been carrying evaporated like mist in the morning sun. I could float with the happiness I felt.

"You made it," I breathed, staring at Finn. "You did it."

He didn't look as bad as Primus or Celia. He was covered in a slimy, clear substance. There were scratches on his arms. His pants had a few rips. His black hair was wet and messy. But beyond that? He was *fine*.

I grinned at him.

"Move, body." Wolfgang shoved past me, stalking down the hall.

Finn started to smile back, a happy curve of his lips, but when he looked at my face, the smile turned to a swirling, stormy, frightening sort of rage. The navy in his eyes darkened and consumed the lightning.

A violent shudder pulsed through him, and his upper lip lifted in a snarl.

I hurriedly stepped back.

As quickly as the rage appeared, it was gone, consumed by the blissfully blank gaze of solange. Finn's posture relaxed. That smile that had abruptly cut off curved on his lips. He blinked at me, one eye closed, then the other.

"You've got . . ." He tapped his head.

I pressed my hand to my cheek. I'd forgotten to wash off the blood. And the bruise. But I think he was pointing out the knot of illusion.

"I know," I said. "I ran into trouble."

Darin snorted. He looked between me and Finn's tilty, swaying form. "Yeah. Okay. Let's go."

He held out an object. The golden lyre. *Holy.* The golden lyre? That meant . . .

That meant Finn had won. He'd won the first game?

"Yeah. He won," said Darin. "Now we've got a giant target on our backs. You've got a target. I've got a target. Dad's got a target. It's about to get fun in here. You think you could move? I'd like to get to our rooms, so we aren't, you know . . . ambushed, killed, maimed."

Darin stalked after his father, conjuring his ring of blue fire to surround himself. Finn followed, turning every few seconds to stare at the friendship knot on my forehead.

We turned down halls. Climbed stairs. Avoided the main living areas and the suites of the other families.

I was all right keeping quiet, letting the sound of our footsteps echoing in the servants' stairwell fill the silence, but as we neared the sixth floor, Finn squinted down at me. He stopped on the stair above me and asked quietly, "What is it, exactly?"

I lifted a shoulder. Whispered so Darin wouldn't overhear. "Last Clark planted a history. Wove memories to make me believe we'd been best friends since we were young."

Finn frowned. His jaw tightened, and he turned away.

"What?" I asked.

He shook his head. "Nothing. Just thinking about history. Memory. How easy it is to create a false past."

Didn't I know it. But . . . "I took care of it."

He swallowed. Nodded. He stared down at me, his eyes swirling with a thousand memories of his own. He lifted his hand as if he wanted to press his fingers to the knot on my forehead.

I stepped away. Down two stairs. Out of reach. "You shouldn't touch me. The solange will disintegrate the illusion. I need it to stay, so she doesn't suspect I . . ."

"Right." He dropped his hand.

Darin shoved open the door at the top of the stairwell. Finn gave me one last tilty, sleepy look and then turned and followed his brother. I hurried after him.

Inside the suite, Darin had dropped the lyre onto the coffee table. He'd pulled out his phone. When we came in, he grinned.

"Okay, before debriefing . . . pizza. Right? We're having pizza. Friggin' Bards." He pointed at Finn. "Pepperoni? Yeah." He turned to me. "And you . . . you . . . what? You look like an anchovies-type person."

I literally had never eaten anchovies in my entire life. Roumelade would die.

"What? No anchovies? Tell me you aren't vegetarian. Smiths aren't vegetarian. Neither are their bodies. If you don't like meat, you can have chicken—the vegetable with legs."

"I like cheese," I said, shrugging. When Darin lifted an eyebrow, I frowned. "Double cheese?"

"Meat. Pizza must have meat." He was spelling it out for me.

He really was an annoying brother.

"Okay. How about bacon?"

He grinned. "Now we're talking."

Suddenly, there was a clatter from mine and Finn's bedroom.

Darin and I looked at each other, then we sprinted toward the noise.

While we'd been arguing about pizza, Finn had slipped into the bedroom without us noticing. He was sprawled on the silk rug, staring at the ceiling, a joyfully drunk smile on his face. A silver thimble clattered across the wood floor and then rolled to a stop. The bottle of solange was tipped over, leaking its iridescent liquid across the rug.

Darin stared at his brother. "Is this normal? Does he do this every time?"

Oh.

Oh no.

I'd forgotten that I'd poisoned Finn's solange.

"No," I said, shaking my head. "Finn?"

Finn pushed up on his forearms, swaying dizzily. "Mmm?" He smiled at me, blinking happily.

"How much solange did you have?"

"Lots," he said. "Lots and lots."

"What is this?" Darin asked, appalled.

Finn grinned and rubbed his hand through his hair, pushing it back from his forehead. His cheeks were rosy-pink. His eyes were glassy. He swayed like a sailor on shore leave.

"This is . . . I like you." He pointed at Darin. "I like my brother. And you . . ." He stretched out a wobbly hand and pointed at me. "You, I love."

"This," I said in answer to Darin's question, "is Dainty Drink."

32

"What do you mean, 'Dainty Drink'?" Darin scowled at me and then growled at Finn, "Get off the floor!"

Finn wobbled on his forearms and shook his head. "Can't. Don't have legs."

"Dainty Drink," I said, edging closer to Finn, toeing the rug, "is a . . ." —*poison*—"liquid that makes people . . ."—I waved a hand at Finn— "inebriated."

"He's inebriated all the time! This isn't inebriated. This . . . this is . . ." Darin pulled himself into his military posture. He was the lighter, paler, chestnut-haired version of Finn, but right now, they looked like polar opposites. He threw off the guise of affable brother and cloaked himself in hard-eyed military precision. He snapped at Finn, "Get up."

Finn grinned at him and stayed comfortably sprawled on the floor. "Thought you were ordering pizza."

I held out my hand to Finn. He was big, broad, and while I *could* toss him over my shoulder and roll him, I couldn't lift him off the floor. But I could *help* him stand.

"Come on," I said, extending my open palm.

It was interesting, the way Finn looked on the soft cream and navy silk rug. He sat just at the end of a beam of sunlight shining through the window. It fell over him like milk poured from a ceramic jug. Because he was black-haired and navy-eyed, a dark bit of night, he seemed to soak in all the setting sun's light so that he glowed even more, all luminescent and night-sky bright.

He was the opposite of his brother. Darin stood at the diffused edges of sunlight, and with his fairer skin, his lighter hair, and his cloud-gray eyes, the sun didn't sink into him and turn him luminous or make him darkly shine. Instead the light reflected off him like a mirror, or like polished armor. The light scattered away, reflecting elsewhere.

Bathed in that light, lounging in the warmth, Finn stared at my outstretched hand. He studied it as if it was disconnected from my body and had magically appeared in front of him. Then he followed the line of my hand, up my wrist, up my arm, to my face. He smiled a happy, puppy-in-love, fistful-of-daisies smile.

"Mari," he said, and there it was again: the way he said my name was a caress; a hand stroking lovingly over bare skin.

I stepped closer. "Let's go. We'll get you cleaned—"

Quick as lightning, he gripped my hand and yanked me down on top of him. I hit hard. Hip to hip. Chest to chest. My breath whooshed out. My hands smacked the silk fabric of the rug. Finn was a hard line of muscle and heat. Every inch of me pressed against him, knotting and tying as if he was wrapping himself around me—inside, outside, everywhere. There was no illusion—none that I could see—only the feel of an invisible knot tying two threads together.

Finn's grip tightened on my wrist. His clothing was wet and cold, but his skin was hot. His hand circled my wrist and wrapped around the rapid staccato of my pulse.

What was this?

Where was the knot?

I could *feel* it. But it wasn't there. There was nothing there.

I stared into Finn's eyes, riding the rapid rise and fall of his chest. His heart boomed under me. Thunder sounded in my mind. The smell of a summer rainstorm surrounded us, and my skin tingled as if it had been bathed in lightning.

"What—?"

I broke off. Finn sent his calloused hands through my hair and tugged my mouth to his.

His lips were soft, tender, and sweet. He was cranberry and allspice; rainstorm and thunder. His fingers dug through my hair, pulling the knots of my braid free. He groaned against my mouth, and the vibration of the deep, longing noise reached inside me and plucked a thread that shimmered and glowed.

He ran his tongue over my lips, and when I gasped, he quested his tongue into my mouth. Stroking. Seeking. Knotting with mine. He held me in place—not with his hands, but with the knots he was tying around me . . .

No. There were no knots.

But—

He clung to me. Stroked me. Moved his mouth over mine as if he knew the contour of my lips and he'd loved them for years. The line of my hips was his home. The taste of my lips was his dream. I was the sunlight he walked in, the starry night he yearned for. I was—

"Mari." His mouth whispered over mine, smooth and allspice-tinted. "I love you."

"While this is sweet . . ." Darin said, clearing his throat loudly. "I'm still here. And you still need to get up."

I gasped and shoved at Finn.

He didn't budge, just kept ahold of me, one hand cupping my cheek, the other pressing into my lower back. His hand stroked in a slow circle over my spine, building a warm need wherever he touched. He stared at me with his starry-sky eyes.

"Let me go," I hissed.

He smiled. "Can't."

"Finn. We've done this before. You didn't like the result." While this time I couldn't flip him, I could use other tactics. Ones he wouldn't like.

I tensed, deciding between knee, elbow, and a gouge to the eyes.

Finn's forehead creased in a confused wrinkle. "Wait. I . . . You . . . you poisoned me?" he asked, sounding more bemused than upset. He wrinkled his nose. Blinked. Shook his head. His hair was still damp from the game, his skin slightly sticky. "Mari? Did you poison me again?"

"Again?" Darin asked. Then, when I looked over my shoulder at him, he scowled. "Wait. *You* did this to him?"

I turned back to Finn. "Shh," I whispered.

"Okay." He smiled.

His cheeks were flushed red, and his lips were glossy from our kiss. The look on his face gave me an uncomfortable itch. It was similar to the smile I'd worn when thinking about how much I loved Last. Was this what Dainty Drink had done to Finn—made him think he was desperately in love with me?

Was it the poison mixing with the effects of this new face? I already knew Finn was yearning for his love. Was this face and the Dainty Drink confusing him?

"Finn, I don't want to hurt you. Let me go." I shifted my hips, trying to break free from the pressure of his hand, but that movement only resulted in a spark lighting where our hips met and a strangled grunt from Finn.

"You," Darin said, "are literally the worst body in the history of Smith bodies. You're supposed to take care of him, not poison him. Will it kill him?"

"No," I snapped. "He'll be fine in a few hours. It was an accident." I shoved at Finn. "Let me go. You love Cora. Think about how upset you'll be in a few hours."

Darin stepped closer and peered at Finn. "Who's Cora?"

Finn frowned, blinking at me. "No. I love you. I've loved you from the second I first saw you."

I sighed. "That was yesterday."

Finn gave a happy rumble as if he were reliving a beautiful memory. "Only yesterday? Feels like years ago."

I couldn't agree more. "Tell me about it."

Darin cleared his throat. Nodded at the door to the bedroom. I lifted my eyebrows. *What?* He nodded at the bedroom door again.

Wolfgang was standing at the threshold, a dark expression on his grizzled face. How long had he been there? By the slanted line of his eyebrows and the thinness of his mouth, I'd say long enough.

He stared at Finn and me for a moment and then turned his hard gaze to Darin.

"There was an incident." He spaced out his words with hard precision. "The Bards have—secretly—called a physician. For whom, I don't know. I'm going to . . ." He paused, considered his words, then said, "See what I can learn."

Darin stiffened. All amusement fled from his expression. "An assault? An assassin?"

The Smith shrugged. There was shrewd calculation in his gaze. "We'll see."

Darin shifted his weight. Pondered his father's announcement. "I'll prepare."

The Smith nodded, then his eyes flicked to me. I held still. There was something wolflike in the way the Smith watched me. He was a predator staring with cold eyes from the edge of a dark forest.

Finn didn't seem to notice his father. He slowly ran his fingers through my hair, stroking the ends, watching the dark strands glitter in twilight's golden light.

"If you harm our chances of winning the games," Wolfgang said in a low warning growl, "I will send you in pieces back to your master. It's a true death I'll deliver."

Well. Here was the Smith I'd always imagined. Direct threats. Perfect understanding. Get in my way. Die.

"Understand, creature?" he asked.

I nodded. I understood. There wasn't much difference between his threats and Jagger's. They both gave promises, and you'd better believe they'd deliver. For example, when Jagger promised, "If you fail to lockpick the Clark's record of the 700th game, I will sever your left hand"—well, let's just say that for the last few months of my fifth life, I only had one hand.

So yes, I understood Wolfgang perfectly.

I glanced down at Finn. He watched me with a small smile, his expression separate from the events in the rest of the room. It was as if we were tucked under the mossy oaks and ferns of a forest together, bathed in filtered light and loamy scents, a cool, clear spring gurgling nearby.

"Harm a hair on her head . . ." Finn murmured—so quietly I didn't think Wolfgang could hear him. "Deliver a true death, Father, and I will become your destroyer of worlds. I will end this earth in flames of retribution."

Finn sifted his hands through my waterfall of hair and then tugged a strand free. A shiver raced over me as he smiled and looped the strand around his finger.

I stared at him, a band tightening around me, like the dark loop of my hair tightening around his ring finger. My chest constricted. I was still pressed against him, the sheath to his knife. If I was gone, would he unsheathe and destroy the world?

But that didn't make sense. He couldn't. He was a null. He was a solange addict. He was . . . nothing. No one. Just a pawn. Jagger's pawn. Wolfgang's pawn. My . . . pawn.

In a way, he was my pawn. If he won, I'd be free. Jagger had promised this, and Jagger kept his promises.

He wins. He dies. I'm free.

He loses. He dies. I'm not free.

In both scenarios, he dies. A pawn. Not a destroyer of worlds.

Wolfgang was gone. He'd cut Darin a glance—a "take care of this" look.

There was a strange tightness in my chest, a hollow space that constricted and contracted, that knot that wasn't a knot twisting in the empty space. I pushed at Finn, and finally, his hands fell away, as if he didn't know why he'd been holding me in the first place.

"I wonder," Darin said, staring at the empty threshold where his father had stood. "What happened with the Bards?"

Oh.

Luvic!

"I . . ." I scrambled off Finn and stood hurriedly, backing across the rug. I looked sheepishly between Finn and Darin. "I may have poisoned Luvic."

Darin cut a surprised glance my way.

I held out my hands. "It was an accident!"

Darin ran his hands through his short hair and shook his head. "You

... you are literally ... How do you accidentally poison two people in one day?"

I lifted a shoulder in a half-shrug. Finn pushed himself to a sitting position. He gave me a disappointed look, as if he was saying, "You really shouldn't have done that."

"Dainty Drink?" Darin asked.

"No." I felt a little horrible admitting it. "Assassin's Hourglass. I'd say he has ... twelve hours to live. Tops."

Darin rubbed his eyes. Tugged his hand over his face and shook his head. "All right. Two options. One, we let him die. Not a bad option. He's fair game—"

"No," I said, remembering Luvic's eyes as he'd struggled to breathe, Primus's noose around his throat. For some reason, he'd trusted me to save him. "What's option two?"

Darin shrugged. "Easy. We give him the antidote and demand something in return. You have the antidote, right?"

Finn let out a small snort, and I glared at him. Darin ignored him.

"No, not exactly ..."

Darin crossed his arms over his chest. "Okay?"

"I don't have the antidote." I smiled. "But I know someone who does."

33

THERE WOULD BE WINKING STARS, HIGH IN THE ATMOSPHERE WHERE THE summer air cooled, far past the thick cloud of city lights. There would be the smiling moon, less than half-full but still bright enough to swim in. There would be the freedom to race through the night, gusting through the forest of steel and concrete buildings, skating over black-gloss rivers, shooting through the open air.

The wind left the boy in the company of his mother—the woman whose mind tilted and spun like a tornado dying and reforming—and another woman—the old, fleshy one who smelled of cod liver oil and had been the boy's caretaker as a child. She rubbed ointment into his cuts and clicked her tongue while the mother muttered, "Where is the key? Where is the lock? How is there a shadow without the sun?"

The wind had tickled the boy's earlobe and left when he smiled in response. Now it spun dizzily down the hallway, drifting over the bristled hair of thick wool rugs, along the smooth, waxed legs of tables, and over the cold, round bellies of porcelain vases. Ahead, a velvet curtain whispered and ruffled as air flowed through an open window.

Summer smells. City smells. Hot concrete. Air-conditioner fluid dripping freely. Subway steam and urine. The smoke of a cigarette. A woman's vanilla perfume. Wet newspaper and mint gum stuck to a rusted newspaper rack.

The wind moaned happily and slid over the soft brush of burgundy velvet, inching toward the lip of the open window.

"Your son is surprising," a man said, his voice melodiously soft.

The wind stilled under the folds of the voluminous curtain. Footsteps echoed, one pair of feet only, but a second voice answered.

"Not so surprising." It was a crisp, hard voice—one the wind knew. It knew both voices well. It peeked out from beneath the velvet curtain folds.

Only one man passed, but the air currents of two men rode through the hall. Ah, illusion. The wind smiled. It stretched out toward the two conjurers, principals both. It rolled in their power, careful not to be trod upon.

You may wonder, who were they? Which principals? The wind wouldn't say. This is all it relayed. Capricious, mischievous wind.

"The question of your daughter. She nearly died during the game . . ." The visible man held out his hands, his words trailing off like a stiff gust dying suddenly on the open sea. Then he stopped walking, and the wind skittered around his ankles, weaving past the tingle of the other's illusion.

"And she will again," the invisible man said, his voice melodious and mournful. "It is how this game is played."

The wind drifted back toward the curtain, and the velvet folds rustled and shifted. The man turned, narrowing his eyes on the moving fabric. "Later. There are ears here, even when there are no eyes."

The man moved away at a steady clip, leaving the invisible one to stand silently in the hall.

The wind waited, sniffing the summer air, longing to rise to the open window and float free. It would stretch toward the Hudson; run through the curl of green leaves and the scratch of rough bark. The man strode forward and snapped the window shut.

The wind moaned as the man strode away, still unseen but not unheard.

It would have to seek another way out. A crack, a crevice, a mouse hole, a metal vent, a creosote-soaked brick chimney, a front door.

The wind slid along the floor toward the cold, marble-tiled entry, humming a song about winking blue stars and skating on moonlight. When it was close—but not too close—to the entryway, the wind heard a sharp cry.

It hesitated.

Outside was near. But . . . there it was again. A muffled, worried sound. An ocean sound, salt-tears and conch shells, stormfronts and sea mist.

The wind slid under a closed wooden door, through an open courtyard, and beneath another closed door. It found the citrus and pearl dust scented woman. She was with the musician. The trickster too.

But when the wind slid over the trickster, it realized something was wrong.

Humans were strange creatures. They had an animating spirit, just like the wind. Sometimes their spirit blew and stormed; other times it lay still in quiet repose. But occasionally, the spirit sank deep and curled in on itself. Often, when it did that, it would flee the human shell and never come back.

The wind ran along the trickster's cheek, scratching at his stubble and feeling the cold of his skin.

He needed more air. Anyone could see that.

"Deloure—the physician—is almost here," the musician said, his words a broken melody. "Don't worry. He'll be fine."

The woman gripped the trickster's hand. The wind ran over the salty tears on her cheek. Noted the sting.

"No! He isn't fine—"

"He's survived worse."

She looked away, thrusting the tears off her cheeks. The wind rode down her arm, touched her collarbone, and then noticed what it had missed with its attention fixed on the trickster.

She smelled of antiseptic and blood, not citrus and pearl dust. A long tube ran from a plastic bag hanging on a metal pole. Deep, ruby-red blood, copper-penny blood, flowed from the narrow tube into the woman.

The gray-haired man, the grim-faced, gray-uniformed one, grunted and squeezed the blood bag. The woman winced.

"She'll need more," the man said, his voice a dispassionate scrape. This had been a frequent occurrence since they were small children, this thing where the musician and the trickster gave their sister their blood.

The musician rolled up his sleeve. "Then get her more."

The gray-haired one went about it, tightening a powdery latex tourniquet around the musician's arm and jabbing him with a long needle, hooking it to a bag to fill.

The woman closed her eyes. Bent her head. The wind realized she was small—much smaller than the other humans. With her sigh, she seemed, to the wind, even smaller.

"Primus said Luvic gave the paladin the death-axe pomegranate. I almost died in there, Raggie. I was supposed to be a siren, and instead I was a damsel in distress. Remember, Luvic said . . ." She shrugged.

"Celia. Primus is trying to get in your head. Make you doubt."

"Still . . ."

The musician scowled at the gray-haired man when he wiggled the needle deeper into his vein to speed the flow of blood.

He turned back to his sister. Shook his head.

"No, Celia. Whatever you're thinking, no. Luvic plays deep—you know this. Whatever he did, he did it for a reason. If you stop trusting him . . ." The musician looked at the trickster. His mouth flattened, and his fist clenched. "If we can't trust him, we can't trust anything. We may as well end it right here, right now."

The woman swallowed. Her hand shook. She reached out and rested her fingers against the trickster's cheek.

Would they kill him? Conjurers had been killed for being suspected of less.

Then the woman looked back at the musician. "You know I trust him. Even if he betrayed me, I'd trust him while he was shoving the killing knife into my chest. I trust him. We're family."

The musician nodded. The gray-haired man grunted and yanked the needle from the musician's arm.

"And so," said the musician, "here we are."

"Wake up, Luvic," the woman whispered, brushing his black hair back from his forehead.

But the wind knew the trickster's spirit was far, far down in the cave inside himself. He wouldn't wake without a forceful wind shoving him out.

The wind sighed. The winking stars could wait. Skating on moonlight could wait. Freedom could wait.

The wind tickled the trickster's nose, slid down his esophagus—deep into his diaphragm—and went in search of his spirit.

34

THE ANTIDOTE REQUIRED PIZZA. OR THE APPEARANCE OF PIZZA. PEPPERONI, meat lovers, and double cheese with bacon.

The scent of spiced sausage, fennel, and rosemary tickled my nose as I lifted the lid of the delivery box. The night was muggy, late-June's humidity rising off the night-pale concrete. I wondered where the wind was. It was too still, the air clinging like itchy, damp wool. Not even the movement of taxis, mopeds, or the rushing sound of a horn blaring and fading could ease the night heat.

I smiled hesitantly at Justice, aware the jackaltooth doorman was only a few feet away. That unnerving rattle sounded in his throat.

Justice didn't seem to notice. He was a different man today, broader-nosed, paler, red-haired.

"Awright then?" he asked—not about the pizza, but about everything else.

Even with the smooth paleness of Justice's minor illusion, there were still tension lines around his mouth and fatigue around his eyes. Sometimes he looked like this when Jagger sent him out on weeks-long "cleaning" sprees. I wondered what he'd been doing in the short time since I left. I'd been around long enough to know the answer was most likely "a lot."

In twenty-four hours, Justice could clean out households of Jagger's enemies. He'd done it once in Jersey City. That was another one of those times that Justice refused to talk about. So I didn't ask why he looked so tired, or why the knot of his illusion was so loosely tied. Instead I softened my hesitant smile. Gave him a soft hug in my mind.

The tension around his mouth lessened, and he ducked his head. A block away, a bus's hydraulic brakes hissed, and a car horn sounded. There were city noises, but the Bard Mansion, illusioned and hidden to all, sat in residential apartment-building quiet.

The heat of the cardboard pizza boxes scalded my fingers. I pretended to smell the steam rising from the pizza, and then, aware of the doorman's stare, I quickly whispered, "I need the antidote to Assassin's Hourglass."

Justice nodded. "That'll be forty-two fi'ty." Then, in a quieter, near-lethal voice, "You've been poisoned?"

I snapped the lid shut. "No. I did the poisoning."

His expression relaxed. "Then let them die. Unless it's the fool. Yet . . ." He shrugged. "Even then."

I stared at Justice. Tightened my mouth and gave him my "you did not just take the last scone off the plate" look.

His mouth twitched. He considered me for a moment. Two. But I knew he'd help. Just like he'd always split the scone in half—or thirds, if Griff was there too.

"Yer order wasn't right?" he asked loudly. "Is that it? Hang on then."

He turned, stepped away, pulled a phone from his delivery-uniform vest. He spoke in a low, quick voice, his words as quiet as cold mist slipping over a rocky shore. He'd called Roumelade. I was surprised she could hear him, but she could hear the sound of the Atlantic's waves even miles away, so I suppose that explained it.

My arms were loaded down with the three pizza boxes, and the heat was like pressing bare skin against a hot radiator in the summer. I was flushed, and sweat trailed down my neck and my chest. My silk uniform stuck to my damp skin.

Behind me, the mottled-skinned doorman's gaze pressed into my back. Earlier, when I walked to the front door, he'd only said, "May I help you?" and again, I'd said, "I have a delivery."

I'd left Darin and Finn upstairs. Finn had promised to take a shower and change into a clean outfit. Darin had muttered something about needing to prepare defenses for assassination attempts, frontal assaults, and accident-prone bodies. I'd claimed pizza was the key to getting the antidote.

Really, Rou was the key, but pizza was the path to her.

I'd had to use this circuitous route because, first, Jagger didn't allow mobile phones in Hell Gate. There was only one phone line: the rotary in Rou's kitchen. Jagger was a technophobe. Rou had installed the rotary back in 1952, and thankfully, he still hadn't noticed. She hid it in a cookie jar, because leggerocks don't eat sweets. If he ever heard the jar ringing, she claimed it was full of "bell cookies." Stranger things have existed, so Jagger never questioned it.

Second, whenever a nine was out on a task, Jagger allowed no communication between us and the denizens of Hell Gate. When you were out, you were on your own. It was the whole sink-or-swim mentality. If he was in a boat next to you and you were drowning, he wouldn't throw you a line; rather, he'd tie an anchor to your ankles and hurry you to the bottom of the ocean, fool that you were to ask for help.

That was why I wasn't sure if Justice was here because Jagger wanted eyes on me and Finn, or if Justice was keeping tabs on me because he . . . cared. Really, it was better not to ask. That way, if he was doing this of his own volition, I wouldn't have knowledge that might get him in trouble if Jagger probed.

"Awright," he said, drawing out the word and shoving the phone back into his vest. He turned back to me and gave a sheepish smile. "T'make it right, we'll get you free dessert. I'll be back in three hours wit' it." Then he ducked his head and murmured quietly, "The whisper of a butterfly's wings. A ribbon length of a baby's laugh. Hair plucked from a virgin's head. A pound of fire. A liter of wind. Vodka."

I frowned. "Vodka?"

Behind us, the doorman's throat rattle grew louder, competing with the roar of a motorcycle's engine echoing through the streets.

Justice shrugged, his gaze sweeping over me, illusioned red hair glinting under the streetlight. "You've got two hours. Drop the ingredients in the newspaper rack at the end of the block. Rou will bake your antidote, and I'll be back in three. Yeah?"

I nodded. Yeah.

He stepped back and said loudly, "No charge, awright?"

"Thank you."

"Don't worry 'bout it."

Then he was gone, and I went upstairs to deliver the pizza.

The Davis Family Butterfly Vivarium was located in the Natural History Museum on the Upper West Side. It was the only place in the entire city where I knew we'd be certain to find the whisper of a butterfly's wing at short notice.

If Darin or Finn found Roumelade's list of ingredients strange, neither said anything.

Darin had merely shrugged and said, "I'm coming."

When I'd raised an eyebrow, he added, "If you think I'm letting you two,"—he pointed at me—"the incompetent body"—he pointed at Finn —"and her inebriated charge, wander the city alone in the middle of the games, you've got another think coming."

Finn, clean from his shower and happily eating his third slice of pepperoni pizza, had merely grinned at his brother. The Dainty Drink seemed to have worn off a little, so instead of being a handsy-in-love drunk, Finn was merely … happy.

He kept reaching over and taking my hand, linking his fingers with mine. For the whole cab ride, where I was shoved tight between two overlarge men, then for the walk down Central Park West, slipping through the spill of streetlights, and even while Darin broke us into (okay, stealthily conjured us into) the museum and the vivarium, Finn had held my hand.

Every now and then, I tugged my hand free. When I did, he looked down and frowned as if he didn't know we *were* holding hands. But then, seconds later, he'd have ahold of my hand again. It was like he didn't even realize he was doing it.

When Darin pointedly stared, I shrugged and said, "He thinks I'm his girlfriend."

It was easier to just go with it. In a few hours, Finn would be back to himself and in love with his actual girlfriend/wife-to-be/good luck charm.

Now, his hand was warm and solid, and he ran his thumb over my skin, tracing a slow figure-eight pattern. I ignored the shiver it sent through me and instead looked around.

I'd always wanted to come to the vivarium, but I never had. Maybe it was because a room full of moths and butterflies would remind me of what us orphan wards of Hell Gate had lost. Maybe it was because I'd never had anyone to come here with.

But here I was, and it was everything I'd imagined. The room was a warm, tropical oasis, with soft, eggshell-white walls, domed ceiling lights, and cascading concrete islands of micro-rainforests.

Tall grasses, fat, glossy leaves, thick, aloe-tinted fronds, heart-shaped leaves, spiky leaves, forests of humus and loam scented foliage. There was the lingering hint of sugar water and orange—butterfly food—as well as the memory of the colognes and perfumes of the hundreds of people who'd passed through before closing.

The lights were low. The outdoor city glow from the large windows overlooking trees, scaffolding, and streetlights shone into the vivarium. The quiet hum of the HVAC vibrated through the room.

It's interesting. Butterflies are diurnal—they fly during the day—but moths are nocturnal and fly at night. So while all the museum visitors saw the butterflies at their most active, we were witnessing the hidden side of the vivarium.

The Atlas moth, with its wingspan wider than Finn's outstretched palm, slowly fluttered its wings. White, nearly translucent moths fluttered around us. Large, jagged-winged beige moths rose off the red and green striped grasses. A spring-green curling leaf trembled and then flew into the air—a moth, not a leaf, after all.

As we moved into the vivarium, surrounded by Darin's illusion of darkness, the moths swept around us like a blown dandelion seed head, all the white fluff catching the wind and flying free.

I paused next to a bright purple and yellow plastic feeding dish labeled "Please Do Not Touch the Fruit" and held out my palm. A delicate white moth hovered over my hand, the tickle of air currents teasing my skin. Then it fluttered away.

"I've always wanted to come here," I whispered as a moth flew past. "Have you been?"

Finn was staring at a tall glass cylinder where long strands of golden rope hung, giant triangular winged moths fluttering on the strands. There was a strange look on his face—one I couldn't quite place.

"Once. Years ago." He kept his gaze on the moths inside the glass column. "They only live two weeks. Atlas moths." He nodded to the encased moths. "They don't eat. They don't sleep. Their only goal is to find their mate. Then they die."

Darin moved closer, peering at the column of rope and the moths tied to it. "Kind of depressing."

Finn gripped my hand, thinking maybe of his Cora. "No. They're focused."

"Speaking of focus, how did you win the game today?" Darin asked. "We'll have our debrief tonight, but just give me a taste. What, did you fight? Did you kill? Did you—?"

"The game?" Finn asked, turning away from the Atlas moths. "I walked the wire of Mneme. Before that . . . a pack of three dozen jackaltooth hounded me. They seemed especially attracted to me—"

"Jackaltooth? Nice touch, Bards." Darin grinned as if an attack from a pack of jackaltooth was all fun and games.

Finn lifted an eyebrow, and I flushed. Apparently, the stolen Bard button didn't ward off jackaltooth; it lured them closer.

"Sorry," I mouthed.

Finn smiled. "It took me a while to . . ."

"Slaughter them?" Darin asked.

Finn tilted his head in a slow nod. "After that, I walked a lifetime of memories."

I frowned at how casual, how easy, he made it sound. "But people get lost in Mneme. You don't just stroll through it. Mneme would've been the most dangerous of the three paths."

Finn shrugged. "Not for me."

"Why?"

"Because." Finn turned back to the Atlas moths. "Memory is only dangerous to people who are afraid of the past yet can't face their future. Memory will never be dangerous for someone like me."

I took in Finn's profile—his sharp nose, sharp cheekbones, slanting eyebrows, and the deceptive softness of his inky-black hair. There was a grim set to his mouth, and I wondered, had the Dainty Drink worn off? But if it had, why was he still holding my hand?

I pulled free, and when I did, Finn shook his head, tugging himself out of whatever memory had momentarily snared him. He stared at his empty palm.

"The whisper of a butterfly's wings," I said, pointing to a butterfly quietly tucked beneath a palm frond.

According to the glossy placard detailing the names and images of the butterflies and moths in the vivarium, this was the Starry Night Cracker butterfly, named after Vincent van Gogh's famous painting.

The butterfly's wings were deep navy blue, the color of a summer night sky. They were splotched with starry swirls of light aqua and pearlescent moons of sky blue. It looked as if God had taken one look at Finn's eyes and then painted them onto a butterfly's wings.

I held out a glass vial, unstopped the cork, and then shooed the butterfly until it shivered, fluttered, and flew away. I shoved the cork into the bottle, stoppering the sound.

"One down."

As we left the tropical warmth of the vivarium for the quiet hallway of the museum, I asked Finn, "Just wondering, what color were your eyes before solange?"

He peered down at me and smiled. "I always thought they were brown, but someone once told me they were hazel. Like my mom's."

After that, we spilled out onto the wide sidewalk of Central Park West, an hour left to collect the remaining ingredients.

"A pound of fire?" I asked. "A liter of wind?"

Darin shrugged, holding out his hands in a "beats me" gesture. "I'm going for baby's laugh and vodka."

So we walked north, heading toward the nearest liquor store and straddling Central Park, keeping an eye out for nannies or parents pushing strollers.

There were playgrounds nearby, walking paths, and the giant schist boulders that sparkled with quartz and mica in the evening lamplight. Here on the edge of the park, thick-trunked oak trees arched over the green park benches lining the cobblestone sidewalk, and ferns grew from weathered cracks in the great boulders.

The evening shadows were lengthening, and time was leaking away.

"There," Darin said, veering toward the short stone wall edging the park.

A young mother drank a cup of iced coffee as she pushed a stroller over the honeycomb-shaped cobblestones lining the sidewalk. Her baby contentedly chewed on his fist as he watched the headlights of the buses and taxis pass.

I pulled another vial free of my pack and unstopped the cork. Darin stepped in front of the mother and stuck his tongue out at the baby.

And—

Okay.

Well, you have to understand. Darin is big. He has to be nearly a foot taller than me. He's built like a truck. He has a hard face, and when he walks, he looks like he's looking for someone to kill, or he's thinking about someone he just killed.

Sure, he's funny. And sometimes he acts like an annoying big brother. But he's also a Smith, and he's kind of scary. Okay, very scary.

So it isn't surprising that the baby started wailing and the mother screamed, threw her cup of iced coffee in Darin's face, and then shoved past us, knocking Darin aside.

I stopped the cork back in the vial.

"So," I said, waiting for Finn to stop laughing and Darin to wipe his face off with his T-shirt. "That didn't work."

Darin scowled, licked his lips, and said, "I hate hazelnut."

"Forget about it." I pointed down the sidewalk. A short man scrolled on his cellphone, pushing a double stroller with two twin babies wearing lacy pink dresses and matching headbands. "I'll do it."

I unstopped the vial.

"You? You're not funny," Darin said. "In fact, you are so *far* from funny, you've almost circled back to funny."

I ignored him. When the babies neared, I danced in front of the stroller and crossed my eyes.

Unfortunately, Darin was right, because the baby on the right started to whimper, and then the baby on the left started to sniffle, and I could tell they were working their way up to a wailing-banshee baby cry.

"What are you doing?" the short man asked, looking up from his phone. "Can you move?"

Darin smirked, but before I could put the cork back in the vial, Finn stumbled, tripped, and then fell in front of the stroller.

The baby on the left hiccupped in surprise. Finn tried to stand, wobbled, and then fell again. The baby on the right threw her pink pacifier at him. It hit him in the eye, bounced off, and left a drip of milky slobber on his cheek. The baby gave a high, delighted baby laugh.

I jabbed the vial forward, collecting a ribbon's length, and then stopped it with the cork.

The short man grabbed the pink pacifier from Finn and pushed the stroller past, muttering about drunk idiots and sidewalk-hogging tourists.

Finn sat on the sidewalk grinning up at us. "And *that* is how it's done."

Darin yanked him upright. "He gets the women. He wins the games. He makes babies laugh. Null or not, this is Smith blood at work."

I snorted. Right.

After that, the vodka was easy. Darin came out of the liquor store with two paper bags. When I stared questioningly, he shrugged, "For later. We're celebrating the win. So, virgin's hair?"

"Easy." I wrapped a finger around a strand of my hair and tugged.

Both Finn and Darin watched as I placed my hair in a vial. Darin's face was carefully neutral, but Finn seemed dubious.

"What?" Just because he was a hedonist who grew up in the Night Den and dreamed of weeks and weeks of sex, it didn't mean everyone around him also had lots of lust-hazed, sex-filled nights.

At my frown, Finn looked away.

I shook the vial. Roumelade had a trick. She said you could confirm hair had come from a virgin by dropping a bit of lint from your bedsheets and ashes from a half-smoked cigarette onto it. If it was virgin hair, it would turn rose gold. If it wasn't, it would turn red.

I'd prepared the mix in advance, just so Roumelade wouldn't need to test it herself. As soon as I shook the vial, my strand of hair turned bright scarlet.

I stopped. Nearly dropped the vial. "That's impossible."

A couple shoved past, steering their yellow lab around us. I stared at the bright red strand of hair, holding it up to the streetlight's yellow glow. Maybe it was too dark to tell. Maybe the traffic lights were shifting the color.

"What color is this?" I showed the vial to Finn.

"Red."

Darin peered at it. "More like burgundy."

"But I'm a virgin! I've never had sex!" I nearly shouted it.

A woman passing covered her toddler's ears and hurried by.

"Yeah. We get it. Sorry you're sad." Darin frowned at me. "We have forty-five minutes. How about we get some wind and fire?"

"No, you don't understand. Red hair means I'm *not* a virgin. Which isn't possible."

Finn was staring at my strand of hair, closing one eye and then the other. "Neat trick."

My cheeks flamed. "How can I be a virgin but *not* be a virgin?"

Darin shrugged. "Probably somebody put an illusion over your memory."

My hand flew to my forehead. It was then I remembered Finn's hands stroking through my hair when he'd kissed me. His solange-touched fingers. He'd unraveled Last's final knot. *No.* She'd *know.*

I scowled. "That's not possible."

"Sure it is," Darin said. "It's easy. You just—" He held out his hand in the conjurer's pose. Made a little motion, demonstrating the technique. "Like that."

I shook my head. Now that Finn had brushed free Last's illusions, there weren't any more knots in my mind. "Trust me. That's not it."

I frowned as Finn walked over to a woman standing at the nearby bus stop.

"Excuse me?" He smiled sweetly at the woman.

"Yeah, handsome?" The woman, close to forty, held the handle of a rolling cart full of grocery bags. She beamed at Finn, sizing up his long legs, muscled arms, and wide shoulders.

"I need your help," he said.

"Uh-huh?"

"I'm trying to find a virgin in New York. Are you one?"

What? What! He asked *what?*

Ridiculously, he sounded kind of adorable, in a lost-kid-in-the-big-city sort of way. Clearly, the Dainty Drink hadn't completely worn off.

The woman laughed as if this were the funniest question she'd ever been asked. "For you? I could be."

The bald man on the bench next to her looked over sadly. "I am." He raised his hand. "Forty-two yesterday and still a virgin. Probably the last one left in Manhattan."

"Aww, honey," the woman said, handing him a potato from her grocery bag. "Have a baked potato for dinner. It'll make you feel better."

"Thanks," he mumbled, staring morosely at the potato.

The woman turned her brilliant beam on the sad, bald virgin.

Bald. No hair.

Darn it.

Darin sighed. Flagged a taxi. "Let's go."

"But we have to find a virgin," I whispered. Because clearly, according to bedsheet lint and cigarette ashes, I wasn't one.

Maybe Roumelade's trick was broken.

Or my hair was broken.

A yellow taxi swung to the curb, stopping in the bus lane. Darin yanked open the back door. Gestured for Finn and me to climb in.

"But—"

He scowled. Blushed. "It's fine. You can stop looking for your virgin."

"But—"

The tips of his ears turned red. "Get in."

"But—"

"Mari. Get in."

Oh. Ohhh. "You're . . . ?"

He nodded once. "Tell anyone, and I'll use your head as a football and your intestines as the goalpost."

Sure.

Finn and I got in. Darin's hair passed the virgin test.

The taxi slid away, driving noiselessly down the block of yellow brick apartment buildings. After the blast of air-conditioning and pine scented air freshener, the muggy weight of the still night was jarring.

So was the quiet. The taxi driver was a Ragnor Bard fan and had blasted his latest platinum love song for the entire drive north. My ears were still ringing from Ragnor's silken voice and soulful strumming. I usually avoided his music, but sometimes—like in taxis, coffee shops, or grocery stores—I couldn't escape.

Roumelade was a secret fan. Not that she'd ever admit it. But I'd heard her singing some of his songs to herself in the kitchen while she stirred a pot of soup or chopped up vegetables from her rooftop garden.

Finn's fingers brushed against mine, and I thought he was about to grab my hand again, but then he sort of shook himself and stepped away.

The Dainty Drink was fading then.

I licked my finger and held it up to the muggy night. "Still no wind."

And still no idea how to collect or even measure a liter of wind.

Darin scratched his chin and stared at the apartment buildings lining the block.

Many of the lights in the windows were on, and I could see the lives within—a man folding laundry, a couple cooking, an old man watching the glowing lights of his TV, a toddler knocking over a tower of blocks.

It was interesting. The people living in those buildings had no idea the apartment next door was really a Beaux-Arts-style mansion full of murderous conjurers, sitting on top of a nightmare-filled cave system, all of them holding puppet strings tied to our world. And inside that mansion, one of those puppet masters was dying.

He would die if we didn't collect wind and fire.

"Any ideas?" I asked.

Darin stared at the cars parked along the curb, some jammed so tightly together their front and back bumpers kissed. A bicyclist rode past, his reflective vest flashing under the streetlights.

"Flamethrower and compressed air," Darin said. "Measure it out, we're good to go."

"Well . . ." I didn't think that was quite what Rou's recipe meant.

"It's spirit," Finn said.

Both Darin and I turned to look at him. He had his hands in his pockets, his shoulders were slumped, and he was staring up at the haze-clouded half-moon. He swayed a bit, and I wondered what tightrope he was currently walking.

I stepped closer. Looked up at the moon too. "What do you mean?"

The haze, the muggy heat, it was all so thick that the moon was merely a blurred, milky glow behind a thick veil.

"Wind can't be measured. Fire can't be weighed. Not in the physical world. It's the spirit you need. The wind when it exists but doesn't. Fire when it's fire but not."

Darin peered at Finn, his eyes narrowing thoughtfully. For a moment, he had that shrewd gaze his father wore, but when I looked at him, he shrugged, and it cleared.

"I don't exactly understand . . ." I said, pulling a vial free. "What you mean and how we get it in here."

Finn shifted his attention from the blur of hazy moonlight to me. He blinked as if surprised to find me standing in front of him.

Then he smiled, and stupidly, my face burned, and my cheeks prickled. I'd said he was beautiful when he smiled. I was wrong. He was heartbreaking when he smiled. I wished, like with Last's memories, I could wipe the potency of his kiss from my mind.

Finn, though, didn't seem to remember we'd done anything at all. His smile was back to that vacant, solange-filled, starry look.

"What are we?" he asked.

I shook my head.

Finn nodded at the sky, the veiled moon, the still trees, and the glowing window lights. "Do we exist?"

"Sure hope so," Darin muttered.

Finn grinned at his brother. "No. We don't. And yes. We do."

Was this what growing up in the Night Den did to you, or was this all solange?

Finn gently took the glass vial from my hand, loosening my fingers one by one.

"What are we but God's thoughts made manifest? The love words of God's soul, spoken into being. But before you speak, do the words exist? If I say 'I love you,' did those words exist before they left my mouth and reached your ears?"

"No," Darin said at the same time as I said, "Yes."

Finn nodded. "Exactly. Actualization and nullification. Spirit before birth. The nothing of everything. Fire. Wind. That's what we need."

Finn rolled the glass vial between his fingers, pondering the still night air. Yet I was stuck on the question he'd asked. *If I say 'I love you,' did those words exist before they left my mouth and reached your ears?"*

Did love exist before it existed?

Did we exist as ourselves before we existed?

Did Finn . . .?

I had the strangest feeling. There was something inside me—it existed, but it didn't. I couldn't name it. There were no words yet. But did that mean it wasn't there?

Was it real? Was it illusion?

Darin snapped his fingers. "I get it. It's conjuring. We pull the idea of something into physical reality. There's the universal idea we all pull from, and there's the physical form. You want me to call up the thought of a liter of wind but not conjure it? The idea of a pound of fire?"

Finn grinned at his brother. "That's right."

Darin nodded. His gray eyes unfocused, and he pulled himself into that place I knew and used too. The place where you left the outer world and focused completely on the space above and outside of yourself.

He held his hand out in front of him. Then he touched his second and third finger to his thumb, and a tingle of static electricity raced over my skin.

Darin's power pulsed around him, a shock of lightning and a lick of flame. He may have been the weakest Smith heir in generations, but he was still strong.

He didn't twist his hand. He didn't conjure. No gust of wind appeared. No explosion of fire.

Yet floating above his palm was a translucent silver thread waiting to hitch and knot. I knew instinctively that it was wind. A liter of wind.

I pulled the vial free from Finn's hand and swept it through the translucent thread. It coiled in the glass bottle, and I quickly stoppered the bottle shut.

"Did it work?" Darin asked, frowning at the bottle.

To him, it'd look empty. To me, a small coil of thread pulsed in the glass. "It worked."

Finn stared at the bottle, smiling to himself. He put his hands in his pockets, slumped his shoulders, and watched as I uncorked another bottle and Darin pulled up the thought of a pound of fire.

Once we'd dropped all the ingredients for the antidote into the newspaper rack, Darin asked, "How'd you know to do that? I've been conjuring my whole life, and I've never thought of it in that way."

Finn shrugged. "I've only ever thought of it that way. What is a null but a conjurer who can't speak the words in their soul and can't give birth to their thoughts? We only have the spirit of a memory that doesn't yet exist."

For some reason, at that last sentence, I wanted to reach over and take Finn's hand. But Darin slapped Finn's shoulder and laughed.

"You sound like my tutor, Clerwell."

"That's because he was my tutor too." At Darin's surprised look, Finn grinned. "You think the Smith would let me live without making certain I was trained in the fine arts?"

Darin let out a surprised breath. "Don't know what I think."

"It's why I thought he'd welcome me with open arms when I turned fifteen. I was winning every philosophical argument, every sword fight, every sharpshooter contest—"

"He skewered you, didn't he? That's what he did." Darin laughed, and it made me wonder about the sanity of all the Smiths. "I didn't know about you, but if I did . . ." He got a faraway look in his eyes. "Maybe if we both survive the games, you can come on campaign. We control dozens of armies. Pick one, lead it into war. Europe. Asia. Africa. Sweep them all. We'll be the greatest brothers to war since Hannibal and Mago. Imagine the—" He broke off suddenly, his grin fading, realizing probably at the same time as I did that Finn was in solange free fall, so even if he survived the games, he wouldn't live much longer.

There would be no Smith carnage. No domination and world war. At least, not one led by Finn and Darin.

"I've imagined it," Finn said, his voice low.

I shivered, not able to tell if in his imagination, carnage, war, and untold death were something to be revered or reviled.

Later, after checking in at the suite to see if the Smith was back and not finding him, we decided to wait outside in the muggy embrace of the becalmed night.

We sat in a row of three on a low concrete wall, a dozen feet from the now empty newspaper rack, passing a bottle of vodka between us. It burned my throat and made my eyes water as I tilted it back and took a quick swallow.

I coughed.

Darin grabbed the bottle and took a long swig. It was expensive vodka. Supposedly, *the best*. To me, though, it just tasted like fire and future regret.

Finn waved the offered bottle away, and Darin swallowed another chug.

"Ask him for a future favor," Darin said. "One of our choice, at a time of our choosing. Don't give him the antidote until he agrees."

"And if he refuses?"

Darin shrugged. "Then he dies. No terrible loss."

Finn sighed. Reached for the bottle and took his first swallow. Then he handed it to me, and my hand brushed his. I jerked away, and he frowned at me.

"What?"

I shook my head. "Nothing."

Finn narrowed his eyes. Considered me. Came to a conclusion. "It's because I kissed you."

"It isn't."

"It is," Darin said. "You've been weird."

"You don't even know me!"

"I know you well enough to know when you're being weird. You're stiff and awkward now, and your face keeps going red."

I gestured to Finn. "Well, he *kissed* me, but he has a wife—an almost-wife—and . . . and . . ."

And it was incredible. It was the kind of kiss you never forget.

"Sorry," said Finn, pressing the vodka bottle into my hand. "If it makes you feel better, I was lost in a memory. I wasn't seeing you. I was . . . It won't happen again."

Darin snorted. "Unless she poisons you a third time."

"There is that."

I tipped back the bottle and let the burn slide down my throat. I was sitting between Darin and Finn again, and by the time I'd put the bottle down on the concrete slab, Darin had gone deathly, scarily still.

"Don't move," he hissed.

It was a command, and he expected to be obeyed.

Finn tilted his head and peered down the silent residential street. It was nearing midnight, and there hadn't been a car, a bicycle, or a pedestrian since we'd begun our night watch.

The leaves in the trees were black ink splotches dripping from the branches, with no wind to rustle them. There was the noise of car engines far-off, an occasional siren streets away, even an infrequent shout, but mostly, the night wore a thick coat of silence.

With our conversation cut short, the section of street where we sat was tucked into the blanket of quiet draped over the rest of the city.

Darin stared at the end of the block, a wolf with his hackles raised.

I followed his line of sight and watched a man emerge from the shadows. He moved fluidly, rolling from darkness to deeper dark.

Watching the way he moved, I could tell he could—and would—deliver death in seconds. He kept his hands free, his body a coiled spring over muscle, his movements a study in brutal efficiency. He was—and I've never admitted this before—a terrifying sight.

"*That* is a killer," Darin said, unfolding from the concrete step and placing himself in front of me. He held his hand out, ready to conjure. What, I didn't know. A fiery sword. A pit to swallow. Darkness to shield and consume. Darin didn't take his eyes off the approaching man. "Brother? Shall we?"

Finn raised his eyebrows, still lounging on the concrete wall. He'd noticed something Darin hadn't.

I wasn't scared. I wasn't worried. I was smiling.

"*That,*" I said, "is my friend. With the antidote."

"Are you kidding me?" Darin asked, keeping his hand extended. "Mari. That creature is dangerous."

Yeah, okay. Thanks for that. I'll take note and remember that when this *Smith burns and pillages a dozen nations* for fun.

I shoved past Darin and hurried down the sidewalk. There was no way I was letting him and Justice within twenty feet of each other. Finn, meanwhile, seemed content to watch, slouching lazily on the concrete slab, sipping from the bottle of vodka.

As I closed in on Justice, a light entered his eyes, as if he knew the effect he was having on Darin. A whisper of humor flickered across his shadowed face. He'd come as himself, but with a cloak of darkness illusioned about him.

He wouldn't stay, I knew. He wouldn't talk or laugh or pretend to be a delivery driver with a Brooklyn or Long Island accent. He wouldn't even be the Justice I knew—the one who slung his arm over my shoulder and tucked me close. Instead he was darkness. He must be on his way to a job.

As I neared, I noticed a small, crystal-cut turquoise and gold-speckled glass bottle in his hand. His gaze slid over me, past me, like he didn't notice me there. Then we were passing each other, two whispers intersecting in the night, and the bottle was in my hand, then in my hidden pocket, and in less than a breath, Justice was across the street, in a shadow, and gone.

In case there were any curious eyes watching from apartment buildings or the Bard Mansion, I kept walking. I meandered to the newspaper rack, bent down, opened it, pulled out a damp paper. It smelled like ink and cigarettes. I snapped it open and pretended to read the first article as I walked back to Darin and Finn.

Darin was seated again, taking a long swig of vodka. I lifted an eyebrow.

When he put the vodka bottle down, he scowled at me. "Forgot you were a creature too."

Ah.

Okay.

"I have it," I said, my mouth a tight line. "We can go." I crossed the street, angling toward the Bard Mansion, where we had targets on our backs, and where at least one Bard lay dying.

35

FREEDOM TASTED LIKE SHADOW MEETING LIGHT AND THE DECISION THAT LAY between. It was a pomegranate so tart and sweet that it burst over the wind as it gleefully raced from the trickster's lungs and out the hastily flung-open window.

"Luvic! You're awa—" The woman's voice was cut short as the wind spiraled down the tickle of illusion covering the mansion and scraped on the rough stubble of sidewalk concrete.

Oh, the joy. The bump of limestone stairs. The wild roulette spin of a bicycle's metal spokes. The swish of a woman's skirts, and the bristled fur of her short-haired dog. The wind rode over the smooth, engine-hot hood of a taxi and flew past a slammed restaurant door, carried on chili paste and tamarind. It reached into the humid, cloaked night and *stretched*.

Where first?

The Hudson, with its stone and mud scent and its star-tipped rock-a-bye waves?

The spired metal and glass skyscrapers to the south, where the wind would rip down their sleek sides like a sheet of paper torn in half, screaming gleefully the whole way?

Or the forest in the park, for the soft sweep of sleeping grass, the hush of petals closed, and the curl of sweetly scented leaves whispering as the wind danced through the trees?

Where—where—where—?

There.

As the wind played chutes and ladders with a fire escape on an old tenement, it heard a familiar voice.

The voice drew the wind up the metal ladder one rusted rung at a time, until it snuck through a crack in the crumbling brick and plaster and found itself in a wide-open room.

There were human things here—old things—wobbly chairs, dusty trunks, a broken Formica table, a painting of a woman with a hole through one eye. All sorts of musty things were layered in dirt, and chalky plaster coated the room like ghost dust. It was a sneezy sort of place, lit only by the streetlight glow trying vainly to press through the thick gray grime permanently etched into the windows.

"Don't kill me," a man's voice whined. It was a dying storm whine. An almost done, blowing out over the ocean whine.

The wind curled around the edge of the room, sifted through a thick layer of dust, and stirred a pile of motes to float in the gray half-light.

"Why would I kill you?" asked the man whose voice he knew. It was a hard voice, deep and unyielding. It reminded the wind of the cold caverns beneath the Bard Mansion.

"Because that's what you do," whined the man, but the wind knew he meant "because that's what you are."

The wind crept close to the russet-haired, solemn man—the one with only one tiny, painful shard of good left in his heart. He was cloaked in shadow, that sprinkle of conjurer trickling through him.

"Tell me," the man said, his voice a knife thrusting through the other man's plea.

"You'll do it quick? Painless?"

"Tell me."

The wind slid up the whining man's trembling voice. What did he know? What secret was he about to let into the world?

"It was a Bard." The whining one closed his eyes. Waited for the death blow.

The solemn man stilled, as quiet as a deep pool beneath the earth, glossy, black, and unmoving. "Not a Smith?"

"A Bard. I swear it."

The russet-haired, solemn one watched the other as if he were reaching inside him, digging for answers. "Which Bard?"

The wind tickled the whining man's mustache, making him twitch and shiver. He shook his head. Pressed his lips tight. The skin around his mouth went white.

"Which Bard?" the shadowed, solemn one asked.

The wind circled the room, stirring the dust. It watched the dust motes float in the dark gray, tomb-like room. A closed-up room. A forgotten room. It skipped through the smudges of footprints in the ash-like dust, sweeping the floor while it waited.

The solemn one waited too.

Finally, the whining one let out a great gust of bereaved breath and caved in on himself. "The youngest," he half-choked, half-cried. "The youngest Bard is the one who killed her."

It was quick after that. The wind knew it would be. The solemn one wasn't like the Clarks, who enjoyed taking their time; he wasn't like the Smiths, who enjoyed a good fight; he wasn't even like a Bard, who enjoyed a good show, or a Ward, who liked mind games. No. He was always—when he was allowed to be—quick.

A splash of copper scent hit the wind, and the whining man hit the floor. A whoosh of dust flew outward, like a white sheet blown in a summer breeze.

It was done.

The solemn man sighed. Cleaned his knife. Put it away.

When the solemn one sighed again—weary, perhaps—the wind tapped one of the freckles on his cheeks, then another, bouncing on the man's sprinkle of fairy kisses until he brushed at his cheek and shook himself off.

"Justice."

The wind whooshed in surprise at the sound of another voice. It'd been closed up for too long in the caverns. It hadn't noticed the stone scented, rocklike one appearing in the room.

This one, the wind didn't like to be near.

It didn't have a spirit like men. It didn't even have a spirit like the wind. It was a shriveled, devouring, rocklike thing. It was a hateful thing, and it ensnared and consumed those with spirits to sustain itself. The rocklike thing smelled of its favorite spirit drink and hard, deep earth.

The wind shivered and slipped toward the crack in the crumbling brick.

"I haven't been keeping you busy enough? You've had time to . . ." The rocklike one waved his clawed hand at the whining one's body. "I see you've been watching Mari. I see you've been finding answers."

The wind slipped into the wall's crack. It nudged aside newspaper shavings, chewed plastic, and the soft pigeon feathers of an abandoned mouse nest.

The solemn one didn't respond. He merely stood quiet, muscles tense, eyes cold, hands relaxed.

The rocklike one moved close, towering over the other. He was even more gray in the darkened room, his skin more wrinkled and stony in the dust and the grime. His flat black and gray eyes traveled over the solemn man. He smiled coldly when his gaze reached the man's freckles and once soft face.

"Ah, Justice. What did you find? Who was it that killed Mari?"

At the question, the man's hand curled into a loose fist. "The youngest Bard."

The rocklike one smiled. "Who?"

The russet-haired man's gray eyes burned with the promise of retribution. He snarled the name. "Luvic."

The wind itched to flee. It itched to scramble out of the crack and tumble down the fire escape to rush through the streets and—

"You won't touch him," the rocklike one said.

The man's head jerked toward him, showing his first true emotion.

"No. You won't touch him. You won't hurt him. You won't kill him. You won't tell Mari by word, action, or deed that it was Luvic who killed her."

The solemn man stiffened, his body jerking as if he was on a rack, yanked tight, strung between two opposing forces.

"Justice?"

"I won't touch him. I won't hurt him. I won't kill him. I won't tell Mari by word, action, or deed that it was Luvic who killed her."

The rocklike one studied the man. Smiled. "I know you won't."

They were quiet for so long the wind thought all the secrets had been told, but then the man asked, "Why?"

The rocklike one shrugged. "You remember when he was our guest?"

The man nodded.

The wind remembered it too. It had been when the trickster was still young—still learning how to *be* a trickster, and how to carry secrets. The trickster had learned a lot in the time he'd been at Hell Gate.

"We have an understanding," the rocklike one said. "There are games, and then there are games. Did you think I would play without knowing I would win?"

The man didn't respond. He didn't need to. He'd already lost the only game he'd ever played with the rocklike one.

"When the time comes, you will do what I asked of you." This was said in a crumbling, rockslide voice. An avalanche that made the wind tremble.

The russet-haired man closed his eyes. There was the twist of pain on his face—perhaps the knife shard of love in this heart twisting and hurting. It was a struggle for a human, the wind knew, to keep a shard of light when the rest was dark.

"Justice. You know how this ends. When the time comes, you will do what I demanded of you. Say it."

The man opened his eyes. Blazing, steel-gray, tormented eyes. "I will do what you demanded. Your will is mine."

The rocklike one nodded, satisfied. That was what happened when a nine died their final death. They went from a nine with free will to an extension of the rocklike one's will. They were no longer their own. They were his.

He called the first his nines. After, he called them *mine*.

"Go," the rocklike one said. "You've had too much idle time. There are five Bards, fourth cousins of the family, holed up at the Regis. Here for the games, but not staying at the Bard home. Kill them. Make it messy. Make it loud."

The russet-haired man nodded. He'd pulled the shadows about himself again.

"As you know, the only good conjurer is a dead conjurer. Or . . ." The rocklike one smiled at the solemn one—the one with a trickle of conjurer in him. "A leashed conjurer."

The solemn one nodded again and moved across the room, his steps so light the dust didn't even stir.

Before he slipped through the door, the rocklike one called, "Make them scream. You know I dislike quiet, painless deaths. You know I dislike mercy."

The solemn man was gone, and the wind was about to slip away—rush to the cool, cleansing waters of the Hudson—when the rattle of dry branches and the whisper of the executioner's tree climbed the stairs.

This abandoned, forgotten, tomb-like room was a busy, busy place.

"Thought I saw you up here," the dark-haired, pixie-like woman said. She spun around, wrinkling her nose, and the wind inched deeper into the crack, burying itself under newspaper shavings.

The woman smiled, her gaze roving over the disintegrating human treasures and the rotting wood. She paused when she saw the painting and laughed, "Look! Isn't that a painting of the last lockpick? What was her name again?"

"Winnie . . . Why are you here?"

"Hmm? Why am I where?"

The rocklike one curled his hands into two massive fists, but the pixie-like woman didn't notice. She was prowling around the room, poking at piles of books that sighed and crumbled when she touched them, and prodding at moth-eaten sheets draped over wooden furniture that had rotted and caved in on itself long ago.

"Oh. Here. Well, as I told you 300 years ago, when 107 tormented souls stained the branches of my tree, my trunk split in two, and I was born from blood and grief—"

"Why are you here? In this room. Right now."

The rocklike one wasn't necessarily afraid of the woman with grief and wind in her voice, but he was leery, just like the wind was leery.

She smiled at him like she knew it. "You're having fun, are you, Jagger? Having fun using your knife?"

The rocklike one leaned close and focused his flat black gaze on the woman. He ran a finger over the obsidian knife hanging from his throat. "He is my knife."

She nodded, sniffed the dusty air, and wrinkled her nose. "Yes. But knives are funny. You forge them in red-hot fire and thrust them into cold water to make them strong. But if you do it too coldly or too quickly, they'll be brittle. Maybe they'll have one tiny defect. Then, when you direct them to strike, they'll break. I think you may want to be careful not to break your knife."

The rocklike one laughed his avalanche laugh. "If my knife breaks, I'll throw it out. It's only a knife. There is always another."

The rocklike one's laugh boomed through the ghostly dust and shoved the wind from the crack in the brick, spiraling it back onto the muggy city street.

The wind shivered, shook itself off—flinging dust motes and newspaper shavings into the air—and then rushed down the open street, hurrying, hurrying, hurrying, west toward the river.

36

THE BARD SUITE WAS ON THE FIRST FLOOR, DOWN THE MARBLE, STATUE-lined hall, near the cornucopia of poisoned fruit. I knew this because Darin had told me when we decided it'd be best if I went alone to deliver the antidote and demand a favor in exchange.

Apparently, it would be considered poor etiquette for one player to approach the suite of another player during the games. So Finn was out. And if Darin went, the Bards may see it as an attack or a chance to attack. Now that Finn had won the first game, Darin was convinced it was open season on him, his dad, me, and any other Smith within spitting distance.

I couldn't disagree. There had been a few games in the past where a winner's entire family was killed before the games were done. There were other games where the winner of the first game would bow out of the contest after a few key members of their family were slaughtered. Nobody, though, had ever lost or dropped out because their body was harmed or killed.

In the grand scheme of things, bodies were disposable.

"Try not to get killed," Darin had muttered, pointing me down the long, gilded hallway.

Finn had merely smiled at me, although maybe he was smiling at the nude statue behind me. His eyes were a little unfocused, so I wasn't entirely certain.

Regardless, when I knocked the harp-shaped golden door knocker at the Bard's suite, I was expecting a *slightly* warmer reception.

"Why do you want to speak to Luvic?" Celia asked, blocking my entry to the suite. Her voice was raspy and as frigid as the Arctic Ocean, and although she was small—only topping five feet by an inch or two—she managed to fill the door.

Maybe it was the diamondback rattlesnake she'd conjured. It coiled around her feet, its head cocked, fangs ready to strike. Its yellow eyes tracked my every breath. And while the rattler had been conjured with a simple overhand knot, its bite would still kill.

It was funny—conjured food couldn't sustain, conjured healings wouldn't cure, but conjured death always killed. Why? I didn't know. Maybe it was because while life was truth, death was only an illusion.

I tracked the cobra's movements, careful to stay relaxed and nonthreatening. Celia was on high alert—that much was clear. Probably because Primus had gone primal rage on Luvic, and now I was knocking on her door.

I smiled at her, but let's be honest, I didn't have much practice with friendly, neighborly, knock-on-the-door-type chats, so I think it came out more bared-teeth, get-your-freaky-snake-off-me than the "Hi! Let's be friends!" smile I was going for.

Celia snorted. She twisted her hand, and the diamondback drew back its head.

I dropped the smile. Tactful directness was a better route. "I have a message from the Smiths."

The rattler stilled. Celia narrowed her eyes. She had tiny butterfly knots of illusion around her. I knew they were for her appearance. Celia always had knots enhancing her appearance. Complexion, makeup, hair. Tonight it was heavier than usual. She looked too dewy-fresh, too rosy-cheeked, too perfectly coiffed, to be anything but illusion. Remember the state she'd been in after the games, when I saw her in the hall crouching over Luvic?

"Which Smith?" she asked.

Oh. Hmm. Darin? Finn? The Smith? Which would get me past the rattlesnake?

I peered over her shoulder. I could only see the entry. I had a feeling the Bard suite was a lot more luxurious than the Smiths'. This was their family home. But all I could see was an entry hall, its creamy wallpaper stenciled with gold leaves and berries made of—I think—tiny chips of diamonds and rubies. There was a tall mirror, a table with a vase full of perfumed lilies, and a thick, cream silk rug.

"The Smiths," I said, wondering if it'd be obvious if I untied the knot of her rattlesnake. "All of them."

She didn't believe me. Or . . . She twisted her hand, and the rattler was suddenly wrapped around me, its teeth pressing into the thin skin of my wrist. I couldn't move—she'd bound me with air—and now the six-foot-long rattlesnake was climbing my legs, climbing my waist, wrapping itself around my arm.

"Was the message perhaps," she asked, "meant for me? Did the Smiths send their body to finish what was started? Were they expecting such easy prey that a body could dispose of my brother?"

I shook my head. "You're pretty far off base. Like, out of the stadium off base."

She raised an eyebrow. The snake's fangs dug deeper into my flesh.

"Look. While I appreciate that you want to protect your brother, I think—"

"Why are you *really* here?"

The rattlesnake held still, its scales strangely soft, the heavy column of its body firm and almost hot. Nearly all my attention was focused on the pressure of its fangs. I had the strongest desire to untie the butterfly knot. Just a little tug. A tiny pull on the thread.

But what had Jagger always taught me?

Don't let them know what you are.

Never let them know what you can do.

Finn knew. Somehow.

And maybe now Luvic knew. Although, I hoped, between the confusion, the explosion, and the chaos, it wasn't obvious *exactly* what I'd done. Maybe he'd think Primus had destroyed his own illusion.

"I'm here . . ." I said, thinking Celia's expression matched the one she wore in a sci-fi movie where she played a coldly beautiful cyborg assassin, "to talk to Luvic. I have something from the Smiths for him. He gave them a pomegranate . . ."

Celia's gaze shifted uncertainly, and the rattlesnake's grip wavered, so I pressed my advantage.

"And now they want to give him something in return." I held still, gripping the butterfly knot so that, with one quick tug, I could undo the rattlesnake's bite right as it struck.

"All right," she ceded, nodding. "But body? If you harm my brother, I will remove your head, put it on a stick, and use it as a prop in a play."

She twisted her hand, and the rattlesnake disintegrated. I held myself upright as the air bonds unraveled.

She'd already begun walking down the entry hall, expecting me to follow. I hurried after her, and the front door slammed shut behind me.

The suite was exactly like I imagined and more. When we left the hallway, it opened into a room that spired high. The ceiling reached at least three stories. Each floor surrounded a courtyard, the hallways wrapping around the center, so all the levels were open and airy. There was a Roman fountain in the center of the courtyard, blooming bougainvillea and lush, potted palm trees, a gold and turquoise ocean mosaic on the ground surrounding the fountain, and divans where the Bards could . . . I don't know . . . lounge and strum their lyres?

The suite was massive, a mansion inside a mansion, all gold, marble, and turquoise mosaics. It smelled like grapes warming in the sun, and the wisteria that wrapped around the marble columns. It was warm, and the sound of the fountain was as sweet as a child's laugh.

Celia cut diagonally across the courtyard, her heels clicking on the tile as she swept through without looking right or left.

There were other Bards here. Some on the divans. Two sitting on the fountain's stone edge. A few leaning against the railing on the third floor, looking over the courtyard. There were more Bards here than any other family.

The Smiths had come alone. The rest of their extended family were back in Queens, at their ugly, military-like stone mansion.

The Clarks had brought many of their crow-like, dour relatives, but they weren't as colorful and conspicuous as the Bards.

The Wards? It was just Jacob and his parents. The Wards tended to spread out. They were like those great cats that were territorial and needed a large range just for themselves. There were plenty of them out there, but they were mostly solitary.

We moved from the color and bubbling noise of the courtyard into a long, quiet marble hallway, and then, finally, into a second smaller courtyard with a marble fountain and an ivy-covered wall, plus a wooden door surrounded by vining purple clematis.

This, I realized, was the actual home of the Bards. The showy Beaux-Arts splendor out there was all theatre and drama and appearances.

Celia led me through the front door, past a comfortable living room full of plush white couches, and down a hallway with closed doors.

Finally, at the end of the hall, she knocked on a door, and when a muffled voice called, "What?" she hid a smile and called, "I have a visitor, but I'll kill her if you'd rather?"

When Darin had threatened to rip off my head and use it as a football, I'd known he was joking. Probably. Celia was dead serious.

"Who is it?"

"The Smith body."

There was a quick rustling, something being knocked over, a harsh swear word, and then, "Send her in."

Celia raised her eyebrows and then narrowed her eyes on me. "Remember what I said."

Yeah. I didn't think I'd be forgetting that she'd offered my head a starring role in her next play. "Sure."

She pushed open the door, and I hurried inside, closing it after me.

Then I stopped.

Surprised, I suppose, to find Luvic in bed.

He looked terrible.

I don't know what I was expecting. Maybe the Luvic I'd seen before Primus attacked him. The one from the gala, wearing a tuxedo, smooth and impossibly handsome, a Bard through and through.

But no. Here he was, in his bed. It *was* his bed, clearly. His room. There wasn't much illusion here—not like the rest of the house.

I could see, for the first time since entering the Bard suite, that we were on the first floor, facing the street. There was a window, and outside was the spill of yellow streetlight, the flat-fronted brick apartment buildings, and the gray-brown trunks of the maples planted uniformly in the sidewalk.

It was a strangely ordinary room, and an ordinary view.

His bed was neat. It had a light blue comforter and two pillows. Two nightstands and a thick paperback—the latest thriller, dog-eared near the middle—which made my heart give a slow, painful thud.

There was a framed photograph of him, Celia, and Ragnor, all their arms slung around each other, wearing shorts and T-shirts, standing on the edge of an ocean cliffside somewhere, the sun washing out the background.

He followed my gaze and smiled at the photo. "Crete."

"Oh. Uh-huh."

He lifted his eyebrows, but when I didn't say anything more, he smiled and propped his two pillows against the headboard, sitting further upright.

"Sorry. I'd offer a seat, but . . ." He shrugged. The only place to sit was his bed. He studied my face, moving his gaze over my forgettable, unnoticeable, temporarily beautiful features. "What can I do for you?"

"Well." I shifted, scratching the toe of my shoe against the ivory-colored carpet. "Do you remember when you said that you like me?"

He narrowed his eyes. His face was all right, but his neck had a raw red and purple necklace around it where Primus had tied illusion's rope. Still, he was pale, drawn. His breath was shallow, and his lips and fingertips had a slight bluish tinge.

It was the Assassin's Hourglass. Soon he'd be struggling for breath.

Already, it seemed he was having trouble remaining upright. I imagine he thought it was the aftereffects of Primus's attack. Soon, he'd realize it was something worse.

"Yes," Luvic said. "And I was right. You saved my life." His lip curled in that mischievous smile, although it wasn't as bright as usual.

"How did you know that? I can't figure that out. How'd you know the future?"

He laughed and then winced and touched his throat. "I didn't. I planted a seed to see if it'd sprout."

When I raised my eyebrows, he shrugged.

"Any human can plant a seed. Sometimes the idea grows into reality, and sometimes it doesn't. You don't have to conjure to make things happen. I didn't know Primus would attack me, but I figured I had a high chance of being targeted in the next few days, and . . . perhaps, if I planted a seed, it'd grow into a flower." He smiled. "And look. I was right."

Hmm.

"So," Luvic asked, his smile still in place, "has the Smith sent you to kill me? Is that what we're doing tonight?"

I let out a surprised breath.

He nearly laughed, but he stopped himself. "Try it, Mari. Try it and see." His smile moved to a grin. "You're fun like this. You know that?"

I scowled at him. "I want your promise that you won't hurt me when I . . . tell you what I came to say." I nodded to his right hand, where his second and third fingers were pressed to his thumb.

He shrugged and let his hand relax.

"Your promise."

He thought for a moment. Sighed. Winced. His lips were even more blue than they'd been just a minute before. He really didn't have much time.

"Please," I said.

I really, truly didn't want him to die. Or at least, I didn't want to be the one who killed him.

He studied me, a small line on his forehead. "All right. I promise. I won't hurt you when you tell me what you came to say."

"Now or as restitution later," I added.

His eyes widened. He tilted his head to the side. "What're you up to?"

I held out my hands. "Promise."

"Yes," he said impatiently. "Fine. Yes. I promise."

Okay. I know. A conjurer's promise lasts about as long as the time it takes to leave their mouth and reach your ears. It's practically worthless. What does Roumelade say? *"Don't gather promises. Deliver threats."*

Still.

"All right. When you met me in the hallway . . . when I was bloodied . . ."

"Ah. The great hallway incident. I see you worked that out."

Did he know? Was that why he'd told me to comb my hair? Did he know what I was?

"Do you . . . ?"

He tilted his head. "Do I what?"

I couldn't say it. I shook my head. Continued. "When you were helping me, I may have . . . accidentally poisoned you."

I waited for Luvic to conjure. For him to erupt. For a display of rage or violence.

Instead he held perfectly still. All his focus turned inward. It was as if he'd stopped breathing. His mind was working—I could practically see it churning.

Finally, he breathed out. "That's why I feel like I'm nearing death's embrace."

"Right. Because you are."

"Which poison?"

"Assassin's Hourglass."

He gave me a warm, admiring smile. "If this is how you treat friends, I'd love to see how you treat enemies."

I shrugged. "We're not exactly friends."

He made a questioning noise and then held his thumb and forefinger an inch apart. "Maybe a little bit friends."

"You know, I think I've had enough friend invites for one day."

He laughed, then he winced and coughed. "Last. She was dropped on her head as a baby. I know. It's in the records."

I held back a smile. It seemed Luvic was keeping his promise. He hadn't yet attempted revenge or retribution. Instead he was watching me as if I was infinitely interesting.

"I assume," he said, "since you're here, you aren't leaving me to the tender embrace of an early grave. I have to admit, I'm a bit hopeful you're not just here to brag. Or to battle it out with Celia. If so, I'd avoid Ragnor —he doesn't fight fair."

"No." I took a step forward, and Luvic watched me, seemingly relaxed. "I have the antidote—"

"Thank God."

"—and I'll let you have it for a trade."

"A trade?"

I nodded.

"And if I say no?"

"You die."

"But Mari. If I die, you die. Do you think my family would let you live?"

I shrugged. "I have plenty of lives."

Sort of. Not really.

Luvic smirked. Like he knew. "But . . . you'd be sad. Trust me. If I died, you'd be very, very sad."

I tapped my foot on the carpet. "Because we're friends?"

He grinned. "Now you're getting it."

"I'm not sure I want to be your friend. Actually, I'm pretty sure I don't."

His eyes gleamed with restrained humor. How could he be laughing when he was practically dangling by a thread over death's pit? "Tell me your favor."

"Two, actually," I said, ignoring his raised eyebrows. "First, the Smiths ask that you repay them with a future favor of their choosing, at their time of choosing."

He shook his head. A quick, dismissive cut. "No. A future favor only during the period of the games. Of their choosing, but only within my power, and only one that won't hurt me, my family, or someone I love."

That was fair. "Deal."

Luvic smiled.

"Second favor. Finn's solange dissolved Last's illusion. Her . . ." I waved my hand at my head. "You noticed it. She made a . . . history for us. She called it a memory crown."

For the first time, Luvic's blasé smile and mischievous grin turned to a harder, sharper-eyed mien. His lips flattened, and he held himself still. "And you want . . . ?"

Did he expect that I was going to ask him to kill her? Maim her?

"I need you to put a similar illusion on me. Just a small one. A few harmless memories, so she doesn't realize it's gone . . . so . . ." I trailed off at Luvic's grunt of surprise.

"You want . . . Ah, Mari. You're playing a game with Last. That's . . . fun."

You could call it that. If you were a maniac.

"I'll know what memories you plant," I tell him. "Nothing harmful. Nothing that influences my behavior. Nothing meant to sway or seduce. Nothing—"

Luvic waved a hand. "I don't need to make you like me. You already do. I don't need to make you do what I want. You're already doing it. Deal. We have a deal."

I sighed. Let out a relieved breath. He'd live. For some reason, it mattered. He'd live, and I'd have a favor and knots of illusion in my mind.

I freed the little turquoise and gold cut-glass bottle from my pocket.

Luvic stared at it, his gaze burning my hand.

"First, the illusion," I said.

His eyes flicked to mine. "Are you sure you want me in your head?"

"Just do it."

He twisted his hand, and I felt the slide of a delicate thread tightening around my skull, sinking into my mind. It was a lark's head knot, shimmering, the strands flapping like feathered wings on a cool breeze. The false memory soared into my mind, swooping in. It was only a fragment, the quick glide of sight and sensation.

It was a picture—or frames—of a movie. Twenty, thirty, slowed and viewed one by one. It was Luvic. He grinned at me. His eyes were scrunched, his hair a mess, and there was grass on his shirt and mud streaked across his cheek. The strong smell of freshly cut grass surrounded us. "Tag," he said, his voice melodious. "You're it."

Then he was tying another knot—this one a blood knot. It slid quickly into my skull, stabbing behind my right eye. I winced as the memory sliced into me. It was dark—so dark I couldn't see. I could only smell dirt, wet stone, and musty, stagnant air. The flash of a knife caught a dull glow and arched down toward me. "Luvic. No!" I yelled, thrusting my hands in front of me. "I swore I'd kill you," he said. Then the knife plunged into me, and I screamed.

I stumbled across the bedroom. Hit the bed and fell to my knees. Luvic slid another thread into my skull: a butterfly knot that fluttered and dusted my mind with its wings.

There were tears in my eyes. When I looked down, I was in an ivory dress, and when I reached up, I felt a crown of soft, cool roses. My lips quivered as I smiled at Luvic. He wore a gray suit with tails—one you'd wear to wedding—a white rosebud tucked in his lapel. He smiled at me. Not a mischievous smile, but a smile full of love. He put his hands to my cheeks and pressed a cool, happy kiss to my mouth.

I gasped and shoved back from the bed, stumbling to my feet. My heart pounded wildly as the illusions settled in my mind, flying, stabbing, and fluttering. I pressed a hand to the space between my shoulder and my heart, where I could still feel the sting of the knife.

Luvic watched me, his face blank. "Three memories," he said, his eyes lidded. "One for the past. One for the present. One for the future."

I shivered. They were illusions. Non-memories. Not real.

"Thank you," I said stiffly. These weren't like Last's illusions. They didn't twist my emotions or make me want to please. They were just . . . there.

Seeds planted to see if they'd grow.

Luvic smiled and held out his hand. "If you don't mind, I'd rather not die tonight."

"Right." I stepped forward and dropped the vial into his palm.

He unstopped the cork, tipped back his head, and swallowed the antidote in one go.

His eyes watered, he coughed, and then the blue tinge in his lips and fingertips fled. He dragged in a deep breath and coughed again.

He was all right. It was clear. Rou's antidote had worked. He was all right.

Although, considering the memories he'd shoved into my mind, I wasn't as happy about it as I'd thought. I was especially leery of the knife in the chest bit.

"So . . ." I said. "That's that."

Luvic swung his feet over the side of the bed, rolled his shoulders, and stretched. "That's better. To think, I thought it was all Primus. By the way . . ." He cut a glance at me out of the corners of his eyes.

I froze, worried he was about to threaten me because he'd figured out I was a lockpick.

But he only said, "Thank you. For . . . whatever you did."

I shrugged. "I didn't do anything. Just a bit of distraction. Enough that Primus let go of his illusion."

Luvic nodded. "Right. Well."

I gestured to the door. "I'd better go. It's late. The Smiths will . . ."

Luvic smiled. "Worry? Are they pacing the suite, worrying for you?"

Maybe.

Probably not.

I mean, why worry? Someone was either all right or they weren't. That was what happened when you went out on jobs. And what was this but another job?

"I'll walk you back," Luvic said, standing a little unsteadily. He shook his head, took a breath, and then said, "I'm all right. Just . . . fine."

He was still shaky. Wobbly from being strangled, slammed against a wall, and knocked unconscious. Anyone would be.

"You don't have to. I know the way."

"Trust me. If you walk out of here alone, there's a ninety-nine out of a hundred chance that you won't make it out of the courtyard alive. We Bards enjoy . . ."

"A good show? A murder mystery? A thriller?"

He grinned and opened his bedroom door. "A tragedy. We enjoy a good tragedy."

When he offered his arm, I took it. He delivered me safe and sound to the Smiths' front door.

37

THE SILENCE STRETCHED OVER ME, A COOL SHEET THAT FLUTTERED AND sighed as I shifted on the hardwood floor. The bedroom was lit by half-light—that whispery time between the dark night past and the bright morning to come.

I lay on my back on the floor, in front of the locked door, staring at a crack in the plaster ceiling—one not hidden or smoothed by illusion. The bedroom was warm and scented with warmed cranberry and allspice.

When I returned from the Bards' suite, the debriefing between Finn, Darin, and the Smith was finished, and Finn was lazily heating himself a thimble of solange (from a sealed/untampered bottle) before falling into bed.

Although the day had been long and tomorrow would be longer, I couldn't sleep. Instead I traced the crack on the ceiling, shifted on the hardwood, and listened to the silence. On the bed, Finn rolled onto his back and let out a sleep-filled sigh. His breathing was as steady and soothing as an ocean wave rolling onto soft sand and then washing back to sea.

"Are you awake?" I whispered, stretching my senses.

The sheets rustled, and Finn shifted.

"No," he mumbled.

I smiled into the dark. "Didn't think so."

It was quiet again. All except the stretch of skin over sheets, a low sigh, and a night moth fluttering and tapping against the windowpane. After a moment, it flew away, seeking brighter light.

We had at least four hours until morning. Perhaps I'd be able to fall asleep if I curled on my side.

"Mari?"

I tucked my head onto my curled arm and pressed my back against the door, staring at the shadowed bed. I could just make out the shape of Finn, his bare skin, the rumpled, kicked-away sheets.

"Can't sleep?" His voice was a soft rumble in the darkness, like distant thunder over the still, silent grass of a summer meadow.

"No." I sighed. "I can't stop thinking. I'm having . . . thoughts."

I couldn't see it, but I was certain he was smiling. He shifted, and I saw the pale flash of the underside of his arm as he folded his hands behind his head and stared at the four-poster bed's starry-night canopy.

"Would a bed help? You could—"

"I'm not sharing a bed with you."

"Have it."

Oh.

"No." I shifted on the floor, punched my pillow, and then wrapped my arms around myself. "If you gave me the bed, I'd like you more, and that's a problem, isn't it? I'm not supposed to like you."

He made a small, rumbly noise and then moved so one leg was bent. The curve of his knee glinted in the dull half-light. He was all angled form and half-shape, sleepy and relaxed.

"No, I wouldn't be able to sleep in that bed. I'd have nightmares about all the things that might crawl through the door to slaughter us while I slept comfortably on a too-plush feather mattress. It's my job to watch you. Make sure you survive until the end."

Finn scrubbed a hand over his face and then sent it through his messy black hair, rumpling it further. What was his expression? Exasperation? Fatigue? The vacant, glassy-eyed stare of solange? Or were his eyes lit with a starry, understanding light?

"I know someone," he said slowly, "who has trouble sleeping. Sleep is her elusive lover—the harder she chases it, the faster it runs."

I understood that. Too well.

At Hell Gate, sleep wasn't a refuge. It was an acknowledgement of defenselessness. An invitation for injury or harm. How could someone sleep deeply when they didn't feel safe?

Deep sleep, I think, is only for the ignorant or the blessed. Or, I suppose, the dead.

"What does your friend do, when she can't sleep?"

Finn sat up, leaning against the glossy wooden headboard. His chest was bare and shadowed, his arms folded behind his head. Maybe she curled against him. Maybe she laid her head on his warm chest, pressed her ear to his heart, and fell into the lulling rhythm of his breath.

"She'd talk," he said, a smile in his voice. "I'd make her a mug of chamomile tea. A spoon of honey. A tiny splash of milk."

All my senses stretched out to him, toward the warmth of his voice.

"Sometimes, while she talked, she'd pace. Or, if she was very tired, she'd sit with me, and I'd . . ." He paused, and I waited, feeling the curl of hot tea steaming through the room, and the warmth of a voice in the dark. "I'd listen. After an hour, sometimes two or three, all the thoughts, all the words . . . they were let out. Once she'd said the words, the emotion they were born from could rest. And so could she."

I waited for him to say more, but the room sank back to silence. Just the quiet rustle of a long sigh, the whisper of sheets, the scrape of my back against the wooden door . . .

And my thoughts.

"Could I . . .?" I stopped, started again. "Do you mind if I . . .?"

"I don't mind."

Maybe it was because Finn already knew my greatest secret. Maybe it was because I knew he only had a matter of weeks to live. Or maybe it was that he was already practiced in the art of listening to nighttime confessions. Whatever it was, I opened to him.

"You know I'm a nine?"

Finn made a soft noise of acknowledgment.

"Right. I'm a nine. I've been one since the day after my fourth birthday. I've always been a ward of Hell Gate, but I wasn't anything but human until…" Until what? What exactly happened? "I died. It was an ordinary death, I guess, as deaths go. Justice, my friend, wanted to kick a ball in the park, so I ran to my room to get this rubber ball that Rou, my … sort-of mom … gave me for my birthday. It was blue with a red star. Stupid thing to remember, but I clearly remember the red star and the powder blue color. I even remember the rubber smell of it and the bumpy feel of the cold rubber. I was at the top of the stairs. These big old stone steps they have in grand houses, you know?"

I didn't wait for his nod or acknowledgment; I was too lost remembering. "Justice and Griff were at the bottom of the stairs. I held up the ball, waving, and started to run down. Then I tripped. I thought I tripped. Later, Griff told me something invisible had shoved me. Flung me down the steps. I bounced down, just like that ball. But instead of bouncing harmlessly across the stone, I broke bones, I cracked my head, I … I hit the ground. And then Jagger was there. And he was saying, 'Mari. Mari, you're dying. You don't want to die, do you?' And I didn't, because I'd grown up hearing about how my parents had been murdered by . . . the conjurers . . . and how terrifying death's embrace was. 'You want to stay, don't you? You want to live, don't you?' I was choking on my own breath, and the pain was so much I could barely think. But I knew one thing. I *didn't* want to die like my parents. I wanted to live. So I nodded. 'I can give you nine lives,' Jagger said. 'I can give you nine, and then after, you'll be mine.' I knew what that meant. Even at four, I'd met some of Jagger's nines. Justice was already a nine. Griff too, and they both seemed fine. I'd even met one mine—this terrifying man who came in and out of Hell Gate at all hours. I was slipping away. Even a four-year-old knows what dying is. So I nodded again. 'Say it,' Jagger said. 'Say I give my death into your keeping, I give you mine.' I said it. Choking on air and blood, I said it. Then I died."

I shivered, thinking about the first time I'd left my body and moved as a shade through the shadowed valley of death. It was after, when I came back and lay paralyzed in my bed, unmoving, unseeing, crying with fear inside myself, with only Justice and Griff to keep me company, that I realized exactly what I'd done.

Justice had promised that someday he'd fix it. That he was sorry he hadn't warned me what Jagger might do. That someday our parents would come and rescue us—me, him, and Griff—and we'd go to our house in the Catskills with our white picket fence and our two gray kittens.

"When I came back, I had seven black lines tattooed on my wrist. Every time I died, another disappeared. Once there aren't any lines left, I'm on my ninth death. There won't be tattooed lines. Instead there'll be a rose, a thorn, and a drop of blood. Then, after that final death—my ninth —when the rose disappears, I'll not be a nine anymore."

Finn had sat up in bed during my story. He was no longer stretched out or relaxed or idly folding his hands behind his head. Instead his gaze was focused on my dark form. Even if I couldn't see him clearly, I could feel his attention on me. It wound itself around me and tied me tight, pulling all the worry knots and secrets out of me. I unraveled myself to him.

"After that, I'll be Jagger's. That's the price of the bargain. You get nine lives, but then your will is Jagger's. You aren't yours anymore. It's like he takes out a piece of your soul and puts a tiny seed of his own in its place. It takes root and strangles and sows . . . Do you know evil? How evil came into this world from one tiny seed? One little seed sewn into the heart of man?"

Finn nodded. A slow nod in the dark.

"Look at how much suffering and destruction that one seed caused. So, even with a heart of good, after my ninth death, what . . . what will I become? I'm terrified of it. Remember how it felt to be in the inquisitor's chair? How it compelled?"

"I remember," Finn said, his voice quietly reaching through the darkness.

"It's like that, but more. His will becomes yours. You are his. Entirely. Until . . . until you have your final, true death. I've wished . . . sometimes I've wished I never made that bargain. It terrifies me, the thought that someday I'll do horrific things. But then I've always comforted myself with the idea that while Jagger is evil, he's not as evil as the conjurers.

That by being his nine, I was able to fight against something worse than the cruelties of a leggerock.

"It's made my life easier, painting all conjurers as my parents' murderers—sadistic sociopaths, the originators of the greatest evils in the world. But . . . if that's the case . . . then why do I . . . almost . . . sort of . . . like you? You're half-conjurer. And why, after a day, do I find myself softening toward Darin? Even if he could or might kill me without a second thought. Why do I want to help Luvic, a Bard, when his family has sewn so much strife around the world? Why do I want to help you, help Luvic, help Darin, when helping you could mean I die another death? I only have two deaths left. After that? I'm not mine anymore. I'm his."

Finn's gaze pinned me to the door. "He can't have you."

I jerked back, pulled from the deep dark that had wound itself around me. "What?"

"He won't have you," Finn repeated.

I sat upright, letting the blanket fall away. Through the dark, there was the glint and swirl of Finn's cosmic eyes. A low hum of energy pulsed around him.

"You don't really have a say," I said quietly. "It's a bargain I made. It's the price I have to pay."

"If I win the games, Jagger promised me a nine of my choice. I've decided. I choose you."

I held still, my heart pounding against my ribs. "If you win the games, Jagger has already promised my freedom." Then I remembered the condition attached to my freedom. "If I kill you. That's the key . . . if I kill you."

"How about," Finn asked, an enticing promise in his voice, "we skip the killing, and I'll just choose you?"

I smiled, although I wasn't certain he could see me. He leaned back against the headboard, relaxed once more.

The quiet fell around us—the hush of plaster walls, old brick, and thick silk rugs. It was a comfortable, secrets-opened-and-aired kind of quiet.

"It's all right, Mari," Finn mused, tilting his head to look up at the embroidered canopy of gold and silver stars. "It's okay to love good when you see it. As long as you remember that sometimes good isn't good; it's a lie masquerading as truth. But true good? Don't feel conflicted about softening toward that."

Finn knew all about lies masquerading as truth. After all, he was a solange addict in the middle of an illusioned world. He could see through all the illusions. Unfortunately, it didn't give him the power to see the illusions in people's motives—true good, falsehood, lies, or truths.

I peered at him through the dark. "And if the good is in a Bard? Or a Smith? If I believe it's true?"

"Ah. Well. Half of me is Smith. I would say . . . it isn't necessarily my blood or my name that makes me who I am. It's the fork I come to every minute of every day, and the choice I make—which path?"

"Are you telling me not all conjurers are bad? That I should trust some of them?"

He breathed a quiet huff, an almost-laugh. "No. Never trust a conjurer. Just . . . trust me."

"Not a chance."

He hummed. "Trust me to choose you?"

"And if you lose? If you die? And if I become a mine and my deeds become more evil than all the conjurers combined? What then?"

He sighed. Mused, "What then?"

I swallowed, frightened at the prospect of Finn dead, the crown in a Clark or a Ward or even a Bard's hands. Me under Jagger's will.

"What then?" I whispered.

"I'll just have to win. We'll have to make certain you don't die."

He made it sound so simple. So certain.

"Why would you care? Why would you help me? It's not . . . it isn't to your benefit."

He stood. Padded across the hardwood floor, then the soft rugs, until he was standing over me. He was lean, a tall shadow of muscle and wide shoulders. He wore only a pair of shorts, nothing else. He held out a hand.

"Up. You can have the bed. I'll sleep here."

"Why?" I stared at his hand.

He smiled, and this close, I could see the exact curve of his lips and the spark in his eyes. "I know it isn't to my benefit. Go climb into bed. Sleep."

I took his hand. Let him pull me upright. I held on a little longer than necessary. Felt the warmth, the callouses, the strength and sinew. His warmth flooded down my arm and into my chest, curling softly, like a purring cat circling and lying down in a warm, contended ball.

As I held his hand, I asked, "Do you ever wish you could change the world?"

His eyelashes drifted down, and his smile widened. "All the time."

"And what do you do?"

He shrugged. "Change myself."

I stepped closer. The heat rolled off his bare skin; the rainstorm scent of him wrapped itself around me.

"I would've been very lucky to have known you," I said, my throat tight, "for longer than two weeks. I would've considered myself very lucky to be your friend."

"Thank you." He tilted his head, his eyelashes lowering to cover his expression. It felt as if there was more, as if there was a precipice with a great, yawning expanse of words yet to be said. But instead Finn raised his head, gave me a soft smile, and said, "Night, Mari."

He stretched out in front of the door.

I curled up on the feather mattress, in the warmth he'd left behind, and slept like the blissfully ignorant. The safe and protected. Like the dead.

38

THE DAY PASSED IN A HAZE OF ERRANDS THAT TAUGHT ME EXACTLY WHAT IT meant to be a body. While Wolfgang, Darin, and Finn congregated in the sitting room I'd dubbed "the war room," I ran downstairs, upstairs, down halls, and around halls.

According to Wolfgang, I'd been lax in my duties. He gave the terse, disapproving lecture of a commanding officer to his negligent soldier.

My duties were—and this is a pared-down list—strip the bed, wash the linens, confirm the linens hadn't been soaked in poison, remake the bed. Repeat, but with Finn's clothes. Sweep the floors. Mop the floors. Clean the bathroom. Draw Finn a bath with a tincture for sore muscles. Rub his shoulders and any tight muscles while he took said bath (refused. I refused). Tend to any wounds. Stitch, bandage, or medicate. Empty the bins of trash. Tidy the room. Dust. Prepare the family breakfast from their store of food (sesame bagels, cream cheese, fruit). Clean up. Prepare lunch (chicken, potatoes, asparagus). Clean up. Prepare dinner (udon noodles with thinly sliced sirloin and sesame dressing). Clean up. Serve hot coffee, iced coffee, hot tea, iced tea, and any other beverage any of them wanted, whenever they wanted it. Above all, see to Finn's comfort, health, and safety. In all ways. All the time. And, as an afterthought, I, myself, should try to stay alive.

Let's just say, my gray silk uniform was sticky with sweat, my arms and legs were sore from a day of scrubbing and carrying, and I was short-tempered from how many times Darin had told me his coffee was too hot, then too cold, then too hot again, then . . . too bitter, make it again, then too weak, make it again, then . . .

I'd have dumped the pot on him if Wolfgang weren't there.

The grizzled Smith often held out his mug when I passed through the sitting room with an armful of something to wash, not looking at me, just expecting I'd fill it—immediately, without fuss. No words. No thanks. He was a principal. I was invisible.

Which was a good thing to be when it came to conjurers. So that wasn't terrible. It wasn't even too terrible when Darin told me to remake the coffee for the fourth time.

What was terrible was how Finn murmured, "Thank you," when I set a drink in front of him, and how he gave me distracted half-smiles when I walked through the sitting room. And how, when he tasted the chicken I'd sautéed on the Smith's hot plate, he made a surprised humming sound before murmuring happily, "This is . . . I love thyme. Thanks, Mari."

That thanks tugged at the warmth that had curled and settled in my chest last night. It pulled and stroked and made me tingle and glow. Something as inane as a thank you. That was stupid. That was terrible.

Meanwhile, throughout the day, Wolfgang and Darin strategized in tense, quiet voices, while Finn lounged on the low leather couch, his gaze unfocused, contemplating . . . who knew? Solange? His almost-wife? The games and all the machinations?

It seemed last night, while Finn, Darin, and I were out and about, five Bards had been viciously, bloodily, noisily slaughtered in their hotel suite. The police, thanks to a bit of manipulation by the Bards, believed it to be drug violence. But the conjurers were looking amongst themselves.

"Did you do it?" Wolfgang asked.

There were many in the hallways whispering that it was Darin and his null half-brother who'd attacked them. After all, they'd been seen leaving the Bard Mansion late last night. No one, apparently, remembered me in the group—thanks, I supposed, to my being so forgettable. Or maybe they just didn't think a body was worth mentioning.

"No, I didn't." Darin studied the photos Wolfgang handed him. Squinted at the thin, bladelike slashes on the bodies. "Looks like Clark work."

Wolfgang nodded. Scratched his chin. "Or a Bard play-acting as a Clark. We still don't know who killed Secondus and Morjorie."

Darin nodded. "Not Phillip."

"Not Phillip."

So it'd been obvious to more people than just me. Which made me wonder, was it meant to be obvious?

Then Wolfgang turned to the prospect of the next game and how Finn could win it. "You won the Bard game through sheer luck," he claimed.

I heard him as I passed through with the bedsheets in my arms. I gave Finn a quick glance. He smiled at me, his eyes crinkling.

Then I remembered Cora pressing her fingers to his lips and saying, "All my luck is yours." Was that it? Was that how he'd won the first game? His good luck charm had helped him?

"Now we have the Clarks to contend with. Luck won't do you much good there—their games are more savagery than skill. You'll need ruthlessness more than luck."

I didn't hear Finn's response.

I only wondered, could he be ruthless if needed? Could he be like Justice? Like Jagger? Even like Darin and Wolfgang? Could he be like them? Or was he *already* like them?

The first game was the Bards. On the compass, they were the west. The games were always played counterclockwise. The next direction was the south. The Clarks.

From the records I'd read, they usually replayed some twisted version of history. They seemed to believe there was no reason to think of a new game when history held so much inspiration. It was why I'd been plunged into the East River by Herman Clark, iron chains wrapped around me. It was why I was banking on the fact that they'd be pulling something from the past.

And when I met up with Last, I was determined to find out as much as I could.

I'd take whatever advantage we could get. Even if it meant having a slumber party with my enemy.

At ten o'clock sharp, I knocked on the blue door next to the Caesar statue on the third floor. I'd barely gotten half a knock in before the door was flung open and Last had yanked me inside.

All day, I'd been prepping myself, catching my expression in every mirror I passed, attempting a glassy-eyed, worshipful look.

I thought of how I'd felt, what I'd said, when I believed we were friends. I let myself luxuriate in the faded, photocopied memories Last had stapled into my past. I flipped through the scrapbook of memories and let myself feel all the good feelings, all the joy, all the warmth.

So when I knocked on that primrose-blue door, I'd stoked all the good feelings until the photocopy was a vibrant photo in front of me again, and I was Last's dear friend. I couldn't think or feel anything else. My life, and maybe Finn's, depended on it.

"Mari," Last laughed, her bright gaze raking over me.

She was in brown wool pants and a brown Oxford, her dark hair in a tight knot. She was pale, with blue shadows under her eyes. Blue-green veins stood out on her thin skin. She was so skinny that her joints stuck out at sharp angles. Immediately, a spurt of worry pulsed through my chest. Hadn't she been eating? Sleeping?

"Last, let me do something for you," I said.

She still held my hand. Hers was cold.

"You look tired. Hungry. Let me make you something to eat. Please? I've missed you. Let me do something for you."

I couldn't help it—there was still that spark there that I'd kindled into a flame. I wanted to take care of her. I wanted to love her.

A grunt sounded from the far side of the room. I noticed the Clark body was here again, shaking his head and rolling his eyes.

"Mush," he muttered. "She mushed her."

"What does it matter?" Last snapped. "She's *my* friend—aren't you, Mari? You'd let me do anything to you, wouldn't you?"

I nodded, thinking of the night we'd stayed awake until three, eating popcorn and watching *Spartacus*. I smiled at her, imagining the taste of butter and salt, cuddling under blankets together.

"Yes. Anything."

Another grunt. But this wasn't from the body. The noise came from the corner. It was Primus.

He was leaning over a large, wooden table—the thick, heavy-legged kind you see in castles from the fourteenth century—dressed in black, the spill of lamplight absorbed by the inky dark of his clothes. On the table were dozens of open ledgers, leather-bound record books, and other archive documents I recognized from the times I'd stolen from them.

Primus didn't look at me or Last. He merely scowled down at the record he was reading and said mockingly, "Would she die for you, sister?"

Last looked at me, her eyes turning limpid, a question in them.

My heart thundered in my chest, beating painfully down my arm to where she gripped my hand. My lips were numb, but I held her gaze—held the feeling of what it meant to love her. My hand shook.

"Does he . . . does he want me to?" I whispered. A tear dripped down my cheek, and, surprised, I wiped it away.

"Would you?" Last tilted her head, birdlike and curious.

I nodded. "Yes."

I would. I had to believe it so she would believe it. And maybe that meant I really would. Who knew? More curious things had happened in the world.

"Maybe I should get a friend," Primus said, tossing aside a thick record book. "Except, no. I like fear better than friendship. What is your name?"

I froze.

Last smiled at me encouragingly. We were one happy family here. Happy in the way that only Clarks could be.

Last paraded me in front of Primus, tugging me after her. I was forced to keep up, and then to stand in front of him like a student in front of the harsh-faced schoolmaster.

The room was all dark, wood-paneled walls, bookshelves, red carpet, and bronze fixtures. Dim light, drawn curtains. It smelled of parchment, mothballs, and dry earth.

Primus stood, shoving his stiff-backed chair away from the table. He towered, a gaunt giant, over me and his sister. His fingers tapped against his thumb as if he were contemplating all the illusions he'd like to conjure.

"Mari," I whispered.

"That is *not* your name," he said, scraping his hollow gaze over me. "Take note—the body does not know her name. Your name is One. That is the name of my sister's first friend. Just as his name"—he pointed to the Clark body—"is Twelve. As he is my twelfth body. Do you understand?"

Twelfth body? Eleven bodies came before that one? What happened to them all?

No. Never mind. I knew.

My hand shook. My throat was tight as I said, "Yes."

"Yes, what?"

What did he mean, "yes, what?"

"Yes, sir?"

"No. Not yes, sir. Take note—One does not know how to address her betters. Take note—the Smiths do not know how to train a body. You will call me Heir Clark. You will call my sister Friend Last. Do you understand?"

"Yes, Heir Clark."

I have to admit, I almost broke into a hysterical laugh right then and there. It itched my throat; it climbed through my chest. I'd never been so scared and confronted with such ridiculous sociopathy in my life. Not even in Hell Gate. The Clarks were the conjurers I'd always imagined.

"One." Primus waited.

Last pinched my side.

"Yes, Heir Clark?"

"My sister tells me you are to poison Heir Ward and Paladin Smith. Have you done so?"

I dropped my head, my cheeks flushing. That spark I'd kindled, the love for Last, made me feel shame. "I poisoned Paladin Smith, but not yet Heir Ward."

"And what happened to Paladin Smith?"

"He became sloppy and confused. Sedated and drunk. It wore off, Heir Clark."

Primus frowned. "Do it again before the game tomorrow."

"Yes, Heir Clark."

"You must poison Heir Ward before the game as well."

"Yes, Heir Clark."

He liked that. He smiled, thin and tight. "Sister, your friend is a delight."

She nodded and then said, her eyes narrowing, "You can't have her."

Primus ignored her. "My sister tells me you are meant to kill Luvic Bard and Ragnor Bard. Have you done so?"

He knew darn well I hadn't done so.

I kept my gaze limpid, thinking of marshmallows and chocolate and riding bikes with Last in Central Park.

"I haven't seen Ragnor Bard. I poisoned Luvic Bard with a deadly poison. However, he recovered."

Primus smacked his desk. I jumped. A cloud of dust flew into the air, and the record books shook.

"Take note—One does not remember how to address her betters. One does not know how to kill. One is an incompetent friend."

I dropped my head, cheeks flushed red. "I apologize, Heir Clark."

"One, what is the definition of kill?"

"To . . ." I stuttered. What was he looking for? "To . . ." I looked over at Last, wondering what she thought of her brother taking over her friend.

"Twelve, define 'kill' for One. She is a stupid body. The Smiths do not know how to train or utilize their bodies."

"Yes, Heir Clark," Twelve said in a gratingly eager voice. "To kill. End life. Remove head. Stop brain. Stop heartbeat. Stop animation. Stop breath. Remove spirit of being from corporal form. Kill."

What the . . . ?

"One, take note. That is the definition of kill. When you are asked by my sister to kill Luvic Bard and Ragnor Bard, you will do so."

I nodded. "Yes, Heir Clark."

I shivered. That oil-slick, dirty feeling that coated the Clark body was wrapping itself around me like a ragged cloak. I wanted to shrug it off. I wanted to take a bath and scrub it away.

"Are we done?" Last asked, her voice a high whine. "I want to play with my friend."

"Sister?"

She sighed. Restrained the veiled hatred I'd seen her aim at Primus's back at the opening ceremony. "Yes, Brother?"

"Principal Clark asked that you be punished for your failure to find Secondus's killer."

Last gasped. "He dares!"

Primus smacked his desk again. "He is your principal!"

My nose itched from the dust motes flying in the air. I held back a sneeze.

"I'm looking," Last hissed. "I'll find whoever did it."

"Meanwhile," Primus said, "what shall your punishment be?"

He circled his hand, spinning, spinning, inviting an answer.

"Perhaps One would give a suggestion."

I swallowed, a hard lump in my throat. "No, Heir Clark."

"Take note." He smiled coldly. "One does not know that One may never say no to a Clark."

He conjured an ivory-handled letter opener, its dull blade milky in the low light.

"This isn't fair," Last said. "I found her. I made her my friend. You can't kill her just to punish me. It's not fair."

"Thank you, Last," I said, feeling all sorts of warm fuzzies toward her.

She gasped and slapped my cheek. "*Friend* Last. My brother told you to call me *Friend* Last."

"Take note," Primus said, holding out the letter opener. "As punishment for my sister's failure, and as punishment for her own transgressions, One will carve 'Friend Last' into her thigh. Proceed."

I stared at the letter opener.

"Proceed."

Last sniffed. Her eyes grew teary. "I hate punishments. They hurt me so much."

"Proceed."

I took the cold, ivory-handled letter opener from Primus. I pushed down the silk of my uniform and carefully carved "Friend Last" into my thigh. The blood ran down my leg and soaked into the silk.

Last watched with wide, hungry eyes. Primus didn't watch at all—he'd gone back to flicking through the dry vellum of the record books, ignoring everything but the ancient writing in front of him.

When I was finished, Last smiled, sated and happy. "Would you like to watch a movie with me?"

I nodded, my leg stinging and burning, eyes watering. "Above all things."

We watched a comedy. Last conjured me a box of chocolates. I ate all twelve truffles and got numbingly, dizzily drunk on them. The TV lights played over the wood paneling, the bookshelves, and the red carpet, flickering happily to the sound of mine and Last's laughter.

The body, Twelve, stood in the corner, watching us with his oil-slick stare. Primus sat at his desk, ignoring us, scratching notes into the side margins of the record books.

At midnight, Last hugged me, and I hugged her back, nearly too dizzy to stay upright. My bones buzzed, my blood fizzed, and I smiled drunkenly at her.

"I had the best night, Friend Last."

She stroked my hair. "One? If you die, will you still love me?"

I tilted my head. It felt as if it might float off my neck and bob against the ceiling. "I don't know, Friend Last. I don't know what happens when I die."

She looked disappointed at my answer. "I'll find you," she said. "My father says you're a creature. That you'll come back. I'll find you so we're always friends. Would you like that?"

I smiled, my lips wobbling. The room spun, the bookshelves spun—maybe even I did too. She held me tight.

"Don't forget to poison Jacob and the paladin tomorrow, before the game. My brother is counting on you."

I nodded, my head heavy, the room spinning. I was buzzy and happy. The room was floaty.

"Send One on her way," Primus demanded from the corner, not

looking up from his records. "She has a busy day tomorrow. It will be eventful for her."

There was something in his voice that made my skin crawl. It dimmed the warm glow Last's chocolates had infused in me.

"Goodnight, One," Last said, patting my cheek. "I'll miss you."

When I stumbled into the Smith suite, Finn was the only one still awake. He took one look at me, then his eyes blazed with a cosmic, fiery rage. He'd been sprawled out, sleepy-eyed and twirling a thimble of solange in one hand, humming a familiar tune. What was it? What . . .? But then he practically fell off the couch, stumbled upright, and snatched me to him.

"What happened?"

I hiccupped and then giggled.

His gaze narrowed on the blood on my silk pants, and there were, I swear, explosions in his eyes. The stars, the nebula—they collided in a terrifying cosmic storm.

"What happened, Mari?"

"You like me," I said, my words slurring as I slumped against his chest. The tingle from the chocolates was riding through my skin, and when I touched him, my whole body lit and sparked. "You like me lots. I can tell, 'cause you're angry, and that means you like me."

He gently took my arms and held me away from him. I swayed, smiling up at him.

"Hi, Finn."

He let out a long breath—trying, I think, to bring all the rage swirling inside him under control.

"Hi, Mari," he said, his voice a quiet rumble. It was filled with the threat of lightning and destruction. But not for me. I was standing in the eye of the storm, where it was calm and quiet and safe.

"Don't be angry," I said, blinking at him.

He was out of focus, and his features were shifting. His eyes moved from navy blue to greenish-gold and brown. Hazel? His face blurred. Became softer. His mouth was full and reminded me of strawberries and cream, cinnamon and sugar, shaded glades and stretching out on cool gray boulders to kiss and kiss and . . .

"Do I know you?" I squinted.

His features rearranged, swirling and shifting.

"I think I know you. Finn. Hazel-eyed Finn Alterra."

He grunted. "You're drunk. What did they give you?"

"Conjured chocolate. I love it."

He made another noise. Guided me through the sitting room to the bedroom, and then to the en suite bathroom I'd cleaned earlier that day.

"Stay here."

I stood in the tiled bathroom, in the stark white light, staring at my reflection. As I looked at the perfectly symmetrical features, the upwardly curved lips, the high cheekbones and wide eyes, I began to yearn.

It was a dizzy, chocolate-infused, stupid, beautiful face yearning. What was I yearning for?

Finn.

I'm ashamed to admit I was yearning for Finn.

He came back in, unaware that the bright red splotches on my cheeks were because I'd pictured him in only his shorts, his chest slick with sweat, his (hazel) eyes burning with love. I'd pictured him over me, in me, kissing me, loving me.

It was the chocolates. They'd fried my brain. Made it mush.

He handed me a cold bottle of water. The condensation ran down the plastic and dripped over my hands.

"Drink it," he said softly. "I'm going to clean you up."

"That's my job," I said as he kneeled on the tile in front of me. "I'm s'posed to take care of you."

He made an irritated noise. He had a warm washcloth, a bowl of soapy water, and antiseptic. Ointment and bandages. "I'm just going to . . ." He cleared his throat. "Is it all right if I inspect where you're bleeding?"

Inspect.

Inspect?

I smiled down at him. "Uh-huh."

He frowned at me and carefully untied the drawstring of my silk pants. Then he gently slid them down my legs. I winced as the fabric scraped over the cuts on my thigh.

"What the . . .?" Finn stiffened, and I thought perhaps he was about to lose control. The cold tiled bathroom filled with a strange, pulsing energy. A violent, solange-tinted storm. "Who did this?"

I touched his shoulder.

He looked away from the blood on my thigh. His features were stony. His body taut. "Mari. Who did this?"

The buzzy dizziness of the chocolates faded. The effervescent fizz slowed to a trickle. "Me." I squeezed his shoulder reassuringly. "It was a job, Finn. It was just a job. I've been hurt worse."

He closed his eyes. "I don't want you hurt at all."

I smiled. What a funny statement. "You can't live without getting hurt. That's how life works."

He nodded. Dipped the washcloth into the warm water and then slowly dabbed the cuts on my thigh. It stung, but I held onto his shoulders and let him wipe away the blood.

He sighed as he pressed the washcloth to the cuts, cleaning out any chance of infection. My skin tingled as he ran the warm, scratchy cloth over my thigh. He wrung out the washcloth, and the sound of tinkling water cascaded over me. He concentrated, his brow puckered, as he wiped free every smear and speck of blood.

I smiled down at his bowed head, the dark gloss of his hair, the slight wave at the ends. He was kind. He was good.

A true good. I was sure of it.

"Thank you," I said as he gently pressed antibiotic ointment into my cuts.

He shook his head like there was nothing to thank him for.

"Thank you," I said again, squeezing the broad width of his shoulders, thinking how they'd be wide enough to carry so many of life's burdens. "I'm glad you like me," I said as he bandaged the cuts. Then I admitted, because I was drunk on conjured chocolates, "I'm a bit jealous of your Cora. Your almost-wife. She's very lucky. I bet she doesn't know how lucky."

He finally looked up from his kneeling position. I was struck by the sight of him. My breath went tight in my lungs.

He smiled, and I knew he was thinking about the woman he loved, because he looked as if he was reliving their first kiss.

"Let's get you to bed," Finn said.

I thought maybe he meant us, together, which didn't make sense—but then he scooped me up and carried me to the big four-poster bed and laid me gently on it.

"I'm not sleeping here again."

He shrugged. "I'm sleeping in front of the door. You can sleep where you like."

Oh. Okay. Well, that was all right then.

I closed my eyes. Finn turned out the lights. He padded to the door. I started to sink into sleep. Then I jerked up in bed, eyes open, wide-awake.

"Oh!"

Finn jumped to his feet as if someone had just burst into the room, sword drawn, ready to attack.

"What? Where?" He spun around, light on his feet.

"Finn. No. I know what the game is."

He paused. Stared at me with wide eyes.

I nodded. "Exactly. I know what game the Clarks made. Last told me. I know what you're playing tomorrow."

"You do?"

I nodded again.

Finn grinned, and I smiled back.

39

THE CLARKS GAME WASN'T UNTIL TWO, WHICH GAVE FINN, DARIN, AND Wolfgang an entire morning and an early afternoon to work through what I'd learned. Though I didn't think Last had lied about the game, we couldn't be certain, so they'd also prepared for other scenarios.

While Darin had a lifetime of education and preparation—even knowing he'd lose—Finn was walking into these games as ignorant as a baby. "Fool," Wolfgang had called him. "Fool," the Bard had laughingly sneered. "Fool," the Clarks had recorded in their books. "Fool," the Wards believed.

"Fool" had been shot around so often I'd stopped hearing it.

It seemed to me that the conjurers had all forgotten there was more than one type of illusion. I kept those thoughts to myself. If they couldn't see the knot, I wouldn't untie it for them.

Meanwhile, Wolfgang decided I'd stay useful as a spy by continuing to ingratiate myself to the Clarks. Which meant I had to poison Jacob with Dainty Drink before the game.

He said it casually, in the middle of contemplating the walking dead. I filled his coffee mug while he spoke.

"... the catacombs are full of bones. Body, go do the Clarks' bidding. You are marginally useful as a spy. The bones will rise, I think, as they did in the 700th . . ." He frowned at me, a grizzled bear, cranky and impatient. "Body, *go*."

I left.

It was fine. I'd told Finn everything I knew about the Clarks' plan and the layout of the catacombs last night. We'd leaned against the door and talked into the shadows while I told him about the one and only time I'd been to the catacombs. While we pondered history.

After a while, I'd drifted off, my head falling to his shoulder. In the morning, I'd woken up in the bed.

Now I was at the Wards' suite. I peered left. I looked right. There was an eerie statue of a satyr with horses' legs and horses' ears but a man's leering face. The statue watched me with a Dionysian smirk—an invitation to mischief and revelry.

I imagine the satyr's placement at the Ward's door was a joke from the Bards. The Wards weren't known for revelry, or for the wild, drunken orgies satyrs loved. It would've been more fitting to have a statue of the minotaur and his labyrinth, or Arachne weaving her silken web.

I'd been watching the hallway for an hour when I saw Jacob and his father hurrying past. The Ward looked over his shoulder as if he'd heard or seen someone watching. Then he murmured something to his son, and Jacob searched the hallway. My heart thudded as I remembered the painful constriction of his illusion. But then he shook his head, and they were gone.

I didn't know where the body was. Or Uliea. But I had to take a chance.

Their door was painted a deep forest green. It was locked, of course, but a lockpick didn't just unlock illusions. I pulled out my tools from the bag I'd looped over my shoulder, and in seconds, I had the door open. I slipped inside and quietly shut it after me.

I'd found that each of the suites matched the personality of the family. The Wards played in the mental realm. They believed reason, wisdom, and mental acuity were the highest ideals. The good Wards— the rare ones in history whom I'd read about—were the conjurers who helped shine a light through prejudice, superstition, or fear by using the illumination of reason. Of truth.

Remember what Roumelade said? That after the flood it was the youngest Ward who drank from the well of knowledge? If that story is true, it would've had to have been a Ward, because they're the one family who value knowledge, truth, and reason above all else.

Matching that, the suite had cool white walls and light birchwood floors. It was airy and open, with wide windows overlooking an illusioned field, where the sun shone and the wind blew a rippling sea of golden wheat. The curtains shifted and danced, and a soft breeze tickled the silk of my uniform.

Other than that, there were white couches, a coffee table with a bowl of fresh fruit, a glass vase of pink freesia. It smelled of wind, sunshine, and fresh air. The only noise was the soft whisper of the curtains brushing over the hardwood.

I tiptoed across the room, keeping my eyes open for anything that would help Finn in the games, and searching for how I might slip Dainty Drink to Jacob with his lunch.

"Who are you?"

I froze.

The suite wasn't empty. I'd gambled and lost.

I was halfway across the entry room. The door was twenty feet back. There was a wide hallway to the right, and an arched entry to another room to the left.

Uliea stood in the entryway. She held a silver tea tray. It held a pot of tea—the ceramic kind, with painted violets, bluebirds holding ribbons, and swirling vines. There were three teacups, saucers, a bowl of sugar cubes, and a small pitcher of milk.

I held still. She peered at me as if she were underwater and I was blurred by ocean waves. Or perhaps she thought I was a figment—one of the figures that danced in and out of her madness.

"Ah." She smiled, her confusion smoothing and her gaze focusing. "You came back. I knew you would. I told them you would. Have you come for tea?"

I could've said no. I should've said no. But Uliea wasn't the terrifying woman from before the first game—the one vowing death and destruction by her daughter's hands. Instead she was placid calm, gentle smiles, and warm invitation.

She walked forward, her cool-blue silk dress rustling in the breeze. Once you looked past the ruin of her grief and the twisted maze of her madness, she was beautiful, in a pale, airy way. She looked so much like her son that you knew exactly how he'd age. Slight, pink-skinned, golden haired, green-eyed. I wondered if Viola had looked just like her too. Supposedly, she was Jacob's mirror, and since Jacob looked just like his mom, I imagined Viola did too.

Uliea slid the silver tray onto the coffee table, the saucers and cups tinkling. "Sit. Sit down. Have you seen Jacob?"

Okay. So Uliea seemed to be under the impression we'd met. That we were friendly. I wasn't going to disabuse her of this notion. In fact, if that tea was for Jacob, I was going to poison his little bluebird cup and then hurry out before he and his murderous father returned.

I touched my earlobes, reassuring myself Roumelade's earrings were where they should be—just in case.

"I . . . umm . . . no. I haven't seen him."

Uliea frowned, her forehead wrinkling. "That's too bad. He's been so lonely. Since . . . since . . ." Her forehead smoothed out. "Since his fourth birthday. When he . . ."

Exploded his sister. Yeah.

"Shattered his mirror . . ." she finished.

That was one way of putting it.

She perched elegantly on the couch and patted the cushion next to her.

"Thank you." I sat. The cushion was stiff—the antique, not-too-comfortable type of seat. "Are you expecting Jacob to be back soon?"

"Of course. We're having tea before the game. Jacob likes tea. And shortbread. He likes shortbread. Do you know what I think you should do?"

I shook my head slowly. I was tense, my heart a jackrabbit, racing through my chest, but I kept my face relaxed and happy. "No. What?"

"You should find the key."

"Sorry?"

Uliea blinked. Stared as if we were underwater again and the currents were swirling around us. "Who are you?" she asked finally.

Her eyes were no longer placid, her features no longer calm. Her left hand twitched as if she were about to conjure a nasty surprise.

A shrill whistle pierced the quiet. I jerked and looked around the room.

"Ah. The water's ready. That's for Jacob's pot. He prefers gunpowder tea, while I prefer Darjeeling. Will you be a dear and retrieve it for me? He'll be back soon."

The pot was still whistling. It was a sharp warning. Jacob and his dad would be back any second. Yet . . . here was a chance to drop Dainty Drink into his beverage.

"Of course."

Uliea smiled at me as if I'd just granted her dearest wish.

I moved carefully from the couch and then across the room, into the kitchen. I poured the steaming kettle into a second tea pot and dropped in the gunpowder leaves to soak. Then I poured in enough drops of Dainty Drink to make Jacob as drunk as a lightweight at his bachelor party. There was a plate of shortbread, so I grabbed that as well and hurried back to the sitting room.

Uliea sipped a cup of tea and smiled at me when I returned. I was focused on the seconds ticking by, on saying goodbye and hurrying away, on carrying the hot teapot and the plate of shortbread. Which was why I didn't notice the illusion in my path.

It was a trap—one the families used regularly to guard private spaces from intruders. I'd been avoiding similar traps for more than a decade. They were like mouse traps: a bit of cheese, a little bait, and then—*snap* —your neck was broken. Or they were toothy steel traps, where jaws clamped down on you, and the only way out was to gnaw off your own leg.

I stepped into the loop. It was a constrictor knot. As soon as my foot hit the illusion, a steel bear trap sprang into existence. One move, and the jaws would clamp around my leg.

"Oh dear." Uliea set the teacup down and wiped her hands on a linen napkin. "My husband leaves his toys all over the house. I always tell him not to, but . . . men."

"Well." I smiled and held out the tea and cookies. "If you don't mind. Could you disable it?"

She stared at the plate of shortbread and said, "Dear, just step out of it. It won't hurt you."

I wasn't so sure, but clearly, she wasn't going to be any help. I followed the rope of illusion, found the knot—the impossibly tied constrictor knot. If I worked it very, very carefully, with a marlinspike and . . .

"No, no," Uliea said. "Just step out." She cocked her head.

Outside the door, I could hear loud voices—the sound of people passing by.

"Ah. Here they come." She motioned for me to drop the tea and shortbread on the table.

I didn't have time to untie the knot. I was well and truly trapped. But maybe Uliea was telling me the trap wasn't real; that it was disabled or fake or . . .

I stepped out of it.

The jaws didn't snap. The teeth didn't clamp my ankle and slice through bone. Instead the steel jaws dissolved.

A tingle of relief washed through me. What kind of place was this? Who purposely set traps that didn't spring?

Uliea smiled. It was blindingly brilliant. Her green eyes grew watery. "You're going?"

I'd set the pot and shortbread down and was already hurrying to the door. "Yes. Thank you for the visit."

That's me. Always polite.

She waved. "Don't stay away for so long next time."

I opened the front door. Looked left and right. Jacob and Philoneas were at the end of the hall, their backs turned, speaking to Primus.

When Primus saw me, his eyes narrowed, and then he smiled. He drew Jacob and Philoneas's attention close, and I slipped from the Ward suite and hurried in the opposite direction.

It was nearly noon. I'd need to make lunch for everyone before the game. I hurried toward the stairs. The Wards were on the fourth floor, above the Bards and the Clarks, but below the Smiths.

At the fifth-floor landing, three turns and one flight up from the Ward's suite, toward the center of the mansion, I paused and then carefully crept forward. There was the hushed murmur of two men talking: a scraping, eager voice, which was an oil slick on my skin; and a quiet, demanding rumble.

The fifth floor didn't have a family suite. It housed overflow rooms for all the family members and guests not staying in the main suites. There were plenty of conjurers rooming on this floor. But there weren't any conjurers with voices so recognizable.

I peeked around the corner. Jerked back.

It was Finn.

And Twelve.

They were huddled close. Finn was clearly giving directions. He gestured with his hand and spoke in a low, demanding tone that was *just* like his father's. Twelve, the gaunt Clark body, seemed just as eager to please Finn as he was to please Primus.

Was Finn in league with Twelve? Or with the Clarks? What *was* this?

I peeked around the corner again. Finn was stalking away from Twelve—not a sway, not a stumble, not a trip to be seen. He disappeared around the corner.

Twelve, for his part, walked toward my end of the hallway, his face blank, steps hurried.

An itch tickled the back of my neck. Something was up. Something was odd. As Twelve rounded the corner, I fell into step beside him.

"Hi, Twelve."

He sniffed and stared forward, refusing to look at me. "One."

"What were you talking to Finn about?"

Finally, Twelve looked down from his gaunt height and glowered at me. "Finn?"

Oh. Right. The Clarks didn't use informal address. "Paladin Smith."

Twelve's shoulders tightened. "I have never spoken to Paladin Smith in my entire existence."

Okay. While I didn't think Twelve and I were friends or confidants, I at least thought we were bonded by our . . . Clarkness.

"You were literally just talking to him." I gestured down the hall. "I saw you."

Twelve jerked to a stop. Loomed over me. While he wasn't a conjurer, he was something else. Not human. Not exactly. A dirty, drippy, leaky feeling coated my skin every time he was close. Perhaps the Clarks conjured their bodies. Maybe that was what this feeling was.

"One is a liar," Twelve said in a near-perfect imitation of Primus. "I have never met Paladin Smith. I do not know Paladin Smith. I have never spoken to Paladin Smith. If One continues this lie, she will be punished by Heir Clark."

Twelve said this with pure conviction. It sounded like the absolute truth. Either Twelve was a double agent playing a deep game or he was having a laugh trying to gaslight me. My bet was on gaslighting. It seemed to be a Clark trait.

"Okay. Sure thing," I said, giving a small wave. "Bye."

Finn and Twelve.

Finn and Twelve?

Or . . . Finn and the Clarks?

In the end, did it matter? No. The game had to be played. I had a job to do. Would I ask Finn about Twelve? No. I'd keep my own counsel. Most of the time, it was wiser to keep secrets unaired.

I ducked around the corner and took the stairs two at a time. All the same, the dirty, oily feel of Twelve stuck to my skin long after I'd left him.

40

Years ago, I swore I'd never set foot in the Clark catacombs again. No matter how much Jagger hinted, demanded, or punished, I refused. I was still at the point that I *could* refuse. It wasn't wise to, but sometimes fear overrides wisdom.

And because the catacombs were where my second death occurred, and why to this day Roumelade stays with me while I drift back into this world, Jagger doesn't push too hard. It's not because he's kind. It's because he knows in time I won't be able to refuse him.

That time came earlier than I thought.

We were under the Clark Mansion, at the bottom of Manhattan, at the hollowed-out, gaping-skull mouth of the catacombs. It was a large, circular room, with dirt and cobblestone walls—except the smooth cobbles were parchment-yellow and bone-white. There was no reason to pretend I didn't know what sort of brick and mortar had built these catacombs. We all knew.

My skin puckered, and gooseflesh rose. Whether it was from the damp chill or the memory of what I'd seen here when I was still young and scared of things like figments and boys who exploded their sisters—well, I didn't know. Either way, I moved closer to Finn and the heat of him.

We'd arrived not by taxi but in one of the Smiths' armored Range Rovers. Darin drove. (As an aside, he is *insane*. Literally *insane*. On the drive from the Bards' down to lower Manhattan, he nearly killed us about three dozen times. Every time someone swerved, honked, or flipped him off, he laughed like a maniac. I swear, his driving was scarier than an invite to Sunday dinner with the Clarks.)

"When we're done here," I murmured to Finn, cutting a glance at Darin, "we're taking a taxi back. Promise me I won't have to ride with him."

Finn restrained a smile and studied Darin, who was leaning casually against a bone wall, pretending to ignore every other conjurer in the room while probably plotting the best way to kill them all with a fire sword. He probably thought he could do it too. Three Smiths with swords against forty other conjurers. *Insane.*

Darin noticed Finn looking and gave him that maniacal driver smile.

Finn turned back to me. "I promise."

Who am I kidding? I was trying to distract myself. You know me well enough to realize it. I was using any tactic I could to keep from noticing the long dirt tunnel leading deep under the Clark Mansion. I didn't want to think about the conjured green candlelight that flickered and flamed and cast trick-the-eye shadows. I didn't want to think about the smell. It was the same. Tightly packed dirt, damp bones, parchment, and rotting wood. I hated it.

Across the room, Last watched me with a small, private smile. I didn't acknowledge her, Primus, or Twelve. She'd told me to pretend I didn't know her when we were in public. Although, I did wonder if Herman, the Clark, knew about our "friendship."

The Clarks were closest to the tunnel, all of them dressed in loose black clothes. While the Clark spoke with a few members of his family (a cousin, two nephews, three second cousins), Primus watched Jacob with a satisfied, gloating air.

I couldn't blame him. Jacob was a mess. His T-shirt was stained with a tea-colored blob, his shoes were untied, and his blond hair was sticking up as if he'd raked his hands through it a dozen times.

It seemed he'd had a cup of gunpowder tea—or, more likely, the entire pot. He swayed; he slumped. He shook himself off, stood rigidly upright, then swayed again. Philoneas grasped his arm and propped him up, speaking quickly into his ear. Jacob shook his head and swatted at the air as if Philoneas were an annoying fly that needed to be shooed away.

When I turned away from Jacob's red cheeks and too-bright eyes, I saw Luvic watching me. He nodded at Jacob then lifted an eyebrow in question, as if to ask, "Was that *you*?"

I kept my face carefully blank. Luvic grinned. Winked.

I didn't wink back.

The knife-in-my-chest memory he'd planted was still way too vivid for me to be trading winks.

He looked better today though. Not 100 percent, but better. He hadn't used illusion to cover the red rope burn and the purple and green bruises around his throat, and he hadn't used it to cover the paleness of his skin. Instead, it was almost as if he was flaunting the marks, saying, "Do you think you hurt me? Really? Try again. Try it and see."

There was a whole host of Bards. Twenty at my last count. Ragnor was in a military-style coat. I'd never seen him so tense. He looked like someone had peed on his favorite guitar and he was out for blood.

The Bard was his usual showy, laughing self, but Celia was cold and focused. She was in a white, very tight, partially sheer one-piece jumpsuit that wrapped around her and showed off her curves. Her long black hair was in a crown braid. Her lips were fiery-red, her eyelids smokily shadowed, and she had a gold watch on her wrist.

That must be the item she was bringing into the game.

Finn was carrying a military-style steel knife, which he'd pulled out of his backpack. After I outlined the Clarks' game for him, he said the knife was just the thing.

He didn't seem at all concerned at the prospect of being buried alive, lost in a maze of catacombs, or fighting reanimated skeletons. I supposed, considering some of the Clarks' past games, it *was* tame in comparison. Surprisingly tame.

Herman Clark clapped his hands. Three sharp claps that cracked across the room. The twenty Bards, the fifteen Clark relatives, the three Wards, and the Smiths all quieted and turned to the front.

"Take note," the Clark said, and I held back a snort. So that was where Primus got it from. "Let it be recorded that the second game begins now. The players will descend into the catacombs. Learnedness, a knowledge of history, and a respect for the past will guide you well. What is the past but a map for our future?" He spoke in his dry, husky voice, his words blowing free like air leaking through a thin straw. His hairless head and eyebrow and eyelash-less face glowed in the dim light like a polished skull baking in the sun.

Darin yawned loudly. I could practically hear him begging, "Make it stop, I'll buy you a pizza."

"Heir Smith," the Clark said, casting his eyes in our direction, "you mock, but where do you stand? In your null half-brother's shadow."

The Bard laughed, and some of the others joined. Ragnor didn't. Luvic didn't. He was murmuring to his sister, who was nodding, her fists clenched.

The Wards weren't paying attention. Jacob was slumped against Philoneas. Uliea was staring at the catacomb entry, clasping and unclasping her hand, that lost, grief-stricken look on her face again.

The Clark waited for the laughter to stop echoing off the bone walls. A cold draft swept through the crowded room, blowing the conjured green candlelight and making macabre shadows dance on the cobbled walls.

"We Clarks have waited 300 years to wear the crown again. This is the year we will."

"Not a chance," Darin muttered, too quiet for anyone but me and Finn to hear.

"When we rule, humans remember the truth of their existence. Why are we here? What is it we're here for? What is it that is required of us?"

The wind blew again, tugging the silk of my pant legs. I shivered at the chill and the parchment scented damp.

"Sacrifice," the Clark said. "When a Clark rules, the world remembers the importance of sacrifice."

A prickle of unease crawled over my skin. I could feel the pressure of Last's gaze. What did she say? That the world hadn't changed. Humans still sacrificed each other, even in this day and age.

"Do you remember the grand eras, when blood ran in a sacrificial river? Do you see us working now? I imagine you do." He smiled—the cold, death-mask smile he'd worn when he conjured iron chains around me. "Where today do you see us? Look around. Sacrifice is a noble virtue. A celebration. The very people who once defended life are offering it up for sacrifice. Oh yes, the people love it. When a parent offers their son, their daughter—when they celebrate the sacrifice of their child—do you see us there? When they offer up their old? The weak. The unwanted. The strong. The desired. They are all ours. Imagine if a Clark wore the crown. *Imagine*. The nature of this world is sacrifice. There cannot be spring without the sickness of autumn and winter's death. Plants cannot grow without the worm-chewed necrosis that feeds the soil. There *must* be death for life. This is the way of the world. Every time a human celebrates this, know that we may have pushed them to the ledge, but they were the ones who willingly flung themselves off. We are merely the ones smiling behind them."

I had a bad feeling—a very bad feeling—about this. I glanced at Last. She was wearing funeral black, and her dark eyes glistened. When she saw me looking, she lifted her hand and wiggled her pinkie in a small wave goodbye.

"Finn?" I whispered.

He moved closer, his arm brushing mine. "Yeah?"

"I don't think I learned everything last night."

"The greatest virtue"—the Clark gave his thin-lipped smile—"is sacrifice. Not self-sacrifice. No. That is not a virtue. That is a fault. A weakness that should be eradicated. No. I mean sacrifice of . . ." He smiled out at the room crowded with conjurers. "A warm body."

I stiffened.

I felt Finn drawing into himself—that particular stillness he wore when he pulled all of himself into a tight ball, ready to explode in a violent attack. I'd yet to see him unleash it, but I could feel him preparing.

I brushed my hand against the back of his. It was okay. I was *okay*.

"Once the players have reached the end of the game, they will find a warm body. Take note, to finish the game, they will have to sacrifice said body. If they fail . . ." Herman winced. Held out his thin, vein-lined hands. "After one hour in the catacombs, 100 human or humanlike creatures will be sacrificed somewhere in the world. After two hours, one thousand. After three hours, ten thousand. An earthquake. An avalanche. A building collapse. You see?" He waved his hand in a continuing circle. "You each hold the lives of thousands in your hands. Once you sacrifice your warm body, the clock stops ticking. The sacrifices end. I know . . . I know . . . some of you may want to take your time so that your count is higher, but I implore you, think of the game. Think of winning—"

"Are you . . .?" Ragnor stepped forward angrily. "Are you suggesting that the players kill their bodies? Is that what this is?"

The Bard cut his hand and hissed, "Ragnor, stand down."

The Clark chuckled a dry, raspy laugh. "Kill? No. No, no. Sacrifice, Ragnor Bard. Sacrifice. What is a victory without sacrifice?"

Ragnor's eyes blazed. Celia gripped her brother's hand and tugged him back. Their body—the short, gray-haired man—growled something in a low voice. At his words, Ragnor and Celia nodded. Luvic put his hand on the body's shoulder, bent his head, and whispered something. The body smiled. It was the first time I'd ever seen him smile.

What had Luvic said to him? Or promised him?

Next to me, Finn was dangerously still. He hadn't moved. I wasn't sure he'd even breathed since the Clark had confirmed the end of this game was . . . my death.

There was a strange, almost homicidal light in his eyes. The stars were colliding again, and I think he was either envisioning a way to end every single conjurer in the room or he was trying desperately to think of a way for me to not get hurt.

What had he said? I remembered it, even though I was drunk on conjured chocolate.

I don't want you hurt at all.

"It's okay," I whispered. "Finn. It's okay."

He could hear the shaking in my voice. I knew he could.

He didn't believe me. In fact, he looked like he was about to do something rash. Something we'd all regret. Wolfgang eyed him as if he were considering conjuring his fire sword and plunging it through Finn's gut if he so much as stepped out of line.

"You'll do it," Wolfgang growled, gripping Finn's arm and yanking him to face him. "Do you hear me? You'll do it, or after, I'll kill her myself. I won't be kind." He shook Finn and hissed, "Coward? What are you fighting for?"

Finn stiffened as if he'd been struck. Then he said in a cold, dangerous voice, "Step back."

Wolfgang grinned, baring his teeth. "That's better."

The Clark lifted his hands. His black sleeves fell, revealing his thin, sticklike arms and his hairless skin. A deep bell gonged twice.

"The game begins!"

Primus swept toward the catacomb entry, his black clothes rippling in the sudden draft. Celia followed, her head high, her stride iced-over fury and determination. Jacob stumbled forward, blinking at the tunnel entrance, tripping over his own feet. He was pale, and for the first time since I'd met him, he looked spooked.

When he passed by me, another draft blew through the room, and he tripped on a rounded bone sticking up from the dirt floor. Surprised, I reached out to steady him but pulled back at the last minute. What was I thinking, trying to catch Jacob Ward?

He righted himself and then turned to stare at me. His pupils were wide, nearly swallowing his green eyes, and his cheeks were bright red.

I held still and waited for the prodding, the poking, the choking and tearing apart feel of him. But instead, he just looked at me for a long moment, and then, at another gust of wind, he turned and stumbled into the tunnel.

"Finn. Go," Wolfgang said.

Finn brushed the back of his hand against mine—a warm, reassuring touch. He stood still and quiet for a moment. Then, without looking at me or saying a word, he walked through the flickering green candlelight and into the bone-lined walls of the catacomb.

41

I'M GOING TO ADMIT SOMETHING. I KNOW YOU WON'T BE TOO HARSH IN YOUR judgment of me—at least not for this. For other things? Yes, perhaps. But maybe not for this.

Here it is.

I'm scared.

Telling this part of the story scares me. I've dreaded it since the beginning. It's a coil of fear roped in my belly, sliding and twisting so I'm sick from the feel of it.

You wouldn't be afraid. You burned away fear in a giant blaze, and all the dread flew away from you in ashes. But me? I don't have a blazing fire, conjured or real; I only have the ability to unwind and untie. But this knot of dread? It's as tight as a constrictor knot.

But I'll tell you this part, because if I don't, if I abandon you here at the mouth of the catacombs, then we'll never get to where we are now. We won't see the end. You'll never decide what I am and who you are.

I can't abandon a story in the middle of its telling, just like I couldn't abandon Finn to face this game without me.

I thought about it for half a second. Once the catacomb had swallowed the four players and Finn's figure was lost to shadow . . . I thought about it.

Last watched me with dark, teary, pain-hungry eyes. Luvic glanced my way, but his face was tight, and he didn't wink. Darin gripped my shoulder, but for once, he didn't have a joke or anything funny to say. He just sighed and gave a curt nod. It was the type of nod a soldier gives another before a suicide mission.

I wanted to run. I *knew* what was in those catacombs.

Yet I couldn't run. Not because there were forty conjurers in the room, and they'd easily overpower me even if I foolishly untied their illusions. Not because Jagger would kill me himself if I returned to Hell Gate without finishing the games. Not even because of the way Finn brushed his fingers reassuringly against mine.

I had to enter the catacombs because of the people. There were a hundred people. A thousand people. Ten thousand people. They were all strangers. They were people I'd never met and would likely never meet. But if I didn't go into those catacombs, then they wouldn't see the sun set. There would be a mom who cried for her son. A husband who wept for his wife. There would be . . . a girl who would never remember her parents' faces or voices or . . .

It's easy to discard death when it's a large number. Oh, a hundred people. Oh, a thousand. It's objective. It's unemotional. They cease to be individuals and are just a number.

But what if they weren't a number? What if they were a friend or someone you loved?

I used to wish, when I was younger and still had wishes left, that there was someone in the world who was thinking of me, who wanted me safe, who was wishing for me like I was wishing for them.

What I'm trying to say is that I willingly went into the catacombs, because I can't think of a person—even a stranger—as a number. As a necessary sacrifice.

Not when I can do something to stop it.

What did you tell me? *Mari, I won't see you become less.*

So I didn't resist when the Clark bound me and the other bodies in illusion. I walked with only slightly shaking hands, blindfolded and secured as I was prodded down an uneven, dirt-floored, cobwebbed and must scented tunnel.

I didn't even flinch when I heard the scratching of nails against bone, the shrill whistle of the nameless, faceless, hungry thing that crawled in the catacomb walls. I just took one breath, then another, and another. One step, and another, and another, until the Clark shoved me, knocked me flat, and I landed on my back on a cold stone slab.

Ah.

So.

I knew. Well, I'd suspected. Now I knew.

The stone slabs were one of the Clark's objects of power. They didn't have many objects. The Bards had the most. They liked collecting, and they liked pretty, interesting things. The Smiths had mostly weapons and armor. The Wards . . . I wasn't sure. They were more secretive and didn't ever bring objects to the games or write about them.

But the Clarks had written about these slabs. They were used in a game about one thousand years ago. It didn't work out, because all the players died except for the one who didn't sit on the stone. They hadn't used them since.

Well, not in the games, at least.

There was a copper scent in the air. It smelled like wet pennies, cobwebs, and crumbling bones.

There was the heavy, rapid breathing of someone closing in on panic. Was that me? I didn't think it was me.

I couldn't see the others though. The blindfold illusion was tied tight, so there was only an ever-present shroud of black.

No one knew—not even the Clarks—the genesis of the stones. They didn't even know exactly what their original purpose was. That was common with old objects. It was a guessing game: Were they used as an astronomical calendar? For religious festivals? As military defense?

I swear, in five thousand years, archeologists are going to dig up a satellite farm and hypothesize that the strange objects are evidence of ancient humans worshiping a solar god by constructing giant, circular offering platters.

Anyway, the stones were excavated two thousand years ago, in the time when the Roman Empire decided to build roads zigzagging the world and needed material to do so. The slabs were either uncovered in

Thessalonica, Alexandria, or Deva in Brittania. Even that much was unclear.

I, for one, had always thought the slabs came from Alexandria. I imagined a tutor exasperated with his students, who were always squirming, wanting to jump up and leave the lessons behind, so he made these stone benches you could never rise from.

Never.

As in . . . never.

Until you were dead.

So that was that.

When the Clark shoved me, blindfolded and bound, onto the rough, cold slab, I knew I'd never leave that stone. Not alive.

Immediately, the power clamped over me, gripped me, and held me flat. I knew without even trying that I wouldn't be able to stand. There were no knots, no illusions, here.

I suppose someone could've carved the stone so only shards of the slab stayed connected to you. You could've chiseled away until you were almost—sort of—free.

Maybe that was what students in Alexandria did once they'd learned all their lessons.

It wasn't what the Clarks used it for.

This was the room where Primus had played. Where Herman had made Last watch her mother take her last breath. Whatever the slabs had been used for in the past, they were now only used for one thing.

The hungry, eyeless, mouthless, faceless thing in the walls scratched, scratched, scratched . . .

The Clark ripped free the blindfold to leave me staring into shrouded darkness. Did the same for the others. Then he left, closing the groaning wooden door behind him.

The breathing of the other bodies was loud, the panicking one—was that me?—breathing rapidly.

No one spoke.

No one spoke for a long time.

Do you remember this room? I don't know what you remember, what you know, or what you think you know and what you don't.

The nameless, faceless thing—the one from my second death—pressed itself against the shroud of darkness, tentatively tasting my fear. Then, delighted, it sucked at it, like soft marrow from a brittle bone.

Justice always said there were things he'd never share. I told you I was afraid. I won't tell you anymore. Instead, I'll send you to the wind. You'll be safe with the wind.

42

THERE WAS SOMETHING WRONG WITH THE BOY. THE WIND KNEW IT immediately.

It had spent too long dancing gleefully over foam-crested waves, sliding down suspension-bridge cable wires, and twirling between the stumps of cedars that stood like soldiers, lining the deep sloughs that fed the estuaries that fed the rivers that fed the bay that fed the wild, free, gale-rich ocean. And oh—it had almost forgotten the game.

The wind gusted across the sun-dappled bight, shoving at the steep waves and darting over the smooth-glossed wings of a shearwater. Sometimes, if the wind was feeling courageous, it would hitch itself on the underside of a shearwater's long wings, and when the bird plunged into the cold sea, air bubbles speeding past, the wind would scream gleefully as they hurtled 200 feet down, down, deep into the ocean. And then, on the final gurgling pocket of air under the shearwater's wings, the wind would rise again, darting in a great, gasping expulsion into the bright, cold Atlantic air.

But that was a game for another day.

This day, the wind was using the shearwater's glide to push it faster and further, hitching a ride to Lower Bay, then up Buttermilk Channel.

It swept past the merry-go-round of the red sandstone military fort that glinted red-gold at sunset. Sometimes, the wind would mimic the castle's booming cannon from 200 years earlier, shaking ceremoniously between the stone walls. But not today. It was in a hurry today.

Up the channel, speeding toward the city spires, swooping over the masts of tall ships, bouncing off gusting white sails, and ducking under bridges into the cold tickle of the Upper Bay, where the Hudson and the East River converged.

And there, the old city, where secrets were built upon secrets were built upon secrets. So many layers of secrets that the wind had forgotten many of them.

The cobblestone streets wound, hitchhiked, and piggybacked in a sprawl of unplanned city spread. Churches, theaters, public houses, tenements, and shipyards, all jumbled and built one on top of the other. Until—yes.

There was the solitude of the old church, the sandstone and pink-lit granite. Sometimes, if the wind was close and it heard the great bells ringing, it would speed to the tower and jump onto one of the thick ropes. The ringers would heave the ropes until they sprang up and down, and the wind would rocket around the giant bells, speeding down the dizzying octave, playing pinball with the notes. The bells weren't ringing today. There were only car horns and bus noises and a jay cawing.

It didn't matter. The wind wasn't listening. It sped through the church spire, blasted the leaves of the ghost sycamore—still there, still there— that had stood protecting the church for a century but didn't any longer, and slid past the metal and glass of Wall Street, until it landed at the Clark Mansion.

The fastest way, the quickest way, was to slip under the streets, down through a manhole, into the sewer, and then through a rat's nest, into an old smuggler's cache, through a crack, past the broken pottery layers of an abandoned settlement, and into the parchment scented, weepy gray light of the catacombs.

There.

The wind burst into the wide, bone-built room on a cold draft and then tagged behind the boy as he wended into the dark, secret tunnel.

The boy had never been in the catacombs. The wind had. There was air here. There were plenty of cracks and holes to escape through. There were drafts to ride and some secrets to collect. It had traveled these green, candlelit tunnels.

But the boy . . .

What was wrong with the boy?

He stumbled and groped for the wall, clinging to a shard of bone. It was dark, yes, but not so dark that the boy should be stumbling. The boy had never needed light to see.

He breathed heavily, and the wind tickled his nose and blew across his cheek.

"'M'all right," the boy slurred.

The wind puffed, disbelieving. The boy smelled like sugar cubes and gumdrops—a strange, sweet smell that was a cotton candy tilt-a-whirl. Fun, perhaps. But not fun for a game.

Boys could die in the games. The wind had seen many die over the years. It would have to nudge the boy, carefully push him, protect him if it could.

It tickled the boy's ear. He nodded and shoved off the cold bone wall.

"Wondered where you'd been," the boy said, weaving deeper into the catacomb. "Having adventures?"

The wind did *not* have adventures. The wind was a proud, cunning, intelligent being, above such low things as adventures. It shoved the boy's knees, and he stumbled a bit.

"Oh! Didn't like that? Sorry. Only meant . . ." He cleared his throat. Wobbled. "Missed you."

Well, that was better. Not that the wind cared about human emotions like missing or being missed. But still, it was a fine thing for the boy to miss it.

They came to a fork in the catacomb, the green candlelight dancing between the two paths. The boy paused, his golden hair glinting like the gold-green of aged copper. He leaned one way, then the other. Undecided.

The scuff of a shoe sounded behind them, and the boy stiffened.

He held his hand still, ready to conjure. Even smelling of sugar and gumdrops and tilt-a-whirls, the boy would still be able to conjure, surely?

There were things in this cavern . . . bone things, held together by air that *wasn't* wind.

A man—the solange-eyed one, the Smith—rounded the corner. When the boy saw him, he blinked at him, swayed, and held his hand ready.

"Don't want to hurt you," he said, slurring a bit.

The solange-eyed one nodded, his eyes gleaming in the dull light. The wind held quiet. Still.

"You wouldn't be able to if you tried." The black-haired man's eyes glowed with stars colliding. The wind could see the birth of the universe there.

It tugged at the boy, cautioning him. This was not a man to play with. Not yet. Not now.

The man held a steel knife in his hand. When the wind slid carefully down the metal, it tasted the cranberry and allspice of solange. Ah. A knife to shred illusion. Cunning solange. Cunning man.

"Shall I try?" the boy asked, not heeding the wind's warning.

The black-haired man smiled. Usually, he was the one tilting, swaying, and stumbling; a man buffeted by wind walking a wire between two skyscrapers. But now he was steadier than the wind had ever seen him. It was the boy who was swaying.

"You might," the man said. "But I'd rather you didn't. I have someone I need to find."

Curious. The wind didn't know what he meant, but the boy seemed to understand. He nodded and then waved his hand.

"Be my guest. Your choice is as good as any."

The black-haired man closed one eye, then the other, and as quick as a kestrel's dive dodged to the right, disappearing into the downward-tilting tunnel.

The wind moaned. The right was not a wise choice. The black-haired one would be lucky to see the sky again. The right was where the earth came alive, and where men were buried beneath sediment and hungry stone.

But the wind wasn't there to cling to the Smith or to ride the edge of his knife. The wind was there to make sure he could ride the boy's laugh again—the one that tumbled from him in delighted surprise before his lips snapped shut again just as quickly.

It tapped the boy's left hand, and then again.

Until the boy nodded and then stumbled left.

He hummed. He tilted. He sniffed and wiped his nose. The green candle flames *did* have the sort of acrid scent that made a being's eyes water.

Once, the boy almost fell, but the wind gusted beneath him and steadied him, so instead, the boy gripped a stone shelf holding the moldering bones of a 400-year-dead Clark.

"Thank you," the boy said, because manners were important.

Unfortunately, manners or speaking also woke things. The bones the boy had disturbed wiggled. Shifted.

"Oh!" He was surprised. He shouldn't have been.

The bones flew from the shelf. They congregated into a manlike form. Black, cobweb-covered funeral suit. Mildew and dust. A skeleton with a wind-like (but *not* wind) shriek.

"Wind!" the boy shouted.

He twisted his hand, and the bones blasted apart. The wind ricocheted across the bones as they struck the walls. They cracked against the catacomb shelves, a loud organ of sound.

There was silence for a second. Then the bones yanked themselves back together. They dragged a spine, a disconnected finger bone, across the stone shelves. The tapping shook the shelves until bones that were buried beneath dust and gravel shuddered, heaved, and spilled onto the ground.

The wind did not like the magnetic air that pulled the bones together.

The air tugged at the wind. Wanted it to join the game.

The wind shoved the boy.

"I can burn them!" the boy said, twisting his hand.

Fire hit the bones. Flickered and died.

The wind shoved again.

"Or cut them."

The boy conjured an army of swords. They sliced at the bones. The clang and the noise erupted around them, calling more bones. More skeletons held together by something *not* wind.

The boy stumbled back. Twisted his hand. The swords sliced. Whacked. Batted away bones that raced at him. But even as he cut the bones smaller, they congregated back together, reforming in a plaster-cast, marrow-pasted abomination.

That was the word. Abomination.

The wind shoved again. *Go!*

The boy was in no condition to fight. If he didn't smell of gumdrops and sugar, yes, it would've been easy. But now, the boy could barely conjure a decent flame.

"Or I could go," the boy said.

Finally.

He twisted his hand and built a wall of air around himself, an invisible shield that shoved the bones to smash against the catacomb walls. The boy ran. Stumbling. Nearly falling. Tripping, only to have the wind push him back up.

The wind hated the skeletons and their wrongness so much that it didn't notice the pit.

The boy plunged into open air. The wind dove after him, screaming.

There were spikes at the bottom of the pit. Poison-tipped, impaling spikes.

The wind raced beneath the boy and shoved. Up! Up! It parachuted his fall, giving him half a second to conjure.

A rope wrapped itself around the boy and jerked him to a halt. He slammed against the wall. The breath whooshed out of him.

He was hanging an inch from the tallest wooden spike. The rubber sole of his shoe scraped the sharp, poisoned tip.

The wind moaned and curled against the boy's chest. His heart clanged against the wind, a loud bell booming noisily.

"That . . ." The boy leaned his head back against the sheer dirt wall of the pit and closed his eyes. "That was . . . Did you know, Wind . . . I don't much like falling."

The wind huffed. It didn't like wrong-air skeletons. It didn't like spikes with poison. It didn't like boys who swayed and stumbled and smelled like sugar cubes and couldn't take care of themselves.

The collection of bones clamored at the edge of the pit. Were they being held back by the drop, or was that the limit of their locomotion?

"S'pose we should go."

The boy gripped the rope, set his feet to the dirt, and then climbed the sheer wall, one hand over the other. At the top, he hoisted himself over the edge and then stumbled to his feet.

"Excuse me?"

The boy jerked. Shook his head. Looked around.

The wind purred. It was the woman. The citrus and pearl dust scented Bard who wore silks and glinting jewelry. The one whose voice carried the wind on a lovely, swirling route through the winding halls of a conch shell.

The wind nudged the boy and turned him to face the woman.

She was in white, her little sparks of blue and orange flaming around her. While the boy was covered in dust and had cobwebs in his hair and bone mildew smudged on his cheek, the woman didn't have a speck of dirt on her.

"Are you . . .?" She peered at him. "Are you drunk?"

The boy made a funny choking sound. The wind dragged over his suddenly sunburn-hot cheeks.

"No."

The woman sniffed the air. Leaned closer and sparked a flame in front of the boy's face. She made a clicking noise with her tongue.

"Blown pupils. Pale skin. Can't stand straight to save his own life. Not drunk . . . drugged. Who drugged you?"

Oh. So that was what was wrong with the boy. Who had drugged him?

The boy smiled. "My mom. Put it in my tea."

Once he'd said it, his eyes widened as if he was surprised he'd admitted anything at all.

The wind wasn't surprised. This woman was the type who made men *want* to tell their secrets.

"You have a strange family," she said, crossing her arms. "Why would your own mother poison you?"

The boy shrugged. "She's been a little upset with me since . . ."

"Oh. Right." The woman looked down at the ticking metal band—watch—on her wrist. Then she peered down the length of the tunnel. "I have to go. I don't want to go, but I have to go. It's already been forty-five minutes. Do you . . . do you need help?"

The woman was surprised she'd asked. The wind could taste the surprise in the flush on her skin and in the rapid tapping of her pulse.

The boy squinted at her, swaying slightly. He stumbled and then grabbed the wall. "No." He leaned against the wall before sliding down it, landing on the bone-paved ground.

The woman sighed. Tapped her foot. "If I leave him . . . he could die. He saved me last time. Yes, he made that wall of fire, but . . . he saved me. I should . . ."

The wind slid over the curve of the woman's wrist, vibrating with the ticking second hand of her watch.

"Celia, you're going to regret this," she said.

Then she bent down and grasped the boy under his arms. She was small, so she used a bit of illusion to hoist the boy upright. After that, she hooked his arm over her shoulders and put hers around his waist.

"Come on, charmer." She walked slowly down the bone-lined catacomb.

The boy wrinkled his forehead. Swayed. Kept ahold of her. "Why're you helping me?"

"Because I'm an idiot."

The boy didn't say anything for many steps, but then he nodded. "Prob'ly."

The woman snorted.

Then the boy's head dropped to his chest. He jerked it back upright. He shook himself hard.

When he stumbled, the noise echoed though the catacomb. The shadow creatures on the walls paused, and then a scraping, bone-dragging noise sent out a slow, scratching query.

"You might," the woman whispered, "want to stop making so much noise."

He shrugged. The wind shoved him. Idiot boy.

He smiled. "Why didn't the skeletons bother you?"

"Oh, they did. I just sang them back to sleep. A sweet little lullaby."

That was impressive.

"Really?"

The woman smiled. It was a smile that glowed as bright as the fire lights surrounding her. "No. I buried them. Dust to dust, Jacob. All bones return to earth. Weren't you listening to the Clark? He practically told us what to do."

The boy grunted. Of course he hadn't been listening—he could barely hold himself upright.

"Do you remember . . .?" The woman paused and then said more quietly, "Do you remember the first time we met?"

The boy smiled. The wind drifted close. It was his real smile—the one he didn't show anyone. Maybe he'd forgotten that the woman could see him. Or maybe the gumdrops and sugar cubes had muddled his mind.

"I knew someday we'd be here," she said, propping him up. "That someday I might have to kill you. Or you me. I was eight."

"I thought you were . . . funny," the boy said, not noticing the startled glance the woman sent him at his slurred words. "You made me laugh. Not then. Later . . . because you . . ."

"Conjured a toad in your fruit juice?"

"Mm-hmm. I kept him. Made him a vivarium. Called him Punch. He lived . . ." The boy closed one eye. "Till I was twelve."

The woman frowned into the darkness, and the wind slid over the tight line of her shoulders.

"Do you think I'll have to kill you?" she mused, not expecting an answer.

"Maybe," the boy said in the same tone. "Lia?"

She jerked her head and looked at the boy in surprise. The only people who ever called her "Lia" were her brothers. "What?" This was said in a sharp warning tone, but the boy didn't notice.

"I know your secret," he said, giving her a wobbly smile.

The wind moaned. Why had he told her that? Secrets were *not* meant to be handed out or flashed about. They were to be hoarded, hidden, stored under lock and key until the right moment.

This was *not* the right moment.

The woman kept her face placid, but behind her palm, she twisted her hand and conjured a knife. The blade was sharp and thin.

The wind tugged the boy's earlobe. He shook his head and brushed it away.

"What secret?" the woman asked, her voice featherlight.

The boy smiled at her, his eyes as soft as a spring leaf glowing under the rising sun. "Thala ... thala ..."

The woman paused. Stopped walking. Her knuckles turned white as she gripped the handle of the knife. She kept it hidden from the boy. She'd strike before he knew it was there.

"Thalassemia," he finally said.

The woman would kill him. The wind knew this. It could see it in her eyes. It could taste it in the bitter tang of her emotion and the suddenly steady beat of her heart.

"You have to ..."—the boy squinted at her—"have blood transfusions ev'ry week. From your brothers—only your brothers—or you're too weak to conjure. Then too weak to live ... Your heart'll stop 'cause your blood ..." The boy sniffed. Scratched his nose. Wobbled unsteadily.

The woman lifted the hidden knife; twisted it so it would slide between the boy's ribs.

Would the wind be able to stop her? Build a gust so strong she'd be flung back and the boy could escape?

"Lia?"

"Yes, Jacob?" She angled the knife higher, keeping it out of sight, adjusting the angle.

Would she really kill him? Players were supposed to be protected in the games. It was against the rules to knowingly or purposely kill another player. Yet ... it had happened before. While others didn't know, hadn't seen or recorded the event, the wind had seen it. The wind knew.

The boy sighed. Leaned against her. "If I could, I'd take that burden for you. I would ... if I could."

The woman flinched. Her hand twisted. The knife disappeared.

When the boy looked at her, the woman's face was pale in the green-tinged darkness.

"If you ever need my help," he whispered, "you could ask me."

The woman smiled. The wind, never good at reading subtle human emotions, wasn't able to decipher what the smile meant.

"I don't trust you enough to ask for your help."

"I s'pose"—the boy shrugged—"I don't trust you enough not to kill me. If you'd moved that knife one inch closer, I would've lopped off your head." He nodded to the ceiling.

The woman looked up. There was a gleaming, long-handled axe floating above her. Its angle was perfect for removing a head from a neck.

"I think," she said, carefully stepping away from the boy and his axe, "you are well enough to continue on your own."

The boy nodded. "Probably best."

The woman smiled. Wiped her hands on the white fabric of her pants. Then she reached down and wound the watch at her wrist.

"No—" The boy reached forward. Twisted his hand.

Too late.

A half-second later, he was flung back. The wind flew on the collar of his shirt. Smacked the dirt and bone wall. Curled protectively over the boy as he slumped to the ground, unconscious.

The woman sighed. Stared at the boy's crumpled form.

"I could just . . ." She bit her lip, considering.

The wind knew she was thinking about dust to dust and bones to earth. It made a creaky, groaning, angry sound. The woman looked behind her, shuddered, then turned on her heel and hurried into the dark.

Time.

What was time?

Nothing to the wind.

But it meant something to the boy. So the wind tickled him. Blew in his ear. Whispered and urged. Tugged him until his eyelashes fluttered and he opened his eyes to the dark, bone-dust-settled catacomb.

The green candlelight had burned down, a clock of its own. The light no longer danced but instead crept over the rough dirt floor like a hungry creature. The light didn't brighten; it devoured.

The boy groaned and pressed a hand to his forehead. The wind ran over the bump on his head.

"I'm all right," the boy said. He shook himself off and stood.

"The good things is," he said, sounding more like himself, "I was out for long enough that whatever that drug was wore off. The bad thing is . . . I was out for long enough to . . . well . . . I've lost, haven't I? And Droona, she'll have been . . . well, let's go."

The boy was back to himself. The wind skittered over the bone and dirt and gleefully kicked up dust and mildew as the boy raced through the tunnel. This was more like it!

The boy sprinted, light-footed and sure, through the catacomb. He twisted his hand and sent the rising bones and vengeful skeletons back to their rest. Even the not-air fled before the boy. He shot forward, and a wall of bones crumbling to dust blew after him.

The catacomb narrowed. There was the thick scent of copper, the new smell of fear, and the sound of two heartbeats racing. The boy slowed, and then the wind pushed open the thick wooden door. This was the end of the game.

The wind had been in this room before. It was not a nice room. As the wind knew, there were no secrets in cruelty. But all the same, the wind didn't expect *this* to be the ending to the Clarks' game.

"Droona, I'm here," the boy said. His voice was soft, warm, like it hadn't been in years.

He ignored the other three in the room. Two of them were already cold, their animating spirits gone. One of them was still warm, her head tilted toward the sound of them approaching.

"What took you so long?" the old one asked.

The boy smiled, but it was not his real smile. The wind didn't think it was really a smile at all.

"I'm sorry."

He kneeled at the edge of a stone slab—one with a sticky, tree sap and tar feel that the wind instinctively shied away from. The boy, though, was careful. Smart once again. He didn't touch the sticky slab.

"You missed the first hour," she scolded. "Don't miss the second."

The boy had been lectured by this old woman his entire life. The wind knew she'd rocked him in thick arms when he was an infant. She'd lectured him when he snuck candy before bedtime, and she'd needled him after he stopped sneaking candy once his mirror was gone. She'd fed him soups and meats to keep him strong, and cookies to keep him sweet. She'd pestered and fussed, and the wind knew this old one had stayed up many nights worrying for this boy.

The boy's mouth trembled. He looked away. Wiped the palm of his hand against his cheek. The wind stroked the salt and the heat.

"Don't," the woman scolded. She could never stop scolding. "Don't. You knew this could happen. I knew it too. Now, I'll be quick. The Clark body merely said, 'It has been my honor to serve, Heir Clark.' That was it. Gruesome business. But then the Clark looked at the Smith body and said, 'One, when you come back, we shall call you Two. You've done well.' She's in league, that one is. You know what to do about that."

"Yes," the boy said. "All right."

The old one smiled, maybe glad to see the boy so ready to take her direction without her having to lecture him. "Then the Bard body, he said, 'My blood is yours. Always has been.' Then the girl killed him quick. That was about an hour ago."

"That's all? Nothing else?"

The woman paused. Although her wrinkled face was calm, grooved enough for the wind to sled through the age lines, she wasn't entirely placid. There was a tightness in her bones.

The woman looked hard at the boy, her eyes reaching through the shadows. Searching. Searching. Like the wind when it was rolling over the grassy lawn in Central Park searching for the last dandelion seed, hoping to send the little parachutes into a wishful puff in the air.

"I hope . . ." She paused. Cleared her throat. "Before I die, I wanted to ask that you forgive me. Jacob?"

He looked down. Stared at the sticky gray slab of stone imprisoning the woman.

"What's there to forgive? It was my fault. I did it. Not you—"

"No. You were a child, with a child's understanding. It was not your fault. Please. Since that moment, I've waited for your forgiveness."

"Why would you wait? You always had it. You . . ." The boy glanced at the girl lying across the room, shrouded in darkness. Her breath came in quick, quiet gasps.

He watched the girl for a moment, but she didn't move; didn't acknowledge that she could hear a word. Didn't acknowledge that she would soon be the last one left in this room.

He looked back at the old one. "In my heart, you were my mother. In my heart."

The wind wrapped itself around the boy's hand. There was a hollow sound in his voice—a wind down a long, empty tunnel sort of note. If the boy lost the mother of his heart, who would be left?

"Ah, Jacob. In my heart, you were my son. That's what happens when a body raises a boy. Do you think I'm sorry I'm here? No. I'm not sorry. I'm proud."

"What do you want me to do?" he whispered. "Do you want me to kill them all? I will. When I leave this room, I'll bathe them in darkness. I'll shatter every one of them."

The woman clicked her tongue. "No. Remember yourself! If you do that, then what happens? Everything we've been working for is lost. Only . . ." The woman smiled—a happy, gloating curl. "Only . . . give them each a mirror. Don't bloody your hands for me. Only give them a mirror."

The boy nodded. Smiled back at the mother of his heart. "I will. I promise you."

"Do it then. Do it quick."

And it was done. The boy was fast—faster, even, than the solemn one, who never liked pain or unnecessary cruelty.

After, for a long time, he stared at his hands. His shoulders shook, and he drew in shuddering, gasping breaths.

The wind crouched next to him, huddling against his leg.

A tear splashed to the dirt and bone floor. The sound of it sizzled over the wind and coated it in salt and grief.

The wind moaned. Then the boy—the wind's boy—gathered himself.

Pulled the winds that rushed through him into a mighty, vengeful gale. It was the bitter-ice winds of the Arctic. A wrathful hurricane.

The boy stood. His fists clenched. The wind swept around him, tugging his clothes, blowing his hair. The boy was destruction.

"Are you," he asked, his voice a storm-threat, "for the Clarks?"

"No," the girl whispered.

The boy stared at the girl. Weighing, measuring. The wind rode the coil strung between them. The boy's eyes narrowed.

"Are you frightened?"

She swallowed. The vibration of her pounding heart shook the wind. "Yes."

He nodded. Whispered as he turned, "Wind, stay with her. She needs you more than I do."

The wind settled over the girl's chest, onto the rise and fall of her breath and the drum of her heart.

The boy kicked open the exit door. Stormed from the tomb. The door slammed shut after him. The wind purred at the muffled echo of screams. The boy had made the conjurers their mirror.

The screams, the shouts, the thunderous booms and violent clangs beyond the door had fallen to silence by the time the solange-eyed one stepped into the dark tomb.

He sucked in a breath and walked swiftly to the girl's side.

"Don't touch the slab," she said quickly, her voice a shivery, windy, husky storm the wind happily swirled in.

She hadn't spoken to the wind. She'd only lain in tense, careful silence as the thing scraped in the walls and the scent of hot blood cooled. Even when the screams beyond the door ceased, she didn't make a noise. Only . . . waited, the rise and fall of her chest a tight, frightened rhythm.

The wind tried to soothe her with a rocking, gentle breeze, but it only made her shiver.

This girl . . . the wind knew her. Hadn't it been the one to carry the story of her to Hell Gate? Hadn't it been there when she'd taken her first step; had her first fall? Hadn't it been there when, as a child, she'd been trapped under the water, only a bubble of air left while she fought to unlock her shackles? Hadn't the wind watched for years as the rocklike one cruelly taught her to untie illusions? Hadn't the wind sent her true friend to her? Hadn't it watched as she'd changed faces but always kept the same spirit?

But still, she didn't speak to the wind. Didn't acknowledge the soft curl of it on her chest.

Perhaps she couldn't. Perhaps she didn't know the wind had kept all her secrets.

"Mari." The solange-eyed one kneeled down next to her, much like the boy had kneeled not long before.

He reached out, but the girl said, "Don't. If you touch the stone, you'll never be free. The only way off is death. Be . . . careful."

The man nodded. Pulled his hand back.

The wind swept around him, curling over the coating of dirt and grime. His skin was dark with it, and he smelled of mineral, mud, and rotting things. There were scratches and bruises. Torn nails and torn clothing.

So. He'd been buried. Just as the wind had thought he would. Swallowed by the hungry thing in the catacombs that devoured blood and bones and living things. The wind was surprised the man had fought his way free of the earth's stomach. It hadn't been done before.

Once a being was buried so deeply in the ground, choking on dirt and rock and bone . . . how could they know which way to dig? How could they know up from down; death from life? Soon, the trickle of air would run out, and a being's mouth and nose would be filled with gravel and sand and other things.

"How long has it been?" the girl asked.

"Nearly two hours."

"Then . . ." She sighed. "Don't let two hours pass."

The wind waited. It expected the man to be quick like the boy or the solemn one. But he didn't move. Instead he stared through the dark at the wind-voiced girl.

"I . . ." The man closed his eyes.

The wind scrubbed over his cheek, ran down his pulse, trying to determine what the man was thinking. But this man, he was a Smith, and the wind didn't understand Smiths. And this one, raised in secret, brought up in shadow . . . this one it understood even less.

"Mari. I'm afraid if I do this, you'll never—" He stopped himself.

The wind urged him, nudged him. It wanted him to finish the sentence.

"If you don't do this, I'll never forgive you," the girl said.

He swallowed. Reached out to touch her and then pulled back again. "I don't want to hurt you."

"It's all right," she said, and the wind felt the coldness of her skin, the shaking in her fingertips. "I never expected anything else. You and me? We aren't . . . we aren't friends. We aren't your grand love story. Your Orpheus and Eurydice. I'm not your Cora. I'm just a means to an end. I'd do the same. Finn? If you were here, on this slab, I'd plunge a dagger into your heart without a second thought. I'd do it. Okay?"

The man watched her, a quiet stillness surrounding him. The navy starlight of his eyes swirled as it swept through the illusion of the room. The illusions, perhaps, that only the solange-eyed man could see.

He shook his head. Dropped the steel dagger to the dirt and bone floor. It clattered, and the wind drifted over the solange-soaked metal.

"How many minutes?" she asked, her voice a quiet windstorm.

"Two." The man bowed his head.

The wind rode the man's breath as his chest heaved and he let out a great gust.

"Finn. I will hate you if you don't do this. I will hate you for the thousand lives lost. Do you hear me? I will hate you."

The man nodded. "Hate me then."

"I'll come back! I'll come back in less than a day. You'll see me before tomorrow morning. I'll come back!"

"But you'll be one death closer to his. Didn't you just tell me—?"

"I'm wearing diamond earrings. My . . . Roumelade made them. They're poison. I want you to take them out of my ears, put them in my mouth."

"Mari, I can—"

"Now, Finn."

The black-haired man jerked at the hardness of her voice. Then he carefully, without touching the slab, pulled the earrings free from her earlobes. When she opened her mouth, the wind skated over his clenched hand and loosened his fingers. He dropped the earrings onto her tongue.

It was quick.

The wind knew it would be. The watery one's tears always worked quickly. In seconds, the girl was gone. Spirited away.

The wind settled next to the man. He sat for a long moment, staring at the empty stone slab.

"Mari," he finally said, addressing the wind; the empty, spiritless tomb, "I'm afraid if I do this, you'll not come back. That one of these times, you won't come back."

The wind whistled across the dry bone and dirt. What did he mean? The girl would come back—she always came back. She would have a different face, but she would still be the girl.

Wasn't that what she'd told him? Wasn't he listening?

But the man didn't answer. He only clenched his fist and said harshly, *"Don't look back."*

The wind rushed from the tomb, out of the catacomb, up through the parchment-musty mansion, to the blue-skied city streets. It raced north to Hell Gate.

43

I LAY IMPATIENTLY IN THE TOMB OF MY NEW BODY, WILLING A FINGER TO twitch, an eyelash to flutter, my lips to curve. But—nothing. It would be hours before I settled into myself and came back from wherever it was that nines went when they left themselves.

I landed again in Roumelade's kitchen, right on the old wood table. There was the crash of dishes, the overwhelming scent of butter cookies baking and strawberry jam bubbling on the stove, and then Roumelade cried, "Mari! Not the table. Not again!"

I used to land in my bedroom. Once, I landed in the front hall. It had only been the last two times I'd ended up in the kitchen.

A chair was shoved back, and Griff said, "I'll get her."

"Gone and got herself killed in the games, I see," Roumelade said, "You'd think you'd have more sense. I told you to use the earrings! And Justice gave you a knife. And now what? Now you've only got one life left. Look at that rose tattoo. Soon you'll be . . ." Roumelade tsked.

"Don't say it," Griff said, and my stomach swooped as he picked me up and carried me along the hall to my bedroom. His feet echoed on the wood floors as he hurried me down corridors and up the stairs, growling menacingly at anyone who said, "Is that—?" or, "Oh-ho! She's back—" or, "One left, eh?"

While Griff was basically a puppy-dog in a grown man's body, if someone he cared for was threatened, he could (occasionally) channel his dad's growl. While the Jersey Devil was known for his viciousness, Griff was known for his undiluted innocence. Genetics are a funny thing. But there he was, growling practically the whole way to my bedroom.

I was tucked on my thin mattress, the scratchy cotton pulled over me and Griff on the wooden chair next to my bed.

Roumelade brought in a platter of butter cookies and fresh strawberry jam with clotted cream for Griff to snack on while they sat with me. The homey smell made my chest hurt. It was funny to think I'd miss a place like Hell Gate, especially after only a few days gone, but I had.

"I want you to be more careful," Roumelade lectured. "How are you going to kill the Wards and win the crown if you're lying here lazing about? And then what? Next death, when you're Jagger's? I love him, but he isn't going to let you be anything but his, Mari. He's been gentle with you, but once you're no longer a nine, he won't be anymore. I think Justice has made you believe the transition will be easy, but I've seen other nines after their last death, and it isn't easy, Mari. You won't be you anymore—that's for certain. It'll be an adjustment, and you won't necessarily . . . You see, when you have a river and you want to direct it, you can gently nudge it by building a channel, or you can dam it up and leash all its power for yourself. Right now, you're a channel. Soon, you're a dam, and Jagger will be your operator. That's a fact. You need to win this game before that happens, because . . . well, you might not survive the transition from channel to dam. Some don't. It's a hard thing, and I for one would very much like Jagger to have the crown of illusions before you go and dance with death again."

"Rou," Griff said, his voice thick, "can you not talk about death and channels and dams?"

"Not talking about it doesn't make it less true."

"But we don't even know what happened. Maybe Mari didn't die on purpose. Maybe one of the conjurers . . ." He shuddered. The conjurers were Griff's monsters under the bed.

Rou clicked her tongue, and then I heard the groan of my bedroom door opening.

"So . . . you just couldn't stay away. Did you miss us that much?"

If I could've smiled, I would've. Justice's deep rumble rolled over me. The door snicked as he closed it and moved farther into my small bedroom.

He smelled like wet concrete and rain, and with that, I finally noticed the soft patter of rain plopping against the thick Victorian glass of my bedroom window. I was settling further into myself, the haze and the numbness receding.

"You'll be happy to know," Justice said, amusement tinging his voice, "you aren't beautiful anymore. Not even pretty."

"She is so!" Griff said.

"Have a cookie." That was Roumelade. "The jam's fresh."

"Fine. She isn't." Griff again, an apology in his voice. "You look a lot like you did after your fourth death. Remember, Mari? You had that freckle over your lip and an interesting nose."

He means a long nose.

"It's better this way," Justice said. "No one notices you when you look like this. Rou, Jagger wants a big dinner. He said he wants a feast to celebrate Mari's imminent success."

"Oh, for crying out—" Roumelade broke off. "Dinner is in less than four hours! I'll have to—"

The door swung open and shut behind her.

"Did he really?" Griff asked, sounding doubtful.

"Of course he did. You know I can't speak an untruth about Jagger."

Griff grunted. "Do you two remember? Justice? Mari? Do you remember when Jagger kept conjurers in the basement?"

Justice made a short, rumbling noise in the back of his throat. A yes. Of course he remembered. How could any of us forget?

That was one of the reasons Griff was so terrified of conjurers. He'd snuck down one night—I don't know why—to look, to see, to confront his bogeyman. In the morning, Rou found him huddled on the cold stone floor of the basement, his arms wrapped around his legs, rocking back and forth, just staring blankly at the conjurer in the cage, while that conjurer—a Bard cast-off—laughed and laughed.

"I've been thinking about that," Griff said. "I've been thinking how Mari's in a house full of them, and what if they find out? What if they know what we did?"

By "we," he meant me. Or Jagger and me.

You see . . .

Do you remember this? Do you remember what I did, all those years ago? If I'm supposed to pretend we've never met, then you wouldn't know about it. Of course. I forgot about that.

I'll tell you.

When I was small, Jagger trained me to be his lockpick. You know this. He locked me in boxes, wrapped me in chains, threatened drownings and other wild things. But do you wonder . . . how did Jagger, a leggerock, create the illusions I had to untie?

Leggerocks can't conjure. Neither can humans. The only person who can conjure in all of Hell Gate is Justice.

Justice is only a few years older than me. When I was four, he was seven and just coming into his own power. Jagger had us practice together, but it only took a month before I could untie all of Justice's illusions—those simple, weak, one-tug knots.

After that, Jagger "found" conjurers. He started with the weakest. The cast-offs. The seventh and eighth cousins. The conjurers who could barely perform parlor tricks. He kept them, one at a time, in a metal cage in the basement. It looked like a giant birdcage. It was bronze, and it had a small door, a metal floor, and a hook to hang it from the ceiling. The human-size birdcage was an object of power. Jagger bragged that no one, not even a powerful conjurer, would be able to break out of that cage. And no one ever did.

For years, I practiced untying the illusions the conjurers created in the basement of Hell Gate. They'd throw everything they had at me. Jagger promised them that if they killed me, he would let them go. It was life-or-death for both me and the nameless conjurers in the cage.

Some threatened me. Some taunted. Most merely stared at me with blazing, hate-filled eyes.

"A truth-seer," they'd say. "The Leggerock has a truth-seer? You will die. When the principals learn of you, you will die a thousand agonizing deaths." Or they'd say a variation of that theme. For instance: "Clear vision? A ten-year-old with clear vision? The Wards will devour your mind, child. I may die, but you will die worse."

When I was very young, I didn't know what happened to the conjurers after I'd untied all the illusions they could throw. None of them ever succeeded in killing me, although it was frequently a close call. Jagger liked to push me. But soon after I bested their final effort, the conjurer would be gone from the cage.

When I was eleven, I finally saw what happened to the conjurers afterward. It was a third cousin, a Ward from Bulgaria visiting New York. He looped a constrictor knot illusion—a coffin for my mind. I pried myself free, gasping and desperate, and when I succeeded in untying his knot, the old conjurer cackled wildly. Spittle flew from his mouth, and he ranted, "She's dancing in illusion."

Then Jagger, as quick as a snap, killed the conjurer. When I gasped, he shrugged and said callously, "What did you think happened to them? They aren't playmates, Mari. They are *conjurers*."

Jagger may have brought one more in after that, but I can't be sure. I think . . . after that, he stopped. I'd learned all I could from the cast-offs and the distant cousins, and Jagger didn't want to risk getting too close to a principal's family. If he did, they might find out about me.

So, after that, I had to practice in the real world. The last conjurer, the Bulgarian, had been nearly twelve years ago. But Griff was still terrified of conjurers *and* the basement.

"They won't find out about it," Justice said in response to Griff's fear.

"But what if they do? Imagine what they'd do."

"They won't find out, because all of them but one are dead," Justice snapped. "And that one is Jagger's."

Who? What?

"Oh. Right. Sorry," Griff said, his voice mournful. "I always forget you're part-conjurer. That you helped Mari too."

Justice blew out a breath. "Don't worry about it."

"What does it feel like," Griff asked, "to have people at Hell Gate hate you because you're part-conjurer, and then to have conjurers hate you because you're part Hell Gate?"

Justice made a noise. There was the scrape of a chair moving close to the bed and then the sound of him sitting down. "I don't think about it. But I suppose, if I did, it'd feel just like being the son of a monster who hated the sight of me so much he gave me to a leggerock for half a bottle of Furtig. I suppose it'd feel like that."

Griff sighed. That was how he'd come to Hell Gate. Everyone knew Griff's dad didn't want him. He'd traded him for a half-drunk bottle of liquor.

"I suppose," he said.

"Do you mind if I talk to Mari alone for minute?" Justice asked.

"All right." Griff stood and then sighed again. "See you at dinner, Mari. Try not to take too long getting up. I'm hungry."

After the door closed, Justice scooted close. The coarse bedsheets rustled as he pushed them aside, and although I couldn't feel it, I knew he was holding my hand.

He sat in silence for a long moment. What was it he wanted to say? Had he found who'd killed me with the arrow of fire? Had he learned something about Finn? Was there something he knew from the nights he'd watched over me at the Bard Mansion?

I stretched my senses toward him, my skin tingling, blood flowing, body slowly waking.

"I've been thinking," Justice finally said, his voice so low I could barely hear him, "about that house in the woods. I barely dream anymore, but last night I dreamed about it."

There was a wistful smile in his voice—one I barely heard anymore. I suppose he hadn't learned anything about the conjurer who'd shot the arrow through my heart. Instead, he just wanted to . . . remember.

"It was built from cedar planks, and there was this wraparound porch with benches and rocking chairs. I'd never thought of those before. But they were there. It was in the mountains, like we always said. There were boulders around it, and pines that had dropped their needles in this thick, pine scented carpet."

I could feel the tingle of illusion weaving overhead, and I knew Justice was painting the illusion in the air above the bed, just like he used to weave the stars for me.

"We had our white picket fence. It was bright white, with a gate, and Griff and I were sitting on the porch, and then you walked through the gate. Smiling. You were smiling. It was like we'd lived there a long time. Rou was in the kitchen, making a pie, and there were two kittens lounging in a strip of sun on the porch. I stood, walked across that pine-needle yard, and then you . . . you disappeared. The dream was done."

Justice tied the last knot. The illusion hung above me. I only had to open my eyes to see it.

"I wish . . . I wish we'd taken the risk and run. I wish you, me, and Griff had gone to the Catskills. Just for one day. One hour. Even if it would've only been two minutes before Jagger'd come and taken us back to Hell Gate. If we'd had just two minutes, it would've been enough. You know? Mari?"

Yes.

I wanted to tell him yes. I knew. I understood. But I couldn't. I could only listen as I slowly fell back into myself.

"That's all I wanted to say. That I wish we'd had those two minutes."

He'd stood then, the legs of the chair scraping on the hardwood.

"I made you a picture of the cabin. Untie it before you come out." He moved toward the door, which groaned as he opened it. "Your fingers are twitching—you'll be up in five minutes or less. I'll get someone to sit with you until then."

He knew. Justice understood that even five minutes alone like this was five minutes too long.

"Winnie, you lurking?" I heard Justice murmur.

She laughed, shoved him from my room, and shut the door in his face.

"Ooh, that's pretty," she said, prowling around my room. "He's right— you'll be up any minute. Oh, but Griff's wrong. You don't look anything like you did after your fourth death. You look like . . . hmm . . . this painting I saw recently. Except you have both eyes."

Winnie leaned over the bed. I could feel her gaze scraping over my new features. I could also feel the hard beat of my heart, the pins and needles in my limbs, and the slow chug of blood flowing through my veins.

"I forgot—I was going to tell you." She circled my room, picking up books from my dresser, clicking the lamp on and off. "When you use Justice's knife, you should return it to him."

What?

"He wants it back," she said, opening a book and then closing it with a snap. "So. Make sure you give it back to him. Otherwise . . ." She made the throat-slit noise, as if Justice would be so upset at me not returning his knife that he'd cut my throat.

Unlikely.

Past unlikely.

"Oh. You're awake. I'll let you be. Don't forget. Give him back his gift."

She was gone. I opened my eyes.

Above me, hanging like a vivid tapestry of golden illusion, was the picture Justice had painted for me. It was our home in the woods. Cedar, pine, a porch to sit on, a white picket fence, two gray kittens swatting playfully at a white moth fluttering in the sunlight. I stared at the illusion for a long time before unraveling it.

Dinner was the best kind of feast. Apple stuffing with rosemary and thyme. Roasted chicken (not duck—ducks were waterbirds and off-limits). Just-baked sourdough rolls with freshly churned butter and a sprinkle of sea salt. Roasted parsnips, carrots, and potatoes pulled from Roumelade's rooftop garden. Peppery rocket. Cherry tomatoes bursting with juice. Fresh pea soup with cream and watercress (watercress is okay to eat). And a dessert of cream puffs, filled with chocolate mousse and whipped cream, and as much coffee as we could drink.

Roumelade was in a celebratory mood. Griff, as he'd said, was hungry and ate enough for three people. Justice sat next to me at the table, but he didn't put his arm over my shoulder or let on that he'd painted me a beautiful illusion. Probably because Jagger was sitting at the head of the table.

We were in the kitchen, not in the dining room where all the other creatures of Hell Gate ate. Tonight's dinner was private. Us nines (and former nines) were Jagger's favorite creatures, and the rest of Hell Gate knew it.

After three hours, I'd told them everything that had happened, from poisoning Finn with Smith's Folly to the inquisitor's chair, to the first game, and Luvic's pomegranate.

"Luvic Bard helped you?" Griff asked, surprised, because Bards were not known to be helpful people.

Justice stiffened, and I cut him a glance, but he didn't look at me.

"What?" I whispered.

He stared at his plate, unmoving.

"Continue," Jagger said.

And so I told them about how Primus had attacked Luvic and Celia had defended him, but I didn't mention untying Primus's knot. When I mentioned Luvic owing a favor for the antidote, Jagger gave a glinting, greedy smile. But when I told them about Last crowning me with a friendship history, Jagger stroked the knife around his throat, his black-gray eyes flat. It was a known fact Jagger didn't like anyone playing with what he considered his.

Griff went pale when I talked about the Clarks. They were his nightmare made real. When I told them about the Wards, Roumelade wanted to know more.

"Did you ask"—Rou leaned across the table, her wrinkled cheeks pink—"whether Viola Ward exploded into a million pieces or spontaneously combusted?"

"I didn't get the chance . . ."

"Shame."

At the end of dessert, I'd finished with the tomb and the earrings. I pushed my plate of cream puffs away, unable to eat them.

Jagger grinned, his sharp teeth flashing. "Mari. My Mari. We'll have the crown. We'll have it." His gray claws tapped against the wooden dining table—the one I'd so recently appeared on, crushing Rou's butter cookies.

Now that the second game was done, the players had been awarded more points. As it stood, Primus was in first place with six points, Jacob and Finn were tied with five points, and Celia was last with four points. Jagger was convinced Finn would take the games.

"Especially," he said, "with you there. Do I make myself clear?"

He did.

He'd outlined everything he expected me to do. Sabotage. Chaos. Mischief. Mayhem.

"If I'm in danger, do you want me to untie illusions?"

"No. Not under any circumstances. You're to die rather than allow any conjurer to learn what you are."

Under the table, Justice reached over and put his hand on mine. I took a deep breath and let out a long sigh.

Outside the warm, firelit glow of the stone-lined kitchen, the rain *tap, tap, tapped* against the window, and a gust of wind rattled the pane. The day had leaked away and bled into night.

"I'll go then." I'd given my report; I'd received my orders; I'd rested, settled into my ninth body, and had a warm hug from Roumelade.

"Before you do," Jagger said, humming happily as he sipped a glass of Furtig, "I've decided exactly when I'd like you to kill Alterra. I don't want him to become a problem."

I stilled. I'd forgotten . . . Well, no, I hadn't exactly forgotten—I'd just pushed it aside.

"Yes?"

"I want it done at the closing ceremony. I don't want even the slightest chance Alterra will collect on his bargain." Jagger gave a rasping rockslide chuckle. "You can't collect if you're dead. You'll kill him at the ceremony, lockpick the crown, and I'll be the only winner in this game."

A wave of cold washed over me, from my head all the way down to my toes.

How about we skip the killing and I'll just choose you?

Jagger tilted his head, a cruel smile on his face. "Are you starting to like the solange addict, Mari? Now why would you do that?"

"I wouldn't."

"You would think." He stroked a fingernail down his obsidian knife.

The sagging folds of his skin twitched as he shifted in his seat, staring, staring at me.

"I only wonder . . ." I paused and looked down at the scratches on the old wooden table. "He'll be dead soon anyway. He's in freefall. He won't last more than a month. Why not—?"

Why not let him have what time he had left? Why not let him be with his love?

"He will die. By your hand or another. If you want your freedom, it will be by yours. You'll do it, Mari."

Without looking up, I nodded.

Justice, his hand still on mine, curled his warm fingers around my hand and held me tight. The rose tattoo on my wrist pulsed—a tight, painful thing. The tattoo thorn pressed insistently into my skin.

"All right," I whispered. And even though I didn't have to—not yet—I said, "Your will is mine."

44

The doorman at the Bard Mansion opened the front door after a single hard knock.

It was nearly two in the morning, and while I hardly expected Finn and Darin to be on the stoop, passing a bottle of vodka between them while they worriedly awaited my return, I was a tiny bit disappointed that the only greeting I received was, "May I help you?"

The gaunt, mottle-skinned doorman sniffed the air around me.

If he'd asked Jagger that question, Jagger would've said, "You can help me by dying," and then the doorman would've done just that.

But I only said, "I'm the Smith body. I'm here for the games."

The doorman's throat rattled, but after another sniff, he held the door wide-open.

Have you ever been in a museum after closing? When the lights are dim, the halls are empty of life, and all the statues and the people in the paintings are just . . . there. Staring. Watching. Immobile, silent figures.

Maybe it was because I'd been so recently immobile in my own body —aware but not able to move, feel, or speak—or maybe it was because it was the middle of the night and no one was in the massive entry but me, the doorman, and a circle of marble statues, but for the first time, I felt the hard press of the statues' milky-white eyes and their watchful, silent gaze.

I hurried through the entry, my footsteps loud on the stone, clothes wet from the misting rain. The cold air of the mansion prickled over the damp fabric, and I was thinking of how to convince Finn it was in his best interests to sleep on the floor instead of me when—

I was yanked into a closet, and the door slammed shut after me.

That fast.

One second I was thinking about that feather mattress, and the next I was plastered to the tiny closet's wall, held in place by illusion bonds of air.

The room was empty, just bare walls and wood floor. If I took two steps one way and three steps another, I'd have circled the entire space. It was hot and cramped, and it smelled like dust and dry plaster.

"Mari?"

I squinted into the dark. A sliver of light crept under the closet door, lighting Last's features just enough for me to make out her dark eyes, her thin face, and the black glint of her hair.

Though I said I was a tiny bit disappointed not to have had a welcome party waiting worriedly for my arrival, I take it back. A welcome party is a terrible thing.

"Mari, is that you? I heard you tell the creature you're the Smith's body—"

Note to self: Speak more quietly.

"And although you don't look the same . . ." She raked her gaze over me, and just like my eyes were adjusting to the low light, I knew hers were too. "How does that work?" She smiled delightedly and clapped her hands as if I were a trick pony at the circus. "Do you come back different every time? That is so neat!"

Yeah. Okay.

While Last clapped, I thought about ways to get out of the situation. I promise you, I wasn't exactly looking forward to being her "friend" again.

Unfortunately, I think I conveyed the sentiment, because her smile faded, and when she leaned in close, she said sadly, "Our history crown is gone. Are you still my friend? Still my One?" She swept away the air gag over my mouth and waited for my response.

"Yes," I said, but it came out as a sort of question.

Last laughed—a tinkling laugh that was incongruous with her severe features and her black Clark heart.

"Lie," she sang. "Lie, lie, lie. But I promised we'd be friends forever, and *I* am still your friend. Oh, Mari, now you'll be called Two and we'll have so much fun. I'll just . . ." She pressed her cold fingers to my temples, even though to conjure her false memories she didn't have to. The sharp-thorn weave and tug of her rope slid toward me.

I knew Jagger had told me not to untie knots. I knew that. And I knew if anyone found out what I was, it'd be the end of me, but . . . I considered it. I slid my senses out. Gripped the end of Last's illusion. Thought about tugging it free and then knocking her unconscious and sending her for a nice holiday at Hell Gate.

But . . . I couldn't do it. I knew what happened to conjurers who went for a stay at Hell Gate. While Last was a sociopath, I couldn't bring myself to tug the end of the rope that would lead directly to her death.

Why?

I wasn't ready to cross that line. I still had free will. I had a choice.

"Tonight," she whispered, "I'm going to have you kill the Smith heir in his sleep."

Well, I once had a choice.

The closet door was flung open. The wash of bright light snapped over us, and then, just as quickly, the door was yanked shut, and we were in darkness again.

Last gasped. Her hands flew from my head, illusion rope suspended in the air in front of me.

"Sorry. Is this closet already occupied?"

Luvic.

Luvic.

I'd never been so happy to see a conjurer in my life.

Last held her hand out in front of her, fingers pressed to her thumb. Her upper lip curled, and she made a snarling noise.

"Leave, Bard."

The closet was tiny, barely big enough for a grown person to turn around and touch their toes in. With three people crammed inside, it was suffocatingly small.

"Leave? But I just got here." He slumped his shoulders, stuck his hands in his pockets, and looked around the cramped, near-black closet.

"I'm having an . . ."—he lowered his voice to a whisper—"assignation." Tilting his head toward me, Luvic winked.

It was so dark I barely caught it, but yes, that was a wink.

"Would you like me to make you another noose?" Last asked in a sweet, high-pitched voice. "Leave, Bard. Now."

"I'm afraid I can't do that," Luvic said, a smile in his voice. "You see, this is *my* home. *My* closet. *My* secret spot. And I'm meeting someone here in . . . hmm . . . two minutes."

Last was flummoxed. That was the word. She was flummoxed.

She stared at Luvic. Turned and looked at me. Back to Luvic.

She blew the bonds of air away, and I dropped to the wood floor.

"Come, Two. We'll go elsewhere."

Yeah right.

"I'm sorry," Luvic said. "Did I forget to mention? My home. My closet. My secret spot. *My* girl."

His girl? *His?*

Luvic winked at me again, bared his teeth in a grin, and then turned back to Last.

"*My* assignation. You, Last, are the only uninvited guest."

She twisted her hand. A noose hung threateningly above Luvic. "Two is mine."

Luvic glanced at the noose and then down at Last. I forgot how tall he was, how big, until he was shut in a tiny closet, leaning over crow-like, stick-thin Last.

And while she was tense and—I was sure—ready to conjure an arsenal of history's worst weapons, Luvic merely flicked his hand, a gust of air sending the noose to thud against the wall and fall to the floor.

"You had your fun last game," he whispered, "using the Smith body. Now it's my turn. We let you play. Now we get to play."

"But she is my friend!"

"No," Luvic said, twisting his hand, weaving an illusion. It was a beautiful knot. A butterfly knot. A whisper of gold fluttering in the dark, flying toward me. It settled over my head, perched on my temple, and kissed me. "She is mine."

Last gasped. "No! No, no, no!"

A rain of butterfly wings misted over my forehead—a cool, soft, gentle touch.

"Tell me you love me," Luvic said.

"No! Two is—"

I smiled dreamily at him as his butterfly knots stroked my skin. "I love you, Luvic. I love you so much."

"See?" Luvic turned to Last. Loomed over her. "She is mine. If you touch her, if you conjure in the same room as her, If you look at her . . . I will know. And you will die."

"You can't—"

"Can't I?"

"You're too weak!"

"Am I?"

"Two?" Last's eyes glimmered in the dark. She was a little girl, abandoned and alone. She lifted a hand beseechingly.

"Out," Luvic said. "Out of my closet."

Last snarled. Twisted her hand. A morningstar, that medieval mace, flew through the air.

Luvic threw up his hand, and a whirlpool swallowed the morningstar and splashed harmlessly to the wood floor.

Last blasted a dozen poison-tipped needles. They had only inches to shoot and pierce both Luvic and me.

He twisted his hand, and the needles folded into a dozen death-axe butterflies.

Last shrieked when they turned on her. She flew from the closet. Luvic kicked the door shut after her.

The butterflies burst into blue and orange flame. The sparks floated around us, picking out the highlights in Luvic's dark hair, brushing his gold skin.

He smiled down at me, his eyes sparking mischievously.

He placed a hand on either side of me, bracing them on the wall. He moved close, his warm mouth pressing against my ear, his body caging me to the wall as effectively as Last's air bonds.

"Say it again, Mari," Luvic murmured, his lips brushing my skin, feathering in my loose hair. "Tell me how much you love me."

His voice was low. Melodious, as only a Bard's could be. It was a lulling, seductive tenor. The closet was no longer suffocating and dark. Instead, it was a fairyland filled with floating light, intimacy, and the spiced heat of Luvic pressed over me.

I kicked him in the ankle. Hard.

He jerked back. Made a face and then nodded at the door. He widened his eyes and nodded again.

Oh.

Last was still there. Listening. Eavesdropping. Being Last.

I rolled my eyes. He rotated his hand in a "come on!" gesture.

"Tell me," he said. His voice sounded like the soft glide of silk pants dropping.

For crying out loud. "I love you so much."

He looked to the ceiling as if praying to the muses for patience. As if he thought I could do better. But I wasn't a Bard. I was a lockpick, not an actress.

"Shall I kiss you?" he asked seductively, moving closer, a gleam in his eyes.

I shook my head.

"Shall I make you shout my name?"

I shook my head again.

He nodded. Pinched me.

"Yes," I said, wincing. "Oh yes. Yes. So good."

He flattened his mouth; held back a laugh. Gestured for me to continue.

"Luvic. Oh, yes! Yes! You are . . . so . . . oh . . . so . . . good."

"You like my kiss? You like my—"

I kicked him again. "I love it. I'll do anything for it. You're so good. So manly. So . . ." I was reaching. I was really reaching now. What did you say? What did people say? "So . . . ambidextrous."

Luvic's face twisted. It turned bright red. He closed his eyes and shook his head, shoulders heaving with restrained laughter. He clenched his fist and hit the wall in a rhythmic thud.

"That's so good," I said. "So, so good."

"Stop," he said, laughing. "Stop. She's gone. She's gone."

I shoved him. He didn't budge, just kept laughing.

"Ambidextrous? Is that all I am to you? Good on the left, great on the right?"

I brushed a hand over my head. My fingers tingled at the illusion. "What's this? What did you put up there?"

It wasn't a memory or a history, that was for sure.

He shrugged. "It's something Celia uses. It keeps flyaways down. Makes her hair stay in place. Look nice."

He gave me a hairdo? Some illusion hair spray? "I . . ."

He smiled. "Want to thank me?"

"How did you know I was here?"

"I didn't . . ." He turned to the wall opposite the door and ran his hand over the plaster. A click sounded, and then the wall swung inward. "I really do have somewhere to be."

Oh.

Huh.

"Do you want me to come?" I asked.

He smiled, a laughing spark in his gaze. "No, Mari, I do not want you to come to my secret meeting. I'm weaving plans, spinning plots, making mischief. You can't be part of it."

I shrugged. "Thought I'd ask. Do you still want to kill me?"

"What?" He gave me a quick, startled glance.

"Before." I waved my hand in the air. "The memories . . . the knife, the kiss, the game of tag. Do you still—?"

"Oh." He gave a surprised hum. "Are those the memories I planted? I thought I gave you something different. Hmm. I need to practice that one. Mental illusions are not my specialty."

"What is your specialty?"

He grinned. "It's a secret. Bye, Mari. Get to your Smith. Sleep tight."

I frowned. I'd been gone since the game. There'd been all that screaming after Jacob left the tomb. Who had screamed? Had Luvic been out there? Celia and Ragnor? Darin and Wolfgang?

"But what happened after the game? Is everyone all right? Did—?"

Luvic shook his head. "Sorry, I'm running a bit behind. Gotta go."

Then he was gone, his blue and orange butterfly sparks leaving with him. The plaster wall was a wall once more.

I hurried from the empty closet and ran down the hall and up six flights of stairs to the Smith suite. I was looking forward to a warm welcome.

I didn't get one.

45

THE TRICKSTER MOVED LIKE A COLD STREAM GLIDING SMOOTHLY OVER tumbled rock. He quickly flowed from shadow to deeper shadow, to dappled illusion light, and then back to shadow again. Sometimes, at a sigh from the wind, the trickster looked behind him, but of course, no one was there.

The wind hadn't meant to follow the trickster into the hated watching-stone tunnels beneath the Bard Mansion, but the word "secret" was a lure strung too neatly to resist.

It was the boy's fault. The wind had found him after the game. He'd been curled on his side, lying on his bed, staring at the wall. The wind had tapped his cheek, bounced on a salty tear, and then swirled and curled until it was lying in a thin sheet on top of him.

But the boy had shaken his head and whispered, "No, Wind. I want to be alone."

And so the wind had left the boy alone in his room with his salty tears and his mournful stillness.

It had swept down the hallways, past whispering Bards, shifty-eyed Clarks, and even the solange-eyed one, who'd been stalking down a hallway, not tipsy or wobbly or anything but hard-eyed and moving like an unsheathed knife.

The wind had almost trailed after him, but then the man had passed the trickster, and the trickster had grinned—was it a grin or a snarl?—at the solange-eyed man and said, "Why so glum? Luck ran out?"

The solange-eyed one had hesitated. He'd tensed, and the wind had thought he might spin to the left, cut his hand through the air, and send the trickster into his next life.

The trickster had casually folded his arms, his gaze roaming over the man's dirty clothes. There was scorched fabric. Ash. The black streak of soot. The acrid scent of smoke, burned concrete, and hot metal.

The solange-eyed one's expression had blazed like the fire he smelled of.

"Forget it, Alterra." The trickster's grin—snarl?—had widened. "Don't even think about it." He'd tapped a finger once to his forehead and then slid past the solange-eyed one.

It had left the wind with a decision to make. Stay with the solange-eyed one, who was staring after the trickster with narrowed eyes, or follow the trickster as he glided down the marble hall?

It was an easy decision in the end. The wind liked the trickster. Except the trickster had led it into the tunnels. Which the wind did not like.

This time . . . this time, the wind wouldn't stay long. It wouldn't allow the breathless, airless, empty-lung tunnels to bury it again. This time, the wind ran in the trickster's smooth, cold, flowing-stream shadow, skipping through it like a rock and gliding free. This time it wouldn't sink.

The wind bounced along, deeper, deeper. The trickster didn't speak—not until he came to the hated intersection where the wind had curled into that tiny, breathless ball, and then he only said, "I'm here."

The father stepped out of the wall, the rock an illusion. The wind moaned. Behind it, the slow *drip, drip, drip* of the milky water fell from the rock ceiling.

"Report."

"Two traitors. Illiac and Trenor. Dead."

"Good."

"The Bards at the Regis. It was one of Jagger's creatures. The one they call 'The Knife.'"

The father took a long breath. Pursed his mouth in a tight ball. "And?"

"And . . . 100 dead at the Night Den, 100 in an apartment fire in Astoria, 100 in—"

"Not *and* what did the Clarks do. *And* . . . what will you do if your sister loses the games?"

The wind clung to the trickster's skin, so even though his expression didn't change and his stance remained loose and free, the wind felt the rapid drumming of the trickster's heart.

"What . . . will I do?"

The father smiled. "Yes, Luvic. What will you do? You, of all my children . . . you are the most like me. A loving brother, always doing what *must* be done. Loyal. Cunning. Worthy of power."

The trickster glanced around the shadowed dome of the bulbous, cave-like room. "Are Lia and Ragnor not coming tonight?"

"No. This meeting is for you alone."

"Ah."

The father—the Bard—gripped his son's arm. A human, fatherly gesture. "What will happen if Celia passes on her blood? Is it not a brother's responsibility to think of his sister? If she wins the game . . . she will be magnificent. Regal, beloved like Queen Elizabeth I, the Virgin Queen. Ragnor's children, yours—they would be next in line. But if she doesn't win . . . what story is left? Will she want a family? No. No. That can't happen." The father shook his head. "I've always enjoyed the stories of beautiful actresses tragically lost too young. What is it? The car accident? The overdose? They remain in the hearts of the people for so long, beloved because they were plucked from this life too early."

The wind pressed itself to the trickster's chest. His heart boomed like thunder in a violent storm.

"And Ragnor?"

"Ragnor loves his sister. He'd do anything to protect her. He'd die to protect her."

The trickster nodded. One slow dip of his head.

"Luvic? Is this a triumph, or is it a tragedy? What are you doing to make certain your sister wins?"

The trickster closed his eyes. "Everything."

"And if not . . .?"

"It'd be a tragedy."

He understood exactly what his father was asking him to do if his sister failed. She and the musician would die young.

"*Yes.* You are my son. It will break my heart. If two of my children do not survive the month, oh, Luvic, it will break my heart. Yet having you still? It will be a comfort."

The trickster nodded once more. Then the wind jumped into the swirling speed of his rapid pulse and pounding heartbeat. He didn't turn back the way he'd come, ascending the hollow stone throat of the tunnels, but instead hurried farther down into the deep dark, leaving his father behind.

The wind, strong from the boy's buoying, kept ahold of the trickster. Jackaltooth rattled their throats as they passed, but they let the trickster by, merely watching with glowing orange eyes.

Ahead of the hurried echo of his steps, many-legged insects skittered over the rock and slipped into dark crevices. The stagnant, damp mineral earth pressed on the wind, but so did the trickster's illusion.

He twisted his hand, making something, shifting and flowing, until the tingle ran over the wind so strongly it buzzed. Then the trickster unlatched a hidden door and climbed a narrow set of concrete steps—212 —the wind bouncing after him. When the trickster emerged into the dark, rain-slick city streets, the wind laughed.

He wasn't himself anymore.

The trickster looked just like the solange-eyed man.

Taller than the trickster. Broader. Muscled in the way humans were when they used their bodies as weapons. Black hair still, but longer and messy. Rough stubble. Sharp, hard lines on his face. Midnight solange eyes.

He was wearing the same clothes the solange-eyed one wore when they'd met in the hallway. Dirty, wrinkled, soot-stained jeans and T-shirt. A scrape on his jaw. A bruise in exactly the right spot.

But it wasn't the appearance that made the illusion real. It was the trickster's expression. The way he moved.

He was no longer mischievous and mocking; he was bliss-eyed yet serious, vacant yet focused, determined yet stumbling. He swayed over the glistening, rain-soaked sidewalk, tripped through a puddle, and held his hand in the air when the lights of a taxi speared the misty rain.

The trickster didn't just look like the solange-eyed one; he'd become the solange-eyed one. He was a Bard, a chameleon, and an actor.

The wind laughed as the trickster ducked into the taxi. It sped through the tires hissing over the wet pavement and splashed through puddles. It delightedly sprayed fountains of water onto unsuspecting humans huddled under their umbrellas. It rolled in the wonderful wet of a summer rainstorm, until finally, the taxi glided to a stop near a warehouse at the edge of the Hudson.

The wind was so struck by the mist rising off the black water and the droplets falling in a raindrop symphony over the moonlit night that it almost missed the trickster slipping through the front door of the Night Den.

It sped after him and shoved down the steps, tumbling freely toward the all-seeing eye and its door.

The trickster yanked the door open—it opened to him—and stepped into a room filled with rubble, collapsed concrete, and the acrid, burned-metal scent that had clung to the solange-eyed one.

The wind moaned. It didn't like this. The smoke burned—a weepy, scratchy scent. It wasn't nice like a crackling campfire or a flickering candle. It was mean like twisted, melted metal and burning concrete. The wind crawled carefully over a hill of broken concrete and twisted through a maze of splintered wooden tables.

The trickster moved through the rubble, swaying, tilting, searching. There were many beings here—some human, some not—some with their animating spirits still inside them, some not. The wind was cold suddenly. It wanted, very much, to wend up the stairs and take a dip in the moonlit, raindrop-splashed Hudson.

A woman shouted, "Finn!"

Then she was tripping through the piles of concrete. She flung herself into the trickster's arms.

"They said you were here, but I didn't see you. You came back—" She broke off when the trickster tugged her closer. "Oh!" Her breath came out in a whoosh at the tight squeeze of his arms.

They stayed still, holding each other, while the wind curled around their legs. Beings skirted them, humans sorting through the rubble, some looking purposeful, some lost and confused.

On the city streets above, there was no evidence of the destruction—not even the scent of smoke. The wind knew it was only illusion that kept the rest of the city from knowing what had happened here.

The woman tilted her head back, her long, wavy auburn hair falling down her back. She smiled, although the wind thought it was a sad smile. "Hi there, handsome."

The trickster gave the woman a vacant, night-star gaze. "Hi, Cora."

She gave a dry, wind-choked laugh.

The wind remembered this woman. She'd been there with the solange-eyed one when the girl had come. She'd made the man solange and let him rest his head in her lap. She smelled of luck and new pennies. Not human, no. But not bad like the rocklike one, and not frightening like the executioner's tree come to life.

"How bad is it?" the trickster asked.

"Bad."

The trickster spread his hand over her back and let out a long, weary breath.

The woman's eyes filled with the splash of a penny dropped in a wishing well. A tear trailed down her cheek, and the wind slid over it, tasting the luck of it.

"I thought I wouldn't see you. At least, not until after the games. You didn't have to come—"

Across the rubble-strewn room, the eye's door swung open, and the other rocklike one, the hard one that watched the front door, shot his flat gray gaze around the room.

"What's wrong?" the woman asked. She lifted her hand and brushed it over the trickster's cheek.

He closed his eyes and leaned into her touch.

The other rocklike one moved across the room, watching the trickster and the woman with narrowed eyes. The wind knew he whispered tales to Hell Gate. It knew this meeting would be heard of within minutes. There weren't many secrets in the Night Den.

The woman glanced at the rock scented one and frowned. "Finn?" she said loudly, and the trickster opened his navy-sky eyes.

He smiled. For a moment, it was his trickster smile, but then it smoothed into a blissful, vacant one. "Cora?"

"Yes?"

"I've just been offered . . . everything. All the power. All of it. The only thing I have to do is betray the people who trust me."

The wind held still as the woman spread her fingers over the trickster's cheek. Sent her fingers over his skin in a soothing, questing glide.

"And what will you do?" Her hand slid into his hair, catching the smooth silk of it between her fingers.

He stared at the woman, a bleak light in his navy gaze. "That's the question, isn't it?"

"Is it?"

The trickster looked over the burnt destruction of the Night Den, his jaw firm, eyes filled with a bleak sort of determination.

The woman pressed her mouth to his—a soft kiss that reminded the wind of the gentle glide of the sun over a falling rose petal. It was a lover's kiss. The ocean kissing the shore. Dew resting on grass. The moon stroking the mist.

"Can you stay the night?"

The trickster shook his head. "No. I have to go. Only . . ."

"Only?"

"I came to ask . . . for a bit of luck."

The woman smiled. A beautiful smile that made the wind tingle and forget that it was surrounded by charred remains and acrid smoke.

"Always. You know you never have to ask. I love you. All my luck is yours."

The woman kissed the trickster. The wind dove into the honey-sweet smell wrapping around them. The trickster held the woman tight as her mouth moved over his. Then he smiled against her lips as the cool, golden glow of luck pressed into him.

46

THE SECOND I KNOCKED ON THE SMITHS' DOOR, IT WAS FLUNG WIDE-OPEN. Darin stood on the opposite side, a tower-like figure full of menace, his wide smile hinting at bloodshed. He loomed over me, filling the doorway, his shadow stretching across the hall.

I instinctively took a small step back. When I did, his smile grew wider.

I hadn't seen him look so viciously murderous since the gala, when I'd shot Finn with Smith's Folly. I guess I'd let myself forget that Darin was as much a conjurer as the Clarks, and just as efficient of a killer.

"Sent another, did we?" His deep voice was a growly purr that sent chills up my spine.

This was not a Darin I'd ever met. His shoulders were bunched, his stance wide. If I had to put a mood to him, I'd say it was similar to Jagger's mood right before he tore off someone's arm and gnawed on it while they watched.

Even the chestnut-brown of Darin's hair, the cloud-gray of his eyes, and the broadness of him seemed darker, sharper, more menacing.

This was not the greeting I'd expected.

"Um. Hi . . ." I raised a hand in a half-wave.

His lips curled into a feral "I'm about to carve you open" grin. Clearly, something had happened while I was away, and clearly, he didn't recognize me. His fingers were pressed to his thumb, and I imagined he was about to go full Smith on me.

You know what I mean. The "kill first, ask questions never" philosophy.

No problem—I just had to let him know who I was.

I gave a small smile. "It's me. Mari."

"Really?" He raised his eyebrows, looking me up and down.

"Yeah. I know I look different—"

"No. No, come on in." He smiled politely and made a welcoming gesture with his hand, stepping aside so I could come into the suite.

All the same, the back of my neck itched. There was a strange light in Darin's eyes. A falseness to his smile. It wasn't his "if you make it stop, I'll buy you a pizza" smile; it was . . . a shark pretending to be a minnow while it lured you into its gaping, sharp-toothed mouth.

I'd never seen him smile like this.

If he'd had illusion knotted around him, I would've suspected him of being someone else. Someone like Primus, or even Wolfgang. But there wasn't any illusion. It was just Darin being exceptionally weird.

I gave him a cautious glance, hesitating in the doorway. "Is Finn here?"

Darin's shark smile widened. "Sure is."

I peered behind him. The spartan sitting room was lit by the soft yellow glow of a table lamp, but other than the light edging across the wood floor, the room was empty. Quiet.

"Where is he?"

"Get inside." Darin gestured again. "I'm not a doorman."

Well, that was a little more like the Darin I knew. The tickle on the back of my neck lessened, and I ducked into the suite.

The door slammed shut. Locked.

Crap!

I ducked. A neon-blue fire knife flew over my head. It hit the wall. Stuck.

"Darin!"

Another knife.

I jumped to the right. "Stop!"

The wall of blue flame encircled us. I backed away. Darin stalked closer.

This was not the Darin I knew. The joking, annoying, older-brother Darin. This was a Smith intent on his kill.

His false smile was gone. Instead, he watched me with predatory intent. His muscles tensed, like a wolf right before its jaw-snapping leap. I kept backing away. The blue fire singed the backs of my thighs. I stopped, trapped.

"Darin—" I held up my hands.

He moved so fast he was a blur. Was it illusion? Was he just that fast? He slammed me against the wall. One arm caged me. His other hand held a blue fire knife to my throat. The breath shot from my lungs in a pained wheeze.

"Now," Darin said, smiling his bloodthirsty grin, "before you die, tell me the truth." He pressed the knife's edge against the soft skin of my throat. "Who sent you?"

"No one! I'm Mari—"

The knife pressed harder. "That's what the last one said. She died too."

What the . . . ? The last one?

"At least the first creature looked like Mari. Put up a better fight too. Yet . . . she still died. Now tell me. Who. Sent. You?"

So was this it? Was Darin going to send me to my final death? All I'd wanted was a nice, soft feather bed, and if not that, then a nice blanket and a pillow on the floor in front of the door. And what had I got instead? The worst welcome party ever.

"The last one turned to black liquid when I killed her. Will you do the same? Speak, creature. Who sent you?"

Creature? Again with the creature? He could be such a prick.

I bared my teeth and hissed, "Let me go, you overbearing, sociopathic, homicidal . . . virgin!"

He blinked. The menacing expression in his gaze slipped to confusion. The sting of the knife lessened. "Mari?"

I glared. "What, are you going to cut off my head for a ball and use my intestines as a goalpost? Well, if you are, then do it. Then I'll come back again. But I'll look different, and I won't be as nice. Trust me. I will *not* be nice."

"What kind of pizza do I like?" Darin asked, eyeing me skeptically.

I rolled my eyes. "Meat. All the meat."

The blue flames around us dimmed. "Coffee or tea?"

"Coffee. Black. Two spoons of sugar. Stupidly hot."

His hold on me loosened.

"Boxers or briefs?"

I thought back to the laundry I'd done for them all. "Briefs. Black."

"My favorite song?"

"'Like a Virgin.'"

He held back a smile. "My favorite color?"

"How should I know? You're a homicidal sociopath, so it's probably bloodred."

He grinned. "Hi, Mari."

I didn't smile back.

Behind Darin, the door to Finn's room opened, and he stepped out. He was just out of the shower, his hair wet, T-shirt and pants damp from being thrown on without toweling off completely. He paused when he saw Darin's blue flame circle and the knife still held to my throat. His gaze was solange-blank, all vivid-star bliss and shattered kaleidoscope. I was starting to be able to read how much solange he had in his system by the brightness of his eyes. Right now, I'd bet he'd just downed two thimblefuls.

He focused his gaze on me, and for a moment, it was just the two of us, back in that tomb, him desperate not to hurt me, me desperate to save a thousand strangers.

What had he said? *"Mari. I'm afraid if I do this, you'll never——"*

What? What had he been afraid of? And what would I never do, be, say?

Do you remember when I wished there was someone out there who'd recognize me after I died without me having to tell them who I was? I felt it again in that moment. I desperately wanted Finn to recognize me. To know me.

Not even Justice or Griff could recognize me. They only knew me because—just like them—I'd land in my new body, buck naked, on Hell Gate's kitchen table, in the entryway, or in my bedroom.

I think Luvic had heard Last, or he'd deduced who I was from what Last had said. But . . . Finn? Could he see who I was?

He closed one eye. Opened it. Closed the other. Opened it. What did he see through his solange gaze?

"Hi, Finn. I'm back."

As soon as I spoke, he swayed as if he'd heard a note of music, and then he shook his head, clearing the song out.

"Hi, Mari. What took you so long?"

I grinned at him as Darin's knife and blue flame vanished.

Finn knew me.

He *knew* me.

I wanted to run to him, jump in his arms, and tell him everything was all right. Everything was going to be all right. It was irrational. Untrue. But I still had the strongest urge to hurry across the sitting room and fold my arms around him.

"How did you know it was her?" Darin asked, frowning between me and Finn. "She looks nothing like herself."

Finn tilted his head. Closed an eye. Shrugged. Then he walked across the lamplit room, stumbling only once when he skirted the leather sofa.

I tilted my chin as he stopped in front of me. I was shorter this time. Smaller. Eyes more gray than blue. Long hair more brown than black. But still, essentially, me. My features were a flowing stream for eyes to move quickly past, ignoring and forgetting.

I wasn't yearningly beautiful anymore. Thankfully. Instead, I was as unadorned and forgettable as a plain white dress, no ruffles or lace or embroidered eyelets to make me unique or memorable. The only concern I had was that this face reminded me of a blank canvas.

Sometimes, when people see a blank canvas, they paint their own picture on it. Love. Hate. Greed. Murder. Lust. This face could become a reflection of their own heart.

Finn studied my face; looked into me and through me, just like he'd done that first time in the Night Den. Was he painting his own story onto me, or did the solange let him see me as I was? I didn't know.

His gaze left my face, and then he reached forward and took my hand. His calloused palm rubbed over my skin as he flipped it over.

I closed my eyes as his thumb slowly brushed the tattooed rose. His fingers gently scraped over the rose petals. The thorn hurt. It was a constant stinging pressure digging into my skin. He stroked the spike with warm fingers. Finally, he pressed his thumb into the tattooed blood drop.

"I'm sorry."

I opened my eyes. His shattered gaze stared at where he held my wrist.

"I'm sorry, Mari."

I shrugged, trying to ignore the golden pulse running from where he held me, all the way up my arm, down into my chest. It was that rope again. The rope that didn't exist. The invisible knot that wasn't there. It tightened on my heart and tugged at the sorrow in his voice. I dropped my eyes and pulled my hand free.

"There's no reason to be sorry. It's the games. I told you before, I'll do anything to make sure you win."

Finn dragged in a breath and then nodded.

"Right," Darin said. "Okay. Now that apologies for killing are out of the way . . . and sorry, Mari, for thinking you were a black liquid creature sent to kill us. I didn't realize you were . . . you." He waited, his Darin smile firmly in place.

"Forgiven."

"Thanks." He grinned. Considered me. "So, Mari. We've been on high alert since Jacob went . . ."—he whistled "cuckoo" and wound his finger in a circle at his temple—"so I couldn't order takeout. And none of us can cook like you. Or taste-test for poison. So . . ." He smiled hopefully.

I gave him a disbelieving stare. "You want me to make you a meal at two in the morning? After you just tried to kill me?"

"Would you? You're amazing." He nudged me toward the little half-kitchen area with its portable stove.

I glanced at Finn. "Are you hungry too?"

Finn's eyes crinkled as he smiled.

"He hasn't eaten since lunch," Darin added helpfully. "Neither have I."

"Darin Smith, you are a sad, sad man."

He gave me a little orphaned kitten look, full of innocence and hunger. I scoffed and bent down into their portable refrigerator and box of food supplies to see what I could find. I'd have to go shopping soon if they expected me to keep making them full meals four times a day.

"Can you cook?" I asked Finn, pulling out two thick rib eye steaks.

He nodded.

Darin gave him a quelling look that clearly said, "Don't ruin this gravy train for me."

I smiled as I grabbed butter, black pepper, and seasoned salt. There was a bag of potatoes that I'd been saving for hash browns, but I pulled them out so I could make mashed potatoes. The cupboards were well-stocked for two bachelors coming out on what they'd consider a military campaign.

"Who packed the food for you? The kitchen supplies? You're surprisingly well-set."

"Aska. My body. My . . ." Darin frowned, probably realizing if Aska had come, she wouldn't be alive anymore.

"What happened," I asked, thinking about the screaming I'd heard after Jacob left the tomb. "After Jacob left? I heard the—"

"Screams?"

"Yeah." I handed Finn the bag of potatoes and a paring knife.

He held them in his hands, looking at them blankly. Then he smiled, made a "huh" sound, and dropped to a wooden stool at the kitchenette counter and started on the first potato.

Darin eyed me, probably worried I was about to assign him a task as well. "Well, I guess you saw him during the game."

I nodded, filling a pot with water. I didn't share that Jacob had loved his body like a mother. It didn't feel right to give that piece of him away. I was there for a private moment that I shouldn't have seen, and out of respect for—I don't know—the boy I'd always felt sorrow for . . . I was going to keep his own sorrow hidden.

I put the pot of water on the stove and started to heat a cast-iron pan for the rib eye. Finn had peeled the first potato. He'd peeled the skin in one long, unbroken spiral. The shape of the spiral dropping to the counter and his small, satisfied smile made my chest squeeze.

"Yeah," said Darin. "So nobody except Primus was happy about the game. He came out first, grinning like he'd just won the lottery. Then Celia came out. She was as cold as ice, but you could tell she was upset. Mainly because her brothers stood in front of her, shielding her from the room. When they get protective like that, you know something's up."

Finn dropped another perfectly peeled potato onto the counter. He kept his head bent, listening, his shoulders tense.

"We were all waiting in the room, watching the clock count down. The Clark was rubbing his hands, salivating over the fact that soon we'd hit the two-hour mark. Then—"

He broke off as I flicked water into the cast iron, testing the heat. It sizzled and popped. I lowered a prepared steak into the pan. It hissed and snapped.

Darin smiled. "Then Jacob came out. I don't know exactly what he did. It was some Ward mental illusion. One minute there's forty of us in the room, just watching the clock, and the next . . ."

Finn dropped another spiral peel to the counter. Grabbed his fourth potato. His knife moved quickly across the potato skin.

"The next . . .?" I asked.

Darin shrugged. "Jacob's in a class of his own. I'm surprised he hasn't won every game. He came out, and the room went pitch-black. Then there was a blinding flash, and the room lit up again . . . It's hard to describe. The Smith—Dad—and I threw out shields. So did the Bard and his kids. The Clark. But the rest of them weren't so lucky. Even with our shields, we still felt it."

"What was it?"

The water was boiling. It roiled in the pot. I grabbed the potatoes Finn had peeled and cubed and dropped them in, piece by piece. The steam rose in a cloud, and drops of water hit the cast iron and popped.

I jumped away from the hot skillet.

"He made people . . . I guess you could say . . . he magnified people's inner-self. Whatever trait or emotion is most . . . you . . . he yanked it out and blew it up a thousand times."

Finn cocked his head, and his eyes widened. "How many Clarks were in the room? Bards?"

Darin nodded. "Yeah. Twenty-three Clarks. Eighteen Bards. Then me and Dad and Philoneas."

I flipped the first steak. The bottom half was perfectly charred. It cracked and sizzled as the fat hit the heat.

"Dad and I were fine. We were shielded, and we just felt like . . . you know . . . fighting. Swords. Knives. Fists. Whatever." He shrugged. "Basic sparring we'd done most of our lives. We knew what was happening and just rode it. If it'd hit us full force, my guess is, we'd have gone into a killing rage and tried to slaughter everyone."

Dang. I stabbed a boiling potato with a fork. Not even close to done.

"The Bards, they shielded too. Luvic and Ragnor. Right away, they stepped in front of Celia, weapons out, and made this impenetrable wall. They were so loaded up with 'come near my sister, I'll kill you' that it's pretty obvious the only thing inside of them is family loyalty. If Jacob's illusion magnifies what you are, I'd steer clear of trying to split the Bard siblings. So then it was the Clarks. They weren't prepared. Basically, they're bloodthirsty, torture-mad, history-loving, sacrifice-touting . . ." He held out his hands. "It was a bloodbath. They turned on each other. That's nothing new. Practically a Clark hobby. They also went after any unshielded Bards. And the Bards—the unshielded ones—were weak, so . . ."

"How many?" Finn asked.

"Fifteen dead, Clarks and Bards both. Eight injured."

I stared at Darin. This was by far the bloodiest game in centuries.

"Steak's done," he said, pointing to the stove.

I pulled it off, set it on a plate to rest, and lobbed a pat of butter on top to melt. Then I dropped the next steak onto the cast iron.

"Then," Darin continued, "in the confusion, Philoneas sent a wave of air daggers at Dad. We burst them, of course. But then he sent this wind-zombie creature with poisoned teeth after Dad, and while we were busy with that, Philoneas hit Dad with a poison-tipped dart—"

"Is he—?"

"No. He's all right. Since the gala, I've been carrying the antidote to Smith's Folly on me at all times."

"So inside Philoneas, there's only the desire to kill Wolfgang?" I asked.

Finn stood and moved across the small kitchenette space. As he passed, his arm brushed mine. My body sparked and sizzled at the touch. He poked at the steak, and I flipped it.

"Forgot you like it rare."

"Thanks." The right side of his mouth kicked up.

"Yeah," Darin said. "Pretty much. They've been trying to kill each other my entire life."

"Is this . . .?" I wrinkled my brow, trying to remember the history between Philoneas and Wolfgang. "Is this because of Lucinda Bard?"

"Bingo."

As the kitchenette filled with the smell of charred steak and melting butter, and the sound of sizzling meat and boiling water, I thought about what I knew of Lucinda Bard.

She was the current Bard's younger sister, third-born after her late brother, Dougan. According to Roumelade, she was the most beautiful Bard in generations. She wasn't an actor or a musician or in the arts like the rest of her family. She was something of a black sheep.

"How much do you know?" Darin asked, and I shrugged.

"Love triangle gone wrong. Betrayal. Death. Lifelong vendetta. You know, the usual."

Darin snorted and grabbed the steak off the counter. "I'm eating this now."

I waved my hand in a "feel free" gesture and pulled Finn's steak off the stove. A dab of butter, salt, no pepper. "You don't like pepper, right?"

He smiled in surprise. "How'd you guess?"

I shrugged and speared a potato again. Done. I'd drain them and whip them with milk and butter and a touch of garlic and salt. Maybe parmesan, if they had it.

"It wasn't actually a love triangle," Finn said, and when both Darin and I stared at him, he shrugged. "It wasn't."

"How so?"

"I know the story too. The three of them were best friends," Finn said. "That's not a love triangle. They'd been best friends since they were kids. Both Philoneas and Wolfgang loved Lucinda, but Philoneas as a friend, while Wolfgang loved her . . ."

"This isn't my mom, by the way," Darin said, waving his fork. "My mom came later. Here's the thing. Philoneas and Lucinda were supposed to marry, because their principals had worked out a contract. But Philoneas helped Lucinda and my dad disappear so they could marry in secret. Philoneas was put through some pretty nasty Ward torture by his principal trying to pry out the truth of where Wolfgang and Lucinda had run off to. He held out. Never told. Then, years later, Lucinda comes back. She shows up on Philoneas's doorstep. She's all beat-up, looks like she was attacked by a madman. She has this story that Dad went insane and tried to kill her. Next thing you know, Dad's back in New York with a new bride. My mom. She's pregnant with me. A week later, Lucinda tosses herself off the Brooklyn Bridge. After that, Philoneas made a death promise. Someday, he swore, he'd kill my dad in revenge. Dad grieved. I don't know if he really did attack Lucinda—I've never asked. But I know he still grieves her. He has a lock of hair wrapped in a blue ribbon that he pulls out sometimes. Black, like a Bard's. Nothing like my mom's. Anyway, Philoneas married Uliea. Had Jacob and Viola. You know what happened there. And every few months or so, Philoneas and my dad try to kill each other. I think when one of them finally succeeds, they'll be very surprised. And then, probably, whoever is left alive won't know what to do with their life anymore." He shrugged. He also looked a bit sad, so I plopped a spoonful of the mashed potatoes I'd just whipped up onto his plate.

"Thanks, Mari."

I gave Finn a big spoonful too. "Eat up."

Darin made a happy sound as he tasted my potatoes.

"You conjurers are a tragic bunch," I said, thinking how much Roumelade would love their family dramas. "By the way . . . will Jacob be disqualified? I thought the rules explicitly stated a player can't harm any other player during the game. And the Bards promised safe passage while in their home . . ."

Darin swallowed the bit of mashed potato in his mouth. "No. He didn't harm anyone. While all that chaos was happening, he just stood in the center of it, blank-eyed and staring off into oblivion. Nobody came near him. He didn't raise a hand against anyone. The principals ruled he wasn't at fault. He only grew the seed that was already in everyone's hearts. If he'd done that illusion in a group of kindergarten teachers, they'd have probably had milk and cookies and sung the ABC song in a circle, so no. He's still in it. We're just . . . on high alert. A bit paranoid. Seeing as . . ."

"Someone tried to kill you, disguised as me?"

He nodded.

"I bet it was the Clarks. Last told me to kill you tonight."

Darin stiffened. "Did you just poison my steak?"

"Ha-ha."

He dropped his empty plate to the counter. "What's for dessert?"

When I gave him a look, he started to whistle and looked innocently at the ceiling.

"Thanks, Mari," Finn said, taking his plate to the sink. "That was the best steak I've had in a long time."

"Do you think," Darin asked, "Jagger would let you off being a nine so you can be my body after Finn's dead?"

I shoved him.

"What?"

"Go to bed, Darin."

"I'm waiting up for my dad," he grumbled, walking out of the kitchenette.

That left me and Finn alone in the small space. Finn watched me, a quiet, cautious bent to his mouth. Slowly, he reached out and touched the tips of his fingers to the back of my hand.

Reflexively, I gripped his fingers. When I did, he folded my hand in his own. The warmth of his grip spread through me.

"You've got . . ." He nodded to my head. "More illusion."

"It's for my hair."

Finn gave me a quizzical smile.

I was reaching up, about to touch the stubbled line of his jaw, when I realized what I was doing. My hand froze midair. I dropped it and pulled my other hand free of his.

"I wanted to tell you . . ." I peered up at him. He was seemingly taller than before. It was me, though—I was shorter. "Jagger . . ."

He nodded. Looked down at me with a solemn expression.

"Jagger told me to kill you at the closing ceremony. He has no intention of honoring your bargain. He said a dead man can't collect. I . . . I want to be honest with you. Just know, if it isn't me at the closing ceremony, it's going to be someone else. You need to . . . watch your back."

He smiled, the right side of his mouth lifting.

I frowned. "What?"

"You," he said. "You aren't supposed to tell someone *when* you're going to kill them."

Well, since the beginning, he'd known my role in this game. What harm would it do to tell him the end play?

"Try not to die," I said. "Against my better judgment, I'm starting to like you. I want you to live out your short, blissful, love-filled life."

He hesitated for a moment, a decision tilting him one way, then the other. Then, decided, he pulled me close. Tucked me against him. I sighed and rested my cheek against the solid beat of his heart.

"I'll do my best, Mari."

"Thank you."

I'll admit, I stayed in his arms longer than I should have.

47

QUESTION: WHAT DO YOU DO IF A LARGE NUMBER OF YOUR GUESTS slaughter each other in a violent, mind illusion bloodbath and the rest of your guests are a hair's breadth away from unleashing mass destruction?

If you're a conjurer, you throw a party. There's nothing better than music, alcohol, and fun in the sun to dispel the promise of bloodbath-ery.

I woke up gritty-eyed and exhausted, and when I was grinding coffee beans, Darin came into the kitchenette, threw a beach towel at me, and said, "Beach-party day. Get Finn."

That's right. Beach party.

Even though Manhattan was technically an island, I'd never been to the beach before. I'd never actually been outside the five boroughs. Jagger's leash was short, and his trust was even shorter. So, although I thought going to the beach for a barbecue was absolutely mad, I couldn't help but feel a wild thrill at the sight of frothy ocean waves spreading over bisque-colored sand.

Fire Island was the kind of pristine natural beauty I'd only dreamed about. It wasn't far from the city, but the remoteness, the quietude, the undisturbed, untouched beauty—it was another world.

Not a conjured world. Not an illusion. It was God's work. I'd seen that before, in the delicate heart-shaped leaf of a gingko, or in a spiderweb glistening with morning dew, or in a pigeon's feather caught and fluttering in a gust of wind. But those were small things in a city made entirely of the dreams of men. Here, there was no illusion to hide the wonder of the world.

I'd never seen anything so beautiful. So free.

Was this what happened when you stepped outside the cages of illusion?

Jagger felt so far away. Hell Gate and the fear of my final death. Even Finn's free fall and my task to kill him felt like a distant unreality. As soon as we boarded the Bard's boat and were sailing toward the long, quarter-mile-wide island, the wind swept all my worries away and barred them from clouding the day.

The sky was a sun-bleached blue. Thin, high clouds drew long, frothy tails across the expanse. My hair whipped across my face, and the misty, ocean scented breeze tugged me closer toward the water.

The island was long. Thirty-two miles. It was a barrier island, with steep dunes, wind-flattened, silvery-green shore grass, sunken wetlands, and quiet woodlands. There were no cars here, no roads, only quaint, centuries-old seaside maritime villages and wooden boardwalks winding down to the shore.

The conjurers avoided the villages and the scattering of sunseekers and instead staked out an empty stretch of white sand hidden by mounded dunes and wind-bent juneberry trees. We were miles away from the rest of the world; miles away from the reality that the fate of the world was being played out in a Machiavellian game by the very conjurers on this beach. There weren't any illusions here—except perhaps the illusion that this was a normal June day, with a group of normal friends enjoying a normal beach party.

I grinned at the wash of gray-blue ocean blanketing the sand. It rolled in high waves, breaking and then sliding across the wet sand, hissing, foaming, and receding. Then it would do it all over again. The crash and slide was addictive. Even the salty seaweed scent and the sting of the wind in my eyes was addictive.

I loved it.

The wind shoved me further onto the beach, and I stumbled,

laughing as sand slid into my shoes. I kicked them off. Made a happy sound at the soft, funny feel of warm sand between my toes.

"Where are you going?" Finn asked, his voice carried off by the ocean breeze.

"To put my feet in the water," I said, intent on the crashing waves. "I've never felt the ocean before. Is it cold? Is it warm? Is it . . .?"

I tugged down my silk bottoms. Pulled off my top. Darin, bless him, had conjured me a bathing suit. It was a black one-piece—exactly the sort of thing a Smith would come up with—and I'd worn it under my uniform. I stripped down, dropping the clothes into a pile next to a line of dried seaweed. The sun blanketed my bare skin, and I held out my arms to the wind.

I turned to Finn, smiling widely. "Isn't this amazing? Isn't it—?"

I stopped at the dumbstruck expression on his face. He was staring as if he'd never seen me before. His eyelids drooped and went all sleepy-slumbery. My skin prickled.

"Finn?"

"Hmm?" He swayed toward me, moving closer like the heave and pull of the waves.

He'd dropped solange into his eyes with his golden eyedropper on the way over. Right now, his gaze was as dazzling as the sun prisming off the ocean.

"It's me." I frowned. "Mari."

"Mmm."

Right. He was blissed out of his mind.

"Race you." I shot past him and ran toward the water.

I heard his surprised laugh, and then he was racing past me, throwing off his shirt and kicking off his shoes. I crashed into the water and—*wow!*—it was take-your-breath-away cold. But Finn was just behind me, gaining, and so I crashed into the first wave and dove under.

The salt stung my eyes, and the cold pinched my skin, but it was exhilarating. Currents tugged and tossed me about, and I popped up only to have another wave smack me and pull me under. I spun and bumped into Finn. He grabbed my hand and pulled me farther into the ocean, where the waves rolled and bobbed instead of crashing against the shore.

I laughed, kicking my feet and wiping the wet hair from my face. Finn kept ahold of me as the waves buoyed and rocked us.

"This is amazing." I grinned at Finn, the taste of salt and sea on my lips. "I've never been to the beach. It's . . . I could live here. I could stay here forever. Just be a mermaid in the water . . ."

Finn ducked his head underwater and then popped back up, pushing his black hair back from his face. "Never been?"

I shook my head. "Never. Wow. Look at them. Look at all of them."

I treaded water, floating in the cold current as we both watched the conjurers on shore. It was a sight. The four families were here. The principals, the heirs, the rest of them. There were also a few Bard and Clark cousins.

All in all, there were about thirty conjurers on the beach. I was the only body. The rest of the players, I supposed, hadn't asked their new bodies to come along.

There was a festive atmosphere. Beach blankets, towels, a smattering of striped beach umbrellas sticking out of the sand. Someone—a Bard, probably—had brought music, and the beat pulsed beneath the crash of the waves. A strange truce had been called for the day. Everyone seemed to have thrown aside vendettas and machinations. There was a sort of jubilant mood in the ocean air.

"They're so . . ." I nodded at Celia, Ragnor, and Luvic.

They'd set out towels on a seaweed-free stretch of sand and stripped down to their bathing suits. I was sure a tabloid would pay a million dollars to have a shot of the three of them on this beach together.

All Bards had this unnatural appeal that sort of stunned people when they first met them. It came with their power, but it was disconcerting sometimes. And when they were together, the sight of them was almost like looking right into the sun.

Celia laughed at something Ragnor said, and then Ragnor grinned at Luvic. I hadn't paid much attention to Ragnor. He seemed intent on keeping close to Celia and watching her back. But as he laughed with his sister, I wondered what sort of power he was hiding, and what exactly he'd do to protect her. Luvic looked out at the waves then, as if he could sense my gaze. A smile tugged at his mouth, and then he looked away.

"Do you think they really like each other as much as it seems?" I asked, watching Luvic rummage through a picnic basket and then triumphantly pull out a bottle of tequila.

"Yeah," Finn said, still treading water. "I do."

Celia grabbed the bottle and then trotted across the sand toward Jacob in her tiny gold thong bikini. He was standing in the sand, still in jeans and a T-shirt, staring out at the gulls swooping down over the water.

She conjured a shot glass, filled it with tequila, and handed it to him.

"I wouldn't drink that." I watched, curious to see what he'd do.

"He will," Finn said confidently.

I waited for a wave to roll us up then down again, then asked, "How do you know?"

Finn closed an eye, staring at them. "Because he likes her."

I laughed. "Right."

Finn treaded water and turned his gaze back to me. "Your lips are turning blue."

I shivered. My fingers were going numb too, but I didn't want to leave the rocking ocean or the feeling of wild freedom that floating in it gave me. It was nothing like drowning in the East River. Here, the currents buoyed and tickled, and the waves laughed as they rolled over the shore. I wanted to stay in it forever.

But then Darin waved his hand and called something that was snatched away.

"Can we ignore him?" It'd be nice. He probably wanted me to make him a sandwich or fix him a margarita.

"I like him," Finn said, holding a hand up in a half-wave. "I like him, and I didn't think I would."

I understood that completely. It felt like a new shoe scraping my heel, rubbing it raw and blistering it. I wasn't supposed to like him. Not any of them.

Maybe that was how Finn felt too. Why should he like his half-brother? The heir. The son of the man who'd abandoned him, gutted him, and used him. Was still using him.

Funny—maybe that was how Finn felt about me too. He liked me even though he didn't think he would. It was how I felt about him.

I looked over at the glossy black of his wet hair and the water dripping down his cheeks.

"You know, I didn't think I'd like you," I admitted. "But here we are." I smiled and started to swim back toward the shore.

Finn kept pace with me, and the surf pushed us toward land. Darin was waiting with his arms folded across his bare chest.

"Mari," Finn called before we were within hearing distance of the sand.

I paused and treaded water. "Yeah?"

He watched me for a moment, an ocean of words in his expression. There was something there he wanted to say. A wave pushed us closer, and I bobbed against him. When our legs and hands tangled, Finn shook himself out of whatever it was that had captured him.

Instead, he said, "Don't let liking me stop you from whatever you need to do. It's not going to stop me."

There was something cold in his words. Some kind of warning and hard, icy determination.

I shivered and then nodded. Suddenly, the water felt every bit the freezing temperature it actually was. I swam hurriedly to the beach and dried off with my towel.

Across the beach, Jacob swallowed his second shot of tequila. Celia grinned at him and poured another, which she shot back in one smooth swallow.

Uliea and the Bard's wife, Cressida, were sitting under an umbrella. I hadn't seen Cressida since the opening ceremony. She hadn't come to any of the games, and she didn't venture outside the Bard suite. She was wearing a large-brimmed hat, sunglasses, a long-sleeve shirt, and linen pants, and she stayed completely under the shade of her umbrella.

Uliea was in a flowing white sundress next to her, but neither spoke to the other. Uliea just stared at the ocean, her gaze vacant, mouth moving, although I doubted she was speaking out loud.

Luvic and Ragnor had set up a sort of beach bar and were mixing liquor and juices together in wild, never-before-seen concoctions. Everyone was eating from the spread of fruit, grilled hamburgers (it was a conjured grill, with a flame that wasn't a flame), corn on the cob, and fresh, iced watermelon.

I tugged my uniform pants back on over my wet bathing suit.

"We've got a game going," Darin said to Finn, handing him a towel. "Beach football. You're on my team. The body's on the other side."

"Excuse me?" I asked, tying my wet hair back.

"Sorry, *Mari* is on the opposing team."

"Literally every time you call me 'body' or 'creature,' I think of all the ways . . . all the ways I could hurt you."

He grinned at me. "Aww, you're so sweet."

"Who said I'm playing anyway? I don't know anything about football."

Luvic strolled over, the sun glinting off his bare chest. He thrust a cup full of pink-orange liquid that smelled fruity and alcoholic into my hands. "You don't need to know anything," he said. "You're on my team. I'd never let anything bad happen to you."

"Uh-huh. Funny joke. What's in this?"

"Hey, Bard," Darin said. "How you feeling? You sure you're up for this? You know you have to do more than look pretty to win." Darin gave him a feral grin.

Luvic grinned back. It was a wild, crazy-eyed sort of smile. His throat was still purple and blue from Primus's attack, and while beautiful, he looked a bit unhinged. "Ah, Darin. Your wit is exceeded only by your charm."

Finn stared at Luvic, his head tilted, shoulders relaxed. If he'd been wearing jeans, I was sure his hands would've been in his pockets, ankles crossed as he leaned against a wall, whistling with indifference.

But wasn't that the pose Finn wore when he was tense on the inside, coiled and ready to pounce? I looked between Finn and Luvic, narrowing my eyes. Luvic had given me that pomegranate for Finn. He'd helped me on multiple occasions. Had it been for Finn? Had it been for me? Or had it been, more likely, for some scheme that benefitted him and his family?

I peered into the cup and sniffed. Watermelon juice. Passionfruit. Vodka?

"Vodka," Luvic confirmed, murmuring so only I could hear.

"Watermelon. Guava. Dainty Drink. I permanently borrowed your little poison book while you were conveniently dead."

I gasped.

He smiled and continued. "Tequila and a dash of cayenne pepper."

Luvic had stolen my Grapes of Wrath? He'd stolen my poisons.

I shoved the cup back to him. "Why would you tell me what's in it if you poisoned it?"

He looked at me like it should be obvious. "Because you asked."

Darin glanced impatiently across the beach to where the Clarks were setting up a makeshift football field. "Looks like we're ready. Don't cry too hard when you lose."

"I never cry," Luvic said, dumping the drink he'd made me into the sand. "I'd be more concerned about Alterra crying. Wasn't his home blown up yesterday? Sad. And his body almost got stolen from him by a Clark, and now . . ."—he shrugged and whispered conspiratorially—"she's on my team."

Wonderful.

Awesome.

Luvic gave Finn a hard, crazy-eyed smile similar to the one he'd given Darin, then he said in a threatening tenor, "Don't cry, Alterra. I'm sure it'll all work out." He grabbed my hand and tugged me across the beach. I tried to yank myself free, but he held me tight.

"What . . . what is wrong with you?" I dragged my feet in the sand, but sand, apparently, had zero traction. "I'm not . . . I am *not* on your team." I kept yanking myself in the opposite direction, so when Luvic stopped near the goal line, I stumbled then slammed into him. His bare skin was hot from the sun. I shoved off him, annoyed at the contact.

"I dislike you."

He smiled. "You love me."

"No."

"We're friends."

"Not."

He nodded. "Say what you like. I know the truth." He pointed to his sister, Primus, a Clark cousin I didn't know, and a Bard cousin I didn't know. "They're on our team. Your job is to stay out of the way and not get into trouble. If you do, just call, 'Luvic! Help! I need you!' and I'll come save you."

I crossed my arms and glared at him. The sun was high overhead, bouncing off the white sand, and my glare probably looked more like a squint.

He laughed.

Our team came over and formed a huddle, strategizing as the sun beat down on us. Primus wanted a frontal assault. Celia wanted to focus on defense. Luvic, meanwhile, was all about trick plays and misdirection. Jagger would love him. His mind was . . . a maze of mayhem.

The cousins and I kept quiet and took direction from Primus, who finally said, "Take note, I am the strongest conjurer on this team. The rest of you are inferior." He pointed to Celia. "Woman." He pointed to Luvic. "Useless third-born." He pointed to me. "Body." Moved to the cousins. "Weak."

Well, at least he was clear in his feelings.

"Thus, I am in charge."

"Weak? Me?" Celia, in her gold thong bikini, tipsy from too many shots of tequila, stepped close to Primus and purred, "Primus, dear, do you know your failing? Like most men, you're utterly terrified of a woman's power. Men can only take life, while women create it. For eons, men like you have been trying to convince women that the only power on earth lies in murder. You want us to be like you. Kill instead of create. The lengths you go to. Because you're scared. We are the more powerful sex. Women. Poor Primus. Poor man. Wittle"—she tapped his chest with a long, painted fingernail—"bitty"—*tap*—"scared"—*tap*—"baby." She fluttered her eyelashes.

Behind her, Luvic bared his teeth.

I waited, wide-eyed, wondering if the beach party truce was about to end. But Primus merely threw his head back and laughed. It was a crow-like cackle, and it matched the black T-shirt and black shorts he wore.

I took a careful step away from them all. If I couldn't untie illusions, I didn't want to be anywhere near this battle. But Primus only chuckled a final time and gave Celia's lush figure an appreciative once-over that made Luvic stiffen and hold his fingers threateningly to his thumb.

I shook my head at him. Didn't he remember what had happened last time he and Primus tussled?

Across the beach, the other team—Finn, Darin, Jacob, Last, a Bard cousin, and a Clark cousin—huddled together. All of them were in a heated discussion, except for Jacob, who was swaying and staring at the sand as if it were the most fascinating thing he'd ever seen.

Ha. I'd said he shouldn't drink those shots Celia had offered him.

Then the huddle was done. The strategy was settled upon. Basically, keep the ball with Primus, who was brutal on the field, and Luvic, who was fast. The Bard cousin could throw. Celia was a good catch. The Clark cousin was solid and could hit like a train. And me? I was supposed to be what Primus called "frontline cannon fodder," because if I was injured or maimed, according to him, it was no loss.

I looked longingly at the sidelines where conjurers were lounging and Ragnor was engrossed in the music.

Then as we walked onto the field, Luvic murmured to me, "Just steer clear of trouble."

That was easier said than done. The conjurers' game of football, even "touch" beach football, was nothing like the football played in stadiums.

First, the conjurers used illusion. They passed fake balls around like a game of hot potato. Which was the real one? Only the offensive team knew. They used the wind to throw the ball farther. Pits randomly erupted in the sand, and you either jumped over them or fell in.

At one point, Luvic became Finn, and when Darin passed the ball to him, Luvic spun around, became himself again, and scored.

Primus shook the sand with mini earthquakes, and Celia skated over the shaking sand on a conjured waterfall. Darin and Finn were playing as if they'd been running plays together since they were born. It was like they could sense each other's next move before it happened.

I fell into a pit at one point and clung to the side, the sand landsliding under my fingers. Celia grabbed my arm and pulled me free by jetting a burst of water from the bottom of the pit. She sprinted off before I could thank her.

Then, when I ran past Last, a fake ball in my arms, she conjured a rope around my legs to trip me. Her hand was flexed, ready to conjure again—a history, maybe, or something else even worse. I didn't know. I flew forward, but then Luvic was there. He spun, grabbed me, and sliced the rope free.

"*My* girl," he snarled at Last.

As Celia sprinted past with the actual ball, Last took off after her.

"Thanks," I said.

But Luvic was already gone.

The Clark on the opposite team was headed toward me, shoulder bent, ready to do serious bodily harm. I knew what that light meant when I saw it in a Clark's eyes. I was bracing myself, ready to deflect and hopefully deliver a blow myself, when Finn ran past and clipped the Clark—his own teammate—so hard the man flew six feet across the sand.

"Finn!" Darin yelled. "He's on our team!"

Finn gave a blank solange stare and raised his eyebrows as if to say, "Really?"

Darin laughed and smacked him on the back. "Let's do this."

Even with Primus's earthquakes, Celia's water, and Luvic's tricks, the other team still won. It came down to the fact that Darin and Finn together were . . . physically unstoppable. Add in Last's nasty surprises and Jacob's mind games, where the ball always seemed to be exactly where it wasn't, and . . . we lost.

I still considered it a win, though, because I hadn't been injured, maimed, or given some nasty illusion by Last.

After that, the partying began in earnest. Remember the gala, when there were champagne rivers and chocolates and cakes sprouting from the ground? Naked servers and drunken revelry?

Yeah.

After the sweat and tumble of the football game, the conjurer families got down to the business of making merry. They drank. They danced. They ate the decadent foods they'd brought to the beach on the Bards' yacht. They made an illusion bonfire and cast a windy, rainy, foggy illusion around the party so no one passing by would see or hear us.

Meanwhile, we were drenched in summer sun, hot sand, and the cool, spraying salt of the surf.

The music thrummed so loudly it pulsed through my veins and lured me to the edge of the revelry. My shoulders were sunburned, my cheeks prickled from the heat. I'd stripped out of my clothes and was wearing only my swimsuit. Sand caked my calves and thighs.

I was so thirsty I went to the Bards' makeshift bar and asked for a drink.

"Only juice," I told Luvic.

I didn't trust him, but I'd had the last of my water hours ago, and I was in serious danger of dehydration. Human. That's me. Susceptible to all sorts of dangers, including sunstroke and dehydration.

"Only juice." Luvic smiled and poured passionfruit juice into a cup.

I took a long sip. It was cold. Sweet. And then . . . it hit me.

It hit me hard.

The sand shifted under my feet. I stumbled. The sky flipped upside down and somersaulted me with it. The music yanked at me, tugged me. The world turned dizzily vibrant, and . . . I giggled.

Oh no.

I giggled.

The cup slid from my fingers. I watched as the pink-orange liquid spread over the sand.

"Pretty," I said, smiling at the iridescence of the colors. Then I stared at Luvic in horror. "You . . . you . . ."

He winked.

The sky spun; the ground tilted again. A warm, happy, glowy feeling settled over me. The music thumped over the sand, and the vibrations traveled up my legs and through my blood. I wanted to dance. I wanted to laugh. I wanted . . .

To be free of all my inhibitions.

To be truth.

Luvic grabbed my hand. Tugged me across the beach, toward the blue and orange flames of the bonfire. It was so pretty. So beautiful. It was all an illusion.

Luvic, sometime protector, sometime enemy, full-time Bard, had given me Dainty Drink.

"I always knew I couldn't trust you," I said, stumbling and then righting myself.

He smiled down at me. "Aww, you can trust me." He righted me, held me straight, and then said, "Dance, Mari."

I didn't want to dance. I wanted to jump into the ocean again and roll around in the froth and the waves. I wanted to be a mermaid, free of Jagger, free of the games, free of conjurers.

I blinked at Luvic, trying to bring him into focus. The beach and the mist wall swirled around him. Other conjurers were dancing. Celia, Ragnor, and their Bard cousins. Jacob laughed with Philoneas near the umbrella, where Cressida and Uliea still sat. The Clarks had congregated in a circle doing Clark things. Meanwhile, Finn was with Darin and Wolfgang, their heads together . . .

"Mari, you're not paying attention." Luvic tugged me to him.

I held onto his shoulders. It felt like I was spinning a thousand miles an hour, even though I'm pretty sure we were only rocking back and forth.

"What'd you say?" I asked, licking my lips. They were dry and salty. I was still thirsty. A few sips of juice and Dainty Drink was not enough liquid after a hot day in the sun. "I'm thirsty."

"Listen. Do you have the key?"

"Hmm?"

"The key. Do you have it?"

"Dunno watch're talking about."

"The key you stole from the Smiths. Do you have it?"

Oh. Ohh. So Luvic knew . . . Luvic knew I was . . . How'd he know?

"You know me?"

He tugged me close. Pressed his body to mine and dragged his mouth against my ear. "If you want to live, you'll get the key before the end of the games."

I giggled. It burst out of me. A stupid, high-pitched giggle.

Luvic pulled back, his eyes half-mast, his mouth next to mine. "Mari. I did mean it."

I swayed, clutching his shoulders tighter. "Mean what?"

"To give you those memories." Luvic stared over my shoulder, gave a mocking smile, and then drawled, "Alterra. She's all yours."

He stepped back, nodded, and then Finn spun me around.

He peered at me, and I smiled.

Oh.

Now I knew. Now I knew exactly what he'd felt when I poisoned his solange. He practically glowed with an ethereal golden light. It poured off him in a liquid aura that made me ache to touch him.

"Hi," I said as the sand shifted again.

I tilted and then fell against him. I let out a breath at the heat that coated me in a viscous, luxurious wave. My limbs went lax and heavy, and all I wanted to do was wrap my arms around him and ride the feathering, tingling sensations building inside.

"Mari?" he asked, a questioning line between his eyebrows.

"If you . . ." I whispered, my throat dry. "If you kissed me, I'd be the happiest woman on earth." Then hot tears pooled in my eyes. "But you can't, because you're in love with someone else. And I can't, because I don't . . . I don't . . . steal." I giggled again.

(I do steal. I steal things all the time.)

Finn let out a low swear and then called Luvic a string of words best not repeated.

I nodded and pressed my head to Finn's bare chest. His skin was smooth. The light dusting of hair on his chest tickled my cheek. His chest was wide, the muscles solid yet soft beneath me. I swayed to the intoxicating thump of the music.

The sand tilted again, the sky somersaulted, and I slid deeper into Finn's embrace. Was it an embrace? No—he was just holding me up, his starry eyes full of concern.

He was so *good.*

"Why can't I have someone like you?" I asked, my heart sore and heavy. "I think . . . I think I'd love you, Finn Alterra. If you let me." I shook my head, and the world spun. "No. Not if you let me. I think I'd love you anyway. But I can't. 'Cause I don't know what love is. 'Cause I'm s'posed to kill you. And you're not mine. And you're going to die no matter what."

Finn stared down at me, his gaze solemn. He brushed a strand of hair back from my face. "Come on. Let's get you some water."

"And after you die, I'll miss you," I said. "I'll probably miss you for the rest of my life. Even though I've only known you for a few days. Can you miss someone you've never had?"

Finn opened a bottle of water. Thrust it into my hands. "Drink."

The ice-cold condensation dripped over my fingers. I stared at the bottle in bemusement. "Where'd you get this?"

"Drink it, Mari."

"I'm going to kill you someday."

"I know."

"And then I'm going to turn evil. 'Cause that's what happens to a nine."

"No. You won't. I won't let it happen."

"You can't stop it. You'll be dead."

"Drink the water."

I drank the whole bottle, the cold water sliding down my throat and clearing my head. The world settled a bit, and Finn's features came into focus, the golden haze around him dimming.

I smiled at him.

"Better?"

I nodded. "A little."

He took me for another dunk in the ocean. We bobbed on the frothy, cold waves as the Dainty Drink fizzled out and left me limp and exhausted.

The Bards were still dancing, the Clarks were still drinking, and the Wards and the Smiths were standing together in a strange, daylong death-promise truce.

Finn and I lay in the sand. I stretched against his side and rested my head on his chest.

"All right?" I asked, so tired I could barely keep my eyes open.

"It's fine."

I stared up at the darkening sky—blue to pink to apricot to gold—and then the deep indigo of the night, with the flickering conjured flames, wild, dancing sparks, and finally, right before my eyes slid closed . . . stars.

I saw the stars for the first time in my life.

"Make a wish," Finn said, his arms keeping me warm.

I made a wish.

It didn't come true.

48

THE WIND SLID OVER THE COOL SAND, BRUSHED AGAINST THE TILTED HEADS of silvery-gray dune grass, and skated over the moonlight coating the surf in a pearlescent glow. The ocean tide was a rocking lullaby, the night full of mesmerizing flames and winking stars.

All day, the wind had kite-surfed over the ocean, reveling in the cold sea spray, the rough roll of the waves, and the roar of the water. It had dived with the mischievous gulls that stole bites of food from beach blankets; bobbed with the barking harbor seals that spied the conjurers from afar; and skirted through the exultant spray of a giant fin whale parting the ocean waters.

It had been a blustery, wild, exuberant day, and now the wind was nighttime-quiet and lulled by the soft sound of the receding tide. The cool sand tickled, and a ghost crab snapped as the wind shifted the sand, searching for . . .

There.

There he was.

The boy sat alone on the edge of a sloping dune, staring at the moonlit water. The other conjurers laughed around the flame, or at the water's edge in groups of two or three, sometimes more. Even the solange-eyed one held the sleeping girl in his arms, but the boy was alone.

The wind understood this was because the boy made the others afraid. He wasn't mischievous like the trickster. He didn't smell good like the woman. He wasn't solid and straightforward like the Smith. Unlike the parchment scented ones, he wasn't even cruel, which was an easy emotion for humans to understand. Humans accepted cruelty more than . . . otherness.

The wind didn't mind though. It had felt the boy's power even before he was born, when he was still eclipsing the sun-bright light of his sister. He was the dark that hid the light so the light could survive.

Besides, the boy had been walking the winding labyrinth of the deepest, darkest parts of illusion for so long that he could twist another conjurer's mind into a maze of unbreakable torment. Whispers of the boy had ridden the wind for so long that not many conjurers were brave enough to stay near him for more than a few minutes. Killed his twin, broke minds, tortured enemies, left them husks . . . twisted, dark Ward.

The boy had asked it, when he was still a small boy and not a man, his voice unsure, "Wind, why is everyone so afraid of me?"

The wind had only rubbed along his leg and circled his ankles, unable to answer. People were afraid of the wind too sometimes. It could cool and carry rain, comfort on a hot day, but it could also destroy, ruin, kill. It was the same wind; it was only the human's perception of it that changed.

The trouble with humans was that they needed other people. The wind didn't quite understand it, but it thought it was like how the wind needed the sun to blow. Without the cosmic rays and solar radiation, the wind wouldn't exist. It thought, perhaps, without love, a human wouldn't be able to exist. It was why the wind tried to be just human enough for the boy, a companion, so he didn't wither and die.

The boy had nodded at the wind's reassurance and then asked in a trembling, young voice, "Do you think my sister . . . do you think she would be afraid of me?"

The wind didn't know. It only knew that if humans were afraid of something, they tended to hate it rather than love it.

The boy had never asked the wind about his sister again, although the wind knew it was a fear in him: that the one human who should have understood him would have feared him instead.

The wind slid across the moonlit sand, edging toward the boy. Whispered conversations, half-sentences, and mumblings weaved through the night.

"—poison didn't work—"

"You want the body? Aren't you supposed to—"

"—addict. Die in weeks—"

"—may explode—"

"—talk to him. Play Peitho, goddess of seduction. Find out what you can about the game."

The last was the Bard father, urging the citrus and pearl dust scented woman toward the boy.

She narrowed her gaze on the shadowed form of the boy and then stepped through the firelight, smoothing her hands over the filmy, sheer gold dress she wore.

The wind wrapped itself in her silky fabric, fluttering the ends, and then padded in her soft sand footsteps.

The boy looked away from the ocean as the woman approached.

They were outside the firelight, and the woman had left her orange and blue glowing sparks behind. The moonlight glistened off the woman's skin, and the wind whistled as her features softened, her lips turned up in a slight lush smile, and her eyes turned the warm brown shade of parted lips, searching hands, and hot breath.

The boy hid his smile at the wind's laughing whistle.

The citrus and pearl dust scented woman belonged by the ocean. It was in the sinuous way she moved, the rocking of her hips, and the sway of her stride. The sound of her sea-mist voice. Oh, the wind liked her, but not when she was playing Bard tricks on the boy.

"Celia," the boy murmured, looking back toward the ocean.

"Jacob. Enjoying the party?"

He tilted his head and glanced again at the woman. The wind fluttered her sheer dress, and she looked at the sand next to the boy.

He shrugged. "You can sit."

She spread the fabric of her dress and then settled next to the boy. The wind tickled the back of her neck, and she shivered.

At the shiver, the boy gave a mirthless smile.

"I've always loved the water," the woman said, digging her bare feet into the cool sand. "It doesn't matter if it's the rough, gray northeastern Atlantic, the deep, glacier-cold fjords, the warm, turquoise Aegean, or even the smallest silver-white raindrop sliding across the palm of my hand. Did you know, there's an entire world in a single drop of water? There's infinity in an ocean. I love water. It makes me feel small, which makes everything better. Being big is exhausting."

The boy let out a slow huff of air. The wind supposed the woman was right. Being a puff of wind, a tickling breeze, was easier than being a hurricane.

They both watched the waves slide over the beach, a curtain opening and closing. The music was quieter on the dune's edge, the firelight dim. There were night frogs in the dune grass, and in the wetlands beyond the dunes, singing their night song. The wind blew and carried their noises closer.

The woman reached down and dragged her pointer finger through the sand, drawing a circle over and over, until a small indentation and mound formed.

"That was some game, wasn't it?" she asked, staring down at the sand. "You took it rather ... hard."

The boy turned his gaze on the woman. A flat, warning look. She ignored it and continued tracing her circle.

"I only wish I'd done something similar. If I could ... if I could do half of what you can, I would've ... I would've made them eat their own hearts while they thought they were dining on caviar."

The boy raised his eyebrows and leaned back against the wall of the sand dune.

"You liked your body?" the woman asked.

"Yes."

The boy's answer didn't convey any of the emotion the wind knew he had inside of him.

The woman nodded. "I ... Creok—he was with me for ten years. That morning, I was annoyed with him over something stupid, and then . . . then none of it mattered anymore. All those minor annoyances and little things, they didn't matter." She looked up suddenly. "Are you ever glad you were born who you are, or do you wish . . . ?"

The wind waited, but the woman didn't continue.

The boy stared at the small, indented circle she'd made in the sand. "I'm always glad I was born as I am."

"Why? I only mean . . . doesn't it scare you, being you?"

The boy tilted his head and glanced up at the night sky. "Do you know why I was born?"

The woman shook her head. "The usual, I guess. A bout of sex. A sperm. An egg."

The boy's mouth twitched, and the wind slid along the almost-dimple that didn't appear. "No, Lia. I was born to protect my sister."

The wind felt the air sort of rush out of her. The surprised oomph and the lowering of her shoulders. "You're like my brothers then. That's how they feel. Except . . ."

"Except they haven't failed you yet? Haven't killed you or been killed because of what they are to you?"

She gave him a look the wind could only describe as spooked. Her hand shook. "You don't make it easy for people to like you."

"I never said I wanted anyone to like me."

The wind shoved the boy, rocking him toward the girl. His shoulders hit hers, and he jerked quickly away. He turned to the side and glared into the night.

The wind laughed.

At the boy's abrupt retreat, the woman scowled. "For goodness' sake, Jacob, I'm trying to seduce you right now. Can you at least make it a little easier?"

He turned back to her. Raised his eyebrows. "What?"

The woman waved her hand, showcasing her sheer dress, the curve of her breasts, and the glistening pout of her lips. "Moonlit beach. Ocean waves. Secluded dune. Confidences shared. Sexy woman leaning against you, giving you smoky glances under fluttering eyelashes. I've been practically begging you with my eyes to kiss me for the past five minutes. How much more obvious do I need to be?"

The boy stared blankly at the woman.

The wind agreed. It was hard to understand women.

"Why . . . ?" He narrowed his eyes. "Why do you want me to kiss you?"

The woman folded her arms across her chest. Looked out over the ocean.

The boy's forehead wrinkled as he thought it over. Then he smiled. "Oh. You want to know about our game. Why didn't you just ask?"

"Because," the woman said, flicking a spray of sand, "that's not how these things work. That's not how I work."

The boy frowned at her answer. "Lia?"

"What? Stop calling me that."

The wind rocked the boy closer, and this time, when his shoulder bumped the woman's, he didn't pull away.

"Are you afraid of me?" he asked.

The woman held still, as motionless as the world before it formed, when it was still the sleeping seed of an idea.

"Yes," she finally whispered.

The boy nodded as if he'd expected nothing less.

The wind didn't like her answer. It knew humans killed what they were afraid of.

"I'll tell you," he said, staring past the woman, out over the rest of the conjurers frolicking on the beach. "If you tell me one thing first. A trade."

The woman thought about it for a moment and then nodded. "All right. What?"

The boy finally turned and looked at the woman full-on. He took in the light of the moon on her skin, the fragile lines of her shoulders, the canny intelligence in her eyes, and the seductive tilt of her lips.

"I'll know if you're lying," the boy said. "Only speak the truth, or the deal is off."

The wind tickled his cheek. The boy was lying. He couldn't tell if a person was speaking the truth or lie. But the woman didn't know that. She probably believed everything she'd heard about the boy.

"Fine."

The boy watched her for a moment longer. He looked different in the moonlight. The wind curled onto his shoulder, tickled by the burnished gold of his hair, the dune-grass silver-green of his eyes, and the hard, blond, stubbled line of his jaw.

His voice was not as deep as the Smiths' and not as melodious as a Bard's, only . . . thoughtful, warm . . . It reminded the wind of a moonlit meadow in the middle of a forest, alone except for the wind rushing through.

"What," the boy asked, "did you see when I came out of the tomb yesterday? What illusions did I pull free from your mind?"

The woman gave the boy a startled glance, a deer stunned by the cracking of a dry branch and the nearness of a predator.

"See?"

The boy gave a slow nod. "Answer that, and I'll tell you what's in our game."

The woman stayed silent for so long that the wind grew bored and played a game of shifting the sands back and forth, back and forth, until they formed the pattern of the seabed.

But finally, she said in a quiet voice, "I saw blood. I saw the world covered in an ocean of blood, and I was standing in the middle of it."

The boy nodded. Went to stand. The woman reached out. "You said if I told you—"

He shook his head. "I said if you didn't lie, I'd tell. You lied, Celia. You're always lying."

"I did not! That's exactly—"

"I saw what you saw," the boy cut in. "I saw what *everyone* saw. I visited the darkest corners of your heart. Don't lie."

The woman's face drained of color and shone pale in the moonlight. The wind skated across her cold skin and rode the rapid beat of her pulse.

"Will you kill me for it?" she asked. "Will you be my judge, jury, and executioner?"

The boy held his two forefingers against his thumb. Across the beach, the musician and the trickster looked toward their sister. The musician began to walk quickly their way.

The wind nudged the boy, letting him know their solitude was about to be broken.

The boy twisted his hand, and the woman flinched. Perhaps she expected to be blown into a million fragments or for her mind to be twisted in on itself. Instead, the boy held a glass teardrop out to her. It was as small as a raindrop, as clear as melted snow, and it glistened and sparkled, refracting the stray bits of illusioned firelight. It was strung on a fragile gold necklace.

The boy waited, his hand held out to her. "Here."

"What is it?"

"A drop. Seemingly indestructible. With one weakness that could destroy it."

The woman stared down at the glass teardrop. "Is this a threat?"

The boy shook his head. "It's a gift. If I ever see you wearing it, I'll know you're ready to tell the truth."

"And if I never wear it?"

The boy shrugged. "Then we go on as we are."

She frowned and clutched the gold necklace in her hand.

"By the way," the boy said, staring out over the sand at the revelry, "I'd be careful. Your brother's walking a dangerous line."

"All right, Celia?" The musician strode into the dark shadow of the sand dune, his voice a low note filled with unspoken threat.

The wind laughed as it rode over the musician's calloused fingertips and ruffled his hair. What could the musician do to the boy?

"Fine," she said, her voice stretched thin.

The wind noticed then she was pale, her heart a slow thud, fatigue underlying her movement.

The musician noticed too. He stepped close, placing himself between the boy and the woman.

"Ward," he said curtly.

The boy smiled. It was a darkly cold smile. A smile that eclipsed all the light in the world. "Bard."

The wind nudged the boy's leg, but the boy ignored him. The boy was almost always polite, but when he wasn't, a chill always seeped into the air.

The musician stared at the boy, taller by a few inches, wider, but not close in power.

The woman took her brother's arm and leaned against him. "I'm ready to go home. You ready, Raggie? Had enough fun for one night?"

The musician considered the boy. The wind knew that considering expression. It was a question: Does the boy need killing, and if so, how will I do it? The wind threw sand against the musician. He shook himself off and tucked his arm around his sister's waist.

"Too much fun," he said, his voice a deep song that the wind appreciated.

"Night, Jacob," the woman called as she and her brother strolled away.

The boy watched them for a moment before turning back to the ocean and the moonlight glinting over it. "How surprised," he murmured to the wind, "do you think they'll be when we tell them tomorrow morning that we're heading north?" He laughed, and the wind spun gleefully on the sound.

North?

North!

The wind loved the north. There were forests, and ice-cold, cloud-caught lakes, and mountains full of crags and crevices and moss-lined boulders.

Oh!

North!

The wind spun in a dizzy, gleeful whirlwind as the boy leaned back on the sand, tucking his arms under his head. As the wind waltzed around kicking up sand, the boy stared at the stars and sighed.

"The only thing is," he said, "if she had tried to kiss me, I think I would've let her."

49

"NORTH?" THE SMITH GROWLED FOR THE HUNDREDTH TIME THAT MORNING. "The Ward is mad. They're all mad. North?"

I settled back into the cushioned black leather of the armored Range Rover and grinned. I was in the back seat with Finn. Darin was driving (why? He was insane behind the wheel), and the Smith was in the passenger seat fuming about mad Wards, haunted timber castles, and the massacre that had happened the last time the games moved outside of a city.

Yet all his barking about knowing the field of battle, preparing defenses, and anticipating ambushes couldn't take me out of the sheer joy I felt as we left the city behind and sped north. To the mountains. To the forests. To . . . all the dreams I'd once had and had almost let go of.

Do you remember the rag man that dropped me outside of Hell Gate with a note penned to my infant chest? Rag men are these silent, wraithlike half-men, shadows who never speak. Roumelade says they form when a human's dreams die. As long as there's a sliver of hope or a dream in your heart, then the dream is still alive, and that half-cold ember can be reignited.

But when a dream dies, when someone lets go of their hope, it crumples up and falls from your heart in a blow of cold ash. That's when a rag man forms. They're the silent, wraithlike, wandering things of lost and abandoned dreams.

I often wondered if I would ever walk down 6th Avenue or Broadway and suddenly encounter the shadowed, mouthless face of my own shattered, abandoned dreams. But I didn't. I hadn't.

I still held onto my dreams, no matter how far away and implausible they seemed. Someone who cared. Someone to love. Freedom from Jagger. A light in the dark. An end to illusions. A home in the woods, in the mountains, in the north. To see the mountains—just once.

My smile widened as the sun flashed over the steepled tops of evergreen and pine. A hawk swooped overhead, and its shadow flicked across the window. I was speared with the speed of the car and the *whoomp, whoomp, whoomp* of the tires racing over uneven pavement. I'd never been on an empty highway. I'd never had sunlight shine through a window and spray over me like a wild, cosmic rainstorm. I'd never seen boulders that could be hills; hills that could be mountains; pines that grew like a shaggy green coat over the hunched shoulders of a sleeping rock giant. It was wonderful. It was wild.

And as Darin sped north, leaving behind concrete, metal, and all the illusions I'd lived within my entire life, I felt . . . I felt as if I was awakening.

The scent of pine. The silver flash of a trickling waterfall from a craggy roadside cliff. The surprised white tail of a deer, turning and dashing into the woods.

A deer! I saw a deer!

We were hours outside the city, climbing higher and deeper into the rich, textured fabric of green—moss, ferns, evergreens, and forests of leaves—and I was exuberant. Tingling with expectation.

Wolfgang's curses and dire premonitions, Darin's insane driving, even the awkward reminder of what I'd said to Finn last night (kiss him? Love him?) couldn't dampen the exhilarating feeling of coming alive.

I glanced over at Finn, my cheeks sore from how much I'd been smiling. His expression warmed when he caught my smile.

"Happy?"

I nodded.

In the front seat, Darin passed a motorcycle, swerving around the bike and back into our lane. He hit the gas, and my seat belt tightened.

Wolfgang didn't notice. He only kept on the tirade he'd been on for two hours: "If a man cannot govern himself, he will seek someone to govern him. A weak man will seek a corruptor. A greedy man will seek a thief. An envious man will seek a murderer. We do not wage war to conquer. We wage war to liberate. Govern yourself first, and only then . . ."

I leaned closer to Finn and whispered, "Have you ever been to the mountains?"

He shook his head. I didn't think so. He'd grown up in the Night Den, just as much a city kid as me.

"Me either. It's beautiful, isn't it? I've never seen so much . . ." I waved to the forest flying past the car window. "Green."

"You like it?" he asked, his voice quiet.

". . . do you expect a man who cannot govern himself to govern another . . ."

"Almost there," Darin threw over his shoulder.

"I love it," I whispered back. "I've always imagined it, but it's like I was imagining a photograph—it was all so two-dimensional. I couldn't see beyond the front of the trees. There wasn't any light or wheeling hawks or running deer. There wasn't the leafy pine smell. There wasn't . . . Darin's crazy driving, or Wolfgang . . ." I nodded my head to the front, and Finn smothered a smile.

I cleared my throat, embarrassed at the sudden hot flush that rushed over my cheeks.

Finn hadn't mentioned yesterday. In fact, this morning at breakfast, and while we packed in a wild rush, he'd acted like I'd never made a fool of myself, drunk on Dainty Drink, telling him I wanted to kiss him and love him forever.

That was kind of him, and probably for the best, but I still felt the need to clear the air.

"About yesterday . . ."

The smile flew from his face, and he held still.

Ah. So he felt awkward too.

"You know Dainty Drink makes you say things you don't mean?"

He nodded slowly. The flash of the sun caught his black hair and the shadow of stubble on his jaw.

"Well, just like it made you think I was someone else . . . I thought you were . . ."

"Someone else?" His voice was low, and the lightning storm that kicked around his eyes shot sparks of silver and blue through his navy irises.

I stared at the storm building in them. If I said yes, I'd be telling a lie. There was enough illusion in the world without me adding to it.

"No, not someone else. Just someone . . . If you'd been someone different, and I'd been someone different, and . . . Do you think you could forget what I said?"

He frowned. "You want me to forget?"

"Yes. Forget it."

He let out a sigh and looked out the window. After a moment, he asked, "Do you want to forget it too?"

I wished I could. Except then I'd be forgetting how nice it had felt to fall asleep with the waves crashing and his heartbeat under my cheek. I didn't exactly want to forget that.

I shook my head.

"Ah," Finn said, nodding as if he understood what I was feeling, which wasn't possible. He didn't know me well enough to understand.

Up front, Darin tapped on the brakes.

We'd exited the interstate and were winding our way up a steep mountain road. It was two narrow lanes, with hilly inclines, switchbacks, and the deep, shadowed green of the surrounding evergreen forest.

We'd caught up to the Bards and the Clarks. They were in SUVs just ahead of us, two bulky black shapes slowly snaking up the road. The Wards were probably already at their haunted timber mansion.

Suddenly, the motorcycle Darin had passed earlier shot next to us, passing on the left. The man was in black leather, wearing a helmet with a darkened visor that hid his face. He had a sling on his back, with a long black rod sticking out of the top of it.

I tightened in surprise. It was Justice.

I didn't know how I knew. I just did. It was the way he leaned over the black bike, the long, lean line of him, the tension and the energy captured inside his leather-clad frame, as if he were a cocked gun ready to explode.

Or maybe it was the way his hands curled around the handles of the motorcycle, loose yet firm, in the same exact way he held my hand.

A wave of pure joy flew through me.

I'd called Rou. I'd told her the conjurers were headed north to the Catskills for the Wards' game. Although Jagger probably knew before I did, I still needed to let him know.

I'd hoped—I'd actually prayed—for Rou to also tell Justice. *Let Justice come. Let him see. I could slip outside one night. We could see the stars. We could—*

He bent his knees and stood in the motorcycle stirrups. In one fluid motion, he yanked the black rod from the sling on his back.

"Is that—?" Darin broke off.

"Shield!" I screamed.

A dozen feet away, across the dividing line of the country road, Justice swung one of Jagger's favorite weapons our way.

Jagger called it the Omnibus.

That was because it contained a dozen diverse, high-powered blood and bone missiles in one slim package. When launched, the missiles tore through metal, concrete—anything, really—and then exploded in a bloody, fiery mass.

Jagger made the Omnibus using good old-fashioned gunpowder, Furtig, ground bone, and his own blood. Nasty. Nasty combination.

Justice aimed. Yanked the trigger.

When he did, he came in line with my window.

He didn't see me before. I knew he didn't realize I was in the SUV. His whole body jerked in horrified rejection at me being there.

He yanked the Omnibus to the side. But it was too late. The missiles sped toward the car.

"Yes!" Darin shouted gleefully.

Wolfgang twisted his hand, and a ball of blue fire surrounded the Range Rover. Armored vehicle or not, he wasn't taking any chances. The missiles hit the blue fire and exploded in a violent, lava-red mass.

My ears popped. My eyes watered.

The explosion slammed into the car. Darin jerked the wheel as the Range Rover boomeranged across the pavement. The blue fire shield shuddered, bending inward and buckling as the missiles exploded.

One. Two. Three. Another.

Finn threw his arms over me. Covered me with his body. The windows shattered. They were spiky-hot shards of melted broken glass. They sprayed across the vehicle.

Wolfgang twisted his hand, and the spray turned into harmless, steaming jets of water.

Another of the missiles exploded, and Darin yanked the wheel. The SUV ricocheted into the ditch. He hit a boulder. Tree limbs rammed the blue fire and burst into ash. Acrid smoke and burning Omnibus scorched my lungs.

The car jerked and then launched into the air. My seat belt tightened in a death grip. We were slammed back to the ground. My head snapped forward. I bit my tongue as we bounced again. The sharp sting of blood filled my mouth.

"Hit it!" Wolfgang yelled.

Darin slammed the gas pedal. The car roared as we flew over the boulders and landed on the road.

Wolfgang twisted his hand again, and a giant ball of blue fire sped over the pavement like a missile, heading for Justice.

No. No, no, no, no, no.

Justice wasn't a nine anymore. He didn't have any more deaths. As a mine, any death would be a true death. If this blue fire hit him, he'd be gone. Just . . . gone.

I pushed Finn off me and gripped the back of Darin's seat. The wind whipped through the broken windows. It grabbed my hair and shoved blue sparks, cedar, and crackling Omnibus smoke through the car.

I watched in horror as the five-foot-circumference blue fireball sped toward Justice.

He'd pulled up ahead. The motorcycle sped past the other SUVs, but the fire was faster.

"No!" I gasped.

At the last second, Justice yanked the bike into a swerve. He tilted in a forty-five-degree angle. The bike rocketed to the side. He leaned so far toward the ground he was nearly parallel with it. The bike flew across the pavement.

Then the blue fireball sped over him and crashed into—

The Bards.

They'd made a whirlpool in the road. It swallowed the blue fire and sent a torrential rainstorm at us. The rain shot through the windows.

"Who is this guy?" Darin shouted, laughing. "Did you see that move?"

He was enjoying it. He loved it.

Wolfgang snarled, holding out his hand. "I don't care who he is, as long as he's dead."

Justice swerved past the whirlpool. Dodged an eruption of asphalt and a sinkhole that suddenly gaped in the road.

Darin swerved around the sinkhole too, just missing it.

Clark. It had to be a Clark erupting the road.

Justice yanked the Omnibus again. Fired at the SUV in front. A barrage of fire hit the Clarks.

What was going on? What was Jagger thinking? Why would he send Justice to attack a caravan of conjurers? Did he *want* him to die?

A boulder crashed into the road, yanked out of the ground by someone ahead of us. It raced toward the motorcycle.

Justice swerved. Dropped close to the handlebars and kicked the motorcycle faster. I couldn't take my eyes off him.

Was this it?

Was this the end?

We'd finally made it to the mountains, only to have him die because ... because *why*?

The Omnibus fire slammed into the Clarks' SUV. Unlike the Smiths, they hadn't shielded with blue fire. Instead, they'd tried stone armor. But the Omnibus could penetrate stone. The SUV flipped, flew through the air, and landed in the ditch.

"I like this guy," Darin yelled over the howling wind.

No, Darin. Actually, you don't.

The Bards were pulling a violent whirlpool around them—a black, dark pool of water with raging tendrils and shrieking waves. The black strands of water sped over the pavement, reaching toward Justice.

It'd been how long? Twenty seconds? Twenty-five?

Longer than any other twenty-five seconds in my life.

"We're done here," Wolfgang said. He held out his hand. I knew instinctively he was conjuring an illusion Justice wouldn't be able to escape. This was the end.

I soared outside of myself, entering the space where illusion couldn't exist. I wouldn't let Wolfgang kill Justice. Even if it meant they'd know what and who I was. Even if it meant I'd meet my own true death. No matter that Jagger had told me not to untie any knots—I still had free will. I opened my senses and raced toward the rope Wolfgang was tying. I'd unknot it. I'd untie the illusion and—

Finn grabbed my hand. Shoved me beneath him.

"No!" I shouted as my concentration broke.

I struggled as Wolfgang twisted his hand, kicking and punching Finn.

Then . . . Wolfgang's illusion snapped. Shattered. The rope he'd conjured, the death trap he was about to launch, burst into nothingness.

On the road ahead, Justice blurred, turned to shadow, and then vanished.

"What the . . .? He's a conjurer? He's a . . . Who *was* that guy?" Darin swerved around another boulder, rammed through a spray of water left by the Bards, and punched the gas.

Wolfgang swore viciously. There was a snarl on his grizzled face when he turned to the back seat. He pierced Finn with a stare that promised a violent gutting. "If you *ever* touch me with solange while I'm conjuring again, I swear, I will kill you on the spot."

"Whoa . . . whoa . . ." Darin looked over at his dad and then veered around another sinkhole.

Wolfgang held Finn's stare. I shoved out from under Finn's arms, out of breath and stunned. Finn had stopped my untying only to . . . break Wolfgang's illusion with solange?

But why?

Had he known what I was about to do? Had he been protecting my secret?

"I think, Finn," Darin said, "you should remember your touch breaks illusions and not accidentally bump us when we're trying to keep you alive. All right? Good?"

Wolfgang held Finn's stare. Unlike Darin, I think he was under the impression Finn had intervened on purpose. That was the impression I had too.

"If I ever touch you with solange again, I'll be *ready* to die," Finn said to his father, smiling coolly.

"Uh-huh," Darin said. "That's nice. By the way, we're here."

I let out a sharp-edged, bruised-lung breath.

Darin pulled the scorched, window-shattered Range Rover onto an evergreen-lined, narrow gravel driveway. The trees bent over the drive in a linked-hand, thick-boughed manner. The trunks and limbs were brown-knuckled and thick, and the needles made a curtain of deep, misty green.

With the windows broken, the wind rushed through, blowing in cedar and pine, wet moss, and the fecund scent of bark, fallen leaves, and rich humus.

My ears still rang from the Omnibus, and my heart banged from Justice's near miss, but over that, I could hear the whisper of the wind through the needles, the shrill call of a hawk, and the *tap, tap, tap* of a woodpecker echoing through the forest.

Sunlight played in the shadows, peeking through the deep greens and rolling over us as we crept up the steep gravel drive.

And then the trees opened, and I took my first look at the Wards' timber castle.

50

YOU HAVE QUESTIONS.

I know. You always had questions, and I rarely had answers. Usually, your questions were targeted arrows shredding the skin of illusion and striking the beating, hidden heart of truth.

When I first met you, I believed certain things about the world, and about myself. There were things I *knew* to be true. Irrevocably, irrefutably true.

The sky is blue. Grass grows. Conjurers are evil. Nines become mines. Two and two is four. The world is ruled by conjurers.

But then you showed me that there are physical truths and there are spiritual truths. They are two different types of truth.

A physical truth is only a truth in the physical world. For instance, "the sky is blue" is a truth, because everyone has agreed blue is the color of the sky. But the sky is not actually blue. It is an illusion; an idea of blue.

Another? Two plus two is four. That is a physical truth. But two plus two is not actually four. Why? Because two does not, in actuality, exist. There is no two. There is no four. There is only an infinity of one. So two plus two is actually one, which is infinity.

But here in this physical world? Yes. The sky is blue. Yes. Two plus two is four.

The funny thing about physical truths is that they can change over time. Something that was a truth one thousand years ago may not be a truth today. And what is truth today won't be truth tomorrow.

Sometimes, this confuses people. It causes chaos and anxiety. It's especially horrible when people believe the changing and subjective nature of truth means there is no truth.

"If your truth is valid and my truth is valid, then no truth is valid."

When humanity reaches the point where *every* truth and *no* truth is "truth," they descend into a chaos so terrifying (because truth is an anchor) that they willingly fling themselves onto a hellacious burning prison-barge ruled by a monster just to stay afloat in their own psyches.

The conjurers love when humans deny the absolutism of truth and instead fall into the subjective lure of illusion. It creates a world of fear and chaos, where they rule with gleeful abandon.

The trouble is, they aren't wrong. Physical truths are temporal.

Then what?

What?

You've forgotten spiritual truths.

These are truths that are eternal. They are and always will be true. Some conjurers will try to twist them, cloud them, pervert them, but if you seek them, you'll find them.

How?

It's easy, and it's hard.

Spiritual truths come from God. From the place beyond our physical world. If you listen, you'll hear them all around you.

Humans aren't able to relay spiritual truths succinctly, so instead, they tell them in stories. They've been doing so for eons.

Look at your religious texts. Look at your myths. Look at your fables and fairy tales. They're all telling you the same spiritual truths.

Love is good. Love is kind. Love defeats all.

Evil often has the appearance of good.

The light always comes after the dark.

Even if evil wins battles, it will never win the war.

Hold fast to love.

There are hundreds—thousands—more. All you have to do is listen. *Listen.*

The conjurers never deny the existence of God—he's made manifest in their lives every day. The only thing they deny is that they're beneath him. They seek to rule in his stead.

Here's another truth. All things in their time and in their place.

It's funny—I can hear your question even though you're not here to ask it.

You're asking, "Mari, if you believe love always wins, why are you so scared? Why are you so terrified of the devastation of the past and the devastation yet to come?"

I suppose it's because even though I know it's a truth that the light will win someday, somehow, I don't know if I will live to see it happen. I don't know if *you* will live to see it happen.

And you . . .

Are you in the light? Am I?

They say one of us is, and one of us isn't.

Are you there?

Are you still there?

Can you hear me?

I'll answer the first question you had. The one you were actually asking. The one you did once ask.

The reason solange isn't used against conjurers as a weapon is because . . .

One, it only works to dissolve illusion when ingested by a human.

Two, it only works to dissolve illusion when the person purposely touches the illusion and wills it to dissolve. Otherwise, the illusion merely has a tint of unreality to the solange devotee.

Three, solange cannot be farmed, bred, grown in labs, or synthetically made. It can only be sourced in the mountains from wild sown seeds pollinated by ruby-throated hummingbirds (really), and it's very, very rare (and very, very expensive).

Four, most solange devotees are too blissed-out to be of any concern to conjurers. They don't usually do any harm. Instead, they settle into an ecstatic solange stupor for a few months or years and then die in free fall.

From what I can tell, conjurers find it amusing or pathetic when solange addicts try to fight against their illusions. It's a nonissue for them.

Finn was actually more lucid than I'd thought a solange devotee would be, and also more in control of the illusion-dissolving effects. Maybe it was the fact that he was half-conjurer, since solange doesn't affect conjurers like it does everyone else. Or maybe, because he'd been a devotee for years, he had better control of the effects.

It was hard to say.

All the same, Wolfgang leveled Finn with a dozen "I'm thinking about killing you" looks while we settled into our new rooms.

Darin found the entire episode funny. He couldn't seem to comprehend what his father (and I) understood: that Finn might be more dangerous to the conjurers than they realized.

I cleaned the glass cuts on Finn from where the shards had hit before Wolfgang turned them to water. I put ointment on his bruises. I unpacked the bags, set up the kitchen—bigger this time—and made a dinner of lasagna, meatballs (Darin's request), garlic bread, and salad.

The timber castle—I'll describe it later—was vastly different from the Beaux-Arts decadence of the Bard Mansion. The suite we settled into was what I would describe as "lumber-baron chic." The walls were crafted from smooth, glossy wood aged to honeyed orange hues. The logs that had been used to build the castle were giant. Thick-planked and wide.

When we arrived, Philoneas had mentioned the wood was hemlock. The logs were from when New York still had old-growth hemlock forests, before settlements and logging wiped them from the land.

Our suite was large and airy. Soaring wood ceilings with exposed beams and joists. Honey-colored wood-planked walls, with dark knots that speckled the planks like winking eyes on peacock feathers. Smooth wood floors. Thick wooden tables. Wooden bookshelves. Large, cushioned white furniture with dozens of white pillows. Sheer white curtains over open windows, billowing like clouds as the mountain breeze shifted through the room.

It smelled like evergreens and clouds and wind through the mountains. The windows looked out over green woods, rocky mountain, blue sky, and blue-sky-lit mountain lakes.

I wanted Griff to see it. He'd laugh and run through the woods. I wanted Rou here, so she could dip her toes into the string of blue lakes I spied from our tower suite. I wanted Justice here, so we could explore the forest and find the perfect spot for our dream cabin.

You get the idea. The suite was wood and woods. It was airy, light, high-ceilinged. It felt open and comfortable at the same time. It was . . . very unlike the Wards and their reputation.

Although, I suppose, the wood used to build this castle took its name from one of the most poisonous plants on earth. Surprisingly beautiful, yes. But poisonous things usually are. I kept that in mind as I unpacked and then made our evening meal.

During dinner, after discussing the incident on the road, Wolfgang demanded to know if I knew the man on the bike.

"What do you know, body?" He hit me with a penetrating glare.

Unlike Darin or Finn, Wolfgang didn't particularly like me. He didn't trust me. With him, I felt I was always one breath away from having his fire sword chop off my head. I was an unfortunate necessity that would someday become unnecessary. Wolfgang was a principal. I didn't expect anything less. Especially considering he found his own son disposable.

Under the table, my fingers twitched, tapping my thigh. I didn't want to say anything. We weren't at the Bard Mansion any longer—they couldn't force me to talk in the inquisitor's chair. Yet the Smith or even the Ward could conjure an illusion that would bend my mind and force all sorts of tales free.

So I told the truth, which was what Jagger had demanded I do. Tell the conjurers the truth. Whatever they ask.

I only hoped Justice was far, far away now he had the attention of the families.

"You knew the attacker."

Usually, Wolfgang was a mirror of Finn sped up a few decades, with gray shot through his beard and a few wrinkles at the corners of his eyes, and on his forehead. A hardened-warrior, ultimate-commander version of Finn. But with the threat in his voice—tell me or die—he was nothing like Finn.

Finn didn't want me hurt. Wolfgang didn't mind hurting me if it served his purposes.

"Yes." I set my fork down on my plate. "He's one of Jagger's."

At my admission, Darin's head turned so swiftly my way I think he gave himself whiplash.

Finn didn't show any surprise. He just stared out the timber-lined window, studying the evergreen-covered mountainside.

"A creature like you?" Wolfgang asked, his cloud-gray eyes stormy.

I clenched my hand. "Yes. Like me."

"A creature." Darin's expression shifted. His hand curled tightly around his water glass. I knew he was remembering the night Justice gave me the antidote for Luvic. "Why would he want you dead?"

I shook my head. "He wouldn't."

"He's part-conjurer," Wolfgang said, his eyes narrowing thoughtfully. "A castoff who should've been—" He grunted. "We'll have to dispose of it."

Him.

Not it. Not creature.

Him.

Fury rose inside me.

Finn reached for me under the table. He turned my hand over and stroked his thumb soothingly over my palm. No one would be able to tell. He was still staring blankly out the dining-room window, his half-eaten plate of lasagna forgotten in front of him.

"Darin. If you see it again, take care of it. Conjurers do not, as a rule, let mistakes run wild."

Darin grinned as he sawed his meatball. "How strong is he, Mari? What are his strengths, his weaknesses? Who is his family?"

Me, I wanted to shout.

I am his family.

Neither Wolfgang nor Darin seemed to understand that, or perhaps they did and they didn't care. But no—I suspected they couldn't comprehend two *creatures* could be like family. Have loyalty to each other. Darin wanted me to tell him exactly how he could kill one of my best friends.

At that moment, I hated him. I hated his smile, his older-brother teasing, his easygoing nature and false friendship. I wanted to pick up my dinner knife and fling it across the lasagna, garlic bread, and salad and have the blade pierce his right eye. So *he* died. Not Justice. Him.

Finn's thumb stroked soothingly over my palm, a steady, slow circle. I concentrated on the feel of it, the soft tingle and warm glow. I breathed in the rich scents of marinara, garlic, and roasted meat. I steadied the angry thump of my heart.

My free hand itched to grab the handle of the stainless-steel dinner knife (what damage could a puny knife do anyway?), so instead, I took my glass of wine and swallowed the dry, tannin-soaked red.

"He's . . . not strong," I said, setting my glass back on the table. I knew Justice would want me to downplay his power and strengths. "He can only conjure the most minor illusions. Parlor tricks, nothing more."

Wolfgang grunted. "Far down the tree then. A twig off a branch off another branch."

I guessed you could call it that. I didn't know for sure, but I'd have guessed Justice was about four or five times removed from his principal. And I had no idea who his principal was. Jagger, who could taste those things, had never said.

"He can disappear." I only admitted that because they'd seen it today. "But that's just as much a magic trick as it is conjuring. He uses smoke, shadow, refraction, and reflection."

"What else?"

I shrugged. "He's good with guns."

Darin nodded. "Guns are no problem."

Yeah. That was why conjurers didn't use them against each other. Even the weakest conjurer could twist a barrage of bullets into a harmless rainstorm.

"What else?" Darin asked, taking a bite of his lasagna. "Come on, Mari. If I'm going after this guy, I need to know."

"Perhaps she doesn't want you to 'go after him,'" Wolfgang said, leveling me with a knowing stare.

Darin dropped his fork. It clattered against his plate. "Mari. If you're attacked, you attack back."

"Family?" Wolfgang asked.

I shook my head. "Don't know."

"Weaknesses?"

I thought about the shock Justice had displayed when he realized I was in the SUV. Weaknesses? Me. I was his weakness. Other than that?

"He doesn't have any."

Darin laughed. "Everyone has a weakness."

I shrugged. "He's Jagger's. Jagger doesn't allow weaknesses."

There was a long silence before Finn pulled his hand from mine. "His weakness is obvious. He's under the thrall of a leggerock." He tossed his napkin onto the table. "A man following another's will has no true freedom. He can't adjust his strategy. He can't follow a hunch. He's merely a bullet, shot at a target, with no ability to change the destiny of his predetermined path. *That* is his weakness."

I dropped my eyes to the deep red marinara staining my plate. I didn't want to look at the others.

Wolfgang chuckled his wolf-chuckle and then said, "And how is being thrall to a leggerock and thrall to solange any different, my son?"

I cleared the table, did the dishes, and left them to their discussion.

51

NORTH!

The wind loved the north. It spent its day spiraling gleefully down fir and pine scented spires, knocking pine cones off boughs, and kicking them over crackling dry needles.

It joyfully chased squirrels, shaking the branches they raced across. It startled deer and laughed as they bounded away. It glided across the ice-cold lakes, racing reflections of clouds, tasting the mineral-cold waters.

There were secrets in the woods too. Not conjurer secrets or people secrets but forest secrets. What did the water spirits say? What did the hemlocks with their evergreen tongues say? What did the ants that marched beneath the stone foundation of the boy's forest home say?

They all had secrets too.

Too many to count.

The wind had glutted itself on the wild, piercing call of the north, and now it settled itself on the downy, abandoned nest of some forest bird. It would lull itself to sleep by gently rocking the boughs of the pine and whistling over its silver needles.

The stars were bright, peeking down with interest on the people they saw winking in and out. The wind hummed happily.

Then a shadow that didn't quite belong with the rest of the shadows split from the side of the boy's wooden home. The shadow became its own shadow and then leaped like an acrobatic squirrel skittering down a branch, all the way from the second story to the ground. It took no time at all, only long enough for the wind to perk up and decide it wasn't time to sleep yet after all.

The shadow sprinted, fleet-footed, across the boulder, the scant grass, and the pine-needle-filled ground surrounding the boy's home. They ran like the wind, skating over the water, their feet barely touching the ground.

The shadow dashed to the thick linked boughs of the forest's edge in seconds and then disappeared into the mossy green dark, where the crescent moon and the stars couldn't find her.

Yes. Her. The wind knew. It was the girl.

As soon as she slipped out of the window and dropped to the ground, the wind knew.

It laughed as it sped after her. It had followed her, hadn't it, for years. It knew her tricks. The way she shimmied down drainpipes, scaled limestone buildings, and squeezed through crevices so small she couldn't breathe until she burst free on the other side.

The wind had seen her jump out of five-story buildings and survive. Rocket down fire escapes. Leap from one rooftop to another. It had seen her fight jackaltooth; claw out from beneath tree limbs and boulders that had buried intruders; unlock illusions that held her underwater, where the wind couldn't always follow.

It had watched her use smoke and fire and distraction to make herself invisible. It had watched her play tricks: mind tricks, magic tricks, wily, sneaky, smart tricks.

She hadn't played many tricks during the games. She hadn't run or jumped or leaped from buildings. She hadn't stolen anything interesting. The girl had been hiding. She was playing an old trick. Let your enemies believe you are weak. Until . . .

The wind laughed as the boy detached himself from the side of the house and stealthily followed the girl into the woods, conjuring an illusion of nighttime darkness to hide himself. And behind the boy—did he know she was there?—the citrus and pearl dust scented woman followed.

This was a fun game.

The wind raced after the girl, catching her in seconds. It gusted behind her, and she stumbled over a tree root. She quickly righted herself and then looked over her shoulder to make sure no one was there.

Just in case the boy was making any noise, the wind shook the branches of the trees. It didn't want the girl to know she was being followed. It wanted to know what she was doing.

She moved stealthily, even though she'd never been in the northern woods. Her steps were quiet and her movements fluid. She was air. She was like the wind, and so the wind was content to blow next to her under the dark, shadowed, night-lit trees.

An owl hooted, its eerie call breaking the silence. The girl startled and then shook herself off.

The wind wondered if she was lost. She hadn't walked in a specific direction. Instead, she wandered randomly. East then west. North then east. South then west. After enough time had passed for the wind to think perhaps it was time to settle down on the boughs of a tree and take a rest, the girl found a patch of moonlight.

It speared through an opening in a tall hemlock tree. It was one of the spired trees the wind had raced down earlier. It was old, and it reached higher than the others.

Earlier, when the sun was mid-sky, the wind had shaken its branches, and a family of deer mice raced free from the tree, and a red squirrel that had been burying hemlock seeds chittered angrily. It was a good tree.

The girl stood in the silver sliver of moonlight and slowly turned in a circle. She smelled good. The wind thought she smelled like fresh air, just-picked violets, and a strong gust of wind. What was she doing?

Then the wind knew, because it felt the knife-edge tingle that always followed the solemn one. He stepped out of the dark forest, and the girl tensed.

He was shadow. A tall, unknown figure dressed in black, moving with purpose toward the girl.

Was he here to hurt her?

He stopped a body's length away from her, the spear of moonlight on the forest floor separating them.

The girl sucked in a sharp breath, and then she moved like the wind knew she could move. She lunged. Jabbed her fist, lightning-quick. The wind whistled with the strike. The man slid to the side, and her fist brushed the feathering ends of his hair.

He spun.

She kicked out her leg.

He jumped.

She struck again.

The wind rolled on her punches. Snapped on her kicks.

The russet-haired, solemn man jumped. Dodged. Weaved between her strikes.

The wind loved moving in this dance of theirs.

Then, almost as quickly as it had started, the solemn man caught the girl's arm. He spun her. Yanked her to him. Held her tight.

The girl's chest heaved. Her breath came out in short gasps.

"*Justice.*"

The man stared down at her, his expression hard, pale gray eyes the same shade as the silver needles shining under the moonlight.

The wind tapped one freckle and then another, bouncing from one to the next. This was the hard expression the solemn man wore before he killed.

He was without emotion. Without care. Even that painful sliver of love in his heart was locked deep in a metal vault, where the wind couldn't reach.

The girl tilted her head and whispered, "What were you doing? You could've died! What were you thinking? You could've—"

The man yanked her against him and held her in an embrace that forced all the words and air from the girl's lungs.

The girl stiffened. Then she relaxed, and with a sigh, she dropped her head against the man's chest. "I was so scared for you."

"Mari," he said, and then he laughed. A surprised, unexpected, raw sound. "You were worried about me? I could've killed you. You can't—"

"Who cares about me? What was Jagger thinking? They're after you now. The Smith told his son to kill you on sight. They wanted your strengths, your weaknesses—"

"And what did you tell them?"

The girl tilted her head. The wind whistled, shaking the branches of the hemlock, releasing its scent.

"That you can barely conjure. That you can disappear and are good with guns."

"And?"

"That you have no weaknesses."

The man's mouth lifted in a half-smile. The wind tapped the edge of his lip.

"Guess what?" The man loosened his hold on the girl, but she stayed close.

"What?"

The man's mouth curled into a wide, full smile—one the wind had never seen on him before. "We're in the mountains. And . . . it's just as perfect as I thought it'd be. We're just . . . a few years late."

The girl nodded. Her throat bobbed as she swallowed. "Are you staying?"

The man shook his head. "Jagger wanted the Clarks hit. He didn't like them using you. I thought the SUV . . . They'd illusioned them. I thought I had the right one, but they'd shell-gamed it."

The girl laughed. "So our SUV looked like the Clarks'?"

The man nodded. "Mari, if I failed to kill them . . . I did, right?"

The girl tilted her chin in assent.

"Right. Jagger wants you to find the key. Before the closing ceremony. He wants the key the Clarks took from you."

The girl narrowed her eyes. "Luvic . . . Luvic said something about the key. I'd forgotten . . . he said . . . What did he say?"

The solemn man's back stiffened, but the girl didn't notice.

"Something about . . . if I want to live, get the key."

She looked at the man, but he didn't move or say anything. Instead, he held unnaturally still.

"Are you all right?" she asked.

The wind stirred the air between the two of them. It moved between their legs and climbed the warmth that separated them.

"Justice?"

His mouth twitched; his eyes turned hard. The wind knew this was what happened when the solemn one was fighting the leggerock's hold. The man always lost, but he hadn't yet stopped fighting.

He released a painful breath and whispered, "Fine. I was just . . ." He shook his head. Paused for a long moment.

The girl reached up and touched the side of his face. "It's okay. I know you didn't mean to fire the Omnibus at me. I'm not upset—"

He let out a huff of air. "So the thrown punches and the kicks—"

"Were because you put yourself in danger, you idiot! You—"

"You know it's not my choice what I do or don't—?"

They stood quiet, their words run out. The wind rocked the dry pine needles carpeting the ground at their feet.

"I should go," the girl finally whispered.

The russet-haired, solemn one nodded. Then, before the girl could slip from his arms, he reached out and cupped her face in his hands.

The wind stroked the heat of his fingers brushing her skin. The man's hands curled, and the girl held still.

His pulse rocketed. There was a bittersweet, broken ache in the way his fingers curved over the girl's cheeks.

"Mari," he said quietly, "I'm going to kiss you."

The man leaned down; took a long, breath-held time—long enough for the girl to push him away. Instead, she watched the moonlight over his freckles and the open, yearning silver-gray of his gaze.

The wind swirled softly between them as the man's lips gently settled over the girl's mouth.

His fingers stroked her jaw. Feathered over her face. His mouth moved slowly, coaxing the girl's lips open.

The wind frolicked in the moonlit warmth, the gentle exhale, the quiet stroking of the man's mouth over the girl's.

The man made a soft, rumbling noise. The wind knew it was a pained noise—the noise of a wounded animal and a heart being pierced by a knife from the inside. But the man didn't stop. Instead, he closed his eyes and savored the violet taste of the girl.

The wind brushed the man's hands. Rode his trembling fingers. Felt the warmth of their lips. Then, finally, the man pulled away. Not far. He kept his hands on the girl's face, his fingers stroking her skin.

She swallowed. Blinked into the moonlight.

"Why . . .?" She swallowed again. "Why . . .?"

The man smiled. The wind tapped his wet lips and wondered at the painful curve.

"Because . . . I'll never get the opportunity again. That was my only chance. I had to take it."

At his words, the girl nodded. Wrapped her arms around his middle. Rested her head on his heart. "If you didn't know, I wish we'd had those two minutes too."

After a moment, the girl pulled free of the man. She stepped away, moving back toward the boy's wooden home.

Before she turned fully, she lifted her hand and said, "Be careful. I'll see you back home."

The solemn man didn't say anything as he watched the girl disappear into the forest. Instead, he stood in the shadow of the hemlock tree, a grim line, a dark figure, solemnly watching his only weakness slip away.

The man lifted a hand to his lips and let out a long sigh.

The wind nudged his hand, not wanting him to lose the shard of good still left inside. Maybe it was too late. The wind had seen plenty of men be consumed by darkness.

It fled the hemlock grove, dancing on a mossy log and a bed of sleeping ferns, until it found the boy sitting not far away, on an outcropping of night-cold boulders.

The wind tousled his hair, and the boy twitched and shook his head. Then he whispered, "Well, Wind? What did they say? Shall I kill him?"

The wind whispered in the boy's ear. The boy nodded. Raised his eyebrows. Then nodded again.

"Not tonight then," he decided.

The wind followed sleepily as the boy hurried back toward his mountain-woods home.

~

I had to hurry. But quietly. The wind pushed at me, shaking the pine needles so they made a *shhh shhhh shhh* sound.

It was a risk, sneaking out of the suite. But while I'd been lying in the dark, staring up at the domed wooden ceiling, listening to the loud droning of insects in the forest, I'd thought about Justice, our home in the woods, and our dreams. I knew if he was still here, and if I went out into the woods, he'd find me.

So I'd slipped from the room, careful not to wake Finn, and climbed down to the forest. Maybe you're surprised. Maybe you've forgotten the beginning of my story, when I broke into and out of the Smith fortress. I hadn't yet found a lock on earth that could keep me out, and I hadn't found a place I couldn't break into. Jagger hadn't wasted all the years I'd been alive by letting me lie around.

So I'd taken a risk and left the Smith suite to wander the woods. Was it worth it? Yes.

What can I tell you? There was no reason to hurry through the dense forest—dense with pine and fern, dense with evergreen smells, dense with tree sounds. No reason except emotion.

I had to see my friend for at least one moment in the place we'd always dreamed of.

I reached up and touched the warm curve of my lips. I could still feel the gentle pressure of his mouth on mine. I could taste exactly what he'd been telling me.

It was a goodbye kiss. Or a hello kiss. Probably both. We both knew the forest house he'd painted for us as kids would never happen. We both knew we'd never live in this imaginary home. We both knew the idealized, peaceful world we'd dreamed of wasn't a place either of us would ever live. But for a moment, in that kiss, we imagined what it would be like if it did exist. We said hello to it, and then we said goodbye.

That was what he was telling me. Hello. Goodbye. I'm sorry this wish never came true.

I knew Justice would never kiss me again. He might not ever tell me he loved me again. I only hoped . . . I hoped he'd stay safe, and when I saw him again at Hell Gate, I hoped he'd still remember how to smile.

I paused at the edge of the forest. The softly shaking pine and the bowing ferns shielded me from the dim light of the crescent moon. I'd been gone for twenty minutes. Long enough for Finn to wake up and notice I was gone.

I was counting on the fact that he'd had a thimble of solange before falling into bed; that he was deep in the velvety ties of blissful dreams.

I held still, studying the castle. I told you I'd describe it, didn't I? Do you know the glistening stone castles in Germany and France? The fairy-tale castles, with spires, towers, and grand great halls?

That is exactly what the Wards' northern home looked like. Except their castle wasn't built from pink limestone or gray granite. It was constructed entirely from glossy, honey-colored hemlock. The foundation was stone, but the rest? It was a fairy tale built from wood.

It was tall. Some of the towers reached four stories. It was wide. At least as long as the Met.

There were windows everywhere, letting in light and the ever-present mountain breeze. The castle was perched at the top of the mountain, where rock cliffs collided and then fell in a sheer drop over the expansive forest. In the distance below were ice-blue lakes and a line of blue-green mountains that looked like a fat ribbon unspooling.

There was an illusion of thick, impenetrable trees and mist around the castle. Even the driveway was hidden. No uninvited guests or random hikers would ever wander this way. If they did, I was sure the Wards had plenty of means to deter the unexpected visitors.

I stepped quietly from the forest's edge, keeping to the shadow. I wasn't in the mood to scale the walls back to our suite's open window. Instead, I'd slip through a first-floor window. Perhaps the tall one that led into the library. That room was just around the corner from—

"Hello."

I spun around, thrusting my hand reflexively out in front of me. I was alone. There wasn't anyone near. I *knew* this.

Yet when I turned, Jacob Ward was standing two feet away.

He looked down at my fist an inch from his chest. I held still. Frozen.

Not by illusion, but by the racing of my heart and the adrenaline crashing through me—fight, flight, freeze.

He smiled. When he looked back up, his pale green eyes glowed with amusement.

"Nice night for a walk." He nodded at the panorama of stars glittering above us.

I dropped my arm. Slowly. This was Jacob after all. I'd spent the better part of the week doing my best to avoid him and making myself as inconspicuous and forgettable as possible.

I never wanted to attract the attention of the conjurers. But I especially didn't want to attract the attention of a Ward. Sometimes, I wondered, what was it that made Philoneas kill my parents? Was my mom or my dad a lockpick too? Could the Wards sense it in me? Could they instinctively tell what I was?

Suddenly, I wished Rou had made me another pair of earrings before I left Hell Gate. I may not kill with them, but they at least made me feel safer when facing a Ward.

I realized Jacob was watching me, waiting for me to say something back.

I nodded. My throat was dry and tight when I said, "Beautiful. Really."

We stood for a moment staring up at the towers and spires backlit by the moon and the stars.

Jacob was in his usual gear. His wrinkled jeans and graphic T-shirt "I'm young and harmless" look. I could easily see him sitting in a coffee shop laughing with friends, talking about the concert they were all about to head off to. It was part of what made him dangerous. He was pink-cheeked and fairy-kissed, and while you were awwing over how boyishly cute he was, he was devouring your mind or crafting illusions that made you become your worst self.

I moved an inch away. Then another. If I slowly walked away, he might not notice. In fact, he seemed to have forgotten me altogether.

But then my shoe hit a pebble, and it cracked against a small boulder in the grass.

Jacob looked over and noticed I'd moved a few feet from him. He shoved his hands into his pockets and slumped his shoulders.

"What's your favorite food?" he asked.

I did a double-take. Was this a trick question? Or . . . what? Did Wards use your likes to entrap your mind?

I hedged and then answered, "Freshly baked bread, just out of the oven. With butter and strawberry jam."

He smiled, and the corner of his mouth turned up. Then he tilted his head and looked at the stars. "Do you have a favorite color?"

"Green," I said. Then, when he searched my face for a more thorough answer, I added, "The pale green of a spring leaf when the sunrise first hits it."

Would he use my answers to trap my mind?

But no. He only nodded and asked, "What's your name?"

I swallowed. My throat ached. Naming things gave you power over them. Roumelade had taught me that. Lockpick. Little thief. Mine.

Hadn't God commanded man to name all the creatures on earth? Hadn't God granted man dominion over them?

"Mari," I said.

Jacob let out a long breath. I wasn't sure whether he was going to kill me or ask me another question. That was the thing with Wards—you could never tell what they were about to do. Philoneas, with his nice-guy, bland-professor looks. Jacob, with his cute innocence.

My heart was a painful pounding in my chest. I glanced at the castle, only twenty feet away, wishing I could run inside.

"I'm Jacob," he said, and then he held out his hand.

I stared at his outstretched fingers. It felt as if I was about to reach into grass where a venomous snake lay in wait, ready to strike. My skin went cold, and the breeze tracked over the cold sweat running down my neck.

I reached out and took Jacob's hand.

The illusion snapped around me. It hit so hard I felt as if my insides had been slammed against the castle walls. I hadn't moved an inch, but everything inside me whooshed back in a hurricane of energy.

The air left my lungs. My ears rang as I was gripped in illusion.

Where was the knot? Where was the knot?

I searched frantically.

It was the thread again. The rope that slid around me. Around, around, around. It tightened. I could barely breathe. There were claws shredding. Digging. Searching. My bones hurt. My tendons ached.

Did he know?

He pried inside of me. Found a locked vault buried deep and—

Untie the knot!

Mari, untie the knot!

I gasped. Yanked my hand free.

Trembling, I stepped back. My lips were numb, my limbs heavy.

He'd kill me now. Whatever he'd done, it was the lead up to a Ward death.

But while I tried to force my legs to work, to run, Jacob only stared at me with a deeply furrowed brow. He shook his head and said, "You have a hole in you. It's empty." He pointed at my chest.

I looked down, but there was nothing there. No hole. Just me.

"Are you going to kill me?" I asked, because I'd rather know than not.

Jacob made a surprised noise. "No." Then he asked, more thoughtfully, "Do you think I'm going to?"

Now that he'd asked, I was certain he wouldn't. Not at that moment at least.

"No." I thought for a moment. "Definitely no."

He smiled as if I'd said something funny. "You know, you shouldn't poison people. It isn't polite."

The way he said it, casually throwing it out, made my skin go cold then hot then cold again.

"Sorry?"

Did he know it was me who'd poisoned his tea, or was he referring to any of the other times I'd done it since arriving?

"My tea."

"Ah. Oh."

He raised his eyebrows and then said, "Don't do it again, all right? I can't do what I have to do if you're poisoning me."

What, win the games?

Yet, thinking of that, I remembered the tomb, and Jacob's quiet grief, and then his unleashed wrath. I hadn't said anything then. What could I have said in the moment? But now?

Justice would yell at me, "Don't have compassion!"

Jagger would say, "Learn what you can and then use it against him."

Rou would tell me, "Kill him now. Get your revenge."

Griff would say, "Be careful, Mari. He's a Ward."

I never listened to their imaginary promptings. Instead, I looked at the barren black space between the stars and said, "I'm sorry about the Clark game. I'm sorry for what happened."

Jacob stilled. I don't think he even breathed. But then he let out a long breath. "Why?"

I shrugged. "Because it hurt. Because it shouldn't have been. Because . . . I'm sorry you were hurt."

He stared at me for a long moment. And I saw in him the four-year-old boy who killed his sister. I wondered, had anyone ever told him they were sorry he was hurt? Because he'd been hurt too, hadn't he?

Maybe I was inviting death by saying anything. Maybe showing compassion to a Ward only opened you up for them to come in and destroy you from the inside. But still, I felt it had to be said.

Who else was going to say it? No one.

"I'm sorry," I whispered, "that you lost her. I'm sorry, too, about your sister. I'm sorry if you were hurt."

I knew immediately that I shouldn't have said it.

Jacob's whole body stiffened. He went predator-still, and then he grabbed my wrist and yanked me toward him.

I slammed against him. And then he buried us in a darkness so thick and deep I couldn't even remember what light looked like.

I struggled like a bird with its wings caught in a net.

Jacob gripped my arms and hissed, "Shh!"

I stilled. He wasn't prying my mind open. He wasn't rooting through my bones. Instead, he'd cloaked us in darkness. We were *hiding*.

The darkness was so deep there was barely the hum of illusion around us. It was more an anti-illusion. I wondered if a conjurer would even be able to sense Jacob there. It didn't have the same tingling feeling most illusions had.

A moment later, the Smith stalked around the corner, the Bard with him. Their low voices carried on the wind, just loud enough to make out.

"The attack was the leggerock's doing—" That was the Smith, his voice full of disdain.

"Yet you harbor his creature," the Bard said. His melodious voice matched the moon and starlit night. "For a famed strategist, you made a poor decision in that. What will you do?"

Wolfgang paused, looked across the boulder-strewn grass, and narrowed his eyes. But it wasn't Jacob's cloaked darkness he looked toward. It was the trees.

It was then I saw it: a sheer knot of illusion beyond an old pine. I held back a huff of surprise. Celia. She was tucked behind the trunk, invisible to anyone who couldn't see illusion.

Maybe Wolfgang sensed something, but after a moment, he turned back to the Bard.

"I will do as I've always done. Rule my family. Act with honor. Defend the crown."

The Bard smiled at the last one. At the moment, he was the crown.

They continued walking, moving slowly toward the front entrance. The Bard spoke again. "When Celia holds the crown, I would like you to begin a series of conflicts. War, Wolfgang. I'm asking for war."

Wolfgang ran a hand down his gray-streaked beard. "If she wins, we will give you your wars."

Before they reached the entrance, the Bard said, "How it must pain you to have given life to two weak sons. A man like you. I wondered why you didn't kill him at birth, but then I remembered my own lapse. Compassion is an insidious thing. Will you kill him once the games are done?"

"Perhaps."

"And the leggerock's creature? Once isn't enough. You have to deliver a true death. Send a message to the leggerock?"

Wolfgang waved the question away. "She is nothing. I'll deal with her in the end."

They opened the front door and slipped inside.

Jacob's grip on my arms loosened, and then he stepped back,

releasing the darkness. Moonlight flooded over us, and I took a deep breath. At the edge of the woods, Celia still hid in illusion.

"Thanks," I said, smiling uncertainly.

Jacob nodded and then thrust his hands back in his pockets. "By the way, tomorrow? Tell your paladin it isn't the greatest, it isn't the worst, it isn't the highest, it isn't the lowest, it's the middle road."

I blinked. Waited for Jacob to say more, but he just watched me. "All right. I'll tell him."

Jacob smiled. "Bye, Mari. Go left at the entry. There's a set of stairs around the back that'll take you to your room without anyone seeing."

"Oh. All right. Thank you."

He held up a hand, and I hurried off. When I looked over my shoulder, he was meandering toward the tree where Celia was hiding. So. He'd noticed her too.

Busy night.

I kept to the shadows and then slipped into the house. Once inside, I turned left, found the narrow set of stairs near the back, and hurried on light feet up the wooden steps, pausing at every moan and creak.

I'd almost made it to the top undiscovered, but when I rounded the final turn, I found Finn. He was leaning against the railing, arms crossed, navy eyes practically glowing in the dark. I paused, and a smile edged the corner of his mouth.

"Hi, Mari. Where've you been?"

52

"THE MIDDLE ROAD?" FINN ASKED, THE MOONLIGHT FROM THE BEDROOM window coating the dark shadows of his skin.

"That's what he said." I wrapped my arms around my knees and pressed my back against the wooden door. I was spooked from the encounter with Jacob and heartsore from my time with Justice. My emotions were strangely raw.

"Why would Jacob help us?"

I felt a quick, hopeful pulse at Finn saying "us." In fact, I liked the word so much that I dug my fingernails into my palm so I wouldn't reach over and take his hand.

Finn was oblivious. He'd woken up, gone for another dose of solange, and noticed I was missing. He'd come looking for me and found me sneaking up the stairs.

When I told him I'd gone out for a breath of fresh air and run into Jacob, he didn't doubt my sincerity. It was almost disappointing how easy he was to fool.

In a world where you should trust no one, Finn trusted me too easily.

He leaned his head against the door. He'd settled on the floor next to me after we made our way back to the suite. Darin was snoring in his bedroom, but I didn't think Wolfgang was back yet from his nighttime machinations. I thought about telling Finn his dad was considering ending him after the game, but then he already knew that, didn't he? And what would I say? *"Not if I get you first, ha-ha!"* So . . . no.

"I'm not sure Jacob is helping us," I said. I was very skeptical of his motives. "My guess is he's helping himself. If that means giving you a hint, then he'll do it. Maybe he doesn't want the Clarks to win. Or the Bards. Or maybe the middle road is a trap." I shrugged. "It's hard to say."

I was more concerned with the way he'd acted almost . . . friendly. A lifetime's worth of experience had taught me friendliness was often camouflage for a darker intent. I couldn't brush aside the niggling sensation there was a reason Jacob had sought me out, and it had nothing to do with giving Finn a tip for the game.

"I think he suspects . . ." I cleared my throat and glanced over at Finn. "I'm worried he knows what I . . . am."

Finn looked at me quickly. He studied my face, the moonlight lighting the room. Whatever he saw made him stiffen. "You're sure?"

"No." I shook my head and looked down at my arms clasped around my knees. "It's just a feeling."

How many people knew now? Finn. Maybe Luvic. Now Jacob?

"If he did know . . ." Finn left the final half of the sentence unsaid.

"He'd kill me," I finished. I smiled without humor into the dark. "After he and his dad turn my mind into a hell maze and torture me for a few years. Out of all the conjurers, it's the Wards who scare me the most."

Had I really just admitted that out loud?

Yes. Since Finn reached over and took my hand, I'd say yes, I had.

His hand was warm and his clasp gentle. After a moment, his thumb circled my pulse and the tattoo on my wrist. When he brushed the thorn, the sharp-toothed bite of it lessened to a dull ache.

A soft warmth flowed through me. My eyelids fluttered, and my limbs went heavy. I could lie down, sprawl in front of the door, and enjoy a few hours of sleep before the sun rose over the mountains.

"How's your friend?" Finn asked, his voice soothing.

"Hmm?" I smiled, closing my eyes.

"The one who nearly killed us. I'm guessing that's who you went to see?"

My eyes flew open. I jerked upright, and the relaxed, floaty feeling vanished. "What?"

Finn tugged my hand, and I realized I'd been trying to pull away. He kept stroking the thorn of my tattoo.

"Your friend."

I shook my head. *Deny. Deny. Deny.*

Finn's mouth curved into a smile, barely distinguishable in the dark. "I'm glad he's okay."

So I was wrong. Finn wasn't as easily fooled as I'd thought. But was he truly glad Justice was okay?

"Why?"

Finn gave me a surprised look. "Because he's your friend. Why else?"

"Is that why you stopped Wolfgang—?"

"No. I saw what you were doing."

So that was it. Finn was protecting me. He hadn't wanted me to lockpick Wolfgang's illusion and risk discovery.

He cared.

For some unknown reason, Finn cared.

"Thank you."

Finn nodded. Then he asked with a smile, "Is he the one who'll kill me if you don't?"

"Probably."

His smile turned into a grin. "Good to know."

Fool. Fool man.

I'd reasoned that he wasn't a fool. That it was a disguise. I changed my mind.

Without thinking too hard about it, I quickly stood and crossed the wood floor to the chest of drawers. I opened my pack and pulled free a small white leather box.

Finn watched me, his long legs stretched out in front of him. He was so relaxed you wouldn't think it was three in the morning and he had another game to play in twelve hours.

I padded back to him, the cool floor creaking beneath me. When I reached him, I kneeled next to him and opened the leather box.

Two gold rings fell into my palm. They made a dull clinking noise.

When Finn saw them, he straightened, and a surprised puff of air left him.

"What are those?"

The cold of the metal tickled my palm. The rings were light, and the moon caught the braided yellow glow of them.

"Wedding rings," I teased, but I immediately regretted it when Finn stiffened. "I'm kidding. Just kidding. Sorry. That was thoughtless."

His face had gone pale, and his kaleidoscope eyes looked even more shattered than usual.

"Sorry," I said again. "Sometimes I say things without thinking."

"Don't worry about it." He brushed it aside, but there wasn't any denying his mouth was tight and his gaze unhappy. The easy warmth that had surrounded us had shifted to a strained cold.

He stared at the rings, caught by the glimmer and flicker of the gold in the moonlight. I was close enough that I could feel the air shifting at his long exhale.

"They're callback rings," I said by way of explanation. "A matching pair. When you put the ring on me, you say, 'Mari, whenever I call, you come,' and if you need me, you say, 'Mari, come back.' I'll appear right in front of you. And I'll do the same with you. That way . . ." I paused at the strange light in Finn's eyes. "If you don't want to, that's okay. It was only a sudden feeling I had that you might need me. If you were in trouble, or if I was and you couldn't find me, or . . ."

I swallowed. Waited.

"If we put them on, can we take them off again?"

I shook my head. "I don't know."

Objects of power were strange. They sometimes came with odd side effects or unwanted consequences. Or they worked just like they were supposed to.

"You're giving this to me because . . .?"

I closed my hand around the rings. "Because I'm worried about tomorrow. You can take an object of power into the game—why not this one? The Wards . . . players sometimes don't come out of their games. They get lost. They're never found. If you don't come out after the time's up,"—I shrugged—"I'll call you back to me."

"If I don't come out, I'll be dead. That's the only reason I won't finish a game."

He said it so evenly that it took me a moment to understand what he was saying. He wouldn't want me to call him back.

I opened the box, ready to put the rings back in. "Okay. Fair enough. Let's get some sl—"

"I'd like to wear them." He took my hand before I could put the rings away.

Really?

"Okay." I nodded slowly. "Stipulations?"

He took one of the braided gold rings from my hand and nodded. "Don't call me during a game."

"Agreed."

"Don't call me if it would put you in danger."

I paused. Then nodded. "Agreed."

"Don't call me if I told you beforehand not to."

That one was a little trickier. "What if I learn something that invalidates your request?"

"Even then. Don't."

I sighed. "Agreed."

"And you?" he asked, warming the braided ring in his hand.

"Well . . . don't call me if I'm on a job."

He lifted an eyebrow as if wondering what sort of job I might mean. But then he simply said, "Fine."

"Don't call me if I told you not to."

He nodded like that was obvious.

"Don't call me frivolously. These aren't for fun, only emergencies. And if the rings are permanent, don't call me after the games are done. If you do—"

He smiled. "You'll kill me."

Not what I was going to say, but sure.

"Also," I added, frowning, "I don't know what'll happen if I die my ninth death wearing this ring, so don't call me if I'm dead, all right? And don't call me after."

Who knew what would happen if he tried to find me after? Nothing good.

The room darkened, the shadows drew close, and Finn's eyes narrowed. "You think these rings can call back from the afterlife?"

"I don't know. I doubt they're that powerful."

Besides, I didn't take any possessions with me into death.

So that was that. We'd made our agreement.

"I'll go first," I said, holding the braided gold ring out.

Finn extended his right hand. I hadn't noticed before how quiet the room was. The stillness and the silence. I'd seen the moonlight, but I hadn't appreciated how it painted us in silver. The window was closed, but a soft draft still snuck through the molding and drifted over the wood floor, bringing hints of a sleeping, dreaming world.

My heart thudded softly, and the bedroom took on the silvery, smudged glow of an antique linotype. Finn's breath was a soft, shallow sound as I leaned closer and took his hand.

It didn't mean anything. They weren't promise rings, engagement rings, or wedding rings. All the same, it would be foolish to dismiss the fact that the rings were binding. They were a rope with no beginning and no end, and when you exchanged rings, they symbolized an unbroken connection. There was no knot in rings. No illusion.

Did I trust Finn enough to tie myself to him, even with something as small as a callback ring? Yet . . . this ring could be used against me. I was always warning Finn not to trust me, but when had I stopped warning myself not to trust him?

He smiled as if he could hear my doubts. "It's all right, Mari. I won't hurt you."

That was an easy promise to give and an impossible promise to keep.

Still, I took the warm, braided band and slowly slid it onto his ring finger. The callback ring burned hot and then expanded to fit his finger perfectly. I felt a shudder move through him as I spoke the words, "Finn Alterra, whenever I call, you come."

The ring flashed white and then winked back to dull yellow gold. Finn's gaze went vacant, and for a short moment, he was lost in another world, far away from me and the moonlit room we were kneeling in. But then he was back, and he flexed his hand, adjusting to the feel of the gold ring.

"Now me," I said. I held out my right hand.

In the time it took to take a single breath, he'd gripped my hand and slid the ring over my fourth finger. It burned bright, hot but not painful, and then it shrank to seal around me.

It wasn't pain that had made Finn shudder—I knew that now. Instead, it was the heady, wine-rich, lustrous feeling that swept through my veins. I felt . . . oh, I felt star-kissed and wanton. Lush and needy.

Whatever these rings were first used for, they weren't merely for calling someone back to you. I imagined they were lovers' rings, and the callback was for bedroom affairs.

I made a low, involuntary sound, and Finn watched me from under half-mast eyelids.

"Mari Locke, whenever I call, you come."

His voice rippled through me, and the ring tightened on my finger, sending a pulse through my blood. The call and the answer coursed through me.

Suddenly, I could feel Finn as if I was iron and he was my magnet. Wherever he was—on earth, above, or below—I knew I would be able to turn in a circle and point in his direction. All the iron in my blood now pointed to him.

I ignored the vibration thrumming through me, the soft strum of him, and flexed my hand. The ring was warm, and because I'd never worn jewelry, it felt strange. I rolled my thumb over the braided metal. When I pushed at it, the ring didn't budge.

"I guess that answers that," I said, when I tugged and the ring didn't move.

Finn pulled at his ring. When it didn't come free, he nodded. "Shall we test it?"

"All right." I stood and walked across the room to stand near the far wall, next to the wood-framed bed. "That should be far enough."

The room was large. A city bus length separated us.

I took a breath and said quietly, "Finn Alterra, come back."

There was no time between Finn kneeling next to the door and him standing in front of me. The ring pulsed, tightened on my finger, and then I felt a sharp yank inside of me, like a rubber band snapping and rebounding.

Finn stumbled. I grabbed his arms. The force that had pulled him to me was still yanking. He let out a sharp "oomph," and then I fell backward onto the bed. Finn landed on top of me.

And—*oh*.

I was right. These rings were lovers' rings.

The bed cushioned my back. Finn fell onto me, his thighs pressing into mine, chest scraping against my thin silk top. He tried to steady himself and push away, but the rubber-band snap was too strong.

His mouth landed next to mine, and the heat of his lips curled through me as we both tried to turn away but instead came together.

"Oh!" I let out a sharp breath as his lips fell over mine.

All thought fled; there was only feeling. Deep, exquisite, luxurious feeling. Finn moaned as his lips brushed over mine. His moan captured something inside of me, and I gripped his shoulders, pulling him closer.

We shouldn't—

His lips stroked mine, and then his tongue was running along the seam of my mouth. I wrapped a leg around his waist and held him close. He drove his hand through my hair and tugged me closer. I needed every part of us to touch. Not just our lips, but our hands, our hips, our naked skin.

We should—

Finn parted my lips. He tasted my mouth; sent his tongue in a rhythmic quest. A throbbing, thrumming ache moved with him. His kiss turned from questing and seeking to a driving, mindless need.

His hips moved in rhythm with his mouth, and I held on, burning, needing.

We shouldn't—

"Mari," he whispered against my mouth, his voice pleasure-soaked and rumbly. "Mari."

At my name, my thighs clenched, and I wanted . . . I wanted desperately to . . .

Untie the knot!

Mari, untie the knot!

My eyes flew open. Finn's gaze was heated, bliss-filled, and . . . faraway. This wasn't real.

I shoved at him. He dragged his mouth along my jaw, trailing featherlight kisses over my skin. One. Another. Again.

"Finn."

His grip on me tightened, and he pressed another kiss against the corner of my mouth.

"Finn. Stop."

The ring on my finger pulsed, and a wave of pure lust shot through me. If I'd been standing, my legs would've buckled.

"Stop. Finn."

He held himself over me, his muscles tight, body rigid. He blinked. Blinked again. The blissful, lust-filled haze cleared from his expression.

For a moment, I didn't think he realized where we were. Even worse, I didn't think he knew who I was. He looked down at me with a blank, confused expression. And then, suddenly, although I hadn't thought it was possible, he stiffened even more.

"Get off," I said, refusing to be offended by the horrified look on his face.

He rolled off me and then scrambled upright and took a half-dozen steps away from the bed. I sat up. Smoothed down my hair. Readjusted my pajamas.

He stared at me.

I stared at him.

Finally, he cleared his throat and said, "It looks like they work."

I nodded. The throbbing ache and heavy pulse in my blood was slowly fading. I could still sense where Finn was, but my need for him was subsiding.

"I'm sorry. I didn't know they were . . ." I didn't know what to call them. "Lovers' rings, I guess."

Griff would be surprised. Innocent, funny, happy-go-lucky Griff. He'd be shocked. Thank goodness he hadn't followed through on his original thought and used them for the two of us. Who knew what would've happened if we'd kissed? He probably would've never been able to look me in the eye again.

"I can feel you," Finn said, staring at me with his eyebrows lowered.

"I know . . . it's directional—"

"No." He shook his head. "I can *feel* you. You're . . . confused, amused, embarrassed, and . . . aroused."

I gave him a sharp look. How dare he—?

"And annoyed," he added.

"What . . .?" I stilled, sifted through the feelings inside of me, and then found the ones that were there but weren't mine.

It was hard to say how I knew they weren't mine. I supposed it was like tasting a cup of tea that had a splash of milk instead of honey when you only ever drank tea with honey.

I sorted through the feelings and said, "Tired. Worried. Determined. Aroused."

He shrugged at the last one. I agreed. It wasn't his fault. Just like it wasn't mine. When used, these rings packed a punch.

"And . . ." The largest feeling inside Finn—the one I would've sworn a few days ago I'd never recognize. "Love."

It was big. So big it colored everything else inside of him. It was like a watercolor painting that had been washed in gold. The blues were blue-gold. The reds were red-gold. Everything was tinted with his love.

Finn studied me, and I felt a pulse of worry—not mine, his—that he quickly clamped down on.

"Don't worry," I hurried to reassure him. "Nothing's changed. Like I said, we'll only use these in emergencies."

"Probably best," he agreed.

I had the feeling he was studying the flush in my cheeks; the mess of my hair from him dragging his hands through it while we'd kissed. But when I peered into the darkness, he turned and looked out the moonlit window.

"I'll sleep on the floor," he offered, and where before I would've expected a tinge of annoyance or a spurt of self-sacrifice, I only felt an odd mix of unease and resolution.

I didn't question it. Most of the time, people didn't know or didn't understand their own feelings. How could I expect to understand something Finn probably wasn't aware of himself?

I curled onto the bed, draping the down comforter over me. At the edge of my mind, I could pinpoint where Finn was, and while his emotions were a quiet echo, if I concentrated, I could find them.

The sensation of him wrapped around me was new, and just like the sensation of the ring wrapped tight around my fourth finger, it would take some getting used to. All the same, I fell asleep even before Finn had crossed the room.

53

THE MOUNTAIN WAS AN ILLUSION. SOMETIMES, I WONDERED WHY THE conjurers of today contented themselves with plying the puppet strings of governments, ruling the hearts and minds of people, and waging wars when the conjurers of centuries past had moved mountains and shaken the earth.

Now I knew. They weren't contenting themselves. They still made mountains.

This one towered over the low, age-worn Catskills. Where before the vista was blue-green evergreens, taffy-pulled rolling mountains, and blue-gem lakes, now it was . . . thunderous.

Yes. Thunderous.

I expected a quaking voice to boom from the thick fog and shake the earth. The Catskills had been gentle pines, bowing firs, worn brown stone with ribbons of waterfalls, and strings of lakes. But that had been the Catskills in the light. Now we were in the fog.

It was a gray prison wall, thick and opaque. I told you the Wards were the wardens and prison guards tasked with keeping things out and keeping things in.

Right now, we were being kept in.

I stood with the families at the base of the illusion mountain. The fog that surrounded us was an impenetrable wall, conjured by Philoneas. The chill of the clouded mist seeped through my silk uniform and sank into my flesh. The column rose thousands of feet into the air, a giant fog pillar.

A coldness invaded every part of me. I shivered thinking about the river of power Philoneas must control to conjure a mountain and an impenetrable fog large enough to blanket an entire mountain range.

In that moment, I prayed his attention would never turn to me. I understood why my parents weren't able to escape him, even if I didn't understand why he'd murdered them.

At the rolling in my stomach and the tightened clench in my chest, Finn brushed the back of his hand against mine. A questioning, comforting gesture.

He could still feel me then, just like I could still feel the wall of resolve eclipsing every other emotion inside of him. Except love. That was still there, tinting the resolve in golden shades.

I let his hand drift across mine. To everyone else, it probably looked accidental. Finn, on the outside, looked like his usual wobbly, vacant-gazed, solange-addicted self. Half-there, half-not. But now that I had his knot of emotions inside of me, there was no stumbling, no wobbling; nothing but steady focus and determination.

I left him to his masquerade and studied the mountain and the families gathered at the base.

It was nearly three in the afternoon. Time for the third game. You wouldn't be able to tell from the sun though. We couldn't see it. Instead, it permeated the fog in a weak gray half-light.

There was still the scent of white pine, mossy stone, and damp forest things, but there were no forest birds singing—at least, I couldn't hear them through the gray fog wall. The only sound was the almost hushed blowing of the wind stirring the edges of the misty fog, sifting it like gray silk tassels on a billowing cloak.

I tilted my head up, up, up, trying to see the top of the conjured mountain. It was gray stone, rock-slide gravel, and dirt. There were no trees, bushes, or scrub—not even dying or dead vegetation. It was rock. Only rock.

There were four paths carved into the mountainside. They were narrow. Barely the width of two hands held together. They wound upward at a steep angle. If it were any steeper, the climb would require ropes or carving stairs into the rock.

Perhaps that was what the heirs would do. They'd make stairways or flying machines or escalators to ride to the top.

I didn't know. I only knew the mountain was barren and lifeless. It looked like the smooth, worn surface of a prehistoric beast's giant rib. It gave me the chills. Or perhaps that was the fingers of the ice-cold fog plucking at my too-thin silk uniform.

"This is the third game," Philoneas said, casting his eyes to each of the players.

His voice was the gentle professor's. The kind counselor's. It was the same voice he'd used when I was strapped to the inquisitor's chair. At my involuntary shudder, Finn swayed, tilted drunkenly toward me, and tangled his fingers with mine for a quick, nearly imperceptible moment.

When he pulled back, I felt better. Steadier.

"Don't know about you," Darin muttered, eyeing the encroaching mist and the bone-gray mountainside, "but I think this place is creepier than the Clarks' little basement of horrors."

"Can't disagree," I whispered, even though the Clarks' catacombs were officially my least favorite place on earth.

Darin hid a smile. He'd been trying to get on my good side since last night. I think, belatedly, he'd realized I might not exactly be thrilled with him gunning to kill my friend. He'd made the coffee this morning and handed me a piping-hot mug before asking what was on the menu for breakfast.

He'd looked a little like a puppy that had chewed a favorite shoe and was worried about being scolded. I'd made him a pound of bacon, just to reassure him there weren't any hard feelings. He'd eaten the entire platter to reassure me of the same and said, "No offense, Mari, but your creature friend has to die. Nothing personal."

The thing is, he was right. It wasn't personal. How many times had Jagger sent Justice out on a job where someone had to die? It was never personal.

Darin was a Smith. He was in the business of war and dealing death. At least he was straightforward about it.

"If you kill him, I'll make it personal," I'd said.

Darin had smiled and shoved the last piece of bacon into his mouth.

And that was that. And here we were, back to another game.

Across the clearing, Jacob stood next to his father. While the rest of the players were in tactical gear, hiking shoes, and thick canvas pants, he was casually dressed. He looked as if he'd rolled out of bed a few minutes before the game. His hair was messy, and his T-shirt was wrinkled. In fact —yes, that was the shirt he'd been wearing last night. Maybe he hadn't gone to sleep after we'd talked.

Huh.

He must've felt my attention, because his cool green gaze flicked to me.

I braced myself, expecting the prodding and poking that clawed around in my insides whenever he focused on me, but instead, he tilted his head and frowned. A line formed between his eyebrows. I felt a small tap in the center of my chest. It was like a cautious knock on a closed door.

I stiffened. What was he doing?

But then his attention moved on to the Bards, and the rope that had slid between us evaporated.

"—mountain." Philoneas was introducing the game, and I realized Jacob had distracted me. "You will traverse to the top. To reach the summit, you must travel each path. Once you begin, there is no turning back."

Nearby, the Bards stood in a tight circle. For once, Cressida, the Bard's wife, was at a game. She looked uncomfortable and cold, which wasn't surprising since she'd dressed in a short, strapless ivory silk dress. Next to her was the Bard, looking arrogant and coldly, disturbingly handsome. And then, of course, there was Ragnor and Luvic flanking Celia.

When Luvic saw me turning their way, he lifted one black eyebrow in question, but he didn't wink. The bruises had nearly faded from his throat, but with the fog surrounding him, he looked more menacing than usual. An arrow tightly strung and ready to shoot.

I thought of what he'd demanded: "If you want to live, you'll get the key." Maybe that arrow was pointed at me?

"Are you saying you've created a prison for our heirs? A mental trap that they may never emerge from?" This question was asked by Wolfgang. He had that particular hate-filled growl he used whenever he spoke to Philoneas.

Philoneas turned toward Wolfgang and leveled him with a placid, calm-waters stare. He smiled coolly at his former best friend, and I swear, under that placid lake, I saw the shadow of a retribution and a decades-old death promise in his gaze.

"That's exactly what I'm saying." He gestured to the gray-bone surface of the sheer mountain. It was at least three times the height of any other mountain in the range. "While all of you dream of conquering the world, war and sacrifice, famine and starvation, we Wards dream of . . . other things."

Darin punched Finn on the arm and murmured, "This is where you thank God you were born a Smith."

A flicker of amusement flared in the knot that held Finn's emotions. He really did like his brother.

I smiled at him, but then my smile froze. To our left, the Clarks had congregated in their crow-like murder. Primus was watching me with cold, black eyes. There was something there—some sort of hidden message. When he saw I'd noticed him, his lips curled into a cruel smile.

Behind him was Last. She stared at the ground, her black hair hiding her face. Next to her was their new body. He was as tall, gaunt, and oily as the last body. The only difference was that his eyes were a weak blue instead of brown. I could only presume his name was Thirteen.

The longer I held Primus's gaze, the more his smile grew, as if we were sharing a secret, just the two of us. I clenched my hand, digging my fingernails into my palm, and looked back to Philoneas.

"Humans travel to discover the world. We wonder at the deep blue of the sea, the vast emptiness of deserts, the splendor of cities, and the turning wheel of the heavens above us. We sail sparkling waters, we fly through the air, we travel continents and oceans, we wander the earth, and we wonder. Yet . . . in all this wandering, we humans walk past ourselves every day . . . and not once do we wonder. We never wonder at what lies within. You, my friends, dream of what is without. We Wards dream of what is within."

The thick wall of fog pressed closer—so much so that the cousins and second cousins who had followed the families to the base of the mountain were nearly swallowed by the gray mist.

The Wards stood in the middle of the circle. Uliea leaned close to Jacob and murmured something. She twisted her hands nervously and glanced at the four paths. He nodded and patted her hands.

It's funny—I'd never thought of him as a caring son. I'd never really thought of him in relation to Uliea at all. But there he was, reassuring his mom.

"There are four paths," Philoneas said, looking in turn at each heir and then at Finn. "You will climb this mountain. It's a mountain of illusion. While you climb, your body will remain on the path you chose, while your mind will turn inward. You will plumb the depths of yourself and live four realities: your greatest fear, your greatest desire, your best self, and your worst self. If you can conquer these realities, you will reach the summit. If not, you will remain in whatever life you refuse to leave. Your fear? Your desire? Your worst? Your best?" He smiled then, aiming a gloating look at Wolfgang. "Be careful of the trap that awaits in the agony of bliss and the pleasures of pain. You have six hours. If you return, you will return a new man or woman—one worthy of a crown. If you do not return, you may remain in yourself. You are welcome to the maze of your mind. I, for one, will not bring you from it."

At his words, a large, thundering gong sounded. It boomed over the mountain, sending a rock slide down the smooth edge.

Jacob patted his mom's hand a final time, and then, as if he were going on a stroll through Central Park, he meandered toward the path. As soon as he stepped onto one, he disappeared.

Primus scowled at his father and the rest of the Clarks around him and then shoved his way onto the next path. He was gone in seconds.

Luvic and Ragnor leaned in close to Celia. They were both speaking quickly, and she nodded at whatever they said. Luvic gripped her arms and pressed his forehead to hers. Then Ragnor pulled her to him, and after a quick word, she pulled away and stalked to the third path, her head held high.

Ten seconds had passed. Finn held one eye closed and then opened it, then he closed his other. There was a thoughtful stillness inside of him. A questioning, calm emotion that reminded me of the still, quiet warmth you got from lying on the grass in the sun, with insects droning above and the scent of wild roses washing over you. He wasn't worried at all.

Because of that, I didn't worry either.

If I'd known Finn was hiding his true emotions and sending false emotions along the knot of that ring, I would've felt differently. I would've felt differently about a lot of things. But I didn't know it. At that time, I still thought emotions couldn't lie.

That's naïve, I know. How many times in my life had my own emotions lied and misled me? Too many.

Still, at the time, I thought Finn was confident and calm. So I let that reassure me.

"Take the middle path," I whispered, reminding him of what Jacob had said. It seemed he really had wanted to help, and whatever the words meant, they would aid Finn inside the maze of his mind.

Finn nodded and started forward.

Wolfgang reached out and grabbed Finn's arm, stopping him. "For a man who can't face reality but instead hides in the mists of solange," he said, gripping his son's arm, "I have little faith you'll come out of this alive. You are too much of a coward to face your fears. You are too easily caught and enraptured by the web of your desires. You aren't a man who rules himself. Prove me wrong. Show me you have the blood of a conjurer in you. Show me you are my son."

Finn didn't acknowledge his father's words. He stared through him, and when Wolfgang had finished speaking, Finn shrugged out of his hold and turned away.

He swayed, stumbled over the rockslide gravel, and then, when his foot touched the fourth and final path, he disappeared.

54

Could the wind breach illusion? Could it flutter through mist and enter the mind?

No, it could not.

While the wind had ventured to the dark depths of the earth, riding on the backs of burrowing cicadas and voles; while it had flown into the sea, gliding in air pockets under the wings of an albatross; and while it had soared high above the clouds, buoyed by its own spirit, the wind had never entered the mind of man.

It could whistle in an ear, whisper and moan, but it could not read thoughts or see the contents of a heart.

It chased the mist, brushing through the curtain-like fingers of fog, and panted as it climbed the alabaster mountainside. The narrow path it had chosen to follow—like water in a meandering stream, rising uphill instead of down—was not the boy's path.

The wind wasn't worried about the boy. He wasn't in danger, and there were no secrets of the boy's that the wind didn't already know.

The boy had already faced his worst fear and his greatest desire and had set aside both as anathema to his truth. He had already become his worst and his best self. The worst and the best were the same boy, only separated by intent.

The boy would win this game. The wind knew this, just as it knew the ice crystals in the upper atmosphere were delightful porcupine pinpricks, and that dandelion seeds laughed when it carried them high.

So, instead of following the path the boy had chosen, the wind climbed the narrow trail that smelled of sea and citrus.

The trickster had set his forehead against the woman's and murmured, "You are as you are. Good and bad. I'll take both. Love you, Lia."

Then the musician had whispered to the woman in an urgent voice, "Don't be trapped by the promise of what can never be."

The musician's voice had been tightly strung. Was he frightened or only giving a warning? The wind didn't know.

There were certain things that frightened the musician. He was afraid of the roar of crowds but of the quiet of solitude even more. He was afraid of being seen but more scared of staying unknown. The musician was forever torn between two extremes in himself. But those fears were not what tinged his voice when he urged his sister not to be trapped in her desires.

Perhaps the musician knew something the wind didn't. Something that made him afraid. So the wind followed the smooth, sliding path upward, traveling the mountain of illusion.

By nightfall, the mountain would fold in on itself like a paper tower neatly creased, flattened, and put away. The wind had seen the Wards create illusions like this before. It only had to follow and—

Ah!

Yes.

The citrus and pearl dust scented woman stood at the edge of her first trial. The wind rushed forward and tangled itself in the loop of her shoelace. She hit the wall of illusion and then stumbled as the ground shook, the sky boomed, flashed—and then she blinked, and the mountain was no longer there.

The wind and the woman were surrounded by the projections of her mind.

"Oh." She exhaled, and the wind flew up and wrapped itself around her shoulders, clinging to the thick rope of her braided hair.

The woman was no longer wearing hiking boots, thick canvas pants, or a cotton shirt. Instead, she was in a bloodred silk gown. She was pale, thin; the veins on her arms were blue-green rivers traversing her skin. She looked around cautiously as she descended a dark stone tunnel.

The wind knew this tunnel. Even in illusion, it still disliked the tunnels under the Bards' home.

The cold was there, the *drip drip* of waterdrops, but thankfully, the stones were not the same watchers they were in real life.

The woman paused at the bulbous room where she often met her father and her brothers. It was different. Her brothers were there, the musician and the trickster, but they weren't awake. It was difficult to tell if they were alive.

They were both sleeping on hospital cots. They both had tubes running from them. The room smelled like antiseptic and blood. The wind knew the smell from the times it had visited the woman when her brothers were sharing their blood with her.

The woman's hand flew to her chest, and then she rushed forward to pull the needle free from the musician's vein.

A noise sounded—a scuffed footstep. "I wouldn't if I were you," a man said.

The woman quickly turned. It was the father. He shrugged and winced at his sons.

"You know how they get when they wake. Uncontrollable."

"What . . .?" The woman took a step back. Swallowed uncomfortably. "Why are they like this?"`

The father stepped into the room and sneered at his two sons. "This is what happens when two men betray the woman who wears the crown. They cannot die, but they cannot live."

"Ragnor and Luvic betrayed me?"

The wind pushed at the woman's hair. Her pulse fired rapidly. She'd forgotten this was an illusion. She'd sunk into the depths of her mind, and rage swept through her.

"My brothers betrayed me?" Her voice was low and wrath-filled.

The father laughed. The melodious sound ricocheted around the antiseptic stone room. "Angry again? Don't worry. The Ward wrapped their minds so deep in misery their punishment will last a lifetime."

The wind tugged at the woman's braid. She blinked. Shook her head and swatted at her hair.

"I want to speak to him," she said, pointing at Luvic. "I want to . . ." She pinched her forehead.

"Take their blood, daughter. But don't take their poisoned words—"

"Let me speak to him!"

The father sighed, and then, as if against his own will, he stepped close to the trickster and twisted his hand.

The trickster's eyes flew open. His body went rigid, and he roared. The wind moaned. The trickster's expression was devoid of humanity. He was an animal. He jerked and thrashed, and when he saw the woman, he tore at the invisible bonds that held him.

He hated her. His hate was a cudgel that slammed through the air.

The woman gasped and jerked away.

"Lia!" the trickster screamed. His voice was raw and strangled. "I will slaughter you. I will kill you. I will end you. Die, you blood-stealing—"

"Enough!" She twisted her hand, and the trickster's shout cut off. Not because she'd put him back to sleep, but because she'd turned the trickster to ash.

The wind shivered as the woman's skin turned to ice.

The father chuckled. "I recommend you don't wake the other. I'll call someone to clean up the mess."

The father strode from the stone room. The woman didn't notice. She held her hand out in front of her. It shook. Ash coated the cot.

It smelled of soot and winter.

"Luvic?" the woman whispered. The shaking traveled up her arm and then through the rest of her. "Luvic?" she said again, looking around the room.

The wind yanked on her braid.

"I killed him. Luvic? I killed him. Oh no. No." She shook her head. Twisted her hand.

The musician opened his eyes.

Unlike the trickster, he held still and quiet. All the same, his eyes were filled with a burning hate that exceeded the fire in the trickster's eyes.

"Ragnor," the woman whispered. "I killed Luvic."

The wind tugged on her braid again, but she ignored it.

The musician grew even more still. The hate in him grew even hotter.

A salt scented tear slid down the woman's face. "I don't know what's happened. I don't understand—"

"I'll tell you," the musician said, his voice barely above a whisper. "Come closer. I'll help you understand."

The wind ran up and down the woman's arm, warning her, but she didn't listen. Instead, she stepped closer to the musician and leaned down so she could hear the soft breath of his words.

When she was only an inch away, the musician broke the bonds holding him. He launched upright and gripped the woman's throat.

Her breath wheezed from her, and the wind shrieked. The musician gripped her. Tried to squeeze the life out of her.

"Die. Murderous, evil, blood-stealing—"

She couldn't breathe. There was no air. No wind. She clawed at her brother's hands. Her pulse pounded, and her heart raced. The wind tugged at the musician's fingers.

The musician hated the woman. There was no breath left in her. She twisted her hand, and the musician burned. The flame lasted for a second. Then there was only ash.

Two piles of burned ash.

The woman sat on the floor between her two brothers and stared at the gray stone wall. The wind tugged, pulled, yanked, but the woman ignored it.

The father strode into the room and paused when he saw the ashes. The man next to him laughed.

"You never could control your temper. At least there are the children."

The woman glanced at the man—no, the wind amended—the boy. The wind's boy, but not.

"What children?"

The boy smiled. "Our children."

The woman shook her head. No. No. No.

The wind blew in her ear, whispering the words of her brother, carried up from the base of the mountain: *"You are as you are. Good and bad. I'll take both. Love you, Lia."*

The woman stiffened at the words carried up the mountain path and through the illusion.

"My greatest fear," she said. "My greatest fear."

The two men smiled at her. She ignored them both. Instead, she closed her eyes, looked within herself, and said, "I love you too."

The wind grabbed the woman's braid as the room swirled around her. A whirlwind caught the tunnel and the illusion like leaves in an autumn storm, and then the woman was thrust into a new projection.

She landed on the silk sheets of a bed, the breath knocked out of her.

The wind moaned happily. Silk sheets were better than cold stone rooms. Silk sheets were almost as fun as gliding down rainbow-studded waterfalls and rushing over golden sunbeams at dawn. It loved silk sheets.

The woman sighed and then burrowed down into the bed. She'd forgotten the last illusion already. She'd forgotten this wasn't real.

She pressed her cheek into the pillow and rolled onto her stomach, breathing in the vanilla and spice scent of the warm bed. The pillow next to her had an indent where someone had recently lain.

The room was at the boy's timber home. It was the one the boy slept in. The one in the highest tower, with the view of the twin lakes and the mountains. The wind swirled around the room, pushing open the window to taste the illusion air. It rummaged through the books on the shelves and the purple irises in the crystal vase next to the bed.

The woman made a soft, happy noise and stretched out across the bed. It was dawn. The sun was just rising. It drifted in long, buttery streams across the silk sheets. The woman was no longer in her bloodred dress. Instead, she wore a pink silk and lace negligée, and her dark hair flowed in long, silken waves around her.

The wind was surprised when the boy—but not the boy—padded quietly into the room. He was in an unbuttoned pair of jeans and nothing else. He carried a tray holding a coffee pot, two cups, and a small vase with two delicate freesias. He slid the tray onto the nightstand and smiled at the woman.

She blinked up at him, confused.

"Morning, love," the boy said.

When he climbed onto the bed, the woman smiled. "Love?"

The boy settled over the woman and pressed his thighs to hers. He held her arms above her head and kissed her jaw.

"You prefer wife?" He smiled down at her and kissed her again. "Morning, wife." Another kiss. "Wife." Another. "My wife." Another.

The wind sniffed the freesias on the nightstand. No scent. Not real. It sneezed all the same. The pollen was real enough to tickle.

It drifted to the bed. The woman had relaxed into the silk sheets. Her eyes were closed, and she tilted her head back as the boy—not *the* boy— brushed kisses over her throat.

So this was the woman's greatest desire? The wind would never have guessed. She'd guarded this secret well. Did the boy know it? Had he seen it in the woman's heart?

"Jacob," she whispered as the boy slid his hand over her thigh and lifted the waterfall silk of her nightgown.

"I love you," he said, and the wind rolled around in the silk of the sheets, enjoying the warm slide of them.

Then a faint cry pierced the air, and the boy paused, his hand halfway up the woman's belly.

"What is that?" the woman whispered.

The boy smiled and pressed a kiss to the edge of her mouth. "One of the twins, I expect. Hungry again." He bent down and dragged his mouth over the woman's breast. "They have no respect for the fact that I'm hungry too."

The woman's cheeks burned pink. And when the boy looked up, he smiled.

"I'll get them. You rest. Have coffee. I'll be back, don't worry." He kissed her again, and said, "Wife."

Then, as he did in real life, the boy slipped from the room, as quick as a rushing stream.

The woman stared after him. She pressed her hand to her mouth. "Wife." The word was an aching exhale. "Mother."

Ah. The wind understood now. The woman loved. She loved her parents. She loved her brothers. She maybe loved the boy. And she loved the children she would never have. Her father had never made it a secret that the woman wouldn't have children—not if she wanted to live. Her father had said that even if she didn't pass down her weakness, she was tainted and therefore should never—*would* never—have a child.

This was a human thing, and the wind didn't understand it. What did a body matter? It was the animating spirit that made something strong or weak, good or bad.

Did the woman love the boy because his spirit was strong enough to protect her and their children from her father, or was it something else?

The wind didn't know. It only saw the awe in the woman's eyes. The pink flush on her cheeks. The yearning in her gaze at the sound of the baby's cries.

She would stay here forever. The wind knew it. She would choose to stay in this tower room, with an illusion husband and illusion children, for the rest of her life.

The wind could find its way out of this maze. But the woman would not.

It supposed, since the real boy had told it he would've let the woman kiss him, he'd be unhappy if the woman never found her way free. The wind supposed the boy would want it to help.

So it shoved open the windows and gusted across the room, shattering the crystal vase and spilling the purple irises across the floor.

"Oh!" The woman scrambled out of bed and bent to clean up the vase. A glass shard pricked her finger, and blood welled.

The woman stared at the blood pooling on her fingertip. It domed like a drop of dew on a pliant leaf.

The wind gusted around her and then whispered her brother's words: *"Don't be trapped by the promise of what can never be."*

She jerked. Swung about the room searching for the origin of the voice. She couldn't see the wind. She didn't notice when it tugged on her braid.

Outside the room, the boy's voice filled the hallway as he sang to the crying baby.

The woman's shoulders slumped. She wiped a hand across her wet cheek. Then she pressed her hand to her heart and whispered, "Thanks, Raggie."

The room was torn apart, and the wind and the woman were tossed from the timber mountain tower. On the way down, the wind was torn free. It lost its grip on the woman's shiny braid and was shoved out of the tornado that carried her.

The wind plummeted into the mist and slid wildly down the mountain. A rockslide grabbed the wind, throwing it down a cliff and sending it into the path of an avalanche. Rocks roared. Crashed and tumbled. The wind screamed as it careened down the mountain.

Finally, it slammed into another narrow path. As soon as it hit, it burrowed into a shallow groove. It hid as rocks roared overhead. Then . . . silence. When the wind finally dared lift itself out of the stone path's groove, it was snatched by black, winglike menace and dragged into another illusion.

55

I KNEW I HAD TO SLIP AWAY FROM THE COLD WALL OF THE MOUNTAIN AND the conjurers' game as quickly as I could.

For a while, it seemed like we'd stand in the icy-wet fog for hours, waiting tensely for the players to emerge from their mountain maze.

Everyone stood in clusters, murmuring and sending side-eyed glances around the gathering. There was a hint of trepidation from the Clark cousins and the Bard cousins, as if they were worried that when Jacob emerged from the mists, he'd entrap them again in the hell of their own minds.

Ragnor conjured a guitar and began to strum a haunting melody that put absolutely *no one* at ease.

Luvic sat on a boulder next to him, his chin on his fist, gaze wary. He looked as if he were posing for Rodin's *The Thinker*.

Philoneas and Uliea kept in tense conference with the Bard and Cressida.

Last, her father, and the Clark cousins kept glancing at the mist as if it were about to come alive and swallow them all.

The only people who seemed relaxed were Darin and Wolfgang. They were busy recounting some glorious battle from 1090 AD.

It was the best time for me to get away and search the Clarks' rooms.

Jagger wanted the key the Clarks had taken from me, and even Luvic had mentioned . . .

Well, I needed to find the key. That much was clear.

So when I yawned and Wolfgang growled, "Body, make yourself useful," and Darin added hopefully, "Coffee, Mari?" I gladly hurried away.

By my count, I had twenty minutes before someone would come looking for me.

There was an abundance of sun inside the timber castle, all yellow and warm. It streamed through tall, open windows, along with the cool, forest scented breeze. The castle was far enough away from the conjured mountain and its mist ward to welcome the light summer air.

I ducked through the hallways, quietly padding over glossy wood floors, hurrying toward the Clark suite. The floor was polished to such a high shine that it was a honey-colored mirror, reflecting the sun and the clouds.

My feet whispered over the sky's reflection as I darted through the halls. Not suspiciously, no, but with purpose, as if I were very busy, somewhat annoyed, and had errands to run for someone important. It always seemed to me that if you did that, no one would question you.

I peered around a corner and then jerked back in surprise. When I cautiously looked again, Luvic was still there.

He grinned. "So. What're we up to?"

I brushed past him, channeling busy and annoyed. "Getting coffee."

"Right."

Clearly, he didn't believe me. He strode next to me, keeping up with my hurried pace. The castle, like I said, was as long as the Met, and it took a good while to get from one end to the other.

Luvic whistled a happy tune as I tried to remember which room I'd seen the Clark body hauling their luggage into. At an intersecting hall, I peered right, then left.

Luvic lifted his eyebrows. "Can I help?"

Perhaps if I ignored him, he'd go away.

He smiled. "You do realize ignoring me isn't going to make me go away?"

Darn.

Luvic thrust his hands into his pockets and gave me a questioning glance. "Are we up to mischief?" he asked, a hopeful glint in his eyes.

I frowned. It was hard to remember Luvic was a conjurer with untold power running through his veins. That he could easily kill me. That he very well *might* kill me.

It wasn't hard to remember, though, that he had his own purpose for trailing me. Whatever the reason was, it wasn't to help.

Okay. I needed to get rid of him. I couldn't very well look for the key with a Bard tagging along.

I was going to start with polite and go from there.

"Would you please go away?"

There. That was polite.

Luvic scratched his forehead and frowned. "Go away? Why would I go away? You need me. Your life, I'm sorry to say, would be a sad, gray palette of misery without me. Monotone. Boring. Who would you have without me? Darin?" He scoffed. "Alterra?" He shook his head sadly. "No, Mari. It's me you need."

Right. I needed Luvic like I needed an arrow through the heart.

He saw my expression and clicked his tongue. "Some people don't appreciate a friend when they have one."

I hurried to the left. I definitely remembered the Clark body dragging a stack of suitcases this way.

It was another sunlit, wood-paneled hall with a dozen closed doors. Maybe this wasn't the right hallway. Unlike the Bard Mansion, with its unique and varied decorating style, all the hallways here had a serenely uniform appearance.

This wasn't working. I stopped and slowly turned to Luvic. When I did, his smile widened.

"Hi, Mari. Glad you survived the trip north."

That's right—Luvic and I hadn't spoken since Justice launched the Omnibus at our vehicles.

"You too."

He seemed delighted with my response. The perfectly symmetrical lines of his face, the Bard beauty, and the rich bronze glow of him lit up as he grinned. "Thank you."

It was obvious he was trying to charm me with his sun-bright magnetism.

I tried one last time. "I'm just fetching coffee. Would you mind . . . leaving me alone?"

"Did you know that when you're up to something, you have this little line that forms between your eyebrows? Right"—he tapped a spot above my nose—"here."

I swatted at his hand, and he laughed.

"It's impossible to miss. No matter what face you're wearing, that line always pops up when you're up to no good. I saw it at the mountain, and I thought to myself, 'Mari is about to have fun. I'd better join her.' So here I am."

I glanced at Luvic out of the corner of my eye. I found two things disturbing about what he'd said. One, he'd been watching me closely enough to recognize an expression that had stayed with me even in a new body. Two, he'd been watching me closely, period.

"At the beach," I began, changing direction and climbing a stairwell with a rustic wooden handrail. I looked back, and Luvic nodded. "When you dosed me with Dainty Drink, and we danced . . ."

He remained curiously silent, even when I shot him a censuring glare.

"You told me that if I wanted to live, I'd better—"

He held up a finger, and I stopped. We'd reached the top of the stairs.

He bent close and said in a low voice, "You were hallucinating. We never danced. We never spoke—"

"I was not! You said—"

"You were hallucinating."

There was a hard, dangerous edge to his voice. I stiffened at the predatory way he held himself, as if at one more protest, he would conjure a knife and slit my throat.

I flinched when he lifted his hand. But instead of a knife, he twisted his hand and slid a butterfly knot toward me. It was a sunlit wisp of air, and it landed on my forehead and fluttered its wings.

I thought to untie it. To shove Luvic away. He pressed his cool fingers against my forehead and stared into my eyes.

A vision superimposed itself over the hallway. We were there, standing still and silent, Luvic's hand to my brow, but we were also together in the vision.

"Mari," the Luvic in his illusion said, "if you want to live, you'll find the key."

He clutched me close, and the sand and salt of the beach whipped around us. The music throbbed, and the firelight danced.

"What?" I was thirsty, the tart taste of juice and Dainty Drink coating my dry tongue.

Luvic pressed me closer, swaying to the music, and then said in a low voice that vibrated through my whole being, "This is a hallucination. Forget I said this. Forget I told you this. This isn't real, Mari. This isn't real. It's a hallucination."

I stumbled, dizzy from the drink, and then, when I'd righted myself, I was back at the top of the stairwell. Luvic brushed his fingers across my forehead, pushing back a lock of hair.

"You had something out of place." He gave me an off-center smile and casually dropped his hand away from me. "Better?"

I stared at him, trying to determine what he thought he was doing. Was he warning me, or did he think he'd altered my memory? He hadn't. But maybe he'd tried. He didn't want me to remember he'd threatened me. He'd already admitted mental conjurings weren't his forte.

The only thing for it was to play along.

"Better," I said, tucking the loose strands of hair behind my ears. Then I asked in a confused voice, "What were we talking about again?"

Luvic grinned as if I'd done something incredibly amusing. "Mischief."

Right. Ten minutes had already passed. It was time to ditch this Bard.

I hurried up another set of stairs. Luvic kept pace. He chatted the entire time I rushed through the corridors.

"Noticed you and Alterra have matching rings. Funny—he's a one-woman kind of man. Are you going soft on him? I doubt he'd like that. In fact, I get the distinct impression he isn't interested—"

"Shh." I held my finger to my lips when we reached the door I'd been looking for.

I set my hand on the brass knob and turned the handle. Surprise flashed through me. Once again, the Wards hadn't placed any traps on their front door. They hadn't even locked it.

Luvic grunted when I swung the door wide-open. "How'd you do that? No one can open . . ." He whistled when the Wards' private rooms came into view. "What're we doing here?" he asked with an expectant, appreciative smile.

I stepped into the room, sweeping the area for the telltale glow of constrictor traps like the ones that had littered the floor of the Ward suite at the Bard Mansion.

"Follow me," I whispered. I quietly nudged the door shut and then wound toward a thick circle of illusion hidden on the floorboards.

Luvic's head tilted toward the ceiling. Or where the ceiling should be. Instead of wooden beams, there was only open sky. The Wards' private rooms were unlike anything I'd ever seen before. There were illusion trees: large oaks and hickories growing through the floor. They were surrounded by mossy boulders, patches of grass and marsh violets, and splashes of sunlight falling over gold-tinted hostas and ferns. A stream flowed through the room, and its soothing gurgle filled the air. Birdsong filtered through the trees. There was an upholstered divan and low benches under the branches of a weeping willow. Bookshelves filled to the brim were kitty-cornered against tree trunks. There was a wooden table with three wooden chairs in a small, grassy clearing. It still held teacups, a teapot, and three plates with cookie crumbs.

The Wards' private rooms were a home in a forest. There were painted doors in tree trunks, and I knew they'd lead to bedrooms, studies, or the kitchen.

"I don't know about you," Luvic said, following me across the little stone bridge that arched over the stream, "but I find this place incredibly creepy. Like . . . Hansel and Gretel creepy."

I nodded. We were almost there . . . almost . . .

"Mari, watch out! There's—"

I shoved Luvic.

He gave a surprised grunt and then fell two steps forward. The trap on the mossy floorboards snapped open and swallowed him.

I jumped back, my heart banging recklessly. Back at the Bard Mansion, the Ward trap hadn't sprung when I'd stepped in it. But I figured without Uliea here to disarm them, they'd work just fine. The Wards, after all, were famous for their traps and prisons.

"Mari?" Luvic held his hands out in front of him, unseeing. He was surrounded by a metal cage, similar to the one Jagger had in Hell Gate's basement. "Mari, are you all right? Are you there?"

Luvic couldn't see me. I didn't know what illusion the Ward trap was showing him—I could only tell he couldn't see the forest room in front of him anymore. His hands hit the metal bars. When they did, he flinched. Then a look of pure, terrified panic came over him. I'd never seen such a quick transformation in my life. One second he was cautious; the next, his face leached of color, and his breath came out in frightened pants.

"Mari? Get me out. Mari? Are you there? Get me out."

I took a step back, careful not to make any noise. I'd leave him here. Hurry off to the Clarks' and search for the key.

Luvic gripped the bars of the cage, wincing as they snapped and constricted. The knot of illusion—yes, a constrictor knot—tightened and clamped down. The metal cage shrank, and the bars pressed closer.

Luvic made a small, desperate noise in his throat. It wasn't one I thought I'd ever hear from him. His hands shook, and he blinked quickly, as if he was trying to see through the dark.

He twisted his hand then, attempting to conjure. His illusion guttered, and the cage shrank again. Luvic's breath came faster. Soon, he'd hyperventilate.

I edged closer to the door, passing over the arched bridge and a small smattering of marsh violets.

"Mari? Please."

I paused. I'd reached the door. A half-dozen trees and the small stream separated us. I held my hand above the brass knob.

What was Luvic seeing inside the Ward trap? What conjuring had invaded his mind? It must be terrifying for him to react this strongly.

"Sorry," I said, and his head snapped my way.

He blindly searched the room, looking for me.

"I have to go. But I'm sure the Wards will be here soon. They'll let you out."

His breath came faster. His chin dipped to his chest. "If they find me in their rooms, they'll kill me."

They wouldn't kill him. Probably. Maybe.

His hands shook on the bars, and the cage tightened again.

"Don't move," I said. "The bars shrink when you move or conjure. You'll be fine. Just don't move."

He held still, his gaze focused just to the left of me. "Mari. Let me out of here. You *know* I can't—" He broke off. Searched the room for me and took a shaking breath. "Mari . . ." He closed his eyes. "Don't . . ." His jaw tightened, and the lines around his mouth went white. "Don't leave me here."

I had to. I had to look for the key, and I didn't need Luvic following me while I did it. No matter what he claimed, he wasn't my friend. He *wasn't*.

"Sorry. I have to go."

"Mari! No—"

I slipped out the door and shut it tight, cutting off Luvic's protest.

I brushed off the disquiet I felt at leaving him in the Wards' cage. Justice would've killed him (days ago). Rou would've poisoned him or drowned him. Even Griff would've lured him into a trap. There was nothing to feel bad about. Except . . . I couldn't help it.

There was something about the way his hands had shaken and his voice had trembled, and the pleading desperation in his eyes. As if he was trusting me, counting on me—

No.

He was a Bard. An actor. A liar, manipulator, and conjurer. He'd threatened me twice now. Once in the knife vision, and once at the beach. No feeling bad.

He'd get out of the trap or he wouldn't. What mattered was finding the key for Jagger. Winning the crown. Getting back to the mountain before Finn finished the game. *Not* Luvic Bard.

I ran my thumb over the warm metal of the braided gold ring and searched for that humming awareness. Yes, Finn was there. To the east.

His emotions were muted. Determination. Hardened resolve. Love. No fear. He was fine.

I hurried down a set of wooden stairs, darted down a long hallway, and then sighed in relief when I spotted the Clarks' rooms.

I remembered them because the knot of wood next to their door looked like a crow that had been splattered by a windshield.

Perfect.

I checked the hall, making sure no one was near. I checked the door, searching for any illusions. I unraveled a clove hitch and an angler's knot. Fishing for intruders, I was sure. Then I pulled free my tools from the secret pocket I'd sewn into my uniform. With a quick jimmy and an expert twist, the lock sprang free.

I hurried into the Clarks' rooms.

56

The wind huddled against the smoke and parchment scented pant leg of the cruel and twisted one. His trial sprang up in a vivid, hellscape projection, and as it did, the cruel one laughed.

The wind loved riding on the undulating slides of hearty laughter, but it did not want to ride on this blood and bone carved mirth. The sharp noise crackled over the acrid smoke and dying sounds. There was stinging gas in the air—the kind that blinded and caused humans to wheeze and convulse. A sulfuric haze hung above the earth, more dry-bone alien landscape than lush terra firma.

It was a nightmare the wind had seen before, thousands of years past, when discord and war had been gleefully chased by pestilence, famine, and plague. The cure the conjurers had led the people to was the penance of sacrifice.

The wind thought the horror of that time had been buried deep in the catacombs of memory. How silly to believe that something buried wouldn't be found.

And wasn't it fitting that the cruel and twisted one, who loved the dank dark of the catacombs and the mires of history, would tug this reality into his future?

The wind let out a frightened moan and hid in the fold of the man's black pant leg. It wasn't a stranger to the parchment scented one's delight in cruelty. It had watched him in his catacomb room over the years. But that had not been the worst of the cruel one.

This was the worst of him.

Had the wind missed his fears and his desires? Had it missed the best of him? Or was the best waiting to spring up from the deadened soil of this nightmare?

The world was a wasteland. The wind buried itself in the harsh cotton of the man's pant leg. How long would he stay? How long would he rapture in the worst of himself?

There were some humans who shied away from the evil in their hearts. The proclivity repulsed and frightened them. But there were other humans who invited evil inside like a lost lover and wept with joy as they gave free rein to the unleashing of their basest desires.

The cruel one shuddered with pleasure as he surveyed what the worst of him could accomplish. "Take note," he drawled, his voice scratching over the acrid smoke. "This is what I bring to the world. The subjugation and pain it desires. Man loves his own destruction. I only hold out the knife he rams himself into. Last?"

The wind peeked out from behind the man's pant leg and then quickly ducked into the fold again.

"Yes, Principal?"

The man moaned happily at her words. "What happened to our father?"

"You killed him—"

"And the other principals? What of them?"

The cruel one seemed half-aware, or at least more aware, than the citrus and pearl dust scented woman that this was illusion. That he was living a projection of his own heart.

The wind floated higher, straining to hear the paper-fine whisper of the sister's words.

"Entombed in the catacombs. Imprisoned by earth, chained and buried for ten years now—"

"And my heir?"

The woman dropped her head.

"My wife and heirs?" His voice was hard, and the wind rode on the sharp thrust of him as he threateningly pressed forward. "What of them?"

"Your sons are home. With your wife."

"My wife." The cruel one's voice seethed with pleasure. "Who is my wife."

This wasn't a question, but the woman answered anyway. "Mari Clark. Wife of Principal Clark. Mother of Heir Clark."

"Mari? Mari." The cruel one contemplated this and then asked with surprise, as if tasting an unexpectedly fine wine, "The Smith body?"

The wind moaned. It did not like this projection. It did not like the workings of his mind. The girl was not for this cruel, twisted one. She was *not*.

"The children aren't null? Answer me." The cruel one shook his sister.

"No! No."

He thrust her aside, and she fell to the barren, dry-bone ground. She stayed there, her head bowed.

"Not null?" he mused.

Then he sighed, and the wind blew tentatively at the folds of his shirt. It wanted to leave. It wanted the man to forget this place and the bent of his mind.

"Take note," he murmured, his voice a happy, expectant purr. "This is the reality I desire. This is what I will create."

He would stay. He would enjoy it. The wind didn't know how long the cruel one would play in his hellscape.

Would he, like the citrus scented woman, be lured into staying forever unless someone shoved him out? The wind didn't know. It didn't want to stay to find out.

The girl.

The girl.

Would the cruel one want the girl?

The wind raced away from the man, gusting through the nerve-stinging gases and the acrid, sulfuric haze, searching for the way out.

When the wind reached the edge of the barren landscape, a monstrous roar thundered and shook the earth. The cruel illusion collapsed, and the wind was hurtled down the mountain.

THE CLARKS LOVED HISTORY. THEY LOVED MANIPULATING HISTORY AND perverting the past to suit the aims of the present. They were unerringly constant in this predilection, which made them incredibly predictable.

I kneeled beneath a large wooden table—the kind you'd find in the great hall of a medieval castle. It was conjured, probably by Primus, and it looked identical to the table he'd sat at when he dubbed me "One." Sheaves of papers, old ledgers and documents, were strewn over the worn wooden tabletop. But I didn't look through the things on display. I looked for what was hidden.

For all of history, humans have hidden their treasure. Our original vault was the earth. Safety deposit box? The outhouse. The bank? Your back yard.

The earth wasn't just a vault for our bones. It was a vault for our gold. There's a saying: "Where your treasure lies, so does your heart." The Clarks treasure the past, when valuables were buried, stashed beneath floorboards, entombed in the walls, and hidden in secret compartments.

I ran my hand along the underside of the table, carefully probing the joinery.

In the past, when Jagger had made me steal records from the Clarks,

I'd often found hidden compartments in antique desks and bookshelves. Their Manhattan home was a trove of hidey-holes. There were loose stones in the mortared walls, secret tunnels so well-hidden I wouldn't have noticed them except for the tingle of illusion covering them, loose floorboards in every room, and murder holes above the entries.

Their rooms here were nothing like their home—or even their rooms at the Bard Mansion. Instead, they had the same wood floor, wood paneling, high ceilings, and open windows as the Smiths' rooms. The only difference was, the Clarks had conjured their heavy wood tables and desks and brought along their musty books, leather-bound records, and dusty parchment.

My eyes stung at the overpowering smell of mothballs. My neck twinged at the awkward angle, but I kept tracing my hand over the table joints. The Clarks weren't creative in their hiding spots. If the key wasn't here, I'd check the other conjured furniture and the suitcases in their bedrooms.

I just had to be fast. I'd give myself five minutes before I'd have to race back to the mountain with a cup of (old) coffee.

There!

I paused at a tiny bit of illusion. The entire table was illusion, the knot in my mind's eye a single large clove hitch, but there, along the bottom, I found an angler's loop. The knot was also known as a perfection loop. It could be tied quickly, and it held well, although it did tend to jam badly and could be difficult to untie. Whoever had made the illusion had locked it by tying half-hitches around the loop.

The illusion, from what I could tell, was a thin wood pocket hidden within the table. A secret compartment. I smiled and got to work. It wouldn't take long to untie. I started on the half-hitch lock, which unraveled easily. The angler's loop was jammed, but I only needed to pry it—

The door groaned, and I froze, my hand pressed to the underside of the table.

"'Do this, Last. Do that, Last.' Do you ever think I don't want to do this or that?"

The door shut with a bang, and I held my breath. I was completely exposed. Last was alone, stomping through the room, but all she had to do was look toward the table and she'd see me crouching beneath it.

Not good.

Not good.

"For once, I'd like to tell *you* what to do," she muttered, turning toward the bedrooms.

I let out a slow breath. As soon as she was out of sight, I'd hurry from the room. No problem. Maybe I could even untie the illusion fully and find what they'd hidden. It wouldn't take but a second. All I'd have to do was . . .

Last let out a frustrated shriek, and I jerked in surprise.

My hand hit the pocket illusion, but instead of a wooden secret compartment, the illusion snapped and became something else.

A trap.

A horrible, nasty, terrible Clark trap. My eyes watered at the pain. My hand was stuck between the table and a thick iron plate. The wood and the metal tightened, and when I jerked my arm reflexively, the iron clamped tighter. I hissed in pain. The compartment wasn't to store documents or keys. It was a lure. A trap.

I breathed through the pain. *No problem.* There was still only the angler's knot. *Easily untied.* I pried, tugged . . . *Almost there . . .*

"Well, hello," Last said, crouching down next to the table. "You came back."

I dropped the threads of illusion and slowly looked over at her.

Last looked like she hadn't been sleeping well. Her eyes were bloodshot, and her black hair was limp and uncombed. But when she scanned my awkward, crouched position and my hand stuck between the iron plate and the table, a happy glint filled her bloodshot eyes.

"I knew you'd come back," she said, and I thought for a moment she'd clap her hands with glee. "I'm so glad to see you. I've missed you. What have you gotten yourself into?" She ducked under the table as if we were two kids building a fort or playing make believe. When she saw the iron plate, she clicked her tongue. "Primus made that to see what sort of creature he'd catch. Do you think . . .?" She reached out and touched the butterfly knots of illusion on my forehead.

I flinched, and she frowned.

"Has Luvic Bard sent you?"

Oh gosh. Luvic. This was karma, wasn't it? I'd left him in a trap, and now here I was, in another trap. Last's eyes narrowed at my expression. I was sure she saw guilt and regret.

"I see," she said. "He seems to be using you well. But the thing is, Mari, you're my friend. Mine."

A drop of sweat trailed down my forehead, and my arm shook from being held at an awkward angle over my head. The iron clamp squeezed tighter. How long would it be before it broke my bones?

I only had one little tug. One last quick yank. Just that, and the illusion would disappear. But then Last would know. So we'd have to do this another way.

"Would you mind," I asked, giving Last a careful smile, "letting me go?"

She laughed and clapped her hands. "Oh, I like you. I like you so much. You're never afraid! So many people are afraid, and you never are. Even now, when I could twist your neck. Just pop off your head. You aren't afraid!"

"Well, there isn't much point, is there?" I asked, tugging at my hand, wondering if I could just pull it out. But no. "Fear is an aphrodisiac for your sort, and I don't give out favors for free."

Last gave an earthy laugh and put her bony arm around my shoulder. "That's Primus. He feeds on fear." Then she sobered. "I wanted to take you back, but Primus said I wasn't strong enough to confront Luvic. He said that if anyone would take on Luvic, it would be him. He said since I wasn't strong enough to keep you, you'd be his now. But I don't want you to be his." She looked down at the floor. "He ruins things."

I shivered at the way she whispered the last bit. That Primus ruined things. For Last to believe that, he had to be more monstrous than I could comprehend.

Last glanced back at me, a cold, calculating hardness entering her expression. She glared at the illusion on my forehead. She couldn't know that it was something as simple as an illusion for flyaway hair. Instead, she believed it was mental manipulation.

"What's so special about Luvic Bard?" she asked. "What's so special that a third-born could overpower me? I'm second-born now."

I shook my head, aching to tug free the iron illusion. "Nothing. He's not special." Then, at Last's disbelieving look, I amended. "Well, he is abnormally good-looking."

She nodded, thinking this over. "It's annoying. All the Bards are annoying. They're these showy, fluttering songbirds, and I just want to . . ." She clutched her hand in the air and twisted, as if she'd caught a bird mid-flight and crushed it.

"Yup," I said. Then I nodded at the iron plate. "It's been nice catching up. But I have to get back to the game now. The Smiths will be looking for me. And . . . so . . . could you let me out?"

She gave me her sweet little-girl smile. "Sure, Mari."

Huh. "Thank you."

She rolled her eyes. "No. No, I'm not letting you out. Haven't you been listening? Primus wants you. He'll overpower Luvic, and then you'll be his. To ruin. To . . ." She shuddered. "You shouldn't have come in here. If you'd asked me, I would've told you so."

Then she twisted her hand. The iron clamp over my hand sprang free. I jumped back, but Last conjured again.

Suddenly, I was buried, blinded, cocooned in the depths of the earth. Hard dirt and darkness surrounded me. Cold soil pressed over me, and dirt fell into my mouth at my sudden gasp.

She'd buried me. I was deep underground. Buried in the cold silence of dirt and stone, stretching roots, scrambling insects, and musty, mildewed, clawing, creeping things.

The turning weight of untilled soil pressed down on my lungs, pushing out air, barely letting any back in. The fraction of space between clay and sand allowed only the tiniest trickle of breath.

She'd buried me.

Where did we hide our treasures? In the vault of the earth.

Was I her treasure? Was this where her heart was?

I clawed at the dirt. It caved over me and fell into my eyes, ears, and nose. Blinding me; deafening me.

It was illusion. I was buried alive. It was illusion.

It was *illusion*.

Last had claimed I was never afraid. I wouldn't be afraid now. I could untie the knot. I could escape. I could . . . I couldn't . . . I wouldn't . . .

I remembered my second death. And I started to cry.

58

THE SOLANGE-EYED ONE STOOD ON THE ROOF OF THE CONCRETE FORTRESS his family called home. The sun set in a pale orange blaze over the East River, and the man smiled at the hazy mist of unreality that coated the Manhattan skyline.

The wind blew in unsettled rivulets, twisting around the man's arms and fluttering his black hair. The projection wasn't like the illusions the others experienced. It was the influence of the solange, painting this world in a wavy, impressionist's haze. It was as if the world were being viewed through layers of mist, wavy sea, and glittering sun. There could be no mistaking that any of this was real.

If he were strong enough, the solange-eyed one could reach out and break the illusion without properly passing the trial. Eons ago, the wind had seen solange devotees break even larger illusions, but it didn't know how far the man had descended into his devotion.

"We've taken London," the man next to the solange-eyed one said. It was the brother—the war-happy, battle-minded one who reminded the wind of the whistle of a sword drawn and a sword sheathed.

"And Dubai? Tokyo? Paris? Seoul?"

"We've taken them all," the brother said with a rumble of satisfaction.

"Berlin. Los Angeles. Shanghai. Hong Kong. The world is falling before us."

The wind traveled over the tangerine-flavored sunset beams that fell in wavy lines over the black-haired, navy-eyed man. Then, surprised, it stilled as it caressed the man's face. His eyes weren't navy and starburst anymore; they were a soft brown and green color, gentle like a cool forest glade lit by the summer sun. The wind hummed. This was how the man's eyes had looked before he'd walked the narrow solange path.

Was this his best self?

He wouldn't stay. He wouldn't be caught by the illusion like the others. The man was too cunning for that. Too smart and full of purpose. The wind often thought of him as the gust that blew down from mountaintops, never tiring, never ceasing, driving snowfall, rain, and rockslides. His nature was too direct to be caught in his best or his worst.

The solange-eyed, solange scented one (who did not smell of cranberry and allspice in this illusion) gave his brother a curt nod. And then he twisted his hand. A sword of blue flame appeared.

The wind hummed in surprise and skittered over the sharp edge.

"So," the man rumbled, twisting the flaming sword in front of him, "I am a conjurer here. Is this my best self, or is it my worst?"

"You liberate the world," the brother said.

"And Hell Gate?"

"What of it?"

"What of Hell Gate?" He stared across the orange-painted river, narrowing his eyes at the flicker of the ghost train appearing and disappearing as it sped over the old bridge tracks.

"Gone," the brother said. "As it should be. Along with its creatures."

The solange-eyed one twisted his hand, and the sword disappeared. "I destroyed Hell Gate?"

"You liberated them in death" the brother said, clapping the solange-eyed one on his back. "Come on. Let's go find Cora. It seems to me you need a pick-me-up."

"And Mari?" the solange-eyed one asked. "Is she here?"

But the brother strode from the rooftop without answering.

The solange-eyed one stared at the wavy, distorted steel towers across the river. The lights blossomed and bloomed in flickering-candlelight waves. He narrowed his eyes, looking toward the edge of the river, where an iron gate and an old gothic mansion should stand.

He twisted his hand. Conjured a flame. Blew it out. Conjured another. Smiled. Blew it out.

"As my worst self, I was a conjurer. As my best self, I am a conjurer. All my life, I've felt the call of illusion."

He twisted his hand again, conjuring a great ball of blue fire. It collapsed on itself and became a gently fluttering moth. The wind blew at the moth's fragile wings. It fluttered away, but not before it twisted and folded into a dove. The man watched as it flew toward Hell Gate. Or the ruins of Hell Gate.

The wind knew the man felt the call of illusion. Illusion was a song in the solange-eyed one's blood. He'd been hobbled, tied, and bound, so the power was tantalizingly there, but if he reached out, his hand passed through it. The wellspring of power was something he could never touch.

That was what it meant to be null.

Perhaps the wind had been wrong. Perhaps the solange-eyed one would stay in this hazy, wavy world where he could conjure flames and conquer cities.

It was pleasant. The wind ran over the man's stubble-lined jaw and tousled his hair. It spun around the tightly reined power of his stance and the vibration of physical vitality. Would he stay here? He could. He might.

There was something enticing about tasting what had always been forbidden.

But then the man suddenly stiffened and touched the gold braided metal on his right ring finger. He swiftly turned and searched the wavy lines of illusion. The wind skittered over the man's chest and felt the hard, urgent thud of his heart.

Then the man stilled, and although the wind wasn't particularly good at reading emotions, it knew *this* human emotion.

Rage.

Wild, uncontrolled, unconcealed rage.

It was there, carved into the tensing of his muscles and the snarl on his dark face.

The man held out his hand, and a brilliant golden glow violently erupted from him.

The wind jerked back and scrabbled across the rooftop. Stay away. Stay clear. The wind gusted out of the path of his rage. Safe.

Then the solange-eyed one threw back his head, and the column of golden light enveloped him.

The wind screamed. A sonic boom exploded. The earth shook. The illusion world collapsed.

THE WIND RODE ON THE RAGE OF THE SOLANGE-EYED ONE, CLINGING TO THE knuckles of his tightly clenched hand. The thick fog column reared away from the man like a skittish, frightened animal. He burst into the clearing at the base of the mountain and speared the gathering with his solange-soaked stare.

The boy lifted his eyebrows at the snarl on the man's tight mouth. The wind rushed over and nudged the boy, urging him not to poke at the man. Not now.

The boy frowned and said, "All right. Not now," in the soft, amused voice the wind loved so much.

It had almost decided to stay and wrap itself in the boy's comforting presence. There was the nearby scent of white pine, a family of voles nibbling on pine seeds, the *keer-keer* of a wheeling hawk . . .

It almost stayed, but then the wind caught the murmurings of the steel-hardened, wolflike one growling, "Third. First came Jacob. Then Primus. At least, fool you are, you made it out—"

"Where is she?" the solange-eyed one interrupted.

The wind shivered on the cold, dangerous vibration of his voice. Neither the father nor the brother answered, and when they remained silent, the solange-eyed one stalked past them.

"Better go after him, Wind," the boy murmured, and when the wind moaned, the boy sighed and said, "Go on."

The wind shoved at the boy's knees. It wouldn't mind the company, but the boy shook his head and whispered, "I can't."

So the wind raced through the fragrant white pine, the shadowed hemlock groves, and the sharp-bouldered crags, until it caught the solange-eyed one at a wooden door inside the boy's timber home.

The man had raced through the woods and the halls as if he were tied to a wire and only had to follow the taut string. He was so fast the sword and steel brother, who tried to follow, fell far behind. The wind gripped the man's wrist, bounced over his thundering pulse, and rolled in the solange glow as the man dissolved the illusion coating the door.

Inside the room were two distinct voices. Crackly, breathy, parchment scented voices. Ah. The wind knew who was inside. The cruel one and his sister. The wind shuddered. Had the cruel one taken the girl already? Was that what had caused this rage?

The solange-eyed one snarled at the voices. Then he kicked open the door. The wind shrieked and rushed into the room.

"What? You dare—" The cruel one spun around. He twisted his hand and flung a barrage of poison-winged bat-like creatures toward them.

The wind dodged the sour scented wings and their sharp, stabbing protrusions, but the solange-eyed one merely held out his hands. The bats dissolved.

"Get out," the sister threatened, standing over the girl.

The solange-eyed one had tasted of rage before, but that had been a small sip compared to the flood that washed through him now.

The cruel one twisted his hand, and the ceiling opened. Burning oil poured from a murder hole. The solange-eyed one stalked through the oil. When it hit him, the illusion disappeared. Nothing touched him.

The sister spun a dozen morningstars, and the wind rode on their circling whirlwind. It whistled as the metal spikes clipped closer. The solange-eyed one brushed them aside, and they collapsed like fragile cobwebs. His navy eyes burst with lightning and stars colliding. His gaze was on the girl. The wind rushed to her.

The soft smell of violets was gone, replaced by sweat and the metallic tang of fear. Her pulse sped a rapid, frightened staccato. Her skin was cold and clammy, and the wind rushed over it, trying to wake her.

But she was already awake. Her eyes were open. Unseeing. She was staring at the ceiling, her breath short and pained, gaze searching.

Another pulse of rage rushed from the solange-eyed one.

The cruel one blocked his path. He held his hand out and snarled, "Paladin Smith, take note. You will not engage in direct hostilities with an heir and a player in the games. You will remove—"

The solange-eyed one moved faster than the wind had seen a man move in generations. His hand flew toward the cruel one—a blur, a wind-fast vision. He struck his temple. The cruel one collapsed.

The sister opened her mouth and drew in a breath to scream. The solange-eyed one whirled and hit her temple with his second and third fingers. She fell and hit the wood floor and lay in a boneless heap.

The wind moaned and raced around the room, stirring the fabric of clothing, sliding down pale skin, and riding thudding heartbeats. The solange-eyed one drew a deep, shaking breath. The wind rattled over his exhale and relaxed as he drew in a slower, calming breath. Then the man crouched down next to the cruel one. His jaw hardened as he pressed two fingers to the man's temple.

The wind counted three slow breaths. The solange-eyed one's lip curled, and then he moved to the sister. He crouched over her as well, his shadow falling across her face. He pressed his fingers to her temple and narrowed his eyes.

The wind waited as the solange-eyed one's heartbeat slowed and the boiling, violent rage inside him lessened.

What would he do?

The wind nudged him. Tried to blow the wrath free from his veins.

The man dragged the cruel one to the couch. Laid him on it.

He put the sister in a chair, her head tucked on a cushion.

Finally, he moved away from the sister and stared down at the girl. She was still trapped in whatever illusion surrounded her. The wind moaned as it traveled over her clammy skin.

"Mari," the man said, "I'm here."

His voice was still a hurricane of tightly leashed anger. The wind knew this well. Didn't it become a hurricane too?

But it also could be spring-breeze gentle, so it wasn't surprised when the man reached down and carefully lifted the girl. He held her against his chest and stalked from the room, kicking the door shut behind him.

His solange-gold touch drifted over the girl. The wind hovered over her, and when her unseeing eyes cleared and she saw the solange-eyed man, the wind tasted the relieved salt of the tears that slipped from her eyes.

"I was hoping you'd come," she whispered. "Finn."

The wind traced the soft, gentle curve of the man's smile.

60

THE WIND CURLED IN A CONTENDED BALL, WRAPPING ITSELF AROUND THE boy's shoulders. The game was done, the mountain folded away and the fog blown from the forest. The girl was safe with the solange-eyed one. The wind had left the man to carry her through the empty halls.

It had gone back to the boy. He'd been waiting in the foggy clearing, watching the white column thicken as the sun slipped down the sky. Eventually, the citrus and pearl dust scented woman had pushed through the mist. She was the last player free of the game, and when her foot hit the mountain base, the illusion snapped shut.

It was night now. Outside, there was the slice of the crescent moon, the deep pine darkness, and the startling *who-who* of an owl, to which the wind always answered, *meeee*, and then laughed when the owl called, *who?*

But outside didn't tempt the wind. It only wanted to curl into the boy's solid warmth and gently seesaw into its nighttime slumber.

Did the wind slumber? What else was it called when ship sails went lax, leaves hung limp, and the air held its breath? Of course it slumbered, and if the boy would stop pacing the little hickory and oak illusion glade, it would drift off for a time.

Even the trickster was quiet. He hadn't spoken since the boy found him in the metal cage. Not even when the boy said with some amusement, "What have we here? Sneaking where you don't belong, Bard?"

But no—the trickster was in a waking sleep, a slumber the wind could appreciate. It was the deep stillness sometimes found in the middle of the ocean, where the wind wouldn't blow for days and days. The trickster was deep inside himself, far away from the room and the cage he was in. He wouldn't answer the boy.

The wind tapped the boy's ear in annoyance. Would he stop pacing? But then there was a sharp, angry knock on the front door, and the boy did stop. He looked past the oak and the hickory toward the trickster, but the trickster didn't move or blink or . . . anything.

So the boy paced forward and opened the wooden door.

The wind flew, flapping like a flustered bird swept from its nest. The citrus and pearl dust scented woman shoved into the room and thrust a paper note at the boy.

She waved it—not like a white flag, but like a murder weapon.

She spat out the words on the note. "'Dear Celia, I have something that *belongs* to you'?" If she were an animal, the hair on her back would stand on end. She snarled, and the note burst into flames and then rained in ash flakes to the wooden floorboards. "Where is he? Where is my brother, or so help me, I will—"

She broke off when she spied the metal cage through the illusion woods. The trickster hadn't moved when the woman came in—not even when she'd threatened and raised her voice.

She made an enraged sound, and the wind rode over the threat of it.

"What did you do to him?"

The boy raised his eyebrows and then casually closed the front door. "I didn't do anything," he said. "I found him like this. Usually, I dispose of things that wander where they don't belong, but I thought you might like him back."

The boy smiled, and the wind flicked his ear. The woman was not in the mood for humor. She might not even understand the boy's humor. Not many humans did.

"What do you want for him?"

The wind shivered at her voice. It was the icy frost of a winter morning.

The boy stiffened in surprise, but only the wind noticed that. He relaxed so quickly it would only be obvious if you were resting on his shoulder like the wind was. The boy wasn't going to ask for anything—the wind knew this. He hadn't even thought about asking for something. He only wanted the trickster out of his forest home. But now . . .

The wind flicked his ear again. *Don't do it. Don't do it.*

"You know what I want."

He'd done it.

The wind blew in the boy's ear, and when it did, the boy tugged on his earlobe, repressing a smile.

The woman's face turned sunset-red. Was she remembering the trial, her desire, the silk sheets, and the boy's smile?

"I won't throw the games," she said, leaning forward threateningly. "I won't betray my family. I won't help you win the crown. I won't join any twisted Ward mind game. I have honor. Release my brother."

The boy made a noise the wind knew was the one he gave when someone surprised him. He looked toward the night-blue illusion sky and the shifting stars swirling overhead. He thought over her words, a line on his forehead.

Finally, he said, "You have honor, but does your brother?"

"Yes."

The wind rode the boy's shrug. Then he turned, and the woman hurriedly followed as he crossed the arching stone bridge and the little marsh glade.

The wind tapped the metal bars, jumping from one to the next, banging on them like a spoon tapping a metal pot. The bars rebounded and constricted.

The woman rounded on the boy and said, "Stop that! Let him out."

The boy turned his head and whispered to the wind, "You're getting me into trouble."

The wind laughed and went to brush against the trickster's cold jaw. He stared sightlessly ahead, holding incredibly still. Except—the wind hadn't noticed this before—his lips moved soundlessly, the whisper of a breath on them.

The wind brushed close and heard the trickster's words repeated over and over: "Mari. Let me out. Mari. Let me out. Mari." It was a rosary of words, a small bead and then a large bead, repeated over and over again.

The wind fluttered away.

The boy stared at the trickster. "You might tell him, Lia, to stay out of other people's rooms—"

"Don't call me that."

"And you might give him a shot of something strong, because this trap has . . ." The boy tapped his head meaningfully and shrugged.

The woman's face burned red again. "Let him out."

"You'll do something for me when I need you."

"I won't help you win the games."

"You've already lost—we both know it. You came in last today. Besides, I'm not asking you to help me win. I'm asking for something else. In the future."

She stared at the trickster, her face twisting with pain and then smoothing again. "A one-year limit. And you won't ask me to betray or hurt my family."

"Agreed."

The boy smiled and then twisted his hand. The door to the cage sprang open. The woman grabbed the trickster and yanked him free.

He stumbled into her and blinked as if the night-soaked room were blaringly bright.

"Lia?"

"Luvic," she said, gathering him against her as he started to shake.

The wind raced over the vibrations of his skin and the shudders wracking him. His breath flew from him like leaves shaking on a tree, and he bowed his head, dragging in quaking breaths.

"Luvic," the woman whispered, "Jacob Ward is here. Remember who you are."

At her hard words, the trickster stiffened and then slowly straightened, shrugging free of the woman's hold. A transformation worthy of the greatest Bard on the most celebrated stage flew over his features.

He was the trickster again. Tall, invulnerable, mischievous. Untouched by silly human weaknesses like fear or regret or the weight of a buried past. He was the shining sun; the winking, laughing, changeable spring.

The wind stroked the line of his insouciant smile. Although it couldn't be seen, there was a brittle edge to the amused mask of indifference.

Ah, trickster. The wind sighed at the secrets he held.

The trickster turned then, shrugging free of his sister's hold. He nodded at the boy. "Ward. Thanks for the hospitality."

"Anytime." The boy smiled evenly. "We should do it again."

The woman's expression shifted to fire, and the wind wondered at it. After all, the boy was only being polite.

Then the trickster and the woman walked, heads high, from the forest room. The boy tilted his head, narrowing his eyes on the trickster's easy stride.

The wind agreed. The casual, unhurried steps were worthy of the stage. In fact, there had been a Bard in Shakespeare's time that looked almost identical to the trickster. He had paced the boards of the Globe in a nearly identical manner.

"Go after them."

The wind didn't need the boy to tell it so: it was already drifting under the door.

It wound through the hallways, slid down a wooden railing, and bumped over the knots in the wood paneling. When the citrus and pearl dust scented woman shut their room door, the wind slid inside on a quick gust.

She grabbed the trickster and yanked him to her. He stiffened and then relaxed against her.

"What were you *thinking*, Luvic? What were you *doing* in the Wards' rooms?" When he didn't answer, she squeezed him tight and said, "Never mind. Don't worry about it."

He closed his eyes and wrapped her close. The wind swirled around their legs, winding around their ankles. They stood this way, in the quiet, wood-paneled room, next to the closed door, for only a short time.

Then the trickster opened his eyes and said, "Lia?" He stared at the window. The pane was black, and it reflected the illuminated lamplight, the wooden furniture, and their two stark figures.

"What is it?" she asked, recognizing the trickster needed comfort—something he'd never asked for, not since he was very young and she'd been the big sister he'd cried for.

"Did you win?" The question was hopeful.

She shook her head. "No. I came in last."

A thousand calculations ran through the trickster's eyes, and the wind traced all of them. None of the answers made the trickster smile.

"Then . . ."

"I've lost," she said, "unless all the other players die in the final game. I've lost."

The trickster's eyes grew as bleak and barren as the windswept tundra, where the wind gusted so harshly trees couldn't grow. The woman dropped her head against the trickster's shoulder.

"It's all right," she said. "Did you know, there are things besides the crown? Like . . . family. I've always wondered . . . wanted . . ."

The trickster nodded and squeezed the woman. "Right."

The woman went to step back, but the trickster stopped her and asked, "Lia? If I asked for a favor, would you give it to me?"

The wind traveled over the woman's pulse. It stopped then started again at the trickster's question. Her skin went cold. Was she remembering the trickster's betrayal in her trial? Was she remembering his death?

"Of course I would," she finally answered.

"No matter what the favor was?" The trickster stared at his stark reflection in the darkened glass.

The woman made a decision. She nodded. "No matter what it was. I trust you, Luvic."

The trickster nodded. "Good." His mouth flattened into a hard, grim line. "Good."

I LAY IN THE SOFT FOLDS OF DARKNESS, MESMERIZED BY THE QUIET RHYTHM of Finn's breathing, for a long time.

He settled me in the hollow of his arms and ran his fingers over the curve of my back—a soothing, gentle circle that mirrored the calm echo of his emotions. I clung to the placid knot of him, hanging onto the rope until I was able to pull myself up out of the stricture of panic.

It took a while for me to recognize I was lying on top of Finn, on the plump bed in our wooded bedroom, with the windows letting in the gloss of moonlight.

I might've been embarrassed. I was tangled up in him, riding his inhales and exhales and clinging to his soothing cranberry and allspice scent. I might've jumped free of him—this wasn't what our relationship was—but the feel of him was so safe, so comforting, I couldn't bring myself to leave the haven of his arms. If I'd felt from him anger, worry— even arousal—I would've scrambled out of the bed in a second, but from the moment I found myself being carried out of the Clarks' rooms, I'd only felt his wall of calm.

It comforted me, that he didn't feel anger or fear or any of the things I did. It was reassuring. It let me follow the rhythm of his breathing back to myself.

His hand stilled, and the cool air stirred the silk of my shirt. I shivered, and he began the steady, soothing circling again.

"You're all right?"

His voice was a deep thunderstorm rumble in the darkness. Sweetgrass, summer heat, and the promise of rain. I closed my eyes and shoved aside the lurch in my chest, knowing he'd be able to sense it.

"I'm sorry," I said, not wanting to untangle myself from him.

"Mari?"

"I'm okay. I'm just . . . Thanks for coming." I opened my eyes and tilted my head, peering at the darkened lines of Finn's face. It was too dark to see much. It didn't matter. I could feel him still, that small, ring-size space that held my awareness of him. He was calm. Just calm. I couldn't even sense the love anymore.

"I felt you," he said, staring up at the ceiling beams, black lines bathed in dark. "I felt you even inside the game."

"Did I distract you?"

"No."

"Did you . . . ?"

"No. I was third."

When I stiffened, he shifted, and the blankets rustled and whispered.

"It's fine. Next game, I just have to win. Don't worry—"

"I'm not." I broke off at his disbelieving exhale, realizing he could sense my worry. I changed the subject, dropping my head to his chest and letting his heart drum against my cheek. "Did you have trouble with Last, or . . . ?"

"No. No trouble." His hand drifted to my head and stroked gently over my loose hair, smoothing it down.

I suddenly had the strangest longing. I wanted to lie splayed on the bed with him forever. I wanted to stay cocooned in this soft, warm space, just the two of us and nothing else, for the rest of eternity.

What a funny thing to want. What a stupid thing to desire. But I couldn't remember a time when I'd felt so safe, so at home, in my entire life. Maybe that was what I wanted: to feel at home.

I swept aside the longing, like a cat's paw swiping a napkin from a tabletop. The wind caught it on the way down and blew it away. There. No more longing.

I curled my hand into the bedsheets and asked, "So, what, Last just said, 'Oh. My mistake, Finn. Feel free to take Mari. Sorry for the trouble'?"

Somehow, I couldn't picture that. Last was extremely territorial.

I caught a faint flicker of amusement from Finn. He ran the smooth strands of my hair through his fingers and made a grunt of agreement. I resisted the urge to push myself away from his chest and study his expression. I wouldn't be able to see anything in the dark, glossy moonlight—not any more than I could already gauge from his emotions.

Remember, this was before I knew he was hiding his true emotions behind a wall of calm, with only tiny cracks to hint at his true self.

"Do I need to worry?" I asked, my voice only giving a slight shake to betray the aftershocks of panic at being buried alive.

"No. They won't bother you again." Then he amended. "Unless you wander back into their rooms uninvited."

There was that subtle hint of amusement again, as if he expected me to go back looking for trouble—which, of course, I would. Even scared, even terrified, I would.

"Thank you." I closed my eyes and let out a long breath.

His hand stilled, just for a moment, and then he resumed the soothing caress.

I imagine we could've stayed that way for the rest of the night. Sleep was a sweet cradle I was rocking toward, gently entangled in Finn's arms. If I'd let myself, I could've fallen asleep and then woken up in the morning completely refreshed. I would've locked away the fear I felt and the desperate prayer that Finn would come for me. If I'd wanted to, I wouldn't ever have had to think about it again.

There.

That was what was bothering me.

All my life, I'd lived by Jagger's rule. Every man for himself. You're on your own. Always. If you die, you die. If you're in trouble, no one's coming to help. And you'd better not go help anyone else either. The only person you can count on is *you*.

So why was it that when I was buried under a mountain of dirt, suffocating on soil, I could only think, *Finn, Finn, Finn, please, Finn?* And then, *He'll come, he'll come, Finn will come.*

Why was I so sure he'd come when I'd known my whole life no one would ever come? And then, what, after a few days' acquaintance, I was convinced a man I barely knew would come for me?

Yet, he had.

He had.

I didn't know if I should be scared of the fact that I'd thrown out a lifetime of experience and knowledge and trusted Finn, or if I should be grateful he was worthy of my trust.

Would he always be?

I wanted to think so. Maybe that was what scared me. For a short time, I had someone I could trust.

So I wasn't going to fall into the lull of sleep and the forgetfulness of dreams. Instead, I was going to speak truth into the darkness.

"I was looking for a key," I said, and because it had been long minutes since either of us last spoke, Finn stiffened beneath me.

But then he relaxed and asked, "Why?"

Why? That was a good question.

"Jagger wants it. I don't know why. He's not one to tell you why he wants something. If you ask . . ." I laughed dryly. "You don't want to ask. But the Clarks have the key. It's about the size of an old-fashioned skeleton key. Gold. Simple design. I thought I'd poke around their suite while everyone was at the game. You saw how that turned out."

He shifted me closer, and although he'd stopped stroking my hair, the warmth of him was still comforting. "What happened?"

I shrugged, knowing even if he couldn't see it, he could feel it. "Last came in. I was caught in a trap. In the past, I never would've been in a situation like that. I would've come in at night, or when I was certain everyone was away. I would've lockpicked the trap and been out in seconds. But here . . . I'm hobbled. I'm taking risks I wouldn't usually take. I can't lockpick in front of conjurers. Not if I want to live—"

I broke off. It still felt frightening, having Finn know what I was. Yet he'd known for days and hadn't told anyone. Instead, he'd actively protected my secret.

"So you let her put you in an illusion."

I nodded. I could still feel the rope of panic tightening around my throat. "My worst fear. You felt it."

He brushed his hand over my back, and I buried my face in the warmth of his chest.

"I've never told anyone this," I admitted. "I've never told anyone my greatest fear, because if you tell someone what you're afraid of, they'll use it against you."

I'd never trusted anyone enough to tell them my worst fear. Yet there I was, trusting Finn.

"Not everyone," he said, his voice a quiet whisper. "Not everyone will use it against you."

"What was your greatest fear?" I asked, knowing he'd just come out of the Ward trial, where he'd had to face his greatest fear and his greatest desire.

A rumble—like thunder, like laughter—came from him. The vibration rolled through me, and I smiled into the darkness.

"Are you asking this so you can use it against me?" A spark of amusement lit in the ring-shape knot of him.

"No," I quickly assured him.

He laughed, and the sound of it scraped over my skin. "Mari, I can tell when you're lying."

"I won't use it against you," I said, sobering. "Not unless I have to."

At my promise, he shifted and rolled me off him, untangling our arms and legs. The mattress groaned beneath us, and the sheets made soft, whispery noises as I rolled onto my side.

I curled into a comma and rested my cheek on the palm of my hand. Finn stretched out next to me and faced me, so we were only inches apart. I was wrapped in the scent and the heat of him. Swallowed in the moonlight glinting off his eyes.

"I failed," he said, and there was a thick despair in his words, even if I couldn't feel the emotion. "I failed everyone I loved. I wasn't strong enough. Fast enough. Good enough. I did everything I could, and I still failed."

"Your greatest fear is failing?"

"No." He shook his head. "No. My greatest fear is that there aren't any second chances. There isn't forgiveness. There isn't redemption. I have one chance. One. If I fail? That's it. I may as well have killed the people I love myself. Failing them is the same as killing them."

"That's not . . ." I paused, unsure of what to say. I wanted to say that wasn't true, but what did I know? I didn't know anything about Finn's life. Maybe failing was the same as killing.

Still. "If you fail . . ."

"You'll be the first to stab me in the chest?" He smiled—a crooked, funny smile.

"No. Well, maybe." I smiled back. "No, what I mean to say is, there may not always be a second chance, but there's always forgiveness. I think if your loved ones love you as much as you love them, they'll forgive you if you fail. Besides, what would there be to forgive? You'll have done your best. You'll have done everything you could. I mean, look at you—you've entered a devil's bargain, you're comforting the woman sent to murder you, all the odds are against you. If you fail, it won't be for lack of trying. It won't be for lack of love—"

Lightning-fast, he pressed his fingers against my lips, cutting me off. His second and third fingers brushed against my mouth. I let out a startled breath and then held still as his fingers drifted over my bottom lip.

It wasn't like a kiss. It wasn't a soft, sensual stroke. Instead, it was as if he were trying to make the words become unspoken. As if he wanted them to be swallowed by the darkness, unheard.

There was a distant concentration in his gaze as his calloused fingertips pressed against my mouth. I wondered, was this his secondary trait? Could he call back all the spoken words he regretted?

Wouldn't that be a nice power to have?

"Finn?" My breath brushed over his fingertips, and I tasted the salt and the sweetness of his skin.

He blinked, and his gaze settled on me. He seemed surprised to find his fingers pressed to my lips. "Sorry." He pulled free.

"It's fine. Only . . . it's okay if you fail. I'm sure all the people you love will still love you back."

A barely-there tremor moved over him, and then he slowly nodded, although I could tell he didn't necessarily believe me.

That was all right. Fears were like that. They made it impossible to believe in anything but them. They were insidious, and if you let them, they'd grow like cracks in the foundation of a house. They'd spread and spread, and then, eventually, they'd cause the whole house to collapse.

"When I was little," I said, rolling onto my back and staring at the cool, silvery line of moonlight drifting across the ceiling, "I died for the second time. Jagger sent me to the Clarks'. Into the catacombs. He wanted a document, and he told me I'd either come back with the document or I'd come back dead. There was no alternative."

I took a long, deep breath of the cool, mountain and wood scented night air. Finn rolled onto his back and reached over to take my hand. His grip was loose. I could pull away. Instead, I threaded my fingers through his.

"I wasn't quite eight years old. I didn't have enough experience to be going into the catacombs. But Jagger, he was . . . *is* . . . trial by fire. You know, sometimes, fire makes people stronger. Other times, it burns them up and destroys them. But you won't know what type you are until you're in the fire."

Finn squeezed my hand, and the reassurance loosened the pressure building in my chest.

"He wanted to see what I was . . . what type of nine I'd be. So . . . I nearly had the document." I smiled at the memory.

Little me, jumping between shadows, unraveling illusions, my breath loud in the dusty, musty catacombs. I was terrified of all the bones stacked like books on the stone shelves lining the corridors.

"I was in the room. I saw it on the Clark's desk, and then . . ." I closed my eyes, and the darkness of the room mimicked the darkness of underground. "The ground swallowed me. It was an illusion made real.

The Clark had created a trap that buried uninvited guests alive. I don't know how deep I was—I only remember the weight of the soil. The inability to move. The darkness. I tried to unravel the illusion. I did. I think I did. But even unraveled, I was still buried. I screamed for help. For Jagger. For Justice. For Rou and Griff. But every time I opened my mouth, it was filled with dirt. I choked on it. It didn't take long to die. But when I came back, I was still in the dark. I couldn't move. I couldn't . . . It was like I was still buried. Alive, but buried. That's . . . There, you can use it against me now. If you want to make me suffer, all you have to do is bury me."

I lay rigid next to Finn, feeling the cold chill of coarse soil and the pressure of a thousand pounds of dirt. He drew in a breath and then, coming to a decision, gathered me to him. I let him pull me close. I let him wrap his arms around me. I let him. I'm sorry to say I let him.

"Don't worry," I whispered. "It wasn't so bad this time around. That first time, I knew no one was coming. This time, though, I somehow knew you would."

He tensed beneath me and then sighed.

"Don't worry, Finn. You don't have to add me to the list of people you love. You don't have to worry about failing me."

He gave a short half-laugh, half-acknowledgment. "Do you know something funny? When I was in the Wards' game, my best self was a conjurer who conquered the world, and my worst self was a conjurer who destroyed the world. But in both, I failed the people I love. Even with all that power, I still lost. I wonder. I wonder what went wrong."

I made a sleepy sound and then stretched out on top of him. He wasn't as comfortable as the plush bed or the warm, down-fluffed comforter, but he felt . . . safe. Trustworthy.

"Be glad you aren't a conjurer. I'd never trust you if you were."

"And you trust me now?"

I smiled. "No."

But we both could feel my emotions, and we both knew that was a lie.

"In the morning," I said, my eyelids heavy, eyelashes sails pulled down in the windless night, "when we wake up?"

"Yeah?"

"Don't be sorry for holding me tonight. I need it. I know it doesn't mean anything. So . . . don't be sorry for being kind. I'll be sorry for the both of us. You . . . don't be sorry."

I closed my eyes and drifted off on the gentle waves of Finn's breath; the rocking motion of his beating heart. I inhaled the fresh air, the cranberry and allspice, and the cool moonlight. When I dreamed, I dreamed of Finn with hazel eyes and a sword of blue fire, and Luvic trapped in a metal cage, begging to be set free.

62

THE HOT NOON SUN SLID OVER THE GRAY CONCRETE, AND THE SIZZLE OF condensation hitting the sidewalk fizzled and rattled. The wind skittered over the waterdrops as they plunged from window air-conditioning units and hit the sidewalk in hissing pops.

This was a hot summer game. A city game. It was a hopscotch game that often led the wind from the baked sidewalks of Lower Manhattan, all the way to the broken asphalt of the Bronx.

Although the wind loved the North, it also loved the city. It thrilled at the jarring roar of an impatient car horn, the violent thrust of a subway's locomotion, the lusty steam piped from underground tunnels, the curling smells to ride, the skyscrapers to slide, the lightning rods to shoot across as storms speared their metal columns.

Oh, it was happy to be back. If the wind could admit to feeling happy. Happiness was for humans. Yet happiness had its perks, so the wind *might* admit to being happy.

All the families were back. They'd left just after the sun yawned a big, bright orange "O" and peeked sleepily over the pine-tree valley.

Unlike the drive north, the drive south had been a tired, slow-moving caravan, like a row of camels swaying lazily across a long stretch of heat-hazed desert. As soon as the four families pulled up in front of the Bard

Mansion, the wind slid over the hot black hood of one of the vehicles, spiraled around the slowing tire tread, and then jumped into a sizzle of condensation.

Oh, what fun!

It could hop and skip from one spittle of condensation to the next for days on end. It loved to play this game on the hottest days of summer.

Sometimes, when it was so hot humans dripped with sweat and hid inside, someone would pry open a fire hydrant, and then the wind would roar through the rapids that gushed free like a violent waterfall into the street. It would rush over the frothing water and spin on the glistening wet sidewalks as children ran and screamed and played.

The wind liked these hot city summers—never mind the cool, pine scented forests of the North. It was good to be back. It could play hopscotch on air-conditioning condensation for days. But that was when there weren't conjurer games being played or secrets being told.

The wind could scent a secret from miles away. So, when all the families had hurried inside the mansion—the Clarks with careful, darting looks; the Wards with cool distance; the Smiths with bold swagger; the Bards with their elegant grace—the wind stayed outside to play, and to wait.

Patience wasn't necessary. In the time it took a dozen waterdrops to fall and sizzle away, the front door swung open, and the trickster strolled out. He didn't look left or right. There was no mischievous light in his eyes nor funny tilt to his lips. Instead, his expression was as grim and serious as the hard-planed lines of the cliffs that hung over the Hudson.

Ah. So today, the trickster was on one of his father's errands. The wind didn't know if the trickster liked doing his father's bidding. It didn't matter. He always did what was asked of him. Liking didn't come into the equation. It was like asking the wind if it liked the destruction of a hurricane. Liking didn't matter. It merely was.

The trickster's role was retribution. That was the part he was playing today. The wind could taste it in his tight-handed fury and the cold-steel taste of him. It echoed in the hard thud of his feet and the sharp, erect stiffness of his stride.

At an intersection, the trickster thrust his arm into the air and flagged a speeding taxi.

While the musician preferred the dark, tinted confines of sleek, chauffeured, leather scented vehicles, and the citrus and pearl dust scented woman only traveled in hulking, thickly armored SUVs, the trickster had always loved the vinyl and air freshener scent, the wildcard jostle and street roulette, of yellow taxis.

The wind tagged along, swirling on the whistle of the taxi's open window as it sped south and then east. The whole while, the flat screen on the taxi's back seat showed images of the trickster's sister, and the stereo played a raucous noise that was more like rain and thunder and roaring than music.

The trickster left the window open, letting the wind ruffle his black hair and tug at his open shirt collar. But even with the wind blowing his hair in his eyes and shouting wind-nothings in his ear, the trickster didn't smile. His mouth tightened to a hard, flat line, and his brown eyes went winter-night cold. The wind shivered as the taxi pulled to a stop.

Ah.

Hell Gate.

No wonder the trickster was a hard granite tower. The wind patted his cheek, trying to comfort him as he strode along the sidewalk and then stopped at the tall iron gates.

Even if there weren't any secrets to be found, the wind wouldn't leave him. There were certain things a human shouldn't face alone. Going into something you were afraid of was easy compared to going back to something that had broken you.

The wind patted the trickster again and then slid down the rough stubble of his jaw, rubbing his cheek fondly, as it had seen the citrus and pearl dust scented one do when the trickster was young and still had night terrors.

The trickster didn't acknowledge it. That was all right. No one noticed the wind but the boy. All the same, the wind tried to soothe him as the trickster's pulse picked up speed, reminding it of the war drums of years past, thudding its hard, relentless pace.

Finally, the double front doors of Hell Gate swung wide-open. The trickster stiffened grimly and stared through the metal bars at the russet-haired, solemn one as he stalked down the stone steps to the iron gate.

The sun glistened in his chestnut hair and highlighted the freckles on his cheeks. It also sparked on the metal blades strapped to his chest. The wind laughed. The solemn one was wearing more weapons than the wind had ever seen him wear. The solemn one wasn't subtle. Not at all.

The man stopped at the locked gate, and his right hand curled into a fist. The wind could taste his desire to kill the trickster. It could feel the battle raging inside the man. It was a violent, desperate fight to overcome the rocklike one's command—do not harm, do not kill, do not maim—but the solemn one fought it. He fought, and when his shoulders sagged, the wind knew he'd lost.

"I'm here to speak with your master," the trickster said. It wasn't his teasing, light voice but a hard, menacing cut.

The solemn man put his hand to the gate. He leveled the trickster with a look that spoke of a hundred ways to die, all of them delivered by his hand.

The trickster's lips curled with amusement. "You could try," he said softly, "but I don't think you'd like the results."

The solemn one didn't respond. Instead, he swung the gate open and let the trickster onto Hell Gate's grounds. The wind rushed with the trickster, shoving him a bit so he'd stumble into the solemn one. But the trickster was a Bard and light on his feet, so instead, he swayed and steadied himself in a fluid motion, like a dancer gliding on a rocking boat. The wind hmphed. The trickster smiled at the man's back and followed him up the stone steps.

"You're the one they call the Knife?" he asked, and the wind laughed, because the light was back in the trickster's eyes. He was poking at the man, prodding and pushing, to see what would make him respond.

The solemn one didn't answer. He shoved open the front doors of Hell Gate and motioned the trickster inside.

"I've heard of you," the trickster mused, as the wind tripped after him, hurrying through the cold entryway and rushing down a long, dark corridor.

Figments, water spirits, and creatures rushed past, scurrying out of the solemn one's way. A door opened. A creature stepped halfway out, but when he saw the man and the trickster, he slammed the door shut. Soon, the hall was cleared of life.

The solemn one's back was rigid when he stopped at a large wooden door. He knocked twice.

"Wait," a gravelly, rockslide voice said. The wind rolled over the rumble of it.

The man stepped back and folded his arms over his chest. He stared at the trickster, his expression hard.

"You don't like me," the trickster said, a smile tipping up the corner of his lips.

He was taller—not by much—than the solemn one. The wind jumped from the trickster's shirt sleeve and tapped the solemn one's freckles. First one, then another, and another. His nose twitched, and the wind tapped another freckle. The little copper freckle on his right cheek.

"That's fair," the trickster mused, "but why do you want to kill me?" He smiled. "I know the look."

When the solemn one still didn't say anything (although he wanted to —the wind could tell he wanted to), the trickster spoke again.

"Don't worry. Lots of people want to kill you too. Me included. You killed my cousins at the Regis. That was you, wasn't it?"

The solemn one's jaw tightened, and a muscle twitched on his cheek. The wind tapped the tight line.

The trickster waited for him to respond, and when the man didn't, he said, "I won't kill you though. What would hurt worse—killing you, or killing someone you love?"

The wind rode down the solemn man's arm and then tapped on the white of his knuckles. His hand was clenched in a painfully tight grip. His pulse drummed, and his breath was constricted. Ah. So. He was still fighting the rocklike one's command. The wind wondered what the solemn one was imagining. What sort of death he was planning to avenge the girl.

"Yet who do you love?" The trickster waited and then asked, "Mari?"

The wind skated on the solemn one's indrawn breath. It waited as he held his breath for five, ten, fifteen seconds.

"No?" The trickster tilted his head. Waited.

Finally, the solemn one let out a slow breath. The wind rode the flutter of it. It felt just like the slow receding of the tidal waters before a tsunami crashed over a vulnerable shore.

"Someday," the solemn one said, "I will put you in a cage and keep you there until you go mad. You'll wish you were dead."

The trickster smiled—a brilliant, stage-worthy, glorious smile. "Well, hello there. Happy you joined in. I was tired of playing by myself. What kind of cage? Will I get two meals a day? Three?"

"I remember you," the solemn one said. "I remember when you cried."

"Yes. Funny. I don't remember you. Were you hiding? Were you scared? Were you sorry when I left?"

"No. I'd like to have you back."

The wind whistled as the two men grinned death promises at each other.

"I doubt you'll want me back after today," the trickster said.

Then the rocklike one shouted, "Enter!"

The solemn one's fist clenched, and the wind traced the tremble of his arm as he fought the command to go for a knife and kill the trickster. Finally, he turned and opened the door.

"Luvic Bard," he said to the gray, rocklike one.

The wind slipped into the room, following the trickster's footfall. It had been here before. The room was like the inside of a mountain. Cold. Gray. Windowless. It was the empty stone heart of a barren, lifeless being. It was where the rocklike one squatted and drank the spirits of the dead and the hopes and dreams of the living. There was a biting chill that nipped at the wind and caused a frostbitten ache to spread through it.

The rocklike one stood, thrusting back his chair and placing his clawed hands on a large stone table. His flat gray gaze traveled over the trickster. The wind swirled around the cold stone table legs and traveled up the table, avoiding the bitter scent drifting off the glass of Furtig and instead rustling a stack of records. Parchment and catacomb scented. Stolen, no doubt.

The rocklike one was as tall and wide as one of the gray boulders the wind rolled down in Central Park. His skin had folds and crags and cracks that might have been tempting, except for the hard, soulless feel that chilled the wind and made it shiver every time it touched the rocklike one.

"The crown sent me to deliver a message," the trickster said, his expression losing the mischievous tilt of earlier.

"Ah," the rocklike one said, dragging a dark claw down the obsidian knife hanging on a cord from his neck. "But what is it they say? Kill the messenger?"

The solemn one leaned forward eagerly. The wind whirled around the table, curling the edges of the old papers.

The trickster's eyes glinted as if the rocklike one had just told a fantastic joke.

"Our bargain," the rocklike one said. "How goes it?"

"Well," the trickster said.

The rocklike one nodded and then rolled a hand. "Deliver your message."

The trickster stood tall, straightened, so he reminded the wind of a young beech tree in the forest, golden and unbowed by wind or storm.

"You reside here due to the crown's benevolence," the trickster said, his voice matching perfectly the casually cruel cadence of his father's. "You and your creatures live due to the crown's benevolence. You have murdered five of our cousins. Therefore, we exact retribution. Five times five. We exact retribution. It is done."

The rocklike one lunged, jumping over the stone table, but the trickster had already twisted his hand. The wind shrieked as Hell Gate shook. A blast of heat exploded outward, and the wind tumbled along its razor-sharp edge.

Hell Gate was burning, consumed in an invisible fire. The hungry flames, the skin-blistering heat, the acrid smoke. Then the heat was gone, replaced by cold, dry air. The trickster was surrounded by a wall of swirling water. A shield wall.

Through Hell Gate's plaster walls, there was the muffled echo of screams.

"I believe," the trickster said, "you have a kitchen fire."

The solemn man jerked as if he'd been kicked. "Rou!" He sprinted from the room, shoving past the swirling water, not even flinching when the waves cut his arms and left wave-patterned slices of blood.

The rocklike one narrowed his eyes after the solemn man, and the wind knew he wasn't happy. What did he say? Never help another.

Maybe the solemn man had sprinted like the wind so the rocklike one wouldn't command him to stop and leave the soon dead to their fate.

Perhaps the solemn man had more good in him than the wind had weighed and measured.

Perhaps.

The rocklike one bared his sharp, pointed teeth at the trickster in a gruesome smile. The trickster stared at him through his maelstrom of waves. The wind circled the cold water, whirling in the waves, wondering at the power hiding in the trickster's blood.

The rocklike one focused on the trickster's expression and then, finally, laughed. It was a cold, rockslide avalanche. The wind shivered. Perhaps if the trickster stayed long enough, his swirling water storm would freeze and become a blizzard.

"Retribution exacted," the rocklike one said, laughing again. It was a slippery-edged, jagged laugh. "Five times five, Luvic? Only twenty-five dead? Your crown is weak. But not you. Not you. Message delivered."

The trickster gave a tight smile. Turned to go.

"I look forward to the fulfillment of our bargain," the rocklike one said, grabbing the glass on his desk and raising the liquid spirits.

"As do I," the trickster said.

The wind rode the cold waves of the trickster's shield as he stalked from the burning, blazing heat of Hell Gate on fire.

63

THE CITY WAS BURN-THE-RUBBER-OFF-YOUR-SHOE-SOLES HOT, AND WHILE the Bards had managed to create a Beaux-Arts palace worthy of any of history's flamboyant emperors, they hadn't managed to clinch the greatest luxury of all. Properly functioning air-conditioning.

It was those old, turn-of-the-century stone buildings. I swear they sucked up the heat of the sun and then baked you like a clay oven. Hell Gate was the same—it gifted you with the extremes of all the seasons.

In the winter, there was a bone-deep chill that settled into your marrow and didn't leave until the first narcissus poked its head above the melting snow in the spring. In the summer, there was a blazing fire-blanket of heat that suffocated your senses and made you feel like a steaming rag dripping sweat.

Jagger could never be bothered to install air-conditioning. Leggerocks didn't feel the heat or the cold like humans did. I imagined they felt it like a slab of granite, soaking up the sun or freezing with the cold, not much bothered by either state.

But the Bards? Look at their verdant family suite, with its garden courtyard and tinkling fountains. Maybe they had cool, breezy air blowing in their rooms. Maybe they'd left our suite a humid sweatbox as a present.

I scrubbed my hand over my forehead and wiped away a line of sweat. I'd hauled a half-dozen suitcases up the six flights of stairs (the elevator was a little too 'death trap' for my taste), taking six trips to carry the oversized Smith luggage back to their suite. Then I'd unpacked, checked the suite for bugs (found three, discarded them), and made a quick lunch of roast-beef sandwiches on sourdough, because it was too hot to use the little portable stove, boil water, or make anything warm.

I sat at the dining table, a wilted flower baking in the heat. Don't get me wrong—I love the city. It's what I've always known, and it's as comfortable as an old sweatshirt, threadbare-soft and soothing in its familiarity. But oh, my heart had ached a bit when we'd pulled down the hemlock-lined driveway early this morning and left the birdsong, the wind in the pines, and the quiet, sunrise-tinged mountain forests.

I'd stayed quiet the whole drive back, just watching as the sun wheeled higher in the sky and the hills flattened like dough under a rolling pin, squishing into long, river-furrowed plains. The scattered boulders had disappeared, the spired trees had turned into buildings, and the cool, lake-tinted wind had become slow-river, sunbaked-concrete hot. City hot.

Darin was quiet the whole drive south—not one joke, not even one crazed driving maneuver. Wolfgang had closed his eyes, and while some might have believed he was sleeping, I knew better. There was so much energy buzzing around him I imagined he was building futures in his mind, playing chess games of worldwide proportions, strategy upon strategy.

Finn had sat next to me, and for the entire drive, he'd watched the blur of green and blue that finally shifted to gray and brown. When the city first came into view, he'd turned to me, and I suppose he saw the wistful longing in my expression, because he gave me a soft half-smile that had made me think he understood exactly how I felt.

I imagined he could feel what I felt. I could still feel him—a placid mountain pool of calm, love tinting the waters a golden hue.

When I'd woken up in bed still sprawled on top of him, I'd stolen a moment to imagine it was real. That I lived in the woods. That I had someone I trusted. That I'd never heard of nines or lockpicks or illusion. That I was a regular person with someone to love who loved me back.

But it was a stolen moment. It wasn't truth.

So I'd whispered, "I'm sorry," and untangled myself from Finn. For a moment, while he was still wrapped in the arms of sleep, he'd tightened his hold on me, but then he'd woken up, and I'd pulled free.

I'd had coffee with a side of regret. He'd shot back a thimbleful of solange. The day had begun.

Now we were back at the Bard Mansion, Wolfgang, Darin, and Finn were walking through strategy for the final game. The game, like all Smith games, was a battle. And now that Finn had a chance at winning the crown, Wolfgang was determined he would finish first.

"The great equalizer," Wolfgang said, leaning back in his dining chair, "is the null effect. We've made it so no one will conjure while in our game." He smiled at his sons. "This will be a game of strength, cunning, and courage."

Darin grabbed another sandwich from the platter in the center of the table. He'd eaten two already. This wasn't unusual. The Smith men, I'd found, required a large amount of protein and calories—probably because they were towering walls of muscle that burned through food fast.

"Celia will come in last," Darin said, chewing on his sandwich.

"Likely," Wolfgang agreed.

"She'll be lucky to get through the game alive." Darin finished the first half of the roast-beef sandwich and seemed surprised it was already gone. "Primus will be a challenge. He's trained in combat."

Of course he was. The Clarks, for all their love of scholarly pursuits, also loved martial history and the application of it in modern day.

"And Jacob?" Finn asked, and Wolfgang smiled. He considered Finn, weighing his placid expression, the half-eaten sandwich, the mess of his hair, the wrinkled T-shirt, and the star-studded solange gaze.

"He'll be a challenge too," Wolfgang finally said.

"Mari could poison him again," Darin said, a hint of laughter in his voice. "Turn him around so much he won't know enemy from friend. He'll probably try to pet a war elephant and end up skewered on its tusk."

I squirmed in my seat, the sweat-soaked silk of my uniform sticking to my skin. I didn't want to poison Jacob again. What had he said? *"Don't do it again, all right? I can't do what I have to do if you're poisoning me."*

"It won't work," I said, shifting uncomfortably when both Wolfgang and Darin turned to me. "He figured out it was me the last time. He'll be expecting it."

"And you're still alive?" Darin asked.

I held out my hands, gesturing to my new face. For all they knew, Jacob was satisfied with my death during the Clark games.

Wolfgang grunted and then rubbed a thick hand though his silver-streaked black hair. "We don't know if Jacob is trained in combat. I believe no one outside of Philoneas and Jacob knows if he can wield a sword, shoot an arrow, or throw a knife. However, we do know he is the most powerful heir in centuries. We know he's toppled three governments."

Huh. I thought it was two.

"We know he's connected to fifteen *confirmed* assassinations. We know he's left a trail of conjurers imprisoned in their own minds. We know he is cunning. We know he is ruthless."

"Anyone who kills his sister and takes her power is ruthless," Darin said in an aside to me, maybe thinking I hadn't heard the story.

"We know he has courage," Wolfgang continued. "The only thing we don't know is if he is strong. If he can fight. He's physically at a disadvantage. Wiry. Small."

Only a Smith would call a man of average height and build small.

"But . . . there have been many men in history who've led armies and conquered nations and weren't—"

"Giants?" I asked, then I bit my tongue when Wolfgang's attention swung to me.

Finn spoke before Wolfgang could remind me he was looking forward to gutting me at the end of the games. "Jacob can fight."

"How do you know?" Darin asked.

Finn lifted a shoulder. "You can see it"—he closed one eye, peering at Darin, and then he closed his other—"in the way he moves. He's been training since he started walking. It's in his gait. A man can hide many things, but he can't hide his nature. If you want to know what sort of person a man is, first listen to his laugh. Second, watch his walk. Those will tell you everything."

I hid a smile. It had been a while since Finn last pulled out his solange philosophizing. I'd missed it.

Wolfgang gave Finn a tight-lipped look. "Let's hope you're wrong. A Ward who can fight as well as a Smith would be a dangerous thing."

There was a hard knock on the suite's door. At the interruption, we all went quiet. Then Wolfgang waved his hand, and I hurried to open it.

There was no one there, just a thick, cream-colored envelope, with gold wax sealing the flap and the name "Smith" written in flowery calligraphy on the front.

"Open it," Wolfgang said, and I imagined he was only asking me to do so because poison powder might shoot out, Smith's Folly might be lining the paper, or there could be some other delightful surprise awaiting him that was best handed to a body.

I cracked the wax seal, opened the envelope, and pulled out a thick ivory card with gold-scripted writing.

"It's an invitation," I said, scanning the words. "For tomorrow night. The Smith, his heir, and his paladin are cordially invited to the Hundred Year Gala."

When I looked up from the paper, Wolfgang was scowling, Darin was grinning, and Finn's brow was furrowed.

"The gala," Darin said, an anticipatory gleam in his eyes. "I'd forgotten about the gala. Excellent. Maybe the one who tried to poison Dad with Smith's Folly will be back and we can dance."

By dance, he meant kill. That was obvious by his happy, feral grin.

Then he smiled at me. "Do you think it was your friend—the one on the motorcycle? I think it was." He shrugged, apologizing for the fact that he was still gunning for Justice.

"Pretty sure it wasn't," I said.

He smiled. "I'm pretty sure it was."

Nope. It was me. Sorry.

"In the meantime," Wolfgang said, shoving back from the table, "Finn. Darin. Clear the room. We train."

64

Finn and Darin spent hours chopping at each other with sharp objects, trying to poke holes in each other and then swiping at each other in hand-to-hand combat.

Within the first thirty minutes, they'd stripped down to only shorts. Wolfgang had conjured a sparring ring in the cleared room and was barking at them from the sidelines, sometimes darting in and slamming his fist into one of his sons just to illustrate a point.

I'd seen Finn shirtless before, but I'd never seen him sweat-slicked and moving with such a tightrope, wire-walking grace. He moved as if he existed outside of time.

The first time Darin urged Finn forward, he had a cocky grin. Then, lightning-fast, Finn had knocked him flat. Darin laughed as if he'd just been handed the best present of his life. He sprang up and bounced on his feet, joyfully spitting out a bit of blood. After that, he didn't have a cocky grin; he had a "kid playing with his best friend" type of grin.

I once walked past the dog park in Carl Schurz Park and saw two huge, muscled dogs snapping and growling and rolling across the dirt. I thought they were going to kill each other—the snarls and barks were vicious. I'd stopped to stare, and their owner, the lone man in the dog park, saw me and said, "Oh, don't worry. They're brothers. They do this all the time. They're just playing." Sure enough, thirty seconds later, the two dogs had broken apart with the biggest doggy grins on their faces, tails wagging, licking each other's cheeks. They'd run off to the water dish and shared a drink. Best friends.

Finn and Darin were a lot like that, but more so. Each hit taken, each strike dodged, each fluid move elicited an urge to fight harder, to move faster, to do more. Maybe Darin had liked Finn before but never respected him. He did now.

"You trained with Xelius?" Darin asked.

Finn kicked his feet out from under him. Grinned.

Darin sprang upright. "That's a yes."

They hammered at each other for hours. Wolfgang demanded sequences, commanded moves mirroring famous historical Smith fights, shouted out stances like a caller at a dance. He never smiled. He never seemed impressed. Even when Darin nearly took off Finn's head with a blue fire sword, and Finn did an impossible back bend and then recovered by springing upright and kicking the sword from Darin's hand —not even then did he look impressed.

Me, though? I was impressed.

I was a little too impressed. When Finn pulled his shirt over his head, my body went all heavy and buzzy, and that invisible rope I once felt between us coiled in my abdomen and tightened. I had the strongest urge to reach out and touch the lines of his back, his shoulders; to span my hands over his biceps and run them down his forearms, tracing the veins until I ended at the firm grip of his hands. I wanted to see if his bare skin was as soft as it looked.

My mouth was dry, my skin tingling, and I was dizzy when Wolfgang snapped, "Body. Make yourself useful."

So I brought out jugs of ice water and lemonade, dried fruit, nuts, and more sandwiches. Then I slipped from the suite and did what Jagger had demanded the last time I saw him. Mischief. Chaos. Confusion.

Dainty Drink sprinkled on the oversized fruit cornucopias in the hallways. A thunderer set at the Clarks' threshold, ready to explode on the first person who opened the door. A note next to it that read, "I know who killed Secondus."

I didn't, but apparently, Jagger did, and he wanted to taunt the Clarks. I supposed that meant Justice had killed Last's brother.

I left a box of poisoned chocolates outside the Bard suite. If they were silly enough to eat them, that was their fault. More likely, they'd grow paranoid. Paranoid people made stupid mistakes. Celia had nearly zero chance of winning, but Jagger didn't like *nearly*; he liked zero.

For the Wards? Jagger wanted me to leave a small mirror—the kind that comes in a makeup compact case—outside their door. It was to taunt Jacob for killing his own mirror. Except, when I walked close to the suite, Uliea opened the door, blinked at me, and said, "Hello, dear. Are you coming in for tea?" From inside, I heard Jacob call, "Who is it?" I made my excuses and hurried away without leaving the mirror.

All in all, it was a busy day back. Tomorrow was the Gala. The day after was the final game. The end was rushing closer, gathering speed and bearing down on us all. Looking back, the avalanche had already begun, and the rockslide was crashing down the mountain, about to bury us all. Was there a way to divert it? At what point could we have stopped it? You would tell me the avalanche began before we were born, that it wasn't my fault, but I suppose I'm susceptible to that small human failing: the egoism to think the events in my world are caused by me—that I am always the cause, and never the effect.

We all want to be the arm that throws, and never the knife.

What did Jagger once say to me when I was young and still fighting being a nine? "Do you really think you're in control?" Do you know what I learned from that? Probably not the lesson Jagger intended. I learned I *was* in control, because while Jagger could force me to do something against my will, he could never force me to *believe* something against my will. As long as I stayed firmly rooted in truth, as long as I unraveled illusion, I was the sole proprietor of my own heart.

Outside the bedroom window, the moon was ticking down. Each night, a slice of it was cut off, so that when the crown of illusions was passed on, the moon would be gone, and the sky would be black. A new moon for a newly crowned heir.

I shivered and stared out the window at the white crescent slice. I stretched out on the wood floor and listened for the steady, slow rhythm of Finn's breath. He'd showered earlier. I'd batted away his protests and wiped an ointment over his bruises and cuts. Then he'd fallen into bed, not even arguing when I told him I'd sleep on the floor.

His breath had fallen into a quiet, sleep-filled rhythm within seconds, his muscles loosening and his face smoothing out. His hand lay on the white sheets, palm open, fingers outstretched. I found that was how he always slept. As if he were reaching for someone.

During the day, I'd only felt little sparks of happiness and steely determination from him. Now, there was only that placid pool—not a ripple of emotion. He must be so deeply asleep he'd descended to the space beneath dreams.

My muscles tensed, and ever so slowly, I sat up. I reached for my backpack and quickly pulled on black pants, a long-sleeve black shirt, and my canvas jacket. I'd already put in place everything I'd need. I laced up my shoes.

Then I stood and ever so quietly turned the door handle.

"Mari."

I jerked and spun around.

Finn stood only a few feet away, barefoot and bare-chested.

"Do you really think you should leave without me?" he asked, not a hint of sleep in his voice, or in his face.

"You were awake the whole time?"

He nodded. "Just waiting for you to decide it was time to go."

I sighed. Tugged at the ring on my right ring finger. It didn't budge. The stupid thing had given me away.

Finn's lips lifted into a smile. "You've been wound tight since dinner. You were like a kid waiting impatiently to open a stack of birthday presents. Did you really think I'd be able to sleep with you feeling like this?"

"I wasn't that obvious."

I watched as a host of expressions shifted over his features. Amusement. Disbelief. Humor. Finally, he landed on agreement.

"Right. You're very discreet."

I snorted. "Come on then. But you have to do what I say. This is a job."

It wouldn't be terrible having Finn come along. Unlike Luvic, he already knew I was a lockpick. He'd never threatened me. And I . . . *ahem* . . . sort of trusted him. At least, I trusted him to help me out of a situation if everything went sideways. He wouldn't leave me to my fate, and that was saying something.

"We're headed to the Clarks'?" he asked.

How'd he know that?

"Apparently, I *am* that obvious."

He grinned and tugged a shirt over his head. "Only to me."

I narrowed my eyes as he laced up his shoes. "Do I have a line," I asked, pointing to the space between my eyebrows, "right here, when I'm up to something?"

Finn looked up and frowned at the spot I was pointing to. Then he shrugged. "Sure."

"What do you mean, 'sure'?"

"Yes. You do."

Great. Apparently, everyone and their cousin knew I got a wrinkle between my eyebrows when I was planning on making mischief and having fun. I'd have to work on that.

"Did I have that wrinkle tonight?"

Finn strode across the room, cat-paw quiet, and grabbed my hand. "You have that wrinkle every night. Come on. I want to get back before three."

Every night?

"Why three?"

"Because if I don't get at least four hours of sleep, I get cranky."

Huh. "There's always coffee."

He scoffed and pulled me after him.

We slipped from the suite like two shadows. At the front door, the jackaltooth doorman let us out. After he opened the door, Finn stayed back to speak with him. I walked down the darkened sidewalk and pretended not to notice him pressing his fingers to the doorman's temple.

When he caught up to me, I asked, "That thing you did to the doorman—"

"What thing?"

"Pressing your fingers to his head."

Finn lifted an eyebrow. "Mari?"

"Yeah?"

He leaned close, and my heart skittered in my chest. Oh. Was he . . . was he going to kiss me? The moon hung above us. The blanket of heat thrown over the city tucked itself tighter around us. The streets were lined with sleeping cars and quiet sidewalks. Even the wind was still.

My lips tingled. I drew my tongue over my bottom lip and swayed close.

No, Mari. Bad. This is bad. Don't kiss Finn Alterra. Don't kiss—

Finn reached up and brushed his fingers over my temple. The pads of his fingers were calloused, and I shivered at the soft feel of him stroking my skin.

There was a pulse of heat. A delightful throb that worked itself through me.

The illusion Luvic had woven disintegrated under his touch. I gasped as the knots slid free.

Finn hadn't been about to kiss me. He hadn't been about to work some hidden mental trait on me. He'd just been dissolving illusion.

"Dang it, Finn!"

He smiled and pulled his hand free.

My cheeks burned. *Kiss me?* Right. I didn't even want him to kiss me. Not *really*.

"Now I'll have to ask Darin—"

"No." Finn shook his head. "You don't need it. The Clarks will leave you alone."

I sighed. Was that what Finn was—a walking, talking destroyer of illusions? Did he reach out and brush illusions off people like clearing cobwebs from a windowpane? Did he just brush against people and swipe away all the illusions cluttering their mind? I wondered what illusions the jackaltooth doorman had clogging his brain.

"All right. Let's go." I stalked toward the subway. Finn followed, and although I didn't look, I swear he was smiling.

65

THE BOY DANCED ACROSS THE FIERY, BURNING FIELD, DODGING FLAMING missiles and jumping over molten rivers that exploded from the steaming ground. The wind seesawed on the swipe of his sword and spun with him as he cut the arm from a giant.

The wind laughed as the boy dove beneath the giant's fist and then cut it behind the knees, causing it to topple over and crush the four men in its shadow.

The boy dripped sweat. His wheat-field hair was darkened and wet, and his shirt was soaked.

The wind had played in his illusion while he'd cut down fifty—no, sixty—attackers. It remembered this battle; had been there in history, eons ago, when war horns had shaken the earth and cities had collapsed under the weight of illusion. The sky had burned a violent orange for days while sun-flaming balls were hurled between armies. That war, before the flood, there'd been a Smith who'd taken on 300 men with only his sword and come out the victor.

The boy would never match the violent hunger of that Smith. He was a Ward, after all, and his strength lay down the narrow cobblestone pathways of his mind, not on the wide expanse of a battlefield. All the same, the boy danced through the battlefield, spinning from one partner to the next, leaving them all bloodless on the flaming ground.

The roar of the battle was hurricane-loud; a freight train screaming as it rushed down its track. The fire balls whistled and hissed and tore apart the earth.

This was one of the boy's favorite illusions. He played here often. Sometimes, he would fly over the battle, his hand looped around a giant raven's claw, shooting firebolts from the sky. Other times, he'd stand in the hand of a giant metal construct, like the giant bronze man Hephaestus built to defend Crete, throwing boulders at the vast army. Once in a while, the boy would shove a dark wind through the illusion, and thousands of soldiers would explode, their mirrored shards shooting across the world, capturing thousands of illusions as they burst into dust.

It was whispered on the wind that the Wards always left their enemies trapped in the darkest corners of their minds, chained by their own apostasies. What was hell, if not the eternal absence of God? What was torment but the shackle of shame and the redaction of redemption? The wind had learned enough of humankind to know that when they lost themselves in that labyrinth without love, they were doomed to eternal suffering.

But how did it know that? It had never seen heaven nor hell.

But it knew the boy. It knew the wind that blew through his veins and the spirit that flowed in his blood. It knew that while the Wards left their enemies shackled and tormented by the conjurings of their minds, they reserved the worst of their powers for themselves. They regularly trapped themselves in their own nightmares, shackled themselves to their monsters, and let their deepest fears run riot over their weaknesses.

Why?

The boy had once told the wind that the most terrifying thing in the world was a good person who denied their capacity to hate. The seed was there in humans: what if it was ignored, pushed down, denied? There often came a time when a good person was given *permission* to hate. Then it erupted as violently as a volcano that had lain dormant for centuries. Before, it had simmered and stewed, but it had been held back, unnoticed. What happened when good people were given permission to hate?

Hate the rich, the boy said. Hate them. You have permission. Do you like the thought?

Hate the poor, the boy said. You've been given permission.

Hate the people you think will harm you, kill you, hurt you. Hate them. You have permission. It is to protect yourself. It's to protect your family. It's your right. Hate them.

There, the boy said. You see, Wind?

What happens?

Millions die. Millions will die, Wind, when a good person is given permission to hate.

So what does a Ward do? What does the boy do?

He dances with his demons so they won't one day overpower him and lead him down a path that destroys the world.

The battle always ends the same. The wind, settled by the boy's feet, bubbling on the hot flow of a nearby lava stream. The boy's mirror standing in front of him.

"Viola," the boy said, dropping his sword. It vanished before hitting the ground.

The wind sneezed at the smell of sulfur and then went to rustle the frilly ends of the mirror's white dress. It climbed the lace and ribbon and poked at the pale smoothness of her cheeks.

Always the same. Green eyes like the boy's. Wheat-field-colored hair like the boy's, only long and wavy. A freckle over her lip, in the same spot as the boy's. A dimple and a smile, just like the boy's. She aged in the boy's illusions, mirroring him as she always had.

"Jacob," she said, echoing his greeting.

"How many times do I have to kill you?" he asked, and the wind left off playing with the lacy tassels of her dress and went back to the boy, nudging his hand.

The mirror smiled at the boy and asked, "How many times do *I* have to kill you?"

"Why am I afraid of you?" he asked, and the wind tapped his hand again, disliking the way his fingers trembled. "You wouldn't be here if I weren't afraid."

Her smile grew, and it wasn't a reflection of the boy's expression. The wind shivered. Even the lava pools and the fiery landscape couldn't keep away the chill.

"Why am I afraid of you? You wouldn't be here if I weren't afraid," she mimicked.

"So you aren't going to give me an answer? If not—" He held out his hand, and her lips curved into the boy's half-smile.

"I'll come back."

The boy nodded. "You always do. But only here. Not in real life."

"This is real life."

"No. This is illusion."

She laughed, and the noise was distorted—a shattered-glass tinkling, overlaid by the earth being torn apart. "No. This is real life. If you shatter your mirror, do you shatter yourself? Poor Jacob. Lost his mirror, lost his friend, lost his sister in the end."

The boy snarled. He flung out his hands and twisted his fingers. The wind dove across the fiery plane and slammed into the mirror. The pieces of her shattered. She exploded in a million sparks. The lava and firelight prismed violently over the battlefield. The illusion flashed as hot and as bright as the sun.

The mirror shards vanished. The battlefield vanished. The boy stood in the empty basement beneath the Ward home. It was four gray concrete walls. Concrete floors. Bright lights. Cold air. The echo of a heartbeat and ragged breath. Nothing else.

The basement was wiped clean of the boy's illusion. He reached up and wiped at the sweat dripping down his brow. The wind drifted over the salt and the wet rivulets. Perhaps the boy would ride the subway back to the Bard Mansion. Perhaps the wind would roar through the tunnels, shooting between the rattling, speeding cars. It would like that. It loved it when the boy rode the subway, thumbs in his pockets, rocking back on his heels, pretending he was just an ordinary boy out for an ordinary ride, listening to music and reading a book, while the wind jostled the car and slipped in and out of the subway doors.

The boy let out a long breath and rubbed his T-shirt over his face. Then he said, "You know secrets, Wind. What's mine? Why am I so afraid of killing her that I have to do it again and again?"

The wind thought through the pathways of the boy's life. It listened to the memory of his heartbeat twined with his sister's in his mother's womb. It traveled over his first cry. It remembered the babble of his first laugh. It rode the boy's terrified, plaintive screams on his fourth birthday. It padded through all the secrets, all the confidences; walked through the years of the boy training his mind to become a sharpened knife, forcing his body to become a deadly sword. It traveled down the halls of focus, where the boy had only one thought, one goal.

He wasn't afraid of killing her. He'd never been afraid of that. The wind told him so.

"Then what?"

When the wind didn't answer, the boy nodded and left the basement, turning out the lights.

The wind stayed in the dark for a moment and whispered the answer, so that it might echo around the concrete room and reach the boy when he needed it.

The boy—the wind's boy—the only thing he'd ever been afraid of was solitude.

Of being one instead of two.

66

THE CLARK MANSION WAS A SILENT SPECTER BURIED IN THE MISTS OF ITS own morbid history. The bright lights of the surrounding apartment buildings and office towers shied away from the hulking mansion, skittering free like cockroaches fleeing from a flashlight.

The mansion ate light. That's all there was to it.

The catacombs were infinitely worse.

"I sort of hoped I'd never have to come back here," I joked, nudging Finn with my elbow as I lockpicked the thick wooden door. "Dying here twice was enough, thank you very much."

Finn grunted and held out a hand to stop my progress when the door sprang open on well-oiled hinges. He stepped over the threshold first, wary and light on his feet. He swayed a bit—the solange—but I'd never doubt his physical abilities again. Not after seeing him take down Darin in one blurred punch.

I waited while he tilted his head, probably viewing the dusty bowels of the catacomb tunnel through one eye and then the other.

The house was empty. All the Clarks were settled at the Bard Mansion, and while they kept bodies, I'd never known them to have staff. That seemed odd. As lovers of history, you'd think they'd keep an army of servants, but I think they preferred the emptiness of a dusty cavern and a history book over the bustle of people interrupting with food or drink or dust mops. Besides, conjurers could locomote dusters and vacuums and brooms. Or they could live in a dirty heap and conjure new clothes rather than go to the effort of washing their dirty laundry. They could order every meal for delivery and pay with money they thought into existence.

I, for one, wasn't particularly curious about how Last did her laundry or what Primus ate for breakfast. I was only glad the hulking mansion was deserted.

It was easy to enter. For me.

Like most overpowered conjurers, the Clarks scoffed at things like deadbolts and alarm systems. Instead, they locked their doors with illusion and left illusion traps for intruders.

I know. I know. You're reminding me I was just caught in one of their traps.

However, that was when I couldn't lockpick in front of Last. Now, I could untie any illusion I came across.

I'd cast Finn a side-eyed glance as I lockpicked their conjured security system. We'd entered through the side door, hidden in the shadow of a giant green dumpster.

Finn didn't look curious. He didn't study what I was doing. He wasn't shocked. He didn't say, "Aha! I knew it! I've been waiting to confirm it, and now I'm going to hand you over to the Wards so you can die a million deaths!"

Instead, he'd waited patiently, and when I held open the door, he gave me that smile that made my stomach flip over itself, like I was diving from a high tower and hadn't yet hit the ground.

When he'd smiled, I poked at the ring-shape space where his emotions hid. Calm. A hint of pleasure—the sort you get after you drink that first sip of morning coffee. Love. That was there again, the golden hue not chased away by the Clark Mansion.

Nothing to alarm me. Nothing to make me unravel that thin thread of trust that had wrapped itself around me. So I'd led him through the house, unraveling what I needed to and leaving what I didn't.

And there we were. Back in the catacombs.

"It's clear," Finn said, nodding me in.

I stepped over the threshold and smiled. "Thanks. Don't know what I'd do without—"

The ground opened beneath me.

I screamed.

There had been hard-packed dirt. There had been the stone shelves holding moldering clothes, bones turned to dust, and blankets of cobwebs. There had been the ever-present sickly-green conjured illumination and the dry earth and parchment scent that always lingered.

There had been a ground.

And then there wasn't.

My scream tore free, and I threw my hands toward Finn.

His eyes went wide, and then—I can't believe this—he dove into the pit after me.

I slammed into a hard dirt floor covered in bones—yes, those were bones—just as the ceiling of this little prison snapped shut.

Finn landed next to me, hitting the bones with a hard grunt. A thick cloud of dust blew over us, and I coughed, tried to suck in a breath, and coughed again.

The thin green light was gone, and we were entirely consumed by darkness.

From what I'd seen, we were in a round stone space about four stride-lengths in circumference and two stories deep. The floor was dirt and covered in the bones of about . . . if I had to guess . . . ten or fifteen unfortunates who had rotted here long, long ago.

The dust tickled my nose, and I tried not to think about the fact that I could be breathing in someone's femur. Or tibia. Could be a tibia.

I sneezed.

"Bless you," Finn said, and then there was the clatter of bones knocking together as he shifted and stood. "All right?"

"I'm fine. Some trap. It's not illusion. I think . . ." I closed my eyes. Sniffed the air. "Do you smell that?"

"Sickly-sweet," Finn said. "Like embalming fluid and dried flowers."

Right.

"That's Embalmer's Rest. Okay. Don't panic, but it's going to make us sleepy, and if we fall asleep, we dream until we die. Finn?"

"Hmm?" He made a tired noise and then yawned.

"Don't fall asleep!" I kicked through the bones, holding my hands out. When I stumbled into him, I grabbed his shoulders and shook him. "Don't fall asleep."

"Mmm not."

He was. He definitely was. *What to do? What to do?* He swayed and yawned again. Desperate measures. I pulled back my arm and slapped him. The crack echoed off the stone walls.

He startled. A bright spray of surprise hit me through the ring's connection.

"What?" he mumbled, and then he stumbled backward. "I'm tired, Mari."

Gosh, I was tired too. My limbs felt heavy, and the little room was swaying like a lullaby. The bones didn't feel hard and knobby; they felt soft, like rubbing a mink fur coat along your cheek. The dirt floor was a welcoming mattress, and the dark was a blissful invitation to sleep.

But.

I'd experienced Embalmer's Rest before. When I was twelve, Jagger had caught me napping when I was supposed to be studying, and he'd shoved me into a box and told me if I wanted to sleep, I could sleep for forever. If I managed to stay awake for ten minutes, he'd let me out. Otherwise, he'd see me when I was back from the land of the dead.

He didn't let me out after ten minutes. He let me out after twelve, right when I was about to succumb to the sickly-sweet perfume parading through my veins. He'd laughed and told me I'd held out longer than anyone he'd ever known.

Fun and games.

So while I was tired, I wasn't going to fall asleep. Not yet.

"Just gonna close my eyes for a second." Finn yawned again. It was a loud, jaw-splitting yawn. I knew he was tired, but still . . .

"Stay awake! I'm getting us out of here."

The trap wasn't made with illusion. In fact, it'd probably been built with the original house.

Maybe it was where they'd stored their ice and kept foods cool long before the era of refrigeration. Maybe it'd always been a dungeon. All the same, there had to be a way out.

"Tell me a story," I told Finn. "Talk to me. Don't stop talking."

I shook him again, and he startled and stiffened. "Hmm?"

"Tell me a story. I'm scared of the dark. Tell me a story, and don't stop talking."

"Ah," he said, his voice a sleepy rumble. I heard the scrape of his clothing as he (I think) leaned against the stone wall. "A story. Okay."

I felt for the stones and then began feeling my way around the circle, searching the cold protrusions.

"How do you want it to start?" he asked.

"I don't know. Start it with something exciting. Some action. No tragedies. I don't like tragedies."

I'd made a full circle, feeling around Finn's warmth. There was no doorway, and although I didn't think there would be, I was still disappointed. I reached out with my senses, floating outside of myself, searching for illusion.

There.

High above.

There was a bit of illusion beyond the closed mouth of the ceiling. It was an old knot. A sailor's knot, rigor mortised into rigidity. It would take some time to unravel. It was like an old, thick, ropy knot crystallized from years of soaking in saltwater, dried as stiff as bone.

I wasn't certain it was connected to the trap, but right then, it was our best bet.

I set to work prying at illusion.

"Did I ever tell you," Finn asked, smothering a yawn, "the story of the first time I got caught in a Clark trap?"

"No," I said, not breaking my concentration. "Tell me."

"Mmm . . ." He yawned again, and the bones rattled as he sank to the ground. "We were out . . . messing around . . . We were kids." He yawned. "I was . . . I wanted to pick this flower. It was my mom's favorite. Forget-me-not. The blue ones. I wanted to give . . . the flowers . . ."

He trailed off, and when he didn't continue, I urged, "And then what?"

"Hmm? Oh. Then . . . they were growing in the grass alongside the

Clarks' house. And I didn't think . . . Everyone always said, 'Don't go near the conjurers, Finn. They'll kill you.' But I never thought . . . I thought they were just saying that. Like kid's stories. Like scary bedtime stories. The conjurers that came in the Night Den never hurt me. They just drank or gambled or went off with one of the pleasurers. So I wasn't scared. Yeah? I thought I was invulnerable. The Smith was my dad. I could fight. I was strong. Even when you . . . you told me . . . What did you tell me?"

His breathing steadied, and then he let out a long, sleep-filled sigh. I reached over and shook him roughly.

"What? What did you tell me?" he asked, his voice thick and deep.

"I told you not to fall asleep. I told you to tell me a story. Finn!"

He made a rumbly noise in his throat, a sleep-stretched sound, and then said, "Right. So you told me not to fall asleep, and I went on the Clarks' grass, and I picked the blue forget-me-nots. And then the grass wasn't grass anymore. It was chains, and we were caught. And the air wasn't air. It was water. I would've died. All of them were right. My mom was right. 'Don't go near the conjurers until you're ready, Finn. Don't go near the conjurers until you know the truth.' So she had to choose. Me or her."

"Your mom?" I asked when he went quiet. I was tugging at the knot as quickly as I could, pulling, yanking, prying, but the rigor mortis of it was centuries in the making.

"Hmm? Do I know the truth? Mari?"

"I don't know," I said, pulling harder. *Almost there. Almost there.* "Then what happened?"

"She chose me. There was only enough time . . . for me. I burst free from the illusion, gulped in fresh air. Dove down. But she was dead. She was already dead. She hadn't wanted me to pick the flowers. She said forget-me-nots were the saddest flower, because they meant someone had already forgotten. Forget-me-nots were the tears of the forgotten. I don't . . . I don't remember what my mom looked like. Mari. I don't remember her smile. Do you remember it? Did you ever see her smile?"

"I never met your mom. Finn?"

"Mmm tired, Mari. I'm going to . . . I'm just gonna close my eyes . . ."
There!

I yanked the knot free, and the illusion above the ceiling crumbled. The ceiling groaned, heaved, and then swung open. Dull green light flooded over the circular prison. Finn was slumped against the wall, his chin to his chest, eyelashes fluttering.

He was seconds away from falling asleep. While fresh air was flowing around us, there wasn't enough to clear out the Embalmer's Rest already flowing through his veins. He needed out of here, and he needed out fast.

"Finn." I shook him again. "Stay awake. A little longer. Stay awake."

He frowned and shook his head. "Don't wake me. I'm dreaming."

I grabbed the wall. It was made of cobblestone. An easy climb, even with heavy limbs, sleepy eyes, and the overwhelming desire to lie down and fall asleep. I grappled hand over hand and threw myself onto the dirt floor of the catacomb.

No wonder I hadn't noticed the trap door. The trigger had been buried by cobwebs and dirt, sandwiched between cobblestone and mortar. It probably hadn't been set off for at least a century. We'd been lucky enough to stumble into a trap left by the Clarks of yesteryear.

I dragged in a breath of dry catacomb air, free of the sickly taint of Embalmer's Rest, and said as quickly as I could, "Finn Alterra, come back."

The hot draw of him rushed over me. I'd braced myself, ready for the waterfall of need, but still, it rocked me as it poured through me. The cord between us snapped, yanked like a rebounding rubber band, and Finn landed in the dirt next to me.

He'd been leaning against the stone wall in the prison, and with the wall gone, he fell over me. The snap of the ring brought us together. I landed against the dirt with Finn pressed over me. His eyelashes fluttered, and he looked down at me with a sleepy expression.

Then his navy eyes lit with lightning, a summer-night heat storm rolling through him. The air rushed out of my lungs, and Finn smiled as he stretched over me.

"Mari," he said, his voice a soft rumble. "This a dream?" His hand brushed over my cheek; cupped my jaw. Then he quested his thumb over my lips and pressed closer. "I kiss you in my dreams?"

Was that a question?

Or was it a request?

I was still sleepy, still rocking with the fall-asleep dreaminess of the Embalmer's Rest. I wanted to rock against him and mimic the sweet, need-filled call between us.

Instead, I pressed my hands to his chest and shoved. "Not a dream."

"Hmm?" His mouth hung an inch from mine. His lips curled into that air-stealing, gut-kicking smile.

"Not a dream. Get up." I shoved again.

His hips shifted over mine, and I scowled at him. He felt too good. He felt too right. It made me so angry, how right he felt.

He blinked.

"You're angry in my dream?"

"This isn't a dream." I shoved again, but it was the wrong move, because that shifted us closer, and Finn's eyes lit with sparks. And then a flood filled me. It rushed at me from the space where his emotions lay. It was as if they'd been muted before. Hiding and hidden.

When he looked down at me with a sleepy, dreamy look, all I felt was . . . Let's face it, if want and desire had a scale, Finn's desire in that moment would've blown that scale up with an atom bomb. The width and height of it rocked me, and I vibrated with the aftershock.

"Finn?" I said, my voice quivering.

He smiled, questing his hand over my cheek. I peered at him, trying to match the supernova of desire exploding inside of him with his sleepy, placid, dream-filled gaze. It blasted through me and coated me in a liquid-gold aura.

"This isn't a dream," I repeated. "You need to get up."

He blinked again. Squinted through the pale green light. Closed one eye. Then another. "Not . . ." He cleared his throat. Looked down at where our bodies were connected. Noted our prone positions on the dirt floor of the musty-dusty catacomb. "You used the ring."

His voice was flat. Unemotional. But a wave of alarm washed through me—an echo of his emotion. Then, all that lust, all that love, snapped away and disappeared. It was like a thunderer: a brilliant flash, a thundering boom, and then nothing. There was just that wall of calm. With a hint of relief and gratitude.

"You saved us."

I nodded as he rolled off me. He tottered a bit when he sat up. Clapped his hand against a stone shelf and shook his head.

"Wow. Yeah. Okay. I'm good." He blinked over at me. "You good?"

I sat up, dusted myself off. Nodded. "I'm fine. Let's . . ." I kicked the dust-covered knob that had sprung the trap. The door closed, sealing the dreamy prison. "Let's go find the key."

We looked for hours. I was certain it would be in the catacombs. The hidey-holes, the peekaboo vaults, the rat nests and mouse-hole spaces, were favorites of the Clarks. Besides, they loved burying their treasure in earth's tomb.

We found other treasures. Objects of power I wouldn't touch and hastily backed away from. Old parchment that crumbled at the wind's touch. Wedding rings that bound for better or worse, waiting—I was sure —for Primus's bride. A list of the strengths and weaknesses of all the heirs in the games.

Finn scanned it, smiling when he saw it didn't list him but instead noted Darin's weakness in conjuring illusion, and his penchant to rush into action without forethought. Celia had one word next to her name: "brothers," with three question marks. Jacob's weakness was listed as chivalry to the weaker sex as penance for murdering his sister. I could almost hear the derision in the slant of the writing.

At four in the morning, Finn and I left the catacombs. But not before I set a gift in the room where I'd lost my eighth life. When Finn and I stepped onto the deserted street outside the mansion, I held out my hand with a gesture for him to wait.

Five.

Four.

Three.

He lifted an eyebrow in question.

Two.

One.

The street rumbled. It was the exact vibration of a subway train passing below. A tremor. A roar. A shaking. Except there were no subway tunnels on this old city block. None near enough to feel.

"Did you . . .?" Finn gave me a searching glance. Then he grinned in the soft, milky glow of the streetlight. "Mari. Did you just blow up the Clarks' little room of horrors?"

Should I deny it?

Finn's grin grew, and I had the feeling he wanted to laugh. An exuberant, happy laugh.

"If, by 'blow up,' you mean leave leggerock blood, gunpowder, and Furtig as a special present, then yes . . . yes, I did."

He laughed then. He laughed long and loud.

And I remembered what Finn had said earlier. That you could tell what sort of person someone was by the way they laughed. His laugh was joyful, warm. It felt like somersaulting down a grassy slope, bathed in sunlight, and then landing in a field of wildflowers, arms flung wide, chest bursting with happiness. It was a good laugh.

I smiled back at him. "I've been wanting to do that for a long time."

"Me too."

Thinking about it, I guess he had. Hadn't the Clarks killed the girl he loved? Hadn't they tortured him too?

"Glad I could help."

Although I was sorry we hadn't found the key.

Finn could maybe read minds, because he said, "Tomorrow. I mean, today, I'll see what I can find. I'll get the key for you, Mari."

I gave him a surprised look. "Why?"

He shrugged. "Because it's important to you."

The sad thing was, I realized he was becoming important to me too.

It was then I had a wild idea. I began to think not about winning the crown and saving myself. I thought instead about saving Finn Alterra.

67

When Finn and I arrived back at the Bard Mansion and he brushed his fingers across the doorman's temples again, I didn't bother to wonder what sort of illusion he was wiping away. There were too many possibilities to count.

At the door to the suite, there was a note pinned to the wood. It read, "So do I."

Finn looked at the note, then at me, and asked, "Know what that's about?"

Maybe he felt my splash of surprise. Maybe not.

"No idea."

The left-leaning slant of the spidery writing was the exact scripted penmanship that had recorded the heirs' strengths and weaknesses. Last? Primus? So they knew who'd killed Secondus, and they knew I'd left them the note.

Fun.

Following Jagger's orders inevitably led to sticky situations.

I slept until seven, long after the sun had risen and bathed the room in its bright golden glow. The wind tapped at the window, and a pigeon fluttered on the sill. A muted car horn blared across the city noise, and I stretched, achy from sleeping on the floor and falling into a pile of bones.

Darin already had coffee made when I stumbled bleary-eyed into the tiny kitchenette. He and Finn watched my progress—Finn with bemusement, Darin with a welcoming smile.

"Breakfast?" Darin asked, like I was the magical breakfast fairy. "Bacon? Eggs? Mmm, omelet."

Finn scoffed and shoved a mug of steaming coffee into my hands. "Morning."

He'd lied. He didn't need a minimum of four hours sleep. He'd had two max, and he was bright-eyed, wide-awake, and in a fantastic mood. What was he—superhuman?

"How about a bacon omelet?" Darin asked, but then he shook his head. "No. Never mind. It's better with ham." He smiled sweetly, his big-brotherness firmly in place. "I was thinking, Mari, what's a nine worth? Would the leggerock trade you for the lyre?"

I scowled and took another sip of the steaming brew. "No."

The lyre was an awesome object of power, but Jagger had plenty of powerful objects. Besides, I was a lockpick. He wouldn't trade me for anything.

You know how Finn had bargained that if he won the crown, he could have a nine of his choosing? I bet that was why Jagger wanted him dead before he could collect. Jagger wouldn't give me to anyone else. He'd promised me my freedom if I got him the crown, but . . . well. We'd just have to see, wouldn't we?

"Hmm." Darin opened the mini-fridge and pulled out a tray of eggs, nudging them across the counter toward me. "What about . . . a sword that can cut through granite like it's slicing butter? Would he trade for that?"

I glanced at Finn to see what he thought of his brother. I didn't think he was listening. Instead, he was staring into the mug of coffee he held in his hands, a deep look of concentration on his face. What did he see in the tar-like black surface? Maybe this was one of those times when he was tilting on that tightrope, skirting between the lure of solange and the here and now.

"He won't trade me for anything," I told Darin, grabbing a pan and flicking on the portable stove. "It doesn't work like that."

"Ah. Once a creature, always a creature?" Darin asked.

I yanked ham, cheddar, and green pepper from the mini-fridge. "We're almost out of food. Someone'll have to go to the store."

"Do you think," Darin asked, leaning against the counter, "when this is all over, the leggerock'll make trouble, you'll try to blow me up with that killer Omnibus, and I'll have to come after you, and I'll be all, 'Hey, Mari, before we do this, can you make me another omelet?' Is that how it's going to be?"

I cracked eggs in rapid succession. *Crack. Crack. Crack.* They slid into the oiled pan, and I whisked them with a little more violence than necessary. "Probably."

Darin nodded. "That's what I thought. It's too bad. I like you."

I sliced ham and pepper and tossed them into the eggs. "Aww. Thanks. I sort of like you too."

We waited, sipping black coffee, then I slid the omelet from the pan onto a plate. The steam puffed out from the perfectly cooked eggs.

"Do you like being a creature?" Darin asked, and while I wanted to ignore his question, he seemed to be concerned. For me.

Darin, after all, was a Smith. He conquered, but he also liberated.

"If you don't, just tell me. I'll do what I can to free you. Mari? Do you want me to free you?"

Did you know, no one had ever asked me that question? Not that I could remember. Not ever. And while, as a nine, I had free will, I didn't have the ability to ask to be free of Jagger. I couldn't ask anyone to harm him or kill him. And I couldn't ask anyone to free me from him. That was the nature of the leggerock's symbiosis.

So I smiled at Darin, while inside I was twisted up and kicking the walls of my prison, and said, "No, Darin. I don't want you to free me. I want to be a nine."

At my words—or maybe at my emotions—Finn jerked. The coffee in his mug sloshed over his fingers.

"Whoa. Okay?" Darin asked.

Finn dropped his mug to the counter, and without looking at either of us, he stalked from the half-kitchen.

"What . . .?" I watched as Finn hurried through the sitting room and slammed the suite's front door.

Darin stared at the closed door. A questioning silence hung between us.

"What just happened?" Darin finally asked.

"I'm not sure."

I thought maybe Finn had felt my emotions when I'd told Darin I liked being a nine. If he had, he would've known I was lying. But that couldn't have been it. Finn wasn't even paying attention to our conversation.

"Maybe he doesn't like omelets."

I nodded. "Should I go after him?"

"Probably. We probably both should."

Darin looked longingly at the steaming omelet. I handed him a fork.

"Bring it with you."

The pull of the ring led me through hallways, stairwells, the library, the ballroom—all the open rooms in the maze of the Bard Mansion. I trailed Darin without letting him know I could sense Finn's location like a plant turning toward the sun. But then, before we could find Finn, we found trouble.

68

The wind hummed a summer melody. It dashed under sheer cotton drapes and made a *thrum thrum* sound as it buzzed against loose window screens. It skipped down the hall, following the lazy gait of the trickster, and sent up puffs of acrid smoke that it'd kept from the fire at Hell Gate.

Every time the faint perfume of smoke rose, the trickster's nose wrinkled, and the wind whistled in delight. The wind could play tricks too. Who better to appreciate its tricks than this human?

It had left the boy eating breakfast. The boy liked eating crumpets. Even more, he loved watching the butter melt in the pockets and drizzling clover honey on top. It was a slow, boring process, even with the golden glint of honey dripping over the edge of the steaming crumpet. Not even that viscous, sticky slide or that puff of sweet steam could lure the wind to stay with the boy while he took a full morning to eat his breakfast, drink his breakfast tea, and read the pages of his latest paperback.

The wind didn't understand books. Was there a spirit in them? Did they conjure illusions in humans' minds? Was that why the boy loved them? Sometimes, the wind would shove the boy's paperbacks off his nightstand or flutter the pages so the boy lost his place. The boy would just laugh, though, or say, "Not now, Wind. This is a good part," and go back to reading.

That was why the wind abandoned him and went in search of fun. The trickster would lead it to fun.

But so far, all the trickster had done was try on a black tuxedo, tease his sister, and tell the musician not to worry so much. That no matter what, crown or not, they had each other. The musician had grunted and watched the trickster with an expression that reminded the wind of one of his haunting, melancholic melodies.

Then the trickster left his home's flower-filled courtyard and meandered the winding hallways. Aimless. He was aimless, like the wind on a warm June day, no purpose except to blow any which way.

Until . . . ah. Yes.

The trickster's gait caught, hitched, and then became smooth again. It was the solange-eyed one. The trickster hummed happily, and the wind perked up. A tense current snapped as the man saw the trickster. He adjusted his course, veering toward him.

"Alterra," the trickster said, blocking the solange-eyed one's path.

The wind skipped to the solange-eyed one and rode over the tense muscles of his forearms, up the thick line of his bicep, and onto the hard edge of his jaw. He smelled like the girl. Like they'd been wrapped around each other and had twined their scents together. Cranberries and allspice mixed with crushed violets and fresh spring air.

The wind feathered the black ends of the man's hair. It remembered when his mother had smoothed the messy ends out of his eyes. It remembered what she'd whispered to him, in the dark depths of the Night Den. "Hide, Finn. Hide. Don't let them see you until you know the truth. I'm keeping you hidden. I'm keeping you safe. You have to hide."

He'd disregarded his mom's warning at fifteen and was nearly murdered by his father as a result. But what were young humans except certain they knew better than their parents? It was a human thing to convince themselves they were wiser and better than the humans of the past. The wind, at least, was always and only itself. Never better. Never worse.

Had the solange-eyed one finally realized the truth?

He'd found it. Yes. But had he realized it?

The wind hadn't told him. It wouldn't. It had promised it wouldn't, and the wind had never broken a promise.

So instead of whispering the truth into the man's ear, the wind tickled the back of his neck and rustled his black hair.

The man scrubbed the back of his neck and then said, "Luvic."

The trickster grinned—bared his teeth?—at the solange-eyed one. He casually placed his hands in his pockets and slouched, as if to say, "You're so weak I don't even need to conjure to defeat you."

"Having fun?" the trickster drawled. "Pickled your brain yet, with all that solange? Almost hit bottom yet? Falling too fast?"

The wind bounced on the drumming of the solange-eyed one's pulse.

"How's your sister?" the man asked.

The trickster straightened. "Fine." His smile widened. "How's your girlfriend?"

The wind darted around the two men, riding the waves of tension. Oh, how it enjoyed this. This was better than crumpets. Better than tea.

"Fine," the solange-eyed man said.

The two men stared at each other. The wind whistled between them, waiting while they threw words at each other without saying anything at all.

Then the trickster straightened, took his hands from his pockets, and brushed past the solange-eyed one. As he passed, he murmured, "By the way, Cora says hi."

The solange-eyed one drew in a quick breath. Spun around. He watched the trickster's back with narrowed eyes.

The wind stayed with him, twirling around the tight line of his jaw. He was up to something. It was clear in the way he swayed and tilted, wending down the hall, circling, circling . . .

The wind circled too, whirling around and around the solange-eyed one. It was like the tops children played with, spinning in a circle until they finally wobbled, wobbled, and fell still.

The man fell still outside the cruel one's door.

The wind was dizzy, and so it didn't bother to ride the hard knock —*bang, bang*—but instead slipped beneath the crack under the door. It swung wide, and the wind pushed over the threshold into the parchment scented room.

"Paladin Smith," the cruel one said, his voice the pleased snap of a book page quickly turning. "To what do I owe the displeasure?"

The wind huffed, sneezing at the dust motes covering the records on the cruel one's desk. A spray of dust flew through the air like a storm of cottonwood pollen snowing in summer. The wind puffed again, blowing the dust free.

If it could read, what secrets would it find here?

The solange-eyed one stepped over the threshold and kicked the door shut. Somehow, he made it appear an accident, as if he'd stumbled over an invisible crack and fumbled until the door had closed behind him.

The cruel one sighed, and the wind rode over the sound. This was the sigh the cruel one gave when he was tired of playing in the stale depths of his catacomb, right before he cut free a body's animating spirit.

The solange-eyed one didn't notice. Instead, he swayed, wobbled—

"You're in the wrong suite. If the rules didn't forbid it, I'd kill you and rid the world—"

The solange-eyed man spun so quickly that the wind could only ride the whir of speed. The wind flew on the sharp razor of the man's thrust. It was faster than the shadow of a leaf flickering over the sun. The solange-eyed one pinned the cruel one to the floor.

The wind bounced on the hard thud and the harsh exhale of the cruel one's breath. He slammed. Bucked. Struggled. But the solange-eyed one held him, hands immobilized, unable to conjure.

Once in a while, his fingers connected, but the illusion dissolved in a wash of gold. It was the solange touch. It yanked out illusion before it rooted itself in reality. The cruel one hissed and flailed while the solange-eyed one held fast.

The wind rushed on the struggle. Laughed. The cruel one often pinned humans in the same way. He watched them like they were butterflies pinned to a corkboard, their frail wings spasming as he played his cruel games.

The solange-eyed one waited patiently, his hold unyielding, gaze vacant, waiting for the cruel one to stop struggling. His pulse was steady, gaze placid, as if he could wait eons.

Finally, the cruel one snarled, spit flying from his pale mouth. "Take note, Paladin Smith. You will die as soon as the closing ceremony is complete. Your lifespan is limited to days."

"I'm looking," the solange-eyed one said calmly, "for a key you stole from the Smiths."

The cruel one stiffened and then smiled like a weasel peering over the edge of a cuckoo's nest. "I'll leave you alive long enough to cut out your organs and snack on them. You'll smell your own liver sautéing with onions and garlic."

The wind didn't like the smell of onions or garlic. The smell reminded it of watering eyes and swampy, sulfuric tears. If it could eat, and if it were to eat liver, it would eat it with honey. Or maple syrup, which was nearly as good as honey. It would never eat onions and garlic. But no one asked the wind's opinion.

"Four inches long. On a golden chain. You stole it from a thief."

"Kidney pie," the cruel one said. "You'll watch me eat your kidneys in a pie. Then I'll wrap your intestines around your throat and cut off your air. So sorry. You'll die before your free fall ends."

"Where is the key, Primus?" the solange-eyed one asked, and the wind ruffled the ends of his hair.

"Why didn't Principal Smith kill you when you were born? Why aren't you in the records?"

"The key, please."

The wind hummed its approval. Just like the boy, this one knew how to be polite.

The cruel one made a phlegmy, hacking noise and then spat in the solange-eyed one's face. "After I kill you," the cruel one said, "I'm going to take your body. She'll be mine. I've decided I want her."

The wind rode over the hard thump of the solange-eyed one's pulse and then the rushing-river rage of his heartbeat. The solange-eyed one liked the thought as much as the wind did. Not at all.

He leaned close and whispered a few short words. His voice was a harsh, quiet rumble.

"—killed Secondus."

Ah. The boy. The solange-eyed one was speaking of the boy.

"He'll come for you too," the man promised. "He'll keep you trapped in the terror of all your victims' last moments for decades."

A chill fell over the cruel one's face. His dark eyes grew darker, and his face bleached to bone-chalk white.

"You lie."

"I have no reason to lie," the solange-eyed one said.

The cruel one's lips became a cold, deathly pink as he said, "This is a certainty?"

The solange-eyed one didn't answer. He only stared at the cruel one, his gaze unyielding.

"The Wards . . ." the cruel one said. "How I hate the Wards."

The wind pinched the cruel one, not liking the light that entered his eyes. It was fear, hatred, and the desire to extinguish and kill.

"Where is the key?" the solange-eyed one asked.

The cruel one smiled. A cold, calculating, "I'll enjoy eating your liver" smile.

The cruel one told the solange-eyed one the key's hiding spot. The wind laughed. The girl was right: the Clarks were the least creative humans on the planet. Their hiding places were less original than a squirrel stuffing acorns in the hollow of an oak tree.

"Thank you," the solange-eyed one said.

When he released the cruel one's hands and stood, wobbling slightly, the cruel one smiled. He rolled upright, yanked a dagger from inside his suit coat, and flung it at the solange-eyed one.

Mid-stumble, the solange-eyed one knocked the dagger aside— waved away a tomb of dirt, a wall of poison needles, a flood of hot oil— and then he struck the cruel one against the temple.

The cruel one stopped conjuring. He stood still. His eyes rolled back. His shoulders slumped. His eyelashes fluttered as the solange-eyed one pressed his pointer and his third fingers to the cruel one's temple.

Then the solange-eyed one dropped his hand and stepped back. He opened the wooden door. Stood in the entry.

The cruel one blinked. Scowled at the solange-eyed one. Rubbed his head. "Paladin Smith. To what do I owe the displeasure?"

The wind drifted over the threshold, dusting the wooden floors, pushing dust motes on the air.

The solange-eyed one swayed, tilted, wobbled, and gave the cruel one a befuddled smile. "What are you doing in the Smith suite?"

"This . . ." The cruel one scowled. "This is not the Smiths' suite. You are in the wrong place. Why didn't the Smith kill you when you were born? Fool. Get out. Solange-addled idiot."

"But . . ." The solange-eyed one blinked. "Are you *sure* this isn't the Smith suite?"

The cruel one shoved the solange-eyed one out of the suite and slammed the door. The wind laughed as it rode the current down the hall.

The solange-eyed one smiled. Then he made his way in circles and spins back to the girl.

69

I TOLD YOU TROUBLE FOUND ME AND DARIN, BUT "TROUBLE" HAS MANY different meanings. For some, it's fun and games. For others, it's a harbinger of doom. For the residents of Hell Gate, trouble is the bread and butter served at our communal table.

I'm not unaccustomed to trouble, obviously.

The third floor was deserted. Finn had been here—I sensed him—but he was above us now. On the fifth or sixth floor. Probably headed back to the suite.

So let's just say it startled me when Wolfgang stalked around the corner and snapped, "Where have you been?"

I can practically hear you arguing, "Mari, Wolfgang isn't trouble. I thought you meant real trouble, like a pack of jackaltooth chasing Griff down the hall while he donned his father's form, Last hurling a morningstar at Darin's head, Justice shattering a window and lobbing in a hellfire bomb."

Well, no. All of those things could've happened. Maybe they did. Not in this story, but in someone else's.

In this story, Wolfgang was trouble. Why? Have you forgotten? He's a principal. He's started more wars and military conflicts than any other man alive. The weight of a million deaths (more?) rests on his head. And if a million deaths is just a number that doesn't hit home, need I remind you, he gutted his own son? And more immediately, he proclaimed his intent to kill me and send me back to Jagger as soon as the games are done.

While he looked like a grizzled, harder version of Finn, I couldn't soften toward him. The silver-streaked black hair and closely trimmed beard, the domineering gaze, the sharp, military mind—perhaps this was what Finn would become if he lived a few more decades. If he was a conjurer too. Although I wasn't sure. There was a ruthlessness in Wolfgang that I hadn't seen in Finn.

I hadn't seen it in Darin either though. Unless you counted the few minutes where he'd attempted to kill me.

"Looking for Finn," Darin said, snapping upright, coming alert. "What is it?"

Wolfgang's upper lip curled, and his son stiffened. Looked around for trouble. The hallway was still deserted, not a conjurer, body, or cousin in sight.

I could feel Finn above us, probably on the sixth floor in our suite. He hadn't moved for a while now. We should've just waited for him to come back. I could've finished my cup of coffee. Maybe had a second cup with some cream and sugar. I would've made a cheese omelet and toast with strawberry jam. It would've been amazing. My stomach rumbled at the thought.

Wolfgang scowled at the empty plate and fork in Darin's hands, and Darin shoved them onto a side table.

"What happened in the fifty-first games?" Wolfgang asked, his gaze hard.

I thought through the records I'd read. *Fifty-first. Fifty-first. Fifty-first?* I came up blank.

But Darin's wrinkled brow smoothed out at the same time as his jaw hardened. "Ah. You think ..."

"It's a possibility."

"Then"—Darin glanced around the hallway—"we should ..."

"Yes."

Wolfgang held out his hand and conjured. The illusion snapped in front of me. I flinched. I couldn't help it. Even though I relaxed as soon as I saw the white envelope in Wolfgang's hands, he'd still caught my fear, and he was happy for it.

Darin frowned like I'd failed a test. Like he was wondering why I'd be afraid of his dad. I think, being Darin, he figured as long as the games lasted, we were all on the same team, and none of us would harm the other.

Ha.

Ha ha.

Funny.

"Deliver this to Luvic Bard. Immediately." Wolfgang flicked the envelope toward me, and I caught it.

Then he turned to his son and jerked his head down the hall. "Let's go."

They stalked away, two towering Smiths. Only Darin looked back. He shot me a smile, and I waved, realizing breakfast would have to wait.

$\sim$

I didn't have to find Luvic. He found me. That was probably a good thing, because I wasn't looking forward to knocking on the Bards' door considering the previous warm welcome I'd had from "I'll use your head as a prop" Celia.

I was only a few turns away from their suite, my stomach rumbling, when Luvic rounded the corner. He was whistling a tuneless melody— one that was vaguely familiar—and had his thumbs in his jeans pockets. He walked with a casual, Bard-like glide, like he was out for a lazy stroll in Central Park.

I hadn't seen Luvic since I'd left him in that cage in the Wards' forest home. It was hard not to remember the desperation on his face, the panic, and his hoarse plea. After the fact, I'd realized why the trembling of his hands and the whiteness of his knuckles on the bars had felt so familiar. It was a mirror of what I'd felt when the Clarks buried me, and what I feel when I lie in the coffin of my body, unable to move.

I recognized I'd found Luvic's greatest fear. And then I'd left him in its jaws.

I'll admit, I was a tad bit worried about how he'd react when he saw me. In centuries past, it hadn't been the Clarks who were known as the cruelest of the conjurers. It was the Bards. Although, that being said, they were also easily bored or distracted.

Luvic's whistle broke off with a surprised downward trill, and then he smiled. It was a delighted, warm, I'm-so-happy-to-see-you sort of smile—one you'd give a dear friend you hadn't seen in a long while when you were looking forward to dinner, good conversation, and a few drinks to catch up.

"Mari," he said in his smooth, lilting tenor. I thought about how Last had declared her dislike for all things Bard, especially Luvic and his good looks. He tilted his head, and his smile widened. "Morning."

Okay. Of all the responses, this wasn't one I expected. Anger? Yes. Revenge? Possibly. Threats? Definitely. But a smiling "good morning"? No.

I needed to clear the air.

"Look," I said, peering at him, looking for cracks in his smiling façade. "The other day, I had things to do, and you wouldn't leave me alone. I asked politely, and you didn't listen, and you really can't blame me . . ."

Luvic raised his eyebrows, so I finished.

"I'm . . . well . . . I'm glad you're okay. Glad the Wards didn't kill you."

I waited for anger, hostility, a veiled threat, but Luvic just smiled.

"No harm done."

A draft blew through the hallway, blowing my braided hair across my cheeks. I shoved it back and caught the way Luvic eyed the callback ring on my finger. It was a reminder that while I felt guilty for locking him inside his greatest fear, he wasn't a friend, and it had to be done.

The Bards were for the Bards and no one else.

This was the games, not a picnic.

"I think," Luvic said, brushing his black hair down when a strong draft rustled it, "you've always had a soft heart. I think it could get you into trouble. People with soft hearts don't last long, Mari. They get broken." He twisted his hand but didn't conjure.

Surprisingly, I didn't flinch. Not like I had with Wolfgang.

"I don't have a soft heart," I said, even though it was Rue's biggest complaint about me, and even Griff sometimes told me I had to look at the world more cynically.

"If someone realized that, they could use it against you," Luvic mused. "Gain your sympathy and then betray you. I'd . . . be careful."

I narrowed my eyes. The draft had an acrid scent, like smoke and ash. Luvic wrinkled his nose, sniffed, and then, for a moment, looked at me with an almost guilty expression.

Was he admitting he was trying to gain my sympathies to betray me?

Was that what he had to feel guilty about?

Or was I misreading his expression?

"Careful of you?" I asked.

He pushed his hair back, but it fell back into the same messy arrangement. "No. You can trust me. I told you, we're friends. I'm speaking in generalities. What's that?" He pointed to the white envelope in my hand.

I held it out. "It's from the Smith. For you."

"Ah." Luvic took the envelope, flicked it open, and read the white card. As he read, his lips twitched.

I stood on my tiptoes and tried to peek over the paper's edge, but I couldn't see the writing.

Luvic chuckled when he saw me trying to peek and then conjured a flame that swallowed the envelope and the note. The paper folded up like a fire moth, its wings consumed by flame. The note drifted in tiny ash flakes to the marble floor. A draft running over the tiles swept it away, and in seconds, there was no more envelope and no more note.

"What was it?" I asked, thinking Luvic would either tell me or not, but there was no harm in asking.

"The favor," Luvic said, his mouth still twitching with that almost-smile. "Don't you love it when a favor is called in and it's something you were already planning to do anyway? Then it's not really a favor, is it? Except . . . it is."

Hmm.

"I wouldn't know. What were you going to do?"

"Oh, nothing much. Are you going to the gala tonight?"

"I wasn't—"

"You'll save a dance for me."

"—invited."

"Yes, you are."

"I don't have a dress."

"Sure, you do."

"I'm not—"

"Going to argue. I'll see you there. Someone always dies—it's tradition. If you dance with me, you'll be all right. If Darin asks to dance, refuse. Celia tells me he breaks women's toes."

"Really, I'm not . . . Wait. Someone dies?"

"Sure. Don't worry about it. See you there?"

If someone was going to die, I had to be there. That someone wouldn't —couldn't—be Finn.

"I'll be there," I said.

"I know."

I turned to go, but Luvic placed a hand on my arm, stopping me. I looked back at him.

He gave me that same big, warm, happy smile. Then he said, "Lock me in a cage again, and I promise, you will regret it."

70

THE HUNDRED YEAR GALA BEGAN AT MIDNIGHT. THE MOON WAS A THIN slit in the sky, like a knife had punched a hole in a black sheet and only a sliver of light could shine through. The new moon would arrive soon, and with it, a new conjurer would bow beneath the crown of illusions.

If I had my way, Finn would win the crown for Darin, and then I'd lockpick the crown from under the conjurers' noses. I was still working out a way to avoid Finn's death either by my hand, Justice's hand, or another creature's while still gaining my freedom. *That* was the tricky part.

But three games in, with Finn in the running to win, I could practically feel the crown in my hands. We could actually win this. We could win.

What would that mean? Everything. Not just my freedom but humanity's freedom. Sure, the conjurers would still exist, spinning their deceptions and illusions, but without the power of the crown behind them, the conjurer's lies would be easier for people to unravel. At least, that was my hope.

Although, one thing I've realized after a lifetime of lockpicking is that most people don't want to be told they're surrounded by illusion.

Oftentimes, they despise you for it and turn on *you* rather than the one who created the illusion.

When I was young and first unraveling the knots of illusion, I would eagerly tell the other denizens of Hell Gate if they'd been fooled. Then I realized they hated me for it. Once in a while, someone would try to take my life as repayment.

When someone realizes they've fallen for a lie their entire life, they'd rather stay in the lie than accept an uncomfortable truth. A comfortable lie is preferable to an uncomfortable truth. So what do they do? They kill or silence the truth-teller.

However. I had hope. I thought, without the crown, the people of the world would stand a fighting chance against the conjurers' machinations. We'd all be free.

And yes, I knew Jagger wanted the crown, but there was nothing he could do with it. *Nothing.*

So all I had to do was keep Finn alive until the final game and help him win in any way I could. Keeping him alive was the reason I was at the gala.

I held Finn's arm as we swept into the ballroom, Darin and Wolfgang striding in front of us. Nothing could've prepared me for the sight that greeted me. Not the frenzied revelries at Hell Gate, not the opulent bacchanalia on the opening night of the games—not even my wildest imaginings could've matched the sight and the sounds laid out before us.

Finn swayed, let out a short huff, and then said in a laughing undertone, "We're swimming in it now, Mari."

I could only assume he meant we were swimming in illusion. The ballroom was so thick with it that it was as if we were in a fish tank full of water and the water was illusion. There were knots everywhere: butterfly loops, lark's heads, Prusik knots, bowlines. There were splices in the illusions: back splices, chain splices, eye splices, and pigtails. The room was swimming with cords and cords of illusions and all the chains, loops, and splices.

But if I ignored the knots and the splices, then, oh . . . oh, it was beautiful. It was a feast, and my eyes were starving. The ballroom glittered and sparkled. The walls were coated in gold dust, diamond dust, ruby, sapphire, and emerald dust. The gem dust was painted in scenes that rivaled Michelangelo's finest work.

The sky was a cherubic blue, the clouds a heavenly gold. There was the light of illusion extending from the heavens, spreading over a lush emerald earth. There were scenes of conjurers from the past: the greatest poets, philosophers, and musicians; the heroic and the villainous; the conquerors and the conquered. There were animals painted in gem-studded brilliance: peacocks with indigo and emerald feathers; starlings with onyx wings; leopards inlaid with ruby and jet; dolphins in seabed opal and pearl.

Beyond the gem-dust fresco, the ceilings were painted with constellations set in a light blue sky, while puffy clouds floated overhead. The clouds, I suspected, were made of one of the vapor drugs that caused a rush of lassitude, hedonism, and ecstasy. There was the taunting scent of lilies and champagne; jasmine and sugared frosting.

"The clouds are vapor-drugged," I murmured to Finn.

He eyed them and nodded.

Then we glided into the tumult. Because that was what it was. While dozens of conjurers had accepted the Bards' hospitality and were staying in the mansion during the games, there were still many, many more conjurers in the city awaiting the closing ceremony. It seemed they'd all been invited to the party. There were at least 300 conjurers in the ballroom. They were from every family, every nation, every corner of the earth . . .

Darin looked over his shoulder and grinned at us. It was a wild, laughing grin. He was unaccountably excited. Probably because he figured there was a high likelihood of chaos, and maybe Justice would swing by to play.

Back in the suite, he'd tested how well he could move in his tuxedo, swinging a conjured sword and then nodding with satisfaction.

Wolfgang looked dour in his tuxedo. As we neared the cacophony of the ballroom, he'd commanded, "Stay close. Stay alive."

I sort of missed Hell Gate's parties, where you only had to worry about Rou crying into the soup with poison tears or Jagger literally biting off someone's head.

The perfumed heat of the ballroom crashed over me and jumbled with the sound of hundreds of people laughing and shouting. There was music—Bard music. It petted your ears, stroked your skin, and made you want to do wild, uninhibited things. There were prism lights and gem-flashed rainbows dancing overhead.

Finn tucked me close and clasped our hands together. I sensed a wariness coming from him, but I wasn't sure what it was for.

It had begun when I walked out of the bedroom after putting on the dress I'd found laid out on the bed. When I'd asked Finn about it, he'd shrugged and said he'd picked it up for me and thought it should fit.

I'd reverently run my hands over the fabric. It was spiderweb-soft, moonglow-silver, and it flowed like a rippling stream of moonlight over a velvet night sky. The dress was silk, with two thin straps on the shoulders, an open back, and slits that rode high enough on my thighs that I could run, kick, spin, and climb. Or dance. I was sure it had been made with an eye for fluidity and grace.

I loved it. I'd never worn anything so beautiful. I'd never worn anything that stroked my skin with each breath; ran over me with soft silk kisses. I'd never worn anything that felt like a prelude to love.

When I'd looked in the mirror, I was surprised to see I didn't look like a blank canvas anymore—a rippling stream that gazes glided over. Instead, I looked like a beautiful, loved, desired woman.

I'd blinked at myself and then twisted my hair into a knot and pulled free a few tendrils.

And that was it. I'd put on the sparkling silver shoes that were tucked by the bed, and then I'd walked into the suite's main room. Darin had been swinging his sword. Finn was leaning against the wall, rolling a thimble of solange between his fingers.

I'd cleared my throat. Finn had looked toward me with his vacant solange smile. Then there was a splash of surprise, cold like a spring rain shower. It had hit me and then washed over me with bright, sunlit pleasure. Then, just as suddenly, there was wariness.

I'd frowned at Finn, and then Darin had vanished his sword and said, "Wow. Nice, Mari. Is that a stiletto in your hair?"

It was. It had a thin mother-of-pearl handle and a narrow blade.

I'd smiled at him, and he'd laughed, enjoying the bloodthirsty adornment. When I'd looked back at Finn, the surprise and the hint of pleasure were gone, leaving only wariness behind.

"All right?" I'd asked.

He'd nodded and then tipped back the thimble of solange, downing it in one swallow.

The wariness had stayed. Was still there.

Wolfgang and Darin strode into the thick of the gala. There wouldn't be any slinking around the edges like the Clarks or slow, careful progress like the Wards. No—the Smiths would always cut right to the middle, into the beast's belly.

There were rivers of champagne again, and golden bubbles of it flew through the air. Some people caught the champagne bubbles in their mouths and laughed as they burst on their tongues. I just fanned them away, imagining all the poisons that would fit in those floating balls.

There were exotic foods, conjured and real, served on golden platters carried by the illusions of gold-dusted historical figures—Julius Caesar, Shakespeare, Pliny the Elder—tied with knots set to unwind in a few hours' time. By the river, a gold unicorn lay in a bed of spun sugar, and when it neighed, it made the sound of a harp.

If this were Hell Gate, the unicorn would be snacking on someone's arm, but since this was a Bard creation, it was nibbling on pink sugar.

Across the room—beyond the unicorn, past the golden trays full of dormice stuffed with dates and olives and tiny chocolate books where each page was a different flavor that dissolved on your tongue—past all that, I spied Last, Primus, and the Clark.

Primus and the Clark watched the revelry with sneering contempt, but Last had a small, delighted smile on her face. When she saw me, she lifted her hand and curled her pinkie in a wave.

"Hi," she mouthed. She was in a black lace sheath that made it look like an inkpot had tipped over and spilled spidery ink lines over the pale, cracked parchment of her skin. When I didn't wave or mouth "hi" back, her smile grew.

I turned away, and soon, the mass of conjurers separated us so that the Clarks weren't visible anymore. We'd almost made it to the center.

Finn tilted and swayed more than usual. I think the last thimble of solange had been his fourth—fifth?—of the day, which was . . . a lot.

It made me wonder, even if I could save him from Jagger's knife, could I save him from solange? No one had ever survived free fall.

He leaned close and murmured, "What is it?"

I shook my head.

"You're tense. Do you see something?"

Oh. While I remembered I could feel his wariness, I'd forgotten he could feel my tension too.

My gaze slid over the Ward and then stopped on Jacob. He was twenty feet from us, separated by a raised dais in the center of the room. He wasn't looking my way. Instead, he was focused on something across the ballroom. I followed his line of sight, and—ah, it was Celia.

He watched her . . . well, he watched her like I would sometimes watch the ghost train. Like I was the only one who could see it, and I was sorry that it would soon disappear. And, well, you can't ride or touch or interact with a ghost train, can you? You can only watch it pass by.

I turned back to Finn. "Has anyone ever lived through free fall?"

He tilted, swayed, and I steadied him.

"What? Lived through—" He shook his head.

"Survived free fall."

His wariness settled under a heavy blanket of determination. That emotion was familiar.

"No. Not that I know of."

Well.

"Just because you don't know of it doesn't mean it hasn't happened," I said.

He studied my expression as if that would tell him more than what he felt from me.

Ahead of us, Wolfgang and Darin stopped at the edge of the dais.

"You're here to help win the games, not to save me from free fall."

Finn and I paused next to Darin. There were other Smiths here tonight. A lot of them. They were calling greetings to Wolfgang.

"I know," I said. "It's just . . . I want to help you."

He smiled, but I didn't feel happiness from him. I only felt wariness, determination, and then a wall of calm. His eyes glittered with starry skies and nebula bursts, and suddenly, I wished I could've known him before he'd walked down that solange road. Maybe even before he'd met Cora, and before he'd turned fifteen and decided to introduce himself to his father.

Maybe if I had, I could've stopped him from traveling this path.

I felt so wistful for a past that didn't exist it nearly overwhelmed me.

"Mari?" Finn began, looking down at me with a wrinkle between his eyebrows.

I nodded.

"Tomorrow, after the game. During the closing ceremony. Trust me. Okay?"

He'd asked this before, and I'd said no.

Automatically, I responded, "You know I don't trust anyone."

"I know. But . . . trust me, Mari. Trust me."

He sighed at the easing inside of me. I could feel the stream of him carving away at the hard rock inside that kept me safe. I could feel the trust growing. Unfurling.

What had Luvic said? I had a soft heart. Someone could use that. Play to my sympathies and then betray me.

"Why do you want my trust? Are you going to betray me?" I waited to feel a flicker of emotion from him. Instead, there was only the wall of calm—nothing else. Not surprise, not outrage, not denial. Just calm.

"No," he said.

Too calmly. Too easily.

A seed of suspicion sprouted in me, peeking its head up. I cut it down. Luvic was a menace for planting this thought. Finn was . . . Finn. He was good.

"Don't worry," I murmured. "I already promised to talk to you before I killed you, remember?"

His eyes lit with amusement. "I remember."

Then the bright, gem-studded light of the ballroom dimmed, the music stopped, and there was a clap of thunder. Finn tugged me under his arm.

The conjurers around us shifted with anticipation. The Smith looked like he was contemplating conjuring a sword.

Then the Bard mounted the steps of the dais, held up his arms in a showman gesture, and said in an amplified voice, "Welcome to the Hundred Year Gala. We've prepared a little entertainment. Enjoy the show."

At that, the ballroom pitched into darkness.

71

THE DARKNESS WAS A VELVET CURTAIN THAT OPENED WITH A LOW, HOLLOW note that pierced the ballroom. Mist curled in long, blue-gray tendrils across the room, and stars winked in and out of existence. Around me, conjurers gasped in delight, and the Smith relaxed his "I'm going to kill something" stance.

The single note deepened, became richer, and joined with another, then a third. They formed a triad, a chord so beautiful I wanted to stay wrapped in the noise forever. It echoed inside of me and mirrored the beat of my heart. Someone started weeping at the beauty of it.

The Bards had a family legend that when the universe was thought into existence, the thought took the form of three musical notes. They say that if you listen closely, you can still hear the notes' harmonious vibration. It's in the rustling of leaves, the babbling of streams; in the cry of a newborn as it enters the world.

As the triad of notes reverberated through us, binding us in their beauty, I swayed toward Finn, wondering if this was what he felt under solange's bright glow.

Finn's grip on me tightened, and as it did, the pull of the notes faded, the beautiful illusion of them now a haunting echo of the universe's birth.

Then, overhead, the illusion of a crackling, brilliant, neon supernova formed, collapsed, and exploded. Gemstone dust and gold dust rained over us, coating us all in glitter.

Then the show began.

I'd never really watched Celia's movies. I didn't seek out Ragnor's music. I'd never seen Luvic on Broadway. I understood their Bard appeal—I'd just never been interested. They were Bards after all.

But, oh, was this what I'd been missing, or was this reserved for conjurers alone?

The music began. A lonely, tentative, searching song. It was the sound of a single star shining in the darkness, and the darkness not knowing or recognizing what the star was. With the music, Celia floated from the bright light, drifting on illusion, spinning in a brilliant, glowing wave.

She was the birth of the universe. She was life. The Bards were recreating the story of our world.

Celia was clothed in a dress that was the primordial ocean. It was yards of frothing blue tulle; a sea of turquoise, cerulean, and cream. Her bodice had been painted on. Pasted onto the sea-blue paint were thousands of sapphires in every shade of blue, from morning sky to midnight-dark. Diamonds peeked out from between the sapphires. A thick band of pearls hung around her neck and were draped in a circle around her coiled hair. She was a siren. A sea goddess.

She landed on the dais and began to dance. The music swelled—a crashing, a dawning—and then Ragnor rose from the darkness, clashing with his sister. He was draped in gold. He was the earth to Celia's sea. They spun and swirled, and then Luvic flew above them, the blue, blue sky.

They were the triad. The water, the land, the sky. With them, the universe was born.

The music changed then. It grew faster, more urgent, and the illusion of animals, creatures, and man flickered to life around them. The images were like shadows cast on a cave wall from the light of a blazing fire. They were projected over the dancers and became one with them.

With the birth of man, the Bards began to sing. Celia with her siren voice, Ragnor with his haunting tenor, Luvic with the purity of a melancholy angel mourning the loss of man's place in Eden.

I'd been to a Broadway show once. Griff had bought tickets, back when he'd wanted to try out the things normal people did. He, Justice, and I went.

We sat high, high up, in tiny, uncomfortable seats, our knees pressed to the backs of the seats in front of us. We were so far away from the stage we couldn't see the expressions on the actor's faces. Justice ate a box of nonpareils and then fell asleep, but Griff and I watched the actors flying on invisible wires, the dancing, the singing, the costume changes, and the pyrotechnics, with wide-eyed awe.

When Jagger found out we'd gone, he'd forbidden anymore Broadway field trips. After all, the theater was the playground of the Bards. But Griff had talked about that show for years. He loved to recount the stunts, the flight, the color, and the sound. Yet that show was a child's production compared to this.

The Bards had moved on to the first conjurers. The mythos that surrounded them. The first love. The birth of envy. The first murder. The birth of hate. The first wars. Then, with mounting speed, crashing sound, and violent upheaval, the three Bards finished the war of the conjurers. An illusion of water rushed over the ballroom. The wave crashed through the crowd.

Some screamed. Some ducked.

The waves rushed over me with the cold chill of a winter wind.

Then the waves were gone, and Celia, Ragnor, and Luvic stood on the dais with their father. Four conjurers for the four families. The crown of illusions floated between them.

Not the actual crown. If it had been, I probably would've considered nabbing it right then and there. Even with 300 conjurers surrounding me.

The crown lifted into the air and spun, spun, spun, and then it exploded in a brilliant bright white light. The music crescendoed, and the lights flashed.

We were bathed in the glow of illusion.

I blinked into the brightness. The Bards all gripped hands and then bowed as if they were on stage and expected hundreds of red roses to rain down on them.

The conjurers shouted, cheering, stomping their feet, and clapping. It was thunderous. The Bards rose as one and bowed again.

And then, with a cue from the Bard, the music began, the clapping stopped, and everyone decided it was time to dance.

The party snapped into motion, and everyone threw themselves toward enjoyment, as if it were a cliff and they were happy to fly off the edge.

"Well . . ." I glanced at Finn, then at Darin and Wolfgang, wondering, *What now?*

Luvic jumped off the dais and strode toward us. As he did, the shifting sky blue of his outfit darkened until he was wearing a plain black tuxedo. He wound past drinking Bards and back-slapping Smiths and then smiled widely as Darin stepped in his way.

"Bard," Darin said, baring his teeth. "Nice dance."

I peeked over Darin's shoulder. Luvic's expression was full of laughter.

"Did you think so? I practiced lots and lots."

I snorted. I couldn't help it. Luvic grinned, and Darin sent me a look that told me he thought I was a traitor for finding a Bard funny.

"Practice doesn't help if you're doing it wrong," Finn said philosophically. "Then you're just practicing the wrong thing, over and over. Haven't you heard? Practice makes worse."

Luvic looked at Finn, noted how I was tucked under his arm, and smiled. "You know, I think I've heard something like that. Mari. Let's dance."

His smile had a cold steel sort of edge. It made the hairs on the back of my neck stand on end.

"She doesn't dance with Bards," Darin said, going all big-brother protective. Apparently, he'd sensed the steel in Luvic's smile too.

"Ah. But she does." Luvic winked at me. It was barely-there, but it was a wink.

I ducked out from under Finn's arm and pushed past Darin.

"It's fine," I told him when he started to protest.

Luvic smiled at Darin, and then at Finn. It was his mischievous, sly grin. He took my hand and kissed it. Then he looked over my shoulder and said to Finn, "You'll dance with her next."

It wasn't a question. It was more an order. Finn just tilted his head and peered at Luvic through one closed eye and then the other. I didn't feel annoyance from him. I didn't sense anger or frustration. Not like I was sure I would've felt from Darin, considering the tightness of his shoulders. Instead, there was just that calm, with a lingering hint of wariness.

Before I could say anything, Luvic grabbed my hand and spun me toward the dance floor. We whirled onto the floor, joining the dancing conjurers. I'd never danced, but I had fought in hand-to-hand combat for my whole life, and dancing was a lot like fighting. Luvic thrust. I parried. He jabbed. I ducked. He spun. I whirled. It was heart-pounding, foot-stomping gliding and weaving.

Luvic grinned. "Looking forward to tomorrow?" He dipped me, and I arched my back, tilting my head to the ceiling.

Around us, dozens of conjurer couples spun in multicolored, gem-studded gowns. It was like we were dancing in a windstorm of flower petals. I was the only blade-colored petal amongst all the purples, pinks, blues, and reds.

"I'm looking forward to winning," I said when he pulled me back up.

We spun again. Luvic yanked me close. "So sure Alterra will take the game?"

No. "Yes."

Luvic flung me out in another spin and then snapped me back to him. He leaned close, pressed his cheek to mine, and whispered into the fall of my hair, "Do you remember what I showed you?"

I nodded so subtly I wasn't sure he caught it. But then he pressed me tight and said, "I'm counting on you, Mari. Don't let me down."

I frowned, but when I stiffened and tried to pull away, Luvic tightened his hold.

"Careful," he said, steering me across the dance floor. "It's just about . . . right . . . now."

There was a scream. I looked over my shoulder. One of the crystal chandeliers fell from the ceiling, landing precisely where we'd been dancing. It had to weigh at least a ton. A woman in a pea-green dress threw her hands over her head, attempting to conjure. The chandelier crushed her.

"Oh." Luvic made a surprised grunt. "Shame. I'm always telling my father those old chandeliers could fall and hurt someone. Now look what's happened."

The conjurers had stopped dancing. Everyone stood quietly as the Bard strode to the broken crystal, the twisted brass, and the woman buried beneath the chandelier.

He twisted his hand and lifted the brass chandelier, sending it from the room. The woman was . . . I won't describe it. You can imagine it. In fact, you saw it, so you don't have to imagine it. You know how messy it was.

"Oh dear," the Bard said mournfully. "Look what happened. What a terrible accident. What a sad, sad event. What tragedy. The only thing to do is . . . honor death by living life to the fullest." His somber expression lifted, and he smiled, displaying white teeth and bountiful charm. "Let's enjoy the evening. Let's dance!"

The Bard twisted his hand, and the woman—dead—was ferried from the ballroom. The blood, the shattered glass, all of it was swept away in seconds.

"What . . . the . . .?" I stared as everyone went back to dancing and drinking with a renewed frenzy. The jasmine and lily scented mist tendrils expanded and wound their way through the crowd, pumping sunshine and laughter.

"Was she a Bard?" I asked.

Luvic lifted a shoulder. "Not anymore."

"What did she do?"

"Stood under a chandelier."

"No. What did she do for you to drop it on her?"

"I didn't—"

Fine. He didn't. He hadn't conjured while we were dancing. But he knew who had. He knew it was going to happen.

"What did she do?" I pushed.

The edge of Luvic's lips lifted into a false smile. "Trusted the wrong person."

He stood back from me and bowed. I curtsied. That's what you do, isn't it?

Then I went to find Finn.

I walked past Jacob and Celia. They were dancing, but it wasn't a dance like mine and Luvic's, or anyone else's either. Instead, they stood close and swayed, feet barely moving. They were staring into each other's eyes, tense and stiff-backed, as if one wrong move would send either of them into a killing frenzy.

They were speaking, but I couldn't read lips, so I had no idea what confidences they were sharing. By their body language, I'd say it was going like this:

"I dream about killing you."

"Oh yeah? I dream about locking your mind in a pit of despair that you'll never escape from."

"That's neat. I dream about dipping you in melted gold and then sticking you on my shelf and pretending you're an Oscar."

"Wow. I'd love that. But first, I'd like to make a labyrinth where you relive all the gruesome things you've ever done. For eternity."

"Fun. You're a great dancer."

"Thanks. I like your dress."

Well, that was what I imagined they were saying. I'm not saying I was accurate.

I grabbed one of the tiny chocolate books off a silver tray and peeled out the first page. I popped it into my mouth. The sugar paper melted on my tongue. It was passionfruit. Sweet and tart. I smiled and tore out the next page. Raspberry. Then orange liqueur. Salted caramel. Earl Grey tea. This was the best book ever.

"Enjoying yourself?"

I stopped and swallowed the sugar page flavored like lemon meringue pie.

Last winced at the nearly devoured chocolate book melting in my hand. "You do love chocolate," she said, as if we were bosom friends and she knew all my secrets.

"Yup. Having a great time," I said, then I nodded toward Finn. He was only the length of two buffet tables away. "Got to get back to the Smiths."

"I liked your note," she said.

So it looked like it was Last who'd left the reply on the door for me. She knew who killed Secondus?

"I liked your flashy bomb even better. Caught Primus right in the face. He's covered the burn up, but it's gruesome." She shuddered, but it was a gleeful sort of shudder, like one you'd give when someone brushed your hair aside and kissed you on the nape of the neck. "This is why I like you. We're a lot alike. Someday, I'm going to take you back from Luvic."

I decided to ignore the last bit and asked, "You know who killed . . . ?"

She nodded, a happy twist to her mouth. "But I didn't tell anyone. That way, if he kills Primus too . . . oops."

He. So it was a man. But who? And why? And did it matter? It wouldn't hurt to ask.

"Why would he kill Pr—?"

"How should I know? I find answers, not reasons. I wish you'd come visit." Under the brilliant gemstone glitter, Last looked more sallow and grim than usual. "I've waited. And waited. Is it Luvic? Do you love him? I saw you dancing. Is that why you haven't come again?"

"Umm." Was she serious? The last time I visited, she buried me alive.

"Didn't you like being my friend?"

"No."

Well. That was a lie. When I was her friend, I liked it very much.

She knew that. She smiled her murderous crow smile. "You should come by our suite. Before the games are over."

"You know, I'll have to pass. The last time I came by, it didn't work out so well for me."

Last frowned, her brow knitting together. "Because of Primus? But after that, we watched a movie. And I gave you chocolate. You like chocolate." She looked pointedly at the melting chocolate book.

But . . . wait.

What?

"You don't seem to appreciate everything I've done for you. Mari?"

Hold on.

This didn't make sense. Last was acting like she hadn't caught me in their suite and buried me alive. She was acting like the past hadn't happened. She was pretending the last time I stopped by was when we'd watched that comedy together and I'd carved up my leg under Primus's cruel direction.

"What about . . .?" I paused, thought about what I'd say, and then asked, "What about when I came by and you buried me alive?"

Last laughed. It burst from her like a startled bird taking flight after a gunshot. "Oh. I wish. Wouldn't that have been fun? Is that what you like? Should we do that?"

A lump lodged in my throat. I spoke around it. "The last time I visited, we watched a movie?"

"You aren't as sharp as I thought. Maybe I don't want you."

I nodded. There was something strange going on. "Right. You don't. Thanks . . ."

I backed away. Dropped the mostly eaten chocolate book on a silver tray held aloft by Marie Antoinette.

Either Last was lying or she didn't remember. I was leaning toward her not remembering. People like her didn't miss a chance to reminisce over a cruelty. That meant . . . What did that mean? Finn had rescued me. He'd told me there was no trouble bringing me out. Was that because . . . he could remove memories? Could he do that?

Conjurers could plant memories. I was well aware of that power.

But could nulls—could Finn—have a secondary trait that removed memories?

Once that thought occurred, I had another.

If Finn had this trait, had he used it on me?

The raucous din of the gala swelled. I backed up another step and then hit a hard body. I startled and turned. Finn gripped my arms to steady me.

"All right?" he asked, smiling.

I swallowed. "Yeah. Good." My heart sped, the rapid thump rising in my throat, my pulse skittering. *Calm down, Mari. Calm down. It's no big deal. So he might be able to remove memories. So what?*

Concern pulsed through the ring, and his smile turned into a frown.

"Did Luvic . . . ?"

"No." I shook my head. "No. I ran into Last."

"Ah." His kaleidoscope eyes darkened.

"It's funny," I began, tiptoeing into the question. "She didn't seem to remember the last time I was there. When she buried me in illusion. Isn't that strange?"

I cleared my mind and focused on the ring-size hole in me that held Finn's emotions. There. A bright flash of wariness quickly hidden behind a wall of calm. Then a touch of surprise. False. It was *false* surprise. It lit on his features a millisecond after the quickly hidden wariness.

I kept my breathing even, my emotions steady.

What was he playing at?

What was this?

"That is strange," he said finally, his expression thoughtful. "She didn't threaten you?"

"No."

He looked over my shoulder. Frowned—maybe at Last, maybe at Luvic. Should I ask him? Should I demand he tell me what was going on?

But then what? He could admit everything and then wipe my memory. I'd forget everything.

Perhaps I'd already done that. Confronted him. Lost my memory of the confrontation. Maybe there were entire swathes of time since I'd met him that were missing. I searched my memories, looking for holes, blank spaces. I couldn't find anything. I was poking at my memory like it was a block of cheese, expecting to find lacy, hole-filled Swiss.

Nothing. There was nothing.

I didn't sense any loss of time or missed memory. Nothing.

Finn's brow wrinkled. He stared at me through solange-filled eyes as if he too were seeking the truth. Seeking what he couldn't see.

Did he suspect that I knew?

Maybe he felt about this trait the same way I felt about lockpicking. You had to keep it hidden. A talent like that could get you killed. Except . . . had he used it against me?

And if so, why?

"I'd like . . ." he said, giving me a smile that was tinged with wariness. "Would you like to dance?"

I sensed there was more there. So many unspoken things. Then again, maybe he really did just want to dance.

I nodded. Held out my hands. "All right."

His smile was sunset-sad, his gaze curtained, as we swept across the dance floor. He didn't tilt, sway, or wobble. Instead, he danced like he was part of the music. While Luvic's dance had been a fight, Finn danced as if each step, each spin, each touch was the prelude—or perhaps the epilogue—to love.

His hands glided over my bare back, the callouses dragging across my skin. His thighs pressed to mine, then away. His stubbled cheek brushed mine for a kissing moment and then pushed back. We whirled through the frenzy, and Finn kept me balanced on the tightrope with him.

"I know where the key is," he said once he'd pulled me close.

I felt the boom of his heart against my chest. My hands clutched his shoulders, and the heat of him pressed into me.

"You . . . you found it?"

He smiled. It was no longer tinged with end-of-day sadness. "Should we go get it while everyone's distracted?"

He'd done it. He'd found the key.

"Yes. Yes, we should."

He spun me to the edge of the ballroom, and then we glided out of the glitter and the raucous noise into the cool marble hall. He put his arm over me, and when we passed a couple (Smiths?), one of whom offered Finn a job after the games as a mercenary, we feigned inebriation and gave a laughing wave. When another couple (Bards?) cast us a curious glance, Finn buried his face in my neck and nibbled at my pulse. His lips sent a tingling heat over my skin, and my cheeks flushed. The couples tittered, and we rounded the corner.

When we reached the grand stairs at the entry, most of the noise had faded, and the room was deserted except for the jackaltooth doorman and the legion of marble statues. Finn mounted the stairs, grasping my hand. At the top, he turned down the hall to the elevator. Pressed the button.

While the lights flashed, I had a thought. "I forgot something. Stay here. I'll be right back."

Before he could respond, I raced down the hall, then down the stairs.

The doorman stiffened and tugged the sleeves of his suit coat. "May I help you?"

I lowered my voice to a whisper and asked, "Last night, around four in the morning, did you open the door for me?"

The doorman scowled, his mottled gray skin darkening.

"Or at midnight yesterday. Did you open the door for me?"

"I did not."

I nodded.

"You didn't see me last night?"

"I did not."

Okay. That settled it. Finn could remove memories. It must happen when he brushed his second and third fingers across people's temples.

I remembered Twelve, the Clark's body, and how he'd denied ever speaking to Finn. Even though I'd *seen* them. Had Finn been removing memories for the entirety of the games?

The question was, did it matter, and had he done it to me?

I raced back up the stairs to where Finn was waiting.

"Everything okay?" he asked.

"Yeah. Everything's fine."

He glanced at me out of the corner of his eye. I wasn't certain he believed me. He could read me better than I could him.

The elevator pinged, and then the doors slid open. I shivered. I didn't like elevators. Not at all. They were enclosed spaces without escape. Death hatches.

"Actually, do you mind if we take the stairs?"

"You don't like elevators," Finn said, and it wasn't a question.

He led me down the hall, to the stairwell, and as we climbed, off to find the key, I came to a decision. It didn't matter if Finn could remove memories. It didn't even matter if he'd removed some of mine. What mattered was winning the crown. Keeping him alive to the end of the games. Gaining my freedom. Then . . . then we'd see.

If he hadn't told me his trait, then there was a reason. The thought sent an itch up and down the back of my neck, but, coming from Hell Gate, I knew people had all sorts of reasons for hiding things. The most likely reason was that he wanted the crown, his solange, and his almost-wife. I was a complication at best and his killer at worst.

And I wanted . . .

The thing was, I wanted to save him. Even with this. I wanted to keep him alive.

But most of all, I wanted to trust him.

So that was what I'd do.

72
___

THE WIND BLOWS WHERE IT BLOWS, AND NO ONE KNOWS WHERE IT GOES. But one can be certain that if there are secrets whispered and confessions forced, the wind will be close.

It filtered through the billowing lily and jasmine scented mists that made humans giggle and dance with unconcealed relish. It slid over the taint of blood and broken light, rubbing over the cold marble. It bounced off the reflection of silver platters and vibrant gemstones.

There were so many scents—mist, chocolate, champagne, meat and vegetables, fruit and wine. There were so many sights—billowing clouds of dresses, tightly gloved suits, fluttery peacock feathers, and glittering gems. There was so much noise—sawing and zigzagging music, forced laughter, bellowing voices, titters and shouts and whispers. The wind liked the whispers the best. But it had to sift through all the sounds to find them, like a child at the beach sifting coarse sand, searching for that tiny pink shell.

This was the kind of night the wind liked best, where there were so many secrets aired and ventilated that it became dizzy with the expulsion of them.

The wind had passed the girl when it had slipped under the front door, leaving the nighttime city heat for the splash of cool marble. It had tickled the girl's ankles and ruffled the quicksilver waterfall of her silk dress when she'd asked the doorman whether or not he'd opened the door for her last night.

Why was she asking? Hadn't humans learned that there were some questions they didn't truly want answered?

The wind nudged her, poked the throat-rattling doorman, and then left them to float down the hallway toward the lure of hundreds of voices speaking at once.

Imagine. Imagine all the things the wind could hear on a night like tonight.

"Take note, sister," the cruel one said. "Tomorrow, I will rule them all."

The wind huffed a laugh and splashed champagne over the rim of the flute so that it spilled on the cruel one's fingers. At the man's curse, the wind kept drifting, searching.

There was the boy. The wind knew the look. He'd rather be in his comfy chair, his nose in a book. He had a distant expression, not paying attention to the wild revelry around him. Leave it to the boy to drift off into the library of his mind when there was the scent of fresh blood on the floor and secrets to be aired. The wind rushed past, tugging on the boy's bow tie and mussing his hair.

"Hey." The boy smothered a smile. "Watch it."

The nudge had served its purpose. The boy was yanked out of his head and was back in the ballroom, his gaze sharp and focused. He'd remembered where he was and what he was there for.

The wind moved on before the boy thought to send him after the girl or the trickster, or off into the heat of the city to stalk the solemn one. It sifted through the voices, caught ahold of whispers, carried single words on its sweeping tendrils. Then it was caught up in the frothy spin of the citrus and pearl dust scented one's dress. It didn't mind. Dancing on her dress was like spinning in a funnel cloud over the turquoise Caribbean Sea. It swirled up and glided over the mellow ocean of her voice.

"—have to kill Delilah?"

The trickster held his sister loosely, dancing with an easy glide. "Anyone who sells your secret dies."

"Yes, but . . . we played together as kids. Do you remember the doll house with—?"

"Lia."

"I know. It's only, I wonder if it wouldn't be so bad if everyone knew—"

"A weakness in our world is like blood in the water. You know this. If everyone knew, Ragnor and I would be on the top of every hit list in the world. You'd be . . . We destroy the weak, Lia. That's what conjurers do."

The wind glided over the trickster's smile, still held in place as if he and his sister were speaking of easy things, like days at the beach and champagne brunches.

That morning, the wind had found the trickster alone in his bedroom staring at the barrel of a gun, his eyes bleak, pulse thudding, one hard beat to the next. The wind had glossed along the gun's black surface, testing the trigger, bouncing on the barrel. Tapping out a little percussion. Then the trickster's jaw had tensed, and his eyes had hardened. He'd loaded the gun. The bullets had an odd taste. The wind didn't like them. So, once the trickster had hid the gun away, the wind left him to his mourning.

The gun was a secret—one the trickster wouldn't give up until he pulled the trigger. Some people gave up secrets when they were running out of breath, their life counted in exhales. They used their final breath to free the secrets inside of them. Not the trickster. The wind knew him, and it knew that when he died, he would use his last breath to laugh or cry or laugh while crying.

So the wind twirled on the citrus and pearl dust scented woman's dress, tapped the trickster's sleeve, and then flew off, aiming toward the edge of the ballroom. There was a familiar, beloved face. A worn, weary smile. The wind rushed through a cloud of mist, jumped on the bubbles of champagne, and whooshed down a hall, rushing into a closeted room just as the door closed.

"Are you here?" the man asked, his voice a melodious, comforting sound.

No one answered.

The wind hummed.

"Good. I need to speak with you about tomorrow."

The small room was dark, the closeted space empty and dust-covered. A tiny sliver of light edged from under the door, and the muffled noise of the party swept through. The wind shifted over the dust and swept it from the cedar scented paneling.

There was a long sigh and the heavy sound of breathing. The rustle of tuxedo fabric.

"If I fail," the man whispered, so quiet the wind could barely hear the words, "to kill him, will you help me?"

The wind moaned. The man had never failed at anything. Not in his entire life.

"And when he dies, will you follow and tell him I loved him? Tell him nothing has ever reached the depth of love I have for him. But if it goes wrong, and I'm the one who dies? You have to send him after me."

The wind shuddered. Could it follow? Would it? The wind would do anything for the man, but would it do this? There was the shifting of feet. A long exhale.

"Do you remember when Lu first told us what was going to happen? Well, we'll see. We'll see, won't we? Remember your promise."

The door swept open, scattering dust motes and spearing the wood-paneled closet with light. The man left under a hazy cloud of illusion, drifting insubstantially from mist to mist, until he blended in seamlessly with the glittering crowd.

The wind drifted, fluttered, then settled as the dust sighed over the tile floor.

Then a shape separated from the wall and stepped into the light.

The wind sneezed at the dust that kicked up as the tall, broad-shouldered, steel-bladed man stalked silently from the room.

73

I closed the door of the Clark suite behind us, the soft sigh of air pushing away from the doorjamb. They'd left the lights on, a half-eaten dinner on the coffee table, and parchment strewn over Primus's desk. The room smelled like boxed mashed potatoes and wet cardboard.

I wrinkled my nose and scanned for illusion. Finn nodded to a fountain pen on the coffee table, lying on top of a manila folder. It was heavily wrapped in illusion. Probably another medieval-style trap.

Speaking of . . .

I glanced at the ceiling, checking for a murder hole. Nothing.

"It's in Primus's room," Finn said, nodding toward the hall that branched off the sitting area.

I studied the dark gloss of his hair, messy and finger-combed, even though he was in a tuxedo. He had a five o'clock shadow, sleepy, bliss-filled eyes, and that unsteady, tightrope-in-a-windstorm gait.

While we'd climbed the stairs, I'd decided Finn's (probable) trait wasn't going to affect my tiny sprouting trust or my actions over the next day. Just like Griff's ability to change into his father's form, or Rou's ability to become liquid, or even Justice's ability to conjure, didn't change my opinion of them or how I interacted with them.

Sure, if Finn reached for my temple, I was going to flip him faster than he could blink. But beyond that? He had to use everything he had to stay in the games, didn't he? Besides, he was up against Jagger. Maybe Finn was planning on using his trait on Jagger.

My stomach dipped hopefully at the thought. Was that how he was going to come out on top in the bargain? Was that how he thought he'd gain my freedom?

Maybe.

Or maybe . . . maybe he was playing me.

Either way, I was going to be cautious, but I was also going to help him. That was what I was here for.

"No traps I can see, except the one on the desk."

Finn nodded, and we crossed the sitting room. The half-eaten dinner was a congealed mess of mashed potatoes and solidified gravy. A few smashed peas lined the edge of the plate. There was a hardened, burned disk of some meat-like thing.

"Did I ever mention," Finn asked quietly, "how infinitely grateful I am for your cooking?"

I smiled and checked Primus's door for any traps, alarms, or security. Nothing. "You're welcome."

Finn smiled back, and I felt a softening in him—a lifting of the wariness and unease. Or maybe I felt it in myself. Sometimes, it was hard to tell.

I opened the door, and when Finn went to switch on the light, I grabbed his wrist. Nodded to the light switch. There was a half-hitch there, hastily tied, that I was certain would lead to some sort of inelegant torture.

Unlike the sitting room, Primus's room was filled with illusion: one knot piled on top of another, all hidden, all traps. But knowing where to step and where not to step made things a little easier.

I looked at the twin-size bed with its brown comforter, as boring as a monk's. "A safe under the bed? You're sure?"

He nodded. "I'm sure."

"He's so creative with his torture but so obvious with everything else." I crossed the room, stepping over knots, slipping around ropes of illusion, until I was kneeling down at the edge of the bed. I flipped up the comforter. "Or maybe it's arrogance. I think . . . yeah. Arrogance." I shook my head.

Finn was right. Under Primus's bed was a metal safe too large for me to move, covered in a thick rope of illusion. There were clove hitches, sheet bends, angler's knots, sailor's knots, all of them tied together in one of the longest, thickest knots I'd ever seen. It was as if Primus had thought to himself, "I want an impenetrable safe that no one can break," and these were the knots that had formed.

Unfortunately, he hadn't realized a lockpick would sneak into his bedroom.

"You got this? I could just . . ." Finn held out his hand and mimed touching the safe with solange.

I waved him off. "Stay over there. I have to open the safe too. It's not illusion." As far as I knew, Finn wasn't skilled in the art of safe-cracking. Unless . . . "Do you know how to break into safes?"

He frowned. "Explosives?"

Ha.

I got busy unraveling all of Primus's knots. I crouched on my knees and bent under the bed, hovering in that mental space where I could untie knots—one, two, another—until all twenty-four knots were untied.

"Got it." I peeked out from under the comforter.

Finn was leaning against the doorframe, his eyes sleepy. When my hair stuck up straight from the static of the blanket, he smiled.

"Good job."

I grinned and ducked halfway under the bed again. There were a lot of ways to crack a safe. Many, many ways. This one was easier than most, because Primus, brilliant man that he was, had forgotten safes often had factory codes.

I tried it. The door swung open.

There it was.

Gold key looped on a gold chain.

A final illusion was spiderwebbed over the key. I unraveled it and pulled the key free.

The metal was cold. I gripped it tight and then scooted out from under the bed.

Finn stood straight and gave me a searching look. "All right?"

I nodded. Stood and then held open my hand. The gold glinted dully in the half-light. When it did, something caught my eye. I hadn't noticed it the night of my seventh death. I'd sort of been running for my life. But now that it was just me, Finn, and a dark room, it was easy to spot.

The key had the smallest figure-eight knot wedged between its teeth. I stared at it, bemused. The figure-eight knot was usually used by the Smiths, although sometimes the Wards used it. This was the Smiths' key, so it made sense there'd be a figure-eight. Still, it seemed odd. Maybe because it was almost as if it had been spliced and then mended, which was what Bards did.

I shook my head.

"What is it?" Finn asked.

"An illusion. I . . . I'm going to . . ." I pulled at the end of the knot, and it unraveled as easily as a loose shoelace.

The key glimmered, flickered, and then disappeared. In its place, I held a two-inch-by-one-inch photograph. It was poor quality, like the kind you take in a photo booth. Glossy, cut with scissors, snipped from the photo strip.

"It's . . ." I squinted into the dim light. "Is that . . .?"

Finn leaned close. I looked from the little boy in the photograph back to him.

The boy was sitting in a woman's lap. He was about three years old, with shiny black hair, hazel eyes, chubby cheeks, and an impish smile. His face was covered in the red sugar of a lollipop. The woman holding him was beautiful. She had the same glossy black hair, the same hazel eyes, bright red lipstick, and elegant, aristocratic features. She was pale, porcelain-fragile, and something about her smile made my heart ache.

Finn reached out and then stopped, his hand hanging over the photo. "Me," he said, sounding confused. "Me and my mom." He stared at the photograph, his eyes glassy, gaze drinking in all the details of the captured moment.

What had he said? He couldn't remember his mom's smile.

"Finn . . ." I ran my fingers over the photo's surface. "Are you the key?"

"What?" He shook his head.

"The key. Jagger wants the key. Luvic wants the key. Even . . . Uliea said something about the key. Are you . . .?" I frowned. "Are you the key?"

He looked at me blankly.

"And if you're the key," I asked, closing my hand over the photograph, "then where's the lock?"

74

THE NIGHT WAS DARK, THE LAST SLIVER OF MOON SHROUDED BY A THICK, black veil of clouds.

Finn was the key. Or his mom was the key. Or . . . I didn't know. I didn't even know what the key was, or why everyone wanted it. Thinking about it made my head hurt. There was a throbbing ache over my right eye that felt like a rock hammer chiseling away.

It was my job to get Jagger the key. But was I supposed to hand over the photograph or Finn? On the back of the photo, someone had written, "Unlock when you know the truth."

I lay awake, staring at the ceiling, for so long the sounds of the party downstairs faded, and the mansion fell eerily quiet. Darin stumbled in at around 3 a.m. He made a lot of noise, banging against the low wooden coffee table and then swearing at it, promising death for the ankle bruise. Wolfgang came in shortly after, barely making a sound.

Finn slept through it all, his sheets untucked, hand flung out, palm open. His face was soft and relaxed, his eyelids fluttering as he lived in his dreams. Maybe he was seeing his mom again. Maybe he was dreaming of her smile.

He'd been quiet when we came back from the Clarks' suite. He'd asked if he could see the photo of his mom, and when I'd asked if he had any pictures of her, he'd said no. He'd looked at it for a long while, a sad pulse of emotion came from him—the sort you feel when you're thinking of an old favorite song and suddenly realize you can't remember the melody anymore. Then, without a word, he'd got up, taken a shower, and climbed into bed.

"*Are* you the key?" I'd asked into the quiet, dark bedroom.

"I don't know. I don't even know what the key is," he'd said, and I believed him because I wanted to.

I lay in the bed next to him, on top of the sheets, feeling the soft rhythm of his breath. He'd sleepily told me to climb in next to him, that we'd both need to be well-rested for tomorrow. After all, it was the final game.

Finn had a game to win. I had a crown to steal.

But what was the key?

What was I missing?

I drifted a bit, my eyelids fluttered, and I sank deeper into the mattress. Finn was warm, and I unconsciously moved toward him, rolling onto my side. I exhaled and was falling into that half-awake slumber when I heard a *tap, tap, tap, tap.*

At first, I thought it was part of a dream, but then the tap sounded again: one long tap, two short taps, one long tap again. I came awake instantly. Lay still, listening.

There it was again.

That was Griff's signal. As a five-year-old, he'd been obsessed with secret codes. For two months straight, he only spoke in code words. It would've continued, except he told Jagger one of his creatures was dead, which in code meant Rou was baking bread (it wasn't a great code), and after Jagger had raged, he'd told Griff to never speak in code again. This tapping signal was the only holdout from that short childhood obsession.

I peered through the pitch-darkness, checking to make sure Finn was still asleep. His breathing stayed steady. His eyes still moved under his eyelids. His hand twitched every now and then.

Slowly, I shifted, inch by inch, until I'd rolled off the mattress and onto my bare feet. I tiptoed toward the window, barely breathing, stepping carefully over the cool wood floor, avoiding the squeaky boards.

Once at the window, I ducked behind the velvet curtain. Its folds creased around me, closing me in a muted, fabric-darkened space.

Griff was crouching on the six-inch-wide brick ledge outside the window. When I appeared, he grinned at me, relief spearing his smile. He was dressed in black, his dark hair hidden by a beanie, and he crouched in shadow—but still, this was a stupid risk. An idiotic risk. What was he thinking?

Besides, this room was on the sixth floor, and Griff wasn't the best climber, which meant he'd taken his father's form and flown up. He should've stayed in that form. At least then, if he was spotted, he might be mistaken for a gargoyle.

He gestured, motioning for me to open the window. I glared at him. What if one of the conjurers saw him? There were hundreds lurking here tonight. Or what if Wolfgang or Darin . . .?

I shook my head. He made a puppy-dog face and gestured for me to open the window again.

I had to admit, I was glad to see him. I was always glad to see him. He was the happy one. The innocent. The one who, no matter how dark Hell Gate was, always managed to seem sunny.

I peered at him, checking for illusion. Remember what happened the last time Griff appeared out of nowhere? It wasn't Griff. Then I'd died.

Carefully, I turned the latch, then I slowly lifted the window. One inch . . . another. It stuck, creaked, and a breath of muggy wind fluttered the curtains. I crouched down and put my nose to the two-inch gap I'd made.

Griff flattened himself against the brick and whispered, "Hey."

I grinned and whispered, "Hey, yourself."

I looked behind me, listening. There was no noise from beyond the curtains.

"What are you doing here?" I whispered once I'd assured myself Finn was still asleep.

"Thought you'd be worried," Griff said. "I wanted to let you know I got out okay yesterday. And Rou's better now."

I frowned. Shook my head. "What? Got out? Rou?"

My heart skipped over itself, a heavy, anxious beat.

Griff's forehead wrinkled. "Yesterday, when the jackaltooth chased me. When Rou was—"

I held up my hand. "Start over," I whispered. "You were here yesterday?"

He looked at me as if I'd lost my mind. A prickle ran over my neck, and the hair stood on end. Maybe . . . maybe I had lost my mind.

"When I came to tell you Luvic Bard came to Hell Gate and tried to burn it down. Twenty-five died, and Rou was caught in the fire—"

I tilted. Swayed. Dizziness washed over me, and I gripped the windowsill. I couldn't hear Griff anymore—there was only the sound of my own blood rushing in my ears. What did Rou always say? The games were bad, but what was worse was that they always washed over onto us.

"Luvic Bard came to burn down Hell Gate? He hurt Rou?" My mouth tasted like ash, and the words were laced with fury.

"I told you that yesterday," he whispered, glancing over his shoulder at a noise from the street. "You swore you'd kill him. Did you . . .?"

I shook my head. Had I really just said I didn't care if Finn could remove memories? Was he the one who'd done this? Or was it Luvic? Or . . .

"Tell me what else happened."

Griff frowned. "The thing is . . . are you all right?"

I nodded. "I'm fine."

"Because . . . Mari. I told you yesterday that Rou was vaporized in the fire. But she's coming back," he added quickly. "But Justice ran to the kitchens to rescue her—"

Oh no. My hands tightened on the sill. Jagger would've punished him for that. Sometimes, he even killed those who broke that rule.

"—and Jagger took him to the basement, and I haven't seen him since."

Griff wouldn't go to the basement looking for him. Griff couldn't even look at the stairs to the basement since Rou had found him huddled down there next to the conjurer's cage.

"But Rou's okay? She'll be okay?" I couldn't ask about Justice. I wouldn't know until I got back to Hell Gate.

Griff nodded. "That's what I came to tell you. I got away from the jackaltooth all right, and Rou is coming solid again. It's just a little . . . I guess like water vapor condensing. She's very cranky. And . . ." Griff gave me a worried, almost frightened, sort of look.

"What?"

"I heard something."

I waited. Griff was easy to overlook. He was so puppylike, so nonthreatening, that people often forgot he was around. So sometimes he heard things.

He leaned so close his breath steamed the window glass. Then he whispered, "Before Jagger threw Justice in the basement, Jagger commanded him not to go after Luvic Bard for the fire. And then Justice said he didn't want revenge for the fire—he wanted to kill Luvic for killing you. And then . . ." Griff swallowed. "Jagger laughed."

I stared at Griff, my heart crashing around in my chest. My skin went clammy, and the humid breeze licked over it, causing a chill to rush up my skin.

Luvic . . . Luvic had set my home on fire. He'd killed twenty-five people. He'd hurt Rou. He'd killed me? He was the conjurer who shot me through the heart? Luvic?

"Trust me, we're friends" Luvic?

"You have a soft heart" Luvic?

"Watch out for betrayal" Luvic?

"Mari?" Griff asked. He shifted on the sill, searching my expression. "You don't look so good."

Beyond him, the street was dark. The streetlamps bled downward onto the sidewalk but didn't climb up or reach the sixth floor. Across the street, the apartments were dark, and the moon, as you know, was buried.

"Yesterday . . . was Finn here when you told me . . . ?"

Griff nodded. "I was just telling you, Jagger said to kill him at the ceremony even if he doesn't win. Then he came in, stumbled across the room, and I had to run, because . . . jackaltooth."

"All right. Okay. I'm glad you're okay. I'm glad . . . I'm glad Rou's okay."

I gave Griff a tight smile. He didn't buy it.

On the street, there was a shout, then a laugh, and finally, the kick-started engine of a motorcycle.

My skin prickled. Then I heard the rustle of sheets and an indrawn breath. I put my finger to my lips and opened my eyes wide. Griff gave a quick nod. A flash of a smile. Then, faster than a blink, he jumped off the window ledge.

The curtain was pulled back, and the grommets scraped on the metal rod. I stood, feigning casual, telegraphing my emotions: calm, calm, sleepy, calm.

"Mari?" Finn asked, rubbing his eyes. "Everything okay?"

I nodded. Slowly shut the window. "I thought I heard something, but . . . I guess I was dreaming." I shrugged and padded back to the bed. The whole time, I felt Finn's eyes on my back. Judging the truth of my words. Weighing the sincerity of my emotions.

Sleepy. Tired. Lethargic. I willed myself to feel those things. To be them.

I yawned and slipped under the warm bedsheets.

"Coming?"

Finn stood at the edge of the bed. He slept in shorts only, so the darkness painted his bare chest and ran over the hard lines of muscle. He frowned and ran a hand through his hair.

Finally, he shook his head. "I'll sleep by the door. Maybe you did hear something."

I settled back into the bed. It was still warm from Finn's body heat. It smelled like him. Cranberry and allspice. I ran my hands over the satin of the sheets and closed my eyes.

Thoughts pinballed through my mind, keeping me awake. I was tense and uncomfortable, but I kept trying to telegraph sleepy and calm.

Luvic. He was a Bard. I'd always known he was a Bard. I'd just . . . Why had he killed me? Why had he befriended me? Why . . . why did any conjurer play games?

Because they could.

Maybe it was him who had altered my memory. But . . . I swiped at my head. Drifted into the space that saw illusion. There was nothing there. No butterfly knots. No blood knots. No loops or splices.

Which meant it wasn't Luvic who'd altered my memory. It was Finn.

He must've heard what Griff had said and decided he'd rather I didn't kill him even if he lost, thank you very much.

Although, weren't the terms of the bargain that his life would be forfeited if he lost?

I sighed. Kicked at the sheets. It was too hot. Sweat dripped down my neck.

"Can't sleep?" Finn asked, his voice a quiet rumble in the dark.

"I'm thinking too much," I admitted.

I felt Finn's smile. It was dark. He was across the room, lying in front of the door, but I could feel it. It felt so long ago that he'd offered to listen to me talk out my worries so I could fall asleep. Was he thinking of that moment now?

"I'm worried about tomorrow." I whispered this, telling him as well as myself.

He shifted, and I think he sat up. Then he said, "It'll be okay. Trust me, there's nothing to worry about. We'll just . . . You don't trust me."

I blinked. Swallowed.

"But I trust you, Mari. You'll do what's right. I'll do what's right. If you could just . . ." He let out a long breath, and I tensed, listening for him to continue.

"Just?"

"Just know I'm going to win."

"How do you know? You sound so confident." I stretched out, spreading my arms and legs over the empty expanse of the bed.

"I'm a Smith." There was a smile in his voice. "Smiths are always confident."

"Half-Smith."

He gave a low, laughing assent. "Yeah. Half-Smith."

"You still . . . you're still going to ask for my freedom? When you win?"

"Yes, Mari. So don't kill me right off."

"And if you lose?"

"I won't lose. I know something all the other conjurers don't."

"What's that?"

There it was again. That smile. "The truth."

"Unlock when you know the truth."

I frowned. "Solange?" Wasn't that what some devotees called it?

"Solange," he agreed, his voice a rough sigh.

I was quiet after that, contemplating games inside of games inside of games. By the time Finn fell back asleep, the sky was leaking dusty gray through the curtain. My bones ached with fatigue, so I finally gave in, slipped out of bed, and lay on the wooden floor next to him.

With a tired, sleepy sigh, he pulled my back against his front and wrapped an arm around me. He was asleep. Dreaming.

You might be wondering, how could I go to a man who'd erased my memory; who I didn't trust?

Well, moths are attracted to the light, aren't they?

I fell asleep in seconds.

75

The armored car swayed in the Midtown traffic, a great, lumbering beast that heaved and bullied, lurching from one traffic light to the next. I sat with Finn in the back seat, in the cold leather belly, rocking with the lumbrous stop-and-go of the vehicle.

A cold breeze blew from the air-conditioning, fogging the windows of the sunbaked black car in July. I wiped my hand across the glass and watched the mass of people pushing down the sidewalk, and the line of cars at a near standstill, all unaware that today, the conjurers would play their final game.

In the front seat, Darin and Wolfgang spoke in low tones. Ever since we'd woken up and Darin had shoved coffee everyone's way, Wolfgang had been grim and contemplative. More so than usual. When Darin had reminded Finn he had to come in first, Wolfgang had asked, "And if he wins, what will you do?"

If Finn won, Darin would be crowned.

Darin's jaw had locked, and he'd said, "Whatever the crown asks of me."

"You'll serve?"

"Yes."

He said this as if the crown were sentient or the conjurer who wore it could communicate with it. Or . . . who knows?

Wolfgang had studied his son for a long moment, and then he'd nodded and asked Finn to recite the twelve positions of attack and the thirteen positions of defense.

Now we were on our way to the Smith Mansion in Queens. The rest of the conjurers were following closely behind.

At four o'clock, the final game would begin.

I was wearing my usual gray silk uniform, but today, underneath, I'd strapped on Justice's knife. The matte-black of the handle and the cold, thin blade was reassuring. If anything went topsy-turvy, I wanted to be prepared. I'd also worn poison darts and thunderers. If nothing else, I was ready.

The window fogged again, and the sea of people wading through Midtown, the spear of skyscrapers, and the line of traffic blurred behind the fog and became a misty watercolor.

Next to me, Finn was quiet. He'd refused the coffee, instead swallowing thimble after thimbleful of solange. It scared me to think of the amount he'd drunk, and although I couldn't be certain, I thought he'd also used the eyedropper to drop solange tears into his eyes.

His eyes were lit navy, shattered silver, a glowing kaleidoscope, more brilliant than I'd ever seen them. His skin glowed like it had at the opening ceremony, when he'd been bathed in that stream of golden light. And his hair—it ruffled on a breeze that wasn't there. It was almost like he was generating his own wind, or his own electricity. The air around him crackled and buzzed, and my skin vibrated with it.

If he were anyone else, I think he would have been dead already. The amount of solange running through him should've killed him. He was Icarus: much too close to the sun, flying way too high.

I looked down at my clenched hands.

The crash at the end of free fall was a millisecond away—I could feel it. This final dose was like the last burst of air; the final current pushing Finn up before he hit the ground.

Slowly, I loosened my hands, letting the blood rush back through them. I'd dug nail prints into the meat of my palm.

Finn looked over and gave a small smile. It was distant. A bit vacant. He looked like he was enraptured by the faraway echo of eternal bliss. Yet after his twelfth shot, he stopped swaying, he stopped wobbling, and he became steadier and more focused than I'd ever seen him. Perhaps the tightrope had become a wide paved road.

He reached over and tucked his hand around mine.

My breath was tight in my chest, and even the blast of cold air couldn't loosen it. I didn't want him to die. *I didn't.*

I was so conflicted about Finn, but one thing was certain: I didn't want him to die.

Thinking of him crashing from solange, dying in the games, dying because of Jagger . . . all of it made a swell of anger—no, rage—sweep over me.

Yet I was conflicted. My head, my heart, and my gut were in battle over him.

My head said he was a liar and a manipulator.

My heart said he was good, and I should trust him.

My gut said I shouldn't trust anyone.

"Kill him," Rou would say.

"Kill him," Justice would say.

"Aww, Mari," Griff would say, "you're supposed to be ruthless. Don't you want to be free? You'd better kill him."

"What are you thinking?" Finn asked.

I was over-aware of the weight of his calloused hand resting over mine.

In the front, Wolfgang and Darin were busy discussing one-on-one combat strategies.

"I'm thinking about what happens if you win."

Finn nodded. His hand tightened on mine.

I looked out the window. We'd left the mass of people and the snarl of traffic and were funneling toward the bridge, leaving Manhattan for Queens.

"I was thinking about what I'd do if I were free . . ." I glanced at the front of the car and amended. "If I were free to do whatever I wanted."

Finn stilled. Tilted his head and asked, "What would you do?"

I smiled as we left Manhattan and crossed onto the bridge high above the East River. Why was it that when you were on bridges, you felt both exhilarated and terrified? Was it because you were suspended between the unchangeable past and the unknowable future? It was a precarious present tense.

"I'd . . ." I smiled as Darin sped over the river. "I'll go to Grand Central. I won't pack a bag or bring anything along—I'll just go and not tell anybody I'm going. I'll . . ."

Finn leaned closer, listening quietly as I whispered, burying myself in the dream.

"I'll buy a ticket to the first place I see. Someplace far. Someplace I've never heard of. I'll ride the train across the country . . . just going . . . just . . . I never got to go before. I mean, I never got to leave. I was never allowed to just go. So I'll go, and I'll keep going until I don't feel like going anymore. Then I'll get off the train in a town or a city, or in the middle of nowhere. And then I'll walk. I won't know which way. Or where. But I'll walk until I don't feel like walking anymore. And then . . . I'll sit down, maybe on a rock, maybe on the curb, and I'll look at the sky, and—" I looked over at Finn.

There was a curious emotion flowing from him to me. I couldn't decipher it. I didn't understand it. It wasn't anything I'd ever felt before.

"And?" he asked.

I shrugged. "And that's when I'll know I'm free. Just looking at the big, open sky. Someplace I've never been. Far away."

The car swayed, bumped, then hit a pothole as we left the bridge and entered Queens. Back on land.

I sighed. "The thing is, I've been picturing that for years, but I've never pictured what happens after I look at the sky. It always ends there, like a movie with the credits rolling. That's it. Happily ever after. She gets to see the sky. It's like I'm incapable of picturing what happens next. What I'd even do if I was free. "

Finn's eyes flashed with lightning, the silver striations swirling. There was a rigidness to his face, and he was holding himself tightly, as if he was stopping himself from saying or doing something.

"Maybe," I said, "it's because someone is supposed to be there with me. You could come," I half-joked. Then I shook my head. "No. Never mi—"

"Yes," Finn said. "I'll come. I'll be there."

Suddenly, the vision of myself sitting on the curb, staring up at the sky in some faraway, unknown place, was replaced by another image.

I was on a flat, grayish-brown boulder. It was shot with quartz, glittering in the sun, and there was grass bunched at its edges. A soft breeze blew over me, and the sun shone down, warming my skin. There was a robin hopping at the edge of the boulder, a squirrel scurrying up an old oak tree, and a dragonfly buzzing overhead.

The image was so real I could smell freshly cut grass and newly laid mulch. The warmth of the sun-glazed rock pressed into my bare thighs as I turned to this picture I had of Finn.

He was on his back, staring up at the blue, blue sky, and I was tucked against him, my head on his chest. His hand drifted over my back, lazy and unhurried, as if he'd stroked me that way a thousand times before. I was sleepy and happy, and the soft thud of his heart was comforting. Then I turned back to the sky, stared at that wide expanse, and smiled. I felt the smile all the way down to my toes.

I blinked out of the vision and frowned at Finn. "Did you just . . .?"

He smiled. "I'll come with you."

I shook my head. "What about Cora? What about your free fall? What about . . .?" *Your impending death.*

"It's a dream," Finn said, glancing out the window as Darin slowed in front of the Smith compound. He looked back at me. "It's your dream. You can make it whatever you want. If you want, I'll be there."

The car pulled to a stop. Wolfgang opened his door.

I nodded. "I want you there."

Finn gave the happiest, widest smile I'd ever seen from him. A sunlit rush of warmth flowed through me. A gold-tinted, happy sunrise.

My heart had won. My head and gut had lost. I wasn't going to kill him.

76

I HADN'T BEEN IN THE SMITH COMPOUND SINCE THE NIGHT OF MY SEVENTH death. That night, I'd snuck in with the shadows, slipped through the rooms as invisible as a gust of wind, bypassed their security, untied their illusions, and stolen their key. It had been a tricky, hidden, tiptoeing sort of Tour de Smith Mansion.

This time though I walked in through the front door right behind the family.

The compound/mansion/estate was the same during the day as it was at night. It was a massive stone-gray, unadorned, unembellished, solid square building, meant not to impress but to serve as a barracks/armory/headquarters/seat of power/et cetera.

The floors were buffed concrete, sometimes stone, and rarely wood. The walls were painted light gray or white. The décor was swords, shields, banners, or centuries-old tapestries woven with scenes of great historical battles. Leather and heavy wood were the preferred furnishings. Every sound echoed off the hard surfaces, making it feel as if I'd entered the stone-echoing halls of a medieval castle.

Castles were built to overtake, to defend, to withstand sieges, and to bring death to invaders. Portcullises. Murder holes. Arrow loops. Narrow, winding, steep stone staircases to shove attackers down or corral them for slaughter. Ramparts. Secret tunnels.

The Smith compound had that exact feel. A home built for war.

Now that I knew Wolfgang, Darin, and even Finn personally, I could see the compound wasn't just a flat, square, gray building, uncompromising in its stoic, military-esque façade. Instead, it was a reflection of what the Smiths valued. It was hard, unyielding, and direct without frill or fantasy. A stalwart, solid bastion that would stand long after everything and everyone else fell.

It was interesting—as soon as we strode through the front doors, Darin's entire demeanor changed. Wolfgang stayed the same—he was always ruthless, grim, and stoic—but Darin underwent a complete transformation.

It only took one step, one boot hitting the entryway concrete, for the laughing tilt to his mouth, the relaxed slope of his shoulders, and the teasing big-brother light to vanish. He became, in short, a military commander. A hard-eyed, hard-edged, hard-faced man who commanded armies, directed assaults, and conquered nations. I tried not to stare, but I don't think I succeeded. In front of my eyes, Darin had become a man who, like Alexander the Great, lived solely for the unrelenting drive to conquer the world.

The Smith cousins in the entryway stood in stiff formation, all at attention. I'd expected Wolfgang's stride to cut through the welcome, but I didn't expect Darin to become so Smith-like; so remote and hard.

Finn ignored the silent formation of Smith relatives. He, at least, stayed the same. He swayed a bit, blinking at the concrete and the display of ancient armor and weaponry lining the hall. He smiled vacantly at the Smith cousins. None of them smiled back. It was clear they were all military or mercenary.

I kept my head high and strode after Darin and Wolfgang, keeping Finn in the corner of my eye. The last time he was in this entryway, his dad had shoved a sword through his belly.

After that, it was a blur of preparation. Finn was kitted out in lightweight body armor. All-black. Two swords, both long. I was skeptical.

"Isn't having two swords a bad idea—something only for movies and fiction? Wouldn't you rather a shield?"

Darin laughed, and Finn sheathed the swords.

Apparently, throughout history, certain masters had yielded two swords. The technique was called dual wielding, and it required an enormous amount of training. Not many people could achieve the skill needed: intricate footwork, immense coordination and balance, incredible hand strength, and intense concentration. Dual wielding meant sacrificing deep, powerful cuts for lighter, lightning-quick whirlwind attacks and counterattacks.

Darin seemed to think Finn would look like an eight-armed warrior, his arms like the relentless, blurring blade of a helicopter, as he danced through an army and killed everyone in his path. So. Two swords.

If they could do it in sixteenth-century Italy, then they could do it in New York City hundreds of years later.

Now we were underground, once again beneath the earth, hidden below the Smith compound, about to begin another game. We were standing in an antechamber that felt more like an underground bunker. Concrete floor, concrete walls, and two tall, metal double doors leading to the arena.

Do you remember when the Romans flooded the Colosseum and staged naval battles? There were war ships, thousands of men (doomed to die), and reenactments of famed battles for the gory glory of ancient Rome. The Colosseum was where these bloody battles played out.

The Smith arena, their massive underground hall, was a modern Colosseum.

The antechamber was uncomfortably hot. There were too many people crowded together. The Smiths. Darin, Wolfgang, and Finn, but also, for the first time at a game, about two dozen Smith cousins. They stood behind Wolfgang or lined the edge of the room, stiffly postured. There was something about them that made me feel like they were on the edge of a battle frenzy. It drew an itch over the back of my neck.

Unconsciously, I stepped closer to Finn.

The Clarks and all the cousins, of course, were grouped near the back, dressed in their scholarly browns and blacks. They'd been attempting to snarl and stare down the Smiths since descending to the basement. The Smiths had ignored them.

That morning, everyone had been informed there would be no conjuring in the game, no objects of power, and that the players were allowed only two weapons. No shields.

Primus held a double-bit axe with a long handle and a long dagger. Without illusion, his face held the evidence of my thunderer's burn. When Last saw me studying him, she held back a smirk. I could see the workings of her mind. She was hoping, at least a little, that he'd die today.

The Bards had nearly as many family members crowded into the antechamber as the Clarks. It seemed everyone was showing their power for the final game. The Bards especially, since the only way Celia could win was if all the others died or were disqualified.

Right now, as far as the scores stood, Primus and Jacob were tied at nine points, Finn had seven points, and Celia had five points. For Finn to win, he had to come in first, and Primus and Jacob had to come in last and third, with a final duel to determine the winner. Darin had explained it all while Finn was getting dressed. He hadn't needed to though—I remembered from reading the records. If two heirs tied in the games, they would engage in a conjuring duel to determine the winner. Sometimes, the duel ended with the loser incapacitated. More often, it ended with the loser dead.

So the Bards had turned out in force. They were dressed in bright colors, high fashion, as if the runway or a movie premier were just around the corner.

Celia was the only one dressed in black. She was wearing an outfit similar to Finn's: tactical armor, lightweight, impact-resistant, bullet and flameproof. Her hair was braided and tucked tightly around her head. She wore no illusion because of the Smiths' game rules. It was rare to see her without illusion, but the only difference was that her complexion was paler, almost translucent, and she was perhaps a little frailer and less fleshed-out. She had dark smudges under her eyes and deeper hollows at her cheeks. Maybe her dark hair had more flyaways too, a few short tendrils sticking up at her temples. But other than her pale coloring—

almost anemic in its shade—and the slight loss of her curves, she was basically the same.

I guess Hollywood had higher standards, and "almost perfect" meant the same thing as "not perfect." Maybe that was why Celia hid behind illusion.

She had a longsword and a knife. The longsword was a good choice for a small woman. They were very light and held with both hands, made powerful thrusts. And they made up for a shorter reach by being . . . yes, long.

I wondered if all the heirs had received training in sword fighting, axe wielding, spear throwing, and archery in preparation for the Smith game. After all, the Smiths inevitably chose melee.

Celia reached up and brushed her finger over her necklace. It had a thin gold chain and a crystal pendant shaped like a teardrop. Not an object of power, just a necklace made real with illusion. She rolled the teardrop between her thumb and pointer fingers, her eyes thoughtful.

I looked away, toward the Wards. Jacob's gaze was riveted on Celia. Well, not on her, but on the necklace and the way she was rolling the crystal between her fingers. It was as if he were willing Celia to look at him. She didn't. She kept her eyes on the Smith, who I swear was recounting the entire history of war.

"The Punic Wars were a time of great . . ." He marched on, filling the antechamber with a martial history lesson.

I turned my attention back to Jacob. He'd looked away from Celia and seemed to be engrossed in Wolfgang's oratorical address. Unlike the others, he had a glaive and a shortsword.

The glaive was like a pole arm or a war scythe. It was a Grim Reaper sort of weapon. The handle was metal, about six feet long, and the blade was long, single-edged, and curved, with a sharp hook on the reverse side. Jacob, unlike Finn and Celia, was in his usual jeans and a long-sleeve T-shirt, but the addition of his scythe-like weapon made everyone in the room remember exactly who and what he was.

I'd seen a glaive used once, by one of Jagger's creatures. In combat, it was used like a quarterstaff, and it could kill opponents from a distance or yank them from horseback. This was an important consideration if you were about to be thrust into the middle of a battle somewhere in the annals of history. Jacob was smart, and if Finn had been right in his assessment, he also knew how to fight.

Jacob and Philoneas were the only Wards in the antechamber. Not even Uliea was there. It was as if they were saying, "That's right. We're not concerned. Two Wards can take on fifty conjurers from any family and come out ahead."

Wolfgang's voice increased in volume, and I glanced back at him. Darin, for once, wasn't making jokes or begging for the speech to end. Instead, he stood military-stiff and hard-eyed.

Finn swayed a bit, and the back of his hand brushed mine. My heart jangled and jumped, and when it did, Finn stilled. He'd felt it through the ring, I was sure. Despite this, he kept his hand pressed to mine.

"It isn't the ability to conjure," Wolfgang said, spearing each heir with a hard glance, "that makes you worthy of wearing the crown. You must prove that you are worthy even without that power. Will I bow to a leader who wields power through the gross application of fear?" He sent a withering look toward the Clarks. "Should I bow to one who hoards power through hedonistic manipulation and the perversion of ego?" He lifted an eyebrow at the Bards. "Or perhaps you expect me to bow to one who would have us all locked in the shell of our minds, forfeiting the physical world for a mental hell masquerading as paradise." He cast a contemptuous look at Philoneas, a death promise in his eyes. "The aims you have, the world you envision—why would I follow? Being born a human doesn't make you human. You can choose to be a beast or a man. A beast gives in to his desires. A man ascends. A beast lives for his own pleasure, thinks only of the immediate. Plunders, lusts, kills. A *man* loves."

I jerked, surprised that Wolfgang, a Smith, would mention "love" in a speech about war.

Darin's jaw stayed hard. He didn't even blink at the word.

Finn swayed closer.

"Just because you were born a conjurer doesn't mean you are one. You choose. Conjurer or monster. Man or beast. Honor or dishonor. Courage or cowardice. Loyalty or lies. Truth or treachery. Who are you without your power? Are you a monster? A beast? Or are you a conjurer, with or without the power of illusion? Win our game, and I will bow to you. Finish this game, and I will nod. Fail, and you are not a conjurer. You aren't worthy of the name."

I felt a pressure on the back of my neck, a poking sensation, like someone was staring, trying to get my attention. I scanned the concrete room, glancing at all the varied expressions—bored, determined, aloof, annoyed—until I found one person who was watching me.

He was smiling, amused, his eyes hooded, lips curved. He was focused on me and where the back of my hand touched Finn's.

When Luvic's eyes rose back to meet mine, he lifted an eyebrow as if to say, "I see what you're doing." And then, "Did you find the key?"

Yes, we'd found the key. What it meant? We hadn't figured that out. Not that I was going to tell him any of that.

I flattened my mouth, trying and failing to hide the flash of anger that flowed through me. I'd avoided looking at him. I'd even avoided thinking about him since we'd arrived at the Smith compound.

He'd killed me.

He'd betrayed me.

I know, I know, what did I expect? Nothing less.

Besides, can you betray someone you aren't technically allies with? No. No, you can't.

Luvic had even given me that vision where he'd killed me in cold blood. It wasn't as if he were subtle.

At the angry heat in my eyes, his eyebrows lowered, and his expression clouded with confusion. He frowned and shook his head, silently questioning, "What?"

Someday, I telegraphed, *you will get exactly what you deserve.*

His frown deepened, and a line formed on his brow. He looked away.

I turned my attention back to Wolfgang. He was describing the game.

"—no conjuring. Even one minor illusion. The tiniest illusion, and you are disqualified. No objects of power. None. Once you pass through those doors, you will enter a gauntlet. There are four. All the same. Once through the gauntlet—if you survive—you will enter a historic siege war.

The first through the gauntlet, over the siege walls, and to the top of the stone tower, wins. You have four hours. That is all."

There was no elaborate end to his long war-history speech. There was just, "That is all." Then he strode through the conjurers and yanked open the metal doors.

A riot of noise hit the room. Screams. Clashing metal. Booming thunder. The smell of smoke, char, and blood. I couldn't see anything beyond the doors—the smoke and the haze was too thick, orange-red and gray from thick fires burning somewhere beyond.

I swallowed and glanced at Finn. It would be a lie to say dread wasn't thick and heavy in my veins.

"Win," I whispered.

He nodded and then strode, strangely steady, to the door.

Celia, Primus, and Jacob met him there. Then, as four, they entered the arena.

Wolfgang locked the doors behind them.

77

THE WIND SPED THROUGH THE THICK, ACRID SMOKE THAT REACHED LIKE talon-tipped fingers to claw at the humans' eyes and throats. It blew it aside, shoving the smoke claws away from the boy so he'd have a clear view of the gauntlet and the battle ahead.

It was the same but not the same. The wind had seen many, many skirmishes, battles, and wars.

There were some things that never changed, no matter how young or old the earth was.

The unfurling of a new spring leaf. The careful unfolding of a butterfly's wings after its deathlike chrysalis. The first shaft of sunlight spreading over the dark horizon.

And this. The scent, the sounds, the taste of war.

It was a human thing, war.

The wind knew fury—it was a hurricane, wasn't it? The wind knew frenzy—it was a tornado, was it not? The wind knew wrath—it flattened forests and destroyed cities, did it not? Was war the hurricane of the human soul? The frenzied wrath of a tornado?

It seemed to the wind that some humans were born to clash and war; a violent gale battering a rocky shore until it blew itself out.

Sometimes, these men questioned their fate. But the wind thought a warrior should never grieve that they'd been born a warrior. Wasn't it God's prerogative to make humans as he saw fit? Some for peace. Some for war. Some for riches. Some to be poor. Who would grieve their destiny? This was something the wind didn't understand.

The boy had never grieved his destiny. He wouldn't today, either, when he was so close.

The wind blew furiously, shoving the thick, snaking smoke away.

"Wind," the boy whispered, reaching his hand out to brush his fingers through the river-quick breeze. "You're here." He smiled, and the wind skated over the soft turn of his lips.

Then the boy sprinted, like an arrow loosed, toward the violent clash.

The wind shrieked in surprise and rushed after him.

This illusion wasn't like the illusions the boy created to play inside. Instead, it was a strange conglomeration of dozens of battles, all plastered together and melted into one, like a sedimentary stone layered with centuries of gneiss, granite, quartz, feldspar, and pyrite, all glued together with iron-tinged calcite so the rock dripped bloodred. The worst, the most violent, the most deadly of historic battles. All here.

If the wind spread out in a diffused blanket, it could feel the edges of the arena. It was a city block, two—maybe three—long, but the length and width didn't matter. The illusion was made so the players would run in circles for hours, believing they only ever ran forward.

The wind skittered over the sharpened edge of a longsword and whistled down the stinging metal. It spun as a mace whipped past the boy's cheek. The boy fluidly dodged the assault. He sprinted further into the arena. The wind huffed. It shoved at the spray of dirt as a boulder hit the ground a body's length from the boy.

"Look. The gauntlet." The boy laughed, and the wind flicked his ear. The boy always laughed at the wrong things.

The smoke cleared, parting like hands drawing back a dusty curtain.

Here were the accoutrements of war. The wind had tasted them before. The illusion held a flavor it knew well.

Terror had a taste. Panic too. Adrenaline tasted like a leaking battery, acidic and copper-tanged. Sweat, sharp and biting. The sweat of man was always more pungent than the sweet sweat of warhorses. Blood was a metallic, salty seasoning. Urine. Tears. Smoke. Charred wood and grass.

What else? Sometimes meat over fires. Sometimes wine. Sometimes the scent of dirty blankets or unwashed uniforms, or even the smell of a desperate coupling before the end.

Terror. Panic. Adrenaline.

But then rage, wrath—those things had flavors too. And above that, another emotion.

The wind loved this emotion, although it was rare to find. It was the calm at the eye of the hurricane. Rarely, the wind would find a man who fought with the silent power of the eye; with the violent winds of a hurricane shooting out from him. The eye tasted like destruction.

The wind raced over the trampled grass and slipped over the blood-soaked mud. It glided on the long staff of the boy's weapon as he hurled himself into the illusion.

Sounds ricocheted through the wind. Thunderous booms vibrated it as trebuchets launched boulders and flaming spheres of tar. Men screamed, and the wind rode over their pained undulations. Somewhere far-off, past the gauntlet, a drum heaved a steady, pulse-like boom. Weapons clashed in a metallic discord. The noise sent the wind into a vibrating frenzy. It spun wildly on the sound.

Steadying itself, it grabbed onto the boy's shirt and clung tightly. Ahead, a long line of men faced each other. It was a tunnel of men— longer than the tunnel underneath the river that humans sent their cars through. It was one of the four gauntlets. The wind moaned at the glint of metal as the men held their weapons aloft. Would the boy hurtle himself through the tunnel, dodging and cutting his way to the end?

There were three other tunnels. The cruel one cut through one of the tunnels like a man chopping down saplings. He roared, and the wind shuddered.

The solange-eyed one didn't cut, chop, or draw a weapon. Instead, he moved like a rushing stream. He glided through the swinging swords and thrusting spears. He tilted to the side. Swayed a breath's width to miss a morning star. Dodged to the right and jumped to miss both a club and a mace. He spun in a cosmic dance that mesmerized the wind.

The citrus and pearl dust scented woman hesitated at the tunnel next to the boy. Her sword sang a high-pitched cry as she pulled it from the scabbard.

The boy glanced over. The wind couldn't read his expression. Doubt? Hope? Self-castigation? Determination? The boy's pulse tripped, stuttered, and then raced. Then, mid-sprint, he veered across the blood-soaked mud and dove into the same gauntlet as the woman.

The wind laughed in surprise and spun around the two of them. The boy pressed his back to the woman's and blocked a giant axe rushing toward her head.

"What are you doing!" she yelled, her voice caught in the clash.

"You wore the necklace."

"So?" She swung her longsword. Parried a thrust.

"So." The boy grunted. Knocked aside a war hammer. Kicked a screaming attacker back. "I'm here."

The woman's cheeks flushed red. The wind rubbed over the heat. It rode the bright color and bounced on the violent trembling of her pulse. She swallowed and ducked. A man swung a club over her.

"Okay." She pressed her back to the boy's. Then she said again, "Okay."

The boy grinned as he thrust his glaive into a man's belly. He yanked out the weapon. Then the boy and the citrus and pearl dust scented woman dodged, ducked, and cut their way down the tunnel.

The wind rode over their pulses. Skittered down the sweat that dripped from their foreheads. It vibrated with the thrum of their heartbeats and the boom of the drum. It tied them together as it circled around their legs. The boy seemed to have eyes in the back of his head. Even though the wind knew he did *not*. All the same, sometimes the boy blocked thrusts meant for the woman without even looking or turning.

"Thanks," she'd gasp.

The wind knew the woman would've died if the boy hadn't joined her in the gauntlet. It could see that now. This wasn't a game that favored her kind of power. The wind wondered if the boy or the woman realized that too.

Her arms trembled, the weight of the sword growing heavier with each hacking thrust. Across the field of flaming grass and blood-soaked mud, the cruel one burst free of his tunnel.

How much time had passed? There was no sun here. No shadow or sloping light to tell the wind what humans instinctively knew. How long did they have to fight?

"Ward!" the cruel one thundered, lifting his axe high. "Take note. Your weakness is my strength. A woman will always be your downfall!"

The wind shrieked and shoved a club, nudging it, just to the side. It slid past the woman's skull. The whoosh of it brushed her hair.

"Prick," the woman spat.

Far down the smoke-filled field, the cruel one launched himself into the battle, charging toward the high, gray stone walls.

"He can't win," the boy said. He ducked. Parried.

"What?" The woman dodged a blow. There was a bruise blooming on her cheek. It was swollen, opening like a purple flower. One hit. Only one. But afterward, the boy had brought down twenty men on either side of the tunnel.

The wind blew in the boy's ear, reminding him of his duty. The boy ignored the wind and thrust his shortsword. The tunnel had narrowed, and the glaive was too long for close-quarter fighting.

"Primus can't win. I've seen the hell of his mind. Lia, he has a taste for blood. It's not right—"

The wind rode the edge of the woman's sword. It clanged and screamed as a blade scraped down the sharp metal.

The woman gasped. "I'm kind of focused on staying alive here."

"I'm saying it's time to get out of this gauntlet. So follow me, and *don't die.*"

Then the boy did what he did best. The wind skated on the whir of his blade. It spun in the darkness. The boy didn't need to conjure to be what he was. He was the darkness that hid the light. He was the darkness that preceded the light. He devoured the gauntlet.

The wind laughed. It shoved smoke and dirt. It blew flame and fire. It was a whirlwind that sped through the gauntlet. It rode the boy's blade and danced on the dying illusion. The wind loved this. The wind loved riding on the wings of the boy's darkness.

The citrus and pearl dust scented woman stayed close, hugging the edges of the massacre. She flew in and out, darting through the melee. Then, in the time it took to sing one simple love song, the boy and the woman were free.

Oh, it'd been a risk. Before, the boy had been cautious, protecting the woman. But he was right: the cruel one couldn't win.

"Alterra." The woman pointed toward the clash of armies.

The boy grinned. There was a wild, adrenaline-soaked light in his eyes. "Well, let's catch up to him."

They rushed the battlefield. It was a river of men, roiling limbs, frothing weapons coated in red. Catapults and trebuchets fired. The ground exploded. The mass of men fought with a boiling frenzy.

The wind knew this war-soaked place, the conglomerate of it. There below the churning battle was slippery, sulfur-yellow clay, iron-red volcanic ash, sharp shards of obsidian, soft pink dolomite, and coarse, yellow-gold sand. War always sinks into the soil; here, it was the soil. It knew the dirt of these ancient wars.

The boy cut into the river of men, thrusting his long glaive. The woman spun with him. They rushed through the rapids of it, gaining on the cruel one.

Through the glint of a silver axe handle, the wind caught what the cruel one meant to do. It shoved at the boy, drawing his attention to the solange-eyed one.

He was across the mass of fighting men. The battle was thicker, hotter, louder than even the throb of Times Square when the boy had made the wind join him for the wild human celebration of time passing on New Year's Eve.

The solange-eyed one had chosen a different route than the rest. He'd sprinted free of his gauntlet just after the cruel one and leaped into the center of the field, where the fighting was thickest. It was the shortest route to the walls but also the most difficult. While the fighting on the outer edges was thinned and frayed, the middle was still tightly packed with shoulder-to-shoulder battle.

The wind moaned and tugged at the boy. Yet, what did it expect him to do? The boy couldn't do anything to stop what was about to happen.

The cruel one had used enough hammers and wedges in his cruelty to know how to utilize them in battle. As he fought past a unit of horsemen—ancient Macedonians?—he roared at them to charge. They did. Of course they did. The cruel one was often obeyed for no reason except that he expected to be.

The cavalry descended on the field. Their powerful chests and iron hooves smashed skulls. Broke bones. Men and horses screamed. The solange-eyed one fought. Dodged. Whirled past horse and man like they were paper cutouts. But the wind knew the horses were a distraction. They were funneling the solange-eyed one exactly where the cruel one wanted him to go.

The cruel one leaped atop a wooden siege engine. He threw three men from the top into the mud. Then he aimed a copper tube at the fight. The wind knew the air that leaked from the tube would smell of gas fumes, bitumen, and sulfur. It had danced on the hiss and crackle of this fire-thrower centuries ago. It burned through armies, lit ships on fire, danced on water, and scorched every living and non-living thing it touched.

The cruel one sent the flame toward the army. An orange-yellow lance of fire burst from the copper tube. It was twelve men wide, and it engulfed everything in its path. The explosion of fire was so bright the boy turned away, shielding his eyes.

The solange-eyed man was swallowed by fire.

It consumed illusion. It burned through men. Screams and black, hungry smoke writhed over the boiling mass of men. The smoke and flame were too thick for the wind. If it rushed in, it would only feed the fire and fan the flames higher. It was best if it stayed away.

The solange-eyed one. He was either dead, his spirit fled, or he was alive and fighting his way through fire and smoke.

Nothing could be done for him.

"Wind!" the boy shouted.

But no, the wind wouldn't leave the boy. Not even for the solange-eyed one. Not now.

The cruel one jumped down from the siege engine. He swung his axe, chopping men as he shouldered toward the gray stone walls. He tore toward the finish. It was a facsimile of a castle. A wall. A rampart. A high tower.

The wind shoved the boy. He growled. Then he and the woman connected gazes, and for a split second, the wind thought they could read minds. They turned together and shoved in a frenzy toward the cruel one.

Strike. Block. Dodge. Hit.

They gained. Inch by inch. Blood-soaked mud. Slipping. Striking. There. They'd almost caught the cruel one.

The walls loomed, their gray casting a shadow over the writhing smoke and flames. Almost.

The cruel one glanced over his shoulder. Snarled. The wind knew the workings of his mind. It shuddered at the calculation in his eyes. The cruel one dodged an attack and then cut across the rubble-strewn ground.

He thrust his axe into an archer's head. Stole the crossbow. The boy wasn't watching. The woman wasn't watching. This wasn't right. This wasn't how the games were played. But no one was there to see what the cruel one did. Only the wind.

He aimed. Fired. The bolt sped through the screams and cut through the smoke. In a second, it would pierce the citrus and pearl dust scented woman's fragile skin. Not her body armor but the bare skin of her throat.

At the last second, the wind shrieked.

The boy spun. The bolt was speeding toward the woman. He grabbed her arm, held her like he did when they danced, and snapped her behind him. The arrow flew past.

The woman's face drained of color. She was so pale that if you cut her, she might bleed moonlit-white.

The boy gripped the woman's arm and held his glaive with the other. The wind had seen the boy murderous. It had never seen him enraged.

The woman exhaled violently, her eyes wide. "You keep saving—"

She broke off at a screaming, roaring noise.

The wind rushed against them. There was scalding heat. Flame and shadow. The woman threw her arms over her head. The boy looked up.

A fireball crashed through the air.

The wind couldn't tell time, but it did know that in the time it took to blink, the fireball would hit the woman. It would bury her in flame.

There was no time to dodge. No time to jump. It was three hands away. The flames had already sparked and smoldered in her hair.

The wind rushed at it, singeing and burning itself. But it didn't slow it —it only fed the molten flames.

Maybe later, the boy would believe he'd made a conscious decision. Maybe later, he'd reason he'd purposely decided to give up a lifetime of working toward a single goal. Maybe he'd tell himself he'd done so willingly, knowing the consequences.

And the wind would let the boy believe that. After all, humans liked to believe they were in control. But in truth, in moments where there is only death, life, and a split-second decision, there is no thought. There's only feeling.

The decision comes from the deepest, darkest depths of a human's soul.

If it had been the cruel one standing next to the woman, he would've let her die. At the base of the cruel one's spirit, there was cruelty and hate, and nothing more.

But at the base of the boy's spirit, where the darkness lived, he'd always held a flame of hope and a degree of kindness. And so, without thought, he twisted his hand.

The fireball disintegrated. It splashed over the woman's face, brushing her cheeks with warm, tropical air and flower-blossom wind.

The boy had saved the woman's life and coated her in flowers. Orange chrysanthemums drifted over her, little flame-colored petals curling and catching in her braid.

They stared at each other as the battle clashed around them. The wind shoved at attackers, keeping them at bay.

"You . . ." The woman paled. "You're out. You're disqualified."

Was that disbelief?

The boy swallowed. The wind pressed against the hard, dread-filled beat of his pulse. His jaw hardened. He gave a hard nod.

"Go. Win."

"But . . . you saved me. You . . ."

"Win. I'm out. Alterra . . . who knows what happened?" He swore. Then he looked at Primus mounting the stone wall. "There's only Primus. Win, Lia. *Win*. You're better than him. Knock him out of the game and *win*."

The woman glanced back at the stone wall. She clenched her hand around her longsword. Nodded. "All right. Yes."

Then, before she spun into the battle, she grabbed the boy's shoulder, yanked him close, and kissed him.

The wind rode on the salty-sweet taste of their lips. It tested the heat and the resolve. It slipped on the quick thud of the woman's pulse and the surprised exhale of the boy. It caught the way the woman tugged the boy close, and how the boy sent his hand into the woman's hair. Then the woman shoved away from the boy. Grinned. And rushed into the fray.

The boy stared after the woman, his heart pounding. "Wind," he said, his voice hoarse, "I think we're in trouble. You know what to do. Go."

Then, when the wind didn't leave but instead tapped his cheek, he urged, "Go!"

The wind rushed after the woman.

The woman climbed faster than the cruel one. She scaled the sheer gray stone wall as if she were climbing a set of stairs. Fire arrows, fireballs, and bolts flew around them, and the wind batted them away. The woman didn't know the wind was there helping, but humans rarely realized the help they received from unseen sources.

Her breath came out in ragged gasps as she boosted a leg over the stone ledge. Finally, she mounted the rampart. A line of men blocked the elevated stone walkway. Her only route to the tower.

"Men," she spat, hefting her sword. "Always getting in the way."

The wind tugged at the end of her braid in reprimand. More like she'd gotten in the boy's way. It was that sea-tide voice and the citrus scent. The boy hadn't stood a chance.

But there was a smile hovering at the edge of the woman's lips, so the wind figured she was having kind thoughts about the boy. It stopped yanking on her braid and swept over the rampart. It was an easy push; a gentle nudge. All it had to do was gust and blow. Then, suddenly, the men blocking the woman were unsteady and clumsy, their footing unsure. The wind laughed. It ran along the coarse stone and shoved at booted feet. It was too easy.

The woman was sure-footed. She ran across the stone rampart, swiping and cutting. Her footwork was practiced, her strikes sure. She was running on adrenaline. The wind could taste it.

There was one soldier left. He barred the entrance to the tower. The citrus and pearl dust scented woman charged. The wind screamed. The cruel one barreled over the wall and threw himself at the woman.

She spun to the side.

The cruel one grunted and swung his axe.

Was it at the woman, or was it at the soldier?

Both, perhaps.

The woman jumped back.

"Primus! The rules forbid assault on other players!" She gasped and leaped away as he swung again.

His reach was longer, his bulk and momentum greater. "Heir Bard," he said, holding his axe in front of him, "you may have wrapped Heir Ward in your false allure, but . . . I am not so soft. Or pathetic."

He lunged, and the woman jumped back again.

"If you attack—"

"What? What will you do? Who will you tell? Who will believe you? Poor Celia Bard. Failure. Lost the games. The worst score in history. Attempted to save face with lies. Perhaps, when I win, I'll bring you back to the catacombs, and we can play together in the—"

The woman charged the man, swiping her blade. The cruel one blocked her attack. He grunted in surprise.

The woman's arms trembled. The wind knew the sword had grown heavy. The adrenaline was draining, leaving her exhausted and heavy-limbed. The wind bolstered her arms and helped hold her sword aloft.

"Paladin Smith, dead in fire. Heir Ward, disqualified due to weakness of character. Heir Bard . . ." The cruel one smiled grimly as he swiped his axe again.

The woman stumbled. She tripped on an uneven stone and fell to the ground. The air rushed from her lungs. Her sword skittered across the stones and then fell from the rampart.

The cruel one chuckled. It was the dry, crumbling-parchment chuckle he gave when he was about to do something especially cruel. He stepped over the woman. Loomed. She scrambled away. Her back hit the stone edge of the rampart.

"Take note," the cruel one said.

"I'll kill you," the woman promised. "When we get out of here, I will drain you of blood and feed it to the rats that wander your precious catacombs."

The cruel one laughed. "We? Take note. *We* are not getting out of here. *I* am."

The cruel one raised his axe. The wind screamed. It shoved at the cruel one. At the same time, the woman burst from her crouching position. She shot upright, a bullet released. She tucked her shoulder and slammed into the cruel one. The woman and the wind hit the cruel one with combined rage.

He grunted at the impact. Flew backward. His legs hit the edge of the rampart. The stones knocked the backs of his knees. The wind gusted. Shoved again.

The cruel one flew off the rampart.

He didn't make a sound.

The woman grabbed the gray stone and dug her fingers into the wall. She watched, wide-eyed and breathing hard, as the cruel one hit the ground, twenty feet below.

She winced. "Perhaps," she said, "*your* weakness is women. You always underestimate us. You psychopathic prick."

Then, when the wind brushed her cheek, she let out a shaky breath. Frowned.

"Ugh. He's still alive. He's coming."

The wind peeked over the edge. The woman was right. The cruel one was tearing through the soldiers lining the walls. He had a limp, a bloodied temple, and the posture of an enraged bull.

The woman shook her head and tugged her knife free. When she turned, the solange-eyed one was on the wall, fighting the final soldier.

He cut through the man in one swift thrust and sprinted up the stairs.

"Dang!" the woman said. She raced after the solange-eyed one.

The wind rushed behind them. The stairs wound like a corkscrew. The steps were narrow, only a hand's width wide, slippery and crumbling. The turns made the wind dizzy. It flashed back and forth between the woman and the solange-eyed man as they raced toward the top.

The woman tried to shove past the man, but he was moving too quickly.

She jabbed. Shoved. Tried to duck under his arms and sprint past him.

The climb was as high as the highest lighthouse. Sometimes, the wind would crash on ocean waves, drawn by the searching light of a lighthouse. It would glide up the bright light and then spiral up the stairs, spinning, spinning in a tight coil, until it reached the blinding top.

Once, the wind had heard a lighthouse keeper say there were 365 stairs in the lighthouse, and just like the number, it felt like it had taken a year of his life to climb to the top.

It was the same now. The dark tower, barely lit by thin slits in the stone walls. The dizzying, coiled stairs. The heart-pounding scramble to the top. The wind pushed the woman, giving her a boost. The cruel one was still behind them.

A soldier rocketed down the stairs. The solange-eyed one shoved his blade into him and jumped over the man. The woman scrambled after him.

Perhaps she thought she could still win. Perhaps she thought the cruel one wouldn't make it. That the solange-eyed one would collapse. Or perhaps she was just like she'd always been: a woman who still fought even when she knew the only outcome was losing.

Another attacker. Another leap. And again.

The wall slits became more spaced out. The stairs fell to darkness.

The solange-eyed one was faster, but the woman kept after him. Her heart rammed against her chest, and she took in gusty, violent gasps of air. The wind massaged her lungs and nudged her heart. This was what it had warned the boy about. This was the weakness her father hated.

A salty tear gathered at the corner of her eye. She tripped. The wind pushed at her bruised and cut hands. Her blood stained the smooth, cold stone stair.

The solange-eyed one paused a dozen steps above her. The wind whispered into the stone walls. Its breeze echoed across the dark and the cold.

The woman gave a phlegmy, blood-soaked cough.

"Get up," the solange-eyed man said. The wind thought his voice was kind, but the woman stiffened.

She made a crude gesture.

The wind tugged her braid. That was *not* polite.

"Your brothers are counting on you. Get up."

The woman glared at the solange-eyed man. "Who are you to—?"

"No one," he said gently. "I'm no one."

He was next to her then. He gripped her arms and pulled her up. In her left hand, she clutched her knife. Her hand tightened on it, and the wind rode over the tension in her arm. She was poised to strike. It would be a swift glide into the man's exposed jugular.

"Let's go," he said. "Trust me."

She snarled, and her grip tightened on the knife.

The solange-eyed man blinked at her. The silver striations in his eyes glowed in the dark.

"Why should I trust you?" she asked.

The solange-eyed man smiled, and the wind laughed. He let her go and sprinted up the stairs again. The woman swore before taking a breath and racing after him.

It wasn't long then. At least, not long enough for the woman's heart to start laboring and faltering again. The wind rushed ahead to find the solange-eyed man at the top of the tower. There was a doorway there. It was wooden. There was an eye carved into the wood.

The wind hummed.

The eye looked exactly the same as the all-seeing eye on the door of the Night Den.

He brushed his fingers over it and then looked back as the woman burst into the room.

"I could kill you," she said, gripping her knife as if she were about to throw it. "Walk through that door a winner."

The solange-eyed man closed one eye and then the other. "You could try."

The woman smiled. The wind tugged her braid and waited for her heart to regain its steady rhythm.

"If the Smiths win, I want an alliance."

"If the Smiths win, I have no power to give you an alliance."

She frowned. "Why do you care so much about winning if it's not for you, and you're only going to die anyway?"

The wind sought the solange-eyed man's pulse. It was a hard, slow beat. His skin was sweat-slicked and his muscles tense. He cared. He cared as much as—maybe more than—the boy.

"You can care about something, even knowing you won't see the result. Why do people plant seeds, knowing they might not see them sprout?"

The woman laughed. "You sound like my brother. He's always going on about seeds."

After her laughter faded, soaked up by the old stone, the woman scuffed her boot on the uneven floor.

The solange-eyed one watched her. Then he decided his course of action.

"I'll give you an alliance with me," he said, "if you still want one after the duel."

"Duel?" The woman lifted her eyebrows. Shook her head. "What good are *you*? You're just a soon-to-be-dead null. I want the Smiths."

"Your choice." The solange-eyed man shrugged. "Come through right after me—"

"What?"

The man ducked through the door. The eye blinked.

"Son of a—" The woman threw her knife at the wood. It quivered in the closed door, then stilled. Slowly, the woman smiled.

Far, far below, there was the sound of an angry bellow. She glanced over her shoulder and then hurried to the door.

The eye blinked when she touched the iron handle.

"Jacob," she said, "you'd better get out of this alive."

Then she swept through the door and out of the final game.

The wind went to make trouble for the cruel one.

And then it went to find the boy.

78

THE ANTECHAMBER WAS CROWDED WITH SILENCE'S WEIGHTY PRESENCE. IT was heavy, expectant, and it pushed at every person in the room and filled every bit of space. The taut, bowstrung expectation shoved into the narrow space between conjurers. It bulged upward toward the ceiling. It even pushed against the closed doors, so the room felt as if it were about to explode.

It'd been three hours and twenty-three minutes since the players had entered the arena, and everyone knew it.

More than an hour had passed since we'd given up pretending not to care about the outcome. Before, the Bards had laughed, chatted, and smiled. The Clarks had debated the merits of different classification systems. The Wards—well, it was just Philoneas, and he'd made chummy with the Bard. The Smiths had even loosened their military postures and spoken in quiet rumblings amongst themselves.

But then the two-hour mark had passed, and everyone had slowly turned toward the metal double doors.

Tense expectation rolled through the room and chased out talk, laughter, and pretense. There wasn't enough air to do anything but stare at the doors so you'd be the first person to see the handle turn.

A new era was about to begin, and it would all start when those doors opened.

At some point, Darin had made his way over to stand next to me. He didn't smile, joke, or even speak. He was still stiff-backed and hard. He didn't even look at me. But I was happy to have him standing next to me.

I could barely breathe with the amount of tension pressing through the room. Finn had to be the first one to walk through the doors. If he wasn't, it was all over. He had to come in first.

If he didn't, the game—for me, at least—was done.

You might be wondering why it mattered. Couldn't I just lockpick the crown at the closing ceremony, no matter who won?

The answer is no.

If Finn won, I'd be on the dais with the crown. In some ceremonies in the past, when the principal was incapacitated, the body had even placed the crown on the heir's head. I'd be *right* there.

If Finn lost, there would be hundreds of conjurers standing between me and the crown. By the time I'd fought my way to the dais, they'd have caught me, skewered me, and trapped me in my own mind. Not to mention, they'd have had plenty of time to send the crown back to whatever hidey-hole they kept it in.

The closest anyone in the world got to the crown was during the exchange. That thirty-second period every 100 years when a new heir was crowned.

When we first agreed to this game, you made it very clear I should *not* attempt to take the crown unless you were on the dais. To try anything else would be unwise. Borderline insane.

I appreciated your caution.

While we waited, I resisted the urge to reach up and touch the knife hidden under my uniform. If I pulled it free and jabbed it through the air, would it pop all the tension in the room? Probably not.

So, instead, I stood still, my gaze stuck to the iron door handle.

If Jacob came through first, he'd won. If he came through second or third but still beat Primus, he'd won.

If Primus came through first, he'd won. If he came through second or third but still beat Jacob, he'd won.

If Celia came through first and all the other players were dead or disqualified, she'd won. It was a long shot, but the Bards loved a story with a long shot.

If Finn came through first, he could only win if Celia came through second and Primus and Jacob came through third and fourth. Then he'd have to duel whichever one had come through third.

The chances of Finn coming in first and Celia second were . . . slim. Maybe that was why my shoulders were tight, my right temple was throbbing, and my breath was short.

"If he wins this game," Darin said quietly, leaning close so no one could overhear, "I'm buying . . ."

He trailed off, and I pulled back to look at him. Everyone in the room was hyper-focused on the door, but their eyes shifted quickly to us and then away again.

Darin, for his part, looked as Smith-like and military-stern as he had five minutes ago. For all anyone knew, he'd just given me a command to remember antiseptic and bandages.

I leaned close, and my lungs expanded just a bit, relieving some of the tension. "Double cheese pizza," I whispered. "None of that meat lovers crap."

I pulled away, my face expressionless. Darin's gaze flicked to me, then away, and he gave a curt nod. A flicker of amusement darted through me.

We both went back to staring at the door.

I poked at the space in me where I could feel Finn's emotions. There'd been nothing but determination and calm since he'd walked through the doors. At one point, the determination and calm had fled, and there was only a blank, floating, empty space. It had scared me at first, the silence. I'd thought for a minute he'd died. But then I'd caught a hint of that gold-tinged love, and the determination had come back. After that, it was only that wall of calm.

A trickle of sweat dripped down my forehead and caught in my hair. The temperature of the antechamber had climbed since we'd all crowded in. The air was stagnant and hot. I let the sweat fall. I didn't want to reach up to wipe it away.

Someone cleared their throat. A boot scuffed against the concrete floor.

Luvic tried to catch my eye. I ignored him.

Come on. Come on.

I sent a message of emotions through the ring.

Come on. Come on.

You can do it.

You can.

Suddenly, there was a noise at the door.

My nails pressed into my palms, and I leaned forward, my shoulders tensed. The handle on the door turned.

Everyone in the antechamber held their breath.

The door opened.

Finn strode out.

The Smiths roared. Some shoved their fists in the air. Others stamped their feet. The room, which had been eerily silent, erupted into a booming, thunderous celebration.

I exhaled in a violent rush. *He did it. He did it!* I clenched my hands tighter and resisted the urge to shove my way past the conjurers and run into Finn's arms.

I wanted to jump up, wrap my legs around his waist, hug him, and never let go. I wanted to scream and cry and laugh. The tense expectation in the room burst, and in its wake, all the air that had been missing rushed around us, filling the room with frenzied glee.

Finn didn't seem to notice the shouting Smiths or their raised fists. Instead, he blinked, swayed a bit, and looked around the room with that blank, vacant, solange-filled gaze I'd come to love.

No.

Not love.

Like.

Tolerate.

I shook my head. Not love.

Finn searched the room, ignoring the shouting and the hard celebratory punches. Finally, he stopped searching when his eyes met mine.

I smiled. He smiled back.

A warm heat spread through me. It was like the sun on a spring day, gliding over bare skin, kissing it with welcome heat. I didn't know if the feeling was mine or his. I didn't care.

I grinned. "You did it."

He couldn't hear my words—the shouting and celebrating were too loud—but he nodded anyway.

Next to me, Darin grinned. "He did it," he said, his voice thick. "The son of gun did it."

Then, as if everyone had realized the same thing at the same time, the room quieted. While Finn strode through the thick crowd to me and Darin, everyone else turned back to the door.

If possible, the tension that had so quickly burst flew back into the room and ratcheted even higher.

Across the room, the Bards were grim-faced. The long shot had been shot out of the air. Celia would not wear the crown. The Bard's face was mournful, proud, and melancholy. It was an act. How did I know? He was using illusion to paint that picture. Who knew what he really felt?

Ragnor was easy to read. He looked like a man who sensed a threat, and he was preparing to tear the head from any man who approached his sister. Luvic, on the other hand, was strangely expressionless and still. For a man who thrived on mischief, lies, and misleading people, he was oddly, eerily calm.

The Clarks, unlike the Bards or Philoneas, pressed toward the doors. I could almost feel the eager heat of their breath on the back of my neck. "Primus," they whispered. "Primus."

Finn reached us. Darin gripped his arms. Finally, his military bearing broke, and he grinned at his brother. There was a wild jubilance in his eyes.

"I would've loved to have seen you fight in there."

Finn swayed and gave him a blank solange smile. He was still riding high on the dozen thimblefuls he'd swallowed before the game. I checked his eyes—the wide pupils, the silver lightning, the navy sky. I didn't see the light fading. There wasn't a hint of a crash.

I chewed on my lip worriedly. When I did, he turned to me.

"You're all right?" I asked, noting the bloodied slice along his forearm, the cut on his thigh, and the sweat running down his face.

"I'm all right."

Darin released him and shoved him away. "Of course he's all right."

Then the door opened, and Celia strode through. The room . . . I don't have to tell you this—you already know. The conjurers went wild.

Finn kept smiling at me, completely unfazed. He must've known she was behind him. He already knew he'd be fighting a duel for the crown.

I smiled back.

While Ragnor and Luvic formed a sort of "touch our sister and die" wall around Celia, the conjurers waited.

Whoever came through next would fight Finn for the crown.

Primus.

Jacob.

Primus.

Jacob?

Primus.

When Primus stalked through the door, the Clarks shouted with glee, and then the Clark raised his arms high in the air as if a new reign of blood and terror had already begun.

At the door, the Smith cleared his throat. The room quieted. He pierced the room with his cold gaze.

"The game is complete—"

"What about Jacob?" one of the Bard cousins called.

"Jacob Ward conjured during the game. He is disqualified." Wolfgang's mouth twisted as if to say that in doing so, Jacob wasn't worthy of being called a man, much less a conjurer. "When and if he passes through these doors, he will be stripped of his points. He is last in all ways." He looked at the Ward and said with a hard smile, "His shame is your shame."

I glanced at Philoneas. Usually, his looks were neutral, pleasant, forgettably average. At that moment, his expression was so cold and icily lethal that I shivered in response.

No one waited to see if Jacob would survive and walk through the doors.

Not even his father.

79

I SMOOTHED OINTMENT OVER THE CUT ON FINN'S BICEP. IT WAS DEEP enough to have sliced through layers of skin, but not deep enough to have reached muscle.

He'd showered and was wearing only a white towel wrapped around his waist. I'd already stitched the sword cuts in his thigh. I'd put in twelve neat stitches along the first cut, and then seventy-two tiny stitches along the longer, deeper gash.

I was amazed he wasn't limping. I was even more amazed he hadn't bled out. But no arteries had been nicked or sliced, and the tight fabric of his body armor helped.

I rubbed the glossy ointment over the red cut. It was two inches long, and I'd cleaned it well. What was I supposed to do? Wolfgang had snapped, "Body, take care of him. If he loses the duel because of your incompetence, you will die a thousand deaths."

It was good to know you could count on some things always staying the same. The sun rising. The moon's phases. Wolfgang handing out threats like candy at Halloween.

Finn didn't flinch, grunt, sweat, or curse while I stitched him up. I was sure he would have—even Justice had gone pale and sweated when I'd sewn him up—but before I pulled out the needle, Finn downed three thimbles of solange, so when I shoved the needle through his skin, he only gave me a bliss-filled smile. Perhaps, while in the thrall of solange, even pain was an illusion.

My fingers drifted over the heat of Finn's biceps. His skin was soft, but underneath, he was hard. I was smaller in this new body, and so his biceps were the size of my thighs. His hair was wet from the shower, and waterdrops ran over his wide shoulders and fell onto the cut of his chest.

We were on the second floor of the Smith compound, in a private suite of rooms. They were Darin's, I think, although they were so meticulously clean it was hard to tell. Finn sat on the edge of a king-size bed, and I stood next to him.

The lamplight was low, and steam coated the bedroom windows from the damp heat of the attached bath. Finn smelled like soap and ointment—the scent almost covered the cranberry and allspice. He smiled over at me, his lips curving, and my hand paused on his arm.

Darin was in the next room over, sourcing gear for Finn to duel in. No body armor or tactical gear was allowed, just well-made clothing and footwear. Darin could come in at any time. Then Finn would get dressed, and we'd go. Back to the Bards. For the duel, and then the closing ceremony.

So.

This was it.

These were the last few minutes we'd have. After we left this room, Finn would win, or he would lose. I'd make a play for the crown. Then Jagger would expect Finn to die. And I'd either be free, or I wouldn't.

But in all that, Finn and I wouldn't talk. Or touch. Or . . . anything.

And after, we'd go back to what we were. Me, one of Jagger's nines. Finn, a solange-addict in free fall, in love with another woman. There was nothing to say between those two people.

But between the Mari and Finn of right now, right here?

I had something to say.

I couldn't not say it.

I spoke before I could think better of it.

"I want you to know," I whispered.

Finn stilled, and when I went to pull my hand away, he reached out and held it in place.

I swallowed and continued. "I'm going to do whatever I can to make sure you come out of this alive. I want you . . ." I stopped.

I wanted him.

That was all there was to it.

But I wanted him in a way I'd never wanted anything before. Not in an ownership kind of way, or an "I have to have you" kind of way. In a . . . "I want you to be happy, to be loved, to be okay" kind of way.

I knew he wasn't perfect. He'd lied to me, hadn't he? Erased my memories of Griff's visit. Maybe erased more. But all the same, he'd always done exactly what he'd said he would. He was here to win. And if I could believe him, he was going to save me while he was at it.

Finn's hand moved gently over mine. "Mari," he said, and the way he said it reminded me of the first day we met, when he'd sighed my name as if it were a song in his soul.

I closed my eyes. It was hard to look into the shattered navy of his gaze. It was even harder not to see the naked gold of his skin, practically glowing from solange, or the shadow-carved muscles of his abdomen. A coil wound in my belly, and it tightened and throbbed. The invisible thread, there but not, pulled me closer to Finn.

When I opened my eyes, my throat hurt. My eyes burned. I swallowed painfully and said, "Whatever happens next, whether we become enemies or—"

"You'll never be my enemy." He shook his head.

"Or worse—"

"Mari. You'll never be my enemy."

I pulled my hand from under his, but when I went to move away, he grasped it tightly. I sighed and settled into the steady feel of his grip.

"I might be," I said. "You don't know what I'll have to do. What will happen if I become a mine? What if I destroy the world? What if I'm a sword, and the world is my victim?"

"Then,"—he squeezed my hand—"when I'm standing next to you, refusing to believe you're evil, stab me in the back. Kill me first. Let me die believing in you. I won't ever be your enemy, Mari. Besides, didn't I tell you?" He closed one eye and then the other, studying me. "I see the truth of you."

My throat tightened, and I nodded. Then, unable to resist, I wrapped my arms around his shoulders and squeezed my eyes tight.

My throat was so thick and pained it was hard to speak. "Thank you," I said. "Finn, whatever happens next, thank you. I'm so grateful that fate let me know you. I'm so glad to have . . . that you . . ." I buried my head against his neck and the warm heat of him. "That you showed me what love means. I didn't believe in it until you."

That warm, golden glow that tinged his every waking hour. That determination he had for his almost-wife. The way he talked about her and lived for her. That was love.

"I won't ever forget you," I promised.

Finn dropped his head against mine. "That's not an easy thing to promise."

"I know. But I suppose while people can lose memories, they don't lose feelings. Win today, okay? Win. That way, when we have the crown, we'll save the world, and somehow, I'll save you too."

Finn pulled free of my arms then. He studied me, a strange smile on his face. I wished I could read the lightning in his eyes.

Across the hallway, Darin shouted, "Found them."

Finn stood. He squeezed my hand, and I tried to find where the knot that bound us was hiding. That way, if I needed to, I could cut it. But there was nothing. Just the feeling of connection and warmth.

"If everything flips," he said, looking quickly at the door, "and nothing makes sense, do something for me."

He was oddly urgent. Darin was nearly at the door.

"All right."

"Trust your feelings," he said. "Not your head. Not what you see or think, or what you think you know. Trust your feelings."

I nodded. "Okay."

He let go of my hand and stepped back. I looked away. Darin walked in, a happy grin on his face and a load of clothes in his arms.

It was time to duel or die.

80

THERE WAS NO MOON. THE THIN KNIFE-PUNCTURE OF LIGHT HAD FLED, AND the night sky was as empty as the universe before thought created heaven and earth.

In the darkness, there were no stars, no planetary bodies, and no satellites nor airplanes to be seen through the thick night clouds. The underbelly of the clouds did reflect the city lights, but the reflection was ash-gray and soot-black, and instead of illuminating, the gray light added to the darkness.

The thirty-foot-tall arching windows were darkly opaque, and in them was the mirror image of nearly 300 conjurers gathered to watch the Clark heir and the Smith paladin duel. All the cousins who had stayed in the mansion, and all the ones who had descended on the city for the games, were here tonight.

Brightly dressed Bards. Studious Clarks. Military-stiff Smiths. There was even a dozen or so Wards, old and young, even though they rarely congregated together. They all stood at the edge of the hall, quietly taking in the buzz of energy crackling over the room.

It had been a while since I'd felt that curl of fear in my belly. The survival instinct that warned me conjurers were predators, and I was their favorite prey. But it was there now, snaking through me, tightening my chest.

It was how many of them there were. At the opening ceremony, there'd been about seventy. Now, there were 300. And every single one of them could conjure.

My skin was clammy, and a drop of sweat trailed down my neck, sticking to my gray silk uniform. I kept my face impassive and channeled "forgettable" with everything I had. It was definitely in my best interests for no one to notice me. At least, not until I'd grabbed the crown. Then they could notice me all they liked while I *ran*.

I stood at the front of the marble hall where, not too long ago, the opening ceremony had taken place.

It was before midnight, but not by much. The Bard didn't think the duel would take long. From the whispers, nudges, and murmurings, the general consensus was that Primus would annihilate Finn in seconds. Apparently, the conjurers as a whole still hadn't seen past Finn's stumbling, swaying, and vacant-eyed gaze.

Even Primus, who rarely smiled, strode into the hall with a confident smirk.

The families had entered the hall in the same order as before. The Bards. The Clarks. The Wards. The Smiths.

Ragnor strummed out a song on his stringed instrument, illusion dancing at his fingertips. The notes lit in the air like dancing fireflies. Each sound had a glowing spark—red, yellow, blue, green—that lit and then died in time with its chord. The music was mournful and melancholy, and I couldn't help but think it was because Ragnor was grieving his sister's loss.

The conjurers parted, and we strode down the mosaic-lined aisle. There was no moonlight to glint over the lapis and mother-of-pearl tiles. Instead, they were lit by the song. The gold-shot marble columns were no longer cracked from Finn's solange-filled oath at the opening ceremony. Instead, they were twined with laurel and holly leaves.

The hall was filled with illusion. The gold in the marble was brighter; the mosaic tiles were luminous; the glass of the three-story arching windows was waved like the surface of an inky black lake. It seemed the entire hall had been built and bolstered with illusion. Even the conjurers were covered in it—their clothing, jewelry, hair, and makeup.

Behind me, the dais was empty. The water in the black marble pool was still.

The front of the hall had been cleared and a circular area marked off for the duel. Philoneas, as a Ward, had already conjured an impenetrable barrier to prevent any illusion from backlashing onto the crowd. Whatever happened during the duel would stay within that twenty-pace-wide ringed circumference.

Primus was already inside the ring. He wore a brown long-sleeve shirt and black canvas pants. He had the same axe he'd taken into the final game, but it didn't look like he was planning on using it. Instead, his hands were free and ready to conjure. He rolled his shoulders and turned his neck until it cracked. Then he smirked at Finn.

Finn wasn't paying any attention. Instead, he was gazing around the marble hall with a slight frown. "This whole thing is held up by illusion," he murmured. "Why would they do that?"

"He's aiming to kill you," I whispered, nodding to Primus. "He won't strike to incapacitate. He wants to kill. Finn?"

Finn blinked and then turned to look as Primus's smirk widened into a grin. I'd seen that look enough to know exactly what it meant. You didn't grow up in Hell Gate without seeing your fair share of "I'm about to kill you" smiles.

"He's not playing. His first illusion will be to kill."

Finn smiled back at Primus. "Good."

Wolfgang stepped in front of Finn. He looked him over, disapproving, annoyed, hard. It always felt like there was a fifty-fifty chance Wolfgang would decide he was done with Finn and shove a sword through his gut. Right now, by the look on his face, the odds had shifted to eighty-twenty in favor of gutting. He gripped Finn's forearm and leaned close. The only reason I heard his words was because I was standing inches from Finn.

"When your mother told me about you, I promised her I wouldn't acknowledge you unless you could win the games without illusion. The fool believed in you. I didn't. I still don't. Prove me wrong." He shook Finn, gripping his arms. "Wake up. Prove me wrong."

Finn stepped away from his father, freeing his arm. He tilted his head and said with the quiet of a stone thrown into a pond, "Since when did proving anything to you come into the story? It was proven before I was born. Call my mother a fool again, and you'll regret it."

Wolfgang's mouth twisted into a vicious grin. "Go fight."

Finn stepped across the circular threshold of the ring. The air in the room popped as the barrier sealed itself around him.

He and Primus stared at each other from opposite sides of the circle. Neither moved.

The Bard raised his arms, quieting the ripple of murmurs that moved through the crowd.

"We are here, for the first time in 2,300 years, for a duel. The rules . . ." He smiled. His forehead shone with perspiration, and his mouth was tight. The Bard, even dressed in his plum-colored suit, and with his fingers ringed in gold, looked like he was oscillating between hysteria and rage. His mask was not firmly in place.

I didn't think he'd imagined Celia would lose. The crown would only stay with the Bards for a few more minutes.

"The rules." He waved his hands, and the room filled with a deep silence. "Conjure to incapacitate your opponent. This is a duel of skill, mastery, and cunning. Use whatever capabilities you have to subdue. Keep the conjuring within the ring. Physical weaponry and violence are permitted. The duel is won when your opponent is incapacitated or dead."

"Dead." Primus smiled.

The Bard ignored him. "At the completion of the duel, we will pass on the crown of illusions. We began these games with four players. Celia Bard—"

I glanced at Celia. She held her head high. She was wearing a long, skintight, black crepe dress and her crystal teardrop necklace. There was a pomegranate-size purple bruise on her cheek that she hadn't covered with illusion. She'd fixed her dark hair in a thick crown braid twined with pure gold thread. If she'd wanted to look like a queen, she'd succeeded.

Ragnor and Luvic flanked her. They were both in black tuxedos, less colorful than the Bard cousins surrounding them. This would probably be the last time I saw the three of them together. I stole a moment to take in their dark-haired, dark-eyed beauty. Luvic saw me watching. His face stayed grim, but ever so slowly, his right eye closed in a wink.

I stiffened.

He winked again.

What was he playing at?

"Jacob Ward," the Bard said, and I tore my gaze from Luvic and searched for Jacob.

He stood across from the dais, next to his father. Unlike the Bards or the Clarks, Jacob had abandoned formality and gone back to jeans and a T-shirt. When the Bard said his name, there was a distinct rippling through the hall. Some conjurers craned their necks or moved to the side to see him.

There was a palpable delight at his loss. A schadenfreude at the shame of the once feared Ward, now the lowest of all the players. They were hungry to see him drop his eyes, or to catch a hint of color on his cheeks.

I didn't expect any of that. This was Jacob Ward. Maybe they'd all forgotten he was the boogeyman of conjurers, but I hadn't.

He looked over the hall, a small smile on his lips, as if he was silently laughing at everyone for peeking at him like he was on display for their enjoyment.

Then, as he swept his gaze over the room, his eyes passed over me. He didn't stop. He didn't acknowledge me. But I felt it. That poke, like he was tapping a finger against my sternum. Testing. Questioning.

It stopped as quickly as it began.

"Primus Clark," the Bard said, swinging his arm toward the ring.

Outside the ring, at her brother's back, Last smiled sweetly. Well, if a carrion-eater opening its maw to eat a rotting corpse could be considered sweet.

"And Darin Smith."

Next to me, Darin stiffened as all eyes swung to him. That's right. Finn was the paladin. Darin was technically the player. He stared back at the 300 conjurers, looking like he just might challenge all of them to a duel.

"And now," the Bard continued, "the Clarks and the Smiths duel for the crown. At the conclusion, we will pass on the crown. We look forward to another 100 years of guiding and shepherding humanity. We look forward to 100 years of prosperity."

Uh-huh.

I bet.

I was sure he was excited about world peace and everyone living in harmony.

He thrust his arms in the air and shouted, "Let the duel begin!"

Darin reached over and grabbed my hand. He grinned down at me, his big-brother smile firmly in place. "For luck."

I nodded. "Right. For luck."

Primus leaned forward, twisting his mouth into a cruel smile. "I saw you consumed by fire. I wonder how you survived."

Finn blinked. Swayed. Tilted dizzily. "I'm a Smith. Did you forget? I was born in fire."

Primus laughed. "Let's see how you survive this."

He twisted his hand. Pressed his second and third fingers to his thumb. Then he snarled, and as he twisted, an illusion engulfed the ring.

It roared at Finn. It was a violent, hungry, flaming abomination. The creature was bones of lava and tendrils of fire. It was as wide as the ring and nearly as tall as the fifty-foot ceilings. It looked like it was born in hell and thrived on hate.

Someone gasped. A woman screamed.

Even though there was an impenetrable barrier around the ring, I swore I could smell sulfur and feel the scalding burn of unquenchable fire.

Finn smiled.

He *smiled*.

Then he stepped into the flames.

They dissolved. No—they snapped out of existence. The flames raced at Finn, the creature bellowed with fire breath, and in Finn's smile, it died.

"Holy," Darin said.

I think he was laughing, but I couldn't look at him to be sure. I couldn't take my eyes off Finn.

The lava illusion was gone.

Finn crossed the ring. He looked, once again, like a man walking a wire high above the earth, with winds buffeting him from every side. It seemed he might fall from the heavens at any moment and crash to earth.

Primus roared. He twisted his hand, and a mountain of earth rushed toward Finn. It was gone in a blink. Finn kept walking toward him. Unhurried. Solange-eyed. Smiling.

Primus twisted both hands and threw . . . I wasn't sure, but I think he threw antimatter at Finn. Or a black hole. Or . . . whatever it was, it was nothingness. A black depth of nothingness that writhed with the absence of light and the death of all things good.

Finn stepped through it, and the nothingness exploded.

My pulse rocketed. I held Darin's hand with a death grip.

He was going to do it.

He was going to win.

Finn was going to win the crown.

He'd made it across the ring. Primus must have realized Finn's solange addiction meant he wouldn't succumb to any illusion, no matter how powerful, because he yanked the axe free and raised it over his head.

Finn had his two swords. They were still sheathed. Was he going to yank them free and fight?

Or . . . ?

I didn't think Finn saw it. The axe.

He stared blankly ahead, closing one eye, tilting his head to look at Primus.

Primus roared and swung the axe in a powerful downward arc. It was an executioner's blow. Meant to kill.

Look out! Look out! I couldn't shout—my voice was lost in the panic.

The axe was a hair's breadth from Finn's head.

He didn't look out.

Instead, he moved so fast he blurred. He was as fast as light. As fast as cosmic rays shooting from the sun. He was lightning.

He twisted. Spun. Thrust his hand. It was one hard, deadly jab.

The axe fell to the marble.

Primus fell after it.

He hit the marble with a dull thud and folded into a crumpled heap.

Finn stared down at him for a moment and then looked out at the crowd.

No one moved.

I imagine no one breathed.

Then Finn turned around, found me, and smiled.

A SWELL OF TRIUMPH ROARED THROUGH ME. IT CHARGED THROUGH THE RING and caught me in its tide. Finn's emotions rushed through me so quickly that the stunned silence in the hall was covered by the ocean of blood rushing in my ears and the violent pounding of my heart.

He'd done it.

We'd done it.

I grinned at Finn. My smile was so wide my cheeks burned.

We stood there for I don't know how long, staring at each other with wild, triumphant smiles on our faces. In that moment—one second? Two seconds?—I let myself feel all the things I usually avoided.

The golden sheen of Finn's love. The invisible connection between us. The comforting warmth. The persistent hope.

It was during those short seconds that I let myself love Finn. I let myself feel it. I let it overwhelm me and consume me. And once I acknowledged it, it was like a locked door inside of me was flung open, and all the feeling I'd suppressed tore through me with hurricane force.

It struck Finn too. He stumbled backward. He hadn't anticipated the emotion. His eyes widened, and when he steadied himself, his features tightened.

I couldn't feel anything from him anymore. No triumph. No victory. No love. Just calm.

It would've made me wonder, but at Finn's stumble, I remembered the 300 conjurers in the hall. Less than three seconds had passed since Finn had defeated Primus, but a lot had changed in those three seconds.

Most notably, the Smiths had won the crown.

Perhaps even more notable, every conjurer in that room had realized Finn was a threat to their very existence.

I saw the exact moment Finn went from being a foolish solange-addict to an accident who had to be removed. Immediately.

After all, Darin could be crowned now. What use was there in keeping the paladin around?

The cavernous marble hall was dead silent. And I say this phrase in the way it was meant to be used. The dead are never silent. They weep. They rage. They demand justice. Remember the figments in the East River? They've never been silent. Only, most people can't hear them with their ears. They hear them with something else.

My muscles went taut. All 300 conjurers—all of them—were silently thinking the same thing.

Kill the paladin.

Finn righted himself. Shook his head. Was he completely unaware of the decision 300 conjurers had just simultaneously reached?

Maybe. But somehow, I doubted it.

Darin scowled. "We've got a problem."

He released my hand and held his own out, ready.

In that moment, I decided Darin was a good man. Instead of thinking about the crown and his own future glory, he was worried about his brother.

At the edge of the ring, the Bard raised his arms in the air. He was shocked. His expression hadn't yet cleared. But it was pretty obvious in the look he cast Finn that he was about to announce a winner and a celebratory execution.

"The Hundred Year Games are hereby declared at an end! The crown of illusions now passes on to a new heir. It is a night for renewal, and a night for death . . ."

Darin swore. "He's going to do it. He's going to kill Finn."

"But—"

"The games are over," Darin said. "He's not protected anymore."

But hadn't Darin seen the duel? Could the Bard even kill Finn? Or did Darin mean the Bard was about to set loose 300 conjurers on Finn?

Behind the Bard, the water in the black marble pool began to swirl. Fog rose in clawed eddies. The misty fingers of gray wove together and formed a thick whirlwind. Then the whirlwind shifted from gray to gold, and the crown of illusions rose out of the mist.

The crown was gold. It was old. Very old.

Crowns have been around for as long as humans have been around. Why? I don't know. They're a symbol of power that every human recognizes to their core. It's instinctual.

There's something in our marrow that tells us a crown is meant to rule.

A few years ago, I toured a museum collection in the city and saw a copper crown that was six thousand years old. That crown was an infant compared to the crown of illusions.

It was a thick golden circlet set with forty-four gemstones. Eleven rubies. Eleven sapphires. Eleven emeralds. Eleven diamonds. The stones symbolized the four houses and their four directions. They were united in one crown.

When the crown appeared, the Bard's lip curled. I reached up and touched the knife strapped under my silk shirt.

I was fifteen feet away. I was so close I could practically feel the weight of the crown in my hands. I could feel the smooth glide of gold and the cold surface of the rough-cut gemstones.

Seconds had passed. Primus was still unconscious on the floor. The Bard's arms were raised. Darin held his hand out, ready. Finn swayed. Tilted his head. I looked between the Bard and the crown.

I should've been watching Wolfgang.

He moved nearly as quickly as Finn. One second he was next to Darin; the next, he was inside the ring, a sword of blue fire in one hand.

I didn't know what I'd expected. For Wolfgang to kill his son? Maybe. For Wolfgang to protect his son? No. Definitely not.

He didn't do either.

Instead, he swung the sword at Finn. He lunged across the ring. His moves were fluid, fast, and I think everyone in that hall felt the same awe. This was Wolfgang Smith as he was meant to be.

Darin swore. He started to conjure but then aborted halfway through. He couldn't—wouldn't—interfere. Not if it was his dad.

The Bard laughed. His glee was so loud and bloodthirsty it raised the hair on the back of my neck.

The Clarks, of course, shouted approval. They thought it was a worthy sacrifice: paladin for heir.

The conjurers, as one, had the same reaction to Wolfgang's descending sword. Approval.

Except Luvic. I caught his expression at the last second. He had a grim, solemn look. And then, as the blue fire sword arched, a flash of panic darted across his face. He twisted his hand, and I saw threads of illusion shooting toward the ring.

They hit the impenetrable wall and disappeared.

Was he trying to help?

It was too late. Wolfgang's swing had already connected with Finn.

For Finn's part, he didn't do what I expected him to. He didn't pull free his own swords. He didn't dodge, tilt, or sway. He didn't duck, jump, or fight. In fact, he'd watched his father charge him as if Wolfgang were moving in slow motion.

I felt for fear, surprise, or anger. Finn didn't have any of these emotions. Instead, it was just a wary waiting.

He'd had plenty of time to move or counterattack. Instead, Finn had stood still and allowed his father's strike. I waited for the sword to disappear, like all of Primus's illusions did.

It didn't.

Finn let his father cut him.

He didn't move an inch. He didn't even flinch. He just stood there and watched the sword descend.

Wolfgang grinned as the sword connected. Blood splashed through the air.

A wild wind ripped through the crowd, and the whirlwind fog

surrounding the pool grew more violent. The crown pulsed with a golden glow.

A maelstrom grew over the black marble pool.

I stumbled as the wind shoved me from behind. I wasn't sure where it had come from—there were no open windows or doors. Darin caught my forearm and steadied me.

"Look!" a conjurer shouted.

They didn't have to. We were all looking.

Wolfgang's cut had sliced the back of Finn's right hand. There was now a long line of blood dripping onto the marble tile.

He hadn't killed him.

Instead, Wolfgang grabbed Finn's arm and held it high.

"Second son for heir," Wolfgang shouted. "Blood for blood. Life for life."

Next to me, Darin drew in a sharp, pained breath and clutched his right hand. A line of blood had formed on the surface.

The wind howled and raced through the hall. The conjurers shoved forward, pressing toward the impenetrable wall and the crown of illusions.

"I, Wolfgang Smith, declare Finn Alterra my heir—"

"You cannot!" the Bard shouted. "He is null. He is nothing—"

Wolfgang continued. "He will wear the crown of illusions—"

The entire hall erupted. It was a volcano of noise. Protests. Shouts. Chaos.

Finn stood next to his father, his bloodied hand thrust in the air. He didn't react to his father's words, he only kept his gaze on me.

Wolfgang's voice rose above it all. "As my firstborn child. Born from my wife, Lucinda Bard—"

The wind grew and ripped away the rest of Wolfgang's words.

"Holy," Darin said. "He's . . ."

Darin didn't finish. But I finished the thought for him.

"A conjurer."

Wolfgang dropped Finn's arm. He stalked through the impenetrable wall. He was ready to lead Finn to the crown and to . . . what? Smith glory? Endless wars? What was going on?

Perhaps we'll never know, because the second Wolfgang left the protection of the ring, he was attacked.

There was no warning. No feeling of foreboding. Nothing.

One second, Wolfgang was striding toward the dais; the next, Philoneas Ward had unleashed a windstorm of icy daggers. Hundreds of knives flew across the room. They rode the screaming wind.

Conjurers screamed and flattened themselves against the floor.

Wolfgang snarled and twisted his hands. The daggers burst into flame. The wind rushed toward Wolfgang, and the flame licked around him.

He bared his teeth and snarled, "Nice try."

Then his eyebrows lowered. He blinked. His hand came clumsily to his chest.

Then he dropped to his knees.

Not everything Philoneas had sent at Wolfgang was an illusion. There had been 500 daggers, and then there'd been one true knife, probably coated in Smith's Folly, hiding in the lies.

Wolfgang's hand fell away from the knife, and his eyes widened. His face turned deathly pale, and then, eyes unfocused and death-glazed, he smiled at Philoneas Ward.

It was a smile I imagined he'd given him when they were still friends. Before they'd sworn a death promise and vowed to kill each other.

Then the smile slipped from his face.

Wolfgang collapsed to the marble floor.

Dead.

82

CHAOS.

That was what happened next.

Absolute, utter frenzied chaos.

The sound of Wolfgang hitting the marble floor caused an unleashing. Before, the conjurers had been playing by the rules of the game. Now, the games were over, and there were no rules.

Was Finn crowned? I didn't know. Was I going to steal the crown? I was going to try.

Darin raced ten paces across the hall, dropped to his knees, and reached for his father. Two seconds later, everyone knew exactly what Darin had found. His howl of rage was one of the most terrifying things I'd ever heard.

When he rose, blue fire crackled around him. His muscles bulged, and I thought, if he was like Griff, he would've taken on his true form: a monster of vengeance that slaughtered everything in its path.

His gaze swung to Philoneas Ward, and then he lifted his hand and said, in a rage-slicked voice, "You want blood? Come and get it."

I dropped to the ground. What do you do in a fire? You drop to the ground so you can crawl under the smoke. This was the same.

At Darin's words, hundreds of illusions flew through the air. Darin and Philoneas were locked in a deadly exchange of wind and fire. Around them, the Smith cousins went after Jacob, Philoneas, and their few Ward relatives. The Clarks had decided it was another free-for-all. The Bards were attacking the Clarks *and* the Smiths.

I crawled toward the dais. The crown was still floating in the mist. The gemstones winked, and the gold glistened.

Finn stood in the center of it all. He stared at his dad's body. Then he looked down at his bloodied hand.

I wondered what he was thinking in that moment. His dad had just been murdered by the same man who'd killed my parents. He'd just been declared heir and winner of the crown. What were the thoughts in his heart and his mind?

Had he always known what all this was leading to?

He twisted his hand, but nothing happened. When he looked up, he found me crawling through the chaos. He focused on me and said one word. I couldn't hear it over the roar in the room, but I knew what he'd said.

"Mari."

He took a step toward me.

All the illusion racing overhead hit the impenetrable wall and disappeared. That wouldn't last long though. I was sure the Bard—or many Bards—would try for Finn's head soon.

Finn didn't seem to notice the fighting around him. Instead, he was completely focused on me.

Then Darin roared with pain and rage. Finn jerked and turned toward him. An illusion spear had been thrust through Darin's shoulder. Blood poured from the wound. A Clark swiped at him with a mace.

Darin thrust back with a wall of blue fire.

He was surrounded, but still, he pushed forward, fighting to reach his father's murderer.

Suddenly, I saw how this would end. Wolfgang dead. Darin dead. Finn, probably dead.

Darin's fire flickered weakly and then grew strong again. I realized now why everyone had always said Darin was the weakest heir in Smith history. It was because he wasn't the heir. He'd always been second-born.

There was no way he'd be able to stand against Philoneas, much less his son, his wife, his relatives, and the wall of bloodthirsty Clarks.

Darin was going to die. Probably within the next two minutes.

But then Finn did something no one expected.

While fire, lightning, illusion arrows, lances, abominations, and murder weapons flew through the room like a flock of vicious birds, Finn held up his hands as if he were about to conjure.

I thought to myself, *Here it is. Here's where he finally shows his true self. He's been lying all along. He isn't a null. He isn't even half-human. He's a full-blooded conjurer, and he's about to conjure a mountain of lava to swallow everyone.*

But that wasn't what happened.

Finn didn't conjure. Instead, he called on solange.

The black marble pool exploded. A whirlwind howled and spun across the room. The crown was swept up in the maelstrom. The whirlwind raced through the conjurers, knocking people over and throwing them into confusion.

Suddenly, the whirlwind stopped at the edge of the ring, and then, as if gaining momentum, it burst through the impenetrable wall. It consumed Finn. It wrapped itself around him and yanked at his clothing and his hair. He was in the center of a vortex. The crown floated above him.

I was still on the ground, a few paces away from the dais. The Bards were so close I could reach out and touch the plum fabric of the Bard's suit.

As the crown began a slow descent toward Finn, his head jerked back, and he stared at the ceiling. The whirlwind disappeared, and he and the crown were consumed by a golden column of light.

But unlike at the opening ceremony, the column didn't fall over Finn like a golden river. Instead, Finn gathered the light in his hands. He formed a giant golden ball. It pooled above his hands, a huge droplet forming from the liquid waterfall raining from the sky.

Then Finn looked over the conjurers, nodded at his brother, and shoved the ball of solange across the hall.

It hit like a sonic boom. The air compressed and then contracted. My ears popped at the explosion. The walls shook violently as the entire hall and all 300 conjurers were hit with undiluted solange.

I wasn't a conjurer, but I felt it hit my bones. The impact was like being slammed by a semitruck going lightspeed. It tore through me and ripped me open.

Every illusion in the room shattered and fell apart. Screams tore through the room.

And then the hall began to crumble.

Finn had been right earlier: the entire hall *was* being held up by illusion. Now that the illusion was gone, it was collapsing.

The Bard flicked his hands, attempting to conjure. A lot of conjurers did. They all realized at the same time that Finn had filled the hall with so much solange the place was coated in it. There would be no illusion here. Not anymore.

Everyone knew solange destroyed illusions. But no one had ever seen solange do this.

Darin laughed. If there was no more illusion, then there were only fists and steel. That was where the Smiths loved to play. He yanked his dagger free.

Then, shoulder dripping with blood, teeth bared, he shoved through the crowd, aiming for Philoneas.

Six Clark cousins, who'd been at the edge of the impenetrable wall, decided now was the perfect time to slaughter Finn.

Finn blinked and then raised his eyebrows as if to say, "You really want to do this?" Then, in a fluid motion, he pulled free his twin swords.

When the Clarks rushed him, he spun at them, the blades a blur in his hands. I knew he could move. Of course I knew. I'd seen it. But I'd never seen him like this.

He sliced through the six Clarks in seconds, his two blades moving so quickly it looked as if he were holding eight blades, or sixteen. He moved with such violent force it didn't feel like I was looking at a man but at a force of nature. He was beautiful. He was terrifying. Every

Clark, every Bard, every conjurer who rushed him met the same quick end. There was no passion. There was no rage. There was only Finn, the eye of a storm, delivering death to any conjurer who stepped into his path.

I was frozen. I couldn't move as I watched him cut his way across the marble toward me. My heart thundered, matching the boom of columns collapsing. Finn dealt death, and the whole while, his gaze stayed trained on me.

What . . . ?

What was this?

He was a conjurer. He was a Smith. He was slaughtering every conjurer who attacked. And he was coming . . . for me?

Then Darin shouted again, and Finn turned toward his brother.

My skin went clammy. Cold then hot. Now that Finn had turned away, I unfroze. I scrambled back.

What was happening? Everything was upside down. Everything.

Yet one thing remained: I was here to steal the crown.

Where was it? Could I still grab it?

The solange was still falling in a waterfall over the room. The crown floated in the center of that golden column. Okay. All I had to do was weave through a mass of conjurers, grab the crown, and run. No problem.

I tucked my chin and crouched, ready to sprint toward the crown.

Then I heard Luvic. He wasn't far from me. He was just past his father, next to the dais. He and Ragnor were a wall in front of Celia.

"Lia," he said, his voice had that desperate note I'd heard only once before. When he'd begged me to free him from the cage.

"What is it?" she asked.

"Do me a favor," he said.

I glanced over. Luvic's face was pale, his jaw hard. There was something funny about his expression. I didn't like it. He stared at his sister with an intensity I'd not seen before.

Celia nodded and curled her hands in the black crepe of her dress. I was sure she thought he was about to tell her to get out of the hall before it collapsed. That would have been a logical favor for him to ask.

Instead, Luvic reached into his tuxedo and pulled free a gun.

He aimed it at Celia, and when he smiled, it wasn't his mischievous, twinkling grin; it was cold and grim.

"Die for me," he said.

Then he pulled the trigger.

The noise was louder than I expected. The sharp bang punched through the air.

Celia cried out. She twisted her hand. Of course, nothing happened. Finn had made it so no one could conjure.

Ragnor wasn't as slow as Celia. He didn't try to conjure. Instead, he threw himself in front of his sister.

It was too late though. Luvic pulled the trigger a second time. Another loud, merciless punch.

He was feet away from both of his siblings. He didn't miss.

Both Celia and Ragnor dropped to the floor within a second of each other. It was as if they were puppets on a stage and their strings had been cut.

Celia landed on her side. Her head ricocheted off the marble and then fell still. Her black crepe dress fell around her like a funeral shawl.

Ragnor collapsed on top of her, his arms out in an aborted attempt to save her, his head titled to the side, eyes open and unseeing.

They were dead.

Celia and Ragnor were dead.

Luvic Bard had just killed his siblings.

He stood over them, his gun hand steady, a small, grim smile on his lips.

The echo of the gunshot still rang in my ears.

I shoved away from the Bards, crawling on my hands and knees, praying neither Luvic nor the Bard could see me nearby. Some of the Bard cousins who had been close by were screaming; others were fighting nearby Clarks. A few of them stared, open-mouthed and stunned, at the slaughter of the heir and the second-born.

Luvic gave one last look at his brother and sister. They were boneless, empty-eyed, dead. He'd shot them in their chests, not their heads, so their dying expressions were easily read. Shock. Fear. Betrayal.

Then Luvic turned and sprinted toward the center of the hall.

He raced toward Finn, dodging Clarks, weaving past Smiths.

Was he going to kill Finn too?

Finn saw him coming. He lifted an eyebrow and then cut through another Clark, shoving him aside. Luvic pulled a long knife free from his tuxedo and charged Finn.

Then, at the last second, when Luvic was only a foot away and a clash and a death was inevitable, Luvic stopped, grinned wildly at Finn, and Finn . . .

He grinned right back.

They smiled at each other like they were the best of friends.

Then they spun around, pressed themselves back-to-back, and absolute carnage began.

They cut through everyone in their path. In seconds, they reached Darin, and at seeing Luvic and Finn fighting together, he laughed and joined them.

They cut their way through the Clarks and aimed toward the Wards. Plaster chunks from the ceiling rained down. They struck the floor and exploded. Four of the twelve marble columns had already crumbled, and the ceiling above them had caved and smashed to the floor.

In minutes, the entire room would be buried.

I didn't understand what was going on. I'd read about many, many games. I'd never read anything like this.

Were the conjurers denying that Finn would be crowned? Were they rejecting the Smiths' win? Or was it Finn who was denying the conjurers? Was he planning on slaughtering them all?

But . . .

Finn was a conjurer.

Luvic was his friend.

Finn and Luvic were friends.

You could tell by the way they fought together. You could tell by the way they grinned at each other. A cold chill raced through me.

Luvic had killed me.

Luvic had burned Hell Gate and hurt Rou.

Luvic had threatened me.

Finn had erased my memory so I wouldn't know what Luvic had done.

Finn was friends with Luvic.

Finn was a conjurer.

There was only one conclusion.

I'd been played. I'd been watching the wrong shell for the entire game, and when I'd tapped the container with my guess, it'd come up empty.

Do you remember when Justice warned me about betrayal? He'd told me betrayal often came from friends, and it came from the last place we expected. Even Luvic had warned me that I was too soft, and that people would use my softness against me.

Here was the proof.

Finn wasn't good. He was a full-blooded, death-wielding conjurer, and he was on a mission to kill everyone in this room.

Luvic wasn't good. He'd killed me, and he'd just cold-bloodedly killed both his siblings.

I had to get the crown, and I had to get out. No conjurer, not even Finn Alterra, was going to wear that crown. Not ever again.

It was still hovering in the mass of streaming gold. I just had to reach it.

I hopped up and ran toward the golden light, dodging and weaving. The wind shoved and shrieked, and when I stumbled, a chunk of plaster the size of a taxi smashed onto the marble tile where I'd been.

Darin had reached Philoneas. He was cutting at the Ward with his long dagger. Philoneas didn't have a weapon. Instead, he was blocking Darin's thrusts with a chunk of marble from a crumbled column.

Jacob was next to him, a piece of plaster in his hand, his face a furious mask. He shoved Darin back, but when Philoneas saw me run past, he snapped, "Jacob. Your sister! Go!"

I kept running.

I have to admit, when Philoneas said, "Your sister!" I didn't realize he was talking about me.

But then Jacob saw me. His face transformed from rage to

determination. He shoved the plaster at Darin, leaped past Finn and Luvic, and sprinted after me.

He caught my hand, and before I knew it, we were sprinting toward the windows and the only exit. The back door was blocked. The ceiling there had already caved and buried it. Even now, more plaster chunks were falling.

But even with the hall collapsing, marble columns tumbling, and absolute carnage in the Bard Mansion, I yanked on Jacob's hand. He was a Ward. He was a conjurer. He was—

"Viola!" he shouted, his voice eclipsed by the wind. "We have to go! Remember the fifty-first games? The Smiths, Luvic—they're going to kill everyone. No one's coming out of this room alive. We have to go!"

The fifty-first games?

Wait.

Was this what the Smith and Darin had been talking about? Was this the favor Wolfgang had asked of Luvic? Absolute carnage? To slaughter everyone?

"No." We sprinted past the column of gold, and I tugged, yanking at Jacob's hold. "Let me go."

"We have to get out—"

Then the importance of what Philoneas had said and what Jacob had called me finally hit. It slammed into me as hard as a marble chunk bashing my skull.

Viola.

Your sister.

Viola.

"You're . . ." I couldn't get a breath. I couldn't breathe. I thrust out with the last of the air in my lungs. "You're my twin brother."

The edge of Jacob's mouth lifted into a smile, and then the poking, prodding I'd felt from him before was no longer a tap against my sternum. Instead, that hole he'd mentioned inside of me opened wide and snapped, and as he reached out, it caught the thread of him in its jaws.

The connection between us yanked taut, and it was as if the illusion of plaster and marble columns that had been built inside of me collapsed at once. They caved in on themselves and were swept aside too.

In their place, I felt myself reconstructing, grabbing hold of Jacob's thread and weaving a new rope for myself. That thread had lain dormant and unused my entire life. It had been hidden and buried. Locked away. Unseen. Undiscovered.

Now, it rose up and filled me.

Someone (Philoneas?) had carefully constructed an illusion inside of me—one that had been with me from birth, or even *before* birth. It was so familiar, so much a part of me, that I'd never realized it was there. Hiding me. Hiding me from everyone, including myself. I'd been my own warden; my own jailer.

What had Jagger always called me? A ward of Hell Gate.

He hadn't meant that I was a ward; he'd meant I was a *Ward*.

I was—oh no—I was a Ward. A conjurer. A full-blooded truth-seer. Philoneas Ward's daughter. Jacob Ward's sister.

"But . . . you killed your sister. You—"

"No. I shattered my mirror. She was an illusion. Dad made her to—"

An explosion sounded, and Jacob threw his arms out to block the marble shrapnel that flew at us. He glanced back.

Finn had left Darin and Luvic and was cutting his way toward us. There was a violently thunderous look on his face.

I swear, in that moment, Finn looked like he would slaughter everyone in that room to reach me.

"I'll tell you later. We have to get out of here," Jacob said. He grabbed my hand. "Trust me. Okay?"

I started to shake my head. But I stopped. I did trust him. That thread that coiled between us? It was a sibling bond—one I'd never felt before but had felt the absence of. I realized I *knew* Jacob. I knew him. Not literally, but in the sense I could understand him and predict his actions. I knew him like I knew myself.

He'd opened something inside of me when he'd shoved away all that metaphorical rock and plaster. He'd unlocked my truth. My power—the ability to lockpick—had just received a massive upgrade. I could feel it bursting within me. Before, it had been a trickle leaking from a dam. Now, the dam was gone, and my abilities were a rushing river.

Second-born. I was a second-born conjurer. The only thing was, I had the once-in-a-hundred-generations ability to untie illusions instead of weave them.

I shook my head. The heat and violence of the hall pressed in on us. Jacob tugged my hand, wanting to run.

But I had to know.

"Why don't you want to kill me?"

That was what I'd always been told. What I'd read in countless records. A Ward would kill anyone who could untie illusion. They ruthlessly executed lockpicks.

Jacob frowned. "Kill you? I've spent my whole life keeping you alive. I've spent my whole life waiting to meet you."

We stared at each other, and I knew the truth of his words, even if I didn't know the how or the why. I nodded, and Jacob smiled.

"Okay," I said.

His smile grew. "Okay then."

Then he started to run, and since my hand was in his, I ran too. We flew past the gold column, and as we did, I looked back at the crown.

I reached out with my mind. It hung in the air on a draft of illusion. The knot that held it up was simple. A figure-eight knot, symbolizing eternity. All I had to do was slip it free, and I could grab the crown. We'd take it while the hall fell and buried all the other conjurers. Perhaps we could escape and end the latest 100 years of bloodshed before it even began.

Would Jacob want that too?

"Wait." I tugged my hand. "I have to—"

I didn't finish the sentence.

One second I was holding Jacob's hand, right next to the crown, and the next, I was hurtled across the room into Finn's arms.

He'd used the ring.

The room tilted, spun, and jerked. The snapping rubber-band retraction yanked me to him. A wave of lust slammed into me as I hit Finn's chest.

He shuddered and pinned me to him with his left arm. I shoved at his chest, but he held me against him. He was still swinging one of his swords with his right arm, holding off a Clark.

My blood sizzled, my skin puckered, and I wanted to wrap my legs around Finn and bury my face in his neck. I wanted to kiss him while the world collapsed around us.

Hateful, horrible ring.

I shoved against him again. His arm tightened. No matter how much skill or talent I had, and no matter how many times I'd practiced with Justice, Griff, and all the other creatures in Hell Gate, I wasn't getting out of Finn's hold.

Why had he used the ring? Did he think he was protecting me, or was this the end? Maybe while Jagger had told me to kill Finn, he'd told Finn to kill me. Perhaps that was part of their bargain too. I wouldn't put it past Jagger. And now I wouldn't put it past Finn.

I looked over my shoulder, searching frantically for Jacob. He was fighting, wielding a broken piece of wood he'd grabbed from the splintered dais, surrounded by five bulky Smiths. They were intent on killing him—there wasn't any doubt about it. They taunted him and lunged, like a group of wolves playing with the prey they'd run to ground.

Philoneas had killed the Smith, so the Smiths were going to kill Philoneas and his son. Probably his wife too. And, come to think of it, his long-lost daughter, if they found out who I was.

Jacob caught my eye, and his jaw hardened. One of the Smiths stumbled, and Jacob stabbed him with the wood and grabbed his shortsword.

I shoved at Finn again, throwing my elbow and trying to twist free. His chest was a wall and his arm unmoving. His skin was hot and slick with sweat. While I tried to break free, he held me against him and shoved back a wild-eyed Clark.

I jammed my foot into his. "Let go!"

He skewered the Clark and spun to block a chunk of marble thrown by a Bard.

"Mari," Finn growled. "Are you—?"

I kicked him.

"Mari! Stop."

I wouldn't. Those Smiths were about to kill my brother. My long-lost, didn't-kill-his-sister, been-protecting-me-his-whole-life twin brother.

"Let me go!"

He didn't. Instead, he gripped me tighter. He pressed me against the heat of him and the rough thundering of his heart. He kept me locked behind his arm and the wall of his whirring sword. I was about to try to twist out of his grip again, but then I heard a shout above the rumble of the collapsing ceiling that I didn't expect.

"Mari!"

It was Justice. I jerked and turned my head toward the shout.

Justice stood at the edge of the broken arched windows. He was higher than the rest of the conjurers, standing on a pile of broken marble. The wind tore at him, shoving against the black canvas of his clothes.

He was dressed in his assassin's gear. Black from head to toe. Plaster and marble dust rose around him, and I swear, he looked terrified. I'd never seen Justice so scared in all my life.

Griff, sure. Griff was scared all the time.

But Justice? He'd never been this scared. Not ever.

His face was bleached white. His freckles, even from a room away, stood stark against his skin. His eyes were wide—what had he seen? What did he know?—and his hands shook as he aimed a crossbow at Finn.

"Mari! The knife!" he shouted.

Somehow, I heard his words above the wind, the chaos of the fighting, and even the crumbling walls.

I elbowed Finn, trying to free my arms, but he'd already loosened his grip.

When he saw Justice, he stiffened. Then he drew back his sword arm. I could see it in his eyes; in the bulge of his muscles and the concentration in his gaze. He was going to throw his sword. And somehow, unbelievably, it was going to hit Justice. Not just hit. Kill him.

Finn was going to kill my best friend.

He was a Smith. He'd decided. He'd already envisioned it in his mind. It was going to happen.

Conjured or not, it was reality.

Justice—my friend; the brother of my heart—was going to die a true and final death.

And Finn Alterra was going to be the one to deliver it.

So I did what Finn had asked of me. When things were flipped upside down and nothing made sense anymore, I didn't trust my thoughts. I didn't trust my heart. I trusted my feelings.

I couldn't let Justice die.

I couldn't.

I yanked my knife free and stabbed Finn in the heart.

83

Hero or villain? That's the question, isn't it? Will I be your hero, or will I be your villain?

Or will I only be yours? Nothing less. Nothing more.

The knife was lightweight, the metal handle warm from being pressed against the hot skin of my abdomen. The blade was thin and sharp.

When Justice had given it to me, he'd told me its name: Heart's Death.

He'd said it never missed.

So, while I aimed for Finn's arm, while I arched to hit his bicep and divert the path of his sword, the knife had a different trajectory.

In the life-or-death chaos of the moment, I'd forgotten objects of power had their own rules. If you used a knife called Heart's Death, you could expect that knife to hit the heart. And you could definitely expect it to kill.

In my world, it's easy to become cavalier about life and death. For many, life somehow becomes less than sacred. Perhaps in the beginning, in the realm where reality is spoken into existence, life is pure, golden, and truth-filled. But once it passes through the gray curtain that separates thought from reality, life becomes tattered, dirty, and worn. In

Hell Gate, life is a faded black and white photocopy of itself, and it's so, so hard to find the sacredness you know is at its core.

Yet I'd always clung to the fervent belief that life was sacred. Because once life wasn't sacred, nothing was. I'd avoided killing, even when Jagger had pushed, prodded, and demanded it. I'd always, always avoided crossing that line.

Heart's Death twisted in my hand. As soon as I gave it the intent to stab Finn, his life was over.

The heart is more difficult to stab than most people think. There's the breastbone. The ribs. A whole lot of bone and cartilage shielding that fragile organ.

But none of that mattered with an object of power. It slipped between two ribs and slid into Finn's chest. The knife went easily, like a hand dipped into warm water.

I felt the moment the knife hit his heart.

He'd let go of me to pull back his sword. His right arm was drawn back. His chest was wide-open. He was completely vulnerable.

My hand tightened around the hilt.

Finn jerked. His eyes widened, and he drew in a jagged, shocked breath. When he looked down, his sword fell from his hands and clattered against the marble floor.

I couldn't let go of the knife. I wasn't sure if my hand was locked to it, or if the hot blood pumping from Finn's wound had shocked me so much that I was numb and frozen.

He took in the knife in his chest. My hand on the blade. His blood running free, coating my hand in red. There was a stunned, disbelieving expression on his face. I knew right then that he hadn't believed—not once—that I would ever kill him. He'd trusted me. Completely.

I knew then that no matter what I'd felt or thought during the chaos, the revelations, the deaths, I still wanted Finn to come out of all this alive. I wanted him to have his happy ending, out there somewhere, with his almost-wife. I wanted him to have his patch of sky to look up at.

It didn't matter if he was a conjurer. Funny enough, I was one too. It didn't matter if he was in league with Luvic, my one-time murderer. We all had our loyalties, didn't we? It didn't matter if he'd erased my memory or played me. Hadn't he told me to do what I needed to do, and he'd do what he needed to?

None of that mattered. I still wanted him to live.

His chest spasmed, and he shuddered.

"Finn," I said, yanking at the knife. "Finn?" I didn't know what I was expecting to do. Pulling it free would only speed the blood loss. But it wouldn't budge.

Finn coughed. Choked on a breath. He tried to say something, but no words came out. There was only the sound of a man with no air left in his lungs and no words left to give.

He struggled to speak, and my vision blurred.

I shook my head. "I'm sorry. I'm sorry. I didn't—"

Finn looked past me. The silver in his eyes was shattered, and the navy was clouding over. The golden light in his skin was leaking away.

He swayed as if he'd had too much solange, and his skin drained of all its color. Then he grabbed my arms and tried to yank me to the side.

He was clumsy though, his limbs weak and heavy with the weight of death. I'd experienced it enough to know. You lost the ability to control your body. You floated outside of yourself, and all the threads that had kept you attached to yourself were methodically snipped away, one by one.

He was fighting it, but it wasn't enough. No matter how strong a man was, he wasn't stronger than death.

So exactly two and a half seconds after I shoved a knife through Finn's heart, Justice shot an arrow through mine.

The bolt hit me from behind. It punctured my ribs, punched through flesh, and slammed through my right lung. The pain tore through me. The force of the crossbow bolt slammed me against Finn. He wasn't strong enough to stand anymore, so when I was hit with the bolt, Finn crashed to the floor, and I fell on top of him.

Numbness tore through me. The ability to breathe leaked away. Breath rattled in my lungs, but I couldn't hold onto it long enough to form any words.

My body was cradled by Finn's. The heat of his blood soaked into my thin silk shirt and wet my skin. I pushed against the marble floor and tried to lift myself off him. I had to tell Finn . . . I had to tell him I was sorry.

I was so sorry.

Justice hadn't been aiming at Finn; he'd been aiming at me. His was the betrayal he'd been warning me about in the only way he could. I think . . . I think he'd given me the knife to protect myself from him.

But instead of stopping Justice from killing me, I'd stabbed the man trying to save my life.

I coughed and wheezed, pulling in air that somehow didn't make it to my lungs. I managed to push myself up enough to look down at Finn.

His eyes were clouded. The navy and silver striations were no longer the birth of the cosmos. Instead, they were a night sky filled with gray ash. Sweat soaked his skin, and his face was drawn. His body convulsed and stiffened, and he tried to speak, but no sound came out.

He reached out, trying to close his hand around mine. When he caught my blood-soaked fingers, he held them in a loose, shaking grip.

His gaze moved from the tip of the bolt protruding from my chest, back to my face. There was wrenching, agonizing grief in his expression. More than that, there was the desperate urging to be forgiven.

But what did he have to be forgiven for? I was the one who'd killed him.

I realized then that for the past two weeks, the Finn I'd known had been a lie. A cleverly and carefully fabricated lie.

That wall of calm I always felt through the ring? It crumbled. It fell, and the wreckage let through a tsunami of emotion.

Finn's emotions roared through me. Love. Sorrow. Fear. Need. Pain. Regret. Yearning. Love again. So much love.

He tried to speak again, but no sound came out. At that, a tear trailed from his right eye. He knew he was dying. A man has a certain look in his eye when he knows he's about to cross from this world to the next.

Another crossbow bolt hit me. It punched through my back and splintered my ribs. If I could feel, I knew the pain would be extreme. But I'd already passed beyond the pain of flesh and blood. I fell forward, collapsing over Finn, my lips pressed against the hard plane of his cheek.

His skin was cold. Already, the warmth of life was fading, even before his soul had fled.

His hot, salt-filled tears trailed down his cheek and pooled at the corner of my lips. I could taste the salt and the sorrow. I could taste his pain.

And then . . .

"What will you do if you win?" Philoneas had asked while Finn was strapped to the inquisitor's chair.

"Cry." The word had burst from Finn as if he didn't want to answer.

I gasped, the salt of Finn's tears spreading through me like the golden glow of solange.

Why?

Because Finn's tears unlocked all the memories he'd taken, and suddenly, the taste of his tears opened a floodgate inside of me.

I was torn from the moment, riding on a wave of memories.

"Mari!" the boy pleaded. "Mari! Untie the knot!"

And I knew—because of course I knew—that boy was Finn. We'd been outside the Clark Mansion. He'd wanted to pick me forget-me-nots. Instead, we were trapped, and if I saved him, there wouldn't be enough time to save myself. While Finn had tried to pull me free of the Clark illusion, he'd begged, "Mari! Untie the knot!"

I hadn't.

I'd died for him.

Why?

Because I loved him.

My life—my entire life—came back to me.

While Finn and I lay on the floor, bleeding red on the white marble, I remembered my past. Another marble column crumbled. The plaster walls shook and caved. The roar of the impending collapse was violent, like a thousand men screaming at once. Dust and marble shards flew across the room. It wouldn't be much longer before the entire ceiling caved and crushed everyone inside.

I wouldn't live to see it.

Most of the conjurers were either dead or fleeing. The hall was thick with dust, screams, and violent shaking. Another chunk of ceiling fell, revealing the deep black-purple night sky.

No moon.

I spent the last five seconds of my ninth life reliving a night I'd forgotten.

I sat on the soft white sheets of Finn's bed, my legs crossed, hands in his. The window was open, and a soft summer breeze blew off the Hudson and cooled Finn's room in the warehouse above the Night Den. I wore a white summer dress, and the breeze tugged at the cotton and blew my hair across my cheeks.

He gripped my hands and stared into my eyes.

His were hazel still. The woodsy green and gold color I loved.

He hadn't yet taken his first sip of solange.

That night was only a month ago. Two weeks before the games had begun.

I'd been happy that night. Happier than I'd been in my entire life. The moment had swallowed me whole and left me glowing as bright as the sun.

I'd been wrapped up in Finn and what we were doing. The soft moonlight had spilled through the room and coated me in silver-tinged elation.

"I promise," Finn said, his voice low and urgent, "to honor you and cherish you and love you. In the name of God, I vow to protect you and shield you, help you and love you, all the days of my life. I take you, Mari Locke, to be my beloved wife. You will never be cold, because I will be your warmth. You will never be lonely, because I will be your friend. You will never be alone, because I will be your beloved. I will love you and cherish you until we are parted by my final death. This is my solemn vow." Then, with a small smile, he said, "And even in death, I'll love you still."

We didn't have rings. No one in Hell Gate could know what I'd done. But I'd told Finn we didn't need rings; we'd make a knot of love and tie it tight between us. An eternal knot. One that could never, ever be untied.

"I promise," I vowed, my heart pounding, trying to reach out and connect with Finn's, "to honor, love, and cherish you. In the name of God,

I vow to stay by your side in all things, in all ways. I take you, Finn Alterra, to be my beloved husband. You will never be cold, because I will be your warmth. You will never be lonely, because I will be your friend. You will never be alone, because I will be your beloved. I will love you and cherish you until we are parted by my final death. This is my solemn vow."

"And even in death?" he asked.

I smiled and reached up to run my hand down the stubble on his cheek. "I'll love you still," I promised.

He leaned into the warmth of my hand as I cupped his cheek.

"I just married you," Finn said. He turned his head and pressed his lips to the center of my palm. "Wife."

The warmth of his kiss spread through my hand, up my arm, and tied itself around my heart. I felt it—the rope that wasn't a rope. The knot that wasn't a knot. It slid around my heart and tied me to Finn so that, no matter what happened, our love would never be broken.

I sent my hands into the warm fall of his hair and pulled his mouth to mine.

"Husband," I whispered, feeling the word wrap itself around me. "Husband."

I fell back onto the cool sheets, and the mattress dipped as Finn landed on top of me. His mouth sought mine, and when I opened to him, he made a hungry, yearning noise. I tugged his mouth closer and rocked against the heat of him.

He worshiped me. With his hands. With his mouth. With his words. He spent the night worshiping me.

When he slowly untied the ribbons of my dress and pushed the fabric free, I could've lived on the look in his eyes forever.

His calloused hands scraped over the skin of my hips. He reverently brushed my lips with his. He bared himself to me, and even if we were two people, that night, our lives became one.

We loved like the world had never seen lovemaking before; like we were the ones to first discover it. It was as if we'd been waiting our whole lives for the sun to rise, and it finally had. Fourteen years of friendship. Nearly as many years of love. And there we were. Promising forever.

When the sun finally followed the breeze and rode in through Finn's window, I was cuddled in his arms. Heavy-limbed, sleepy-eyed, and happier than I'd ever been.

There was nothing that could bring me down from the high of being in Finn's arms and living in his love.

His love was the sun, and I was basking in its warmth.

Did I fly too close?

Less than an hour later, it all came crashing to the ground. Wings burned, free falling, death approaching.

I didn't think about that though. For the final five seconds that I bled out, my heart shuddering in my chest, its blood falling over Finn, I thought about the night we'd secretly married.

"Was it real?" I'd asked the next morning, wondering how something so wonderful could be true.

"Trust me," he'd said, pressing a kiss to my head, "it was real."

The hall shook, and another column fell. Marble shards hit my skin, but I'd long passed the point of feeling. Finn's breath rattled, and I knew this was his last moment here.

I could feel him through the ring. I knew he thought he'd failed me. That he didn't blame me. He only blamed himself. His grief and sorrow and fear for me nearly overwhelmed him.

So I reached out like I always reached out. I went outside of myself and floated in that space above my mind.

It was different this time though. I was different. I wasn't the Mari whose power was locked and hidden behind a dam. I was the Mari who knew now that she was a Ward.

Jacob had opened something in me.

So when I reached out, I found in Finn something I'd never seen or sensed before. I poked at it, curious. It was a knot. Sort of. An illusion made real. It was inside of him. It almost seemed to be a part of his blood; a hitchhiker on his essence. It was similar to what had been done to me but completely different. I followed the illusion through his veins, all the way to the core of him.

There are some people who say a human's soul is in their heart. Others say it's below their belly button. Still, others claim it hovers around the body like a cloak. I'm not sure where the soul is, but I did find, right in Finn's chest, beneath the knife, a strange, curious thing.

The illusion ended in a lock. In my mind's eye, it looked like an old-fashioned iron padlock. I poked at it. Found the knot that tied it. And then my mind flinched back in surprise, because when I poked the lock, I felt the prodding within myself.

Was I the lock?

Did Locke mean, quite literally, "lock"?

Whoever had tied this illusion had meant for me to find it—that much was clear.

Quickly, with my mind fraying around the edges, I untied the knot. As I untied, I felt a releasing in me. I didn't understand it. I only knew there was a lock in Finn, and that lock was connected to me.

The knot was a Ward knot. A double constrictor. But instead of tightening, it loosened, until finally, when it broke free, I gasped in relief.

Then, beneath me, Finn jerked and convulsed.

His blood filled with what had been locked away his entire life.

It filled with illusion.

He was a river rushing with power. The principal of the Smiths. I could feel the rapids roaring through him.

His power was immense.

A splash of shock swept through the ring.

And then, a second later, a desperate, final, gasping emotion. The love I knew so well.

Then Finn's body went lax. The space where I'd felt him through the ring stilled. Emptied. His soul fled his body.

I'd killed my beloved. My husband.

I fell into an abyss of nothingness.

I died.

84

The wind sped through the violence, riding on the sharp edge of screams and spinning across clashing blades. There was too much happening. The wind couldn't spread itself thin enough to be everywhere it needed to be.

Where was the boy?

Where was he?

The wind slammed against a marble column. The marble shook as if the wind had been a giant's fist. The column splintered and crashed to the floor. The wind spun wildly in the explosion. It coughed on the dust as it was flung across the hall, spinning, spinning.

It grabbed a marble shard and held on, just as the shard sliced across the trickster's cheek. The trickster snarled and spun. He ducked under a fist-size chunk of marble wielded by a black-clad man and then lunged with his knife.

The wind shrieked, tasting the spray of hot, copper-tinged blood. It sped past.

The wind wasn't concerned about the trickster. He fought with a violent fury that reminded the wind of a tornado lifting homes and leveling entire towns. Eventually, the tornado would lose momentum, but not before it had destroyed everything in its path.

The wind slammed against the sound of an anguished roar and then rode the pain through the clash of bodies. It knew—because it had heard similar agonized shouts for centuries—that the brother of the solange-eyed one had finally seen him fall.

Perhaps he'd watched the girl thrust her knife into the solange-eyed one's heart?

Or maybe he'd seen the russet-haired, solemn one shoot the girl.

Or maybe he could only see the girl and the solange-eyed one now, curled together, limbs tangled, faces pressed together, as if they were cuddled in a field of grass, whispering lover's secrets, unaware of everyone and everything around them.

The roar broke off, and the wind powered through the maze of blades and marble and dust. It spun on curses and promises and threats. It darted over blood and grabbed knives and jumped across marble chunks used as weapons to bludgeon and attack.

It was looking for the boy.

The boy. The boy. Where was the boy?

It would get the boy out of this marble sepulcher alive. It would even —if it had to—gale and gust and shove him through the glass windows.

It hadn't saved the girl. It had never been able to save the girl—not since she was first conceived and then pushed into the world. But the boy? It could still save the boy.

The wind raced through shards of marble and tripped over the splintered wooden dais. The air was bitter here—bitter death—and the wind shrieked when it saw the citrus and pearl dust scented woman and the musician staring blank-eyed at the hall that had become a marble tomb.

The wind slid over the black funeral crepe of the woman's dress and bounced on her cooling skin. It tapped the musician's cold, calloused fingers. The ceiling above them shuddered, and the wind, not wanting them to be buried beneath marble and plaster, blew and blew until the cracked and splintered floor of the dais caved over them and covered their bodies. It was as solid as a sarcophagus lid.

There.

The wind rushed on, sniffing as it passed the crumpled form of the cruel one. His father, his sister, and other black and brown clad ones circled him. They fought, but the wind didn't care. It was searching . . . searching . . .

Where?

Then the wind heard a quiet, pained exclamation. The boy!

It darted through heat, bounced off a cruel laugh, and landed on the tip of a shortsword drenched with blood.

The boy was surrounded. Eight bulky, warlike, sword and knife and blade-wielding conjurers pressed close. The boy could only spin and whirl and duck so fast. He'd already raced through a gauntlet and fought one war today, and now he was surrounded, and . . .

Oh, the wind knew what this was.

It saw it in the forests when it flew north. This was what happened when a pack of wolves surrounded an injured deer. The quick lunge and the bloody slaughter. This was the coyotes snapping and howling before they ravaged the hare. This was the raptor grasping the mouse and devouring its flesh.

This, the wind knew, was nature's game. Hunter and hunted. Predator and prey.

The boy cradled one arm to his side. Broken? No. Bloodied. He held his other arm aloft, barring the sword like a long fang. He tasted of blood, sweat, and anguished fury.

The predators taunted him.

". . . not so scary without illusion . . ."

"Murdering coward. Kill our principal—"

"You may be a Ward, but you'll die as easily as a Clark—"

"Say hello to your little sister. I bet after all these years, she'll be happy to see her murderer."

The wind hissed and then tapped the boy on the cheek. He took the warning and swung his sword, blocking a thrust from behind.

The boy circled. Blocked. He had seconds—the wind knew. This game would only last seconds more.

"Wind," the boy whispered, his voice raw and pained. "I failed her."

The wind moaned and rubbed the boy's sweat and blood soaked cheek. It felt the rage in the boy's jaw.

"They've killed my sister. They killed Ragnor. Celia—" The boy's voice cracked on the citrus and pearl dust scented woman's name. "Wind. This is the end."

The wind shrieked.

It would *not* be the end.

It spun around the boy. It filled itself with all the rage, violence, and anguish riding in the crumbling hall. It consumed the screams and explosions and sucked in the dust and the marble and the shuddering, collapsing walls. It spun and spun, growing and growing.

It may not know human emotions, but it knew it would *not* let this be the end.

The boy stood in the center of the wind's fury. His clothes tore and whipped around him. His gold-spun hair flew around his forehead. The predators surrounding him covered their faces and braced themselves against the maelstrom.

The wind roared and raged, and as the whirlwind built, the boy's feet were lifted from the ground, and the wind held him high in the air.

The predators screamed.

The boy laughed.

One of the predators threw a dagger at the boy, but the wind furiously shoved it aside. Another thrust his sword, and the wind slammed him against a marble column.

No one hurt the boy.

No one.

The wind's rage collapsed another marble column. Another. The walls crumbled beneath the wind's onslaught.

Across the hall, the trickster fought, and the solange-eyed one's brother fought with him. They thrust through the conjurers, side by side, cutting toward the man.

The wind's beloved man.

Ah.

It wasn't just the boy who was in danger. His father was too.

The wind threw the predators aside and carried the boy through the hall. It knocked conjurers over. They fell like untested saplings bowing under a hurricane.

The wind dropped the boy next to his father. The wind would take the both of them out of this death-soaked hall.

"Wind," the man said, his beloved voice weary and grief-stricken.

The wind slowed to listen, its rage-fueled maelstrom lessening.

"You promised," the man whispered. He knew the wind would hear his words. "Have you forgotten your promise? Go after him."

The wind shrieked. It would not. It wouldn't go after him. It wouldn't leave the boy.

"Go!" the man said. "You promised."

The boy smiled. The wind traced the curve of his lip.

"Thank you," the boy whispered. Then he added, even more quietly, "Come back quickly."

The wind blew a great, gusting breath. The hall shuddered, and all the conjurers, except the boy and the man, fell to the marble floor.

It would go.

It would keep its promise.

The wind always kept its promises.

But how?

The wind was spirit. But the wind was also physical. Not in the way of man, or even the way of water. But it was still both spirit and body.

Could the wind follow death without dying?

It would try.

It would leave the boy and try.

With one final gust, the wind raced toward the golden column of light that stretched from the cracked and falling ceiling to the rubble-strewn floor. That light extended farther up and farther down than anyone knew. The wind sped across the hall, flying toward the light.

At the final gust, the wind felt the solange-eyed one's spirit leave his body. The girl's fled hers right after. The both of them died within a breath of each other.

The wind couldn't find the girl's spirit, but the solange-eyed man's was a brilliant white light. It raced toward the golden column, and the wind grabbed ahold of him.

The solange soaking the hall vanished with his death, and as the wind left the world, the man and the boy plunged the hall into darkness.

The wind left a dark world flooded with screams.
It fell into the golden light and followed death.

85

THE LIGHT SWALLOWED THE WIND. THERE WAS ONLY LIGHT, AND THE WIND was the light, and the light was the wind. Time never existed for the wind, but it had existed for man. Yet in the light, there was no time, no beginning, no end. There only *was*, and the wind was.

It flowed with the golden light, a cosmic stream that ran from the mouth of eternity in diffused rivulets across the universe. It was eternal bliss, endless love, the light of spirit, and the light that lit dark places. The wind had known the tempests of the past and had seen the tempests charted in the future, yet in the pool of light, there were no tempests; there was only peace.

Until the wind—the light—felt the ripple and the nudging of the solange-eyed man.

The man was with the wind. No. The wind was with him. It clung to the shining spirit of him.

The wind remembered itself. Who and what it was.

The solange-eyed one flew through the light like a cosmic ray shot from the sun, speeding toward earth. His pace, instead of slowing, quickened. The wind knew that soon, the solange-eyed one would travel so far into the light that the wind would never find its way back to the boy.

It pushed at the solange-eyed man and tugged at his spirit, but the wind had no form here nor air to shove. It only had its voice. It only had its secrets.

The solange-eyed one flickered. Fought. The wind suddenly realized the man didn't want to fly like an arrow through the column of light. He threw out his senses and dragged his mind and shoved against the magnetic pull. The man used the strength and the pulse of golden light inside of himself to throw out anchors and ropes and threads that tied him to the physical world.

What would that do?

The wind didn't know.

It wouldn't work though.

Soon, both the wind and the solange-eyed one would be lost to the world of man.

The wind would never see the boy again. It wouldn't curl in his lap as he read a book or flutter the pages in annoyance. It wouldn't tap his cheek to make him smile or be the one to keep him from never being alone. More, the wind wouldn't race over moonlit rivers or dive down bell towers or storm through spruce-filled mountains. The wind was, but it wouldn't be.

A moment longer—two—and the wind and the solange-eyed man would never see the world again.

The wind whispered urgently to the man. It told him a secret that had been buried since the world was first destroyed. It was something the wind had witnessed when water had buried the earth and all the thoughts that had built and then broken the world had been swept away. It had followed the families down to the edge of the world. It had seen what they'd found there.

The wind shoved the truth at the solange-eyed man.

He grabbed it.

He understood.

With that secret, the solange-eyed one and the wind tumbled out of the light and slammed like a flaming meteor into a misty gray tunnel.

The impact shook the wind, knocked it about, and it shrieked as all the warmth and peace was ripped away. The tunnel was cold and damp, and it smelled like the tunnels where the stone watchers lived.

The solange-eyed one crashed into the ground and skidded across the cold stone. The mist curled around him and grabbed at his spirit. The solange-eyed one shook himself off and stood. He formed as himself, but more wind-like and less manlike.

The wind curled against the heart of the man. It was warm still, and it pulsed like a heartbeat, while everything else in this misted place was cold and dead.

The wind moaned. Why, *why* had it promised the man it would do this?

Forward, the wind urged.

The solange-eyed one heard and walked down the tunnel, searching the slick gray walls and the fingers of mist crawling above the stone floor.

The wind circled the man's spirit, wondering at the difference between a man who was in a body and a man who was not. To the wind, they seemed very much the same.

The solange-eyed one looked the same, moved the same—he even tasted the same. His emotions were still there, the girl still the image he focused on most. And at the bottom of his spirit, in the well that held his being, he was still as he'd always been.

The wind knew why he'd fought the light. He was meant to be with the girl. She was the lock, and he was the key, and together, they were meant to open the door to a new world.

But the solange-eyed one had died.

There weren't any doors to open here.

The wind urged him on, and the solange-eyed one kept moving through the damp chill. It was a half-lit place. Not light, but not dark. It was that place on the edge of the world where spirits could pass and men could walk. It was a gloaming, half-alive place.

The wind didn't know how much time had passed, but finally, it saw what it had been sent to find.

It sped ahead, brushing aside the tendrils of mist.

"Ah," the steely, battle-hardened Smith said. He gazed mournfully at his son. "I expected to see many pass by, but I didn't expect to see you."

The wind curled around the man. He looked different than he did in life. Younger, perhaps, like he'd looked when he'd first married, and when he and the man hadn't promised each other's deaths.

The wind whispered to him. It told the steely-eyed man what it had promised the man he would say.

The steely-eyed man smiled. "So he won't die today? Tell him . . . tell him it didn't hurt. Tell him I'll wait for him, so he doesn't have to cross over alone. Will you tell him?"

The wind would, if it could find its way back to the man. But first, it told the steely-eyed man something else.

The man turned back to his son. "You failed," he said, as unyielding in death as he had been in life.

The solange-eyed one turned back to his father. He'd been staring at a pool of silvery-gray water at the edge of the tunnel. It was lined by round gray rocks, and it was as smooth as mercury. There was no ripple, no current, no waves. The liquid was opaque; so solid that nothing could be seen in it. Stranger yet, there was no reflection. Not of the mist. Not of the walls. Not of the spirit of the solange-eyed man when he leaned down to peer at the water.

The solange-eyed man smiled at his father. The wind had never been good at reading human emotions, but the spirit was easier to know. This was not a happy smile.

"Have I?" he asked.

The steely-eyed one laughed. The walls and the mist swallowed the sound.

"Yes."

"Maybe. Or maybe it's only one failure on the path to success."

"You're just like your mother. Dead and defeated, but still refusing to stop believing. You're so much like her." The steely-eyed man held out his hand. It flickered, nearly formless, in the half-light. "Finn."

The wind slipped over the steely-eyed man's hand and felt the cool chill of his spirit. The man was struggling to stay in this misty place, but the wind knew he would wait here, by the pool, until the Ward—his friend—came.

It was hard for the wind to look at him. It had been hard to keep its promise. There was something about the steely-eyed one that had always made the wind itch and squirm. Perhaps it was his secrets. They felt heavy and uncomfortable, even for the wind.

But wasn't it said that the dead had no secrets? Yet even now, the man kept his silence.

He watched his son with a mournful gaze as the solange-eyed one studied the silver pool. The wind pushed against the steely-eyed one's hand, reminding him it was still there.

The steely-eyed one had almost always known this moment was coming, and he'd accepted it a long time ago. The wind remembered the secret of it—the one it had promised never to tell. Not until the steely-eyed one was dead, and then, not until it knew the truth would only help, not hurt.

It glided over the steely-eyed one's spirit. He was the same as he'd been as a young boy. Wasn't that the way with humans? They came out essentially themselves and changed very little, unless they were chipped and battered and molded by the violent storms of life.

Yet when he was a young boy, black-haired, gray-eyed, serious and blade-sharp, he'd been best friends with the man—the boy's father—and the fawn-like girl. They were three wild, free, joy-filled things that the wind had loved to race after. It had loved to play in the illusions of their imaginations. It had loved to dance in the sparks and the volleys of their minds.

It had showed them its secret place in the middle of Central Park. The quiet place, where human voices and conjurer eyes couldn't penetrate. It had told them where to hide their friendship. Why? Because the wind liked laughter; the wind liked the man; the wind liked the fawn-like girl. The wind tolerated the steely-eyed one.

The fawn-like girl was large-eyed, gentle, fragile too. She wouldn't live long. After her mother's death, the principal—her brother—would spend decades secretly hunting and killing every Bard who was born with the same blood anomaly that lived in his mother and sister's veins. He'd wipe out the secret of their weakness.

But *this* was a different secret. It was a secret from when the three friends were children. This was before the principal had slaughtered his cousins, and before he'd made his sister promise to never give birth to a child of her own.

"I've seen something," the fawn-like girl had whispered. Her voice had trembled, and the thick, gnarled trees had weaved silence around them.

The two boys had leaned close, and the wind had drifted over.

The fawn-like girl often saw things. She caught glimpses of the future. Disjointed reflections. She said it was like seeing a reflection in a car as it sped past, but the reflection in the blurred car window was of a puddle on the street, and in the puddle was a reflection of the sky, and that bit of sky held a patch that told the future. Usually, the glimpses were illogical and impossible to decipher.

That day, it hadn't been disjointed. The fawn-like girl had told them exactly what was going to happen.

"But . . ." The steely-eyed one, still a young boy, had frowned at the girl. "I don't want to have a baby with you. I don't want to marry you—"

"You will. And you'll love me too."

The steely-eyed one frowned and scratched his elbow. Then he said, "But I don't want to. I don't want . . . Lu, I don't want to die 'cause of him."

The fawn-like girl shoved the steely-eyed boy. "Not 'cause of him. For him. *For* him."

The steely-eyed boy dropped his head. "But Lu. I don't want this. I don't want you to die. I don't want Phil to kill me."

The man—still a boy—reached out and gripped the steely-eyed one's hand. "Maybe she's wrong, Wolf. Maybe—"

"I'm not wrong. Listen. We have to do this. Look, Wolf, aren't you always talking about the heroes of old? Well, guess what? That's what this is. You, Phil, me. We gotta do this."

"But the heroes don't die!" That was the man—still a boy—his voice high and pained.

"Yes. They do," the fawn-like girl said. "Whoever told you heroes don't die? They die plenty."

"She's right." The steely-eyed one frowned at his two best friends. "Lots of heroes die." He glanced around at the gnarled trees, the rough bark, and the thick, woodsy quiet, and gestured for his friends to step closer.

They huddled together under the dark, reaching branches and whispered their plan.

"We never mention this again after today," he said.

They all nodded.

Then the man—still a boy—said, "Wind? Promise. You won't tell anyone this. Not ever."

The fawn-like girl added, "Except our kids. And only after Wolf and me are dead, and if the truth won't hurt and can only help."

The wind whistled its promise.

The three clasped their hands together.

They made their plans.

"When I'm having our baby . . . marry someone else . . . boy . . . heir . . . Phil, you'll have twins—don't you dare kill her—"

"But truth-seers have to die."

"Not this one, Phil. If she dies, everyone dies. Hide her. Hide her where no one will ever think to look. When she's born, lock her up and use her to lock mine and Wolf's boy too."

"I won't love him. I won't even like him—"

"Stop being an idiot, Wolf. You'll love him. Protect them. Hide them both. I won't live long. And Wolf, you can't know our boy. You can't meet him. You can't speak to him. You can't know him until the games. If you do, he'll die. If he dies, everyone dies. He can't ever suspect what he is. He can't use his power. If he does, he'll die. The world has to believe he's a null. He'll have a mental power, a trait, that'll help. And Phil, your girl. No one can know—"

"Obviously."

"No one can know! If she dies—"

"Everyone dies," the steely-eyed one echoed.

The fawn-like one frowned. "When our boy wins the games—"

"How can he win the games as a null? It's impossible."

"He'll win."

"It's impossible."

"He'll win! And when he does, you declare him your heir. You get him the crown. And then, Phil, unlock your daughter, and she'll unlock our boy. You see?"

The two of them nodded.

"And then I die," the steely-eyed one said. "Because he'll need my power. Because he'll need it to fight what's coming."

"What exactly is coming?" the man—still a boy—asked.

The fawn-like girl frowned and squinted at the thick line of trees. "I don't know. I only know it's bad. I only see the world torn and broken, worse than it's ever been broken before. I only know our son and your daughter have to be there. I only know our son is either going to save the world or destroy it."

The wind moaned and slid over the heat of the three children's clasped hands.

"And no one can know?" the man—still a boy—asked.

"No one can know," the fawn-like girl said.

"Are you still a hero if no one knows it?"

The steely-eyed one nodded. "Yes. You can still be a hero, even if no one knows it. Just like you'll always be my best friend, even if no one knows it."

The three of them smiled, and the trees pressed solemnly down on them.

"I don't want to kill you, Wolf."

The steely-eyed one nodded. "It's all right. I trust Lu. I trust you, Phil. You'll make sure it's quick. I'd rather it be quick. Maybe . . . make it something for the records, like a whirlwind of daggers. A thousand of them."

The man—boy still—laughed.

The fawn-like girl shook her head, but she smiled.

"Even if no one else knows," she said, "you both are the heroes of my life. So . . ." She twisted her hand and conjured a small, bone-handled knife. She sliced the blade over her palm.

The steely-eyed one cried out, "Lu, don't! You—"

"Shh. Give me your oath."

She cut the boys' palms. And then they swore their oaths, made their promises, and never spoke of it again.

And finally—finally—the steely-eyed one had fulfilled his promises. He'd died for the son he'd said he'd never love. And now he was waiting in the misty, gray-walled tunnel for his friend to cross over too.

"Finn," he said, and the solange-eyed one looked up from the silver pool. "You're not supposed to be here."

The solange-eyed one nodded. "I know." Then he looked more closely at the misty outline of his father and asked, "Why did you wait so long to tell me who I was? Why was my power locked away?"

The steely-eyed man flickered, as insubstantial as the mist. "I waited the length that was necessary. It was locked away because it had to be. How did you die?"

"Mari." The solange-eyed one smiled, and it was as mournful as the last gasp of a dying breeze.

"Ah. Isn't it like a Ward to tell you they love you and then kill you in the next breath?"

The solange-eyed one looked quickly at his father and frowned. "She's Jagger's now."

"I know."

"I'm going back for her."

"I expect you'll try."

The solange-eyed one pointed at the pool. "Do you think an eye will do, or will it want my heart?"

The steely-eyed one laughed. "Before you siege the walls of Mallia . . . I wanted to love you. Your mother . . . she did."

"I know. I remember."

The steely-eyed one nodded. "She told me you would either save the world or destroy it. Which will it be?"

"Destroy or deliver?" The solange-eyed one studied his father. "What if I have to destroy it to save it?"

The wind shuddered. It knew what the solange-eyed one meant. It still remembered the violent waters of the flood that had buried the earth. The water had destroyed the earth and all that man had thought into existence. It was the only way to save what was left of the world.

"I have something your mother told me to tell you," the steely-eyed one said, "once you knew the truth."

The mists in the cavern stopped writhing, and the wind held its breath.

The solange-eyed one stared at his father, a hungry, yearning look on his face.

"She said, 'The truth will set you free, but first, you have to set the truth free.'"

The solange-eyed one laughed.

His father wasn't finished. "She also said that if you ever stopped loving your girl, then both you and the world were doomed."

The solange-eyed one gave his father a tight smile. "Then it's a good thing I won't ever stop loving her, isn't it?"

He turned then and kneeled on the mist-covered ground next to the pool. When he twisted his hand, a knife appeared in the air above his palm. The wind laughed. They were close enough to the world for spirits to conjure.

And this knife—it was the first thing the solange-eyed one had thought into existence.

It was a replica of the knife the girl had plunged into his heart.

He didn't make a sound as he cut his right eye free.

The pool didn't make a sound when he tossed it into the silver water.

The wind clung to the solange-eyed one's spirit.

"Go," the steely-eyed one said. "Deliver. Don't destroy."

The solange-eyed one didn't answer.

Instead, without warning, he dove into the silver waters.

86

THE WIND TORE THROUGH THE WRECKAGE. FIRE TWISTED AND GRASPED AT the air, greedily trying to swallow the wind. It shoved at the inferno, fanning the flames and shooting billows of black smoke across the burning hall. The wind would not be consumed by the flames. Instead, with a shove, it fanned them higher.

Only a moment ago, it had dived into the silver pool after the solange-eyed one. But instead of following the solange-eyed one to wherever he went, the wind had been hurled at hurricane speed out of the silver water and back into the great marble hall.

To the inferno.

Time had passed while the wind had been chasing death. How much? It didn't know.

All the marble columns had collapsed, and the ceiling and walls with them. The hall was a ruin, its rubble and debris the kindling of a burning funeral pyre. The wind shrieked through the fire. It was a fire of illusion made real. It was hotter than the flames the wind had crackled with before—hotter even than a spear of lightning thrown at the earth. The wind loved to ride the ferocious lightning balls that struck the metal rods at the top of skyscrapers, but this fire was even hotter than the electric blue flames that melted metal.

There were conjurers here—ones whose spirits had fled their bodies. Dozens. More? The wind had never thought to count. What were numbers? There was only more or less. It knew the fire had burned through more conjurers than could fit in a city bus, but less than had been here at the start of the ceremony.

It swept through the flames, shifting bodies, searching desperately for the man. For the boy. When it had left them, they'd plunged the hall into darkness, but someone had lit the darkness with blue fire.

The wind sped over marble, skittered through searing heat that would char the lungs of men, and raced through the prism of flame and fire.

The boy wasn't here. Neither was the man.

The wind burst free from the hall. It soared over the window's twisted, melted glass and shrieked at the flashing lights of a dozen fire trucks. It bounced against a siren's high wail and ducked through a splash of cold water.

So the conjurers hadn't kept the game to themselves. Someone had let part of the illusion crumble, and the fire and wreckage was there for everyone to see. The humans could see a brick apartment building in flames, not a mansion, but the flames were real.

What happened after the wind had left to make the conjurers so careless?

Where were they all? Where was the boy?

He'd told the wind to hurry back. He was hurt. Was he alone?

The wind rushed through the crowd, searching, searching . . .

There!

It heard a noise. A muffled shout from blocks away.

The wind raced down the street. The orange and blue flames cast violent shadows over the humans, and the flashing truck lights created a macabre strobe light dance. The trees bowed, and their leaves curled and shriveled against the fire's heat. The wind blew through them and carried glowing embers and sparks on its breath.

The fire's orange glow spread for blocks, and the wind flew past it, seeking the dark. It fled the heat. It sprinted from the sizzle and pop and roar of the flames. It wanted away from the siren's whine and the shout of the water hitting flame.

The wind rushed westward, listening desperately for another muffled, pained cry.

The farther west it flew, the closer it came to the river's edge. The smoke and fire smell was gone. Now, there was only the familiar cold water and mineral smell of the Hudson. It snaked out below the wind, a black, sinuous line that curved along the city's edge.

The wind spread out, searching the empty streets. It splashed through shadow, swept past streetlights, and squeezed down alleyways. It followed the sound of footsteps and sent a low, questioning call to echo over sleeping buildings.

Then, at its *whooooo?* the wind heard the muffled shout again. The noise was followed by the pounding of rapid footsteps. Someone was running.

Was the boy running?

Why was he running?

The wind raced after the clatter of footsteps. There, on the edge of a building's roof, it spied a black-clad figure.

Oh!

The solemn one. The wind had forgotten him. He'd killed the girl. The boy wouldn't be happy. He'd want the solemn one dead.

The wind rushed after the solemn one, chasing him along the concrete edge of a tall building's roofline. The wind had seen the solemn one run over rooftops and fling himself across empty air countless times. Usually, when he sprinted between buildings and leaped between roofs, he had a weightless exuberance. This time, the solemn one felt as heavy as a boulder dropped into a river.

Sweat ran down his forehead. His face was as pale as the missing moon. His breath came in desperate, choked gasps. The wind dragged itself along the solemn one's cheeks and realized it wasn't only sweat dripping over his skin. That salt was the taste of tears.

The solemn one clenched his hands and then jumped from one building to the next. He landed hard and looked behind him, his expression grim.

The wind looked too. And there! Yes! It was the boy.

The boy raced after the solemn one. He ran along the narrow concrete edges of the rooftops and jumped from one building to the next. But unlike the solemn one, the boy was injured.

What was he thinking?

The wind curled around the boy, tugging on his ear and tapping at his cheek.

"Wind. You're back."

The boy was short of breath, his voice pain-laced. He held one arm against his side, trying to keep it immobile. His face was blood-covered and pale. There were bruises—too many. His clothing was torn.

He jumped across the empty sky and landed on another roofline.

The solemn one looked back again, and then he dropped over the side of the building and disappeared.

The boy swore and raced after him. At the edge of the building, he looked down. It was high. Not too high. But high.

The boy closed his eyes. Took a breath. His heart boomed so loudly the wind was nearly knocked over by the noise.

The boy twisted his hand, grabbed a kite-like thing, and glided from the roof to the street. When he hit the concrete, he dropped the kite and ran.

The wind rushed after him. What was the boy thinking? He had to stop. Even if he caught the solemn one, he wouldn't be able to kill him. He was too weak. It was obvious.

The boy was like the wind.

The wind was powerful. Very. It could destroy entire forests of buildings. It could level mountains of homes. But after it blew and blew, the wind inevitably blew itself out. After a storm, there was always calm. After a display of power, it was depleted and had to rest.

Conjurers—the boy too—couldn't blow and blow and blow endlessly. They only had so much power to use, and then, once it was depleted, they couldn't blow anymore. Not until they'd recovered.

The boy knew this.

All conjurers knew this.

The boy had used up all of himself today. He'd barely managed to make the kite to hold himself aloft. He was barely able to run.

He was weak. He was almost as weak as the wind right now. And the wind felt like the last bit of air leaking weakly from a popped balloon.

The wind sighed and ruffled the boy's hair when he stopped at the edge of the Hudson.

"I lost him," the boy said, and although he sounded desperately sad, shaky, and out of breath, the wind was glad he'd lost the solemn one.

The boy bent forward and pressed his hands to his thighs. He dragged in great gulps of air. He dropped his chin to his chest and waited for his heart to stop slamming against his ribs.

The wind curled around his legs. It was all right. It would be all right.

"She died," the boy whispered. His heart thudded hollowly. It was the loudest sound in the night. Did he mean the girl or the citrus and pearl dust scented woman? Who was he thinking of? Who?

The wind moaned.

The night sounds grew then. They were at the edge of the high cliff over the river. There was the nearly empty street, where one or two cars whooshed past, their headlights swallowed by the trees. There were the scrabbling, digging insects burrowing in the dirt and the bark. There were the sleeping creatures and the awake creatures. There was the wind itself, tossing the tree leaves about and pushing the branches so they groaned into the night.

The cliff was a sheer drop, taller than many of the buildings in the city. The stones were jagged and night-cool. They fell toward the black waters and the current that sped toward the cold ocean.

Usually, the wind liked the sound of the water carving away at the rock. Usually, the wind liked the green smells and the water smells. But tonight, the wind only cared about the muffled, pained, sobbing noises the boy was making.

Did his arm hurt? Was that why he was making that noise?

The wind brushed the boy's cheek, but then it startled and shrieked.

The boy jerked upright and held out his hand.

A twig snapped, and then the brother—the solange-eyed one's brother—stepped into the dark.

"Hello, Ward. Are you all alone?" he asked, and the wind shrieked again. The brother smiled. "Fair warning. I'm going to kill you now."

The boy stared at the brother. The wind wanted to rage. It wanted to build and build and carry the boy away, but the wind was so depleted it could barely blow out a candle.

The boy looked down at his hand and then dropped it to his side.

The battle scented brother laughed. The sound was so cold it made the wind shiver. "No illusion left? That's fine. I'll play fair."

The wind screamed. The brother attacked. He didn't use illusion. He didn't conjure. Instead, he did what he loved to do. He moved in a blur. He kicked at the boy. The boy jumped. He dodged. The first two kicks and a punch missed him. The boy was injured. But the brother was injured too. The wind could taste the blood soaking his shoulder and the pain radiating down his arm.

Even so, the brother was still filled with power. It flowed through him, while the boy was empty. He'd played in a game, saved the woman, unlocked the girl's power, fought for his life, and done many more things the wind couldn't know. The boy couldn't stand against the brother.

The boy dodged, but as he leaned to the right, the brother hit him from the left. The punch left him without air. He fell forward, and the brother slammed into the boy and ripped him off his feet. The boy crashed into a tree, and a sharp branch tore through his skin. The wind shrieked at the sting of blood.

The boy shoved himself to his feet. When he stood, the brother slammed a fist into his chest. The boy's heart stuttered.

No!

The wind pressed his chest, compressing and decompressing. The brother slammed his fist into the boy's cheek. His head snapped back, and the brother hit him again.

The boy stumbled back. The wind tugged on his hair. It poked his cheek. It tried to blow cool air over the tears and the blood. Come on, boy. Come *on*.

The brother snarled and hit the boy again. The wind shoved at the brother's fist, but it didn't do any good. The wind was too weak.

The boy fell. He dropped heavily to the wet leaves and the trampled, muddy grass at the cliff's edge.

"Darin," the boy said. He coughed and spat blood into the grass. He pushed himself up onto his forearms and tried to climb to his knees. He held up a hand. "Don't. You're a good man—"

The brother slammed his foot into the boy. At the violent kick, the boy flew over the cliff's edge. He grabbed at roots, saplings, and rocks.

The wind screamed and tried to boost the boy as his feet kicked at the slick, sheer cliff edge.

The boy grabbed a rocky protrusion with one hand. He dangled from the cliff. His knuckles turned white as he tried to pull himself up. It was his injured arm—the wind could feel the agony in the boy. He reached up with his other hand and tried to pull himself back onto land.

The wind circled, moaning and shoving.

The brother leaned over the edge and stared at the boy.

The boy stilled. Stopped struggling.

"I was a good man," the brother said quietly, "and then a Ward killed my dad."

He shoved the boy from the cliff.

The boy didn't make a sound, but the wind screamed the whole way down.

When the boy hit the cold river, the wind tried to keep his head above the surface, but the boy sank, and when the figments and the water spirits grabbed him, the wind couldn't do anything to stop them.

87

It always takes a long time to fall back into yourself after you've died.

It's never a quick whirlwind, like the last bit of bathwater sucked down a drain. It's not even the moderate descent of a red and purple tinged maple leaf falling from its autumn branch.

Instead, it's the slow progress of the sun crossing over the dark depths of the underworld, passing through night door after night door until it finally presses above the lip of the earth.

Coming back to myself was a long, dark, black-shrouded night.

I waited for the sun.

If I could've wept, I would've wept for you.

If I could've cried, I would've cried out for you.

If I could've spoken, I would've said your name.

If I could've moved, I would've reached for your hand and fought to pull you free from death.

But this moment was the same as all the others. I couldn't speak. I couldn't move. I couldn't feel. I could only lie in the tomb of my final body and listen.

I didn't appear naked on Rou's kitchen table. I didn't inconveniently land in the entry hall of Hell Gate, or more conveniently, in my bed. I landed in the basement—down in the cold, stone, windowless dark. When I hit the ground, one of Jagger's creatures grunted and then dragged me across the floor. I could hear the scraping of my skin against stone and the creature's heavy breathing. Then there was the click of a metal door and a lock turning.

They'd locked me in the conjurer's cage.

Rou wouldn't be sitting next to me telling stories or reciting poems, holding my hand as I came back to myself.

Griff wouldn't come to the basement—he was too terrified of this dark place.

Justice?

I didn't think he'd come, but he did. I knew it was him by the steadiness of his steps on the stone floor, and then by his quick indrawn breath.

"Mari," he said, and his voice broke on my name. "You were supposed to kill me. That's why I gave you the knife. Why didn't you—?" He stopped, and I knew he was fighting something inside of himself. "It's done. If you hate me, hate me with all you are. I don't want a tepid hate—I want one that burns hot. All right? Give me a hate that burns worlds. I think I could survive on your hate."

He waited, but I didn't move or speak. I couldn't. He knew it.

I heard the whisper of his clothing shifting as he moved closer. The groan of the metal cage as he leaned against it. The sound of my hair fluttering as he brushed it away from my face.

"I have to go. No one is supposed to be down here. But before you come back, I have to warn you . . . don't fight it. Don't fight him, Mari. If you fight him, he'll rip out pieces of you until there's nothing of you left, and you're only . . . his. If you fight, you'll die. Or worse, you'll live but as something that isn't you. Do whatever he asks. Be whatever he says. Don't fight it. Mari. Don't. Just . . . take this time and hide yourself. Bury yourself —your good, what you love—bury it deep and lock it away. Don't even bring it out for yourself when you think you're alone. Forget it. He'll come soon. When you wake. He'll rip your good away. It'll hurt. It'll . . . hurt. If you fight him, he'll know you've hidden yourself. So don't fight, Mari. Not today. Not tomorrow. Maybe not a year or ten years from now. Keep it hidden, even from yourself. That way, someday, when the time's right, you can bring it back out and—"

He couldn't say it.

No one under Jagger's control could say the words.

But I knew what he wanted to say.

Someday, when the time was right, I could unleash the good I'd hidden, and I could kill Jagger. Defy him. Defeat him. Free us all.

Finally, the scrape of Justice's retreating steps filled the heavy silence. He was backing away. But before he left, he whispered, "I wish I could've saved you instead of being the one you needed saving from."

He left then. When the basement door closed behind him, the dark filled with a pressing, weighted silence. The stone walls had a sound. It was a watching sound that dragged over your skin and gave your bones a chill. There were rats here. Cockroaches. All the city creatures that lived in dark, damp places. Their scratching and their sniffing was a steady, almost comforting noise.

Even with my world falling apart, there were still rats in the city and cockroaches in the walls.

Bury yourself.

Hide yourself.

Did Justice know that being buried alive was my worst fear? No. Only Finn knew. But I was going to do it. I was going to bury alive everything good in me so that I could survive.

I took a deep breath, floated above myself, and reached back through the lives that Finn's tears had unlocked.

In my mind's eye, I saw myself as I was and as I'd been. I was a floating, glowing spirit. I pulled a cord, and my body fell away. I stepped out of myself, and I was a new body. I unwrapped this body too and stepped out of myself again. I did the same, over and over, until nine times I'd stepped out of myself as a new me. Finally, all the layers of myself had been peeled away, and I was only a pure, shining soul. I was at the center of myself. There was no illusion or body to shroud what I was.

I saw the truth.

I beheld myself for a long moment.

Then I began to build a hiding place. And a lock.

I worked at a desperate pace, my heart pounding, pulse galloping, as I fought to hide my light before it was too late and all the love and all the good was extinguished forever.

As I buried myself, the wind blew across the basement floors and through the bars of the cage. It had slipped under the door and followed Justice down, but when he'd left, it had remained. It whispered to me as I desperately hid my light. The wind told me its secrets.

I've often wondered, when you died a final death, did you lose all the memories of your life? Were you like a blackboard wiped clean, all the memories written on your soul just chalk smudges, erased and forgotten? Was this life a cloak you'd throw off as soon as you passed through the veil of death?

Did you forget me?

Did you forget everything I was to you?

Finn?

Did you forget me like I forgot you, or do you only remember your final moments—me as the woman who shoved a knife into your heart?

I don't know if death stole your memories. I only know that if we meet again, I desperately need you to know I once loved you. That you once loved me.

The wind was here. As I hid our love from myself, the wind was here.

I'm sending it to you, Finn. I'm sending the wind with all the memories I'm burying. I'm urging it with all my being to tell you this story. Isn't that what you asked for? You told me if we were ever separated, I'd only have to tell my story, and it would be like we were never separated at all.

I'm sending you the wind with my memories and with my love.

I can't speak, but I pray that you'll listen.

If you find your way back, if you find your way home, nothing will feel right. I won't be me. I won't be good. But I'll still be yours. Everything else is illusion.

Wherever you are, Finn, remember what we always told each other. Remember this:

Life, my dear friend, is illusion. Some people will tell you different.

Some will have you believe that everything you see and know is true. But I'm here to tell you, everything—*everything*—is illusion.

What can you trust? Nothing.

Who can you trust? No one.

No one.

Except me. Trust me.

I'm burying our love. I'm hiding it behind lock and key. I'm sending you the wind.

Listen—

Listen—

Finn—

88

THE WIND SHIVERED OVER THE STILL, COLD SKIN OF THE GIRL. SHE LAY death-still on the floor of the cage the trickster had squatted in all those years ago. The basement was as black as night, deeply silent, with watching stones and cold, dark things.

This was not a good place. It was not a kind place. The wind shuddered as it tapped against the girl's thundering pulse.

She urged the wind to share her secrets. The wind could sense the desperate desire in the thud of her heart. But which secrets? There were many. Too many for the wind to count—not that the wind did count. But the girl had more secrets than all the summer leaves on a giant, thick-trunked oak tree.

The wind blew and shuffled through her secrets, sending them scattering.

Flying through secrets was the same for the wind as flying through an open window, fluttering a linen curtain, and sending all the loose papers on a desk into the air. It was easy. Sometimes it was fun. The wind flew through memories and secrets as often as it blew through the tunnels leading in and out of the city.

But where to begin?

At the beginning? Before?

The wind rode over the sharp edge of the knife in the man's hand as an illusion woman and an illusion man screamed. The wind spun through the arc of blood and danced on the sharp knife's edge. It laughed as the man killed the girl's illusion parents. Then it moaned as the man dressed himself as a rag man and said to the wind, "Keep it secret, Wind. Keep it secret."

The man left his daughter outside the iron fence, where the creatures and bad things lived. His hand drifted sadly over the bloodied rag she was wrapped in. He disappeared with one last press of his fingertips to her infant cheek.

Then the wind whispered to the rocklike one what it had seen: that the man, the Ward, had murdered the girl's parents; that it had ridden their death screams.

The rocklike one tasted the girl's blood. He knew she had conjurer blood. Ward blood. But he didn't know the girl was the man's daughter and that he'd purposely hidden her away in hell.

But no—this wasn't the secret the wind was meant to share. It was a different secret.

It was when the solange-eyed one had first seen the girl.

If a man lost himself in death, then this was the memory he would need.

The wind slipped along the rough mortar, bumping over the gravelly edge of the dark red bricks. The girl was alone except for the wind. The rocklike one had chained her to the brick wall and left her in the musty, abandoned warehouse for cruelty's pleasure. How long? The wind watched the sun rise and set two times before the solange-eyed one walked past.

He didn't notice her. No one ever noticed the girl. She was like her father. Her features were as indistinct as the wind and as difficult to hold onto. The solange-eyed one (this was before, when his eyes were like his mother's—the fawn-like girl) hurried through the warehouse. It was a shortcut he sometimes used, cutting through Hell's Kitchen, hurrying to the Night Den.

The girl held as quiet and still as a deep, silent pool. She didn't even breathe as the solange-eyed one slipped past. She was going to let him pass by without ever knowing she was there.

But then the wind nudged him and forced him to trip over a pile of broken bricks. When he landed on his knees, rolled in a somersault, and sprung upright, the girl burst into a high, surprised laugh.

The solange-eyed one stared at her, startled. "Who are you?"

The wind rode on his surprise. He was young. Not as young as the girl, but he was just as lonely. He frowned at the metal shackle around her wrist.

"Why're you chained to the wall?"

He stepped forward and went to unlatch it.

"Leave it," she whispered.

The solange-eyed one stopped, his hand inches from her arm. "Why?"

"Because," she said, "I want to be here. If I didn't want to be, I wouldn't be. Do you really think I can't undo it myself? I don't need your help."

The solange-eyed one stared at her. The girl stared back.

The wind blew along the stagnant, musty air that separated them. The warehouse was dark. The rocklike one would be back for the girl soon. She knew it. Her pulse beat a nervous staccato.

"Go away."

The solange-eyed one smiled. He hadn't smiled like that since his mother had died. He leaned closer and peered at the girl's face. He studied her like no one had ever studied her before. He memorized her.

"I feel you," he finally said, pressing his hand to his chest, "right here."

The wind laughed. The solange-eyed one didn't know it, but that was because the girl *was* right there. When she was born, the man had tied her up with the solange-eyed one so that he would be the key, and she would be the lock.

They were tied together even before they'd met.

The girl frowned at where the solange-eyed one pressed his hand. "If you kill me, I'll kill you back."

He laughed. "Let's be friends."

"No."

"I'm Finn."

"Go away."

"You feel . . ." He dropped his hand and frowned. He was older than the girl, although still not old enough to have had a growth spurt. He was short for his age but strong. He had tutors and weapons and everything his father knew he'd need, but he didn't have a friend. "You feel like . . . home. Like my home. Are you sure I can't free you?"

The girl scoffed and turned her face away from him.

The wind shoved at the solange-eyed one. The rocklike one was coming. The wind carried the heavy sound of his footsteps and the creak of the warehouse door.

The solange-eyed one turned quickly, held still, and then, with one last look at the girl, he sprinted across the room and dove through a broken window.

The wind followed the solange-eyed one after that. For months, the solange-eyed one followed the girl. He became her shadow. He followed her to Hell Gate. He ducked behind corners and crept through alleyways. He watched her lockpick and spied on her as she broke into the conjurers' mansions.

The solange-eyed one smiled when she broke illusions, and he worried when she was caught. He left her chains of dandelions on wooden park benches, set slivers of mica on the newspaper stands she passed, and dropped packets of bubblegum on the benches of bus stops she walked past. Sometimes, he would take a handful of pebbles and form words with the stones. The girl would walk past, read, "Hi," and then scatter the pebbles with a brush of her hand.

She ignored him.

Until, one day, the wind shoved the solange-eyed one down the stairs of the Times Square subway tunnel. The wind pushed hard, so there would be scrapes and blood.

When he fell, the girl rushed over. Her heart was pounding, and she cried out, "What's wrong with you? Don't you know how to be careful?"

And when she held the solange-eyed one's hand and helped him clean up, he only smiled at her as if he'd fall down another fifty flights of stairs as long as she'd talk to him again.

Then, finally, one spring day, seasons after they'd first met, the boy left a circlet of daisies on a green park bench and watched the girl pass. She looked at him standing there, and then she stopped and sat on the bench.

The solange-eyed one sat on the other end, as far from her as he could possibly get. They didn't look at each other. The girl curled her hand next to the daisies. She didn't take one, although it was obvious by the curve of her fingers that she wanted to.

"I'm Mari," she whispered, her lips barely moving.

The solange-eyed one hid a smile. He didn't look at the girl. Instead, he stared at a vendor's cart across the park. He dug around in his pocket, searching for change, pretending he was preoccupied.

"I'm Finn," he whispered. "Friends?"

The girl looked in the opposite direction, down the long tunnel of leafy trees.

"Friends," she said, and the wind caught the exhale and carried it to the solange-eyed one.

He smiled.

Then the girl was gone. The solange-eyed one looked at where she'd been sitting. He grinned at the blue sky peeking through the jewel-toned leaves. The daisies were gone.

Was that the memory the girl meant to send to the solange-eyed one?

Or was it the later memories, when they'd meet in the deep, forested places of the park, in the silent thickets where the wind guided them? When they'd crawl laughingly through the wet grass and catch sleeping box turtles and then set them free. Or when they'd run barefoot through the cold springs and splash each other until they were soaking-wet, then lie under the sun and tell make-believe stories about all the places they'd go someday.

"We'll ride the ghost train," the girl said.

"You can't ride the ghost train," the solange-eyed one always replied, and the girl would stick out her tongue, and then the boy would tackle her, and she'd tackle him back.

Or when the solange-eyed one would teach the girl to fight with a sword using branches stripped from saplings.

Or was it . . . ? Perhaps it was later.

The wind sorted through the leaves of memories and found one from when the solange-eyed one was taller. When he'd sprouted like a young tree and grown immeasurably tall in one quick summer. His voice had moved down, into the deep ranges, and the wind had chuffed his shaggy black hair when the girl watched him with wide, luminous eyes.

It was the summer they'd met the trickster.

The girl was hiding that memory. She was tucking it away. The trickster was precious to the girl. She loved him, and she was burying everything she loved.

The wind traveled over the solange-eyed one's protests.

"It isn't safe. He isn't worth—"

"He is! We have to save him, Finn. We have to. Jagger will kill him. He can't . . . He doesn't have any time left. We have to save him. Please." And then, "I'm doing it. With you or without you."

"With me."

Of course. The solange-eyed one would always say that. He'd always be with the girl. Ever since she'd died saving him from the Clark's illusion, something had shifted for the solange-eyed one. Before, he'd loved the girl. After, he *loved* her.

The wind skated over the cold stone floor of Hell Gate's basement. The air was filled with mildew, dirt, and stagnant, desperate things. It was dark, long after the moon had set, and the night creatures above had gone to bed in anticipation of day.

The girl crept over the floor, so quiet that not even the wind could hear her. The solange-eyed one was crouching at the base of the stairs, a knife in his hand. He was tense, alert, ready to kill anything that threatened the girl.

The only noise came from the cage in the center of the basement.

The trickster was there. How long had he been in the cage? The wind didn't know. The rocklike one had stolen him at the beginning of summer, when the wind loved blowing through the park and knocking the cherry blossoms free from the cherry trees. Now, the summer heat was curling in on itself, and the leaves were shading to red, yellow, and orange.

In the beginning, the trickster had talked to the girl. They were the same age. Young. Young enough that the trickster still hadn't grown into an adult body. He was small for his age. Big-eyed and skinny. The cage had made him thinner—more bone than flesh. His eyes nearly swallowed the rest of his face, and his cheeks were hollow. The rocklike one often forgot to feed the conjurers in his cage. He thought they could live on conjured food alone.

At first, the trickster had tried to make friends with the girl. He'd told her that was what he was doing. He'd make her like him so she'd let him go. He told her stories about his family; about his home; about his pet goldfish, who surely missed him. He told her his likes and his dislikes. He liked the sunrise, but not the sunset. He liked swimming, but not running. He liked acting, but not singing. He liked the smell of freshly cut grass in the park, but not the smell of freshly laid asphalt. He liked pomegranates, but not apples. He liked sushi, but not pizza. He liked . . .

One day, the rocklike one came down and heard the trickster talking. After that, the trickster didn't talk any more. He only said, "Mari. Let me out. Mari. Let me out."

That was what he was saying now. He was huddled on the floor, his hands around his knees, rocking back and forth. "Mari. Let me out." He stared at the far wall, dirt and sweat on his face.

"Luvic," the girl whispered. She lockpicked the cage and swept the door wide. "Luvic. Hurry. We're getting you out."

The trickster didn't answer. He just kept rocking back and forth. The wind nudged him, trying to wake him up.

The girl was right: he didn't have long. He'd conjured everything the rocklike one had asked him to, and the girl had untied it all. And while the trickster was the rocklike one's greatest prize—a principal's son!—he couldn't keep him forever. Eventually, like the others, the trickster would have to die.

The girl pulled the trickster to his feet and braced his arm over her shoulders. He was shorter than the girl, but he was a dead weight. She struggled to pull him across the basement. When the solange-eyed one saw her stumble, he hurried toward her.

"Luvic," she whispered, "it's okay. We're getting you out. You're free, you're—"

Something changed in the trickster. Suddenly, his eyes cleared, and he tensed. He blinked at the girl and then looked at the solange-eyed one.

"You're okay," the girl said.

The solange-eyed one reached for him. The wind shrieked. It saw what the trickster was going to do before anyone else.

The trickster grabbed the solange-eyed one's knife and tackled the girl.

"Luvic. No!" she cried.

The trickster shoved the knife into her. "I swore I'd kill you."

The wind rushed across the basement, and when the girl died, it shoved the solange-eyed one and the trickster out of Hell Gate.

A quarter-moon later, when the girl climbed through the solange-eyed one's window at the Night Den wearing a new body, the solange-eyed one smiled at her and said, "Mari. What took you so long?"

The trickster tried to jerk out of bed, but the solange-eyed one held him down. He was still thin, gaunt-eyed, and broken on the inside, but he looked better.

The girl pointed to him. "We're going to be friends."

The trickster took a deep breath and looked between the solange-eyed one and the girl. "Do I have a choice?"

The girl smiled. "Not really."

"You two are friends?"

They nodded.

"And you want me to be your friend?"

They nodded again.

"You want me, a Bard, to be friends with a Smith null—"

The solange-eyed one stiffened.

"It's obvious," the trickster said. He turned to the girl. "And a truth-seer I already killed once and might again—"

"Try it," the solange-eyed one said.

The trickster, even as a skinny young boy, still had a mischievous, laughing smile now that he'd been freed from the basement. "You want me to be your friend?"

"Yes," the girl said.

"Why?"

She smiled. "Because I like you."

The trickster studied her, and then he studied the solange-eyed one. "No one knows about you two?"

"No one."

"And no one will know about us?"

"No."

He smiled then—a laughing, bright-eyed smile. "Okay. We'll be friends. But only because you two need a lot of help. Without me, I think you'll both be dead before you hit twenty." Then he looked at the girl and said, "Well, dead again."

The girl jumped onto the bed, and the trickster winced. He had broken ribs, and every movement hurt him. The wind knew this, but the girl didn't.

"First things first," the trickster said, "you're going to help me so no one knows the leggerock broke me, and so no one ever guesses my weakness. And then I'm going to help you two so no one ever discovers our secret."

He twisted his hand, and suddenly, the girl wasn't the girl. Instead, she was a redheaded, freckled teenager with braces. The solange-eyed one jumped back, and the trickster laughed.

"From now on, Mari, whenever you're around me or Finn, you're going to look like someone else. Me too. It's called acting. Trust me. It's going to save your life."

From that day on, the girl had a thousand different faces. Years later, when she and the solange-eyed one kissed or danced in the mists of the Night Den and the solemn one saw them while passing through, he always believed what everyone else did. That the solange-eyed one was a hedonist, and he'd loved and left a thousand women. No one ever suspected the thousand women were all just one: the girl, covered in the trickster's illusions.

The wind swirled in the memories of the trickster, the solange-eyed one, and the girl. Their friendship was a thick rope that spanned season after season, year after year. With subterfuge and illusion, they'd built a friendship that was a tightly woven bracelet connecting them all.

They went to late-night movies at the theater and threw popcorn at screens filled with Bards. They gorged themselves on pastries while listening to concerts in the park. They sailed on sightseeing tours while the trickster conjured seagulls to dive at tourists and steal their maps or hats, making the girl laugh hysterically and the solange-eyed one hide his amusement. They sped on conjured bikes in summer rainstorms, splashing through puddles. They rode the Cyclone at Luna Park and searched for the best arepas at street fairs. They grew up together and pretended for as long as they could that they were normal.

For a short time, the trickster and the solange-eyed one fought bitterly and often, with fists. The girl would always shove between them and shout for them to stop. But then the solange-eyed one came back from seeing his father, barely holding his abdomen closed and his intestines inside himself. When the girl and the trickster held him down and stitched him back together, the solange-eyed one reached for the trickster with blood-soaked hands and gasped, "I'm sorry, Luvic. You were right. I was wrong. I'm sorry." They didn't fight after that.

The trickster wasn't happy to have been right, but he knew the conjurer families, and he knew what would happen if a null approached a principal.

After that, the trickster was quieter. More solemn. Until he met the lucky one—the woman who smelled of new pennies and wishing wells— and fell in love. But that wasn't a secret for telling here. The trickster and the lucky one had their own story.

What else? What else?

What would the girl want to send to the solange-eyed one? What was the girl burying inside of herself?

Her love for him.

Their first kiss.

It was after the solange-eyed one had healed. After the girl had laid next to him in bed for a whole winter, reading him stories while he grew stronger. It was spring, and the solange-eyed one had walked with her in the park. When he bent over to pick up a feather in the path—good luck —a butterfly landed on his hand.

The girl laughed, and then the solange-eyed one grinned and kissed her.

The wind circled between them and tasted the surprise, and then the sudden awareness.

When they pushed apart, the wind rode on their stunned exhales.

It took until summer for them to kiss again. By that time, the wind could ride on the currents flowing between them as if it were riding on an electric storm.

The trickster had left them in the park—the citrus and pearl dust scented one needed him—and the girl and the solange-eyed one were alone for the first time in a long time.

"Mari," the solange-eyed one said, watching her like he sometimes watched the sun setting over the water, "do you . . .? Can I . . .? I really want to kiss you. You know I love you, right?"

The girl smiled and stepped toward him. "I figured it out," she said, "about three years ago."

Then she gripped his T-shirt in her hands and pulled him close. The wind sighed as the girl pressed her mouth to the solange-eyed one's. She opened to him, and he swore and cupped her cheeks and tilted her mouth so he could taste her and touch her and love her.

When they pulled apart, the girl stared up at the solange-eyed one and said, "I guess you have a girlfriend now."

And the solange-eyed one grinned and said, "No, Mari. I have a girl I'm gonna marry."

After that, the girl and solange-eyed one twined themselves together so tightly that nothing would be able to separate them. If they hadn't already been tied together before they knew it was happening, they would've tied themselves together after the fact.

The wind stored the memory of the first time they held hands. The first time they kissed. The second, and then the third. It held the secret of the first time the girl had cried, and the solange-eyed one had held her. Of the nights she couldn't sleep, and the solange-eyed one would rub her back and let her talk. It stored the memories and the secrets. The kisses, the love, and the promises. It watched the solange-eyed one search for ways to free the girl from the rocklike one without the girl ever knowing. It watched the girl worry for the solange-eyed one and what would happen once she died her ninth death. It watched as they married, just the two of them, in secret.

But what . . . what else?

There was the trickster.

A month before the games, he came to the girl.

"The leggerock wants to make a bargain with me." The trickster's forehead was covered in sweat, and he was pale. He'd spent a sleepless night thinking about the deal.

"What kind of bargain?"

"He says he has a cure for Lia. He'll give it to me if I'm his inside man during the games . . ."

"And?" There was an "and" hanging in the air.

The trickster swallowed, and the wind tapped his windpipe. "And if I kill you after the Smith job."

The girl frowned. "What Smith job?"

The trickster shrugged. "He's sending you after a key. My dad's been talking about it too. There's a rumor that whoever holds the Smith key will win the games."

"But Jagger doesn't care about the games—"

"Mari. He wants me to kill you."

The girl waved that away. "Is the cure real? Will it . . . will it make your sister better?"

The trickster shook his head. "I don't know. Knowing the leggerock, I'll fulfill my end of the bargain, and then he'll kill Lia and tell me the ultimate cure to any disease is death."

The girl laughed. "Yeah. But what if . . . what if you could guarantee it wasn't death? That he really had a cure?"

"I wouldn't," the trickster said. "I couldn't hurt you. Not even for Lia."

"Luvic." The girl reached out and took the trickster's hands. "Yes, you could. For your sister? You could. Do it. Take the bargain."

"But—"

"Take it. Just . . . don't tell Finn."

"Mari, I can't—"

"Don't tell Finn, or he'll kill you. But . . ."

"I won't—"

"You've already killed me once. What's another time between friends?"

The trickster grabbed the girl and yanked her to him. She let out a surprised breath and then relaxed into his hug.

The trickster took the bargain, but only after the solange-eyed one and the girl had taken another.

89

HOW DID WE END UP HERE? IF YOU ASKED THE WIND, IT WOULD TELL YOU our fate was laid out even before we were born. That we would blow down this path, through these alleys, and find ourselves in this exact place, because this was how we were meant to go.

But what if you asked men? Wouldn't they tell you we have free will—that we can choose yes or no, today or tomorrow, forever or never?

If that's the case, we didn't end up here because of what fate decreed before we were even alive. We ended up here because of our own decisions. We could've made a different choice. We could've said no.

But what did you tell me? You wouldn't see me become less.

The blood pulsed through my veins and my heartbeat grew louder as I settled into my final self. The cold of the basement pressed into my skin, and my back ached against the hard metal floor of the conjurer's cage. My fingers twitched, and within minutes, I'd open my eyes and wake to my new reality.

I had minutes.

So I burrowed down, buried myself deep, and hid one last memory.

It was the morning after we married. The last moments I knew you for you.

The breeze blew through your open window, and hints of morning drifted through. There was the rumble of a delivery truck, the clatter of metal gates opening, and the sleepy stop-and-go of early-morning traffic. They were the normal city sounds we heard every day. They felt different, though, because I was different. I was yours.

Sunlight spread through your bedroom and nudged at my eyelids, pestering me awake. I buried my face in your shoulder and burrowed further into your warmth.

When I did, you pulled me close and wrapped your arms around me, dragging in a deep breath. Then you kissed the spot where my shoulder and my neck met, and when I made a soft sound, you dug your hands into my hair and pulled me on top of you.

I didn't know that would be the last time we'd make love. If I'd known, I would've done a better job of memorizing every touch, every feel, every sound, and every taste.

Now, all I can remember is the way your breath caught as your hands scraped over my thighs. I can only see the golden green hue of your eyes as you blinked up at me and raggedly whispered my name.

I can only feel the rough heat of your morning stubble against my cheek, and the hot draw of your breath as you held me close and pressed yourself over me.

And then? I can only remember how, when I lost myself in you, you held me tighter than I knew possible and lost yourself in me too. I can only remember the feel of being lost in you, and then finding myself in your arms.

You brushed your hand against my cheek and said, "I love you."

You'd said it before—more times than I could count. But right then, it felt earth-shattering. Or maybe that's in retrospect.

When Jagger kicked the bedroom door down, you threw a half-dozen knives before I had time to scramble upright. The knives glanced off his rock-gray skin, and then I was on the ground screaming, twisting, in agony.

Every good thing, every happy thing—it all evaporated in the acidic burn of Jagger's wrath.

You froze mid-throw, and I whimpered, the sizzle of Jagger's blood burning my veins. This was what he did—another way he could control. His blood was my blood, and the drop of it we'd exchanged when I became a nine could bring me back to life, but it could also burn me from the inside out. Jagger was hell, and his blood was hell in my veins.

"That's right," Jagger purred, studying you like he studied the creatures who cowered in his shadow. "If you hurt me, I hurt her. If I die, she dies. Put the weapon down."

You dropped the knife. It slid off the bed and hit the wooden floor with a dull, hollow thud.

I curled in on myself, holding my arms around my stomach. Jagger held the pain at the threshold of mindless agony. One nudge further, and I'd black out. Here, I was teetering between agony and awareness.

"Mari," you whispered, dropping to the floor and placing yourself between me and Jagger. "Okay?"

Jagger grinned, his sharp teeth glistening in the half-light. His gray skin was dull, and his wrinkles pooled about him as he gleefully took in the picture of your helplessness.

"When my cousin told me my nine had married a Night Den orphan, I didn't believe it."

I twisted at the flash of pain burning through me.

Jagger smiled. "I said, 'Not Mari. She knows she's mine. She knows better.' Yet Eyetooth was insistent. He'd heard the whispered wedding words. He'd seen your faces through a crack in the wall. He swore my nine had married in secret."

He touched the obsidian knife at his throat and pierced his finger on the sharp edge. The pain of his skin cutting open sliced through me, and I screamed. You lunged forward, but when Jagger pressed harder, my scream broke off, and you froze.

"Stop," you said. You looked back at me. I could barely make out your face. The pain had gathered at the edges of my vision and painted it black. "What do you want?"

"Want?" Jagger took in your bedroom. He narrowed his eyes on the bed, the rumpled sheets, the evidence of our night together. Then, as fast as a rockslide, he pierced your forearm with his nail and stuck his finger into his mouth, tasting your blood.

You held still. I reached out, setting my hand against your back. It was cold. It was as if fear for me had robbed you of your warmth.

"Smith," Jagger said, pleasure infusing his gravelly voice. "And Bard . . . and a little bit of everything else. Conjurer. Null? Mari, is he a null?"

"Yes," I said, my voice ragged and raw from screaming.

"Do you love your null? Don't lie, Mari."

It hurt to speak. "Yes."

Jagger smiled cruelly. "And does he love you?"

When he asked, you stiffened. I knew the pose. You wanted to kill him. You wanted to spring up and rip his throat out and kill him. But you couldn't, and it was killing you.

"Yes."

Jagger watched us both with flat gray eyes. Cold sweat dripped down my bare skin, and I shivered. Jagger didn't love. He'd never felt love. He only saw it as a way to hurt and control. As something he could use to manipulate and destroy. When someone loved, they gave away their power.

He'd once told me he loved a man in love, because the fool would do anything to save the object of his ardor.

"I would like to send you to your final death," he said, stretching out the words.

I pressed my hand to your back, begging you to hold still—to wait.

"I would like to kill you. Then kill you again, while you're vulnerable and comatose. That would be enjoyable. Then kill you again, send you on your way. But . . . I very much want to use you, Mari. And now, look. You've brought me a Smith. And I think I very much would like to use him too. Can I use you? Be careful how you answer."

You held your breath. I felt the tightness of your ribs, and then the slow exhale.

"You want to bargain with me?"

Jagger's wrinkles lifted, and he let out an avalanche laugh. It crashed through the room and pounded against my temples. I flinched.

Then Jagger said, "Yes. I'll bargain with you, Smith. I would like . . . Have you heard of the Hundred Year Games?" Whatever Jagger saw made him smile cruelly. "Good. That makes this easier. I want you to enter the games as paladin for the Smiths. I want you to win the crown for me."

My throat hurt, my bones hurt, but I shook my head. "He can't. He'll die. He's null. He can't—"

I broke off when acid burned through me.

You looked back and gripped my hand. I held onto the comfort of your hold.

"If he dies, he dies. I'll delight in it. I'll delight in your pain, Mari. What is it to me? But Smith—"

"Alterra."

"Smith. How can a null defeat illusion? How might you win? You know." Jagger nodded, urging.

"Solange," you said.

Jagger smiled. "That's right." He pulled a vial from his pocket. The iridescent liquid rolled around the cut-glass vial, and the half-light caught in the golden glow. "You'll take this. You'll become an addict. You'll kill yourself so you can survive."

I shook my head. "No. No, Finn—"

I whimpered at a fresh lashing of pain. You glanced back at me, your eyes a deep, fathomless pool. What were you thinking? What were you trying to tell me?

"If I enter the games, if I win the crown—"

"If you enter, if you take on Mari as your body for the games, if you win and she steals the crown and brings it to me—"

"Then you free Mari."

"Then I free a nine of your choice, and I give you a lifetime supply of solange. See? A fair bargain. You may die an addict, but at least I'll give you enough solange to last until the end."

"And if I say no?"

"She dies today. You die today." Jagger laughed. "You don't think I can kill you? I've killed full-blooded conjurers. I can kill a null."

I pushed past the pain and shoved myself upright. You were going to say yes. I could tell by the way you held your shoulders and the slant of your jaw. I *knew*.

I couldn't let you. I couldn't let you to kill yourself for me.

"Jagger," I said, my voice broken, "I'm sorry. I was wrong. Let's go home. I'll be a mine. You can kill me twice today. I'll never speak of or think of Finn again. I'll be yours, just . . . leave him. Leave him, and I'll do whatever you want. Anything."

Jagger shifted on his feet. He loomed over us, his gray rock presence filling the room like an unmovable, malignant mountain. He tapped his nails together and stared at me the way he often looked at creatures he'd grown tired of and was about to kill. Gruesomely.

"Mari. You are already mine. You will already do whatever I want. You have nothing left to bargain with. While he"—Jagger pointed his long, clawed finger—"has plenty to bargain with. I want the crown. I've wanted it for centuries, and you've handed me a means to get it. What will it be?" He stared at you, weighing how much you loved me; how much you'd be willing to give up for me. Too much. "Your blood is thick with Smith. Is the principal your father?"

"Yes."

Jagger grinned. "Perfect. Do we have a bargain? Will you win the games or die trying?"

He held out the vial to you. It caught the light of the sunrise, a rainbow of colors inside the glass. The prism of it fell over us.

I shook my head. A tear leaked from my eye. *No. Don't, Finn. Don't.*

"Choose," Jagger said. "Your death now, or your death later. Her death now, or her death later."

You looked back at me. Smiled. It was . . . it was a smile I'd seen a thousand times before. It was the smile you gave me the first time I picked up a string of dandelions you'd left on a newsstand for me. It was the smile you'd have when we'd hold hands and walk through the streets at dusk. It was the smile you'd give me after you'd pull away from a long, languid kiss. It was your smile—the one you saved for me.

You reached out and took the vial of solange.

The unstopping of the cork was loud and final.

"Before you drink, say the words," Jagger demanded, watching greedily.

Instead of bowing your head, you looked Jagger in the eye. "If I, Finn Alterra, win the Hundred Year Games with Mari Locke as my body, then

Jagger Leggerock will grant me a lifetime supply of solange and a nine of my choosing. If I lose, my life is forfeited."

"Our bargain is sealed," Jagger said.

You tilted back your head and swallowed the drops of solange.

Jagger laughed, and I cried out, but it was too late. You'd swallowed your death in one quick shot. The room filled with a violent golden light. It burst from you and swept over us like a hot desert wind. Your back bowed. You twisted—in pain?—and then dragged in a gasping breath. You rolled to the floor, and the gold tinge swirled around you. Then, as Jagger laughed, you struggled to pull yourself upright.

You swayed. You tilted. You shook yourself off and fell over, then you shook yourself upright again.

I wanted to reach out and help you up, but every time I moved, Jagger sent a lance of pain through me.

He wanted you to struggle. He wanted you to fall.

Finally, after long minutes of dizziness, drunken swaying, and violent retching, you struggled upright. You listed to the side and then pulled in another shuddering breath.

"How does it feel to have stepped onto death's path?" Jagger asked, eyeing you curiously.

You turned toward me, your black hair falling over your forehead. I gasped at the change in you. Your skin was richer; tinged golden. Your movements were more languid, more fluid, like a rolling wave. And your eyes . . . the eyes I'd loved? They weren't warm hazel anymore. They were navy blue and full of silver stars.

You smiled at me. It was vacant, empty, blissful, and . . .

I shook my head.

It was the stare of a solange devotee.

"Finn?"

Your smile grew. "Mari."

You breathed my name as if it were the most beautiful word you'd ever spoken.

Jagger laughed. "He really does love her. Better and better. How about another bargain? You think love is real? You think your love makes Mari yours? How about . . . you have a trait, don't you? My cousin tells me your trait lets you erase memories."

I held still. I was captured by the bliss in your eyes, the vacant smile on your face, as you swayed first left, then right.

A hint of sunlight glanced off your cheek and lit your skin. I wanted to reach out and brush the hair away from your eyes.

"I can," you said.

"How does it work?"

You closed one eye and then the other, peering at me, a curious smile on your face.

"I don't know. How do you breathe? You just breathe. It's the same. I want a memory, I take it."

"And it's gone forever?"

You paused. Then nodded. "I take it, and it's gone forever."

That wasn't exactly true. You could take memories—you'd inherited the trait from your mom's side—but you could also return memories. You could give them back through your essence. Blood. Tears. A person's essence held memories.

Apparently, Jagger's cousin Eyetooth didn't know you could return what you'd taken.

Jagger nodded. "I'd like to give you a gift, Mari. Never say I'm not fair. Never say I haven't given you anything. Here's a wedding gift." He grinned and brushed a hand over his obsidian knife. "Do you believe Mari loves you? That her love is greater than anything—even my hold on her?"

Don't answer . . . don't answer . . .

You closed one eye and then the other. You smiled. "Yes."

"Yes? Yes. And do you believe love is a part of the soul? That she would love you even if she didn't remember you?"

"Yes."

You didn't even pause. You didn't have to think about it. That was how much you believed in our love.

"Here is what I propose. Take her memories. Take all her memories of you. All of them. Make it so that you've never met. Make it so she is mine again, and only mine. During the games, you may not tell her what you were to each other. You can never let her know who you are to her, or what you were. Do you see what I'm getting at?"

"Not quite," you said, "but I think . . . perhaps?"

Jagger crouched down, and his shadow passed over us. "I want to see what happens. I want to see if Mari is really mine, or if she's yours. If, at the end of the games, Mari chooses to defy me by helping you, then you can have her. But if she chooses to obey me to your detriment, she's mine, as she always has been. But she cannot know who you are. You cannot tell her by word, action, deed . . . She can never know. She must forget you. She must think of you as a hedonist, a solange-addict, a Smith null who has never met her, and . . . hmm . . . who loves another woman. If you encourage her, or if her love blossoms because of your actions, the bargain is dead. But if you can keep her in the dark . . . Ah, we'll see what happens. How about it? If you win this bargain, and in the end, Mari chooses to help you over obeying me, then she'll be free, no matter if you win the games or not. She'll be free even if you lose. See? That's a good wedding gift. Two chances to win your wife's freedom."

I stared at you as you considered Jagger's words. My breath was short. My lungs were tight. I held very still, like a mouse under a raptor's claw. The pain was leaching through me, robbing me of my ability to reason.

But I knew one thing.

"Finn, I'd rather die remembering you than live without."

"Sweet," Jagger said.

You reached out and pressed your pointer and third fingers to my temple. You brushed my hair aside and drifted your fingers across my cheek.

"We can do this," you whispered. "We can do this, Mari. I trust you."

"If I forget you . . ." I blinked away the stinging at my eyes. "If I forget you, then I won't have any good left in me. What good will I have? When I meet you, I won't trust you. I'll hurt you. I might hate you. I'll do things to you that—"

"I trust you. Even if you don't know me, don't like me, don't . . . Mari, I trust you with my life."

That was what you'd be doing, and we both knew it. I was Jagger's creature, and without the light of Finn's love, I was . . . a breath away from night.

You smiled at me and pressed your fingers to my lips. "Think of it this way. I'm going to win the crown, and I'm going to save you while I'm doing it."

I laughed, but it felt more like a sob. "I don't want this."

You swayed, tilted, and shook your head as if the world were swinging and you were having trouble staying upright. "Think about how much better the world will be without the conjurers wearing the crown. Think about all the good this could do. Think about . . . think about us on a train together, just going."

I reached up and placed my hand over yours. "I'm scared I'll hurt you. Don't take my memories. It's not worth it. I can't . . ."

Your hand curved over my cheek, and you said something I couldn't fight. "Mari. We have to do this. You know this. Every time you turn your back on a responsibility that is rightfully yours to bear, you make the world a darker place, and you make yourself a lesser person. I won't see you become less. You have to do this. I have to do this. *We* have to."

I nodded. You were right. This wasn't only about us. If we won the crown, the conjurers would be weakened. If I was free . . . how many lives would be saved? I wasn't so naïve that I didn't realize Jagger would use me to kill once I was a mine. If we won even one of these bargains, we'd be saving the world, and we'd be saving each other.

I stared into your navy and silver eyes. How long did you have? And later, could I find a cure? Was there a cure to solange, or was death the only cure?

That thought made me remember Luvic. I mouthed his name to you, and you nodded. I'd have to forget Luvic too. Everything connected with Finn was connected with Luvic.

Would he help us in the games? Would he be there to keep me safe even when I didn't know him? Or would he play with and for his family and leave Finn and me to either live or die?

You gave me a smile full of confidence and love.

"Trust me," you said.

I nodded. "Always."

"Love me?"

Yes. Forever. "Always."

"I agree to your bargain," you said.

Jagger gave another avalanche laugh. "Ah, Mari. What fun this will be. Say the words then, Smith. Make our bargain. Seal your fates."

You said the words, and as you did, you also said goodbye. The bargain sealed you in its grip.

Quickly, we made plans: tell me your story when all this is done; do whatever you have to do to win; don't attempt to steal the crown unless you're on the dais; don't trust anyone except me; and when all this is done, we'll have a wedding—one with flowers and a cake in a church with our friends, and then after, we'll get on a train and find our patch of sky.

We said our final goodbye.

I kept my eyes on you as you pressed your fingers to my temple. I memorized your face as you pulled all my memories away and wiped yourself from my past. I watched you as you stole away my love.

When I collapsed and the darkness consumed me, I was empty, I was barren, I was alone.

In the dark, I heard a voice calling. "Untie the knot, Mari. Untie the knot!"

90

THE WIND SLIPPED THROUGH THE CRACKS IN THE PLASTER WALLS AND dragged itself over a jagged pile of broken marble. The hall was thick with the acrid scent of smoke. The marble floors and the broken stone still held the warm-oven heat of the illusion fire.

The hall had been hastily reconstructed. A ceiling. Walls. Glass windows. Columns. But the cracks remained, and the rubble had been merely swept to the side. The dais was splintered, the marble pool broken in half and empty of its water. A blue fire burned there instead. No one had been able to put it out.

The conjurers were staring at it now. The wind brushed through the blue flames and fanned them higher.

The trickster's jaw hardened, and he looked away from the blue sparks. His eyes were hooded, his expression cold.

He stood next to his father. There were only the two of them now. The musician and the citrus and pearl dust scented woman were gone. The mother was hidden in a room upstairs. The wind could hear her weeping.

What had happened to make the trickster so cold? The wind brushed through the secret of the trickster and the solange-eyed one from before the games. It riffled through the memory.

"You realize what you're asking me to do?" the trickster had asked, looking worriedly over his shoulder. The Night Den was full of mist and darkness.

"Yes." The solange-eyed one knew.

The wall of mist thickened around them, keeping their secrets close.

"You want me to lie to my family and help you win the games. You want me to betray all conjurers and help you steal the crown. You want me to help keep you and Mari alive during the hell that is the games, all for"—he raised an eyebrow—"our friendship?"

The solange-eyed one put his hand on the trickster's shoulder. "Please, Luvic."

The trickster stared at the solange-eyed one. Then he smiled. Was it a happy smile? The wind didn't know.

The trickster took his friend in his arms. "You already know my answer. On your wedding day, I'm walking Mari down the aisle."

The trickster had kept his promise. But for what? In the end, he'd done everything that was asked of him. Perhaps that was why he looked so grim.

The wind sighed and then trailed through the dust on the floor, stirring up little clouds to float in the blue-tinged darkness.

Only the highest members of the families were in the hall—the ones with the most power in their blood.

One night and one gray-clouded day had passed since the destruction and the bloodied fall of many of their family members. The firetrucks were gone now, the firefighters believing an electric fire had broken out in an old apartment and no one had been harmed. The weaker conjurer cousins were gone, having fled the carnage.

Most importantly, the crown was gone. It had disappeared when the solange-eyed one had died.

"By rights," the solange-eyed one's brother said, in a steel-bladed voice, "it belongs to me. Whether the crown is here or not, the Smiths won the game." He stood alone, his brother gone, his father dead. He leaned forward, a challenge in his gaze.

The trickster scoffed. "Where are the Wards? No one is crowned without all four families present. What did you do to them, Darin?"

The brother focused on the trickster. If he'd had a weapon out, it would've been at the trickster's throat. They'd never been friends. The truce of yesterday, when they'd fought side by side, had already been forgotten. The brother thought the trickster had fought with them because of the note his father had sent, calling in their favor. The trickster wouldn't tell the brother he would've fought by the solange-eyed man's side no matter what.

"I think," the brother said, "you can easily imagine what I did, since you did the very same thing to your own siblings. *Heir* Bard."

The trickster bared his teeth.

The trickster's father sighed. "I will keep the crown until the matter—"

"You have no crown to keep," the cruel one said, and his father agreed.

"My son has as much right to the crown as the Smith. He fought in the duel. The paladin died. Perhaps one would say he died in an extension of the duel. My son lived. Therefore, the crown is his. A Clark will rule."

"I don't think so," the brother said.

"Bard?" the parchment scented father asked.

The Bard nodded. "Yes. I agree. Let's."

The trickster, the Bard, the cruel one, his sister, and the Clark all raised their arms.

The battle scented brother took a step back and conjured a ring of blue fire around himself.

"Take note," the cruel one said. "The Smith had an unfortunate accident after the games. He was unable to vie for the crown due to . . . death."

The brother swore. He expanded his blue fire ring. He wouldn't survive. The wind knew he wouldn't. If the boy were here, he would help the brother. Not because he liked the brother, but because the boy had honor, and he was almost always polite.

This was *not* polite.

The brother backed up against the dais.

The cruel one grinned and conjured a dark, empty hole. A grave with no bottom.

The backs of the brother's knees hit the marble pool. The glowing blue flames that hadn't died connected with the brother's fire. The wind screeched as the flames twisted together. They shot toward the ceiling.

A wall of fire burst from the black marble. The wind shot through it and catapulted around the room. The flames flared as bright as the sun. The fire was hot, but it didn't burn.

The conjurers screamed and covered their eyes.

The fire roared and swallowed the dais in burning blue. The wind ripped through it, tearing about and riding on the frenzied, crackling energy. It burst through the room as violently as a cosmic ray. It was an ocean of power. It rolled through the room so loudly that the conjurers clapped their hands over their ears, closed their eyes, and fell to their knees.

The wind screamed. It spun wildly. It rode the currents and danced on the electric. It was the power of a thousand lightning bolts. It was like chasing the sun. It raced around the room and spun on the birth of . . .

A thunderous boom shook the hall.

No.

It shook the earth.

Across the city, buildings swayed, and the ground rumbled.

The shaking stilled, and when it stopped, the blue fire blazed heavenly bright.

The wind laughed as the solange-eyed one stepped out of the fire. The crown of illusions rested over his head. It flickered in the light.

The fire snapped and then caved around him.

The conjurers stared. They were on their knees. Their eyes filled with tears, as if they'd looked directly at the sun.

None of them spoke.

None of them could speak.

The solange-eyed one looked the same as before. Except . . .

The wind trailed over his face. One eye was navy and lightning-filled. The other eye was hazel. So he'd given an eye to the well. He'd sacrificed for knowledge. Or for truth.

The solange-eyed one took in the conjurers. He saw what had been done, and what was about to be done.

He stepped from the marble pool, out of the blue fire, and back into the physical world.

He smiled at the men before him. The wind rushed over him, blowing his hair, twisting his clothes, cooling the scorching fire in his blood. Perhaps he didn't realize that in coming back, he'd shaken the earth.

Deliver. Don't destroy.

The solange-eyed one stepped in front of his brother and pointed at the conjurers.

"You are all going to die," he said. "The only question is, who's going to die first?"

91

THE EARTH SHOOK BENEATH ME. THE BASEMENT RUMBLED, AND THE STONES shuddered and slid an inch, then two, before settling into an unsteady, watchful quiet. Decades of dust and dirt rained over me, and if I could have, I would've sneezed.

My fingers twitched, and my eyelids fluttered. I was waking. I was almost back in my final body.

An earthquake. Was that an earthquake? In New York?

The basement walls had groaned, and the stone had coughed and scraped. I shivered, and goose bumps rose over my skin. There were no large earthquakes in New York City. The only thing that could cause that was illusion made real. A conjurer like the conjurers of old. The ones who delighted in destruction and despair.

Only the worst, the most destructive, the most horrible conjurers would unleash earthquakes in a city of millions.

Was that what had happened?

Was that the world we lived in now?

Finn?

Are you there?

I told you my secrets. I let the story play out. I told it as best I could. While the dirt and the dust rained down on me, I buried the last of my good. While the earth rumbled and rolled beneath me, I locked my love away.

It's gone. It's hidden. I've hidden it even from myself.

Jagger was there. I could feel the cold pain of him; the cruel anticipation; his short laugh as the stones groaned and the floor shook. His breath was loud, and with each inhale and exhale, I felt myself changing.

Finn.

I've locked away my love. I've locked away my good.

I felt Jagger tearing at me. Ripping away my insides. Consuming my soul.

Finn?

I forgot a memory. I forgot to hide one.

We're in Central Park, lying in the grass on Cherry Hill. I'm tucked against your side. The sun strokes us, and you're lazily running your hand in a circle over my back. We're watching the wind blow through the leaves above us. They're playing in shadows across the grass. You lean over and press a kiss to my temple.

"Hey," you whisper.

"Hey, you," I say.

It's an ordinary moment. An ordinary thing to say. And the happiness is an ordinary, everyday sort of happiness.

And . . . I love you. I . . .

Jagger tore it away. He grabbed it. Shredded it and made it bleed. It hurt. It hurt.

He tore through everything.

He overturned and devoured. He found all my happiness. My loyalty to Griff. My affection for his innocence and his dimpled smiles. My love for Justice, and even my forgiveness. He took it, and he shredded it, and he twisted it, until it was a desiccated, battered thing.

The bargain I'd made, the blood inside me—it changed.

I didn't fight it.

I didn't struggle.

I let it change me.

I let it steal everything good away.

As my eyes fluttered open, I became someone else. I was someone else. From that moment on, lie became my truth, pain became my love, and evil became my good.

From that point forward, wrong was my right.

Finn?

I'm sending you the wind. Can you hear it? Will you listen?

If we meet again, will you know me? When I'm darkness and you're the light, will you see me? Or will you destroy the darkness and devour the night?

Jagger didn't only want the crown, Finn. He wanted war. He wanted the death of the world.

I'm going to help him.

Can you stop me?

I opened my eyes. Jagger was smiling down at me, his flat gray eyes sparking maliciously.

"Ah, Mari. Welcome home. Welcome back to Hell Gate. Aren't you glad you're mine?"

And Finn, I have to tell you.

I was.

I *was*.

Come for me. Come for me before I come for you.

Please, Finn.

I'm sending the wind.

I'm sending it with the last of my love.

I'll bury your memory deep. I'll bury it where no one can find it. I'll keep it hidden. I'll keep it safe. I'll keep it for you.

Finn, until we finally meet again, you'll always be my dear illusion.

END OF BOOK ONE

READ THE NEXT BOOK IN THE SERIES:

My Beautiful Reality

Mari is now a mine, and under Jagger's control. Finn is back, but not as himself. The conjurer families are in chaos, and the two lovers fight on opposite sides of the battle.

When Finn promises to kill Mari, she realizes nothing is the same as it was, and in this new world, one of them is the light and the other the dark.

As the families vie for power, the question remains: will their battle save the world or destroy it?

Welcome to the dangerous and secret-laden world of the conjurers where friends are enemies, alliances are made and broken in a heartbeat, and you never know who to trust.

Book Two:
My Beautiful Reality

ABOUT THE AUTHOR

Multi award-winning author Sarah Ready writes fiction that has been described as "euphoric," "heartwarming," and "laugh out loud."

Sarah writes fantasy romance, including *My Dear Illusion*; stand-alone romances, including *Josh and Gemma Make a Baby*, *Josh and Gemma the Second Time Around*, *French Holiday*, and *The Space Between*; magical realism romance including *Ghosted*, *Switched*, *Fated*, and *Wished*; and romcoms in the Soul Mates in Romeo series, all of which can be found at her website: www.sarahready.com.

You can learn more and find upcoming titles at: www.sarahready.com.

Stay up to date, get exclusive epilogues and bonus content. Join Sarah's newsletter at www.sarahready.com/newsletter.

Novella:

Love Letters

Find these books and more by Sarah Ready at:

www.sarahready.com/